RIVALS OF SHERLOCK HOLMES
Two

RIVALS OF
SHERLOCK HOLMES
TWO

*Forty Six Stories of Crime and Detection
from Original Illustrated Magazines
by*

ANGUS EVAN ABBOTT   CLIFFORD ASHDOWN

ROBERT BARR   GEORGE A. BEST   GUY BOOTHBY

JULIUS CHAMBERS   GUY CLIFFORD   ARTHUR CONAN DOYLE

JACQUES FUTRELLE   GEORGE GRIFFITH   BRETT HARTE

E.W. HORNUNG

CUTCLIFFE HYNE   WILLIAM LE QUEUX

L.T. MEADE & ROBERT EUSTACE

BARONESS ORCZY   C.L. PIRKIS   FRED M. WHITE

VICTOR L. WHITECHURCH & E. CONWAY

Selected and Introduced by ALAN K. RUSSELL

CASTLE BOOKS

CONTENTS

MR. WILLIAM LE QUEUX ON HIS 40-H.P. NAPIER CAR, ON WHICH HE MADE HIS
7,000 MILES TOUR THROUGH ENGLAND AND WALES.

MORE FROM
A GOLDEN ERA
OF
CRIME AND DETECTION

THE STORY THUS FAR. . .

This book presents stories from a Golden Era of crime and detective fiction. As
the title says 'Volume 2', a little elementary deduction will lead you to the
conclusion that it has a companion volume, the first in the series being *The Rivals of
Sherlock Holmes*. So what have you missed? And do you need to read the first
volume before you can read this one? The answer to the first question is that you
have missed forty of the finest stories of their kind; the answer to the second
question is that you need no guide to enter the gaslit world of foggy nights and
horse carriages. Enter with us now, and you will find in this book several dozen
superb examples of the best writing of its day. Here are stories from the heyday of
the illustrated magazine, when the magazine reigned supreme as an entertainment medium. The stories are selected from the leading magazines of their day,
and presented to you exactly as they originally appeared.

In *The Rivals of Sherlock Holmes, Volume 2*, we present more stories by five of
the authors who were so well received in *The Rivals of Sherlock Holmes*. The fact that
we are also able to introduce thirteen new authors is a tribute to the popular

magazines' happy knack of being able to tap seemingly unlimited sources of talent. Between the two books you have the work of nearly thirty authors, all of whom competed with Arthur Conan Doyle's *Sherlock Holmes* to thrill, mystify and entertain. Amongst the new memorable characters you will meet are:

- a literary agent, who is a gentleman crook
- the most famous cricketer and gentleman crook of all, A.J. Raffles and his accomplice, Bunny
- The Prince of Swindlers
- rare true crime stories by Arthur Conan Doyle
- the 'thinking machine' in person, Professor van Dusen
- the criminal Count Bindo di Ferraris
- the gross and unscrupulous attorney, Patrick Mulligan

The stories in *The Rivals of Sherlock Holmes, Volume 2* have been drawn from—and are reproduced for you exactly as they appeared—the original, rare English editions of the following magazines:

Cassell's Magazine
The Harmsworth Magazine (which became *The Harmsworth London Magazine* and then *The London Magazine*, with the subtitle 'A Magazine of Human Interest')
The Idler
The Ludgate Monthly (which became *The Ludgate Illustrated Magazine*)
Pearson's Magazine
The Strand Magazine
The Windsor Magazine

The titles of all these magazines conjure up very vivid pictures of London at the turn of the century. The Strand was, and is today, a central thoroughfare leading to Fleet Street, at the end of which is Ludgate Circus—which gave its name to the competing *The Ludgate Monthly*. (The retitling of *The Ludgate Monthly* was no doubt because *The Strand Magazine* was subtitled 'An Illustrated Monthly'.) *Cassell's, Harmsworth* and *Pearson's* magazines were named after their publishers, each of whom were flamboyant and publicity-conscious entrepreneurs. *The Windsor Magazine* was, of course, named after the Royal residence of Queen Victoria—there was also a *Royal Magazine*. *The Idler* reflected, perhaps, indolent lazy days spent punting on the River Thames at Henley.

But, more than anything else, these magazines presented sheer entertainment; and that is what *Rivals of Sherlock Holmes, Volume 2* and the other books anthologized from them represent. Enjoy this book, and then read the other companion books now available: *The Original Illustrated Sherlock Holmes, The Rivals of Sherlock Holmes, The Collector's Book of Science Fiction by H.G. Wells* and *Science Fiction by the Rivals of H.G. Wells*.

ALAN K. RUSSELL

L. T. MEADE.

THE AUTHORS
AND SOME
BIBLIOGRAPHICAL NOTES

IT IS RARE for an author to have had only one of his stories published. Usually they write more and eventually their works appear in book form. The greater an author's published output, the easier it is to find information about the writer and his other literary offerings. Hence the need for bibliographies and biographical reference studies, even full scale biographies. Fortunately, there are a number of guides that can be consulted when researching authors of detective and crime fiction. This being said, I have to confess that there are some authors in this volume on whom either no further information is available or whose work has not received critical comment. Some did write a number of stories, even books, but they appear to be presented here in anthology for the first time. (We do know that with several of these writers only one of their stories was worth preserving.) So perhaps this sorry state of affairs will encourage some dedicated researcher to delve a little deeper, in the hope of un-earthing more information. The first author in this category is Angus Evan Abbott, whose *The Spawn of Fortune* was published in the July 1896 issue of *The Ludgate Monthly*. Also, George A. Best, author of *The Counterfeit Cashier*, which appeared in *Cassell's Magazine* in May 1902; Julius Chambers whose *Seven, Seven, Seven—City* is taken from *The London Magazine* November 1903; Guy Clifford's two stories are taken from *The Ludgate Monthly* of 1895: *A Clever Capture* from the May issue and *The Wendall Bank Case* from the September issue; Fred M. White, a prolific but critically neglected writer, whose *Mazaroff Rifle* is from a series entitled *The Romance of the Secret Service Fund* and appeared in the August 1900 issue of *Pearson's Magazine*. (Some of White's science fiction stories appear in this book's companion volume *Science Fiction by the Rivals of H.G. Wells.*)

Clifford Ashdown was a pseudonym for R. Austin Freeman (1862-1943) and John James Pitcairn (1860-1936). Freeman was the creator of the brilliant Dr. Thorndyke, described in *The Encyclopaedia of Mystery and Detection* by Steinbrunner and Penzler as the "greatest medico-legal detective of all time." Here, however, we present examples of his early work, which contains the character Romney Pringle whom Freeman created in collaboration with a prison doctor. In fact, the identity of Freeman's co-author was concealed for many years, the truth only being revealed some 44 years after the stories first appeared. Pringle is in the Raffles mould; a gentleman criminal, who uses his literary agency as a cover. The two stories in this volume are from *Cassell's Magazine* for June 1903 ('The Submarine Boat') and August 1903 ('The Silkworms of Florence').

Robert Barr's *The Clue of the Silver Spoons* is taken from *Pearson's Magazine*, 1904. His story *The Mystery of the Five Hundred Diamonds*, taken from *The Windsor Magazine*, appeared in *The Rivals of Sherlock Holmes*. He also used the pseudonym of Luke Sharp, under which he wrote a parody of Sherlock Holmes that appeared in *The Idler*—which Barr founded in partnership with Jerome K. Jerome (author of *Three Men in a Boat*). Barr died in 1912.

Guy Boothby was born in Australia and moved to England when he was 27 years old. He wrote a great many popular novels in a short period, before dying at the early age of 37 in February 1904 (although some works cite 1905). Boothby created the sinister Dr. Nikola, but in this volume we present his gentleman crook Simon Carne, who was perhaps the first of the gentlemen crooks in crime fiction (unless you go back to Robin Hood). Over the years, Raffles, Colonel Clay and dozens more followed in his footsteps. The two stories in this volume appeared in *Pearson's Magazine* in 1897: *The Duchess of Wiltshire's Diamonds* in the issue for February and *An Imperial Finale* in July. The complete series was published in book form in 1898 as *A Prince of Swindlers*.

Four rare stories by Arthur Conan Doyle, creator of Sherlock Holmes, are presented in this volume. The three "Strange Studies from Life" were the only ones published out of a planned series of twelve, and come from *The Strand* of March, April and May 1901. They are Doyle's retellings of real-life crimes.

The name Jacques Futrelle sounds French, but he was, in fact, born in Pike County, Ga. His claim to fame is as creator of one of crime fiction's great characters, the cerebral Professor Augustus S.F.X. van Dusen, Ph.D., LL.D., F.R.S., M.D., etc. Unfortunately, Futrelle's promising career was cut short when, aged only 36, he went down with the *Titanic*. Van Dusen's philosophy was that "two and two always make four—not *some* time but *all* the time", and the power of his thinking was such that he could solve any mystery. Ellery Queen chose *The Thinking Machine* as one of his *Queen's Quorum*—his choice of the 125 most important detective-crime books of short stories. The six stories contained in this volume appeared in *Cassell's Magazine*, between December 1907 and June 1908.

George Griffith (George C. Griffith-Jones, 1859-1906) is best known for his science fiction stories and, at the time, his work was as popular as that of H.G. Wells. As with Wells, being a professional writer, he also wrote other fiction, although reference to his crime stories is rare. Griffith was an adventurer who travelled the world, and claimed to have circumvented the globe in a then-record of sixty-four and a half days. The two stories in this volume were set in South Africa, and appeared in *Pearson's Magazine* in 1897: the first was entitled *Five Hundred Carats* and appeared in the November issue, while *The Border Gang* came out the month following. The series was entitled I.D.B. (meaning illicit diamond buyers) and was published in 1899 in volume form as *Knave of Diamonds*. You will find examples of some of Griffith's popular science fiction in the companion volume *Science Fiction by the Rivals of H.G. Wells*.

Francis Brett Harte's *The Stolen Cigar-Case*, from the December 1900 issue of *Pearson's*, is a rare parody of Sherlock Holmes. It was described, by Ellery Queen in *Queen's Quorum*, as "probably the best parody of Sherlock Holmes ever written". Harte's detective is Hemlock Jones—names chosen by other parodists include Thinlock Bones, Shamrock Jones, Sherlock Kombs, Solar Pons, Holmlock Shears and Picklock Holmes. Ellery Queen also edited an anthology of parodies and pastiches of Sherlock Holmes entitled *The Misadventures of Sherlock Holmes* (1944), but publication was supressed. Other authors who have written parodies of this most famous of all detectives include August Derleth, Agatha Christie, Anthony Boucher, Ellery Queen, James Barrie, Mark Twain and O. Henry—no small compliment! Brett Harte's *The Stolen Cigar-Case* was published in volume form in his *Condensed Novels* (1902). Harte was born in 1836, found sudden fame with the publication of his *Luck of Roaring Camp* in 1870, and died in 1902 in London.

In Steinbrunner and Penzler's *Encyclopaedia of Mystery and Detection*, Raffles is considered "the greatest of all fictional thieves", in addition to being "the greatest cracksman in the literature of roguery". Charles Shibuk in *The Armchair Detective* (a magazine that is essential reading for all mystery fiction buffs) called Raffles "unquestionably the greatest rogue in detective fiction". Raffles was not crime fiction's first hero-thief and he certainly was not the last, for many others have joined the ranks since then. But attitudes have changed. When the Raffles stories were first published, the moral climate of the day demanded that they should be presented under the guise of the wickedness of crime. Hence their presentation in *Cassell's Magazine* (between June and November, 1898) under the title *In the Chains of Crime*. The following year, with their publication in book form, this title was changed to *The Amateur Cracksman*, which was chosen as one of *Queen's Quorum*. It was subsequently retitled *Raffles: the Amateur Cracksman* and combined with a second volume of Raffles stories that had been published under the title *The Black Mask* (1901).

On many of his escapades Raffles was helped by a friend and accomplice called Bunny, who had been his fag (which those familiar with the world of the British public school will know is the term for a junior boy who acts as a sort of servant to a senior pupil). From time to time in this volume you may well find phrases or language reflective of the age in which these stories were written. Raffles was created by E.W. Hornung (1866-1921)—the initials stood for Ernest William—who was related by marriage to Arthur Conan Doyle. In recent years there have been several novels in which Sherlock Holmes has met real life characters; it would have been most interesting if the brothers-in-law had arranged a meeting between their two creations. The Raffles stories have, of course, been adapted for radio, films and television. The first Raffles film appeared as long ago as 1905, and over the years such famous stars as John Barrymore, Ronald Colman and David Niven have played the part of Raffles. In this volume you will meet the famous gentleman cracksman as he was first presented to the public. Another of Hornung's stories is also included: *At the Pistol's Point*, which is taken from *The Strand* for 1897.

For many years C.J. Cutcliffe Hyne (1865-1944) wrote stories about the fiery Captain Kettle and some memorable science fiction—including the novel *The Lost Continent*, which appears in the companion volume *Science Fiction by the Rivals of H.G. Wells*. Presented here in his *Tragedy of a Third Smoker*, from *The Harmsworth Magazine* of September 1898.

William le Queux (1864-1927) was a prolific writer. Ellery Queen's *The Detective Short Story* lists 22 books by him, but they were only part of his output—which included over 140 novels and short stories ranging from detection and mystery, and espionage and intrigue, to fantasy and science fiction.

Indeed, he carried an element of fantasy into his own lifestyle, and it has been said that he wrote stories about secret agents so as to finance his own work for British Intelligence! Le Queux is cited in *Queen's Quorum* for his *Mysteries of a Great City* (1920). This volume includes five of the adventures of Count Bindo di Ferraris, from *Cassell's Magazine* in 1906. Le Queux's enthusiasm for motoring is very evident from these stories, which have a grand touring car as one of the central characters.

Six stories by the prolific Mrs. Meade appeared in *Rivals of Sherlock Holmes*. Here are two more, written in partnership with Robert Eustace, which was the pseudonym of Dr. Eustace Robert Barton, who also wrote under the name of Eustace Rawlins. As Robert Eustace, Dr. Barton aided Dorothy Sayers with *The Documents of the Case* (1930). The name L.T. Meade was a nom-de-plume for Elizabeth Thomasina Meade Smith (1854-1914). *The Secret of Emu Plain* was published in *Cassell's* for December 1898, and is a rare story in that the reader is invited to contribute the answer! We, of course, have included the answer page plus the details of the prizewinners. *Followed* was published in the December 1900 issue of *The Strand*.

Baroness Orczy's story *The Old Man in the Corner* was included in *The Rivals of Sherlock Holmes* and in this volume we include another of this author's remarkable characters: Patrick Mulligan, who was known as "skin o' my tooth"—the sobriquet being devised by one of his grateful clients. Steinbrunner and Penzler described Mulligan as "one of the least physically attractive detectives in literature" and thought that "his nickname is equally unappealing". Perhaps this was why the adventures of the gross and unscrupulous lawyer were not published in book form until 1928, nearly 30 years after their magazine appearance. The five stories in this volume were taken from the June to October 1903 issues of *The Windsor Magazine*.

The character of Loveday Brooke was introduced in *Rivals of Sherlock Holmes*, and we now include two more stories by his creator Mrs. Pirkiss. Both were take from *The Ludgate Magazine* (May and June 1893).

Canon Victor Lorenzo Whitechurch (1868-1933) was a British country clergyman and later an Honorary Canon of Christ Church, Oxford. His series of railway detective stories was published in 1912 as *Thrilling Stories of the Railway*—the book also features in *Queen's Quorum*. *A Warning in Red* was published in *The Harmsworth Magazine* for December 1899.

RIVALS OF
SHERLOCK HOLMES
TWO

I

The Spawn of Fortune

ANGUS EVAN ABBOTT

The Spawn of Fortune.

By ANGUS EVAN ABBOTT.
Illustrated by ARTHUR JULE GOODMAN.

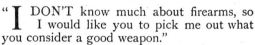

"I DON'T know much about firearms, so I would like you to pick me out what you consider a good weapon."

The salesman ran his eye along the rows of revolvers.

"This one I can recommend," he said. Its barrel glinted blue, its stock was pricked out in nickel, and its hammer filled a glittering cylinder like the nose of a ferret in a rat-hole.

"Ah, yes, that looks all right. Is it loaded? No. Kindly explain to me how the trick is done."

After he had seen the cartridges shoved into the chambers and had paid the price, Arther Bracken-bridge slipped the weapon into his breast pocket, made his way along the Strand, and, turning sharply down Villiers Street, entered the underground station.

"Earl's Court, first return," he said at the pigeon-hole, but he hastily corrected himself. "No, not return, single I mean. Earl's Court, first single."

He pocketed the ticket, grinning ruefully as he said to himself, "The return will be a free journey this time, I imagine." Half-way down the dirty stairs that lead to the platform he suddenly paused.

"What in the world possessed me to take a first ? Third would have done me quite as well. What an ass I am to-day. Ah, well, I have lived in this world first-class, and may as well go out of it first-class."

A few waiting passengers sauntered up and down the platform. Smoke hung in fantastic blue whiffs, writhing and twisting and swirling lazily towards the roof, and the gas burned yellow in the great glass globes that hung above

3

the footway. The ticket inspector at the foot of the stairs, his punch dangling to his fingers, carried on a flirtation with a buxom wench of serving-maid class.

"Besides, it will look better on the evening paper bill. 'Suicide in a Third-class Underground' seems cheap. Few persons of class enter the underground, and none travels third. Substitute 'first' for 'third,' and, well—it should make a rather taking bill, you know."

At this point in his soliloquy Arthur Brackenbridge became aware of a curious growling rumble that rapidly grew into a roar, and as if in fear of this ominous sound the black tunnel began to vomit smoke that gushed out in a dense cloud-bank. At last two yellow eyes trembled and blinked in the darkness, and the next instant a Richmond train came wheezing, rocking, screeching, and grinding out of the blackness, and stopped with a jerk at the platform. Brackenbridge ran nimbly along the carriages and jumped into the first empty compartment. Placing his hat in the rack, he let down the window and stuck his head far out, as though looking for a friend—a trick much resorted to by lovers and school-boys, who wish a compartment to them-selves. On this occasion, however, the stratagem was unavailing. At the moment the train was about to move on a brawny man rushed past the ticket inspector, and, grasping the handle of the door, gave it such a lightning-like twist and pull that had Brackenbridge not drawn in his head with rapidity he must have found himself at full length on the platform. Without one word of apology the stranger shut the door with a bang, and flung himself into a corner, never once glancing at the young man, who stood in the middle of the com-partment looking the anger he felt. To Arthur Brackenbridge's way of thinking, the entrance of this stranger was abrupt to an uncalled-for degree, and the thought of how narrowly he had escaped being flung out of the carriage determined him to remonstrate. So he opened by saying in his decided manner, empha-sised by the anger that was in him:

"My seat, sir."

The stranger glanced up; his eyes were bloodshot, and his features set and hard. He said nothing, however, and sat tight.

"My seat, sir."

This time the stranger did not even condescend so much as a glance.

"For the third time, I tell you that you are in my seat. If you doubt me, my hat on the rack above will prove what I say."

Without a word the fellow flung him-self into the opposite corner.

"Gad, he's a cool customer," Arthur muttered as he took the seat vacated by the stranger.

The man sat, or rather lay along the cushion, his two hands deep into his trousers' pockets and his eyes fixed on his foot as it rose and fell to the rocking of the carriage. He was a man passed middle life, fairly well dressed, and sturdily built.

"I'll startle this cold-blooded fellow before I'm through with him," Arthur Brackenbridge thought. Leaning for-ward he addressed the sullen man:

"I would like you to change compart-ments at the next station."

The man stared angrily at the speaker.

"And I shall do nothing of the kind," he replied decisively.

"I advise you, sir, for your own com-fort, to change."

"I look after my comfort without assistance from others. I shall not change."

"As you please," Brackenbridge re-plied in a careless tone.

The train crunched, and ground, and shuddered and came to a standstill at Westminster Bridge. Arthur Bracken-bridge spoke:

"Allow me, sir, to advise you again to change carriages. It will not put you to much trouble and may save you a lot. I speak in all good faith."

The heavy man ran his eye over the other, and there was unspeakable scorn in the glance. Then he again turned his attention to the dancing boot. When the train disappeared into the tunnel Arthur Brackenbridge sat up.

"As you have seen fit to disregard my advice, given, as I before said, in all good faith, I can only hope, sir, that you do not object to me committing suicide. I intend to blow my brains out before we reach St. James's Park Station."

The surly man leapt wildly to his feet. He threw open the carriage door and the roar of the tunnel drowned Bracken-bridge's cry to "stay." Steam and smoke in a purple cloud, and sulphur smells belched in and filled the compartment. The younger man had grasped hold of the other's arm. At last the door was

"THE MAN LEAPT WILDLY TO HIS FEET"

shut and the two stood facing each other. Brackenbridge grinned.

"I gave you fair warning. It crossed my mind that you might prefer to be elsewhere——"

"What do you mean? You are not going to kill yourself?"

"Ah, but I am."

"Good Heavens, man, you're crazy!"

"You speak like a coroner's jury, sir. As a matter of truth and of fact I am not crazy, but I'm terribly sane, which, as far as I can make out, amounts to pretty much the same thing in this world. It is only the insane that would try to live after the events of this awful day. I'm too sane to attempt to do so."

The elder glowered into the eyes of the younger. He was much the taller of the two and had to stoop low.

"Whom have you done for?" he asked abruptly.

"What do you mean?" The young man felt a trifle uneasy under the other's bloodshot eyes.

"Whom have you made away with? What did he do to you to make you do the deed?"

The fellow stepped hurriedly back into the corner and looked about him as though he feared he had been overheard. Arthur Brackenbridge blurted out:

"What the deuce do you mean, sir. 'Done for?' 'Made away with?' What an idea! You're crazy now, instead of me. It is I have been murdered, foully and brutally murdered. Yes, sir, twice this day. But here we are at St. James's and the little affair not done. I trust to your honour not to say a word to the guard, for as sure as he comes for me I shall fire and in my hurry may make a mess of it, you know. Now, out you get, that's a good fellow, and God bless you, sir. For some reason quite unexplainable I wish to be alone when, when—well, Good-bye."

The surly man stepped out, walked a dozen feet towards the exit, paused for a second or so, and then hurriedly retraced his steps, entered the compartment and shut the door after him.

"No, may I be hanged if I leave you."

Brackenbridge sat wearily back in the cushions. The stranger stood looking down upon him.

"Postpone the deed for just one station more. I want to speak with you. May I?"

Brackenbridge nodded an enforced affirmation, and the heavy man seating himself; a silence followed. At length the stranger said:

"There is but one crime in the long calendar the devil has prepared for us that warrants a man taking his life."

"Yes? What crime is that, may I ask?"

"Murder."

"My dear sir," said Brackenbridge sitting up, and speaking with animation, "My dear sir, a murderer has no need to kill himself."

"You mean Society will do the job for him?"

"Not at all, I mean quite a different thing. A murderer dies the instant his victim dies."

"O! indeed, I did not know that."

"It is so, nevertheless. A murderer may walk about, and be to all outward appearances alive, but, as a matter of fact, he is as dead as Pharaoh. His hold on the world is relaxed. His self-respect is dead, his manliness is dead, his liberty is dead; his ease of mind has been slain by the selfsame blow that slew his victim; everything that constitutes life is slain, and lies dead within him, a rubbish heap with his heart, a core of hateful fire smouldering beneath it all. Breathing, working, walking, talking, seeing—all such things are but the incidents of life. A life of falsehood and subterfuge, of wildly fleeing from a consequence, is death in its most awful form." Brackenbridge spoke rapidly and with bitter vehemence. "I tell you," he continued, "murder changes a man from a living being to a craven coward, a coward who fears to live, and fears to die."

The heavy man sat in silence for some moments.

"It seems to me," he said at length, "that one who contemplates suicide is a still more deplorable creature than a murderer."

"I don't see matters in that light at all."

"Well, I think you will agree that one who has committed murder may, at least, be presumed to have been brave at the moment of the deed."

"I suppose there is something uncanny about taking human life that demands valour of one kind or another," assented Brackenbridge.

"But with suicide it is altogether

different," continued the stranger. " The actuating impulse is cowardice, pure and simple, a weak determination to escape threatened or present pains of body or of mind. But I maintain that to deliberately, with premeditation, slay a fellow-man calls forth one glorious outburst of manhood, one period of physical triumph, of mental exultation, ineffable, supreme ; a moment when a man's feet are on the spheres, when his head is ablaze in the sun, his soul is a great licking, rolling crimson flame, and his arms are reached down through endless space to the spinning world, and his fingers creep among the crowd to clutch his shrieking victim, clutch him, and roll him in the palms, crush his bones, squeeze him, crunch him, and roll him again and again, and work him gradually, gloatingly, towards the finger-tips to hurl him, a pulpy mass, into space and everlasting blackness. Ah! I call that a supreme moment, when the crimson flame of soul-fire leaps through the smoke-clouds of a smouldering life to the very sky !"

The stranger had started to his feet, his eyes great and full of fire, his hands clinched above his head. Whirling round and facing Arthur Brackenbridge he demanded :

" Why would you kill yourself? "

" I have lost my fortune, and —— "

" What is that ? You talk of cowards ! I thought you valiant, you thought yourself so ! Bah ! why waste good powder and ball. You fear to live because, perchance, your circumstances may not be quite so pleasant as formerly. Sordid coward."

" It's not altogether a matter of money," faltered the young man. The stranger kept his eyes fixed upon him. " There's a warrant —— "

" Then you are a criminal ? "

" No, I am not."

" Why the warrant ? "

" My partner has landed us both in fraudulent bankruptcy —— "

" Are you innocent ? "

" Absolutely."

" And you fear?"

" Well, there is as much shame as fear—— "

" You are vain as well as a coward."

" To be the principal in a criminal trial is no pleasant experience; at least, so I gather from the newspapers."

The heavy man sat down again and gazed at Brackenbridge contemptuously.

" Young man, what a craven you would have me believe you. Your cowardice is so great that you are willing to stamp yourself guilty by self-murder rather than face your accusers and confound them. On my soul I am surprised you ventured out alone to kill yourself. I should have thought you would have implored some one to come with you while you took the leap into the dark. Why were you given youth, strength, health, good strong arms and sound heart if they were not intended to overcome obstacles? Think! would it not be greater far to step out before the world and say 'Here am I an honest man : where are my accusers?' rather than to lie on the floor of a railway carriage with a wreath of powder-smoke for a crown ? "

" Yes, but you see, my dear sir, to-day there has been a focussing of all that is unfortunate for me. My whole fortune is gone, the fact that it has been lost causes the police to 'want' me, and the fact that the police 'want' me has lost me—well—— "

" Out with it! Lost you what?"

Arthur Brackenbridge did not intend to say more, but the stranger's commanding gaze and imperative question left him powerless to resist. At every station he prayed that some one would enter the compartment, but the Underground is a contrary line. No one disturbed them.

" What else have you lost?" demanded the heavy man.

" Well, to 'out with it' as you ask— the girl to whom I am engaged—or was."

The stranger threw back his head and burst into a loud fit of laughter, laughter wherein there was no ghost of a trace of mirth. Brackenbridge felt indignant at the sarcastic levity of his new found combatant, but said nothing.

" Girl," the heavy man shouted. " Fine girl, indeed, that will break her promise because you've lost a pound. She gave you her word and now tells you to your face that she will not keep it."

" She has not. I tell you she— she—— "

" But you have just this minute said she told you to go about your business—— " .

" I said nothing of the sort."

" Then how know you that you have lost her?"

Brackenbridge was silent.

"THE GUARDS WERE LIFTING THE CORPSE"

"Let us be honest one to the other. Answer me: How know you?"

"Her guardian, her aunt, told me."

"My young friend, take the advice of one who has seen, experienced, learned. Have no dealings with a woman through a woman—never. Give me that revolver you have in your breast pocket."

The revolver was weakly passed over.

"Now we are coming to Earl's Court Station. Get out; be a man; walk up to the first policeman you meet—or, better still, hail a hansom and tell cabby to drive to the nearest police-station. Say to the Inspector: 'I hear there is a warrant out for me. I have come to give myself up, if you want me.'"

"By George! I don't like to do it, you know, I swear I don't; but I suppose your advice is good. I must say I do not fancy passing through the machinery of justice—the stinking police-cells, the stinking police-court, and maybe the stinking Old Bailey and the stinking Holloway as well. I don't like the idea, I say."

"Nonsense. I have little doubt that you'll find the plank bed in the cells more entertaining at least than the stone slab of the morgue."

"Don't speak of it, sir; not another word. I hadn't thought of that, 'pon my soul I hadn't. You make my flesh creep."

The stranger grinned for the first time. Arthur Brackenbridge reached for his hat and reluctantly left the carriage. He stood for a moment, his back to the compartment and his hand still on the door. Turning, he said:

"Yes, you're right. I'll do it; I'll give myself up and see what becomes of me. My name is Brackenbridge; you will, without a doubt, see it appear often enough in the newspapers during the next month or so. But, whatever becomes of me, you, sir, have saved my life. Whether you have done me a good turn or an evil one has yet to be seen; but to-night at least I am grateful, very

grateful. That slab keeps recurring to my mind, you know, and—well, good-bye, my friend, and God bless you, sir, God bless you!"

The two men clasped hands, gazing into one another's face earnestly and long. The train started with its usual wracking jerk.

The heavy man sat huddled in the corner, his brows contracted, arms folded, and his eyes fixed on his dancing foot. The train arrived at and departed from West Kensington station. He slipped his hand into his breast pocket, and slowly drew forth the revolver. The muzzle smelt blood; it looked blood. Without one glance at the weapon, but handling it as a usurer handles a gold ornament, he muttered:

"Taken one life, saved one life. Surely the one should balance the other. But he says: 'No; not one life, but two you have taken—two! two! your victim's and your own.' I believe he is as right in my case as I was in his, and the balance is against me, against me— hopelessly against me; against me now and for all eternity. He said to me: 'God bless you, sir!' I think that is of good omen. He is the last I shall meet on this earth, and he said 'God bless you, sir!'"

With his thumb he drew back the hammer of the weapon until it "clicked" twice.

"I may as well end my flight by instantaneously putting myself out of reach of my pursuers; and it is better that I do it with the young man's words ringing in my ears. He was flying to his death; I from mine. He found life; I find——"

At Hammersmith station the travellers by the train gathered round the compartment, to stand tip-toe and peer into it while the guards were lifting the corpse up from its sorrowful collapse; and next morning's papers contained the news of the suicide of the Gray's Inn murderer and the arrest of Arthur Brackenbridge.

II

The Further Adventures of Romney Pringle

CLIFFORD ASHDOWN

The Further Adventures of Romney Pringle

THE SILKWORMS OF FLORENCE.

BY CLIFFORD ASHDOWN.

"AND this is all that's left of Brede now." The old beadle withdrew his hand, and the skull, with a rattle as of an empty wooden box, fell in its iron cage again.

"How old do you say it is?" asked Mr. Pringle.

"Let me see," reflected the beadle, stroking his long grey beard. "He killed Mr. Grebble in 1742, I think it was—the date's on the tombstone over yonder in the church—and he hung in these irons a matter of sixty or seventy year. I don't rightly know the spot where the gibbet stood, but it was in a field they used to call in my young days 'Gibbet Marsh.' You'll find it round by the Tillingham, back of the windmill."

"And is this the gibbet? How dreadful!" chorused the two daughters of a clergyman, very summery, very gushing, and very inquisitive, who with their father completed the party.

"Lor, no, miss! Why, that's the Rye pillory. It's stood up here nigh a hundred year! And now I'll show you the town charters." And the beadle, with some senile hesitation of gait, led the way into a small attic.

Mr. Pringle's mythical literary agency being able to take care of itself, his chambers in Furnival's Inn had not seen him for a month past. To a man of his cultured and fastidious bent the Bank Holiday resort was especially odious; he affected regions unknown to the tripper, and his presence at Rye had been determined by Jeakes' quaint "Perambulation of the Cinque Ports," which he had lately picked up in Booksellers' Row. Wandering with his camera from one decayed city to another, he had left Rye only to hasten back when disgusted with the modernity of the other ports, and for the last fortnight his tall slim figure had haunted the town, his fair complexion swarthy and his port-wine mark almost lost in the tanning begotten of the marsh winds and the sun.

"The town's had a rare lot of charters and privileges granted to it," boasted the beadle, turning to a chest on which for all its cobwebs and mildew the lines of elaborate carving showed distinctly. Opening it, he began to dredge up parchments from the huddled mass inside, giving very free translations of the old Norman-French or Latin the while.

"Musty, dirty old things!" was the comment of the two ladies.

Pringle turned to a smaller chest standing neglected in a dark corner, whose lid, when he tried it, he found also unlocked, and which was nearly as full of papers as the larger one.

"Are these town records also?" inquired Pringle, as the beadle gathered up his robes preparatory to moving on.

"Not they," was the contemptuous reply.

"That there chest was found in the attic of an old house that's just been pulled down to build the noo bank, and it's offered to the Corporation; but I don't think they'll spend money on rubbish like that!"

"Here's something with a big seal!" exclaimed the clergyman, pouncing on a discoloured parchment with the avid interest of an antiquary. The folds were glued with damp, and endeavouring to smooth them out the parchment slipped through his fingers; it dropped plumb by the weight of its heavy seal, and as he sprang to save it his glasses fell off and buried themselves among the papers. While he hunted for them Pringle picked up the document, and began to read.

"Not much account, I should say," commented the beadle, with a supercilious snort. "Ah! you should have seen our Jubilee Address, with the town seal to it, all in blue and red and gold—cost every penny of fifty pound! That's the noo bank what you're looking at from this window. How the town is improving, to be sure!" He indicated a nightmare in red brick and stucco which had displaced a Jacobean mansion.

And while the beadle prosed Pringle read:

Cinque Ports to wit TO ALL and every the Barons Bailiffs Jurats and Commonalty of the Cinque Port of Rye and to Anthony Shipperbolt Mayor thereof:

WHEREAS it hath been adjudged by the Commission appointed under His Majesty's sign-manual of date March the twenty-third one thousand eight hundred and five that Anthony Shipperbolt Mayor of Rye hath been guilty of conduct unbefitting his office as a magistrate of the Cinque Ports and hath acted traitorously enviously and contrary to the love and affection his duty towards His Most Sacred Majesty and the good order of this Realm TO WIT that the said Anthony Shipperbolt hath accepted bribes from the enemies of His Majesty hath consorted with the same and did plot compass and go about to assist a certain prisoner of war the same being his proper ward and charge to escape from lawful custody NOW I William Pitt Lord Warden of the Cinque Ports do order and command you the said Anthony Shipperbolt and you are hereby required to forfeit and pay the sum of ten thousand pounds sterling into His Majesty's Treasury AND as immediate officer of His Majesty and by virtue and authority of each and every the ancient charters of the Cinque Ports I order and command you the said Anthony Shipperbolt to forthwith determine and refrain and you are hereby inhibited from exercising the office and dignity of Mayor of the said Cinque Port of Rye Speaker of the Cinque Ports Summoner of Brotherhood and Guestling and all and singular the liberties freedoms licences exemptions and jurisdictions of Stallage Pontage Panage Keyage Murage Piccage Passage Groundage Scutage and all other powers franchises and authorities appertaining thereunto AND I further order and command you the said Anthony Shipperbolt to render to me within seven days of the date hereof a full and true account of all monies fines amercements redemptions issues forfeitures tallies seals records lands messuages and hereditaments whatsoever and wheresoever that you hold have present custody of or have at any time received in trust for the said Cinque Port of Rye wherein fail not at your peril. AND I further order and command you the said Barons Bailiffs Jurats and Commonalty of the said Cinque Port of Rye that you straightway meet and choose some true and loyal subject of His Majesty the same being of your number as fitting to hold the said office of Mayor of the said Cinque Port whose name you shall submit to my pleasure as soon as may be FOR ALL which this shall be your sufficient authority. Given at Downing Street this sixteenth day of May in the year of our Lord one thousand eight hundred and five.

GOD SAVE THE KING.

The last two or three inches of the parchment were folded down, and seemed to have firmly adhered to the back—probably through the accidental running of the seal in hot weather. But the fall had broken the wax, and Pringle was now able to open the sheet to the full, disclosing some lines of script, faded and tremulously scrawled, it is true, but yet easy to be read:

"*To my son.—Seek for the silk-worms of Florence in Gibbet Marsh Church Spire SE × S, Winchelsea Mill SW ½ W. A.S.*"

Pringle read this curious endorsement more than once, but could make no sense of it. Concluding it was of the nature of a cypher, he made a note of it in his pocket-book with the idea of attempting a solution in the evening—a time which he found it difficult to get through, Rye chiefly depending for its attractions on its natural advantages.

By this time the clergyman had recovered his glasses, and, handing the document back to him, Pringle joined the party by the window. The banalities of the bank and other municipal improvements being exhausted, and the ladies openly yawning, the beadle proposed to show them what he evidently regarded as the chief glory of the Town Hall of Rye. The inquisitive clergyman was left studying the parchment, while the rest of the party adjourned to the council chamber. Here the guide proudly indicated the list of mayors, whose names were emblazoned on the chocolate-coloured walls to a length rivalling that of the dynasties of Egypt.

"What does this mean?" inquired Pringle. He pointed to the year 1805, where the name "Anthony Shipperbolt" appeared bracketed with another.

"That means he died during his year of office," promptly asserted the old man. He seemed never at a loss for an answer, although Pringle began to suspect that the prompter the reply the more inaccurate was it likely to be.

" Oh, what a smell of burning ! " interrupted one of the ladies.

" And where's papa ? " screamed the other. " He'll be burnt to death."

There was certainly a smell of burning, which, being of a strong and pungent nature, perhaps suggested to the excited imagination of the ladies the idea of a clergyman on fire. Pringle gallantly raced up the stairs. The fumes issued from a smouldering mass upon the floor, and beside it lay something which burnt with pyrotechnic sputtering ; but neither bore any relation to the divine. He, though well representing what Gibbon has styled " the fat slumbers of the Church," was hopping about the miniature bonfire, now sucking his fingers and anon shaking them in the air as one in great agony. Intuitively Pringle understood what had happened, and with a bound he stamped the smouldering parchment into unrecognisable tinder, and smothering the more viciously burning seal with his handkerchief he pocketed it as the beadle wheezed into the room behind the ladies, who were too concerned for their father's safety to notice the action.

" What's all this ? " demanded the beadle, and glared through his spectacles.

" I've dr-r-r-r-opped some wa-wa-wa-wax —oh ! —upon my hand ! "

" Waxo ? " echoed the beadle, sniffing suspiciously.

" He means a wax match, I think," Pringle interposed chivalrously. The parchment was completely done for, and he saw no wisdom in advertising the fact.

" I'll trouble you for your name and address," insisted the beadle in all the pride of office.

" What for ? " the incendiary objected.

" To report the matter to the Fire Committee."

" Very well, then—Cornelius Hardgiblet, rector of Logdown," was the impressive reply ; and tenderly escorted by his daughters the rector departed with such dignity as an occasional hop, when his fingers smarted a little more acutely, would allow him to assume.

It still wanted an hour or two to dinnertime as Pringle unlocked the little studio he rented on the Winchelsea road. Originally an office, he had made it convertible into a very fair dark-room, and here he was accustomed to spend his afternoons in developing the morning's photographs. But photo-

graphy had little interest for him to-day. Ever since Mr. Hardgiblet's destruction of the document—which, he felt certain, was no accident—Pringle had cast about for some motive for the act. What could it be but that the parchment contained a secret, which the rector, guessing, had wanted to keep to himself ? He must look up the incident of the mayor's degradation. So sensational an event, even for such stirring days as those, would scarcely go unrecorded by local historians. Pringle had several guide-books at hand in the studio, but a careful search only disclosed that they were unanimously silent as to Mr. Shipperbolt and his affairs. Later on, when returning, he had reason to bless his choice of an hotel. The books in the smoking-room were not limited, as usual, to a few timetables and an ancient copy of Ruff's " Guide." On the contrary, Murray and Black were prominent, and above all Hillpath's monumental " History of Rye," and in this last he found the information he sought. Said Hillpath :—

In 1805 Anthony Shipperbolt, then Mayor of Rye, was degraded from office, his property confiscated, and himself condemned to stand in the pillory with his face to the French coast, for having assisted Jules Florentin, a French prisoner of war, to escape from the Ypres Tower Prison. He was suspected of having connived at the escape of several other prisoners of distinction, presumably for reward. He had been a shipowner trading with France, and his legitimate trade suffering as a result of the war he had undoubtedly resorted to smuggling, a form of trading which, to the principals engaged in it at least, carried little disgrace with it, being winked at by even the most law-abiding persons. Shipperbolt did not long survive his degradation, and, his only son being killed soon after while resisting a revenue cutter when in charge of his father's vessel, the family became extinct.

Here, thought Pringle, was sufficient corroboration of the parchment. The details of the story were clear, and the only mysterious thing about it was the endorsement. His original idea of its being a cypher hardly squared with the simple address, " To my son," and the " A. S." with which it concluded could only stand for the initials of the deposed mayor. There was no mystery either about " Gibbet Marsh," which, according to the beadle's testimony, must have been a well-known spot a century ago, while the string of capitals he easily recognised as compass-bearings. There only remained the curious expression, " The Silkworms of Florence," and that was certainly a puzzle. Silkworms are a product of Florence, he knew ; but they were unlikely to be exported in such troublous times.

And why were they deposited in such a place as Gibbet Marsh? He turned for enlightenment to Hillpath, and pored over the passage again and again before he saw a glimmer of sense. Then suddenly he laughed, as the cypher resolved itself into a pun, and a feeble one at that. While Hillpath named the prisoner as Florentin and practically a will. He had nothing else to leave.

Pringle was early afoot the next day. Gibbet Marsh has long been drained and its very name forgotten, but the useful Murray indicated its site clearly enough for him to identify it; and it was in the middle of a wide and lonely field, embanked against the

"SOMEONE HAD BEEN BEFORE HIM!"

more than hinted at payment for services rendered, the cypher indicated where Florentine products were to be found. Shipperbolt ruined, his property confiscated, what more likely than that he should conceal the price of his treason in Gibbet Marsh—a spot almost as shunned in daylight as in darkness? Curious as the choice of the parchment for such a purpose might be, the endorsement was winter inundations, that Pringle commenced to work out the bearings approximately with a pocket-compass. He soon fixed his starting-point, the church tower dominating Rye from every point of view; but of Winchelsea there was nothing to be seen for the trees. Suddenly, just where the green mass thinned away to the northward, something rose and caught the sunbeams for a moment, again and still again, and with a steady gaze he made out the revolving sails of a windmill. This was as far as he cared to go for the moment ; without a good compass and a sounding-spud it would be a mere waste of time to attempt to fix the spot. He walked across the field, and was in the very act of mounting the stile when he noticed a dark object, which seemed to skim in jerky progression along the top of the embankment. While he looked the thing enlarged, and as the path behind the bank rose uplifted itself into the head, shoulders, and finally the entire person of the rector of Logdown. He had managed to locate Gibbet Marsh, it appeared ; but, as he stepped into the field and wandered aimlessly about, Pringle judged that he was still a long way from penetrating the retreat of the silk-worms.

Among the passengers by the last train down from London that night was Pringle. He carried a cricketing-bag, and when safely inside the studio he unpacked first a sailor's jersey, peaked cap and trousers, then a small but powerful spade, a very neat portable pick, a few fathoms of manilla rope, several short lengths of steel rod (each having a screw-head, by which they united into a single long one), and finally a three-inch prismatic compass.

Before sunrise the next morning Pringle started out to commence operations in deadly earnest, carrying his jointed rods as a walking-stick, while his coat bulged with the prismatic compass. The town, a victim to the enervating influence of the visitors, still slumbered, and he had to unbar the door of the hotel himself. He did not propose to do more than locate the exact spot of the treasure ; indeed, he felt that to do even that would be a good morning's work.

On the way down in the train he had taken a few experimental bearings from the carriage window, and felt satisfied with his own dexterity. Nevertheless, he had a constant dread lest the points given should prove inaccurate. He felt dissatisfied with the Winchelsea bearing. For aught he knew, not a single tree that now obscured the view might have been planted ; the present mill, perhaps, had not existed ; or even another might have been visible from the marsh. What might not happen in the course of nearly a century ? He had already made a little calculation, for a prismatic compass being graduated in degrees (unlike the mariner's, which has but thirty-two points), it was necessary to reduce the bearings to degrees, and this had been the result :—

Rye Church spire SE × S = 146° 15′.
Winchelsea Mill SW½W = 230° 37′.

When he reached the field not a soul was anywhere to be seen ; a few sheep browsed here and there, and high overhead a lark was singing. At once he took a bearing from the church spire. He was a little time in getting the right pointing ; he had to move step by step to the right, continuing to take observations, until at last the church weather-cock bore truly 146¼° through the sight-vane of the compass. Turning half round, he took an observation of the distant mill. He was a long way out this time ; so carefully preserving his relative position to the church, he backed away, taking alternate observations of either object until both spire and mill bore in the right directions. The point where the two bearings intersected was some fifty yards from the brink of the Tillingham and, marking the spot with his compass, Pringle began to probe the earth in a gradually widening circle, first with one section of his rod, then with another joint screwed to it, and finally with a length of three, so that the combination reached to a depth of eight feet. He had probed every square inch of a circle described perhaps twenty feet from the compass, when he suddenly stumbled upon a loose sod, nearly impaling himself upon the sounding-rod ; and before he could rise his feet, sliding and slipping, had scraped up quite a large surface of turf, as did his hands, in each case disclosing the fat, brown alluvium beneath. A curious fact was that the turf had not been cut in regular strips, as if for removal to some garden ; neatly as it was relaid, it had been lifted in shapeless patches, some large, some small, while the soil underneath was all soft and crumbling, as if that too had been recently disturbed. Someone had been before him ! Cramped and crippled by his prolonged stooping, Pringle stretched himself at length upon the turf. As he lay and listened to the song that trilled from the tiny speck just visible against a woolly cloud, he felt that it was useless to search further. That a treasure had once been hidden thereabouts he felt convinced, for anything but specie would have been useless at such an unsettled time for commercial credit, and would doubtless have been declined by Shipperbolt ; but whatever form the treasure had taken, clearly it was no longer present.

The sounds of toil increased around.

Already a barge was on its way up the muddy stream; at any moment he might be the subject of gaping curiosity. He carefully replaced the turfs, wondering the while who could have anticipated him, and what find, if any, had rewarded the searcher. Thinking it best not to return by the nearest path, he crossed the river some distance up, and taking a wide sweep halted on Cadborough Hill to enjoy for the hundredth time the sight of the glowing roofs, huddled tier after tier upon the rock, itself rising sheer from the plain; and far and beyond, and snowed all over with grazing flocks, the boundless green of the seaward marsh. Inland, the view was only less extensive, and with some ill-humour he was eyeing the scene of his fruitless labour when he observed a figure moving over Gibbet Marsh. At such a distance it was hard to see exactly what was taking place, but the action of the figure was so eccentric that, with a quick suspicion as to its identity, Pringle laid his traps upon the ground and examined it through his pocket telescope. It was indeed Mr. Hardgiblet. But the new feature in the case was that the rector appeared to be taking a bearing with a compass, and although he returned over and over again to a particular spot (which Pringle recognised as the same over which he himself had spent the early morning hours), Mr. Hardgiblet repeatedly shifted his ground to the right, to the left, and round about, as if dissatisfied with his observations. There was only one possible explanation of all this. Cleverer than Pringle had thought him, the rector must have hit upon the place indicated in the parchment, his hand must have removed the turf, and he it was who had examined the soil beneath. Not for the first time in his life, Pringle was disagreeably reminded of the folly of despising an antagonist, however contemptible he may appear. But at least he had one consolation: the rector's return and his continued observations showed that he had been no more successful in his quest than was Pringle himself. The silkworms were still unearthed.

The road down from Cadborough is long and dusty, and, what with the stiffness of his limbs and the thought of his wasted morning, Pringle, when he reached his studio and took the compass from his pocket, almost felt inclined to fling it through the open window into the "cut." But the spasm of irritability passed. He began to accuse himself of making some initial error in the calculations, and carefully went over them again—with an identical result. Now that Mr. Hardgiblet was clearly innocent of its removal, he even began to doubt the existence of the treasure. Was it not incredible, he asked himself, that for nearly a century it should have remained hidden? As to its secret (a punning endorsement on an old parchment), was it not just as open to any other investigator in all the long years that had elapsed? Besides, Shipperbolt might have removed the treasure himself in alarm for its safety. The thought of Shipperbolt suggested a new idea. Instruments of precision were unknown in those days—supposing Shipperbolt's compass had been inaccurate? He took down Norie's "Navigation," and ran through the chapter on the compass. There was a section headed "Variation and how to apply it," which he skimmed through, considering that the question did not arise, when, carelessly reading on, his attention was suddenly arrested by a table of "Changes in variation from year to year." Running his eye down this he made the startling discovery that, whereas the variation at that moment was about 16° 31′ west, in 1805 it was no less than 24°. Here was indeed a wide margin for error. All the time he was searching for the treasure it was probably lying right at the other side of the field!

At once he started to make a rough calculation, determined that it should be a correct one this time. As the variation of 1805 and that of the moment showed a difference of 7° 29′, to obtain the true bearing it was necessary for him to subtract this difference from Shipperbolt's points, thus:—

Rye Church spire SE × S = 146° 15′, deduct 7° 29′ = 138° 46′.

Winchelsea Mill SW$\frac{1}{2}$W = 230° 37′, deduct 7° 29′ = 223° 8′.

The question of the moment concerned his next step. Up to the present Mr. Hardgiblet appeared unaware of the error. But how long, thought Pringle, would he remain so? Any work on navigation would set him right, and as he seemed keenly on the scent of the treasure he was unlikely to submit to a check of this nature. Like Pringle, too, he seemed to prefer the early morning hours for his researches. Clearly there was no time to lose.

On his way up to lunch Pringle remarked that the whole town was agog. Crowds

"A FEW OF THESE, FRESH FROM A BATH OF WEAK ACID, GLOWED GOLDEN AS THE
SUNLIGHT. . . . SUCH WERE THE SILKWORMS OF FLORENCE"

were pouring in from the railway station; at every corner strangers were inquiring their road; the shops were either closed or closing; a steam roundabout hooted in the cricket-field. The holiday aspect of things was marked by the display on all sides of uncomfortably best clothing, worn with a reckless and determined air of Pleasure Seeking. Even the artists, the backbone of the place, had shared the excitement, or else, resenting the invasion of their pitches by the unaccustomed crowd, were sulking indoors. Anyhow, they had disappeared. Not until he reached the hotel and read on a poster the programme of the annual regatta to be held that day, did Pringle realise the meaning of it all. In the course of lunch—which, owing to the general disorganisation of things, was a somewhat scrambled meal—it occurred to him that

here was his opportunity. The regatta was evidently the great event of the year; every idler would be drawn to it, and no worker who could be spared would be absent. The treasure-field would be even lonelier than in the days of Brede's gibbet. He would be able to locate the treasure that afternoon once for all; then, having marked the spot, he could return at night with his tools and remove it.

When Pringle started out the streets were vacant and quiet as on a Sunday, and he arrived at the studio to find the quay an idle waste and the shipping in the "cut" deserted. As to the meadow, when he got there, it was forsaken even by the sheep. He was soon at work with his prismatic compass, and after half an hour's steady labour he struck a spot about an eighth of a mile distant from the scene of his morning's failure. Placing his compass as before at the point of intersection, he began a systematic puncturing of the earth around it. It was a wearisome task, and, warned by his paralysis of the morning, he rose every now and then to stretch and watch for possible intruders. Hours seemed to have passed, when the rod encountered something hard. Leaving it in position, he probed all around with another joint, but there was no resistance even when he doubled its length, and his sense of touch assured him this hardness was merely a casual stone. Doggedly he resumed his task until the steel jammed again with a contact less harsh and unyielding. Once more he left the rod touching the buried mass, and probed about, still meeting an obstruction. And then with widening aim he stabbed and stabbed, striking this new thing until he had roughly mapped a space some twelve by eight inches. No stone was this, he felt assured ; the margins were too abrupt, the corners too sharp, for aught but a chest. He rose exultingly. Here beneath his feet were the silkworms of Florence. The secret was his alone. But it was growing late ; the afternoon had almost merged into evening, and far away across the field stretched his shadow. Leaving his sounding-rod buried with the cord attached, he walked towards a hurdle on the river-bank, paying out the cord as he went, and hunted for a large stone. This found, he tied a knot in the cord to mark where the hurdle stood, and following it back along the grass pulled up the rod and pressed the stone upon the loosened earth in its place. Last of all, he wound the cord upon the rod. His task would be an easy one again. All he need do was to find the knot, tie the cord at that point to the hurdle, start off with the rod in hand, and when all the cord had run off search for the stone to right or left of the spot he would find himself standing on.

As he re-entered the town groups of people were returning from the regatta— the sea-faring to end the day in the abounding taverns, the staider on their way to the open-air concert, the cinematograph, and the fireworks, which were to brim the cup of their dissipation. Pringle dined early, and then made his way to the concert-field, and spent a couple of hours in studying the natural history of the Ryer. The fireworks were announced for nine, and as the hour approached the excitement grew and the audience swelled. When a fairly accurate census of Rye might have been taken in

the field, Pringle edged through the crowd and hurried along the deserted streets to the studio. To change his golf-suit for the sea-clothing he had brought from town was the work of a very few minutes, and his port-wine mark never resisted the smart application of a little spirit. Then, packing the sounding-rod and cord in the cricketing bag, along with the spade, pick, and rope, he locked the door, and stepped briskly out along the solitary road. From the little taverns clinging to the rock opposite came roars of discordant song, for while the losers in the regatta sought consolation, the winners paid the score, and all grew steadily drunk together. He lingered a moment on the sluice to watch the tide as it poured impetuously up from the lower river. A rocket whizzed, and as it burst high over the town a roar of delight was faintly borne across the marsh.

Although the night was cloudy and the moon was only revealed at long intervals, Pringle, with body bent, crept cautiously from bush to bush along the bank ; his progress was slow, and the hurdle had been long in sight before he made out a black mass in the water below. At first he took it for the shadow of a bush that stood by, but as he came nearer it took the unwelcome shape of a boat with its painter fast to the hurdle ; and throwing himself flat in the grass he writhed into the opportune shade of the bush. It was several minutes before he ventured to raise his head and peer around, but the night was far too dark for him to see many yards in any direction —least of all towards the treasure. As he watched and waited he strove to imagine some reasonable explanation of the boat's appearance on the scene. At another part of the river he would have taken slight notice of it ; but it was hard to see what anyone could want in the field at that hour, and the spot chosen for landing was suggestive. What folly to have located the treasure so carefully ! He must have been watched that afternoon ; round the field were scores of places where a spy might conceal himself. Then, too, who could have taken such deep interest in his movements ? Who but Mr. Hardgiblet, indeed ? This set him wondering how many had landed from the boat ; but a glance showed that it carried only a single pair of sculls, and when he wriggled nearer he saw but three footprints upon the mud, as of one who had taken just so many steps across it.

The suspense was becoming intolerable.

A crawl of fifty yards or so over damp grass was not to be lightly undertaken ; but he was just on the point of coming out from the shadow of the bush, when a faint rhythmic sound arose, to be followed by a thud. He held his breath, but could hear nothing more. He counted up to a hundred—still silence. He rose to his knees, when the sound began again, and now it was louder. It ceased ; again there was the thud, and then another interval of silence. Once more ; it seemed quite close, grew louder, louder still, and resolved itself into the laboured breathing of a man who now came into view. He was bending under a burden which he suddenly dropped, as if exhausted, and then, after resting awhile, slowly raised it to his shoulders and panted onwards, until, staggering beneath his load, he lurched against the hurdle, his foot slipped, and he rolled with a crash down the muddy bank. In that moment Pringle recognised the more than usually unctuous figure of Mr. Hardgiblet, who embraced a small oblong chest. Spluttering and fuming, the rector scrambled to his feet, and after an unsuccessful hoist or two, dragged the chest into the boat. Then, taking a pause for breath, he climbed the bank again and tramped across the field.

Mr. Hardgiblet was scarcely beyond ear-shot when Pringle, seizing his bag, jumped down to the water-side. He untied the painter, and shoving off with his foot, scrambled into the boat as it slid out on the river. With a paddle of his hand alongside, he turned the head up stream, and then dropped his bag with all its contents overboard and crouched along the bottom. A sharp cry rang out behind, and, gently he peeped over the gunwale. There by the hurdle stood Mr. Hardgiblet, staring thunderstruck at the vacancy. The next moment he caught sight of the strayed boat, and started to run after it ; and as he ran, with many a trip and stumble of wearied limbs, he gasped expressions which were not those of resignation to his mishap. Meantime, Pringle, his face within a few inches of the little chest, sought for some means of escape. He had calculated on the current bearing him out of sight long before the rector could return, but such activity as this discounted all his plans. All at once he lost the sounds of pursuit, and, raising his head, he saw that Mr. Hardgiblet had been forced to make a *détour* round a little plantation which grew to the water's edge. The next second Pringle had seized the sculls, and with a couple of long rapid strokes grounded the boat beneath a bush on the opposite bank. There he tumbled the chest on to the mud, and jumping after it shoved the boat off again. As it floated free and resumed its course up stream, Pringle shouldered the chest, climbed up the bank, and keeping in the shade of a hedge, plodded heavily across the field.

Day was dawning as Pringle extinguished the lamp in his studio, and setting the shutters ajar allowed the light to fall upon the splinters, bristling like a cactus-hedge, of what had been an oaken chest. The wood had proved hard as the iron which clamped and bound it, but scarcely darker or more begrimed than the heap of metal discs it had just disgorged. A few of these, fresh from a bath of weak acid, glowed golden as the sunlight, displaying indifferently a bust with " *Bonaparte Premier Consul* " surrounding it, or on the reverse " *République Française, anno XI.* 20 *francs.*" Such were the silkworms of Florence.

The Further Adventures of Romney Pringle

THE SUBMARINE BOAT.

BY CLIFFORD ASHDOWN.

RIC - TRAC! *tric-trac!* went the black and white discs as the players moved them over the backgammon board in expressive justification of the French term for the game. *Tric-trac!* They are indeed a nation of poets, reflected Mr. Pringle. Was not *Teuf-teuf!* for the motor-car a veritable inspiration? And as he smoked, the not unmusical clatter of the enormous wooden discs filled the atmosphere.

In these days of cookery not entirely based upon *air-tights*—to use the expressive Americanism for tinned meats—it is no longer necessary for the man who wishes to dine, as distinguished from the mere feeding animal, to furtively seek some restaurant in remote Soho, jealously guarding its secret from his fellows. But Mr. Pringle, in his favourite study of human nature, was an occasional visitor to the "*Poissonière*" in Gerrard Street, and, the better to pursue his researches, had always denied familiarity with the foreign tongues he heard around him. The restaurant was distinctly close—indeed, some might have called it stuffy—and Pringle, though near a ventilator, thoughtfully provided by the management, was fast being lulled into drowsiness, when a man who had taken his seat with a companion at the next table leaned across the intervening gulf and addressed him.

"*Nous ne vous dérangeons pas, monsieur?*"

Pringle, with a smile of fatuous un-comprehending, bowed, but said never a word.

"*Cochon d'Anglais, n'entendez-vous pas?*"

"I'm afraid I do not understand," returned Pringle, shaking his head hopelessly, but still smiling.

"*Canaille! Faut-il que je vous tire le nez?*" persisted the Frenchman, as, apparently still sceptical of Pringle's assurance, he added threats to abuse.

"I have known the English gentleman a long time, and without a doubt he does not understand French," testified the waiter who had now come forward for orders. Satisfied by this corroboration of Pringle's innocence, the Frenchman bowed and smiled sweetly to him, and, ordering a bottle of *Clos de Vougeot*, commenced an earnest conversation with his neighbour.

By the time this little incident had closed, Pringle's drowsiness had given place to an intense feeling of curiosity. For what purpose could the Frenchman have been so insistent in disbelieving his expressed ignorance of the language? Why, too, had he striven to make Pringle betray himself by resenting the insults showered upon him? In a Parisian restaurant, as he knew, far more trivial affronts had ended in meetings in the Bois de Boulogne. Besides, *cochon* was an actionable term of opprobrium in France. The Frenchman and his companion had seated themselves at the only vacant table, also it was in a corner; Pringle, at the next, was the single person within ear-shot, and the Frenchman's extraordinary behaviour could only be due to a consuming thirst for privacy. Settling himself in an easy position, Pringle closed his eyes, and while appearing to resume his slumber, strained every nerve to discern the lightest word that passed at the next table. Dressed in the choicest mode of Piccadilly, the Frenchman bore himself with all the intolerable self-consciousness of the *Boulevardier ;* but there was no trace of good-natured levity in the dark aquiline features, and the evil glint of the eyes recalled visions of an operatic Mephistopheles. His guest was unmistakably an Englishman of the bank-clerk type, who contributed his share of the conversation in halting Anglo-French, punctuated by nervous laughter as, with agonising pains, he dredged his memory for elusive colloquialisms.

Freely translated, this was what Pringle heard :

" So your people have really decided to take up the submarine, after all ? "

" Yes ; I am working out the details of some drawings in small-scale."

" But are they from headquarters ? "

" Certainly ! Duly initialled and passed by the chief constructor."

" And you are making——"

" Full working-drawings."

" There will be no code or other secret about them ? "

" What I am doing can be understood by any naval architect."

" Ah, an English one ! "

" The measurements, of course, are English, but they are easily convertible."

" You could do that ? "

" Too dangerous ! Suppose a copy in metric scale were found in my possession ! Besides, any draughtsman could reduce them in an hour or two."

" And when can you let me have it ? "

" In about two weeks."

" Impossible ! I shall not be here."

" Unless something happens to let me get on with it quickly, I don't see how I can do it even then. I am never sufficiently free from interruption to take tracings ; there are far too many eyes upon me. The only chance I have is to spoil the thing as soon as I have the salient points worked out on it, and after I have pretended to destroy it, smuggle it home ; then I shall have to take elaborate notes every day and work out the details from them in the evening. It is simply impossible for me to attempt to take a finished drawing out of the yard, and, as it is, I don't quite see my way to getting the spoilt one out—they look so sharply after spoilt drawings."

" Two weeks you say, then ? "

" Yes ; and I shall have to sit up most nights copying the day's work from my notes to do it."

" Listen ! In a week I must attend at the Ministry of Marine in Paris, but our military *attaché* is my friend. I can trust him ; he shall come down to you."

" What, at Chatham ? Do you wish to ruin me ? " A smile from the Frenchman. " No ; it must be in London, where no one knows me."

" Admirable ! My friend will be better able to meet you."

" Very well, as soon as I am ready I will telegraph to you."

" Might not the address of the embassy be remarked by the telegraph officials ? Your English post-office is charmingly unsuspicious, but we must not risk anything."

" Ah, perhaps so. Well, I will come up to London and telegraph to you from here. But your representative—will he be prepared for it ? "

" I will warn him to expect it in fourteen days." He made an entry in his pocketbook. " How will you sign the message ? "

" Gustave Zédé," suggested the Englishman, sniggering for the first and only time.

" Too suggestive. Sign yourself ' Pauline,' and simply add the time."

" ' Pauline,' then. Where shall the rendezvous be ? "

" The most public place we can find."

" Public ? "

" Certainly. Some place where everyone will be too much occupied with his own affairs to notice you. What say you to your Nelson's column ? There you can wait in a way we shall agree upon."

" It would be a difficult thing for me to wear a disguise."

" All disguises are clumsy unless one is an expert. Listen ! You shall be gazing at the statue with one hand in your breast—so."

" Yes ; and I might hold a ' Baedeker ' in my other hand."

" Admirable, my friend ! You have the true spirit of an artist," sneered the Frenchman.

" Your representative will advance and say to me, ' Pauline,' and the exchange can be made without another word."

" Exchange ? "

" I presume your Government is prepared to pay me handsomely for the very heavy risks I am running in this matter," said the Englishman stiffly.

" Pardon, my friend ! How imbecile of

me! I am authorised to offer you ten thousand francs."

A pause, during which the Englishman made a calculation on the back of an envelope.

"That is four hundred pounds," he remarked, tearing the envelope into carefully minute fragments. "Far too little for such a risk."

"Permit me to remind you, my friend, that you came in search of me, or rather of those I represent. You have something to sell? Good! But it is customary for the merchant to display his wares first."

"I pledge myself to give you copies of the working-drawings made for the use of the artificers themselves. I have already met you oftener than is prudent. As I say, you offer too little."

"Should the drawings prove useless to us, we should, of course, return them to your Admiralty, explaining how they came into our possession." There was an unpleasant smile beneath the Frenchman's waxed moustache as he spoke. "What sum do you ask?"

"Five hundred pounds in small notes—say, five pounds each."

"That is—what do you say? Ah, twelve thousand five hundred francs! Impossible! My limit is twelve thousand."

To this the Englishman at length gave an ungracious consent, and after some adroit compliments, beneath which the other sought to bury his implied threat, the pair rose from the table. Either by accident or design, the Frenchman stumbled over the feet of Pringle, who, with his long legs stretching out from under the table, his head bowed and his lips parted, appeared in a profound slumber. Opening his eyes slowly, he feigned a lifelike yawn, stretched his arms, and gazed lazily around, to the entire satisfaction of the Frenchman, who, in the act of parting with his companion, was watching him from the door.

Calling for some coffee, Pringle lighted a cigarette, and reflected with a glow of indignant patriotism upon the sordid transaction he had become privy to. It is seldom that public servants are in this country found ready to betray their trust—with all honour be it recorded of them! But there ever exists the possibility of some under-paid official succumbing to the temptation at the command of the less scrupulous representatives of foreign powers, whose actions in this respect are always ignored officially by their superiors. To Pringle's somewhat cynical

imagination, the sordid huckstering of a dockyard draughtsman with a French naval *attaché* appealed as corroboration of Walpole's famous principle, and as he walked homewards to Furnival's Inn, the seat of his fictitious literary agency, he determined, if possible, to turn his discovery to the mutual advantage of his country and himself—especially the latter.

During the next few days Pringle elaborated a plan of taking up a residence at Chatham, only to reject it as he had done many previous ones. Indeed, so many difficulties presented themselves to every single course of action, that the tenth day after found him strolling down Bond Street in the morning without having taken any further step in the matter. With his characteristic fastidious neatness in personal matters, he was bound for the Piccadilly establishment of the chief and, for West-Enders, the only firm of hatters in London.

"Breton Stret, do you noh?" said a voice suddenly. And Pringle, turning, found himself accosted by a swarthy foreigner.

"Bruton Street, *n'est-ce pas?*" Pringle suggested.

"*Mais oui, Brrruten Stret, monsieur!*" was the reply in faint echo of the English syllables.

"*Le voila! à droite,*" was Pringle's glib direction. Politely raising his hat in response to the other's salute, he was about to resume his walk when he noticed that the Frenchman had been joined by a companion, who appeared to have been making similar inquiries. The latter started and uttered a slight exclamation on meeting Pringle's eye. The recognition was mutual—it was the French *attaché!* As he hurried down Bond Street, Pringle realised with acutest annoyance that his deception at the restaurant had been unavailing, while he must now abandon all hope of a counter-plot for the honour of his country, to say nothing of his own profit. The port-wine mark on his right cheek was far too conspicuous for the *attaché* not to recognise him by it, and he regretted his neglect to remove it as soon as he had decided to follow up the affair. Forgetful of all beside, he walked on into Piccadilly, and it was not until he found himself more than half-way back to his chambers that he remembered the purpose for which he had set out; but matters of greater moment now claimed his attention, and he endeavoured by the brisk exercise to work off some of the chagrin with which he was consumed. Only as he reached the Inn and turned into the gateway did it occur to him that he had been culpably careless in thus going straight home-ward. What if he had been followed? Never in his life had he shown such dis-regard of ordinary precautions. Glancing back, he just caught a glimpse of a figure which seemed to whip behind the corner of the gateway. He retraced his steps and looked out into Holborn. There, in the very act of retreat, and still but a few feet from the gate, was the *attaché* himself. Cursing the persistence of his own folly, Pringle dived through the arch again, and determined that the Frenchman should discover no more that day he turned nimbly to the left and ran up his own stairway before the pursuer could have time to re-enter the Inn.

The most galling reflection was his absolute impotence in the matter. Through lack of the most elementary foresight he had been fairly run to earth, and could see no way of ridding himself of this unwelcome attention. To transfer his domicile, to tear himself up by the roots as it were, was out of the question; and as he glanced around him, from the soft carpets and luxurious chairs to the warm, distempered walls with their old prints above the dado of dwarf book-cases, he felt that the pang of severance from the refined associations of his chambers would be too acute. Besides, he would inevitably be tracked elsewhere. He would gain nothing by the transfer. One thing at least was absolutely certain—the trouble which the Frenchman was taking to watch him showed the importance he attached to Pringle's discovery. But this again only in-creased his disgust with the ill-luck which had met him at the very outset. After all, he had done nothing illegal, however contrary it might be to the code of ethics, so that if it pleased them the entire French legation might continue to watch him till the Day of Judgment, and, consoling himself with this reflection, he philosophically dismissed the matter from his mind.

It was nearing six when he again left the Inn for Pagani's, the Great Portland Street restaurant which he much affected; instead of proceeding due west, he crossed Holborn, intending to bear round by way of the Strand and Regent Street, and so get up an appetite. In Staple Inn he paused a moment in the further archway. The little square, always reposeful amid the stress and turmoil of its environment, seemed doubly so this evening, its eighteenth-century calm so welcome after the raucous thoroughfare. An ap-proaching footfall echoed noisily, and as Pringle moved from the shadow of the narrow wall the newcomer hesitated and stopped, and then made the circuit of the square, scanning the doorways as if in search of a name. The action was not unnatural, and twenty-four hours earlier Pringle would have thought nothing of it, but after the events of the morning he endowed it with a personal interest, and, walking on, he as-cended the steps into Southampton Buildings and stopped by a hoarding. As he looked back he was rewarded by the sight of a man stealthily emerging from the archway and making his way up the steps, only to halt as he suddenly came abreast of Pringle. Although his face was unfamiliar, Pringle could only conclude that the man was follow-ing him, and all doubt was removed when, having walked along the street and turning about at the entrance to Chancery Lane, he saw the spy had resumed the chase and was now but a few yards back. Pringle, as a philosopher, felt more inclined to laughter than resentment at this ludicrous espionage. In a spirit of mischief, he pursued his way to the Strand at a tortoise-like crawl, halting as if doubtful of his way at every corner, and staring into every shop whose lights still invited customers. Once or twice he even doubled back, and passing quite close to the man, had several opportunities of examining him. He was quite unobtrusive, even re-spectable-looking; there was nothing of the foreigner about him, and Pringle shrewdly conjectured that the *attaché*, wearied of sentry-go, had turned it over to some English servant on whom he could rely.

Thus shepherded, Pringle arrived at the restaurant, from which he only emerged after a stay maliciously prolonged over each item of the *menu*, followed by the smoking of no fewer than three cigars of a brand specially lauded by the proprietor. With a measure of humanity diluting his malice, he was about to offer the infallibly exhausted sentinel some refreshment when he came out, but as the man was invisible, Pringle started for home, taking much the same route as before, and calmly debating whether or no the cigars he had just sampled would be a wise investment; nor until he had reached Southampton Buildings and the sight of the hoarding recalled the spy's dis-comfiture, did he think of looking back to see if he were still followed. All but the main thoroughfares were by this time deserted, and although he shot a keen glance up and down Chancery Lane, now clear of all but the most casual traffic, not a soul was anywhere near him. By a curious psychological process Pringle felt inclined to resent the man's absence. He had begun to regard him almost in the light of a body-guard, the private escort of some eminent politician. Besides, the whole incident was pregnant with possibilities appealing to his keenly intellectual sense of humour, and as he passed the hoarding, he peered into its shadow with the half-admitted hope that his attendant might be lurking in the depths. Later on he recalled how, as he glanced upwards, a man's figure passed like a shadow from a ladder to an upper platform of the scaffold. The vision, fleeting and unsubstantial, had gone almost before his retina had received it, but the momentary halt was to prove his salvation. Even as he turned to walk on, a cataract of planks, amid scaffold-poles and a chaos of loose bricks, crashed on the spot he was about to traverse ; a stray beam, more erratic in its descent, caught his hat, and, telescoping it, glanced off his shoulder, bearing him to the ground, where he lay dazed by the sudden uproar and half-choked by the cloud of dust. Rapid and disconcerting as was the event, he remembered afterwards a dim and spectral shape approaching through the gloom. In a dreamy kind of way he connected it with that other shadow-figure he had seen high up on the scaffold, and as it bent over him he recognised the now familiar features of the spy. But other figures replaced the first, and, when helped to his feet, he made futile search for it amid the circle of faces gathered round him. He judged it an hallucination. By the time he had undergone a tentative dust-down, he was sufficiently collected to acknowledge the sympathetic congratulations of the crowd and to decline the homeward escort of a constable.

In the privacy of his chambers, his ideas began to clarify. Events arranged themselves in logical sequence, and the spectres assumed more tangible form. A single question dwarfed all others. He asked himself, "Was the cataclysm such an accident as it appeared ?" And as he surveyed the battered ruins of his hat, he began to realise how nearly had he been the victim of a murderous vendetta !

When he arose the next morning, he

"'WITHOUT A DOUBT HE DOES NOT UNDERSTAND FRENCH'"

scarcely needed the dilapidated hat to remind him of the events of yesterday. Normally a sound and dreamless sleeper, his rest had been a series of short snatches of slumber interposed between longer spells of rumination. While he marvelled at the intensity of malice which he could no longer doubt pursued him —a vindictiveness more natural to a mediæval Italian state than to this present-day metropolis—he bitterly regretted the fatal curiosity which had brought him to such an extremity. By no means deficient in the grosser forms of physical courage, his sense that in the game which was being played, his adversaries, as unscrupulous as they were crafty, held all the cards, and, above all, that their espionage effectually prevented him filling the gaps in the plot which he had as yet only half-discovered, was especially galling to his active and somewhat neurotic temperament. Until yesterday he had almost decided to drop the affair of the *Restaurant "Poissonière,"* but now, after what he firmly believed to be a deliberate attempt to assassinate him, he realised the desperate situation of a duellist with his back to a wall—having scarce room to parry, he felt the prick of his antagonist's rapier deliberately goading him to an incautious thrust. Was he regarded as the possessor of a dangerous secret ? Then it behoved him to strike, and that without delay.

Now that he was about to attack, a disguise was essential ; and reflecting how lamentably he had failed through the absence of one hitherto, he removed the port-wine mark from his right cheek with his customary spirit-lotion, and blackened his fair hair with a few smart applications of a preparation from his bureau. It was with a determination to shun any obscure streets or alleys, and especially all buildings in course of erection, that he started out after his usual light breakfast. At first he was doubtful whether he was being followed or not, but after a few experimental turns and doublings he was unable to single out any regular attendant of his walk ; either his disguise had proved effectual, or his enemies imagined that the attempt of last night had been less innocent in its results.

Somewhat soothed by this discovery, Pringle had gravitated towards the Strand and was nearing Charing Cross, when he observed a man cross from the station to the opposite corner carrying a brown-paper roll. With his thoughts running in the one direction, Pringle in a flash recognised the dockyard draughtsman. Could he be even now on his way to keep the appointment at Nelson's Column ?

Had he been warned of Pringle's discovery, and so expedited his treacherous task ? And thus reflecting, Pringle determined at all hazards to follow him. The draughtsman made straight for the telegraph office. It was now the busiest time of the morning, most of the little desks were occupied by more or less glib message-writers, and the draughtsman had found a single vacancy at the far end when Pringle followed him in and reached over his shoulder to withdraw a form from the rack in front of him. Grabbing three or four, Pringle neatly spilled them upon the desk, and with an abject apology hastily gathered them up together with the form the draughtsman was employed upon. More apologies, and Pringle, seizing a suddenly vacant desk, affected to compose a telegram of his own. The draughtsman's message had been short, and (to Pringle) exceptionally sweet, consisting as it did of the three words—" Four-thirty, Pauline." The address Pringle had not attempted to read—he knew that already. The moment the other left Pringle took up a sheaf of forms, and, as if they had been the sole reason of his visit, hurried out of the office and took a hansom back to Furnival's Inn.

Here his first care was to fold some newspapers into a brown-paper parcel resembling the one carried by the draughtsman as nearly as he remembered it, and having cut a number of squares of stiff tissue paper, he stuffed an envelope with them and pondered over a cigarette the most difficult stage of his campaign. Twice had the draughtsman seen him. Once at the restaurant, in his official guise as the sham literary agent, with smooth face, fair hair, and the fugitive port-wine mark staining his right cheek ; again that morning, with blackened hair and unblemished face. True, he might have forgotten the stranger at the restaurant; on the other hand, he might not—and Pringle was then (as always) steadfastly averse to leaving anything to chance. Besides, in view of this sudden journey to London, it was very likely that he had received warning of Pringle's discovery. Lastly, it was more than probable that the spy was still on duty, even though he had failed to recognise Pringle that morning. The matter was clinched by a single glance at the Venetian mirror above the mantel, which reflected a feature he had overlooked—his now blackened hair. Nothing remained for him but to assume a disguise which should impose on both the spy and the draughtsman, and after some thought he decided to make up as a

Frenchman of the South, and to pose as a servant of the French embassy. Reminiscent of the immortal Tartarin, his ready bureau furnished him with a stiff black moustache and some specially stout horsehair to typify the stubbly beard of that hero. When, at almost a quarter to four, he descended into the Inn with the parcel in his hand, a Baedeker and the envelope of tissues in his pocket, a cab was just setting down, and impulsively he chartered it as far as Exeter Hall. Concealed in the cab, he imagined he would the more readily escape observation, and by the time he alighted, flattered himself that any pursuit had been baffled. As he discharged the cab, however, he noticed a hansom draw up a few paces in the rear, whilst a man got out and began to saunter westward behind him. His suspicions alert, although the man was certainly a stranger, Pringle at once put him to the test by entering Romano's and ordering a small whiskey. After a decent delay, he emerged, and his pulse quickened when he saw a couple of doors off the same man staring into a shopwindow! Pringle walked a few yards back, and then crossed to the opposite side of the street, but although he dodged at infinite peril through a string of omnibuses, he was unable to shake off his satellite, who, with unswerving persistence, occupied the most limited horizon whenever he looked back.

"HELD HIM IN THE ANGLE OF THE PLINTH"

For almost the first time in his life, Pringle began to despair. The complacent regard of his own precautions had proved but a fool's paradise. Despite his elaborate disguise, he must have been plainly recognisable to his enemies, and he began to ask himself whether it was not useless to struggle further. As he paced slowly on, an indefinable depression stole over him. He thought of the heavy price so nearly exacted for his interposition. Resentment surged over him at the memory, and his hand clenched on the parcel. The contact furnished the very stimulus he required. The instrument of settling such a score was in his hands, and rejecting his timorous doubts, he strode on, determined to make one bold and final stroke for vengeance. The shadows had lengthened appreciably, and the quarter chiming from near St. Martin's warned him that there was no time to lose—the spy must be got rid of at any cost. Already could he see the estuary of the Strand, with the Square widening beyond; on his right loomed the tunnel of the Lowther Arcade, with its vista of juvenile delights. The sight was an inspiration. Darting in, he turned off sharp to the left into an artist's repository, with a double entrance to the Strand and the Arcade, and, softly closing the door, peeped through the palettes and frames which hung upon the glass. Hardly had they ceased swinging to his movement when he had the satisfaction of seeing the spy, the scent already cold, rush furiously up the Arcade, his course marked by falling toys and the cries of the outraged stall-keepers. Turning, Pringle made the purchase of a sketching-block, the first thing handy, and then passed through the door which gave on the Strand. At the post-office he stopped to survey the scene. A single policeman stood by the eastward base of the column, and the people scattered round seemed but ordinary way-farers, but just across the maze of traffic was a spectacle of intense interest to him. At the quadrant of the Grand Hotel, patrolling aimlessly in front of the shops, at which he seemed too perturbed to stare for more than a few seconds at a time, the draughtsman kept palpitating vigil until the clock should strike the half-hour of his treason. True to the Frenchman's advice, he sought safety in a crowd, avoiding the desert of the square until the last moment.

It wanted two minutes to the half-hour when Pringle opened his Baedeker, and thrusting one hand into his breast, examined the statue and coil of rope erected to the glory of our greatest hero. "*Pauline!*" said a voice, with the musical inflection un-attainable by any but a Frenchman. Beside him stood a slight, neatly dressed young man, with close-cropped hair, and a mous-tache and imperial, who cast a significant look at the parcel. Pringle immediately held it towards him, and the dark gentleman pro-ducing an envelope from his breast-pocket, the exchange was effected in silence. With bows and a raising of hats they parted, while Big Ben boomed on his eight bells.

The *attaché's* representative had disap-peared some minutes beyond the western-most lion before the draughtsman appeared from the opposite direction, his uncertain steps intermitted by frequent halts and nervous backward glances. With his back to the National Gallery he produced a Baedeker and commenced to stare up at the monument, withdrawing his eyes every now and then to cast a shamefaced look to right and left. In his agitation the draughts-man had omitted the hand-in-the-breast attitude, and even as Pringle advanced to his side and murmured "*Pauline,*" his legs (almost stronger than his will) seemed to be urging him to a flight from the field of dis-honour. With tremulous eagerness he thrust a brown-paper parcel into Pringle's hands, and, snatching the envelope of tissue slips, rushed across the road and disappeared in the bar of the Grand Hotel.

Pringle turned to go, but was confronted by a revolver, and as his eye traversed the barrel and met that of its owner, he recognised the Frenchman to whom he had just sold the bundle of newspapers. Dodging the weapon, he tried to spring into the open, but a restraining grip on each elbow held him in the angle of the plinth, and turning ever so little Pringle found himself in custody of the man whom he had last seen in full cry up the Lowther Arcade. No constable was anywhere near, and even casual passengers walked unheeding by the nook, so quiet was the progress of this little drama. Lowering his revolver, the dark gentleman picked up the parcel which had fallen from Pringle in the struggle. He opened it with delicacy, partially withdrew some sheets of tracing-paper, which he intently examined, and then placed the whole in an inner pocket, and giving a sign to the spy to loose his grasp, he spoke for the first time.

" May I suggest, sir," he said in excellent English with the slightest foreign accent, " may I suggest that in future you do not meddle with what cannot possibly concern you ? These documents have been bought and sold, and although you have been good enough to act as intermediary in the trans-action, I can assure you we were under no necessity of calling on you for your help." Here his tone hardened, and, speaking with less calmness, the accent became more noticeable : " I discovered your impertinence in selling me a parcel of worthless papers very shortly after I left you. Had you succeeded in the attempt you appear to have planned so carefully, it is possible you might have lived long enough to regret it—*perhaps not!* I wish you good-day, sir." He bowed, as did his companion, and Pringle, walking on, turned up by the corner of the Union Club.

Dent's clock marked twenty minutes to five, and Pringle reflected how much had been compressed into the last quarter of an hour. True, he had not prevented the sale of his country's secrets ; on the other hand— he pressed the packet which held the enve-lope of notes. Hailing a cab, he was about to step in, when, looking back, at the nook between the lions he saw a confused move-ment about the spot. The two men he had just left were struggling with a third, who, brandishing a handful of something white, was endeavouring, with varying success, to plant his fist on divers areas of their persons. He was the draughtsman. A small crowd, which momentarily increased, surrounded them, and as Pringle climbed into the hansom two policemen were seen to penetrate the ring and impartially lay hands upon the three combatants.

III

The Clue of the Silver Spoons

ROBERT BARR

THE CLUE OF THE SILVER SPOONS

A Detective Tale.

By ROBERT BARR.

WHEN the card was brought in to me, I looked upon it with some misgiving, for I scented a commercial transaction; and although such cases are lucrative enough, nevertheless I, Eugine Valmont, formerly high in the service of the French Government, do not care to be connected with them. They usually pertain to sordid business affairs that present little that is of interest to a man, who, in his time, has dealt with subtle questions of diplomacy upon which the welfare of nations sometimes turned.

The name of Bentham Gibbes is familiar to everyone, connected as it is with the much-advertised pickles, whose glaring announcements in crude crimson and green strike the eye everywhere in England, and shock the artistic taste wherever seen. Me, I have never tasted them, and shall not, so long as a French restaurant remains open in London; but I doubt not they are as pronounced to the palate as their advertisement is distressing to the eye.

If, then, this gross pickle manufacturer expected me to track down those who were infringing upon the recipes for making his so-called sauces, chutneys, and the like, he would find himself mistaken, for I was now in a position to pick and choose my cases, and a case of pickles did not allure me. "Beware of imitations," said the advertisement, "none genuine without a facsimile of the signature of Bentham Gibbes." Ah, well, not for me were either the pickles or the tracking of imitators. A forged cheque : yes, if you like, but the forged signature of Mr. Gibbes on a pickle bottle was not for me. Nevertheless, I said to Armand :

"Show the gentleman in," and he did so.

To my astonishment there entered a young man, quite correctly dressed in dark frock coat, faultless waistcoat and trousers, that proclaimed the Bond Street tailor. When he spoke his voice and language were those of a gentleman.

"Monsieur Valmont ? " he inquired.

"At your service," I replied, bowing and waving my hand as Armand placed a chair for him and withdrew.

"I am a barrister, with chambers in the Temple," began Mr. Gibbes, "and for some days a matter has been troubling me about which I have now come to seek your advice, your name having been suggested by a friend in whom I confided."

"Am I acquainted with him ? " I asked.

"I think not," replied Mr. Gibbes; "he also is a barrister with chambers in the same building as my own. Lionel Dacre is his name."

"I never heard of him."

"Very likely not. Nevertheless, he recommended you as a man who could keep his own counsel ; and if you take up this case I desire the utmost secrecy preserved, whatever may be the outcome."

I bowed, but made no protestation. Secrecy is a matter of course with me.

The Englishman paused for a few moments, as if he expected fervent assurances ; then he went on with no trace of disappointment on his countenance at not receiving them.

"On the night of the twenty-third I gave a little dinner to six friends of mine in my own rooms. I may say that so far as I am aware they are all gentlemen of unimpeachable character. On the night of the dinner I was detained later than I expected at a reception, and in driving to the Temple was still further delayed by a block of traffic in Piccadilly, so that when I arrived at my chambers there was barely time for me to dress and receive my guests. My man Johnson had everything laid out ready for me in my dressing-room, and as I passed through to it, I hurriedly flung off the coat I was wearing and carelessly left it over the back of a chair in the dining-room, where neither Johnson nor myself noticed it until my attention was called to it after the dinner was over, and everyone was rather jolly with wine.

"This coat had an inside pocket. Usually any frock coat I wear at an afternoon reception has not an inside pocket, but I had been rather on the rush all day. My father is a manufacturer, whose name may be familiar to you, and I am on the directors' board of his company. On this occasion I had to take a cab from the city to the reception I spoke of, and had not time to go and change at my rooms. The reception was a somewhat Bohemian affair, extremely interesting, of course, but not too particular as to costume, so I went as I was. In this inside pocket rested a thin package, composed of two pieces of pasteboard, and between them five twenty-pound Bank of England notes, folded lengthways, and held in place between the pasteboards by an elastic rubber band.

"I had thrown the coat over the chair in such a way that the inside pocket was exposed, and the ends of the notes plainly recognisable. Over the coffee and cigars one of my guests laughingly called attention to what he

termed my vulgar display of wealth, and Johnson, in some confusion at having neglected to put away the coat, now picked it up and took it to the reception room, where the wraps of my guests lay about promiscuously. He should, of course, have placed it in my wardrobe, but he said afterwards he thought it belonged to the guest who had spoken. You see, he was in my dressing-room when I threw my coat on the chair in making my way thither, and, of course, he

"Over the coffee and cigars one of my guests laughingly called attention to what he termed my vulgar display of wealth."

had not noticed the coat in the hurry of arriving guests, otherwise he would have put it where it belonged. After everybody had gone, Johnson came to me and said the coat was there, but the package was missing, nor has any trace of it been found since that night."

"The dinner was fetched in from outside, I suppose?"

"Yes."

"How many waiters served it?"

"Two. They are men who have often been in my employ before; but, apart from that, they had left my chambers before the incident of the coat happened."

"Neither of them went into the reception room, I take it?"

" No. I am certain that not even suspicion can attach to either of the waiters."

" Your man Johnson——"

" Has been with me for years. He could easily have stolen much more than the hundred pounds if he had wished to do so, but I have never known him to take a penny that did not belong to him."

" Will you favour me with the names of your guests, Mr. Gibbes ? "

" Viscount Stern sat at my right hand, and at my left Lord Templemore ; Sir John Sanclere next to him, and Angus McKeller next to Sanclere. After Viscount Stern was Lionel Dacre, and at his right was Vincent Innis."

On a sheet of paper I had written the names of the guests, and noted their places at the table.

" Which guest drew your attention to the money ? "

" Lionel Dacre."

" Is there a window looking out from the reception room ? "

" Two of them."

" Were they fastened on the night of the dinner party ? "

" I could not be sure ; Johnson would know, very likely. You are hinting at the possibility of a thief coming in through a reception room window while we were somewhat noisy over our wine. I think such a solution highly improbable. My rooms are on the third floor, and a thief would scarcely venture to make an entrance when he could not but know there was a company being entertained. Besides this, the coat was there but an hour or so, and it seems to me whoever stole those notes knew where they were."

" That sounds reasonable," I had to admit.

" Have you spoken to anyone of your loss ? "

" To no one but Dacre, who recommended me to see you. Oh, yes, and to Johnson, of course."

I could not help noting that this was the fourth or fifth time Dacre's name had come up during our conversation.

" Why to Dacre ? " I asked.

" Oh, well, you see, he occupies chambers in the same building, on the ground floor. He is a very good fellow, and we are by way of being firm friends. Then it was he who

had called attention to the money, so I thought he should know the sequel."

" How did he take your news ? "

" Now that you call attention to the fact, he seemed slightly troubled. I should like to say, however, that you must not be misled by that. Lionel Dacre could no more steal than he could lie."

" Did he seem surprised when you mentioned the theft ? "

Bentham Gibbes paused a moment before replying, knitting his brows in thought.

" No," he said at last ; " and, come to think of it, it almost appears as if he had been expecting my announcement."

" Doesn't that strike you as rather strange, Mr. Gibbes ? "

" Really, my mind is in such a whirl, I don't know what to think. But it's perfectly absurd to suspect Dacre. If you knew the man you would understand what I mean. He comes of an excellent family, and he is—oh ! he is Lionel Dacre, and when you have said that, you have made any suspicion absurd."

" I suppose you had the rooms thoroughly searched. The packet didn't drop out and remain unnoticed in some corner ? "

" No ; Johnson and myself examined every inch of the premises."

" Have you the numbers of the notes ? "

" Yes ; I got them from the bank next morning. Payment was stopped, and so far not one of the five has been presented. Of course, one or more may have been cashed at some shop, but none have been offered to any of the banks."

" A twenty-pound note is not accepted without scrutiny, so the chances are the thief may have some difficulty in disposing of them."

" As I told you, I don't mind the loss of the money at all. It is the uncertainty, the uneasiness, caused by the incident which troubles me. You will comprehend this when I say that if you are good enough to interest yourself in this case, I shall be disappointed if your fee does not exceed the amount I have lost."

Mr. Gibbes rose as he said this, and I accompanied him to the door, assuring him that I should do my best to solve the mystery. Whether he sprang from pickles or not, I realised he was a polished and generous gentleman, who estimated the services of a professional expert like myself at their true value.

I shall not give the details of my researches during the following few days, because the trend of them must be gone over in the remarkable interview I had somewhat later, and there is little use in repeating myself. Suffice it to say, then, that an examination of the rooms and a close cross-questioning of Johnson satisfied me that he and the two waiters were innocent. I was also convinced that no thief made his way through the window, and I came to the conclusion that the notes were stolen by one of the guests.

Further investigation convinced me that the thief was no other than Lionel Dacre, the only one of the six in pressing need of money at that time.

I had Dacre shadowed, and during one of his absences made the acquaintance of his man Hopper, a surly, impolite brute who accepted my golden sovereign quickly enough, but gave me little in exchange for it. But while I conversed with him, there arrived in the passage where we were talking together, a large case of champagne, bearing one of the best-known names in the trade, and branded as being of the vintage of '78. Now, I know that the product of Camelot Frères is not bought as cheaply as British beer, and I also had learned that two short weeks before Mr. Lionel Dacre was at his wits' end for money. Yet he was still the same briefless barrister he had ever been.

On the morning after my unsatisfactory conversation with his man Hopper, I was astonished to receive the following note, written on a dainty correspondence card :—

3 and 4 Vellum Buildings,
Inner Temple, E.C.

Mr. Lionel Dacre presents his compliments to Monsieur Eugine Valmont, and would be obliged if Monsieur Valmont could make it convenient to call upon him in his chambers to-morrow morning at eleven.

Had the man become aware that he was being shadowed, or did the surly servant inform him of the inquiries made ? I was soon to know. I called punctually at eleven next morning, and was received with charming urbanity by Mr. Dacre himself. The taciturn Hopper had evidently been sent away for the occasion.

While I conversed with him, there arrived in the passage a large case of champagne.

" My dear Monsieur Valmont, I am delighted to meet you," said the young man with more effusiveness than I had ever noticed in an Englishman before, although his very next words supplied an explanation that did not occur to me until afterwards as somewhat far-fetched. " I believe we are by way of being countrymen, and, therefore, although the hour is early, I hope you will allow me to offer you some of that bottled sunshine of the year '78, from la belle France, to whose prosperity and honour we shall drink together. For such a toast any hour is propitious," and to my amazement he brought forth from the case I had seen arrive two days before a bottle of that superb vintage.

"Now," said I to myself, "it is going to be difficult to keep a clear head if the aroma of that nectar rises to the brain. But, tempting as is the cup, I shall drink sparingly, and hope he may not be so judicious."

Sensitive, I already experienced the charm of his personality, and well understood the friendship Mr. Bentham Gibbes felt for him. But I saw the trap spread before me. He expected, under the influence of champagne and courtesy, to extract a promise from me which I must find myself unable to give.

"Sir, you interest me by claiming kinship with France. I had understood that you belonged to one of the oldest families of England."

"Ah, England!" he cried, with an expressive gesture of outspreading hands truly Parisian in its significance. "The trunk belongs to England, of course,

"Let me fill your glass again, Monsieur Valmont."

but the root—ah! the root, Monsieur Valmont, penetrated the soil from which this vine of the gods has been drawn."

Then, filling my glass and his own, he cried:

"To France, which my family left in the year 1066!"

I could not help laughing at his fervent ejaculation.

"1066! Ah, that is a long time ago, Mr. Dacre."

"In years, perhaps; in feelings but a day.

My forefathers came over to steal, and, Lord! how well they accomplished it! They stole the whole country—something like a theft, say I—under that Prince of robbers well named the Conqueror. In our secret hearts we all admire a great thief, and if not a great one, then an expert one, who covers his tracks so perfectly that the hounds of justice are baffled in attempting to follow them. Now, even you, Monsieur Valmont—I can see you are the most generous of men, with a lively sympathy found to perfection only in France—even you must suffer a pang of regret when you lay a thief by the heels who has done his task deftly."

"I fear, Mr. Dacre, you credit me with a magnanimity to which I dare not lay claim. The criminal is a danger to society."

"True, true; you are in the right, Monsieur Valmont. Still, admit there are cases that would touch you tenderly. For example, a man, ordinarily honest; a great need; a sudden opportunity. He takes that of which another has abundance, and he, nothing. What then, Monsieur Valmont? Is the man to be sent to perdition for a momentary weakness?"

His words astonished me. Was I on the verge of hearing a confession? It almost amounted to that already.

"Mr. Dacre," I said, "I cannot enter into the subtleties you pursue. My duty is to find the criminal."

"You are in the right, Monsieur Valmont, and I am enchanted to find so sensible a head on French shoulders. Although you are a more recent arrival, if I may say so, than myself, you nevertheless already give utterance to sentiments which do honour to England. It is your duty to hunt down the criminal. Very well. In that I think I can aid you, so have taken the liberty of requesting your attendance here this morning. Let me fill your glass again, Monsieur Valmont."

"No more, I beg of you, Mr. Dacre."

"What, do you think the receiver is as bad as the thief?"

I was so taken aback at his remark that I suppose my face showed the amazement within me. But the young man merely laughed with apparently free-hearted enjoyment, poured more wine in his own glass, and tossed it off. Not knowing what to say, I changed the trend of conversation.

"Mr. Gibbes said you had been kind enough to recommend me to his attention. May I ask how you came to hear of me?"

"Ah, who has not heard of the renowned Monsieur Valmont?" and as he said this, for the first time there began to grow a suspicion in my mind that he was chaffing me, as it is called in England, a procedure which I cannot endure. Indeed, if this young man practised it in my own country he would find himself with a duel on his hands before he had gone far. However, the next instant his voice resumed its original fascination, and I listened to it as to some delicious melody.

"I have only to mention my cousin, Lady Gladys Dacre, and you will at once understand why I recommended you to my friend. The case of Lady Gladys, you will remember, required a delicate touch which is not always to be had in this land of England, except when those who possess the gift do us the honour to sojourn with us."

I noticed that my glass was again filled, and as I bowed my acknowledgements of his compliment, I indulged in another sip of the delicious wine; and then I sighed, for I began to realise it was going to be difficult for me, in spite of my disclaimer, to tell this man's friend he had stolen the money.

All this time he had been sitting on the edge of the table, while I occupied a chair at its end. He sat there in careless fashion, swinging a foot to and fro. Now he sprang to the floor and drew up a chair, placing on the table a blank sheet of paper. Then he took from the mantelshelf a packet of letters, and I was astonished to see they were held together by two bits of cardboard and a rubber band similar to the combination that had held the folded banknotes. With great nonchalance he slipped off the rubber band, threw it and the pieces of cardboard on the table before me, leaving the documents loose to his hand.

"Now, Monsieur Valmont," he cried jauntily, "you have been occupied for several days on this case—the case of my dear friend, Bentham Gibbes, who is one of the best fellows in the world."

"He said the same of you, Mr. Dacre."

"I am gratified to hear it. Would you mind letting me know to what point your researches have led you?"

"They have led me to a direction rather than to a point."

"Ah! In the direction of a man, of course?"

"Certainly."

"Who is he?"

"Will you pardon me if I decline to answer you at the present moment?"

"That means you are not sure."

"It may mean, Mr. Dacre, that I am employed by Mr. Gibbes, and do not feel at liberty to disclose to another the results of my quest without his permission."

"But Mr. Bentham Gibbes and I are entirely at one in this matter. Perhaps you are aware that I am the only person with whom he discussed the case besides yourself."

"That is undoubtedly true, Mr. Dacre; still, you see the difficulty of my position."

"Yes, I do, and so shall not press you further. But I have also been interesting myself, in a purely amateurish way, of course. You would, perhaps, have no disinclination to learn whether my deductions agree with yours."

"Not in the least. I should be very glad to know the conclusion at which you have arrived. May I ask if you suspect anyone in particular?"

"Yes, I do."

"Will you name him?"

" No, I shall copy the admirable reticence you yourself have shown. And now let us attack this mystery in a sane and business-like manner. You have already examined the room. Well, here is a rough sketch of it. There is the table; in this corner the chair on which the coat was flung. Here sat Gibbes at the head of the table. Those on the left-hand side had their backs to the chair. I, being in the centre to the right, saw the chair, the coat, and the notes, and called attention to them. Now our first duty is to find a motive. If it were a murder, our motive might be hatred, revenge, robbery, what you like. As it is simply the stealing of money, the man must have been either a born thief, or else some hitherto innocent person pressed to the crime by great necessity. Do you agree with me, Monsieur Valmont ? "

" Perfectly. You follow exactly the line of my own reasoning."

"Very well. It is unlikely that a born thief was one of Mr. Gibbes' guests. Therefore we are reduced to look for a man under the spur of necessity—a man who has no money of his own, but who must raise a certain amount, let us say by a certain date, if we can find such a man in that company. Do you not agree with me that he is likely to be the thief ? "

" Yes, I do."

" Then let us start our process of elimina-tion. Out goes Viscount Stern, a man with twenty thousand acres of land, and nobody quite knows what income. I mark off the name of Lord Templemere, one of His Majesty's judges, entirely above suspicion. Next Sir John Sanclare ; he also is rich, but Vincent Innis is still richer, so the pencil obliterates his name. Now we have Angus McKeller, an author of some note, as you are well aware, deriving a good income from his books, and a better one from his plays ; a canny Scot, so we may rub his name from our paper and our memory. How do my erasures corres-pond with yours, Monsieur Valmont ? "

" They correspond exactly, Mr. Dacre."

" I am flattered to hear it. There remains one name untouched ; Mr. Lionel Dacre, the descendant, as we have said, of robbers."

" I have not said so, Mr. Dacre."

" Ah, my dear Valmont, the politeness of your country asserts itself. Let us not be deluded, but follow our inquiry wherever it leads. I suspect Lionel Dacre. What do you know of his circumstances before the dinner of the twenty-third ? "

As I made no reply, he looked up at me with his frank boyish face illumined with a winning smile.

" You know nothing of his circum-stances ? " he asked.

" It grieves me to state that I do. Mr. Lionel Dacre was penniless on the night of the dinner on the twenty-third."

" Oh, don't exaggerate, Monsieur Val-mont," cried Dacre, with a laugh, " he had one sixpence, two pennies, and a halfpenny. How did you know he was penniless ? "

" I knew he ordered a case of champagne from the London representative of Camelot Frères, and was refused unless he paid the money down."

" Quite right; and then when you were talking to Hopper you saw that case of cham-pagne delivered. Excellent, excellent, Mon-sieur Valmont. But will a man steal, think you, to supply himself with even so delicious a wine as this we have been tasting—and, by the way, forgive my neglect. Allow me to fill your glass, Monsieur Valmont."

" Not another drop, if you will excuse me, Mr. Dacre."

" Ah, yes, champagne should not be mixed with evidence. When we have finished, perhaps. What further proof have you ? "

" I have proof that Mr. Dacre was threatened with bankruptcy, if on the twenty-fourth he did not pay a bill of seventy-eight pounds that had long been out-standing. I have proof that this was paid, not on the twenty-fourth, but on the twenty-sixth. Mr. Dacre had gone to the solicitor and assured him he would have the money on that date, whereupon he was given two days' grace."

" Ah, well, he was entitled to three, you know, in law. Yes, there, Monsieur Val-mont, you touch the fatal point. The threat of bankruptcy will drive a man in Dacre's position to almost any crime. Bankruptcy to a barrister spells ruin. It means a career blighted ; it means a life buried with little chance of resurrection. I see you grasp the supreme importance of that bit of evidence. The case of champagne is as nothing compared with it; and this reminds me that in the crisis I shall take another sip, with your permission. Sure you won't join me?"

"Not at this juncture, Mr. Dacre."

"I envy your moderation. Here's to the success of our search, Monsieur Valmont."

I felt sorry for the gay young fellow as with smiling face he drank the champagne.

"Now, monsieur," he went on, "I am amazed to learn how much you have found out. Really, I think tradespeople, solicitors, and all such should keep better guard on their tongues than they do. Nevertheless, these documents I have at my elbow, and which I expected would surprise you, are merely the letters and receipts. Here is the letter from the solicitor threatening me with bankruptcy; here is his receipt dated the twenty-sixth; here is the refusal of the wine merchant, and here is his receipt for the money. Here are smaller bills liquidated. With my pencil we will add them up. Seventy-eight pounds bulks large. We add the smaller items, and it totals ninety-three pounds, seven shillings, and fourpence. Let us now examine my purse. Here is a five-pound note; there is a minted sovereign. Here is twelve and sixpence in silver; here is twopence in coppers. Now the purse is empty. Let us add this to the amount on the paper. Do my eyes deceive me, or is the total exactly a hundred pounds? There is the stolen money accounted for."

"Pardon me, Mr. Dacre," I said, "but there is still a sovereign on the mantelpiece."

Dacre threw back his head, and laughed with greater heartiness than I had yet known him to indulge in during our short acquaintance.

"By Jove!" he cried, "you've got me there. I'd forgotten entirely about that pound on the mantelpiece, which belongs to you."

"To me? Impossible!"

"It does, and cannot interfere in the least with our hundred pound calculation. That is the sovereign you gave to my man, Hopper, who, believing me hard pressed, took it that I might have the enjoyment of it. Hopper belongs to our family, or the family

belongs to him, I am never sure which. You must have missed in him the deferential bearing of a man-servant in Paris, yet he is true gold, like the sovereign you bestowed upon him, and he bestowed upon me. Now here, monsieur, is the evidence of the theft, together with the rubber band and two pieces of cardboard. Ask my friend Gibbes to examine them minutely. They are all at your disposition, monsieur, and you will learn how much easier it is to deal with the master than with the servant when you wish information. All the gold you possess would not have wrung these incriminating documents from old Hopper. I had to send him away to-day to the West End, fearing that in his brutal British way he might have assaulted you if he got an inkling of your mission."

"Mr. Dacre," said I slowly, "you have thoroughly convinced me——"

"I thought I would," he interrupted with a laugh.

"——that you did not take the money."

"Oh, this is a change of wind, surely. Many a man has been hanged through a chain of circumstantial evidence much weaker than this which I have exhibited to you. Don't you see the subtlety of my action? Ninety-nine persons in a hundred would say, 'No man could be such a fool as to put Valmont on his track, and then place in Valmont's hands such striking evidence.' But there comes in my craftiness. Of course the rock you run up against will be Gibbes' incredulity. The first question he will ask you may be this: 'Why did not Dacre come and borrow the money from me?' Now there you have a certain weakness in your chain of evidence. I know perfectly well that Gibbes would lend me the money, and he knew perfectly well that if I were pressed to the wall I should ask him."

"Mr. Dacre," said I, "you have been playing with me. I should resent that with most men, but whether it is your own genial manner, or the effect of this excellent champagne, or both together, I forgive you. But I am convinced of another thing. You know who took the money."

"I don't know, but I suspect."

"Will you tell me whom you suspect?"

"That would not be fair, but I shall now

take the liberty of filling your glass with champagne."

"I am your guest, Mr. Dacre."

"Admirably answered, monsieur," he replied, pouring out the wine; "and now I shall give you the clue. Find out all about the story of the silver spoons."

"The story of the silver spoons? What silver spoons?"

"Ah, that is the point. You step out of the Temple into Fleet Street, seize by the shoulder the first man you meet, and ask him to tell you about the silver spoons. There are but two men and two spoons concerned. When you learn who those two men are, you will know that one of them did not take the money, and I give you my assurance that the other did."

"You speak in mystery, Mr. Dacre."

"But certainly, for I am speaking to Monsieur Eugine Valmont."

"I echo your words, sir. Admirably answered. You put me on my mettle, and I flatter myself that I see your kindly drift. You wish me to solve the mystery of this stolen money. Sir, you do me honour, and I drink to your health."

"To yours, monsieur," said Lionel Dacre, "and here is a further piece of information which my friend Gibbes would never have given you. When he told me the money was gone, I cried in the anguish of impending bankruptcy: 'I wish to goodness I had it!' Whereupon he immediately compelled me to accept his cheque for a hundred pounds, of which, as I have shown you, alas! only six pounds twelve and eightpence remains."

On leaving Mr. Dacre I took a hansom to a *café* in Regent Street, which is a passable imitation of similar places of refreshment in Paris. There, calling for a cup of black coffee, I sat down to think. The clue of the silver spoons! He had laughingly suggested that I should take by the shoulders the first man I met, and ask him what the story of the silver spoons was. This course naturally struck me as absurd. Nevertheless, it contained a hint. I must ask somebody, and that the right person, to tell me the tale of the silver spoons.

Under the influence of the black coffee, I reasoned it out in this way. On the night of the twenty-third some one of the six guests there present stole a hundred pounds, but Dacre had said that one of the actors in the silver spoon episode was the actual thief. That person, then, must have been one of Mr. Gibbes' guests at the dinner of the twenty-third. Probably two of the guests were the participators in the silver spoon comedy, but be that as it may, it followed that one at least of the men around Mr. Gibbes' table knew the episode of the silver spoons.

Perhaps Bentham Gibbes himself was cognisant of it. It followed, therefore, that the easiest plan was to question each of the men who partook of that dinner. Yet if only one knew about the spoons, that one must also have some idea that these spoons formed the clue which attached him to the crime of the twenty-third, in which case he was little likely to divulge what he knew, and that to an entire stranger. Of course I might go to Dacre himself and demand the story of the silver spoons, but this would be a confession of failure on my part, and I rather dreaded Lionel Dacre's hearty laughter when I admitted that the mystery was too much for me. Besides this, I was very well aware of the young man's kindly intentions towards me. He wished me to unravel the coil myself, and so I determined not to go to him except as a last resource.

I resolved to begin with Mr. Gibbes, and, finishing my coffee, got again into a hansom and drove back to the Temple. I found Mr. Gibbes in his room, and after greeting me, his first inquiry was about the case.

"How are you getting on?" he asked.

"I think I am getting on fairly well," I replied, "and expect to finish in a day or two, if you will kindly tell me the story of the silver spoons."

"The silver spoons?" he echoed, quite evidently not understanding me.

"There happened an incident in which two men were engaged, and this incident related to a pair of silver spoons. I want to get the particulars of that."

"I haven't the slightest idea what you are talking about," replied Gibbes, thoroughly bewildered. "You will have to be more definite, I fear, if you are to get any help from me."

" I cannot be more definite, because I have already told you all I know."

" What bearing has all this on our own case ? "

" I was informed that if I got hold of the clue of the silver spoons I should be in a fair way of settling our case."

" Who told you that ? "

" Mr. Lionel Dacre."

" Oh, does Dacre refer to his own conjuring ? "

" I don't know, I'm sure. What was his conjuring ? "

" A very clever trick he did one night at dinner here about two months ago."

" Had it anything to do with silver spoons ? "

" Well, it was silver spoons or silver forks, or something of that kind. I had entirely forgotten the incident. So far as I recollect at the moment, there was a sleight-of-hand man of great expertness in one of the music-halls, and the talk turned upon him. Then Dacre said the tricks he did were easy, and holding up a spoon or a fork, I don't remember which, he asserted his ability to make it disappear before our eyes, to be found afterwards in the clothing of someone there present. Several offered to make him a bet that he could do nothing of the kind, but he said he would bet with no one but Innis, who sat opposite him. Innis, with some reluctance, accepted the bet, and then Dacre, with a great show of the usual conjurer's gesticulations, spread forth his empty hands, and said we should find the spoon in Innis' pocket, and there, sure enough, it was. It was a clever trick, but we were never able to get him to repeat it."

" Thank you very much, Mr. Gibbes; I think I see daylight now."

" If you do, you are cleverer than I, by a long chalk," cried Bentham Gibbes, as I took my departure.

I went directly downstairs, and knocked at Mr. Dacre's door once more. He opened the door himself, his man not yet having returned.

"Ah, monsieur," he cried; " back already ? You don't mean to tell me you have so soon

got to the bottom of the silver spoon entangle. ment ? "

" I think I have, Mr. Dacre. You were sitting at dinner opposite Mr. Vincent Innis. You saw him conceal a silver spoon in his pocket. You probably waited for some time to understand what he meant by this, and as he did not return the spoon to its place, you proposed a conjuring trick, made the bet with him, and thus the spoon was returned to the table."

" Excellent, excellent, monsieur ! That is very nearly what occurred, except that I acted at once. I had had experiences with Mr. Vincent Innis before. Never did he come to these rooms without my missing some little trinket after he was gone. I am not a man of many possessions, while Mr. Innis is a very rich person, and so, if anything is taken, I have little difficulty in coming to a knowledge of my loss. Of course, I never mentioned these disappearances to him. They were all trivial, as I have said, and, so far as the silver spoon was concerned, it was of no great value either. But I thought the bet and the recovery of the spoon would teach him a lesson; it apparently has not done so. On the night of the twenty-third he sat at my right hand, as you will see by consulting your diagram of the table and the guests. I asked him a question twice to which he did not reply, and, looking at him, I was startled by the expression in his eyes. They were fixed on a distant corner of the room, and following his gaze I saw what he was looking at with such hypnotising concentration.

" So absorbed was he in contemplation of the packet there so plainly exposed, that he seemed to be entirely oblivious of what was going on around him. I roused him from his trance by jocularly calling Gibbes' attention to the display of money. I expected in this way to save Innis from committing the act which he seemingly did commit. Imagine, then, the dilemma in which I was placed when Gibbes confided to me the morning after what had occurred the night before.

" I was positive that Innis had taken the money, yet I possessed no proof of it. I could not tell Gibbes, and I dare not speak to Innis. Of course, monsieur, you do not need to be told that Innis is not a thief in the ordinary sense of the word. He has no need to steal, and yet apparently cannot help doing so. I am sure that no attempt has been made to pass those notes. They are doubtless in his house at Kensington at this present moment. He is, in fact, a kleptomaniac, or a maniac of some sort. And now, Monsieur Valmont, was my hint regarding the silver spoons of any value to you?"

"Of the most infinite value, Mr. Dacre."

"Then let me make another suggestion. I leave it entirely to your bravery; a bravery which I confess I do not myself possess. Will you take a hansom, drive to Mr. Innis' house in the Cromwell Road, confront him quietly, and ask for the return of the packet? I am anxious to know what will happen. If he hands it to you, as I expect he will, then you must tell Mr. Gibbes the whole story."

"Mr. Dacre, your suggestion shall be immediately acted upon, and I thank you for your compliment to my courage."

I found that Mr. Innis inhabited a very grand house. After a time he entered the study on the ground floor, to which I had been conducted. He held my card in his hand, and was looking at it with some surprise.

"I think I have not the pleasure of knowing you, Mr. Valmont," he said, courteously enough.

"No. I have called on a matter of business. I was

once investigator for the French Government, and now am doing private detective work here in London."

"Ah! And how is that supposed to interest me? I have nothing that I wish investigated. I did not send for you, did I?"

"No, Mr. Innis; I merely took the liberty of calling to ask you to let me have the package you took out of Mr. Bentham Gibbes' frock coat pocket on the night of the twenty-third."

"He wishes it returned, does he?"

"Yes."

Mr. Innis calmly went to a desk, which he unlocked and opened, displaying a veritable museum of trinkets of one sort and another. Pulling out a small drawer, he took from it the packet containing the five twenty-pound notes. Apparently it had never been undone. With a smile he handed it to me.

"You will make my apologies to Mr. Gibbes for not returning it before. Tell him I have been unusually busy of late."

"I shall not fail to do so," said I, with a bow.

"Thanks so much. Good morning, Monsieur Valmont."

"Good morning, Mr. Innis."

And so I returned the packet to Mr. Bentham Gibbes, who pulled the notes from between their pasteboard protection, and begged me to accept them.

"You will make my apologies to Mr. Gibbes for not returning it before. Tell him I have been unusually busy of late."

IV

The Counterfeit Cashier

GEORGE A. BEST

THE COUNTERFEIT CASHIER

BY GEO. A. BEST.

I.

IT would seem that there are few of the pomps and vanities of mankind more innocent of harm than a well-trimmed moustache or beard, or a pair of (now happily obsolete) whiskers of the "mutton-chop" variety. Yet it was on account of their ability to work mischief to the detriment of the firm, and for no other reason, that these simple adornments were denied to the working staff of the prosperous banking house of Dorrington Bros. To speak more plainly, a cleverly planned and brilliantly executed robbery, resulting in a loss to the firm of £5,000 sterling, was directly responsible for the inauguration of a rule which is still regarded by the banking fraternity in the light of an official absurdity, and somewhat flippantly referred to by Dorrington's employés as the "anti-whisker regulation."

To accomplish their purpose, the thieves chose as an unwilling accessory one Thomas Darwin, a cashier who has long since retired from the firm, and is therefore in a position of independence which might well include side-whiskers among the other luxuries of a retired life in the suburbs. But Darwin still plies his razor with a remorselessness born of habit, and of something else besides. The "something else" in this case represents the gist of my story.

At the time of the robbery Darwin was a tall, somewhat spare man of forty-five. He was bald at the crown of the head, and wore "mutton-chop" whiskers and a heavy moustache. Stooping slightly, yet walking with a short, springy step, strongly suggestive of a high-class marionette, Darwin possessed an individuality which was very marked. He was regarded as a reserved, even taciturn, man, who seldom spoke on any but business subjects during office hours; and some of his colleagues were wont to remark that Darwin always carried his pen as a bit between his teeth in order to curb any desire for conversation, or an exchange of confidences with his immediate neighbours. These little peculiarities of manner and of carriage earned for their owner the nickname of "Automaton Darwin."

On the twenty-eighth day of June, 1881, Thomas Darwin left his home in Rignold Road, Clapton, to catch the 8.55 a.m. train to Liverpool Street. The train left Clapton station neither sooner nor later than usual, but for the first time for many years a certain corner seat on the "off side" of the tenth compartment from the engine was appropriated by a stranger. "Automaton Darwin" was absent.

The circumstances, which for once had proved strong enough to disorganise even the automatic regularity of Thomas Darwin,

47

are interesting, inasmuch as they afford a revelation of the infinite pains taken by their authors to discover the most vulnerable point of an unusually strong character. Darwin was well known in the North of London as a bird fancier of extraordinary enthusiasm ; and an imaginary canary was the only decoy used to effect the capture of the unsuspecting cashier, as the first and most important item on a criminal programme of unusual interest.

Darwin had turned down one of the quieter thoroughfares leading from Rignold Road to High Street, when he was accosted by a working man, who had hurried to the gate of a large and apparently empty house which stood back a dozen yards or so from the roadway. The man wore a plasterer's cap and a long white apron. His face was plentifully besmeared with the whitewash which he had apparently been using indoors, and which still dropped from the brush in his hand.

"Mr. Darwin ! " he gasped excitedly, "there's a beautiful bird, something like a canary, in one of the top rooms of this house. It flew through the open window while I was washin' the ceiling, an' when I saw you comin' down the road I said to myself— 'Here comes the very gentleman of all others who can tell me what the bird is an' what it's worth.' "

Darwin gazed curiously at the speaker for a moment, and then consulted his watch.

"I can only spare a couple of minutes," he said, "and it's a long climb to the fourth floor. Can't you keep the bird until I return from the City this evening ? Or, better still, bring it round to my house in the Rignold Road ? I shall be home by six o'clock."

The honest British workman shook his head sadly.

"I don't think the poor little thing will live as long as that unless it's looked after at once, sir," he replied. "It's beating itself against the walls an' ceiling so vi'lently that there won't be much of it left to identify if I don't open the window again an' let it go. However, sir, I'm sorry to have troubled you ; I thought that you might be interested, havin' read some of your articles in the *Bird Fanciers' Guide*, an' knowing you well by sight. But don't go an' lose your train on my account. P'r'aps it's only an ordinary canary, after all."

For a moment Darwin hesitated. The 8.48, down, whistled into Clapton Station, scarcely a hundred yards away. He had still quite six minutes to spare. The

plasterer was already walking slowly up the weed-grown path towards the open doorway of the house. Darwin flung open the rusty gate, and reached the hall door in a dozen quick, jerky steps.

"This way, sir," cried the workman, mounting the heavy oaken staircase more rapidly, without looking round. "Be careful of the ladder on the second landin'— it's a bit dark up there, for the lobby window hasn't been cleaned for a year or two, an' the paper-hangers—who were doin' the first floor rooms yesterday—have left a lot of things about."

At this momont a heavy clang resounded through the house. The hall door had been hastily closed, and the crash was followed by the ominous shriek of a rusty bolt.

"It's only the wind, sir," explained the plasterer, noticing that Darwin peered suspiciously over the banisters into the suddenly darkened hall below. "A wonderful draughty house this is."

And a "wonderful draughty house" it certainly was, seeing that the heavy door had closed with a reverberating crash, while the leaves of the chestnut trees outside were undisturbed by a single breath of wind !

"The canary's in this room," announced Darwin's guide when the last flight of stairs, liberally strewn with obstacles, had been slowly and carefully ascended. "I reckon it'd be a breakneck job for anybody to rush that last flight," he added impressively, throwing open the door of a small room as he spoke, and respectfully making way for Darwin to enter first.

A rough deal table stood in the centre of the room, and the narrow iron mantelshelf held an empty beer bottle, in the neck of which a lighted candle was fixed. The apartment was as innocent of daylight as a banker's strong room.

While Darwin was peering somewhat impatiently around the room to discover the whereabouts of the imprisoned bird, and the window by which it had entered, the door was softly closed behind him, and, turning sharply round, he was just in time to see the workman turn the key in the lock.

"What are you doing with that door, man ? " he demanded angrily.

"I'm just locking it in case of accidents," replied the workman coolly. "And to prevent any unauthorised person tampering with the lock I've withdrawn the key and taken charge of it myself. We don't want the precious bird to escape after taking all this trouble, do we, Mr. Darwin ? "

With a rapid movement Darwin seized the dusty bottle, and, regardless of the dripping candle grease, raised it threateningly above his head.

"Open that door, you scoundrel, or I'll brain you where you stand!" he cried furiously. "I'm not the kind of man to stand any foolery of this sort. I'll give you exactly ten seconds to——"

The bank cashier stopped abruptly. He was gazing into the barrel of a heavy revolver, very firmly held within a couple of feet of his head.

"Be so good as to replace our candlestick on the shelf, Mr. Darwin," said the plasterer quietly. "You very kindly gave me ten seconds to perform a certain movement in order to retain my brains, and I'll grant you exactly the same time in which to save your own. Replace the bottle on the shelf!"

Darwin shrugged his shoulders and obeyed.

"I suppose it's useless to argue with you—under the circumstances," he growled sullenly.

"Quite useless, Thomas," was the emphatic reply. "I'm glad to find that you realise the utter hopelessness of mere argument—under the circumstances—it will make matters work more easily for both of us. And now I'll show you the canary, for we've no time to spare."

A trap-door in the ceiling of the room opened mysteriously at this moment, and a pair of daintily trousered legs emerged through the aperture, followed by a frock coat, a pair of well-trimmed whiskers, and a bald head. These component parts of Lombardian respectability wavered for a moment in mid air, and the sum total dropped lightly on to the deal table underneath.

Darwin stared wildly at the new-comer for a moment, and every particle of colour fled from his face.

The man was an exact counterpart of himself!

"You devil!" gasped Darwin hoarsely, as the whole of the cunningly devised plot was revealed by a glance at the faultlessly attired figure on the table. "You are going to personate me at Dorrington's and rob the bank!"

"I guess I'm going to try," was the quiet answer. "I think that, instead of using ungentlemanly language, you ought to be really grateful to me for undertaking to do your work for a whole day, Mr. Darwin. I've had ten years' experience as a bank cashier, so I'm fully aware of the exacting nature of the work."

"The get-up is absolutely perfect, Dick!" exclaimed the "plasterer" admiringly.

"Upon my soul you're more like 'Automaton Darwin' than the original is at the present moment. Our excellent model appears to be hardly himself this morning."

Darwin's "double" produced a small mirror from his pocket and surveyed his features critically.

"I must touch up the left eyebrow, Jack," he said, addressing his colleague. "It's scarcely grey enough at the nose end. The right-hand whisker wants darkening a bit, and my scarf is tied too neatly. Get my 'make-up' box out of the cupboard, and be sharp about it. 'Darwin' must not arrive at the office too late; it isn't like him."

"I haven't been a single minute behind time for the last fifteen years!" ejaculated the cashier triumphantly. "You'll be arrested the moment you enter the bank!"

"I don't think I shall," replied the "double" with a bland smile, "touching up" rapidly as he spoke. "I've sent a very discreetly worded telegram in your name, explaining my unpunctuality. One of your colleagues will be, therefore, officiating at your desk when I arrive at the bank, so I shan't have any trouble about keys and locked drawers. I think that when you've seen me walk—so, and bend over an imaginary desk with a pen between my teeth—in this fashion—and grunt 'good-morning,' like that, in the voice of a world-weary parrot, you'll acknowledge that you've been a good master and I an apt pupil."

Darwin gasped. The imitations of carriage, of manner, and of speech were alike perfect.

"What are you going to do with the—the money?" he groaned.

"Pay it over the counter in the usual way, of course," replied the clever rogue cheerfully. "A number of my acquaintances—our mutual friend Jack among them—will call at the bank during the morning and present cheques for various amounts, all of which will be duly honoured, and paid in gold or notes without any reference to the 'signature book.' And while I am attending to these, and to the ordinary customers of the bank, you will be allowed to remain in this interesting apartment, and to amuse yourself as you think best with the somewhat limited means at your disposal."

"I shall amuse myself by trying to escape from this thieves' den!" exclaimed Darwin defiantly. "And as for your plot, it's simply absurd, and the most impracticable thing I've heard of."

"That remains to be proved, Mr. Darwin," said the "plasterer" with a laugh, "and while we are engaged in making a practical test of the scheme you are quite at liberty to escape from what you have ungenerously described as our 'thieves' den'—if you can. We might have had recourse to chloroform, or other less humane measures, to keep you quiet for a while; but we have preferred to trust entirely to bolts and bars, coupled with a little gentle persuasion from the mouth of a loaded pistol.

or the table, or anything else which you fancy. If you turn round or make any movement before that time, I shall be obliged to break about the only commandment which I've taken any pains to keep."

Darwin laughed harshly.

"I have no fear for the safety of the bank, otherwise I might be tempted to defy you," he remarked somewhat weakly.

"Let me see your back," demanded the man with the pistol.

Darwin glared sullenly at the extended

"DARWIN'S 'DOUBLE' PRODUCED A SMALL MIRROR."

And now, as my City friend is anxious to catch the next train up, I must ask you to stand with your face turned towards the wall, so that we may make our exit with as much dignity and as little noise as possible. As soon as you hear the key turned from the outside you may attack either the door,

weapon for a moment, and then turned his face to the wall.

II.

THE apartment in which the unhappy cashier was imprisoned was well chosen by the perpetrators of the Dorrington outrage. The window had been bricked up and the heavy door was secured by a mortised lock, and bolted on the outside. The trap-door in the low ceiling had been carefully locked, and the key removed, after the dramatic entrance of Darwin's "double."

It did not take the prisoner many minutes to realise that any attempt to escape from this cunningly chosen cage without outside assistance would be worse than futile. It was certainly possible that someone might be taking the air in one of the neighbouring gardens far below, and this was the forlorn hope which the situation presented to Darwin's mind ; although the difficulty of communicating with the outside world from an apparently light-proof and sound-proof den on the fourth floor of an empty house appeared insurmountable at first sight. The outlook was by no means an encouraging one ; but Darwin was not the kind of man to rest with folded arms after the first review of a seemingly desperate situation. On the contrary, he took a keen delight in weighing together the few possibilities and probabilities which the case presented, although it was obvious that the former would outbalance the latter on a ten to one scale.

Darwin's first act was to feel carefully for the vesta case which he carried in his waistcoat pocket, and when he was satisfied that the means of obtaining artificial light were available he extinguished the candle. For a moment it seemed that the darkness of night had descended suddenly upon the room, but gradually the prison door was outlined by a single ray of sunshine—a ray so small and so dim that it fell feebly on the lower panels, leaving the rest of the woodwork in deep shadow. Darwin walked to the door and eagerly followed the course of the beam to its ingress. A tiny spot of white light—close to the ceiling—marked the spot at which the cheering ray entered. The cashier climbed on to his table and examined the wall carefully. The hole in the wall through which the light entered was so small that it might easily have been covered with a threepenny-piece. Darwin struck the spot sharply with his clenched fist, and was delighted to find that his hand went clean through the wall-paper and out into the daylight beyond.

At one time the room had apparently been ventilated by the simple expedient of removing a couple of bricks, and there was not even the regulation grating on the outside wall. On the inside the primitive ventilator had recently been papered over, and this was probably the only work

executed on the premises by the sham plasterer.

Unfortunately, the ventilator had been built so near to the ceiling that the imprisoned cashier could neither look through the aperture nor bring his lips to the same level. Standing on the tips of his toes, with his right hand extended to the utmost, Darwin found that he could wave a handkerchief on the outside ; but the movement, owing to lack of space, was so slight that it was scarcely likely to be noticed from below, much less to be interpreted as a signal of distress. For several minutes the excited prisoner stood on the table-top, calling wildly for help, with his head thrown back and every joint of his body racked under the strain of that painfully extended arm, until the very agony of his position forced him to desert for awhile, his only loop-hole of escape.

The clock of a neighbouring church struck ten, and Darwin, returning to the floor of his prison, glanced desperately around the room in search of any idea which might be inspired by the few inanimate objects which the room contained. The inspiration came in the form of a roll of wall-paper which lay on the floor, and Darwin, realising that any plan of campaign was better than none at all, acted upon it without a moment's hesitation. Unrolling the paper on the table, he tore it into half a dozen large squares, and rapidly wrote with his fountain pen a message on the blank side of each square, worded as follows :—

£50 REWARD.

The man who is impersonating me, Thomas Darwin, at Dorrington's Bank, Lombard Street, City, is an impostor. Have him arrested without delay. I am imprisoned in the large empty house on the west side of Dean Street, Upper Clapton. Anyone delivering this message at the Bank before twelve o'clock noon, on this 28th day of June, 1881, will receive the above mentioned reward.

When the last of these remarkable messages had been completed, Darwin climbed on to the table once more, and in another moment the first of the recently written notices had been " posted " through the ventilator, with an accompaniment of piercing yells which caused the staid and dignified cashier to blush for very shame as he uttered them. A dog barked fiercely from a yard on the left, and the freshening breeze carried the released message in the same direction. One by one the bills vanished from sight, and when the last had fluttered away into space Darwin still stood by the tiny loophole, listening hope-

"AN EMPTY BEER BOTTLE CRASHED THROUGH THE CUCUMBER FRAME AT THIS MOMENT."

fully for an answer to his repeated exclamations and interrogations, which appeared to fall on no more intelligent ears than those of the highly exasperated dog in the garden beneath, whose irritating yap rose superior to any other sound in the neighbourhood.

An hour passed slowly by, and the clock of St. John's Church struck eleven. Scarcely had the sound of the last stroke died away before the unmistakable murmur of voices rose faintly, but with sufficient distinctness to enable Darwin to locate the speakers, and to catch the opening words of a neighbourly conversation which was apparently taking place in the garden on the right.

It was simply a polite inquiry as to the well-being of certain cucumbers, which Darwin interrupted by a stentorian " Below there ! " The sensitive hound heard the challenge, and answered it so noisily that the distracted cashier danced on the table-top in a perfect frenzy of rage and excitement.

" Lie down, you brute ! " exclaimed the invisible speaker. " The dog's a perfect nuisance. Speaking of cucumbers reminds me——"

An empty beer bottle crashed through the cucumber frame at this moment. It fell from a great height, and burst with the violence of a lyddite shell at the very feet of the amateur gardener and his sympathetic friend.

With a dismal whine the dog slunk into his kennel, and lay trembling in the darkest corner. His master stepped back to gaze angrily at the upper storey windows of the house next door, but the only sign of movement visible in that direction was a gently waving handkerchief, which flapped weirdly against the wall just below the eaves of the empty house.

"Hallo there! What the deuce are you playing at?" cried the enraged householder. "I'll see that you are punished for this outrage if it costs me fifty pounds!"

"And I'll give you fifty pounds to break into this house and let me out!" came in a strangely muffled voice from the owner of the handkerchief.

III.

WHEN the counterfeit Darwin arrived at Dorrington's Bank he found, as he had surmised, that one of the extra "counter hands" had been installed in the place of the absent cashier. A number of bags of gold and silver from the strong room were being transferred by a bank porter from the bullion trolley to the capacious closets beneath the counter; and the "extra cashier" was engaged in arranging certain bundles of Bank of England notes in their respective pigeon-holes. One of the bullion bags had already been opened, and the contents transferred to the cash drawer in Darwin's desk.

With the utmost coolness and nonchalance the clever impostor replied to the greeting of his unsuspecting colleague; checked the number of bullion bags and the amount of loose cash; and ran through the bundles of bank notes with the firm, yet rapid touch which is only acquired by long practice. He then dismissed the substitute with the laconic remark, "All right," and cashed several cheques for small amounts, cancelling the signatures and filing the forms in a number of quick, jerky movements which were an excellent imitation of Darwin's characteristic business methods. His counterfeit of the absent cashier's handwriting in the entering book was scarcely so successful, although well calculated to deceive a casual observer. Darwin used a broad-nibbed "J" pen, and his entries took the form of a thick, undulating line which was quite illegible at first sight. The impostor's calligraphy, for reasons of his own, was even more illegible.

When the cashier at Desk "E" had negotiated a dozen small cheques, and received a packet of bills from a "bank runner," a draft for a large amount was handed in by a well-to-do farmer, and some £500 in gold were weighed up and shovelled across the counter. A country parson of exceptionally mild appearance followed closely in the trail of the farmer, and this dignitary received in return for the modest cheque of £50 which he presented five Bank of England notes for £100 apiece. This was the first of a long series of similar "errors" made by the fictitious cashier during the course of that exceptionally busy morning. Certain highly respectable and benevolent looking City gentlemen received, without any protest, or even comment, gold and bank notes representing more than five times the face value of the cheques handed in; and these greatly favoured individuals left Dorrington's with all that calmness of demeanour which is said to emanate from a quiet conscience, and wended their way one by one to the Bank of England, where the magic wand of the "Old Lady of Threadneedle Street" converted into bright new sovereigns the crisp bank notes which had so recently been handed to them across the counter of the Lombard Street bank. The mild-looking "curate," the "well-to-do farmer," and the three benevolent and highly respectable "City gentlemen" (who were yet unscrupulous enough to impose upon the absent-mindedness of an overworked cashier of inferior social position to themselves) inaugurated a discreet and well-regulated procession to transact business with the kind "Old Lady" who never breaks her promise to "pay bearer."

So far, the whole of the daring and carefully prepared programme had been carried through without a hitch, and only one of the numerous clients of Dorrington's Bank had reason to complain of any irregularity or want of attention on the part of the cashier at Desk "E."

Darwin invariably left his desk for luncheon at twelve o'clock, and returned with praiseworthy punctuality precisely on the stroke of one. On this occasion, however, the desk was closed and the drawers locked at 11.55, and "Darwin's" immediate neighbours were somewhat surprised to see their colleague don his silk hat and prepare to leave the bank, in spite of the fact that a wealthy client had handed in a draft for negotiation, and was waiting.

As a matter of fact, the counterfeit cashier had just received a telegram bearing a very important message. It read:—

Bird escaped 11.30, make tracks.

So the recipient of this short but startling communication decided to "make tracks" without any unnecessary delay. Even as he walked down the bank with quick, springy steps, a hansom dashed up to the entrance, and a man tumbled out of the vehicle with remarkable celerity—a tall, dark man, with "mutton-chop" whiskers and a heavy moustache. It was "Automaton Darwin" himself!

Darwin met his prototype on the door-step, and throwing his arms round the other's waist called loudly and somewhat incoherently for assistance. Several porters and other employés of the bank sprang forward and tore the struggling men apart.

The head porter gazed from one to the other in speechless astonishment.

"Which is Mr. Darwin?" asked someone from the back of the crowd.

This remark gave the impostor his cue, and he acted upon it instantly.

"Arrest that man at once," he cried, pointing to Darwin. "He is impersonating me for felonious purposes. He intends to rob the bank. Call in a policeman without delay."

The astonished crowd at once turned on Darwin, who struggled fiercely, and most unwisely, with a dozen hands laid roughly on him. He was speechless with rage.

"You fools!" he hissed at length. "What are you doing, idiots? Seize the—the other man; he has been robbing the bank since ten o'clock this morning! Call the manager!"

The manager was already elbowing his way through the crowd.

"What is the meaning of this, Darwin?" he asked sternly.

"The other man!" gasped the cashier incoherently. "Arrest the other man!"

"What other man do you refer to?" asked the manager irritably.

"The rogue who has been impersonating me!" cried Darwin. "He has robbed the bank, and the fools have let him escape! He and his confederates imprisoned me in an empty house in Clapton."

The manager shrugged his shoulders and turned inquiringly to the crowd.

"There certainly was another man here half a minute ago, sir —a man exactly like Mr. Darwin," explained the head porter. "But he must have slipped out after orderin' us to arrest him. And when he struggled so, of course we all thought he was the thief, and the other one the real Mr. Darwin. I hope you understand, sir, but it's rather a difficult matter to explain. It was all so sudden like and unexpected that nobody thought of detaining the two of them; and he was as much like him as his own reflection is in the lookin'-glass. I hope my meaning is clear to you, sir?"

"Not very," said the manager, shortly. "Step into my room, Mr. Darwin; I shall probably hear a more lucid account of this highly complicated affair from your own lips, and in the meantime we'll send a wire to Scotland Yard."

But long before the lengthy and almost incredible story was concluded, a tall, clean-shaven man had cashed a thousand pounds worth of notes at the Bank of England, and afterwards walked home in a leisurely way to burn a pair of "mutton-chop" whiskers and a wig with a very bald crown.

"IT WAS 'AUTOMATON DARWIN' HIMSELF!"

V

A Prince of Swindlers

GUY BOOTHBY

A PRINCE OF SWINDLERS

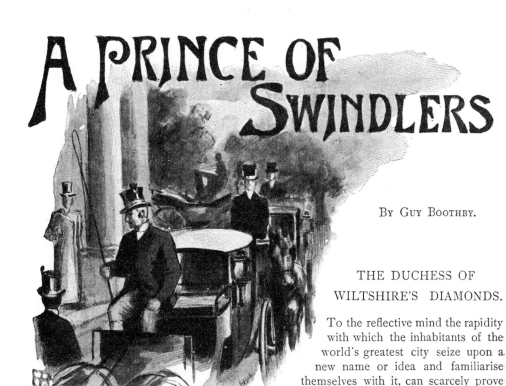

By Guy Boothby.

THE DUCHESS OF WILTSHIRE'S DIAMONDS.

To the reflective mind the rapidity with which the inhabitants of the world's greatest city seize upon a new name or idea and familiarise themselves with it, can scarcely prove otherwise than astonishing. As an illustration of my meaning let me take the case of Klimo — the now famous private detective, who has won for himself the right to be considered as great as Lecocq, or even the late lamented Sherlock Holmes.

Up to a certain morning London had never even heard his name, nor had it the remotest notion as to who or what he might be. It was as sublimely ignorant and careless on the subject as the inhabitants of Kamtchatka or Peru. Within twenty-four hours, however, the whole aspect of the case was changed. The man, woman, or child who had not seen his posters, or heard his name, was counted an ignoramus unworthy of intercourse with human beings.

Princes became familiar with it as their trains bore them to Windsor to luncheon with the Queen; the nobility noticed and commented upon it as they drove about the town; merchants, and business men generally, read it as they made their ways by omnibus or Underground, to their various shops and counting-houses; street boys called each other by it as a nickname; Music Hall Artistes introduced it into their patter, while it was even rumoured that the Stock Exchange itself had paused in the full flood tide of business to manufacture a riddle on the subject.

That Klimo made his profession pay him well was certain, first from the fact that his advertisements must have cost a good round sum, and, second, because he had taken a mansion in Belverton Street, Park Lane, next door to Porchester House, where, to the dismay of that aristocratic neighbourhood, he advertised that he was prepared to receive and be consulted by his clients. The invitation was responded to with alacrity, and from that day forward, between the hours of twelve and two, the pavement upon the north side of the street was lined with carriages, every one containing some person desirous of testing the great man's skill.

I must here explain that I have narrated all this in order to show the state of affairs existing in Belverton Street and Park Lane when Simon Carne arrived, or was supposed to arrive in England. If my memory serves me correctly, it was on Wednesday, the 3rd of May, that the Earl of Amberley drove to Victoria to meet and welcome the man whose acquaintance he had made in India under such peculiar circumstances, and under the spell of whose fascination he and his family had fallen so completely.

Reaching the station, his lordship descended from his carriage, and made his way to the platform set apart for the reception of the Continental express. He walked with a jaunty air, and seemed to be on the best of terms with himself and the world in general. How little he suspected the existence of the noose into which he was so innocently running his head!

A poster setting forth the name of the now famous detective, Klimo.

As if out of compliment to his arrival, the train put in an appearance within a few moments of his reaching the platform. He immediately placed himself in such a position that he could make sure of seeing the man he wanted, and waited patiently until he should come in sight. Carne, however, was not among the first batch, indeed, the majority of passengers had passed before his lordship caught sight of him.

One thing was very certain, however great the crush might have been, it would have been difficult to mistake Carne's figure. The man's infirmity and the peculiar beauty of his face rendered him easily recognisable. Possibly, after his long sojourn in India, he

found the morning cold, for he wore a long fur coat, the collar of which he had turned up round his ears, thus making a fitting frame for his delicate face. On seeing Lord Amberley he hastened forward to greet him.

"This is most kind and friendly of you," he said as he shook the other by the hand. "A fine day and Lord Amberley to meet me. One could scarcely imagine a better welcome."

As he spoke, one of his Indian servants approached and salaamed before him. He gave him an order, and received an answer in Hindustani, whereupon he turned again to Lord Amberley.

"You may imagine how anxious I am to see my new dwelling," he said. "My servant tells me that my carriage is here, so may I hope that you will drive back with me and see for yourself how I am likely to be lodged."

"I shall be delighted," said Lord Amberley, who was longing for the opportunity, and they accordingly went out into the station yard together to discover a brougham, drawn by two magnificent horses, and with Nur Ali, in all the glory of white raiment and crested turban, on the box, waiting to receive them. His lordship dismissed his Victoria, and when Jowur Singh had taken his place beside his fellow servant upon the box, the carriage rolled out of the station yard in the direction of Hyde Park.

"I trust her ladyship is quite well," said Simon Carne politely, as they turned into Gloucester Place.

"Excellently well, thank you," replied his

lordship. " She bade me welcome you to England in her name as well as my own, and I was to say that she is looking forward to seeing you."

" She is most kind, and I shall do myself the honour of calling upon her as soon as circumstances will permit," answered Carne. " I beg you will convey my best thanks to her for her thought of me."

While these polite speeches were passing between them they were rapidly approaching a large hoarding on which was displayed a poster setting forth the name of the now famous detective, Klimo.

Simon Carne, leaning forward, studied it, and when they had passed, turned to his friend again.

" At Victoria and on all the hoardings we meet I see an enormous placard, bearing the word ' Klimo.' Pray, what does it mean ? "

His lordship laughed.

" You are asking a question which, a month ago, was on the lips of nine out of every ten Londoners. It is only within the last fortnight that we have learned who and what ' Klimo ' is."

" And pray what is he ? "

" Well, the explanation is very simple. He is neither more nor less than a remarkably astute private detective, who has succeeded in attracting notice in such a way that half London has been induced to patronise him. I have had no dealings with the man myself. But a friend of mine, Lord Orpington, has been the victim of a most audacious burglary, and, the police having failed to solve the mystery, he has called Klimo in. We shall therefore see what he can do before many days are past. But, there, I expect you will soon know more about him than any of us."

" Indeed ! And why ? "

" For the simple reason that he has taken No. 1, Belverton Terrace, the house adjoining your own, and sees his clients there."

Simon Carne pursed up his lips, and appeared to be considering something.

" I trust he will not prove a nuisance," he said at last. " The agents who found me the house should have acquainted me with the fact. Private detectives, on however large a scale, scarcely strike one as the most desir-able of neighbours,—particularly for a man who is so fond of quiet as myself."

At this moment they were approaching their destination. As the carriage passed Belverton Street and pulled up, Lord Amberley pointed to a long line of vehicles standing before the detective's door.

" You can see for yourself something of the business he does," he said. " Those are the carriages of his clients, and it is probable that twice as many have arrived on foot."

" I shall certainly speak to the agent on the subject," said Carne, with a shadow of annoyance upon his face. " I consider the fact of this man's being so close to me a serious drawback to the house."

Jowur Singh here descended from the box and opened the door in order that his master and his guest might alight, while portly Ram Gafur, the butler, came down the steps and salaamed before them with Oriental obsequiousness. Carne greeted his domestics with kindly condescension, and then, accompanied by the ex-Viceroy, entered his new abode.

" I think you may congratulate yourself upon having secured one of the most desir-, able residences in London," said his lordship ten minutes or so later, when they had explored the principal rooms.

" I am very glad to hear you say so," said Carne. " I trust your lordship will remember that you will always be welcome in the house as long as I am its owner."

" It is very kind of you to say so," returned Lord Amberley warmly. " I shall look forward to some months of pleasant intercourse. And now I must be going. To-morrow, perhaps, if you have nothing better to do, you will give us the pleasure of your company at dinner. Your fame has already gone abroad, and we shall ask one or two nice people to meet you, including my brother and sister-in-law, Lord and Lady Gelpington, Lord and Lady Orpington, and my cousin, the Duchess of Wiltshire, whose interest in China and Indian Art, as perhaps you know, is only second to your own."

" I shall be most glad to come."

" We may count on seeing you in Eaton Square, then, at eight o'clock ? "

" If I am alive you may be sure I shall be

there. Must you really go? Then good-bye, and many thanks for meeting me."

His lordship having left the house Simon Carne went upstairs to his dressing room,

Klimo himself.

which it was to be noticed he found without inquiry, and rang the electric bell, beside the fireplace, three times. While he was waiting for it to be answered he stood looking out of the window at the long line of carriages in the street below.

"Everything is progressing admirably," he said to himself. "Amberley does not suspect any more than the world in general. As a proof he asks me to dinner to-morrow evening to meet his brother and sister-in-law, two of his particular friends, and above all Her

Grace of Wiltshire. Of course I shall go, and when I bid Her Grace good-bye it will be strange if I am not one step nearer the interest on Liz's money."

At this moment the door opened, and his valet, the grave and respectable Belton, entered the room. Carne turned to greet him impatiently.

"Come, come, Belton," he said, "we must be quick. It is twenty minutes to twelve and if we don't hurry, the folk next door will become impatient. Have you succeeded in doing what I spoke to you about last night?"

"I have done everthing, sir."

"I am glad to hear it. Now lock that door and let us get to work. You can let me have your news while I am dressing."

Opening one side of a massive wardrobe that completely filled one end of the room, Belton took from it a number of garments. They included a well worn velvet coat, a baggy pair of trousers—so old that only a notorious pauper or a millionaire could have afforded to wear them—a flannel waistcoat, a Gladstone collar, a soft silk tie, and a pair of embroidered carpet slippers upon which no old clothes man in the most reckless way of business in Petticoat Lane would have advanced a single halfpenny. Into these he assisted his master to change.

"Now give me the wig, and unfasten the straps of this hump," said Carne, as the other placed the garments just referred to upon a neighbouring chair.

Belton did as he was ordered, and then there happened a thing the like of which no one would have believed. Having unbuckled a strap on either shoulder, and slipped his hand beneath the waistcoat, he withdrew a large *papier-mâché* hump, which he carried away and carefully placed in a drawer of the bureau. Relieved of his burden, Simon Carne stood up as straight and well-made a man as any in Her Majesty's dominions. The malformation, for which so many, including the Earl and Countess of Amberley, had often pitied him, was nothing but a hoax intended to produce an effect which would permit him additional facilities of disguise.

The hump discarded, and the grey wig fitted carefully to his head in such a manner that not even a pinch of his own curlylocks could be seen beneath it, he adorned his cheeks with a pair of *crépu*-hair whiskers, donned the flannel vest and the velvet coat previously mentioned, slipped his feet into the carpet slippers, placed a pair of smoked glasses upon his nose, and declared himself ready to proceed about his business. The man who would have known him for Simon Carne would have been as astute as, well, shall we say, as the private detective—Klimo himself.

"It's on the stroke of twelve," he said, as he gave a final glance at himself in the pier-glass above the dressing-table, and arranged his tie to his satisfaction. "Should anyone call, instruct Ram Gafur to tell them that I have gone out on business, and shall not be back until three o'clock."

"Very good, sir."

"Now undo the door and let me go in."

Thus commanded, Belton went across to the large wardrobe which, as I have already said, covered the whole of one side of the room, and opened the middle door. Two or three garments were seen inside suspended on pegs, and these he removed, at the same time pushing towards the right the panel at the rear. When this was done a large aperture in the wall between the two houses was disclosed. Through this door Carne passed drawing it behind him.

In No. 1, Belverton Terrace, the house occupied by the detective, whose presence in the street Carne seemed to find so objectionable, the entrance thus constructed was covered by the peculiar kind of confessional box in which Klimo invariably sat to receive his clients, the rearmost panels of which opened in the same fashion as those in the wardrobe in the dressing-room. These being pulled aside, he had but to draw them to again after him, take his seat, ring the electric bell to inform his housekeeper that he was ready, and then welcome his clients as quickly as they cared to come.

Punctually at two o'clock the interviews ceased, and Klimo, having reaped an excellent harvest of fees, returned to Porchester House to become Simon Carne once more.

Possibly it was due to the fact that the Earl and Countess of Amberley were brimming over with his praise, it may have been the rumour that he was worth as many millions as you have fingers upon your hand that did it; one thing, however, was self evident, within twenty-four hours of the noble Earl's meeting him at Victoria Station, Simon Carne was the talk, not only of fashionable, but also of unfashionable, London.

That his household were, with one exception, natives of India, that he had paid a rental for Porchester House which ran into five figures, that he was the greatest living authority upon China and Indian art generally, and that he had come over to England in search of a wife, were among the smallest of the *canards* set afloat concerning him.

During dinner next evening Carne put forth every effort to please. He was placed on the right hand of his hostess and next to the Duchess of Wiltshire. To the latter he paid particular attention, and to such good purpose that when the ladies returned to the drawing-room afterwards Her Grace was full of his praises. They had discussed china of all sorts, Carne had promised her a specimen which she had longed for all her life, but had never been able to obtain, and in return she had promised to show him the quaintly carved Indian casket in which the famous necklace, of which he had, of course, heard, spent most of its time. She would be wearing the jewels in question at her own ball in a week's time, she informed him, and if he would care to see the case when it came from her bankers on that day, she would be only too pleased to show it to him.

As Simon Carne drove home in his luxurious brougham afterwards, he smiled to himself as he thought of the success which was attending his first endeavour. Two of the guests, who were stewards of the Jockey Club, had heard with delight his idea of purchasing a horse in order to have an interest in the Derby. While another, on hearing that he desired to become the possessor of a yacht, had offered to propose him for the R.C.Y.C. To crown it all, however, and much better than all, the Duchess of Wiltshire had promised to show him her famous diamonds.

"By this time next week," he said to himself, "Liz's interest should be considerably closer. But satisfactory as my progress has been hitherto it is difficult to see how I am to get possession of the stones. From what I have been able to discover they are only brought from the bank on the day the Duchess intends to wear them, and they are taken back by His Grace the morning following.

"While she has got them on her person it would be manifestly impossible to get them from her. And as, when she takes them off, they are returned to their box and placed in a safe, constructed in the wall of the bedroom adjoining, and which for the occasion is occupied by the butler and one of the under footmen, the only key being in the possession of the Duke himself, it would be equally foolish to hope to appropriate them. In what manner therefore I am to become their possessor passes my comprehension. However, one thing is certain, obtained they must be, and the attempt must be made on the night of the ball if possible. In the meantime I'll set my wits to work upon a plan."

Next day Simon Carne was the recipient of an invitation to the ball in question, and two days later he called upon the Duchess of Wiltshire at her residence in Belgrave Square with a plan prepared. He also took with him the small vase he had promised her four nights before. She received him most graciously, and their talk fell at once into the usual channel. Having examined her collection and charmed her by means of one or two judicious criticisms, he asked permission to include photographs of certain of her treasures in his forthcoming book, then little by little he skilfully guided the conversation on to the subject of jewels.

"Since we are discussing gems, Mr. Carne," she said, "perhaps it would interest you to see my famous necklace. By good fortune I have it in the house now, for the reason that an alteration is being made to one of the clasps by my jewellers."

"I should like to see it immensely," answered Carne. "At one time and another I have had the good fortune to examine the jewels of the leading Indian Princes, and I should like to be able to say that I had seen the famous Wiltshire necklace."

"Then you shall certainly have that honour," she answered with a smile. "If you will ring that bell I will send for it."

Carne rang the bell as requested, and when the butler entered he was given the key of the safe and ordered to bring the case to the drawing-room.

"We must not keep it very long," she observed while the man was absent. "It is to be returned to the bank in an hour's time."

"I am indeed fortunate," Carne replied, and turned to the description of some curious Indian wood carving, of which he was making a special feature in his book. As he explained, he had collected his illustrations from the doors of Indian temples, from the gateways of palaces, from old brass work, and even from carved chairs and boxes he had picked up in all sorts of odd corners. Her Grace was most interested.

"How strange that you should have mentioned it," she said. "If carved boxes have any interest for you, it is possible my jewel case itself may be of use to you. As I think I told you during Lady Amberley's dinner, it came from Benares, and has carved upon it the portraits of nearly every god in the Hindu Pantheon."

"You raise my curiosity to fever heat," said Carne.

A few moments later the servant returned, bringing with him a wooden box, about sixteen inches long, by twelve wide, and eight deep, which he placed upon a table beside his mistress, after which he retired.

"This is the case to which I have just been referring," said the Duchess, placing her hand on the article in question. "If you glance at it you will see how exquisitely it is carved."

Concealing his eagerness with an effort, Simon Carne drew his chair up to the table, and examined the box.

It was with justice she had described it as a work of art. What the wood was of which it was constructed Carne was unable to tell. It was dark and heavy, and, though it was not teak, closely resembled it. It was literally covered with quaint carving, and of its kind was a unique work of art.

"It is most curious and beautiful," said Carne when he had finished his examination. "In all my experience I can safely say I have never seen its equal. If you will permit me I should very much like to include a description and an illustration of it in my book."

" Of course you may do so ; I shall be only too delighted," answered Her Grace. " If it will help you in your work I shall be glad to lend it to you for a few hours in order that you may have the illustration made."

This was exactly what Carne had been waiting for, and he accepted the offer with alacrity.

" Very well, then," she said. " On the day of my ball, when it will be brought from the bank again, I will take the necklace out and send the case to you. I must make one proviso, however, and that is that you let me have it back the same day."

" I will certainly promise to do that," replied Carne.

" And now let us look inside," said his hostess.

Choosing a key from a bunch she carried in her pocket, she unlocked the casket, and lifted the lid. Accustomed as Carne had all his life been to the sight of gems, what he saw before him then almost took his breath away. The inside of the box, both sides and bottom, was quilted with the softest Russia leather, and on this luxurious couch reposed the famous necklace. The fire of the stones when the light caught them was sufficient to dazzle the eyes, so fierce was it.

As Carne could see, every gem was perfect of its kind, and there were no fewer than three hundred of them. The setting was a fine example of the jeweller's art, and last, but not least, the value of the whole affair was fifty thousand pounds, a mere fleabite to the man who had given it to his wife, but a fortune to any humbler person.

" And now that you have seen my property,

"This is the case to which I have just been referring," said the Duchess.

what do you think of it ? " asked the Duchess as she watched her visitor's face.

" It is very beautiful," he answered, " and I do not wonder that you are proud of it. Yes, the diamonds are very fine, but I think it is their abiding place that fascinates me more.

Have you any objection to my measuring it ? "

" Pray do so, if it is likely to be of any assistance to you," replied Her Grace.

Carne thereupon produced a small ivory rule, ran it over the box, and the figures he thus obtained he jotted down in his pocket book.

Ten minutes later, when the case had been returned to the safe, he thanked the Duchess for her kindness and took his departure, promising to call in person for the empty case on the morning of the ball.

Reaching home he passed into his study, and, seating himself at his writing table, pulled a sheet of note paper towards him and began to sketch, as well as he could remember it, the box he had seen. Then he leant back in his chair and closed his eyes.

"I have cracked a good many hard nuts in my time," he said reflectively, "but never one that seemed so difficult at first sight as this. As far as I see at present, the case stands as follows: the box will be brought from the bank where it usually reposes to Wiltshire House on the morning of the dance. I shall be allowed to have possession of it, without the stones of course, for a period possibly extending from eleven o'clock in the morning to four or five, at any rate not later than seven, in the evening. After the ball the necklace will be returned to it, when it will be locked up in the safe, over which the butler and a footman will mount guard.

"To get into the room during the night is not only too risky, but physically out of the question; while to rob Her Grace of her treasure during the progress of the dance would be equally impossible. The Duke fetches the casket and takes it back to the

"I see a box," answered the man.

bank himself, so that to all intents and purposes I am almost as far off the solution as ever."

Half-an-hour went by and found him still seated at his desk, staring at the drawing on

the paper, then an hour. The traffic of the streets rolled past the house unheeded. Finally Jowur Singh announced his carriage, and, feeling that an idea might come to him with a change of scene, he set off for a drive in the park.

By this time his elegant mail phaeton, with its magnificent horses and Indian servant on the seat behind, was as well-known as Her Majesty's state equipage, and attracted almost as much attention. To-day, however, the fashionable world noticed that Simon Carne looked preoccupied. He was still working out his problem, but so far without much success. Suddenly something, no one will ever be able to say what, put an idea into his head. The notion was no sooner born in his brain than he left the park and drove quickly home. Ten minutes had scarcely elapsed before he was back in his study again, and had ordered that Wajib Baksh should be sent to him.

When the man he wanted put in an appearance, Carne handed him the paper upon which he had made the drawing of the jewel case.

"Look at that," he said, "and tell me what thou seest there."

"I see a box," answered the man, who by this time was well accustomed to his master's ways.

"As thou say'st, it is a box," said Carne. "The wood is heavy and hick, though what wood it is I do not know. The measurements are upon the paper below. Within, both the sides and bottom are quilted with soft leather as I have also shown. Think now, Wajib Baksh, for in this case thou wilt need to have all thy wits about thee. Tell me is it in thy power, oh most cunning of all craftsmen, to insert such extra sides within this box that they, being held by a spring, shall lie so snug as not to be noticeable to the ordinary eye? Can it be so arranged that, when the box is locked, they shall fall flat upon the bottom thus covering and holding fast what lies beneath them, and yet making the box appear to the eye as if it were empty. Is it possible for thee to do such a thing?"

Wajib Baksh did not reply for a few moments. His instinct told him what his master wanted, and he was not disposed to answer hastily, for he also saw that his reputation as the most cunning craftsman in India was at stake.

"If the Heaven-born will permit me the ·night for thought," he said at last, "I will come to him when he rises from his bed and tell him what I can do, and he can then give his orders as it pleases him."

"Very good," said Carne. "Then tomorrow morning I shall expect thy report. Let the work be good and there will be many rupees for thee to touch in return. As to the lock and the way it shall act, let that be the concern of Hiram Singh."

Wajib Baksh salaamed and withdrew, and Simon Carne for the time being dismissed the matter from his mind.

Next morning, while he was dressing, Belton reported that the two artificers desired an interview with him. He ordered them to be admitted, and forthwith they entered the room. It was noticeable that Wajib Baksh carried in his hand a heavy box, which, upon Carne's motioning him to do so, he placed upon the table.

"Have ye thought over the matter?" he asked, seeing that the men waited for him to speak.

"We have thought of it," replied Hiram Singh, who always acted as spokesman for the pair. "If the Presence will deign to look he will see that we have made a box of the size and shape such as he drew upon the paper."

"Yes, it is certainly a good copy," said Carne condescendingly, after he had examined it.

Wajib Baksh showed his white teeth in appreciation of the compliment, and Hiram Singh drew closer to the table.

"And now, if the Sahib will open it, he will in his wisdom be able to tell if it resembles the other that he has in his mind."

Carne opened the box as requested, and discovered that the interior was an exact counterfeit of the Duchess of Wiltshire's jewel case, even to the extent of the quilted leather lining which had been the other's

principal feature. He admitted that the likeness was all that could be desired.

"As he is satisfied," said Hiram Singh, "it may be that the Protector of the Poor will deign to try an experiment with it. See, here is a comb. Let it be placed in the box, so— now he will see what he will see."

The broad, silver-backed comb, lying upon his dressing-table, was placed on the bottom of the box, the lid was closed, and the key turned in the lock. The case being securely fastened, Hiram Singh laid it before his master.

"I am to open it, I suppose?" said Carne, taking the key and replacing it in the lock.

"If my master pleases," replied the other.

Carne accordingly turned it in the lock, and, having done so, raised the lid and looked inside. His astonishment was complete. To all intents and purposes the box was empty. The comb was not to be seen, and yet the quilted sides and bottom were, to all appearances, just the same as when he had first looked inside.

"This is most wonderful," he said. And indeed it was as clever a conjuring trick as any he had ever seen.

"Nay, it is very simple," Wajib Baksh replied. "The Heaven-born told me that there must be no risk of detection."

He took the box in his own hands and, running his nails down the centre of the quilting, dividing the false bottom into two pieces; these he lifted out, revealing the comb lying upon the real bottom beneath.

"The sides, as my lord will see," said Hiram Singh, taking a step forward, "are held in their appointed places by these two springs. Thus, when the key is turned the springs relax, and the sides are driven by others into their places on the bottom, where the seams in the quilting mask the join. There is but one disadvantage. It is as follows: When the pieces which form the bottom are lifted out in order that my lord may get at whatever lies concealed beneath, the springs must of necessity stand revealed. However, to anyone who knows sufficient of the working of the box to lift out the false bottom, it will be an easy matter to withdraw the springs and conceal them about his person."

"As you say that is an easy matter," said Carne, "and I shall not be likely to forget. Now one other question. Presuming I am in a position to put the real box into your hands for say eight hours, do you think that in that time you can fit it up so that detection will be impossible?"

"Assuredly, my lord," replied Hiram Singh with conviction. "There is but the lock and the fitting of the springs to be done. Three hours at most would suffice for that."

"I am pleased with you," said Carne. "As a proof of my satisfaction, when the work is finished you will each receive five hundred rupees. Now you can go."

According to his promise, ten o'clock on the Friday following found him in his hansom driving towards Belgrave Square. He was a little anxious, though the casual observer would scarcely have been able to tell it. The magnitude of the stake for which he was playing was enough to try the nerve of even such a past master in his profession as Simon Carne.

Arriving at the house he discovered some workmen erecting an awning across the foot-

His hostess and her husband received him.

way in preparation for the ball that was to take place at night. It was not long, however, before he found himself in the boudoir, reminding Her Grace of her promise to permit him an opportunity of making a drawing of the famous jewel case. The Duchess was naturally busy, and within a quarter of an hour he was on his way home with the box placed on the seat of the carriage beside him.

"Now," he said, as he patted it good-humouredly, "if only the notion worked out by Hiram Singh and Wajib Baksh holds good, the famous Wiltshire diamonds will become my property before very many hours are passed. By this time to-morrow, I suppose, London will be all agog concerning the burglary."

On reaching his house he left his carriage and himself carried the box into his study. Once there he rang his bell and ordered Hiram Singh and Wajib Baksh to be sent to him. When they arrived he showed them the box upon which they were to exercise their ingenuity.

"Bring your tools in here," he said, "and do the work under my own eyes. You have but nine hours before you, so you must make the most of them."

The men went for their implements, and as soon as they were ready set to work. All through the day they were kept hard at it, with the result that by five o'clock the alterations had been effected and the case stood ready. By the time Carne returned from his afternoon drive in the Park it was quite prepared for the part it was to play in his scheme. Having praised the men, he turned them out and locked the door, then went across the room and unlocked a drawer in his writing table. From it he took a flat leather jewel case which he opened. It contained a necklace of counterfeit diamonds, if anything a little larger than the one he intended to try to obtain. He had purchased it that morning in the Burlington Arcade for the purpose of testing the apparatus his servants had made, and this he now proceeded to do.

Laying it carefully upon the bottom he closed the lid and turned the key. When he opened it again the necklace was gone, and even though he knew the secret he could not for the life of him see where the false bottom began and ended. After that he reset the trap and tossed the necklace carelessly in. To his delight it acted as well as on the previous occasion. He could scarcely contain his satisfaction. His conscience was sufficiently elastic to give him no trouble. To him it was scarcely a robbery he was planning, but an artistic trial of skill, in which he pitted his wits and cunning against the forces of society in general.

At half-past seven he dined and afterwards smoked a meditative cigar over the evening paper in the billiard room. The invitations to the ball were for ten o'clock, and at nine-thirty he went to his dressing-room.

"Make me tidy as quickly as you can," he said to Belton when the latter appeared, "and while you are doing so listen to my final instructions.

"To-night, as you know, I am endeavouring to secure the Duchess of Wiltshire's necklace. To-morrow morning all London will resound with the hubbub, and I have been making my plans in such a way as to arrange that Klimo shall be the first person consulted. When the messenger calls, if call he does, see that the old woman next door bids him tell the Duke to come personally at twelve o'clock. Do you understand?"

"Perfectly, sir."

"Very good. Now give me the jewel case, and let me be off. You need not sit up for me."

Precisely as the clocks in the neighbourhood were striking ten Simon Carne reached Belgrave Square, and, as he hoped, found himself the first guest.

His hostess and her husband received him in the ante-room of the drawing-room.

"I come laden with a thousand apologies," he said as he took Her Grace's hand, and bent over it with that ceremonious politeness which was one of the man's chief characteristics. "I am most unconscionably early, I know, but I hastened here in order that I might personally return the jewel case you so kindly lent me. I must trust to your generosity to forgive me. The drawings took longer than I expected."

"Please do not apologise," answered Her Grace. "It is very kind of you to have brought the case yourself. I hope the illustrations have proved successful. I shall look forward to seeing them as soon as they are ready. But I am keeping you holding the box. One of my servants will take it to my room."

She called a footman to her and bade him take the box and place it upon her dressing-table.

"Before it goes I must let you see that I have not damaged it either externally or internally," said Carne with a laugh. "It is such a valuable case that I should never forgive myself if it had even received a scratch during the time it has been in my possession."

So saying he lifted the lid and allowed her to look inside. To all appearance it was exactly the same as when she had lent it to him earlier in the day.

"You have been most careful," she said. And then, with an air of banter, she continued: "If you desire it I shall be pleased to give you a certificate to that effect."

They jested in this fashion for a few moments after the servant's departure, during which time Carne promised to call upon her the following morning at eleven o'clock, and to bring with him the illustrations he had made and a queer little piece of china he had had the good fortune to pick up in a dealer's shop the previous afternoon. By this time fashionable London was making its way up the grand staircase, and with its appearance further conversation became impossible.

Shortly after midnight Carne bade his hostess good night and slipped away. He was perfectly satisfied with his evening's entertainment, and if the key of the jewel case were not turned before the jewels were placed in it, he was convinced they would become his property. It speaks well for his strength of nerve when I record the fact that on going to bed his slumbers were as peaceful and untroubled as those of a little child.

Breakfast was scarcely over next morning before a hansom drew up at his front door and Lord Amberley alighted. He was ushered into Carne's presence forthwith, and on seeing that the latter was surprised at his early visit, hastened to explain.

"My dear fellow," he said as he took possession of the chair the other offered him, " I have come round to see you on most important business. As I told you last night at the dance, when you so kindly asked me to come and see the steam yacht you have purchased, I had an appointment with Wiltshire at half-past nine this morning. On reaching Belgrave Square, I found the whole house in confusion. Servants were running hither and thither with scared faces, the butler was on the borders of lunacy, the Duchess was well-nigh hysterical in her boudoir, while her husband was in his study vowing vengeance against all the world."

"You alarm me," said Carne, lighting a cigarette with a hand that was as steady as a rock. "What on earth has happened?"

"I think I might safely allow you fifty guesses and then wager a hundred pounds you'd not hit the mark; and yet in a certain measure it concerns you."

"Concerns me? Good gracious. What have I done to bring all this about?'

"Pray do not look so alarmed," said Amberley. "Personally you have done nothing. Indeed, on second thoughts, I don't know that I am right in saying that it con-

cerns you at all. The fact of the matter is, Carne, a burglary took place last night at Wiltshire House, *and the famous necklace has disappeared.*"

"Good Heavens! You don't say so?"

"But I *do.* The circumstances of the case are as follows: When my cousin retired to her room last night after the ball, she unclasped the necklace, and, in her husband's presence, placed it carefully in her jewel case, which she locked. That having been done, Wiltshire took the box to the room which contained the safe, and himself placed it there, locking the iron door with his own key. The room was occupied that night, according to custom, by the butler and one of the footmen, both of whom have been in the family since they were boys.

"Next morning, after breakfast, the Duke unlocked the safe and took out the box, intending to convey it to the Bank as usual. Before leaving, however, he placed it on his study-table and went upstairs to speak to his wife. He cannot remember exactly how long he was absent, but he feels convinced that he was not gone more than a quarter of an hour at the very utmost.

"Their conversation finished, she accompanied him downstairs, where she saw him take up the case to carry it to his carriage. Before he left the house, however, she said: ' I suppose you have looked to see that the necklace is all right?' 'How could I do so?' was his reply. 'You know you possess the only key that will fit it.'

"She felt in her pockets, but to her surprise the key was not there."

"If I were a detective I should say that that is a point to be remembered," said Carne with a smile. "Pray, where did she find her keys?"

"Upon her dressing-table," said Amberley. "Though she has not the slightest recollection of leaving them there."

"Well, when she had procured the keys, what happened?"

"Why, they opened the box, and to their astonishment and dismay, *found it empty. The jewels were gone!*"

"Good gracious. What a terrible loss! It seems almost impossible that it can be true. And pray, what did they do?"

"At first they stood staring into the empty box, hardly believing the evidence of their own eyes. Stare how they would, however, they could not bring them back. The jewels had without doubt disappeared, but when and where the robbery had taken place it was impossible to say. After that they had up all the servants and questioned them, but the result was what they might have foreseen, no one from the butler to the kitchenmaid could throw any light upon the subject. To this minute it remains as great a mystery as when they first discovered it."

"I am more concerned than I can tell you," said Carne. "How thankful I ought to be that I returned the case to Her Grace last night. But in thinking of myself I am forgetting to ask what has brought you to me. If I can be of any assistance I hope you will command me."

"Well, I'll tell you why I have come," replied Lord Amberley. "Naturally they are most anxious to have the mystery solved and the jewels recovered as soon as possible. Wiltshire wanted to send to Scotland Yard there and then, but his wife and I eventually persuaded him to consult Klimo. As you know, if the police authorities are called in first he refuses the business altogether. Now, we thought, as you are his next door neighbour, you might possibly be able to assist us."

"You may be very sure, my lord, I will do everything that lies in my power. Let us go in and see him at once."

As he spoke he rose and threw what remained of his cigarette into the fireplace. His visitor having imitated his example, they procured their hats and walked round from Park Lane into Belverton Street to bring up at No. 1. After they had rung the bell the door was opened to them by the old woman who invariably received the detective's clients.

"Is Mr. Klimo at home?" asked Carne. "And, if so, can we see him?"

The old lady was a little deaf, and the question had to be repeated before she could be made to understand what was wanted. As soon, however, as she realised their desire she informed them that her master was absent from town, but would be back as usual at twelve o'clock to meet his clients.

"What on earth's to be done?" said the Earl, looking at his companion in dismay. "I am afraid I can't come back again, as I have a most important appointment at that hour."

"Do you think you could intrust the business to me?" asked Carne. "If so, I will make a point of seeing him at twelve o'clock, and could call at Wiltshire House afterwards and tell the Duke what I have done."

"That's very good of you," replied Amberley. "If you are sure it would not put you to too much trouble, that would be quite the best thing to be done."

"I will do it with pleasure," Carne replied. "I feel it my duty to help in whatever way I can."

"You are very kind," said the other. "Then, as I understand it, you are to call upon Klimo at twelve o'clock, and afterwards to let my cousins know what you have succeeded in doing. I only hope he will help us to secure the thief. We are having too many of these burglaries just now. I must catch this hansom and be off. Goodbye, and many thanks."

"Goodbye," said Carne, and shook him by the hand.

The hansom having rolled away, Carne retraced his steps to his own abode.

"It is really very strange," he muttered as he walked along, "how often chance condescends to lend her assistance to my little schemes. The mere fact that His Grace left the box unwatched in his study for a quarter of an hour may serve to throw the police off on quite another scent. I am also glad that they decided to open the case in the house, for if it had gone to the bankers' and had been placed in the strong room unexamined, I should never have been able to get possession of the jewels at all."

Three hours later he drove to Wiltshire House and saw the Duke. The Duchess was far too much upset by the catastrophe to see anyone.

"This is really most kind of you, Mr. Carne," said His Grace when the other had supplied an elaborate account of his interview with Klimo. "We are extremely indebted to you. I am sorry he cannot come before ten o'clock to-night, and that he makes this stipulation of my seeing him alone, for I must confess I should like to have had some-one else present to ask any questions that might escape me. But if that's his usual hour and custom, well, we must abide by it, that's all. I hope he will do some good, for this is the greatest calamity that has ever befallen me. As I told you just now, it has made my wife quite ill. She is confined to her bed-room and quite hysterical."

" You do not suspect anyone, I suppose," in-quired Carne.

" Not a soul," the other answered. " The thing is such a mystery that we do not know what to think. I feel convinced, however, that my servants are as innocent as I am. Nothing will ever make me think them otherwise. I wish I could catch the fellow, that's all. I'd make him suffer for the trick he's played me."

Carne offered an ap-propriate reply, and after a little further conversation upon the subject, bade the irate nobleman goodbye and left the house. From Belgrave Square he drove to one of the clubs of which he had been elected a mem-ber, in search of Lord Orpington, with whom he had promised to lunch, and afterwards took him to a ship-builder's yard near

"I was able to make a regular succession of footsteps in the dust along the ledge."

Greenwich in order to show him the steam yacht he had lately purchased.

It was close upon dinner time before he returned to his own residence. He brought Lord Orpington with him, and they dined in state together. At nine the latter bade him good-bye, and at ten Carne retired to his dressing-room and rang for Belton.

" What have you to report," he asked,

"with regard to what I bade you do in Bel-grave Square ? "

"I followed your instructions to the letter," Belton replied. " Yesterday morning I wrote to Messrs. Horniblow and Jimson, the house agents in Piccadilly, in the name of Colonel Braithwaite, and asked for an order to view the resi-dence to the right of Wilt-shire House. I asked that the order might be sent direct to the house, where the Colonel would get it upon his arrival. This letter I posted myself in Basingstoke, as you desired me to do.

" At nine o'clock yester-day morning I dressed my-self as much like an elderly army officer as possible, and took a cab to Belgrave Square. The caretaker, an old fellow of close upon seventy years of age, ad-mitted me immediately upon hearing my name, and proposed that he should show me over the house. This, however, I told him was quite unnecessary, backing my speech with a present of half-a-crown, whereupon he returned to his breakfast perfectly satis-fied, while I wandered about the house at my own leisure.

" Reaching the same floor as that upon which is situated the room in which the Duke's safe is kept, I discovered that your supposition was quite correct, and that it would be possible for a man, by opening the window, to make his way along the coping from one house to the other, without being seen. I made certain that there was no one in the bedroom in which the butler slept, and then arranged the long telescope walking stick you gave me, and fixed one of my boots to it by means of the screw in the end. With this I was able to make a regular succession of footsteps in the dust along the ledge, between one window and the other.

" That done, I went downstairs again, bade the caretaker good morning, and got into my cab. From Belgrave Square I drove to the shop of the pawnbroker whom you told me you had discovered was out of town. His assistant inquired my business and was anxious to do what he could for me. I told him, however, that I must see his master personally as it was about the sale of some diamonds I had had left me. I pretended to be annoyed that he was not at home, and muttered to myself, so that the man could hear, something about its meaning a journey to Amsterdam.

" Then I limped out of the shop, paid off my cab, and, walking down a by-street, removed my moustache, and altered my appearance by taking off my great coat and muffler. A few streets further on I purchased a bowler hat in place of the old-fashioned topper I had hitherto been wearing, and then took a cab from Piccadilly and came home."

" You have fulfilled my instructions admirably," said Carne. " And if the business comes off, as I expect it will, you shall receive your usual percentage. Now I must be turned into Klimo and be off to Belgrave Square to put His Grace of Wiltshire upon the track of this burglar."

Before he retired to rest that night Simon Carne took something, wrapped in a red silk handkerchief, from the capacious pocket of the coat Klimo had been wearing a few moments before. Having unrolled the covering, he held up to the light the magnificent necklace which for so many years had been the joy and pride of the ducal house of Wiltshire. The electric light played upon it, and touched it with a thousand different hues.

" Where so many have failed," he said to himself, as he wrapped it in the handkerchief again and locked it in his safe, " it is pleasant to be able to congratulate oneself on having succeeded. It is without its equal, and I don't think I shall be over-stepping the mark if I say that I think when

she receives it Liz will be glad she lent me the money."

Next morning all London was astonished by the news that the famous Wiltshire diamonds had been stolen, and a few hours later Carne learnt from an evening paper that the detectives who had taken up the case, upon the supposed retirement from it of Klimo, were still completely at fault.

That evening he was to entertain several friends to dinner. They included Lord Amberley, Lord Orpington, and a prominent member of the Privy Council. Lord Amberley arrived late, but filled to overflowing

He held up to the light the magnificent necklace.

with importance. His friends noticed his state, and questioned him.

" Well, gentlemen," he answered, as he took up a commanding position upon the drawing-room hearthrug, " I am in a position to inform you that Klimo has reported upon the case, and the upshot of it is that the Wiltshire Diamond Mystery is a mystery no longer."

"What do you mean?" asked the others in a chorus.

"I mean that he sent in his report to Wiltshire this afternoon, as arranged. From what he said the other night, after being alone in the room with the empty jewel case and a magnifying glass for two minutes or so,

"But how did Klimo find all this out?" asked Lord Orpington.

"By his own inimitable cleverness," replied Lord Amberley. "At any rate it has been proved that he was correct. The man *did* make his way from next door, and the police have since discovered that an individual, answering to the description given, visited a pawnbroker's shop in the city about an hour later and stated that he had diamonds to sell."

"If that is so it turns out to be a very

"Here's a good health to Klimo."

he was in a position to describe the *modus operandi*, and what is more to put the police on the scent of the burglar."

"And how *was* it worked?" asked Carne.

"From the empty house next door," replied the other. "On the morning of the burglary a man, purporting to be a retired army officer, called with an order to view, got the caretaker out of the way, clambered along to Wiltshire House by means of the parapet outside, reached the room during the time the servants were at breakfast, opened the safe, and abstracted the jewels."

simple mystery after all," said Lord Orpington as they began their meal.

"Thanks to the ingenuity of the cleverest detective in the world," remarked Amberley.

"In that case here's a good health to Klimo," said the Privy Councillor, raising his glass.

"I will join you in that," said Simon Carne. "Here's a very good health to Klimo and his connection with the Duchess of Wiltshire's diamonds. May he always be equally successful!"

"Hear, hear to that," replied his guests.

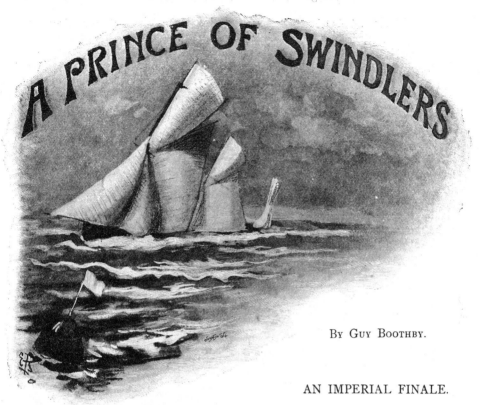

A PRINCE OF SWINDLERS

By Guy Boothby.

AN IMPERIAL FINALE.

(A Complete Story.)

OF all the functions that ornament the calendar of the English social and sporting year, surely the Cowes week may claim to rank as one of the greatest, or at least the most enjoyable. So thought Simon Carne as he sat on the deck of Lord Tremorden's yacht, anchored off the mouth of the Medina River, smoking his cigarette and whispering soft nothings into the little shell-like ear of Lady Mabel Madderley, the lady of all others who had won the right to be considered the beauty of the past season. It was a perfect afternoon, and, as if to fill his flagon of enjoyment to the very brim, he had won the Queen's Cup with his yacht *The Unknown Quantity* only half-an-hour before. Small wonder, therefore, that he was contented with his lot in life, and his good fortune of that afternoon in particular.

The tiny harbour was crowded with shipping of all sorts, shapes, and sizes, including the guardship, his Imperial Majesty the Emperor of Westphalia's yacht the *Hohenszrallas*, the English Royal yachts, steam yachts, schooners, cutters, and all the various craft taking part in England's greatest water carnival. Steam launches darted hither and thither, smartly equipped gigs conveyed gaily dressed parties from vessel to vessel, while, ashore, the little town itself was alive with bunting, and echoed to the strains of almost continuous music.

"Surely you ought to consider yourself a very happy man, Mr. Carne," said Lady Mabel Madderley, with a smile, in reply to a speech of the other's. "You won the Derby in June, and to-day you have appropriated the Queen's Cup."

"If such things constitute happiness, I suppose I must be in the seventh Heaven of Delight," answered Carne, as he took another cigarette from his case and lit it. "All the same, I am insatiable enough to desire still greater fortune. When one has set one's heart upon winning something, besides which the Derby and the Queen's Cup are items scarcely worth considering, one is rather apt to feel that fortune has still much to give."

"I am afraid I do not quite grasp your meaning," she said. But there was a look in her face that told him that, if she did not understand, she could at least make a very good guess. According to the world's reckoning, he was quite the best fish then swimming in the matrimonial pond, and some people, for the past few weeks, had even gone so far as to say that she had hooked him. It could not be denied that he had been paying her unmistakable attention of late.

What answer he would have vouchsafed to her speech it is impossible to say, for at that moment their host came along the deck towards them. He carried a note in his hand.

"I have just received a message to say that his Imperial Majesty is going to honour us with a visit," he said, when he reached them. "If I mistake not, that is his launch coming towards us now."

Lady Mabel and Simon Carne rose and accompanied him to the starboard bulwarks. A smart white launch, with the Westphalian flag flying at her stern, had left the Royal yacht and was steaming quickly towards them. A few minutes later it had reached the companion ladder, and Lord Tremorden had descended to welcome his Royal guest. When they reached the deck together, his Majesty shook hands with Lady Tremorden, and afterwards with Lady Mabel and Simon Carne.

"I must congratulate you most heartily, Mr. Carne," he said, "on your victory to-day. You gave us an excellent race, and though I had the misfortune to be beaten by thirty seconds, still I have the satisfaction of knowing that the winner was a better boat in every way than my own."

"Your Majesty adds to the sweets of victory by your generous acceptance of defeat," Carne replied. "But I must confess that I owe my success in no way to my own

ability. The boat was chosen for me by another, and I have not even the satisfaction of saying that I sailed her myself."

"Nevertheless she is your property, and you will go down to posterity famous in yachting annals as the winner of the Queen's Cup in this justly celebrated year."

With this compliment his Majesty turned to his hostess and entered into conversation with her, leaving his aide-de-camp free to

"Surely you ought to consider yourself a very happy man, Mr. Carne."

discuss the events of the day with Lady Mabel. When he took his departure half-an-hour later, Carne also bade his friends good-bye, and, descending to his boat, was rowed away to his own beautiful steam yacht, which was anchored a few cables' length away from the Imperial craft. He was to dine on board the latter vessel that evening.

On gaining the deck he was met by Belton, his valet, who carried a telegram in his hand.

As soon as he received it, Carne opened it and glanced at the contents, without, however, betraying very much interest.

An instant later the expression upon his face changed like magic. Still holding the message in his hand, he turned to Belton.

"Come below," he said quickly. "There is news enough here to give us something to think of for hours to come."

Reaching the saloon, which was decorated with all the daintiness of the upholsterer's art, he led the way to the cabin he had arranged as a study. Having entered it, he shut and locked the door.

"It's all up, Belton," he said. "The comedy has lasted long enough. and now it only remains for us to speak the tag, and after that to ring the curtain down as speedily as may be."

"I am afraid, sir, I do not quite take your meaning," said Belton. "Would you mind telling me what has happened ? "

"I can do that in a very few words," the other answered. "This cablegram is from Trincomalee Liz, and was dispatched from Bombay yesterday. Read it for yourself."

He handed the paper to his servant, who read it carefully, aloud :

To CARNE, Porchester House, Park Lane, London. — Bradfield left fortnight since. Have ascertained that you are the object.
TRINCOMALEE.

"This is very serious, sir," said the other, when he had finished.

"As you say, it is very serious indeed," Carne replied. "Bradfield thinks he has caught me at last, I suppose ; but he seems to forget that it is possible for me to be as clever as himself. Let me look at the message again. Left a fortnight ago, did he ? Then I've still a little respite. By Jove, if that's the case, I'll see that I make the most of it."

"But surely, sir, you will leave at once," said Belton quickly. "If this man, who has been after us so long, is now more than half way to England, coming with the deliberate intention of running you to earth, surely, sir, you'll see the advisability of making your escape while you have time."

Carne smiled indulgently.

"Of course I shall escape. my good Belton," he said. "You have never known me

neglect to take proper precautions yet ; but before I go I must do one more piece of business. It must be something by the light of which all I have hitherto accomplished will look like nothing. Something really great, that will make England open its eyes as it has not done yet."

Belton stared at him, this time in undisguised amazement.

"Do you mean to tell me, sir," he said with the freedom of a privileged servant, "that you intend to run another risk, when the only man who knows sufficient of your career to bring you to book is certain to be in England in less than a fortnight ? I cannot believe that you would be so foolish, sir. I beg of you to think what you are doing."

Carne, however, paid but small attention to his servant's intreaties.

"The difficulty," he said to himself, speaking his thoughts aloud, "is to understand quite what to do. I seem to have used up all my big chances. However, I'll think it over, and it will be strange if I don't hit upon something. In the meantime, Belton, you had better see that preparations are made for leaving England on Friday next. Tell the skipper to have everything ready. We shall have done our work by that time ; then hey for the open sea and freedom from the trammels of a society life once more. You might drop a hint or two to certain people that I am going, but be more than careful what you say. Write to the agents about Porchester House, and attend to all the other necessary details. You may leave me now."

Belton bowed, and left the cabin without another word. He knew his master sufficiently well to feel certain that neither intreaties nor expostulations would make him abandon the course he had mapped out for himself. That being so, he bowed to the inevitable with a grace which had now become a habit to him.

When he was alone, Carne once more sat for upwards of an hour in earnest thought. He then ordered his gig, and, when it was ready, set out for the shore. Making his way to the telegraph office, he dispatched a message which at any other, and less busy, time would have caused the operator some astonishment. It was addressed to a

Mahommedan dealer in precious stones in Bombay, and contained only two words in addition to the signature. They were:

"Leaving—come."

He knew that they would reach the person for whom they were intended, and that she would understand their meaning and act accordingly.

The dinner that night on board the Imperial yacht *Hohenszrallas* was a gorgeous affair in every sense of the word. All the principal yacht owners were present, and, at the conclusion of the banquet, Carne's health, as winner of the great event of the regatta, was proposed by the Emperor himself, and drunk amid enthusiastic applause. It was a proud moment for the individual in question, but he bore his honours with that quiet dignity that had stood him in such good stead on so many similar occasions. In his speech he referred to his approaching departure from England, and this, the first inkling of such news, came upon his audience like a thunder-clap. When they had taken leave of his Majesty soon after midnight, and were standing on deck, waiting for their respective boats to draw up to the accommodation ladder, Lord Orpington made his way to where Simon Carne was standing.

"Is it really true that you intend leaving us so soon?" he asked.

"Quite true, unfortunately," Carne replied. "I had hoped to have remained longer, but circumstances over which I have no control make it imperative that I should return to India without delay. Business that exercises a vital influence upon my fortunes compels me. I am therefore obliged to leave without fail on Friday next. I have given orders to that effect this afternoon."

"I am extremely sorry to hear it, that's all I can say," said Lord Amberley, who had just come up. "I assure you we shall all miss you very much indeed."

"You have all been extremely kind," said Carne, "and I have to thank you for an exceedingly pleasant time. But, there, let us postpone consideration of the matter for as long as possible. I think this is my boat. Won't you let me take you as far as your own yacht?"

"Many thanks, but I don't think we need trouble you," said Lord Orpington. "I see my gig is just behind yours."

"In that case, good night," said Carne. "I shall see you, as arranged, to-morrow morning, I suppose?"

"At eleven," said Lord Amberley. "We'll call for you and go ashore together. Good night."

By the time Carne had reached his yacht he had made up his mind. He had also hit upon a scheme, the daring of which almost frightened himself. If only he could bring it off, he told himself, it would be indeed a fitting climax to all he had accomplished since he had arrived in England. Retiring to his cabin, he allowed Belton to assist him in his preparations for the night almost without speaking. It was not until the other was about to leave the cabin that he broached the subject that was occupying his mind to the exclusion of all else.

"Belton," he said, "I have decided upon the greatest scheme that has come into my mind yet. If Simon Carne is going to say farewell to the English people on Friday next, and it succeeds, he will leave them a legacy to think about for some time after he has gone."

"You are surely not going to attempt anything further, sir," said Belton in alarm. "I

Carne's health was proposed by the Emperor himself.

did hope, sir, that you would have listened to my intreaties this afternoon."

"It was impossible for me to do so," said Carne. "I am afraid, Belton, you are a little lacking in ambition. I have noticed that on the last three occasions you have endeavoured to dissuade me from my endeavours to promote the healthy excitement of the English reading public. On this occasion fortunately I am able to withstand you. To-morrow morning you will commence preparations for the biggest piece of work to which I have yet put my hand."

"If you have set your mind upon doing it, sir, I am quite aware that it is hopeless for me to say anything," said Belton resignedly. "May I know, however, what it is going to be ?"

Carne paused for a moment before he replied.

"I happen to know that the Emperor of Westphalia, whose friendship I have the honour to claim," he said, "has a magnificent collection of gold plate on board his yacht. It is my intention, if possible, to become the possessor of it."

"Surely that will be impossible, sir," said Belton. "Clever as you undoubtedly are in arranging these things, I do not see how you can do it. A ship at the best of times is such a public place, and they will be certain to guard it very closely."

"I must confess that at first glance I do not quite see how it is to be managed, but I have a scheme in my head which I think may possibly enable me to effect my purpose. At any rate, I shall be able to tell you more about it to-morrow. First, let us try a little experiment."

As he spoke he seated himself at his dressing-table, and bade Belton bring him a box which had hitherto been standing in a corner. When he opened it, it proved to be a pretty little cedar-wood affair divided into a number of small compartments, each of which contained *crêpe* hair of a different colour. Selecting a small portion from one particular compartment, he unraveled it until he had obtained the length he wanted, and then with dexterous fingers constructed a moustache, which he attached with spirit gum to his upper lip. Two or three twirls gave it

the necessary curl, then with a pair of ivory-backed brushes taken from his dressing-table he brushed his hair back in a peculiar manner, placed a hat of uncommon shape upon his head, took a heavy boat cloak from a cupboard near at hand, threw it round his shoulders, and, assuming an almost defiant expression, faced Belton, and desired him to tell him whom he resembled.

Familiar as he was with his master's marvellous power of disguise and his extraordinary faculty of imitation, the latter could not refrain from expressing his astonishment.

"His Imperial Majesty the Emperor of Westphalia," he said. "The likeness is perfect."

"Good," said Carne. "From that exhibition you will gather something of my plan. To-morrow evening, as you are aware, I am invited to meet his Majesty, who is to dine ashore accompanied by his aide-de-camp, Count Von Walzburg. Here is the latter's photograph. He possesses, as you know, a very decided personality, which is all in our favour. Study it carefully."

So saying, he took from a drawer a photograph, which he propped against the looking-glass on the dressing-table before him. It represented a tall, military-looking individual with bristling eyebrows, a large nose, a heavy grey moustache, and hair of the same colour. Belton examined it carefully.

"I can only suppose, sir," he said, "that, as you are telling me this, you intend me to represent Count Von Walzburg."

"Exactly," said Carne. "That is my intention. It should not be at all difficult. The Count is just your height and build. You will only need the moustache, the eyebrows, the grey hair, and the large nose to look the part exactly. To-morrow will be a dark night, and, if only I can control circumstances sufficiently to obtain the chance I want, detection, in the first part of our scheme at any rate, should be most unlikely, if not almost impossible."

"You'll excuse my saying so, I hope, sir," said Belton, "but it seems a very risky game to play when we have done so well up to the present."

"You must admit that the glory will be the greater, my friend, if we succeed."

" But surely, sir, as I said just now, they keep the plate you mention in a secure place, and have it properly guarded."

" I have made the fullest inquiries, you may be sure. It is kept in a safe in the chief steward's cabin, and, while it is on board, a sentry is always on duty at the door. Yes, all things considered, I should say it is kept in a remarkably secure place."

" Then, sir, I'm still at a loss to see how you are going to obtain possession of it."

Carne smiled indulgently. It pleased him to see how perplexed his servant was.

" In the simplest manner possible," he said, " provided always that I can get on board the yacht without my identity being questioned. The manner in which we are to leave the vessel will be rather more dangerous, but not sufficiently so to cause us any great uneasiness. You are a good swimmer, I know, so that a hundred yards should not hurt you. You must also have a number of stout canvas sacks, say six, prepared, and securely attached to each the same number of strong lines; the latter must be fifty fathoms long, and have at the end of each a stout swivel hook. The rest is only a matter of detail. Now, what have you arranged with regard to matters in town ? "

" I have fulfilled your instructions, sir, to the letter," said Belton. " I have communicated with the agents who act for the owner of Porchester House. I have caused an advertisement to be inserted in all the papers to-morrow morning to the effect that the renowned detective, Klimo, will be unable to meet his clients for at least a month, owing to the fact that he has accepted an important engagement upon the Continent, which will take him from home for that length of time. I have negotiated the sale of the various horses you have in training, and I have also arranged for the disposal of the animals and carriages you have now in use in London. Ram Gafur and the other native servants at Porchester House will come down by the midday train to-morrow, but, before they do so, they will fulfil your instructions and repair the hole in the wall between the two houses. I cannot think of any more, sir."

" You have succeeded admirably, my dear Belton," said Carne, " and I am very pleased.

To-morrow you had better see that a paragraph is inserted in all the daily papers announcing the fact that it is my intention to leave England for India immediately, on important private business. I think that will do for to-night."

Belton tidied the cabin, and, having done so, bade his master good-night. It was plain that he was exceedingly nervous about the success of the enterprise upon which Carne was embarking so confidently. The latter, on the other hand, retired to rest and slept as peacefully as if he had not a care or an anxiety upon his mind.

Next morning he was up by sunrise, and, by the time his friends Lords Opington and Amberley were thinking about breakfast, had put the finishing touches to the scheme which was to bring his career in England to such a fitting termination.

According to the arrangement entered into on the previous day, his friends called for him at eleven o'clock, when they went ashore together. It was a lovely morning, and Carne was in the highest spirits. They visited the Castle together, made some purchases in the town, and then went off to lunch on board Lord Orpington's yacht. It was well-nigh three o'clock before Carne bade his host and hostess farewell, and descended the gangway in order to return to his own vessel. A brisk sea was running, and for this reason to step into the boat was an exceedingly difficult, if not a dangerous, matter. Either he miscalculated his distance, or he must have jumped at the wrong moment ; at any rate, he missed his footing, and fell heavily on to the bottom. Scarcely a second, however, had elapsed before his coxswain had sprung to his assistance, and had lifted him up on to the seat in the stern. It was then discovered that he had been unfortunate enough to once more give a nasty twist to the ankle which had brought him to such grief when he had been staying at Greenthorpe Park on the occasion of the famous wedding.

" My dear fellow, I am so sorry," said Lord Orpington, who had witnessed the accident. " Won't you come on board again ? If you can't walk up the ladder we can easily hoist you over the side."

" Many thanks," replied Carne, " but I

think I can manage to get back to my own boat. It is better I should do so. My man has had experience of my little ailments, and knows exactly what is best to be done under such circumstances; but it is a terrible nuisance, all the same. I'm afraid it will be impossible for me now to be present at his Royal Highness's dinner this evening, and I have been looking forward to it so much."

"We shall all be exceedingly sorry," said Lord Amberley. "I shall come across in the afternoon to see how you are."

"You are very kind," said Carne, "and I shall be immensely glad to see you if you can spare the time."

With that he gave the signal to his men to push off. By the time he reached his own yacht his foot was so painful that it was necessary for him to be lifted on board—a circumstance which was duly noticed by the occupants of all the surrounding yachts, who had brought their glasses to bear upon him. Once below in his saloon, he was placed in a comfortable chair and left to Belton's careful attention.

"I trust you have not hurt yourself very much, sir," said that faithful individual, who, however, could not prevent a look of satisfaction coming into his face, which seemed to say that he was not ill-pleased that his master would, after all, be prevented from carrying out the hazardous scheme he had proposed to him the previous evening.

In reply, Carne sprang to his feet without showing a trace of lameness.

"My dear Belton, how peculiarly dense you are to-day," he said, with a smile, as he noticed the other's amazement. "Cannot you see that I have only been acting as you yourself wished I should do early this morning—namely, taking precautions? Surely you must see that, if I am laid up on board my yacht with a sprained ankle, society will say that it is quite impossible for me to be doing any mischief elsewhere. Now, tell me, is everything prepared for to-night?"

"Everything, sir," Belton replied. "The dresses and wigs are ready. The canvas sacks, and the lines to which the spring hooks are attached, are in your cabin awaiting your inspection. As far as I can see, everything is prepared, and I hope will meet with your satisfaction."

"If you are as careful as usual, I feel sure it will," said Carne. "Now get some bandages and make this foot of mine up into as artistic a bundle as you possibly can. After that help me on deck and prop me up in a chair. As soon as my accident gets known there will be certain to be shoals of callers on board, and I must play my part as carefully as possible."

As Carne had predicted, this proved to be true. From half-past three until well after six o'clock a succession of boats drew up at his accommodation ladder, and the sufferer on deck was the recipient of as much attention as would have flattered the vainest of men. He had been careful to send a letter of apology to the illustrious individual who was to have been his host, expressing his sincere regrets that the accident which had so unfortunately befallen him would prevent the possibility of his being able to be present at the dinner he was giving that evening.

Day closed in and found the sky covered with heavy clouds. Towards eight o'clock a violent storm of rain fell, and when Carne heard it beating upon the deck above his cabin, and reflected that in consequence the night would in all probability be dark, he felt that his lucky star was indeed in the ascendant.

At half-past eight he retired to his cabin with Belton in order to prepare for the events of the evening. Never before had he paid such careful attention to his make-up. He knew that on this occasion the least carelessness might lead to detection, and he had no desire that his last and greatest exploit should prove his undoing.

It was half-past nine before he and his servant had dressed and were ready to set off. Then, placing broad-brimmed hats upon their heads, and carrying a portmanteau containing the cloaks and headgear which they were to wear later in the evening, they went on deck and descended into the dinghy which was waiting for them alongside. In something under a quarter of an hour they had been put ashore in a secluded spot, had changed their costumes, and were walking boldly down beside the water towards the steps where they could see the Imperial launch still waiting. Her crew were lolling about, joking and laughing, secure in the knowledge that it would be some hours at least before their Sovereign would be likely to require their services again.

Their astonishment, therefore, may well be imagined when they saw approaching them the two men whom they had only half-an-hour before brought ashore. Stepping in and taking his seat under the shelter, his Majesty ordered them to convey him back to the yacht with all speed. The accent and voice were perfect, and it never for an instant struck any one on board the boat that a deception was being practised. Carne, however, was aware that this was only a preliminary; the most dangerous portion of the business was yet to come.

On reaching the yacht, he sprang out on the ladder, followed by his aide-de-camp, Von Walzburg, and mounted the steps. His disguise must have been perfect indeed, for when he reached the deck he found himself face to face with the first lieutenant, who, on seeing him, saluted respectfully. For a moment Carne's presence of mind almost deserted him; then, seeing that he was not discovered, he determined upon a bold piece of bluff. Returning the officer's salute with just the air he had seen the Emperor use, he led him to suppose that he had important reasons for coming on board so soon, and, as if to back this assertion up, bade him send the chief steward

The first lieutenant saluted respectfully.

to his cabin, and at the same time have the sentry removed from his door and placed at the end of the large saloon, with instructions to allow no one to pass until he was communicated with again.

The officer saluted and went off on his errand, while Carne, signing to Belton to follow him, made his way down the companion ladder to the Royal cabins. To both the next few minutes seemed like hours. Reaching the Imperial state room, they entered it and closed the door behind. Provided the sentry obeyed his orders, which there was no reason to doubt he would do, and the Emperor himself did not return until they were safely off the vessel again, there seemed every probability of their being able to carry out their scheme without a hitch.

"Put those bags under the table, and unwind the lines and place them in the gallery outside the window. They won't be seen there," said Carne to Belton, who was watching him from the doorway. "Then stand by, for in a few minutes the chief steward will be here. As soon as he enters you must manage to get between him and the door, and, while I am engaging him in conversation, spring on him, clutch him by the throat, and hold him until I can force this gag into his mouth. After that we shall be safe for some time at least, for not a soul will come this way until they discover their mistake. It seems to me we ought to thank our stars that the chief steward's cabin was placed in such a convenient position. But hush, here comes the individual we want. Be ready to collar him as soon as I hold up my hand. If he makes a sound we are lost."

He had scarcely spoken before there was a knock at the door. When it opened, the chief steward entered the cabin, closing the door behind him.

"Schmidt," said his Majesty, who was standing at the further end of the cabin, "I have sent for you in order that I may question you on a matter of the utmost importance. Draw nearer."

The man came forward as he was ordered, and, having done so, looked his master full and fair in the face. Something he saw there seemed to stagger him. He glanced at him a second time, and was immediately confirmed in his belief.

"You are not the Emperor," he cried.

"You are not the Emperor," he cried. "There is some treachery in this. I shall call for assistance."

He had half turned, and was about to give the alarm, when Carne held up his hand, and Belton, who had been creeping stealthily up behind him, threw himself upon him and had clutched him by the throat before he could utter a sound. The fictitious Emperor immediately produced a cleverly constructed gag and forced it into the terrified man's mouth, who in another second was lying upon the floor bound hand and foot.

"There, my friend," said Carne quietly, as he rose to his feet a few moments later, "I don't think you will give us any further trouble. Let me just see that those straps are tight enough, and then we'll place you on

this settee, and afterwards get to business with all possible dispatch."

Having satisfied himself on these points, he signed to Belton, and between them they placed the man upon the couch.

"Let me see, I think, if I remember rightly, you carry the key of the safe in this pocket."

So saying, he turned the man's pocket inside out and appropriated the bunch of keys he found therein. Choosing one from it, he gave a final look at the bonds which secured the prostrate figure, and then turned to Belton.

"I think he'll do," he said. "Now for business. Bring the bags, and come with me."

So saying, he crossed the cabin, and, having assured himself that there was no one about to pry upon them, passed along the luxuriously carpeted alley way until he arrived at the door of the cabin, assigned to the use of the chief steward, and in which was the safe containing the magnificent gold plate, the obtaining of which was the reason of his being there. To his surprise and chagrin, the door was closed and locked. In his plans he had omitted to allow for this contingency. In all probability, however, the key was in the man's pocket, so, turning to Belton, he bade him return to the state room and bring him the keys he had thrown upon the table.

The latter did as he was ordered, and, when he had disappeared, Carne stood alone in the alley way waiting and listening to the various noises of the great vessel. On the deck overhead he could hear someone tramping heavily up and down, and then, in an interval of silence, the sound of pouring rain. Good reason as he had to be anxious, he could not help smiling as he thought of the incongruity of his position. He wondered what his aristocratic friends would say if he were captured and his story came to light. In his time he had impersonated a good many people, but never before had he had the honour of occupying such an exalted station. This was the last and most daring of all his adventures.

Minutes went by, and, as Belton did not return, Carne found himself growing nervous. What could have become of him? He was in the act of going in search of him, when he appeared carrying in his hand the bunch of keys for which he had been sent. His master seized them eagerly.

"Why have you been so long?" he asked in a whisper. "I began to think something had gone wrong with you."

"I stayed to make our friend secure," the other answered. "He had well - nigh managed to get one of his hands free. Had he done so, he would have had the gag out of his mouth in no time, and have given the alarm. Then we should have been caught like rats in a trap."

"Are you quite sure he is secure now?" asked Carne anxiously.

"Quite," replied Belton. "I took good care of that."

"In that case we had better get to work on the safe without further delay. We have wasted too much time already, and every moment is an added danger."

Without more ado, Carne placed the most likely key in the lock and turned it. The bolt shot back, and the treasure chamber lay at his mercy.

The cabin was not a large one, but it was plain that every precaution had been taken to render it secure. The large safe which contained the Imperial plate, and which it was Carne's intention to rifle, occupied one entire side. It was of the latest design, and when Carne saw it he had to confess to himself that, expert craftsman as he was, it was one that would have required all his time and skill to open.

With the master key, however, it was the

The entire cabin was strewn
with salvers, goblets . . .

work of only a few seconds. The key was turned, the lever depressed, and then, with a slight pull, the heavy door swung forward. This done, it was seen that the interior was full to overflowing. Gold and silver plate of all sorts and descriptions, inclosed in bags of wash-leather and green baize, were neatly arranged inside. It was a haul such as even Carne had never had at his mercy before, and, now that he had got it, he was determined to make the most of it.

"Come, Belton," he said, "get these things out as quickly as possible and lay them on the floor. We can only carry away a certain portion of the plunder, so let us make sure that that portion is the best."

A few moments later the entire cabin was strewn with salvers, goblets, bowls, epergnes, gold and silver dishes, plates, cups, knives, forks, and almost every example of the goldsmith's art. In his choice Carne was not guided by what was handsomest or most delicate in workmanship or shape. Weight was his only standard. Silver he discarded altogether, for it was of less than no account. In something under ten minutes he had made his selection, and the stout canvas bags they had brought with them for that purpose were full to their utmost holding capacity.

"We can carry no more," said Carne to his faithful retainer, as they made the mouth of the last bag secure. "Pick up yours and let us get back to the Emperor's state room."

Having locked the door of the cabin, they returned to the place whence they had started.

Having detached a line, he began to pull it in.

There they found the unfortunate steward lying just as they had left him on the settee. Placing the bags he carried upon the ground, Carne crossed to him and, before doing anything else, carefully examined the bonds with which he was secured.

Having done this, he went to the stern windows, and, throwing one open, stepped into the gallery outside. Fortunately for what he intended to do, it was still raining heavily, and in consequence the night was as dark as the most consummate conspirator could have desired. Returning to the room, he bade Belton help him carry the bags into the gallery, and, when this had been done, made fast the swivel hooks to the rings in the mouth of each.

"Take up your bags as quietly as possible," he said, "and lower them one by one into the water, but take care that they don't get entangled in the propeller. When you've done that, slip the rings at the other end of the lines through your belt, and buckle the latter tightly."

Belton did as he was ordered, and in a few moments the six bags were lying at the bottom of the sea.

"Now off with these wigs and things, and say when you're ready for a swim."

Their disguises having been discarded and thrown overboard, Carne and Belton clambered over the rails of the gallery and lowered themselves until their feet touched the water. Next moment they had both let go, and were swimming in the direction of Carne's own yacht.

It was at this period of their adventure that

the darkness proved of such real service to them. By the time they had swum half a dozen strokes it would have needed a sharp pair of eyes to distinguish them as they rose and fell among the foam-crested waves. If, however, the storm had done them a good turn in saving them from notice, it came within an ace of doing them an ill service in another direction. Good swimmers though both Carne and Belton were, and they had proved it to each other's satisfaction in the seas of almost every known quarter of the globe, they soon found that it took all their strength to make headway now. By the time they reached their own craft, they were both completely exhausted. As Belton declared afterwards, he felt as if he could not have managed another twenty strokes even had his life depended on it.

At last, however, they reached the yacht's stern and clutched at the rope ladder which Carne had himself placed there before he had set out on the evening's excursion. In less time than it takes to tell he had mounted it and gained the deck, followed by his faithful servant. They presented a sorry spectacle as they stood side by side at the taffrail, the water dripping from their clothes and pattering upon the deck.

" Thank goodness we are here at last," said Carne, as soon as he had recovered his breath sufficiently to speak. " Now slip off your belt, and hang it over this cleat with mine."

Belton did as he was directed, and then followed his master to the saloon companion ladder. Once below, they changed their clothes as quickly as possible, and, having donned mackintoshes, returned to the deck, where it was still raining hard.

" Now," said Carne, " for the last and most important part of our evening's work. Let us hope the lines will prove equal to the demands we are about to make upon them."

As he said this, he took from the cleat upon which he had placed it one of the belts, and, having detached a line, began to pull it in, Belton following his example with another. Their hopes that they would prove equal to the confidence placed in them proved well founded, for, in something less than a quarter of an hour, the six bags, containing the Emperor of Westphalia's magnificent gold

plate, were lying upon the deck, ready to be carried below and stowed away in the secret place in which Carne had arranged to hide his treasure.

" Now, Belton," said Carne, as he pushed the panel back into its place, and pressed the secret spring that locked it, " I hope you're satisfied with what we have done. We've made a splendid haul, and you shall have your share of it. In the meantime, just get me to bed as quickly as you can, for I'm dead tired. When you've done so, be off to your own. To-morrow morning you will have to go up to town to arrange with the bank authorities about my account."

Belton did as he was ordered, and half-an-hour later his master was safely in bed and asleep.

It was late next morning when he woke. He had scarcely breakfasted before the Earl of Amberley and Lord Orpington made their appearance over the side. To carry out the part he had arranged to play, he received them seated in his deck chair, his swaddled up right foot reclining on a cushion before him. On seeing his guests, he made as if he would rise, but they begged him to remain seated.

" I hope your ankle is better this morning," said Lord Orpington politely, as he took a chair beside his friend.

" Much better, thank you," Carne replied. " It was not nearly so serious as I feared. I hope to be able to hobble about a little this afternoon. And now tell me the news, if there is any ? "

" Do you mean to say that you have not heard the great news ? " asked Lord Amberley, in a tone of astonishment.

" I have heard nothing," Carne replied. " Remember I have not been ashore this morning, and I have been so busily engaged with the preparations for my departure to-morrow that I have not had time to look at my papers. Pray what is this news of which you speak with such bated breath ? "

" Listen, and I'll tell you," Lord Orpington answered. " As you are aware, last night his Imperial Majesty the Emperor of Westphalia dined ashore, taking with him his aide-de-camp, Count Von Walzburg. They had not been gone from the launch more than half-an-hour when, to all intents and purposes, they reappeared, and the Emperor, who seemed much perturbed about something, gave the order to return to the yacht with all possible speed. It was very dark and raining hard at the time, and whoever the men may have been who did the thing, they were, at any rate, past masters in the art of disguise.

" Reaching the yacht, their arrival gave rise to no suspicion, for the officers are accustomed, as you know, to his Majesty's rapid comings and goings. The first lieutenant met them at the gangway, and declares that he had no sort of doubt but that it was his Sovereign. Face, voice, and manner were alike perfect. From his Majesty's behaviour he surmised that there was some sort of trouble brewing for somebody, and, as if to carry this impression still further, the Emperor bade him send the chief steward to him at once, and, at the same time, place the sentry, who had hitherto been guarding the treasure chamber, at the end of the great saloon, with instructions to allow no one to pass him, on any pretext whatever, until the chief steward had been examined and the Emperor himself gave permission. Then he went below to his cabin.

" Soon after this the steward arrived, and was admitted. Something seems to have excited the latter's suspicions, however, and he was about to give the alarm when he was seized from behind, thrown upon the floor, and afterwards gagged and bound. It soon became apparent what object the rascals had in view. They had caused the sentry at the door of the treasure chamber to be removed and placed where not only he could not hinder them in their work, but would prevent them from being disturbed. Having obtained the key of the room and safe from the chief steward's pocket, they set off to the cabin, ransacked it completely, and stole all that was heaviest and most valuable of his Majesty's wonderful plate from the safe."

" Good gracious," said Carne. " I never heard of such a thing. Surely it's the most impudent robbery that has taken place for many years past. To represent the Emperor of Westphalia and his aide-de-camp so closely that they could deceive even the officers of his own yacht, and to take a sentry off one post and place him in such a position as to protect them while at their own nefarious work, seems to me the very height of audacity. But how did they get their booty and themselves away again ? Gold plate, under the most favourable circumstances, is by no means an easy thing to carry."

As he asked this question, Carne lit another cigar with a hand as steady as a rock.

" They must have escaped in a boat that, it is supposed, was lying under the shelter of the stern gallery," replied Lord Amberley.

" And is the chief steward unable to furnish the police with no clue as to their identity ? "

" None whatever," replied Orpington. " He opines to the belief, however, that they are Frenchmen. One of them, the man who impersonated the Emperor, seems to have uttered an exclamation in that tongue."

" And when was the robbery discovered ? "

" Only when the real Emperor returned to the vessel shortly after midnight. There was no launch to meet him, and he had to get Tremorden to take him off. You can easily imagine the surprise his arrival occasioned. It was intensified when they went below to find his Majesty's cabin turned upside down, the chief steward lying bound and gagged upon the sofa, and all that was most valuable of the gold plate missing."

" What an extraordinary story ! "

" And now, having told you the news with which the place is ringing, we must be off about our business," said Orpington. "Is it quite certain that you are going to leave us to-morrow ? "

" Quite, I am sorry to say," answered Carne. " I am going to ask as many of my friends as possible to do me the honour of lunching with me at one o'clock, and at five I shall weigh anchor and bid England good-bye. I shall have the pleasure of your company, I hope."

" I shall have much pleasure," said Orpington.

" And I also," replied Amberley.

" Then good-bye for the present. It's just possible I may see you again during the afternoon."

The luncheon next day was as brilliant a

social gathering as the most fastidious in such matters could have desired. Everyone then in Cowes who had any claim to distinction was present, and several had undertaken the journey from town in order to say farewell to one who had made himself so popular during his brief stay in England. When Carne rose to reply to the toast of his health, proposed by the Prime Minister, it was observable that he was genuinely moved, as, indeed, were most of his hearers.

For the remainder of the afternoon his yacht's deck was crowded with his friends, all of whom expressed the hope that it might not be very long before he was amongst them once more.

To these kind speeches Carne invariably offered a smiling reply.

"I also trust it will not be long," he answered. "I have enjoyed my visit immensely, and you may be sure I shall never forget it as long as I live."

An hour later the anchor was weighed, and his yacht was steaming out of the harbour amid a scene of intense enthusiasm. As the Prime Minister had that afternoon informed him, in the public interest, the excitement of his departure was dividing honours with the burglary of the Emperor of Westphalia's gold plate.

Carne stood beside his captain on the bridge, watching the little fleet of yachts until his eyes could no longer distinguish them. Then he turned to Belton, who had just joined him, and, placing his hand upon his shoulder, said :

"So much for our life in England, Belton, my friend. It has been glorious fun, and no one can deny that from a business point of view it has been eminently satisfactory. You, at least, should have no regrets."

"None whatever," answered Belton. "But I must confess I should like to know what they will say when the truth comes out."

Carne smiled sweetly as he answered :

"I think they'll say that, all things considered, I have won the right to call myself 'A Prince of Swindlers.'"

VI

Seven, Seven, Seven—City

JULIUS CHAMBERS

"SEVEN, SEVEN, SEVEN—CITY."

A TALE OF THE TELEPHONE.

By JULIUS CHAMBERS.   Illustrated by A. KEMP TEBBY.

I.

I WENT to my telephone exactly at eleven o'clock on the night of December 30th last winter to call up the editor of my paper. My house was on the west side of Regent's Park, and the wire ran to the City telephone exchange.

Apparently my line was switched into connection with the Fleet Street exchange. But delay followed. I was familiar with the peculiar hum caused by the induction on the wires, but that night the sounds were of an unusual character. The operator at the City office had given me an unused wire.

As I awaited the answering signal to indicate that the desired connection had been made, I heard two people talking in loud whispers, to me unintelligible. Then I heard a door, swinging on a squeaky hinge, hastily closed with a muffled sound—a cupboard door. Then silence. One of the people had entered the cupboard and closed the door. Then a knock, unanswered.

Immediately followed a crash at the other end of the wire. I heard the breaking in of a door.

"John!" exclaimed a woman.

"Ah! my lady, I have caught you at last," were the words of the intruder as he strode into the apartment, slamming the broken door against the wall behind. There was a metallic tone in that voice that made me chilly when he added "Where is the scoundrel?"

"I don't understand!" were the affrighted words of the woman.

"Well, I do. He's in that cupboard."

I heard the door squeak again, and the man in the cupboard step out.

"At your service, sir," said a strange voice, low and with a shiver in it.

"I knew it, woman," fairly screamed the head of the family.

"Make a memorandum of the temperature," said he.

89

"Don't be a brute," said the calm, low voice. "I am here, settle with me."

"You dog!" hissed the first speaker, as he sprang for the offender, overturning a table covered with bric-a-brac, and a mortal combat began.

In a momentary lull, while I could distinguish the breathing of the two infuriated combatants, I heard the rustle of a woman's dress as she swept across the floor, the opening and closing of a door. The unfaithful creature had abandoned her lover. Not a sob nor an entreaty for mercy.

I was as sure of the facts and understood the situation as if I had been in that apartment.

The contest was resumed, and crash after crash of broken furniture attested its savage character.

Who were these men? And where? Unquestionably, in a house where a telephone had been left open, or an interruption had occurred during its use. Had the receiver been hung up, communication with that room of mystery would have been severed. The wire leading thereto was "crossed" with the one given me to use.

The struggle was to the death. I could hear the breathing of the contestants as they lay on the floor, but neither man asked quarter. The door re-opened and to a woman's sobs were added appeals for forgiveness. One of the two men had overpowered the other! Which was the victor?

A pistol shot, sharp and crisp! Then, the stillness of death. It was death! The hush could be felt over the unknown length of the wire connecting me with the murder chamber. I was ear-witness to the crime.

Whispers broke the silence; a window was raised. Now, shall I hear the cry of "Murder!"? No. Somebody looked into the street—presumably to ascertain if the pistol-shot had been heard by passing pedestrians. That indicated the home to be in a populous neighbourhood, although the opened window did not admit sounds of passing vehicles. Then the window was slowly closed.

Next, I heard a match struck. Merciful Heavens! This deadly conflict had taken place in the dark!

The lover had been killed; but would that lighted match reveal to the husband the face of a stranger, or of a well-known friend? What would be done with the body——?

"Are you through?" asked the telephone clerk at the City exchange.

"No, mark that wire with which I am connected. It doesn't go to Fleet Street, but I must know where it runs. Mark it, as you value a five-pound note. I'll be at your office as soon as I can get there."

"All right!" was the prompt reply.

The clerk at the City exchange tied a ribbon round the plug that carried the end of the wire leading me into the unknown house. I related the entire incident and appealed to his curiosity and avarice. As I had divined, he, inadvertently, had switched me upon an abandoned line—it had been put up for a special occasion and "cut out" thereafter. It was a lost wire, and did not lead to the Fleet Street exchange or anywhere else!

After making tests, the clerk reported that communication with "the house of the crime" no longer existed, but, as an explanation, he pointed to a thermometer outside the window.

"Make a memorandum of the temperature," said he.

"What's the use?"

"You understand how you got into that house on the lost wire?"

"No."

"At a certain degree of cold, that house-line contracted sufficiently to 'cut in' on the dead wire and thus connect us, for a brief space, with the chamber of the murder—wherever it may be."

"We must be careful to have this correct," said I, now comprehending the operator's meaning. "What does the instrument register?"

"Exactly zero."

*   *   *   *   *

The body of a young physician of social prominence, Henry Clay Stanage (brother of Dr. Oscar Stanage, so prominently identified with the Jasper case), was found at the side of a path in Hyde Park next morning. He had died from a pistol shot in the right temple, and near the corpse was a weapon with one chamber discharged. Evidence in support of the theory of suicide was so strong that a verdict to that effect by the Coroner's jury disposed of the case in the public mind. I saw the body and found finger marks on the throat and a rent in the back of the dress-coat.

The young gallant had died at the hand of "my murderer." Stanage bore the reputation of a "gay boy." All attempts to establish the whereabouts of the physician on the previous night came to naught.

The ease with which the body might have been placed in a carriage and driven to the spot where it was found became apparent on the most casual consideration.

II.

The only clue I possessed was the abandoned wire. I engaged a telephone-man to find the house of the crime, hoping thereby to bring the murderer to justice, and, incidentally, to secure a piece of sensational and exclusive news for my journal.

The lineman was zealous and over-confident, but at the end of two weeks he had lost the wire near the "Elephant and Castle."

He believed the house we sought to be in Brixton. He sneered at all suggestions from the telephone-operator.

"An ear-trumpet chap can't tell me how to work," said he contemptuously. "I didn't learn my trade that way."

Another wire expert was hired, and I told him the story. Perhaps I had not been sufficiently frank with the first man. The new telegraphist adopted the suggestion of the exchange-operator, and said : "An accidental crossing of the wires, caused by contraction, admitted you to that room, and enabled you to hear the murder done. We have only to wait, Mr. North, until the thermometer registers zero, then ring up that dead wire from the City exchange and ask, 'What number is that ?' You will have landed your game."

That seemed simple. But the winter was unusually mild.

Although I

He had died from a pistol-shot in the right temple.

retained the man in my pay for a month, there wasn't a moment in which the thermometer touched zero. We kept ceaseless vigil, one relieving the other at the City telephone office during enforced absence for sleep and meals. I took a room in a boarding house near the exchange, that I might be within easy call. Nothing must thwart me.

One night the weather moderated, and I deemed it safe to go to Kensington to pay a call I had owed for a long time. While I was away, the temperature fell so rapidly that it was within one degree of the desired point. The clerk at the exchange hurried a messenger to the address I had left with him.

In the warm house of my friend, the condition of the weather had been forgotten, but in the street the night . was bitterly cold. Possibly the hour had come ! At the first chemist's, I saw a thermometer outside the door. Jupiter ! The mercury stood *exactly at zero!* A cab carried me to the City telephone exchange in half an hour. I stepped inside and, connecting the dead wire, rang.

No answer.

Glancing through the window-glass at a thermometer outside, I saw that the weather had slightly moderated ; the reading thereon was two degrees above zero. There it hovered for an hour. Then the mercury slowly descended into the bulb. Now, it stood at one and a half degrees ! Ten minutes later the record was less than a degree above !

I rang vigorously, but did not hear any sound at the other end.

In my anxiety, I forgot the thermometer. When I looked again, the mercury had moved up half a degree.

Another wait succeeded, and I had almost decided to give up the vigil for the night, when the bell connected with the dead wire rang. Snatching up the receiver, I asked, my voice almost tremulous : " Well ? What number do you want ? "

" Who are you ? " was the rejoinder.

" This is the exchange. What number do you want ? "

" You're Kensington," was the cautious query, after a moment's hesitation.

" Yes, what is your number ? " I asked, in hopes of obtaining from an unguarded answer the information I had been so anxiously seeking.

" Ah ! you want to know what number this is ? "

I recognised the voice !

I was talking to the murderer — " my murderer," as I had often mentally designated him, to distinguish him from everybody else's murderer.

And wasn't he mine ? Only one other living person knew him beside me—the woman who had witnessed the killing, and had remained silent as the price of forgiveness !

" What is your number ? " I asked again.

" Find out ! " was the reply.

Then I heard the 'phone hung up. It seemed to me that I had not learned anything new. I was deeply chagrined for the moment ; but, taking stock of my knowledge, I had acquired much valuable information.

First.—I had confirmed the theory that the house I sought had been reached by a wire that hung in close proximity to the abandoned line.

Second.—The short house-wire hung over, not under, the long wire, because the contraction in the copper-wires of which the house connections were made was slight.

Third.—The man and the house I sought were in Kensington, not Brixton, as the first expert had concluded.

Fourth.—" My murderer " was usually at home at night.

Fifth.—His telephonic connection was made through the Kensington exchange.

Sixth.—The man I believed guilty was on his guard and was suspicious of my inquiries. He would probably be wary of the telephone in future. On the other hand, he would not dare to have it removed at this time.

The " dead " wire was the only clue. My next step was to go to the office of the Telephone Company, and secure an appointment as a receiver in the Kensington exchange.

I was inconspicuous, and I donned the remarkable headgear the receivers wear. The wear and worry of the work nearly crazed me the first day. The steel band that encircled my temples completely disorganised my brain. A month passed, and I was no nearer the solution. Despair was overcoming me, when a new suggestion of the greatest importance was made to me.

" Has Moxley tested the wires, as usual ? " asked one of the operators during the day.

" Not this week," replied the Exchange Superintendent.

All customers are frequently called up by an expert to ascertain that the wires are in good order. If I could become Moxley's assistant, I reflected, I might be able to hear " my murderer's " voice again.

I secured the place, and made my appearance at the Kensington telephone exchange as Moxley's " helper,"—not a position calculated to turn the head of any man. I was delighted, and believed success assured. My duties were to carry the galvanometer and rheostat ; but, by dividing my supposed wages with Moxley, he consented that I should test the wires. I was a bachelor, he assumed, and I could live on little money ; besides, he liked to encourage enthusiasm in young men. Moxley guaranteed to make me expert in three years.

" George Reilly is the best lineman in England," said he, " and Reilly began with me as ' helper.' "

Only one operator was in the office when we arrived, because the telephone is not in much demand before ten o'clock. I tested the private lines, of which there were several hundreds.

I sought in vain for " the voice." Sixty-three customers failed to answer when called. I marked these " torpid " wires, hoping that the one I wanted was among them.

Having completed the tests of the private wires, I began making connections with the pay-stations throughout the district.

A curious thing occurred.

I rang up a station on Camden Hill ; I heard the receiver taken off the hook, but no reply came in answer to my summons. I called again and yet again. No reply.

Warm as was the day, I felt a chill down my spinal marrow. I heard a door unlocked, and, an instant later, the squeaking of a hinge. The wire led into a cupboard.

Again I asked for a response. Finally, the 'phone at the other end, wherever that might be, was replaced on the hook, and—silence.

III.

I left the building, called a cab and drove to the address of the number I had rung up. It proved to be a chemist's shop near Holland Park. Showing my credentials, I demanded to know why the inspection call had not been answered. The chemist was civil, and explained that he had observed, the previous summer, that on hot days the communication with the exchange was interrupted at times. He stoutly maintained that the bell had not sounded. I tried it and called up the Kensington exchange without difficulty. The druggist was in nowise nonplussed. He merely pointed towards the street and said, as he turned to wait on a customer:—"You forget that it is raining. The weather is cooler."

True, there had been a heavy shower while I was in the cab, but so intent was I in pursuit of my only object in life that I had hardly observed it. I understood the chemist's meaning. In the case of the first wire I had attempted to run down, the bit of metal I sought doubtless passed *over* the abandoned line; by the same reasoning, the wire that had again led me into this modern Francesca's chamber by another route was strung *under* the one that entered this chemist's shop. Zero weather contracted the metal in one case; summer heat lengthened the line in the other. *Contact* was made at two different places.

The co-efficient to this last problem was unknown to me. The druggist had not noticed the thermometer just prior to the shower, because he took the temperature only at nine, twelve and three o'clock. I remembered the telephone standard at the top of the London Life Assurance Company's building, where Sergeant Dunn had machinery that automatically recorded every change in the weather on an unimpeachable tally-sheet.

That officer received me courteously. I asked the exact thermometrical reading just before the heavy rainfall. Consulting the cleverly-devised instruments, he replied :

"Exactly 90 degrees Fahrenheit."

The degree of summer contact with the lost wire had been established; but that was all.

I must go on. Had I located the section of the city in which the criminal lived? I feared not. This wasn't a crime of the slums; but the use of a telephone did not necessarily indicate respectability. Why not start at the chemist's and run down the wire from that point?

The end of a rainbow never seems far away.

I sent for Moxley and told him what I wanted to ascertain. He looked knowing; said the task would be easy, and he'd take "a day off" to do it. Although he gave a month to the task, he did not find the house, the man or the woman! But he was full of explanations, and showed how, wholly by accident and not by design, the people at the other end of the wire were absolutely safe if they did not make a "break" themselves.

The days drifted along into September. The warm weather was gone, and I could not hope that ninety degrees of heat would recur.

It was equally impossible to restrain my curiosity until mid-winter.

I engaged a room in a boarding-house adjoining the Kensington telephone station. The cables came along thereto underground and were carried up the side of the house in a covered box to the roof; there the strands were separated and strung upon a rack, from which they were conducted to the operating-room below. The discovery that all the wires brought into that station were underground complicated matters seriously. The line I

I recognised the voice. I was talking to the murderer—"my murderer."

wanted was strung aloft at some point of its length, but *where* did it leave the subway and how could I recognise it when found?

I now did what I ought to have done long before—secured the services of George Reilly, the most expert "trouble-man" in the country. When the whole subject was laid before him he pronounced unequivocally in favour of starting at the City office to run down that wire. A long chase was more likely of success than a short one.

Reilly went to work with zest. With his experienced eye, he had no difficulty in following the abandoned wire along Holborn, thence down New Oxford Street, where, without apparent reason, it switched off to the roofs, which it followed to Victoria, where it returned to the underground. By the end of the third day Reilly was in full cry through Lambeth, into Kennington, down as far as Pearl Street. At Brixton Station it made a long jump from the top of a tall building, over the railway bridge to another building. Reilly believed he was close upon a solution of the mystery. Out of Brixton Road, atop a telephone pole, emerged a bright copper wire; it crossed closely above the line he was following. His practised eye told Reilly that the two wires were liable to have contact by the contraction of the long wire. The stretch previously mentioned was more than a thousand feet in length, and, at zero temperature, contraction would be fully two-thirds of an inch. Nothing could have been easier than to tie the two wires together and to ring up the house of the crime. But Reilly thought that course unwise.

"My murderer," as I still called him, was on his guard. Having kept the secret for eight months, he knew exactly what he was about.

I was waiting at the City exchange the following day, when Reilly called me over a public line, and asked me to "ring up" the dead wire.

I did so, and someone exclaimed: "Is that you, John? When will you return? Better come at once." It was a woman's voice—*That of the woman who had begged for mercy!*

Standing back from the transmitter, I asked: "Where?"

"To the——" Buzz! whir-r-r! zip!

The contact was broken. I called up Reilly and told him to tie the two wires together. He did so, but I could not get "my lady's" ear again. I asked Reilly what he thought. In his opinion, the woman lived in Brixton. The wire ran in that direction.

Reilly announced later in the day a change of mind. The copper wire was a private one, running from a city office to a private house in Brixton. He had traced it to an office building in Cheapside. The wire did not go to Brixton, as he had supposed, although it ran in that direction for a good way. Telephone wires are often pieced together, he explained, and a lineman will sometimes appropriate an old wire, though it makes a long detour.

The members of the firm in whose office the line ended were easily discovered. Reilly slung a coil of wire over his shoulder next day and entered the office. He asked for the telephone, and was shown into the private room of the firm—"Gasper, Todd, and Markham."

At his desk sat John Perry Gasper, solicitor, aged fifty-seven.

Reilly was not a student of men; he could not read character as he could a Morse instrument. But the wire was what he wanted, and now that he had found one end of it, nothing appeared easier than to secure the other one. After having made two or three pretended tests of the machine, he went away.

The instant he reached the landing outside the office, his manner changed. He sprang down the stairs and to the bank on the ground floor, where he asked for a city directory. There the residence of John Perry Gasper was given: "Cheapside, and Kensington."

Madly triumphant, Reilly hurried to my address, and rushed breathlessly into my room. In a few words he revealed his success. I was as jubilant as he. We hurried to Kensington to look at the house. We almost ran.

No difficulty was experienced in finding the building. It was a corner house of splendid proportions, and the name, "Gasper," shown audaciously upon the door-plate. While my thoughts were busy as to my next action, Reilly's were occupied with a different text. He had surveyed the building from all possible points, in a thoroughly appreciative way; but when he came back from a hasty walk down the side street, he was pale and trembling.

"What's the matter?" I asked.

"Matter? Why, I'm 'knocked out.'"

"I don't understand," was my reply.

"Can't you see that there isn't a telephone wire entering that house?"

"What wire is that?" I asked, in dismay, pointing upward.

"Oh! that's a district-messenger call. Notice, it runs from the pole opposite the stable, and is of the cheapest iron. There isn't any telephone in that house. See! A reference to the telephone catalogue—which we ought to have made earlier—shows that."

The more he was mystified the clearer became the situation to me. It was a case of another woman—another family! Nevertheless, the other end of the wire and the house of the murder were as far away as ever.

One thing I could establish at once, and I would make the test. Strange that I had allowed a moment to elapse since I had learned of Gasper's connection with the case.

I went to the nearest Call Office, called up Gasper, Todd and Markham, Cheapside, and

asked to speak with Mr. Gasper. I hadn't
thought what I should say, when a voice
answered, "I am Mr. Gasper? What is
wanted?" I had only sense enough to reply:
"When did you take the
telephone out of your
house?"

"Never had any in it,"
was the curt retort; after
waiting a moment, he added
savagely, "And I don't
want any."

This was the voice, and
Gasper's name was John!

Reilly went back to Gas-
per's office to see the telephone. Gasper was not
there and the expert ex-
amined it more carefully.
He discovered that the wires
led through the back of the
little box in which was the
'phone, thence into a large
wardrobe. This was locked,
but a moment's examination
showed that the two wires
left that sealed clothes-press.
They went out by different
windows, but they came
from the same switch—a
switch inside the wardrobe,
by which a private wire
could be "cut in" or "cut
out." The line over which
I had called up the office
obviously was a different
one from that leading to
the mysterious room where
the shooting occurred.

"Look here," exclaimed Gasper, "you're after blood; but, man to man, I
stake my life I can convince any judge or jury that that rascal died at the
right time."

This was really a discovery! I speak of it
as a "discovery," although it was, as yet,
merely an assumption. But Reilly was as sure
that a switch existed in that cupboard as if he
had seen it. As he told me his theory, I
remembered that the office had not responded
when the wires were tied together. The bell
hadn't rung, because the private wire had been
"switched out!"

"One bold stroke," thought I, "and we
shall have this story." My next step was
startling. I had been admitted to the Bar
years before. I called upon a prominent K.C.
friend of mine and secured letters of introduction to John Perry Gasper, and finally wrote
him asking when I might call with a certainty
of a private interview. He named the
following afternoon. I presented my letters.
One was from the Chief of Police. I watched
the lawyer's face, and a tremor crossed it as he
broke the seal of the big blue envelope bearing
the arms of the department.

I waited for an inquiry from him as to my
business; but he was stolid, immobile as marble.

His dull, grey eyes appeared slowly withdrawing themselves inside his skull; the
eyelids gradually closed to a peculiar squint.
Reilly was waiting in the hall, and I knew the
moment had come. Now for audacity!

"Will you let me have an expert examine
the cupboard immediately behind your telephone?"

"There is no cupboard behind it," was the
quick retort.

"Yes, there is—right behind that door against
which the 'phone box sits."

My voice trembled, and I was very pale; but
my "nerves" did not fail me.

Gasper took up the letters, one by one, read
them through more carefully than before, and
then muttered:

"Go to the—deuce."

"Not until I find the other end of that
private wire leading from the next room," I
retorted. "If you refuse, I shall return with
a search warrant and thoroughly turn over
the entire place. The warrant will be based
on the charge that you are defrauding the

telephone company ; but that will not be the real accusation."

" Ah ? "

" Your arrest, which will follow, will mean——"

" What ? "

" That you are charged with the murder of Henry Stanage, who was found dead in Hyde Park last winter, with a bullet in his head, and —your pistol at his side."

I was sure of a sensation ; but it came in an unexpected way.

" That's your game, is it ? " his voice ringing with exultation. " If ever a man deserved to die, that scoundrel did."

It was my turn to be surprised into speechlessness.

" Look here," exclaimed Gasper, rising to his full height behind the desk. " You're after blood ; but, man to man, I stake my life I can convince any judge or jury that that rascal died at the right time. Denounce his murderer, arrest him, indict him—hang him, if you can ; I shall defend him to the last extremity, and with every technicality known to the law."

" But you know the murderer ? "

" As to who killed Stanage," Gasper fairly screamed, " that is for you to find out."

My K.C. friend assures me that the case is not complete, because evidence heard over a telephone is not admissible in a Court of Law. Gasper knows that as well as the Public Prosecutor.

Therefore, I alone, of all living men, know how Henry Stanage died.

VII

A Clever Capture

GUY CLIFFORD

A Clever Capture.

By GUY CLIFFORD.

URNING over the pages of one of my old diaries I come across notes here and there of many curious riddles. Some worked out and ticketed off as solved, others still awaiting the fulness of time when all shall be known.

Amongst the former, and perhaps one of the most curious of them all in the manner of its solution, is that which I have chosen as the title of this remarkable story.

My friend and partner, Robert Graceman, had been almost invisible for several days, shut up in his den engaged on some recondite chemical experiment, appearing only at occasional intervals to restore exhausted nature with a hasty meal. His usually rubicund and jovial face bore evident signs of his continuous and laborious researches. His eyes were heavy and leaden-looking with want of sleep, and his whole demeanour showed most painfully the enormous strain of overwork that he was imposing upon his system.

That evening, at dinner, I took him to task severely on the foolishness of continuing his work without proper relaxation.

"All right, Halton, old fellow," he replied, "a few more hours and then I will promise to take a holiday. Your anxiety, however, is quite unnecessary, for I'm as right as a trivet, except that I feel a bit fagged. To-morrow, however, I will lie in bed all day and catch up my back sleep." So with a nod and a smile he left me to return to his crucibles and evil-smelling chemical mixtures.

Next morning his place at the breakfast table was empty, and looking into his den I was glad to find his apparatus put aside as though done with for the present. Evidently the experiments he was engaged on were completed, for the present at any rate, so cautioning our old housekeeper not to disturb him, I descended to the offices to get through my usual morning's work.

"SKIMMING THE DAILY POST

99

On going upstairs to lunch I found Graceman perched on the back of a chair, skimming the *Daily Post*.

" Hullo, my busy bee," he exclaimed, throwing down the paper, " I've taken your advice, you see, and kept my promise. Now I'm going to dose you with your own physic. We will take a holiday together, turn up business and chemistry and have a good time."

" I can't leave the office at present——" I commenced, when he broke in.

" Well, you'll have to take the office with you then, for go you do, my boy, so there's no use wasting time in discussing that point; the question is where shall we go and what shall we do?"

" I may as well give in," I replied, with more pretence of reluctance than I really felt, for his joyous mood was very infectious and a few days off would do us both good.

" Ah! I thought you wouldn't resist the temptation. Shall it be Brighton—no, too crowded—a few days up the river at Sonning, say, wouldn't be half bad if this weather holds, and it looks like keeping up."

So it was decided that on the following morning we should pack our bags and depart for Sonning-on-Thames, one of the sweetest little spots on our lovely river. We were like a couple of school boys all that evening, for it was seldom of late years that we had made holiday together, and it was a matter of some difficulty to unearth our boating flannels, so long had they remained unused. Graceman, who was a fisherman of more than ordinary zeal, spent hours in furbishing up his rods and tackle. However, at last all was ready and everything packed up.

We determined to start early, and before nine o'clock we were on our way to Paddington. Sonning is an out of the way little river village having no station of its own, so it is usually reached by driving from Twyford. As our train drew into Maidenhead Station, just this side of Twyford, Graceman, who was gazing out of the window, suddenly called out " Why, there's Layman; I wonder what he's doing down here?" and jumping up he thrust his head out of the window and waved his hand.

Layman, or Inspector Layman, of Scotland Yard, to give him his proper title, was somewhat of a favourite of Graceman's.

In a few seconds he was at our door and shaking hands.

" We're playing truant, Layman," said Graceman. " Mr. Halton and I are on the jaunt for a few days; but what's the matter with you man, you look hipped?"

" I am hipped, sir, and pretty badly, too," returned the Inspector. " You no doubt saw in the papers yesterday that there had been a burglary at Lord Lipham's house down here the night before last and all her Ladyship's jewels stolen except those she had on. The usual thing you know, dinner time—entrance gained by ladder to her Ladyship's bedroom—no one about—no trace—no clue—no nothing," wound up the Inspector, laconically. " And the aggravating thing," he went on, " is that this is one of five or six burglaries that have occurred during the last six weeks or so that we can find no clue to; first they are down in Surrey at Woking, then Sevenoaks, Bickley, Harpenden, and Esher are visited, and now they're here. We feel sure it is the same hand at each of these places, for the work is so clean and not the slightest trace left behind to help us."

" Poor fellow," said Graceman, " it's too bad of them to play you such games. We're off now, come and see us next week at the office if you don't catch them and we'll put our heads together. Good-bye," and so saying Graceman resumed his seat as the train moved on.

Our holiday has nothing to do with this adventure, so I will pass over the pleasant days we passed on the bosom of old Father Thames and come to our last night at Sonning. It was Sunday, and we intended returning to London by an early train on Monday morning. We were sitting on the lawn of the White Hart Hotel smoking a final pipe before turning in to bed when Graceman remarked:—

" I haven't seen any account of the capture of the Maidenhead burglars in the papers this week; have you? "

" I had forgotten there were such things as burglars," I replied. " I've scarcely looked at the *Post* which you so thoughtfully ordered."

" What a humbug you are, Halton," he languidly answered. " When I proposed this little trip, oh! you couldn't leave the office, but since you've been down here I don't believe you've thought once of all your multitudinous business obligations. My professional opinion is that at heart you're a loafer, a perfect loafer. Come on, let's turn in."

When we arrived at Paddington next morning, Graceman rather surprised me by saying he wanted to send a wire to Inspector Layman, so making our way round to the telegraph office he despatched the following message to that gentleman :—

" Come and see me to night at Fig Buildings if you have not found your Maidenhead friends—Graceman."

As we bowled along in a hansom I endeavoured, delicately, to pump him on the subject of burglaries in general, and Layman's in particular, but he failed to respond to my insinuating enquiries, and, recognising my want of success, I at last desisted.

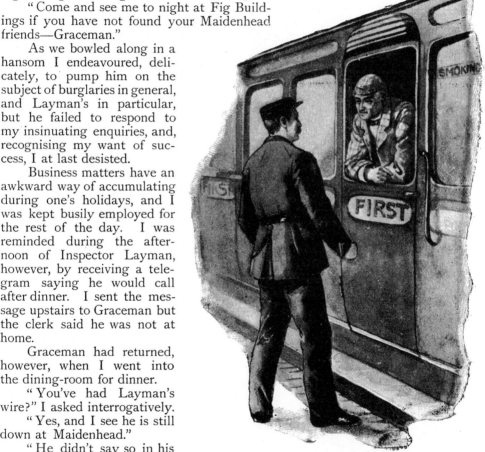

" ' POOR FELLOW ' "

Business matters have an awkward way of accumulating during one's holidays, and I was kept busily employed for the rest of the day. I was reminded during the afternoon of Inspector Layman, however, by receiving a telegram saying he would call after dinner. I sent the message upstairs to Graceman but the clerk said he was not at home.

Graceman had returned, however, when I went into the dining-room for dinner.

" You've had Layman's wire?" I asked interrogatively.

" Yes, and I see he is still down at Maidenhead."

" He didn't say so in his message," I remarked.

" No, of course not, but the telegram is despatched from Maidenhead if you notice, therefore I think it is a fair inference that the man is there also, but we shall presently know what success he has had. Meantime, have you any engagement for Wednesday evening, as I have a little adventure to propose which I think you would like to share? "

As I had nothing special on hand I signified my willingness to participate, and from past experience I refrained from trying to elicit what the adventure was until he was prepared to enlighten me.

When dinner was over we adjourned to the smoking-room, where very shortly afterwards Inspector Layman was announced.

"How's Maidenhead looking, Layman?" said Graceman, with a twinkle in his eye as he shook the Inspector's hand; "you're getting quite sunburnt."

"I was about to make the same remark to you," returned Layman; "both you and Mr. Halton are looking very fit, but as to Maidenhead it's a jolly enough place if you're down there boating and nothing to worry you, but from a professional point of view I'm just about tired of it."

"Then you have made little progress?"

"No, we are just where we were when I saw you at the station; in fact, we are worse off, as there is a week's loss of time with absolutely nothing to show for it. We overhauled several suspicious customers during the first day or two after the burglary, but they were not our men. Personally I don't hope to trace them, as I feel convinced they are well out of the neighbourhood; their mode of work shows me that they are too clever to be caught unless we are able to drop on them red-handed. I cannot even form any definite theory as to who the thieves may be, or how they work.

"'LAYMAN, I WANT YOUR ASSURANCE'"

You've helped me unravel some tough cases, Mr. Graceman, but then we've always had some clue or trace to work on, but now I'm beaten."

"Never say die," said Graceman, as the Inspector finished speaking; "you forget the 'Delford Mystery' and the 'McHenry Will Case,' to say nothing of one or two others, where we had as little to guide us, and yet you pulled them off all right."

"You pulled them off you should have said," returned Layman, "for if you had not put me on the right scent they would have remained mysteries to the present day; but I fear even you cannot pull these chestnuts out of the fire for us."

"Now you want to nettle me, Layman; you know my weak side and take advantage of it," replied Graceman with a smile. "However, I will humour you and accept your challenge, but, mind you, on our usual understanding: my name—I may say our names, for Mr. Halton will help me—are not to appear under any circumstances whatever."

"Of course I shall be charmed to go burglar-catching, but I don't quite see——" I began, when Graceman stopped me with:—

"Wait a bit, Halton. Layman, I want your assurance."

"If you wish it, of course I promise, sir; but let me tell you frankly I would much sooner you allowed me to inform my chief, for I don't much care for false credit, and praise so gained rather rankles here," said Layman, striking his clenched hand on his chest.

"It must be as I say," returned Graceman, "we cannot be known in the matter; you and I have worked together many times and you have previously tried to overcome my desire for remaining *incognito* without success, so you must accept the stipulation. And now to business. ' From information received,' as the newspaper reporters have it, I understand a burglary is to be attempted at Sunbury next Wednesday evening. My information, unfortunately, does not give the address of the victims, nor does it state the numerical strength of the burglars, but I put the number at about three. A very important fact, however, is that the confederates meet at Sunbury railway station at half-past six on Wednesday evening, and they are the same gentlemen you are looking for at Maidenhead." As Graceman finished speaking he leaned back in his seat and surveyed the Inspector, who sat bolt upright in his chair, his face vividly expressing the astonishment he felt at this explicit and detailed exposure of the enemy's plans.

"This beats Maskelyne and Cooke; why if I did not know you so well I should believe you were making a fool of me," exclaimed Layman. "Here have I been in close communication with all our force, half over England, for more than a week, on this job while you return this morning from your holiday, and in a few hours put your hand on the entire band. Yes, it's funny, awfully funny," he wound up, as I burst into laughter at the comical expression which the Inspector wore.

"Excuse me Layman, it's too bad to laugh at your perplexity," I said, "however, I am as much in the dark as you are."

"Can you inform us, Mr. Graceman, the source of this remarkable intelligence?" began Layman.

"I thought I told you, 'from information received.'"

"Is that all?"

"All that I can tell you for the present, but I should like to ask you how you intend to act in the matter; or perhaps you would prefer to hear my ideas first and say what you then think of them?"

"By all means," replied Layman.

"Halton," Graceman commenced, "please give me your attention, for you are as well acquainted with the ground over which we are to travel as I am;" then turning towards Inspector Layman, he continued, "Sunbury, you are probably aware, is a small riverside village a couple of miles or so above Hampton Court; the station lies about a mile from the river, and the best part of Sunbury is situated close to the Thames, along the road from the station to the village are also several large detached houses, and I may mention here that this road is exceedingly badly lighted at night time. I may say that near the station on the opposite side of the line are a number of houses, in fact, another village, but as these are all small cottages I don't think we need trouble about them. You made the remark when we met at Maidenhead that there had been five or six burglaries, all very similar in character, during the past few weeks around London and that they occurred during the time the family were at dinner—was this so in each case?"

"There was only one exception, if exception it may be termed," replied Layman, "and in that case the thieves are presumed to have entered after dinner, as during dessert the lady of the house sent one of the servants up to her bedroom for her vinaigrette, and the girl noticed nothing unusual in the room, but they must have been just at hand, for within an hour the robbery was discovered by the lady's maid when she went to tidy up her mistress's room. For all practical purposes we may, therefore, say each of these robberies was effected during dinner."

"Let us assume then that the plans of our friends at Sunbury are laid on the same lines—what I propose is this, that to-morrow you go down to Sunbury with two or three good men and thoroughly investigate the neighbourhood, find out the habits of all the residents in the near vicinity who may be considered worth these fellows' attention, ascertain if there are any strangers recently arrived at any of the hotels and if anyone is giving a dance or a dinner-party on Wednesday evening. You will have but little difficulty in your enquiries, as it is only a one-horse place and everyone knows everybody else's business. You can leave your men down there if you like, but they must be careful to avoid being conspicuous. They should dress like boating men, flannel shirts and serge suits, and go for a row in the day to blind suspicion. By this means you will gain a good knowledge of the locality; and if you will call here to-morrow evening we will make our plans for Wednesday. If you get back in time come straight on here and have dinner with us."

As Graceman concluded, he rose and stretched himself by slowly walking up and down the room, while Layman, after asking a few questions about Sunbury and promising to see us again the next evening, lighted up a fresh cigar which I offered him and took his departure.

"If not asking too much, Graceman," I remarked, when the Inspector had gone, " I should rather like to have one or two little points cleared up on this affair."

" Say on, my friend."

" Firstly, then, at what time on Wednesday do you require the pleasure of my company? secondly, where are *we*—that is, you and I—going to? and, thirdly, what are we going to do when we get there?"

"Concisely put and with commendable moderation," said Graceman; "and I will reply as tersely. Firstly, three p.m.; secondly, Hampton Court; thirdly, for a row. Having gratified your curiosity I must bid you good-night, for I still feel the effects of the balmy air of Sonning, and am confoundedly sleepy."

Whether this was an excuse to avoid further questioning or no I cannot say, but I rather think it was, for my friend Robert's custom was rather to sit up till the small hours of the morning.

Graceman, after breakfast next morning, informed our housekeeper that we should probably have a visitor to dinner that evening, and a little later on he joined me in the office, where, somewhat to my surprise, he remained the rest of the day, a thing he now rarely did, as I think I have before mentioned.

Inspector Layman, however, did not arrive in time for dinner, and it was past ten o'clock when he appeared. His report of the day's proceedings at Sunbury may be summed up very shortly. As arranged, he had made inquiries as suggested the previous night, and thoroughly surveyed the neighbourhood. The most important facts he had gleaned were that at two houses there would be parties on the Wednesday evening, and that as far as could be learnt there were no persons staying in the village whose movements were at all suspicious. These two houses were both on the road from Sunbury to Hampton, and not more than five minutes apart.

"The chief result attained," remarked Graceman, "is that your knowledge of the ground will be of immense advantage to us when

"'I SHOULD LIKE TO HAVE ONE OR TWO POINTS CLEARED UP'"

we have to work at night. You, of course, particularly observed the situation of the houses which were giving the entertainments?"

Layman signified his assent to this question by a nod.

"Briefly, then," went on Graceman, "my proposal is this: You take down three more good men to-morrow afternoon, and have them just outside the station at a quarter-past six. It will be almost dark at that hour. How many men have you there now?"

"Three."

"Good! Then instruct two of them to proceed, when it gets dark, to watch these houses, and the third man must patrol between the two; if nothing transpires then they are to return to Sunbury station at eleven o'clock. But if the burglars arrive at either house the man must get quietly away and summon his two *confrères*, and secure the thieves as they best can. Mr. Halton and myself are going down to Hampton Court to-morrow afternoon; we shall row up to Sunbury, and will meet you at the Magpie Hotel. We shall be there just before six o'clock, and we will immediately proceed to the railway station, where I hope to spot our friends when they meet. I think that provides for everything?" Graceman wound up, interrogatively.

"It's all right if we can recognise the scamps," replied Layman; "or if they attack the houses we have under surveillance; but I don't see where we shall come in if we miss them at the station, and they break into some other place."

"That's certainly the weak part of our chain," returned Graceman, "but I will show you how we can strengthen it when we meet at the Magpie. From their method of work, however, I think you will find one or more of these burglars are past masters at their trade, and I shall be more than surprised, Layman, if you don't find them to be old acquaintances, in which case you will recognise one or more of them yourself. I need hardly suggest that all your men and yourself should be disguised, as we do not wish the birds to take flight just when we are about to snare them."

Discussing various details of the morrow's campaign it was nearly midnight ere the Inspector left us.

Graceman and I went down early on the following afternoon to Hampton Court, where we hired a light skiff from the boatyard we usually patronised, and informed the man that we should leave the boat at Sunbury that night and he could send and fetch it back next day.

The distance by river to Sunbury is just about three miles, and Graceman suggested that pulling easily we could arrive at our destination about five o'clock and have some tea before Layman joined us.

I must not linger over the scenery of the river, which at that season of the year, for it was the end of September, was full of ripe beauty which always held me with a special charm, and the reach below Sunbury I consider one of the most beautiful on the Thames.

For myself I thought it all too soon when we reached the landing-stage of the Magpie Hotel, and the adventurous enterprise on which we were engaged was forcibly thrust upon me by Graceman's remark to hurry up, or I wouldn't get any tea. However, he had arranged matters so well that we had finished our meal comfortably and lighted our pipes before the Inspector arrived punctually on the stroke of six.

Dusk was fast deepening into the gloom of night as we started for the station, and as soon as we were out of the main street of the village, Layman reported that everything was in order as arranged.

"Good!" remarked Graceman; "and now I will tell you how I mean to make the weak link in our chain right; but first I must look in here," and as he spoke he opened the gate of a tiny cottage, and walking up the short path knocked at the door, which was opened almost instantly.

"Ready, Tom?" we heard him say.

"That you, Mr. Graceman? Right you are, sir."

And as the door shut, and the two men came towards us, I remembered that this was the abode of Tom West, a professional fisherman, who had many a time and oft been engaged for a day's fishing by Graceman.

In a few words Graceman told him as we continued our walk what we were down there for, and then, addressing Layman and myself, remarked that Tom knew every man, woman and child in Sunbury, whether villagers or gentlefolk and that he had written him to be ready at six o'clock that evening when he called.

"You will see presently that his assistance will be of the utmost service," said Graceman, and then he continued his remarks which this addition to our party had interrupted.

"You have no doubt noticed the exit from Sunbury station is through a wooden gate at which a porter stands to collect tickets. You remember that I said my information gave the meeting place as Sunbury station at half-past six? A coincidence, or shall I call it a corollary, is the fact that a train arrives here from town at twenty-six minutes past six—what more probable then, that this train brings one or, perhaps, more of the thieves? Now, Tom West can tell us who are natives and who are not, and if there are any strangers on the platform awaiting the train's arrival we must

THE REACH BELOW SUNBURY

watch them. If, however, there are no suspicious characters about then we must look for them amongst the passengers by the train. You must place your men, Layman, outside the gate where they can be talking together obscured in the gloom. They must watch you, who will indicate to them by a nod to follow any person or persons that Tom West does not know, and which he will point out to me and I will nod to you as the suspected party passes the gate. Your men, after shadowing his suspect, must report to you at the Magpie, where Mr. Halton and myself will adjourn as soon as you are engaged on the track. Here we are at the station and the train's signalled too, so look sharp, Inspector, and arrange your men. We'll go on the platform."

As we passed on to the platform Graceman commenced to chat rather loudly with Tom West on the chance of a day's sport on the morrow amongst the barbel. There was apparently no one there besides ourselves, but still laughing and chatting he kept the conversation from flagging for an instant until the roar of the quickly approaching train drowned his efforts. Then he said sharply "Tom, keep your eye on each person that approaches the exit, and if you don't know him, give me a poke on the arm with your stick. Now look out sharp and keep chattering and laughing at the same time." There were very few passengers by the train, perhaps a score in all, and several had already passed through the gate when Tom West whispered "That fellow in a brown hat gaping round near the gate is a stranger to me."

As I glanced at the man out of the corner of my eye, I saw a look of recognition flash from him, and in a moment another man joined him.

"There's another stranger talking with him," whispered West again.

Both men now gazed among the quickly-thinning group of passengers, when I noticed one touch the other on the arm, and both moved towards the gate.

"Now Halton," said Graceman rapidly, in a low voice, "you walk off to the gate as if you were going out, and when I call out 'Jim,' count five then answer back 'yes' and return to us."

Closely following Graceman's instructions a few steps brought me amongst the last of the people pushing through the gate; the two men I had been watching were just passing the exit, when Graceman called out "Jim."

Waiting to count five, before I replied, another voice outside the gate answered "Hallo" at the same moment I shouted "Yes." Naturally surprised, I looked towards the spot whence the voice came; I saw the two men we had been watching, together with a third man, all turned towards the spot where Graceman stood; they were just through the gate in front of me, and I could have touched them by putting out my hand. Fortunately I didn't forget Graceman's instructions, and turning sharp round I called out, "Well, what is it?" As I did so I heard one of the three give a guffaw, and say "I thought it was you, Jim, the bloke wanted."

This little scene took far less time to act than it does to set down here, and half a minute would more than cover the time occupied.

When I got close to Graceman he burst out into a hearty laugh that might have been heard at the end of the road, and Tom West joined him; but what they saw to laugh at beat me. However, they seemed so tickled that I felt compelled to help them and so we laughed at each other.

"Capital, couldn't have been better," said Graceman, when he had finished making an exhibition of himself.

"I'm glad of that, anyhow," I replied.

"All right, old man, keep your hair on, what kind of a chap was Jim?"

"Tall, darkish beard and moustache, rough, dark-grey overcoat, brownish soft-cloth hat, and he had a largish black hand-bag," I answered somewhat proudly, for I have a woman's knack of taking stock of people at a glance.

"My dear Halton, you're a credit to me. Let us away. Come on Tom, and don't forget we're fishermen only now."

So saying, we sauntered away from the station into the darkness of the night. We had barely gone thirty or forty yards before a figure advanced from the gloom of the hedge at the roadside.

"It's all right sir," said the figure, for it was Layman. "My three men are shadowing them. We know one of the scamps, the one in the brown hat, so there's not the slightest doubt you've given us the straight tip this time. I must be off now after my men. Are you going on to the Magpie?"

"Yes."

"Then I'll come on there directly we've located them." And the Inspector walked briskly off ahead of us.

Nothing more was said on the matter as we returned to the hotel. Tom West and Graceman went deep into the merits of trolling and spinning for jack and the subtle niceties of snap-tackle fishing for that same interesting fish.

"Come in Tom and have a whisky," said Graceman, when we arrived at our destination.

When we were seated in a comfortable corner of the smoke-room, Graceman said: "Would you like to be in at the death, or shall we wait the final act here, Halton?"

"I should rather like to see the capture," I replied; "that is if it's in the neighbourhood."

"All right, we will decide when Layman returns."

It was nearly an hour before the Inspector appeared. He was beaming and as sprightly as a two-year old.

Declining my invitation to have a whisky he drew a chair up to our little table and detailed his movements since he left us. The presumed burglars had walked leisurely down the road we had just come without any sign of uneasiness; they continued through the village in the same easy indifference until they were close to the house where the dinner-party was in progress, here they loitered a bit, as if to see if the coast were clear, then they disappeared over the wall which shut off the side grounds from the road. One of the detectives followed them and returned in a few minutes to say they were ensconced in a summer-house, at the bottom of the garden. The other two detectives had then got over the wall and hidden themselves in some shrubs near the house, whilst the first went back to watch the summer-house.

"When do you start, Layman?" said Graceman when the Inspector had finished.

"As soon as you like, sir; the dinner-party is for eight o'clock, and it's nearly that now, so we ought to be moving."

"Come on, then, let's be off, Halton, if you're coming."

"Yes, I've come so far, so I may as well see the finish," I remarked.

"You must be careful, gentlemen," said Layman, "for one man, I know, is a dangerous customer. Is Mr. West going to join us, too?"

"I should like to uncommonly, if I shan't be in the way," eagerly remarked Tom.

"All right," said Graceman, "you stick close to me; now we're ready." And so saying, we moved off on our expedition.

The night had closed in pitch dark, a heavy mantle of black rain-clouds obscured the heavens and the wind was beginning to blow with some force.

The road beyond the village was dark and lonesome; some little distance before we arrived at our destination the Inspector bade us halt while he went on to see if all was quiet. Returning in about ten minutes he reported all serene, and under his guidance we went forward and clambered over the wall. He hid us away near the two detectives and desired us to remain perfectly quiet unless he called us by name.

The house was a wide two-storied building with a verandah over the ground floor; every room downstairs was a blaze of light, but in the top rooms only two rooms showed a full light, whilst in the others there was only a dim twinkle as though the gas burners were turned down low.

We were barely hidden away when we heard eight o'clock strike from some neighbouring church.

Scarcely breathing, the minutes passed like hours, but it could scarcely have been a quarter-past eight when I saw three shadowy forms approaching from the opposite corner of the house. They halted close to where I was crouching with Tom West on the one side and Graceman on the other.

"Keep a sharp look out, Bill," I heard one whisper, and then the same man said, "Give me a hoist."

Clutching hold of one of the pillars that supported the verandah, the other stooped for him to put his feet on his shoulders; then, slowly rising, the climber grasped the edge of the verandah, and drew himself up; a second man followed in the same manner, and when he was up, the other whispered down, "Now for the bag," and the fellow picked up the black bag, and groping about, presently said in a hoarse whisper "All right," and I saw the bag slowly ascend. It had evidently been tied on to a piece of cord which it was too dark to discern.

From our hiding-place I could see the two men crawl to one of the darkened windows ; then, in about a couple of minutes, I heard a faint click, and presently the window was slowly raised and both men disappeared inside the house.

I was quivering with excitement now and breathlessly waiting the next act in the drama. I had not long to wait. The man watching below stood back a little from the house, where he could command every window. Just behind him was a patch of shrubs, and as I watched him, a dark object crept noiselessly round the bushes ; then straightening itself up, two arms shot out, and clutching the watcher by the throat, threw him on his back on the grass—a dull thud was the only sound that reached me as the body fell. Then another figure joined the first, and in a few seconds the fallen man was drawn out of my sight behind the bushes. Another figure then appeared, and took up the position the captured man had occupied, whilst three other forms crept under the verandah just where the burglars had climbed up.

Ten minutes or so slowly dragged by, then a figure appeared at the opened window, and crawled quietly out, followed by his pal. When they got to the edge of the verandah, one whispered, " Here you are, Bill," and the supposed Bill stepped forward and secured the black bag. Both the men on the roof then lowered themselves over the edge, and dropped right into the arms of those there waiting for them hidden beneath the verandah. There was a bit of a scuffle, and the rest of us rushed up, but the capture was completed without our aid, and without a word having been spoken.

When the handcuffs were on one of the twain said in a bitter tone :—

" Bill's peached, I spose Jim."

" Yes, damn him," replied the other.

" Oh, no, he hasn't," remarked Layman, "we've got him trussed like a fowl on the grass here. We've had our eyes on you since the Maidenhead affair."

" Yes, we've done it once too often," admitted the fellow.

" But let us see what you've got in the bag here," and Layman as he spoke moved closer towards the window and let the light shine into the opened bag, turning the contents over with his hand. "Ah," he ejaculated, " By Jove! but you made a grand haul; we had better go round to the front door, and let them know what's been happening."

"I SAW THE TWO MEN CRAWL TO THE WINDOW

We all marched through the side yard to the front, the prisoners guarded each by two stalwart detectives.

"Let's get in the background —we don't want to be recognised," said Graceman to me as the Inspector knocked at the main entrance.

The servant started back in alarm on beholding the band of men in the porch, but a few words from Layman reassured him somewhat, and closing the door again he went to fetch his master.

"By Jove! it's old Colonel Stanley," whispered Graceman in my ear as a tall, white-haired man threw the door open widely.

"Well, friends, what's the matter?"

"Fortunately nothing very serious," replied Layman, "your house has been broken into while you were dining; but we secured the thieves in the act and have all the plunder here," tapping the bag.

"Good gracious! are you a police officer?" said the Colonel.

"'YOUR HOUSE HAS BEEN BROKEN INTO'"

Layman nodded and the Colonel asked him to go in.

"We may as well toddle," remarked Graceman, taking my arm. "Tell the Inspector, Tom, that Mr. Halton and I have gone back to the Magpie."

It was not long before the Inspector joined us, and when I suggested a whisky this time he did not refuse.

He still retained the black bag.

"I've sent the men up to the railway station," he said, in answer to Graceman's enquiry, "and if you don't object we might catch the next train back to town, as I shall feel more comfortable when these jokers are safe under lock and key."

On our journey to Waterloo, Layman related what had passed when he entered the house at the Colonel's invitation. The old man called his son out from the dining-room and Layman related the affair of the capture, and it was agreed that nothing should be said to the guests till after the dinner was finished. Then the story was to be told and the people in the house were to make a list out of what things they missed and the lists were to be sent on to the Inspector at Scotland Yard—Layman also was to catalogue the contents of the black bag and send the list to the Colonel, who was to attend the police-court on the following morning, when no doubt the Magistrate would order the things to be handed over to him.

When the Inspector had finished relating these arrangements he turned to Graceman and begged him to relate how he had discovered the plans of the burglars which he had forecasted so exactly.

Graceman unbuttoned his overcoat, and taking out his pocket-book, handed to Layman a little slip of a newspaper cutting.

"Have you seen that before?" he asked.

"No," the Inspector replied in a hesitating manner; then suddenly, as a remembrance seemed to strike him, "Yes I have though, by Jove! Didn't it appear in one of the morning papers a few days ago?"

"Quite so; in the *Daily Post* Agony Column," returned Graceman.

"But what's it got to do with this affair?"

"That's my 'information received,' that's all," said Graceman quietly.

"Do you mean that this is all you had to work on?" quickly demanded Layman.

"Yes."

"Well I'm—but I won't swear; please explain it and settle me."

"Don't flurry, there's a good fellow," returned Graceman, as he handed me the cutting, which was as follows :—

O W S N E U H D N A N B L E U F S R P D Y A A S S Y T T N
A S E T I X I X T.—JIM.

Then he continued. "This appeared in the *Daily Post* Agony Column last Monday, and I read it and solved it as we were returning from Sonning; then I wired you to come and see me. Similar notices had appeared in the same paper at different times during the past two or three months, but you put the clue in my hands at Maidenhead."

"Me! how?"

"When you informed me that similar burglaries had occurred at Woking, Sevenoaks, and the other places. Now these little cryptograms have an attraction for me and I had taken the trouble to decipher them; the answer to this one is found by reading every third letter in rotation, thus," and so saying he handed us a slip of paper on which was pencilled the following.

O	W	S	N	E	U	H	D	N	A	N	B	L	E	U	F	S	R	P	D
13	26	1	14	27	2	15	28	3	16	29	4	17	30	5	18	31	6	19	32

Y	A	A	S	S	Y	T	T	N	A	S	E	T	I	X	I	X	T. — JIM.
7	20	33	8	21	34	9	22	35	10	23	36	11	24	37	12	25	38

"If you start at number 1 and read the figures in numerical order the translation comes out, 'Sunbury station, half-past-six Wednesday next, Jim.' Those that appeared in the previous weeks solved themselves by the same rule, but each read differently, the difference being in the place and time of meeting. I looked up the file of the papers and found that on each date a burglary took place in the neighbourhood given. But in two cases the name appended to the cryptogram was 'Bloater,' the others were all 'Jim.' I concluded that it was the practice of these rascals, when they spotted a suitable crib to crack, to communicate the fact to each other by this means, and I think you will admit my conclusions have justified themselves, and by our joint efforts we have outwitted the enemy."

"Joint efforts is good, remarkably good," Layman said, with a half-hearted kind of laugh. "A pretty tale to pitch to my chief. 'How did you manage it, Layman?' he will say. 'Joint efforts with a man unknown,' I answer. Make him smile, won't it?"

"Pooh, you can put your chief right better than that," returned Graceman, " say anything or nothing, but mum's the word as regards Mr. Halton and myself, and now good-night to you;" and shaking hands with Layman as the train drew into Waterloo we left him to look after the safe custody of his charges.

It may be well in conclusion to relate that at the trial it was fully proved that the prisoners had been concerned in all the burglaries mentioned in this narrative, and the sentence was ten years penal servitude, the judge commending Inspector Layman for the smart way in which he had secured his captives.

VIII

The Wendall Bank Case

GUY CLIFFORD

The Wendall Bank Case.

By GUY CLIFFORD.

⟡•◦•⟡

I BELIEVE few professions see so much of the seamy side of life as do solicitors in active practice. Some clergymen in the poorest and lowest districts of our great cities are no doubt oftener brought in contact with sufferers from keen poverty and its concomitants, drink and debauchery; but this class is only one of many that comes under the heading I have in mind. The medical brotherhood, too, have curious and saddening experiences amongst their poorer patients, but to the lawyer is opened out a larger field, embracing all sorts and conditions of men, from the most wretched pilferer to the high class rogue.

"MR. WENDALL WALKED INTO MY ROOM"

The particular case which has brought these thoughts uppermost in my mind may perhaps be recognised by some who peruse this story, but in order to avoid unnecessary pain I shall omit the real names of the chief actors in the scenes.

Among our most lucrative and esteemed clients was Josiah Wendall, the head of the well-known firm of private bankers of Wendall, Holmes and Co.

When Mr. Wendall walked into my room early one morning some years ago, I noticed immediately that some matter of serious importance was troubling him. There was no jovial salutation, as was his wont, but, instead, his face bore the impression of grief and sorrow. Without preamble he commenced, as he sat down by my side. "Mr. Halton, I am sorely upset and want your advice; not so much professionally as privately, as a friend."

I expressed my sympathy in a few words and waited for him to proceed.

Mr. Wendall was a rich man, and his affairs, I had ample knowledge of knowing, were prosperous and thriving, so I did not attribute his worry to money matters.

"I scarcely know how to commence," began Mr. Wendall, "for my story inculpates without a shadow of doubt one whom I have always looked upon as the soul of honour and who is endeared to me as much for his own good qualities as also for his father's sake. Even now, with every circumstance pointing to his guilt, I cannot believe him criminal. However, I will give you the facts so far as they are known and then, perhaps, we may find some opening to work upon.

"You are aware, Mr. Halton, that my nephew, Frank Wendall, holds the responsible position of chief cashier in our bank?"

I signified my assent to this question, and he continued:—

"Now, as such, he has the right to enter the safe-room during business hours. This right is also enjoyed by the manager and myself and my partner Holmes, and no one else is ever permitted to go into that room save the four persons I have just named.

"As it happens, the manager is away on his holiday, and before he left last Saturday the cash, notes, and other securities were checked, and all was correct, so that we can leave him out of the affair, which is now narrowed down to three persons.

"Yesterday, after the doors were closed, the books were made up, and the cash and notes checked in the usual way, when it was discovered that £3,000 in notes were missing."

"Excuse me for a moment," I interrupted, "but are they still unaccounted for?"

My client seemed rather surprised at the question, for he answered somewhat irascibly:—

"Yes, of course, or I shouldn't be troubling you."

At his reply I rang my bell and desired the clerk who answered it to ask my partner, Robert Graceman, to come down to my room if he was in.

While he was gone with his message I explained to Mr. Wendall that I thought Mr. Graceman's advice on such a serious matter would be far more valuable than mine.

While I was speaking, Graceman came in, and these two old friends greeted each other warmly.

"How's my little godchild, Trixie?" asked Robert Graceman.

The smile of welcome passed away from Mr. Wendall's brow at the question, and he replied gravely:—

"I'm afraid, Graceman, that the news she will soon have to hear will break her heart."

Beatrice, or Trixie as she was usually called, was Josiah Wendall's only child, and the apple of his eye. The fact that my partner, Robert Graceman, had stood godfather for her shows the terms of friendship which had existed between the two men for many years.

At the serious, and to him strange reply of his friend, Graceman turned to me with the remark: "What's the matter?"

"Tell him, Halton," said Mr. Wendall.

So I repeated, shortly and as concisely as possible, the opening incidents I had just heard.

As the elucidation of the disappearance of the notes and the final result of the affair passed hereafter through Graceman's hands, I shall set down the rest of the story in narrative form as the various details were unravelled.

"What has all this got to do with Trixie?" asked Graceman.

" Although I have no authority for saying so beyond what my common sense tells me, yet I am sure that Frank and Trixie look upon each other with more affection than their cousinly relationship might justify," replied Mr. Wendall.

" What does Frank say to the loss of the notes?" was Graceman's next enquiry.

" He can give no explanation; he's as much in the dark as the rest of us," replied Frank's uncle.

" When the loss was discovered, it was at first naturally assumed to be a mistake in the counting; but after repeatedly checking no alteration could be made, and Frank sent one of the clerks up to my house for me whilst he remained with those of the clerks who had been engaged with him.

" When I received his message I hurried back to the Bank, and we had all the business done since the last checking gone through, but still there remained that unaccountable discrepancy of £3,000. Frank then suggested we should examine the contents of the safe, in the hope that the packet of notes might have fallen down somewhere; so he and a couple of the other clerks emptied the room whilst I looked on. As each bag of coin or package of notes was returned they were carefully and anxiously scanned; but we had our trouble for nothing. As no one could suggest anything further, we locked up for the night, leaving the watchman in charge.

" When I arrived at the Bank this morning Holmes was already there, and Frank had related the whole of the circumstances to him.

" ' This is a bad business, Wendall,' he began; ' a very unpleasant business.'

" FOR A FEW MOMENTS HE PONDERED "

" Now Holmes, as a rule, is an easy-going fellow—in fact, too easy-going, as I have sometimes hinted to him ; but it struck me somehow that there was more feeling in his words than the occasion at present called for. I suppose my surprise at his manner showed itself, for he went on:

" ' It appears that the books and cash were checked over and over again last night and the £3,000 is still missing. Well, notes don't walk away by themselves, and unless someone broke into the safe-room, of which there is no appearance or suggestion, they must have been—well, to speak plainly, stolen.'

" It was speaking plainly with a vengeance, yet still there was no other way of accounting for their loss. Then he continued:

" ' This cannot be hushed up, for it affects the heads of the Bank too seriously; for there are only three people who have free entrance to the safe-room: you, myself and your nephew, Frank Wendall. Under these circumstances I am sure you will agree with me that the fullest investigation only will suffice, and the sooner the matter is put into proper hands the better for us all.'

"For a few moments I pondered over what Holmes had so clearly reasoned, and I could find no fault with his argument. Somehow I felt that Frank was not the culprit; but if this were so there remains but Holmes and myself, and I should as soon expect to be charged with the theft myself as dream of suspecting Holmes. Altogether, as Holmes says, it's a very unpleasant business."

"Have you called anyone in to investigate?" asked Graceman.

"No; I suggested to Holmes that I should ask your advice as to what we should do, and he consented immediately to our consulting you."

For a few seconds Graceman remained in thought; then he said, "I quite agree with Mr. Holmes that the matter should be gone into without further delay, and if you consent, I will send a note up to Scotland Yard at once, and put the affair into Inspector Layman's hands. He is a cautious, careful man, and you don't want the matter made more public at present than can be helped. Meantime, I should advise you to call in your official accountants, and have your books authentically audited so as to make absolutely sure that there is no other way of explaining the loss."

So Mr. Wendall went back to his Bank, and a note was sent up to Inspector Layman by special messenger, and in due time that official came down to our office.

After he and Graceman had discussed the matter from the facts they so far had, they went together round to the Bank.

"I am very glad you agreed with me, Mr. Graceman," said Mr. Holmes when they entered, "my opinion is, that the sooner an affair of this kind is put into proper hands the better for everyone."

Then they proceeded to the safe-room to see for themselves where the notes were stolen from, and Inspector Layman minutely examined the lock for evidence of tampering. There was no indication, however small, to show that the safe had been forced, so after a short while they met again in the partners' private room.

"The safe has not been broken into, gentlemen," remarked the officer, authoritatively, then he proceeded : "I understand that only you two gentlemen," looking alternately at Mr. Wendall and his partner, "and your chief cashier, Mr. Frank Wendall, were allowed to enter the safe-room."

"That is so," answered Mr. Wendall.

"Is it impossible for either of the other clerks to enter the safe?" asked Mr. Layman.

Mr. Holmes glanced at his partner, who returned the look of enquiry, when the former replied, "It is not impossible to enter it, but I believe it would be impossible for either of the clerks, or any one else, to enter without being observed, and that is really what you mean."

"Yes, sir, that is my meaning," answered the Inspector, "but how do you arrange that no one can enter unseen? Is there always someone watching the safe?"

"Let me explain," said Mr. Holmes. "You saw that the safe stood apart and clear from the clerks' desks, with a large space between it and the nearest desk."

Mr. Layman answered in the affirmative, and Mr. Holmes then continued: "Our strictest injunction and most sternly-enforced rule is that no clerk shall approach or enter the safe-room, unless specially requested, and is accompanied by one of the partners, the manager, or the chief cashier. The penalty for the breach of this rule is instant dismissal, without appeal. Another rule, equally stringent, obliges any clerk or other official to report at once anyone infringing this rule, and to call the attention of those in the office to the offender to corroborate his breach of these regulations. The desks facing the safe-room seat twenty clerks, and I should say it would be absolutely impossible for anyone to enter the safe without being observed."

" I quite endorse Mr. Holmes' opinion," added his partner. " I do not believe the safe could be entered by anyone without being noticed."

" Very well, gentlemen," replied the Inspector, " you, of course, are aware that the only inference that can be drawn from your opinions is that your chief cashier must have abstracted the notes, and I should like to have a few words with him if you will allow me to do so."

Scarcely had the Inspector formulated his wish ere Mr. Holmes rang his bell and requested Mr. Frank Wendall to be sent to them.

" Have you a private room I can see him in?" asked the officer.

" Certainly," Mr. Holmes answered; then, as Frank entered, he said, " This is Mr. Frank Wendall, Inspector Layman," then turning to Frank he continued, "your uncle and I have considered that it is advisable to transfer our personal responsibilities to the proper authority and this gentleman," waving his hand towards the officer, " desires to have a few words with you—take him into the next room."

Inspector Layman closed the door carefully and approaching quite closely to Frank said " I presume we cannot be overheard in any way."

" I think not," answered Frank rather shortly, for he did not quite appreciate the position. Circumstantial facts pointed very inflexibly at himself as the thief, and he knew that unless the notes were discovered the odium and shame would surely rest on him, whether or no Mr. Holmes and his uncle charged him openly. Knowing himself innocent he had hitherto refrained from supposing that the notes were stolen, for the very simple reason that as he hadn't taken them, there were only two other persons who could, namely his uncle or Mr. Holmes, neither of whom could for a moment be thought culpable.

Frank's notion was that by some strange mischance the notes had got mislaid, how or where he hadn't the slightest idea.

All this had been careering through his puzzled brain ever since the notes were proved to be gone.

Inspector Layman noticed the abruptness of Frank's reply and proceeded. " Do not consider me an enemy, Mr. Wendall, simply because I am a police officer and have to ask unpleasant questions." Frank reddened somewhat at the implied rebuke, and then with his usual outspokenness said " I beg your pardon, of course, you are only doing your duty, now fire away and ask anything you like. Meanwhile pray sit down," and Frank drew a chair forward for the Inspector while he sat himself on the corner of the table.

" First of all, can you give me the numbers of the missing notes?" said the Inspector.

Frank drew a slip of paper from his pocket and handed it to Mr. Layman. It contained the numbers of the notes, which were all of the value of ten pounds each.

" Good," replied the officer, as he glanced over the slip, then he added, " what is your opinion as to the missing notes; are they lost, mislaid, stolen, or what? "

" At first, of course, I thought they were mislaid somehow, but that seems impossible now, after the searches we have made. Then comes the question of theft and the thieves." And then Frank went over the same rules that Mr. Holmes had previously enumerated. " So you see that, if they are stolen, there are three possible thieves: myself, my uncle, and Mr. Holmes."

" Have you any reason to think either your uncle or Mr. Holmes guilty," interrogated Mr. Layman, holding up a warning finger as Frank sprang off the table.

Frank choked down the hasty words of denial he was about to utter and reseating himself on his corner answered quietly, " Not the slightest suspicion."

" Humph!" ejaculated the officer looking squarely at Frank, who returned his gaze without flinching and then added:—

" I don't know whether that 'humph' of yours was a question or not, but I may remark that I have not taken the notes."

"I believe you, Mr. Wendall," answered the officer, in a tone of sincerity, then he said, "Now for my last question. Why does Mr. Holmes dislike you?"

"Dislike me," asked Frank, in amazement; "I was not aware that he did. Certainly we have never been particularly cordial with each other, but then he is stand-offish with all the clerks. No, I think you are mistaken, Mr. Layman."

"Well, perhaps I am. No doubt it's only his manner," and rising from his seat he thanked Frank for his confidence and returned to the room where the partners and Graceman were still busy turning over the details of the loss.

"Well," asked Mr. Holmes, interrogatively, as the detective officer entered.

"'NO, NO!' EXCLAIMED MR. WENDALL'

"Mr. Frank Wendall cannot account for the loss," the latter replied; "he practically confirms every point you have mentioned."

"What do you now propose should be done, then?" asked Mr. Holmes.

For a few moments the astute officer did not reply, then he said, "I should like to consider the case for a short time, say until to-morrow morning, then I will give you my opinion, that is unless you prefer to charge your cashier with the theft at once."

"No, no," exclaimed Mr. Wendall, "Frank is no thief."

"Very well, then, gentlemen, I will call in the morning."

Mr. Graceman rose as the Inspector bowed himself out, and in a low tone said to the two partners, "I will go with him and hear what he thinks of the matter."

As the lawyer and detective walked slowly away Mr. Graceman opened the conversation abruptly with :—

"Is Frank Wendall the thief, Layman?"

"I believe not," was the answer; "but he's in a terribly bad hole. I suppose there's not a doubt the notes were there?"

"They all say so," replied Mr. Graceman ; then he added, "le me jot down the numbers of the notes," and the officer handed the slip to his companion from which he rapidly copied what he required.

"Now I must leave you, Layman," said Robert Graceman, as they reached the corner of the street; then, as though it was an afterthought, he added as they shook hands, "I am rather interested in this little affair, and perhaps shall be able to offer you a few suggestions when I've thought the riddle out; but then again I may be working on a wrong scent, so you go ahead with your own deductions, and if I come across anything of importance you shall hear from me." And so they parted.

The detective officer returned to his office, and by breakfast time next morning he had reports and notes from several of his staff, who he had specially detailed to glean information likely to help him.

Frank Wendall's private address had been watched, and his movements dogged during the past few hours. His uncle and Mr. Holmes had also shared a part of the careful Inspector's attention, but so far nothing of importance had been unearthed by the bloodhounds of Scotland Yard. Frank had gone home to his rooms in Russell Square rather later than usual, having had another turn at the books at the Bank ; he had his dinner, and then walked up Oxford Street to Hyde Park and entered his uncle's house, which he left about half-past ten and walked back to his diggings.

Mr. Wendall, Frank's uncle, had gone home direct from the Bank early in the afternoon, and had not since left his house. Mr. Holmes, however, had dined at his club, visited one of the theatres and caught the last train at Waterloo for Richmond, where he resided in bachelor estate.

"Precious little to help me here," muttered the detective, as he threw down the various reports of his satellites. "I don't like Mr. Holmes," he soliloquised, "but that's mere prejudice, for, of course, there's no motive for his stealing the notes—unless—by George I never thought of that," and Mr. Layman hastily·rose and put on his hat and hurried out.

The Bank had just opened when the detective arrived, and Frank Wendall was busily engaged in opening and reading the ordinary business correspondence in his private room when the Inspector was announced.

"You're early Mr. Layman," remarked Frank, looking up, "have you good news ? "

His visitor shook his head negatively, but instead of answering the question asked another.

"Can you inform me if either your uncle or Mr. Holmes is pressed for money? Now don't get angry, there may be nothing in the enquiry, and if it is a breach of confidence why you can please yourself if you answer or no ; but in the latter event it would necessitate my finding out through other sources, which might be still less to the liking of the partners."

Frank sat for awhile with his thoughts rapidly **examining** the motive for the detective's question.

The Inspector saw his advantage and followed it up in a masterly manner.

"Don't forget, sir," he said quietly, "that I have been instructed to investigate this unfortunate affair, and that your position is seriously and gravely threatened if the missing notes are not soon discovered."

"You shall see the accounts of my uncle and Mr. Holmes as they stand in the firm's ledger," Frank replied at last, and without further parley he went into the outer office and brought in the bank ledger. Turning up the account first of his uncle there appeared a goodly balance to that gentleman's credit ; then Mr. Holmes' account was found.

"I thought he had more than that," muttered Frank, as the figures were totted up showing only a few hundred pounds balance, "still this is only his private account, and he appears to have been drawing on it pretty frequently lately, probably he's investing it, I see a good many cheques are payable to Scott and Son: those are his stockbrokers."

"Yes, very likely," answered Mr. Layman, "and now to complete my curiosity, let me see your account."

As the detective made his demand he glanced keenly at the young man by his side.

Frank turned the leaves over rapidly, and without hesitation pointed his finger at the columns which represented his own little account. Then he remarked, with a smile, "I am sorry it is so small, but I rely on your reticence not to publish my poverty to the world."

"You may rely on my treating your confidence with absolute secrecy," replied his companion, and then he bade him good morning, saying he should return to see his uncle later on.

But his morning's work had not discovered any new feature in the tangled skein which had been placed in his hands for solution, and when Inspector Layman, a few hours later, presented himself before the two partners he had practically nothing new to report.

"We must wait till some of the stolen notes turn up," was his last remark as he left the room.

"There's nothing to work on," mused the puzzled detective, as he made his way thoughtfully towards the City, where he proposed to drop into the Bank of England on the off chance of finding some of the missing notes had been cashed.

All the banks in London and the country had been notified of the loss, with the numbers of the notes.

There was no news of them yet, however, so Mr. Layman hailed a hansom and got back to his official quarters to attend to other business.

On the third day after his visit to the City, Inspector Layman received a telegram just as he was leaving to get his frugal lunch; it was from Robert Graceman, and was despatched from the Royal Hotel, Hull. The message was short, but the detective seemed thunderstruck at the contents; then he read it through again. "Bring warrant for arrest of Charles Farnley, Wendall's manager for theft of £3,000 notes, he is detained here."

"Well, I'm ———," he muttered.

Early that night Inspector Layman arrived at Hull and Mr. Graceman met him at the station.

"Have you got your papers?" said Mr. Graceman, as they shook hands. Layman nodded, then he could hold his patience no longer. "How on earth did you trace it to him?" he exclaimed. "Where did you find your clue?"

"Wait till we've got him safe under lock and key, and then you can hear all the details," replied his companion, as they walked briskly towards the police station, which was only a few minutes away.

Charles Farnley was detained on suspicion, and as soon as Inspector Layman arrived with his warrant the prisoner was transferred to the secure custody of a police cell.

"Come now, Mr. Graceman," Layman began, directly they had got back to the hotel and had secured a quiet corner in the smoking-room. "How did you get on his trail?"

"Let me ask you a question first, Layman," said Robert Graceman. "You were present when Mr. Frank Wendall checked the contents of the safe for our edification, did you notice the method in which it was done?"

The Inspector looked at his questioner as though he would read from the latter's face what he was driving at.

At last he slowly replied, "Yes, I believe I remember. Mr. Frank took the packages of notes and bags of coin from one of the clerks, who called out each, and glancing at them placed them in the safe."

"Quite so," replied Mr. Graceman, approvingly; then he continued, "our friend here, Mr. Farnley, went through the operation on the previous checking just before he went away."

"Yes," said the Inspector, still in the dark.

"Therefore, assuming that neither Mr. Wendall, the uncle, or Mr. Holmes, or Mr. Wendall, the nephew, had touched the notes since then, Mr. Farnley was the last person who did so."

"Ah!" ejaculated the Detective, "that set you thinking about the manager."

"Just so, and then I casually enquired where our friend had gone for his holiday, and was told to Scarborough. Now Scarborough, at this period of the year was, so I thought, hardly the place for a man of Farnley's lively temperament—for he's a bit of a masher in his way, and it was dead out of season for that lively seaside resort. I ascertained from Mr. Wendall, on the quiet, what hotel he was staying at, and as I knew you would attend to matters in London all right, I considered the air of Scarborough might do me good, so I caught the afternoon train for that charming place." Then he hospitably exclaimed, as he proffered his cigar case: "Have another cigar; yours is out."

"Thank you," replied Inspector Layman, judiciously hiding his impatience to hear the rest of the story.

Then Mr. Graceman continued. "I was not surprised to find when I arrived at the hotel that Mr. Farnley was out. He had gone away for a few days, the clerk informed me politely, but he did not know where. The porter had carried his bag to the station, so I interviewed that individual and was fortunately able to discover his destination. I say fortunately; you may call it luck, perhaps. He had sent the man with his bag to secure a corner seat in a smoking carriage while he bought his ticket, and then gave the man a shilling for his services and jumped into the carriage. He had forgotten to get a paper, however, and called the porter back to give him a copper to buy one, and in so doing he pulled his ticket out and it fell on the platform. The porter was an observant fellow and his eye caught the name of the station on the ticket. It was Hull. Thus you see what little things lead up to, for that penny paper cost our mutual friend his liberty."

Layman knew his friend too well to hurry him, but he fretted at the prolixity of his narrative, so he nodded his appreciation and pretended to enjoy his cigar as he closed his eyes and waited patiently for his friend to continue.

"Hull I thought a still less attractive place for Mr. Farnley's holiday," Mr. Graceman resumed, "and I was so curious to know what the attraction was that drew him there that I followed at once. It was rather late when I arrived, so I left my investigation till the morning; then I set out to try and trace my man. I was some time before I got on his tracks, and then I discovered he had taken the steamer on the previous day for Rotterdam. This was a still more curious change of plans, so I followed him by that day's boat, and to cut a long story short, with the aid of the authorities I soon discovered what he was up to. He had gone over to change the stolen notes, but we were too late to catch him before he had turned them into coin. The man who had changed them, however, showed me the identical notes which he had changed for ten per cent commission. As I did not want any extradition trouble I kept quiet and waited for the next steamer to sail for Hull. Just before the advertised time for starting arrived my man came on board and I knew that he was safe. When we arrived at Hull I followed him to the hotel, and then I called in the chief inspector and charged him with the theft, and you know the rest."

"You're splendid—simply splendid!" exclaimed the excited Inspector, when Robert Graceman ended his story. "Now, I took it for granted that the notes were safe when the manager left, and never connected him with the case at all."

"You under-estimate your abilities, Layman, and over-estimate mine."

"'HOW DID YOU GET ON HIS TRAIL?'"

"That be bothered," replied the Inspector; "there were the facts for me to see and utilise, just the same as you saw them, but I could not see beyond my nose, while you read them correctly. The force lost a mighty leader when you took to the law, sir."

"Pooh, pooh!" replied Mr. Graceman, smiling at the officer's laudation. "You forget your own many successes."

To say that all at the Bank were amazed at the turn of events would be to speak mildly. Mr. Holmes had considered Frank Wendall's guilt as next door to proved, and he hastened to offer his young cashier his sincere apologies for his doubts, which Frank met in the fullest manner, and thereafter their personal esteem grew and flourished. Frank's uncle also was delighted to find his nephew was freed from the stain which had seemed to compass him round, and shortly afterwards he showed his regard for his kinsman by giving him his blessing when he proposed for his daughter Trixie, and shortly after he was made a junior partner in the banking firm.

IX

Strange Studies from Life

ARTHUR CONAN DOYLE

Strange Studies from Life.

By A. Conan Doyle.

[The cases dealt with in this series are studies from the actual history of crime, though occasionally names have been changed where their retention might cause pain to surviving relatives.]

I.—THE HOLOCAUST OF MANOR PLACE.

N the study of criminal psychology one is forced to the conclusion that the most dangerous of all types of mind is that of the inordinately selfish man. He is a man who has lost his sense of proportion. His own will and his own interest have blotted out for him the duty which he owes to the community. Impulsiveness, jealousy, vindictiveness are the fruitful parents of crime, but the insanity of selfishness is the most dangerous and also the most unlovely of them all. Sir Willoughby Patterne, the eternal type of all egoists, may be an amusing and harmless character as long as things go well with him, but let him be thwarted—let the thing which he desires be withheld from him, and the most monstrous results may follow. Huxley has said that a man in this life is for ever playing a game with an unseen opponent, who only makes his presence felt by exacting a penalty every time one makes a mistake in the game. The player who makes the mistake of selfishness may have a terrible forfeit to pay — but the unaccountable thing in the rules is that some, who are only spectators of his game, may have to help him in the paying. Read the story of William Godfrey Youngman, and see how difficult it is to understand the rules under which these penalties are exacted. Learn also from it that selfishness is no harmless peccadillo, but that it is an evil root from which the most monstrous growths may spring.

About forty miles to the south of London, and close to the rather *passé* watering-place of Tunbridge Wells, there lies the little townlet of Wadhurst. It is situated within the borders of Sussex at a point which is close to the confines of Kent. The country is a rich pastoral one and the farmers are a flourishing race, for they are near enough to the Metropolis to take advantage of its mighty appetite. Among these farmers there lived in the year 1860 one Streeter, the master of a small homestead and the father of a fair daughter, Mary Wells Streeter. Mary was a strong, robust girl, some twenty years of age, skilled in all country work, and with some knowledge also of the town, for she had friends up there, and above all she had one friend, a young man of twenty-five, whom she had met upon one of

"HER BUNDLE OF LOVE-LETTERS UPON HER LAP."

her occasional visits, and who had admired her so that he had actually come down to Wadhurst after her, and had spent a night under her father's roof. The father had expressed no disapprobation of the suitor, a brisk, masterful young fellow, a little vague in his description of his own occupation and prospects, but an excellent fireside companion. And so it came about that the deep, town-bred William Godfrey Youngman became engaged to the simple, country-bred Mary Wells Streeter, William knowing all about Mary, but Mary very little about William.

July the 29th of that year fell upon a Sunday, and Mary sat in the afternoon in the window of the farm-house parlour, with her bundle of love-letters upon her lap, reading them again and yet again. Outside was the little square of green lawn, fringed with the homely luxuriance of an English country garden, the high hollyhocks, the huge nodding sunflowers, the bushes of fuchsia, and the fragrant clumps of sweet William. Through the open lattice came the faint, delicate scent of the lilac and the long, low droning of the bees. The farmer had lain down to the plethoric sleep of the Sunday afternoon, and Mary had the room to herself. There were fifteen love-letters in all: some shorter, some longer, some wholly delightful, some with scattered business allusions, which made her wrinkle her pretty brows. There was this matter of the insurance, for example, which had cost her lover so much anxiety until she had settled it. No doubt he knew more of the world than she, but still it was strange that she, so young and so hale, should be asked and again asked to prepare herself for death. Even in the flush of her love those scattered words struck a chill to her heart. "Dearest girl," he had written, "I have filled up the paper now, and took it to the life insurance office, and they will write to Mrs. James Bone to-day to get an answer on Saturday. So you can go to the office with me before two o'clock on Monday." And then again, only two days later, he had begun his letter: "You promised me faithfully over and over again, and I expect you to keep your promise, that you would be mine, and that your friends would not know it until we were married; but now, dearest Mary, if you will only let Mrs. James Bone write to the insurance office at once and go with me to have your life insured on Monday morning next!" So ran the extracts from the letters, and they perplexed Mary as she read them. But it was all over now, and

he should mingle business no longer with his love, for she had yielded to his whim, and the insurance for £100 had been duly effected. It had cost her a quarterly payment of 10s. 4d., but it had seemed to please him, and so she would think of it no more.

There was a click of the garden-gate, and looking up she saw the porter from the station coming up the path with a note in his hand. Seeing her at the window he handed it in and departed, slily smiling, a curious messenger of Cupid in his corduroys and clumping boots—a messenger of a grimmer god than Cupid, had he but known it. She had eagerly torn it open, and this was the message that she read:—

"16, Manor Place, Newington, S.E.
"Saturday night, July 28th.

"MY BELOVED POLLY,—I have posted one letter to you this afternoon, but I find that I shall not have to go to Brighton to-morrow as I have had a letter from there with what I wanted inside of it, so, my dear girl, I have quite settled my business now and I am quite ready to see you now, therefore I send this letter to you. I will send this to London Bridge Station to-morrow morning by 6.30 o'clock and get the guard to take it to Wadhurst Station, to give it to the porter there, who will take it to your place. I can only give the guard something, so you can give the man who brings this a small sum. I shall expect to see you, my dear girl, on Monday morning by the first train. I will await your coming at London Bridge Station. I know the time the train arrives—a quarter to ten o'clock. I have promised to go to my uncle's to-morrow, so I cannot come down; but I will go with you home on Monday night or first thing Tuesday morning, and so return here again Tuesday night, to be ready to go anywhere on Wednesday; but you know all that I have told you, and I now expect that you will come up on Monday morning, when I shall be able to manage things as I expect to do. Excuse more now, my dearest Mary. I shall now go to bed to be up early to-morrow to take this letter. Bring or burn all your letters, my dear girl. Do not forget; and with kind love and respects to all I now sum up, awaiting to see you Monday morning a quarter to ten o'clock.—Believe me, ever your loving, affectionate,

"WILLIAM GODFREY YOUNGMAN."

A very pressing invitation this to a merry day in town; but there were certainly some curious phrases in it. What did he mean by saying that he would manage things as he expected to do? And why should she burn or bring her love-letters? There, at least, she was determined to disobey this masterful suitor who always "expected" in so authoritative a fashion that she would do this or that. Her letters were much too precious to be disposed of in this off-hand fashion. She packed them back, sixteen of them now, into the little tin box in which she kept her simple treasures, and then ran to meet her father, whose step she heard upon the stairs, to tell him of her invitation and the treat which awaited her to-morrow.

At a quarter to ten next morning William Godfrey Youngman was waiting upon the platform of London Bridge Station to meet the Wadhurst train which was bringing his sweetheart up to town. No observer glancing down the straggling line of loiterers would have picked him out as the man whose name and odious fame would before another day was passed be household words to all the three million dwellers in London. In person he was of a goodly height and build, but commonplace in his appearance, and a character which was only saved from insignificance through the colossal selfishness, tainted with insanity, which made him conceive that all things should bend before his needs and will. So distorted was his outlook that it even seemed to him that if he wished people to be deceived they must be deceived, and that the weakest device or excuse, if it came from him, would

"THEY WALKED DOWN THE PLATFORM TOGETHER."

pass unquestioned. He had been a journeyman tailor, as his father was before him, but aspiring beyond this, he had sought and obtained a situation as footman to Dr. Duncan, of Covent Garden. Here he had served with credit for some time, but had finally resigned his post and had returned to his father's house, where for some time he had been living upon the hospitality of his hard-worked

parents. He had talked vaguely of going into farming, and it was doubtless his short experience of Wadhurst with its sweet-smelling kine and Sussex breezes which had put the notion into his Cockney head.

But now the train rolls in, and there at a third-class window is Mary Streeter with her pink country cheeks, the pinker at the sight of her waiting lover. He takes her bag and they walk down the platform together amongst the crinolined women and baggy-trousered men whose pictures make the London of this date more strange to us than that of last century. He lives at Walworth, in South London, and a straw-strewn omnibus outside the station conveys them almost to the door. It was eleven o'clock when they arrived at Manor Place, where Youngman's family resided.

The household arrangements at Manor Place were peculiar. The architect having not yet evolved the flat in England, the people had attained the same result in another fashion. The tenant of a two-storied house resided upon the ground-floor, and then sub-let his first and second floors to other families. Thus, in the present instance, Mr. James Bevan occupied the ground, Mr. and Mrs. Beard the first, and the Youngman family the second, of the various floors of No. 16, Manor Place. The ceilings were thin and the stairs were in common, so it may be imagined that each family took a lively interest in the doings of its neighbour. Thus Mr. and Mrs. Beard of the first-floor were well aware that young Youngman had brought his sweetheart home, and were even able through half-closed doors to catch a glimpse of her, and to report that his manner towards her was affectionate.

It was not a very large family to which he introduced her. The father departed to his tailoring at five o'clock every morning and returned at ten at night. There remained only the mother, a kindly, anxious, hard-working woman, and two younger sons aged eleven and seven. At eleven o'clock the boys were at school and the mother alone. She welcomed her country visitor, eyeing her meanwhile and summing her up as a mother would do when first she met the woman whom her son was likely to marry. They dined together, and then the two set forth to **see** something of the sights of London.

"SHE SAT IN THE CROWDED PIT WITH
HER SILENT LOVER AT HER SIDE."

No record has been left of what the amusements were to which this singular couple turned: he with a savage, unrelenting purpose in his heart; she wondering at his abstracted manner, and chattering country gossip with the shadow of death already gathering thickly over her. One little incident has survived. One Edward Spicer, a bluff, outspoken publican who kept the Green Dragon in Bermondsey Street, knew Mary Streeter and her father. The couple called together at the inn, and Mary presented her lover. We have no means of knowing what repellent look mine host may have observed in the young man's face, or what malign trait he may have detected in his character, but he drew the girl aside and whispered that it was better for her to take a rope and hang herself in his skittle-alley than to marry such a man as that—a warning which seems to have met the same fate as most other warnings received by maidens of their lovers. In the evening they went to the theatre together to see one of Macready's tragedies. How could she know as she sat in the crowded pit, with her silent lover at her side, that her own tragedy was far grimmer than any upon the stage? It was eleven o'clock before they were back once more at Manor Place.

The hard-working tailor had now returned, and the household all supped together. Then they had to be divided for the night between the two bedrooms, which were all the family possessed. The mother, Mary, and the boy of seven occupied the front one. The father slept on his own board in the back one, and in a bed beside him lay the young man and the boy of eleven. So they settled down to sleep as commonplace a family as any in London, with little thought that within a day the attention of all the great city would be centred upon those two dingy rooms and upon the fates of their inmates.

The father woke in the very early hours, and saw in the dim light of the dawn the tall figure of his son standing in white beside his bed. To some sleepy remark that he was stirring early the youth muttered an excuse and lay down once more. At five the tailor rose to his endless task, and at twenty minutes past he went down the stair and closed the hall door behind him. So passed away the only witness, and all that remains is conjecture and circumstantial evidence. No one will ever know the exact details of what occurred, and for the purpose of the chronicler it is as well, for such details will not bear to be too critically examined. The motives and mind of the murderer are of perennial interest to every student of human nature, but the vile record of his actual brutality may be allowed to pass away when the ends of justice have once been served by their recital.

I have said that on the floor under the Youngmans there lived a couple named Beard. At half-past five, a little after the time when the tailor had closed the hall door behind him, Mrs. Beard was disturbed by a sound which she took to be from children running up and down and playing. There was a light patter of feet on the floor above. But as she listened it struck her that there was something unusual in this romping at so early an hour, so she nudged her husband and asked him for his opinion. Then, as the two sat up in bed, straining their ears, there came from above them a gasping cry and the dull, soft thud of a falling body. Beard sprang out of bed and rushed upstairs until his head came upon the level of the Youngmans' landing. He saw enough to send him shrieking down to Mr. Bevan upon the ground-floor. "For God's sake, come here! There is murder!" he roared, fumbling with his shaking fingers at the handle of the landlord's bedroom.

His summons did not find the landlord entirely unprepared. That ill-boding thud had been loud enough to reach his ears. He sprang palpitating from his bed, and the two men in their nightdresses ascended the creaking staircase, their frightened faces lit up by the blaze of golden sunlight of a July morning. Again they do not seem to have got farther than the point from which they could see the landing. That confused huddle of white-clad figures littered over the passage, with those glaring smears and blotches, were more than their nerves could stand. They could count three lying there, stark dead upon the landing. And there was someone moving in the bedroom. It was coming towards them. With horror-dilated eyes they saw William Godfrey Youngman framed in the open doorway, his white nightdress brilliant with ghastly streaks and the sleeve hanging torn over his hand.

"Mr. Beard," he cried, w' ɔn he saw the two bloodless faces upon ɔe stairs, "for God's sake fetch a surgeon! I believe there is some alive yet!" Then, as they turned and ran down stairs again, he called after them the singular explanation to which he ever afterwards adhered. "My mother has done all this," he cried; "she murdered my two brothers and my sweetheart, and I in self-defence believe that I have murdered her."

The two men did not stop to discuss the question with him. They had both rushed to their rooms and huddled on some clothes. Then they ran out of the house in search of a surgeon and a policeman, leaving Youngman still standing on the stair repeating his strange explanation. How sweet the morning air must have seemed to them when they were once clear of the accursed house, and how the honest milkmen, with their swinging tins, must have stared at those two rushing and dishevelled figures. But they had not far to go. John Varney, of P Division, as solid and unimaginative as the law which he represents, was standing at the street corner, and he came clumping back with reassuring slowness and dignity.

"Oh, policeman, here is a sight! What shall I do?" cried Youngman, as he saw the glazed official hat coming up the stair.

Constable Varney is not shaken by that horrid cluster of death. His advice is practical and to the point.

"Go and dress yourself!" said he.

"I struck my mother, but it was in self-defence," cried the other. "Would you not have done the same? It is the law."

Constable Varney is not to be drawn into

giving a legal opinion, but he is quite convinced that the best thing for Youngman to
do is to put on some clothes.

And now a crowd had begun to assemble
in the street, and another policeman and an
inspector had arrived. It was clear that,
whether Youngman's story was correct or not,
he was a self-confessed homicide, and that
the law must hold her grip of him. But
when a dagger-shaped knife, splintered by
the force of repeated blows, was found upon
the floor, and Youngman had to confess
that it belonged to him; when also it was
observed that ferocious strength and energy
were needed to produce the wounds inflicted,
it became increasingly evident that, instead
of being a mere victim of circumstances,

The horror and the apparent purposeless-
ness of the deed roused public excitement and
indignation to the highest pitch. The miserable sum for which poor Mary was insured
appeared to be the sole motive of the crime;
the prisoner's eagerness to have the business
concluded, and his desire to have the letters
destroyed in which he had urged it, forming
the strongest evidence against him. At the
same time, his calm assumption that things
would be arranged as he wished them to
be, and that the Argus Insurance Office
would pay over the money to one who
was neither husband nor relative of the
deceased, pointed to an ignorance of the ways
of business or a belief in his own powers of
managing, which in either case resembled

"HIS FATHER VISITED HIM."

this man was one of the criminals of a
century. But all evidence must be circumstantial, for mother, sweetheart, brothers—
the mouths of all were closed in the one
indiscriminate butchery.

insanity. When in addition it came out at
the trial that the family was sodden with
lunacy upon both sides, that the wife's mother
and the husband's brother were in asylums,
and that the husband's father had been in an

asylum, but had become "tolerably sensible" before his death, it is doubtful whether the case should not have been judged upon medical rather than upon criminal grounds. In these more scientific and more humanitarian days it is perhaps doubtful whether Youngman would have been hanged, but there was never any doubt as to his fate in 1860.

The trial came off at the Central Criminal Court upon August 16th before Mr. Justice Williams. Few fresh details came out, save that the knife had been in prisoner's possession for some time. He had exhibited it once in a bar, upon which a bystander, with the good British love of law and order, had remarked that that was not a fit knife for any man to carry.

"Anybody," said Youngman, in reply, "has the right to carry such a knife if he thinks proper in his own defence."

Perhaps the objector did not realize how near he may have been at that moment to getting its point between his ribs. Nothing serious against the prisoner's previous character came out at the trial, and he adhered steadfastly to his own account of the tragedy. In summing up, however, Justice Williams pointed out that if the prisoner's story were true it meant that he had disarmed his mother and got possession of the knife. What necessity was there, then, for him to kill her—and why should he deal her repeated wounds? This argument, and the fact that there were no stains upon the hands of the mother, prevailed with the jury, and sentence was duly passed upon the prisoner.

Youngman had shown an unmoved demeanour in the dock, but he gave signs of an irritable, and occasionally of a violent, temper in prison. His father visited him, and the prisoner burst instantly into fierce reproaches against his treatment of his family—reproaches for which there seem to have been no justification. Another thing which appeared to have galled him to the quick was the remark of the publican, which first reached his ears at the trial, to the effect that Mary had better hang herself in the skittle-yard than marry such a man. His self-esteem, the strongest trait in his nature, was cruelly wounded by such a speech.

"Only one thing I wish," he cried, furiously, "that I could get hold of this man Spicer, for I would strike his head off." The unnatural and bloodthirsty character of the threat is characteristic of the homicidal maniac. "Do you suppose," he added, with a fine touch of vanity, "that a man of my determination and spirit would have heard these words used in my presence without striking the man who used them to the ground?"

But in spite of exhortation and persuasion he carried his secret with him to the grave. He never varied from the story which he had probably concocted before the event.

"Do not leave the world with a lie on your lips," said the chaplain, as they walked to the scaffold.

"Well, if I wanted to tell a lie I would say that I did it," was his retort. He hoped to the end with his serene self-belief that the story which he had put forward could not fail eventually to be accepted. Even on the scaffold he was on the alert for a reprieve.

It was on the 4th of September, a little more than a month after the commission of his crime, that he was led out in front of Horsemonger Gaol to suffer his punishment. A concourse of 30,000 people, many of whom had waited all night, raised a brutal howl at his appearance. It was remarked at the time that it was one of the very few instances of capital punishment in which no sympathizer or philanthropist of any sort could be found to raise a single voice against the death penalty. The man died quietly and coolly.

"Thank you, Mr. Jessopp," said he to the chaplain, "for your great kindness. See my brother and take my love to him, and all at home."

And so, with the snick of a bolt and the jar of a rope, ended one of the most sanguinary, and also one of the most unaccountable, incidents in English criminal annals. That the man was guilty seems to admit no doubt, and yet it must be confessed that circumstantial evidence can never be absolutely convincing, and that it is only the critical student of such cases who realizes how often a damning chain of evidence may, by some slight change, be made to bear an entirely different interpretation.

Strange Studies from Life.

BY A. CONAN DOYLE.

[*The cases dealt with in this series of studies of criminal psychology are taken from the actual history of crime, though occasionally names have been changed where their retention might cause pain to surviving relatives.*]

II.—THE LOVE AFFAIR OF GEORGE VINCENT PARKER.

HE student of criminal annals will find upon classifying his cases that the two causes which are the most likely to incite a human being to the crime of murder are the lust of money and the black resentment of a disappointed love. Of these the latter are both rarer and more interesting, for they are subtler in their inception and deeper in their psychology. The mind can find no possible sympathy with the brutal greed and selfishness which weighs a purse against a life ; but there is something more spiritual in the case of the man who is driven by jealousy and misery to a temporary madness of violence. To use the language of science it is the passionate as distinguished from the instinctive criminal type. The two classes of crime may be punished by the same severity, but we feel that they are not equally sordid, and that none of us is capable of saying how he might act if his affections and his self-respect were suddenly and cruelly outraged. Even when we indorse the verdict it is still possible to feel some shred of pity for the criminal. His offence has not been the result of a self-interested and cold-blooded plotting, but it has been the consequence—however monstrous and disproportionate—of a cause for which others were responsible. As an example of such a crime I would recite the circumstances connected with George Vincent Parker, making some alteration in the names of persons and of places wherever there is a possibility that pain might be inflicted by their disclosure.

Nearly forty years ago there lived in one of our Midland cities a certain Mr. Parker, who did a considerable business as a commission agent. He was an excellent man of affairs, and during those progressive years which intervened between the Crimean and the American wars his fortune increased rapidly.

He built himself a villa in a pleasant suburb outside the town, and being blessed with a charming and sympathetic wife there was every prospect that the evening of his days would be spent in happiness. The only trouble which he had to contend with was his inability to understand the character of his only son, or to determine what plans he should make for his future.

George Vincent Parker, the young man in question, was of a type which continually recurs and which verges always upon the tragic. By some trick of atavism he had no love for the great city and its roaring life, none for the weary round of business, and no ambition to share the rewards which successful business brings. He had no sympathy with his father's works or his father's ways, and the life of the office was hateful to him. This aversion to work could not, however, be ascribed to viciousness or indolence. It was innate and constitutional. In other directions his mind was alert and receptive. He loved music and showed a remarkable aptitude for it. He was an excellent linguist and had some taste in painting. In a word, he was a man of artistic temperament, with all the failings of nerve and of character which that temperament implies. In London he would have met hundreds of the same type, and would have found a congenial occupation in making small incursions into literature and dabbling in criticism. Among the cotton-brokers of the Midlands his position was at that time an isolated one, and his father could only shake his head and pronounce him to be quite unfit to carry on the family business. He was gentle in his disposition, reserved with strangers, but very popular among his few friends. Once or twice it had been remarked that he was capable of considerable bursts of passion when he thought himself ill-used.

This is a type of man for whom the practical workers of the world have no affection, but it is one which invariably appeals to the feminine nature. There is a certain helplessness about it and a naïve appeal for sympathy to which a woman's heart readily responds — and it is the strongest, most vigorous woman who is the first to answer the appeal. We do not know

"IT WAS AT A MUSICAL EVENING AT THE HOUSE OF A LOCAL DOCTOR THAT HE FIRST MET MISS GROVES."

what other consolers this quiet dilettante may have found, but the details of one such connection have come down to us. It was at a musical evening at the house of a local doctor that he first met Miss Mary Groves. The doctor was her uncle, and she had come to town to visit him, but her life was spent in attendance upon her grandfather, who was a very

virile old gentleman, whose eighty years did not prevent him from fulfilling all the duties of a country gentleman, including those of the magisterial bench. After the quiet of a secluded manor-house the girl in the first flush of her youth and her beauty enjoyed the life of the town, and seems to have been particularly attracted by this refined young musician, whose appearance and manners suggested that touch of romance for which a young girl craves. He on his side was drawn to her by her country freshness and by the sympathy which she showed for him. Before she returned to the Manorhouse friendship had grown into love and the pair were engaged.

But the engagement was not looked upon with much favour by either of the families concerned. Old Parker had died, and his widow was left with sufficient means to live in comfort, but it became more imperative than ever that some profession should be found for the son. His invincible repugnance to business still stood in the way. On the other hand the young lady came of a good stock, and her relations, headed by the old country squire, objected to her marriage with a penniless young man of curious tastes and character. So for four years the engagement dragged along, during which the lovers corresponded continually, but seldom met. At the end of that time he was twenty-five and she was twenty-three, but the prospect of their union seemed as remote as ever. At last the prayers of her relatives overcame her constancy, and she took steps to break the tie which held them together. This she endeavoured to do by a change in the tone of her letters, and by ominous passages to prepare him for the coming blow.

On August 12th, 18—, she wrote that she had met a clergyman who was the most delightful man she had ever seen in her life. "He has been staying with us," she said, "and grandfather thought that he would just suit me, but that would not do." This passage, in spite of the few lukewarm words of reassurance, disturbed young Vincent Parker exceedingly. His mother testified afterwards to the extreme depression into which he was thrown, which was the less remarkable as he was a man who suffered from constitutional low spirits, and who always took the darkest view upon every subject. Another letter reached him next day which was more decided in its tone.

"I have a good deal to say to you, and it had better be said at once," said she. "My grandfather has found out about our correspondence, and is wild that there should be any obstacle to the match between the clergyman and me. I want you to release me that I may have it to say that I am free. Don't take this too hardly, in pity for me. I shall not marry if I can help it."

This second letter had an overpowering effect. His state was such that his mother had to ask a family friend to sit up with him all night. He paced up and down in an extreme state of nervous excitement, bursting constantly into tears. When he lay down his hands and feet twitched convulsively. Morphia was administered, but without effect. He refused all food. He had the utmost difficulty in answering the letter, and when he did so next day it was with the help of the friend who had stayed with him all night. His answer was reasonable and also affectionate.

"My dearest Mary," he said. "Dearest you will always be to me. To say that I am not terribly cut up would be a lie, but at any rate you know that I am not the man to stand in your way. I answer nothing to your last letter except that I wish to hear from your own lips what your wishes are, and I will then accede to them. You know me too well to think that I would then give way to any unnecessary nonsense or sentimentalism. Before I leave England I wish to see you once again, and for the last time, though God knows what misery it gives me to say so. You will admit that my desire to see you is but natural. Say in your next where you will meet me.—Ever, dearest Mary, your affectionate GEORGE."

Next day he wrote another letter in which he again implored her to give him an appointment, saying that any place between their house and Standwell, the nearest village, would do. "I am ill and thoroughly upset, and I do not wonder that you are," said he. "We shall both be happier and better in mind as well as in body after this last interview. I shall be at your appointment, *coûte qu'il coûte.*—Always your affectionate GEORGE."

There seems to have been an answer to this letter actually making an appointment, for he wrote again upon Wednesday, the 19th. "My dear Mary," said he, "I will only say here that I will arrive by the train you mention and that I hope, dear Mary, that you will not bother yourself unnecessarily about all this so far as I am concerned. For my own peace of mind I wish to see you, which I hope you won't think selfish. *Du reste* I only repeat what I have already said. I have but to hear from you what your wishes are and they shall be complied with. I have sufficient *savoir faire* not to make a bother about what cannot be helped. Don't let me be the cause of any row between you and your grandpapa. If you like to call at the inn I will not stir out until you come, but I leave this to your judgment."

As Professor Owen would reconstruct an entire animal out of a single bone, so from this one little letter the man stands flagrantly revealed. The scraps of French, the self-conscious allusion to his own *savoir faire,* the florid assurances which mean nothing, they are all so many strokes in a subtle self-portrait.

Miss Groves had already repented the appointment which she had given him. There may have been some traits in this eccentric lover whom she had abandoned which recurred to her memory and warned her not to trust herself in his power. "My dear George," she wrote—and her letter must have crossed his last one—"I write this in the greatest haste to tell you not to come on any account. I leave here to-day, and can't tell when I can or shall be back. I do not wish to see you if it can possibly be avoided, and indeed there will be no chance now, so we had best end this state of suspense at once and say good-bye without seeing each other. I feel sure I could not stand the meeting. If you write once more within the next three days I shall get it, but not later than that time without its being seen, for my letters are strictly watched and even opened.—Yours truly, MARY."

This letter seems to have brought any vague schemes which may have been already forming in the young man's mind to an immediate head. If he had only three days in which he might see her he could not afford to waste any time. On the same day he went on to the county town, but as it was late he did not go on to Standwell, which was her station. The waiters at the Midland Hotel noticed his curious demeanour and his vacant eye. He wandered about

"HE WANDERED ABOUT THE COFFEE-ROOM MUTTERING TO HIMSELF."

the coffee-room muttering to himself, and although he ordered chops and tea he swallowed nothing but some brandy and soda. Next morning, August 21st, he took a ticket to Standwell and arrived there at half-past eleven. From Standwell Station to the Manor-house at which Miss Groves resided with the old squire is two miles. There is an inn close to the station called "The Bull's Head." Vincent Parker called there and ordered some brandy. He then asked whether a note had been left there for him, and seemed much disturbed upon hearing

that there was none. Then, the time being about a quarter past twelve, he went off in the direction of the Manor-house.

About two miles upon the other side of the Manor-house, and four miles from the Bull's Head Inn, there is a thriving grammar school, the head master of which was a friend of the Groves family and had some slight acquaintance with Vincent Parker. The young man thought, therefore, that this would be the best place for him to apply for information, and he arrived at the school about half-past one. The head master was no doubt considerably astonished at the appearance of this dishevelled and brandy-smelling visitor, but he answered his questions with discretion and courtesy.

"I have called upon you," said Parker, "as a friend of Miss Groves. I suppose you know that there is an engagement between us?"

"I understood that there *was* an engagement, and that it had been broken off," said the master.

"Yes," Parker answered. "She has written to me to break off the engagement and declines to see me. I want to know how matters stand."

"Anything I may know," said the master, "is in confidence, and so I cannot tell you."

"I will find it out sooner or later," said Parker, and then asked who the clergyman was who had been staying at the Manor-house. The master acknowledged that there had been one, but refused to give the name. Parker then asked whether Miss Groves was at the Manor-house and if any coercion was being used to her. The other answered that she was at the Manor-house and that no coercion was being used.

"Sooner or later I must see her," said Parker. "I have written to release her from her engagement, but I must hear from her own lips that she gives me up. She is of age and must please herself. I know that I am not a good match, and I do not wish to stand in her way."

The master then remarked that it was time for school, but that he should be free again at half-past four if Parker had anything more to say to him, and Parker left, promising to return. It is not known how he spent the next two hours, but he may have found some country inn in which he obtained some luncheon. At half-past four he was back at the school, and asked the master for advice as to how to act. The master suggested that his best course was to write a note to Miss Groves and to make an appointment with her for next morning.

"If you were to call at the house, perhaps Miss Groves would see you," said this sympathetic and most injudicious master.

"I will do so and get it off my mind," said Vincent Parker.

It was about five o'clock when he left the school, his manner at that time being perfectly calm and collected.

It was forty minutes later when the discarded lover arrived at the house of his sweetheart. He knocked at the door and asked for Miss Groves. She had probably seen him as he came down the drive, for she met him at the drawing-room door as he came in, and she invited him to come with her into the garden. Her heart was in her mouth, no doubt, lest her grandfather should see him and a scene ensue. It was safer to have him in the garden than in the house. They walked out, therefore, and half an hour later they were seen chatting quietly upon one of the benches. A little afterwards the maid went out and told Miss Groves that tea was ready. She came in alone, and it is suggestive of the views taken by the grandfather that there seems to have been no question about Parker coming in also to tea. She came out again into the garden and sat for a long time with the young man, after which they seem to have set off together for a stroll down the country lanes. What passed during that walk, what recriminations upon his part, what retorts upon hers, will never now be known. They were only once seen in the course of it. At about half-past eight o'clock a labourer, coming up a long lane which led from the high road to the Manor-house, saw a man and a woman walking together. As he passed them he recognised in the dusk that the lady was Miss Groves, the granddaughter of the squire. When he looked back he saw

that they had stopped and were standing face to face conversing.

A very short time after this Reuben Conway, a workman, was passing down this lane when he heard a low sound of moaning. He stood listening, and in the silence of the country evening he became aware that this ominous sound was drawing nearer to him. A wall flanked one side of the lane, and as he stared about him his eye caught something moving slowly down the black shadow at the side. For a moment it must have seemed to him to be some wounded animal, but as he approached it he saw to his astonishment that it was a woman who was slowly stumbling along, guiding and supporting herself by her hand against the wall. With a cry of horror he found himself looking into the face of Miss Groves, glimmering white through the darkness.

"Take me home!" she whispered. "Take me home! The gentleman down there has been murdering me."

The horrified labourer put his arms round her, and carried her for about twenty yards towards home.

"Can you see anyone down the lane?" she asked, when he stopped for breath.

He looked, and through the dark tunnel of trees he saw a black figure moving slowly behind them. The labourer waited, still propping up the girl's head, until young Parker overtook them.

"Who has been murdering Miss Groves?" asked Reuben Conway.

"I have stabbed her," said Parker, with the utmost coolness.

"Well, then, you had best help me to carry her home," said the labourer. So down the dark lane moved that singular procession: the rustic and the lover, with the body of the dying girl between them.

"Poor Mary!" Parker muttered. "Poor Mary! You should not have proved false to me!"

When they got as far as the lodge-gate Parker suggested that Reuben Conway should run and get something which might stanch the bleeding. He went, leaving these tragic lovers together for the last time. When he returned he found Parker holding something to her throat.

"Is she living?" he asked.

"She is," said Parker.

"Oh, take me home!" wailed the poor girl. A little farther upon their dolorous journey they met two farmers, who helped them.

"Who has done this?" asked one of them.

"TAKE ME HOME!" SHE WHISPERED. "TAKE ME HOME!"

rumour of a disaster. The bearers stopped as they saw the white hair gleaming through the darkness.

"What is amiss?" he cried.

Parker said, calmly, "It is your grand-daughter Mary murdered."

"Who did it?" shrieked the old man.

"I did it."

"Who are you?" he cried.

"My name is Vincent Parker."

"Why did you do it?"

"She has deceived me, and the woman who deceives me must die."

The calm concentration of his manner seems to have silenced all reproaches.

"I told her I would kill her," said he, as they all entered the house together. "She knew my temper."

The body was carried into the kitchen and laid upon the table. In the meantime Parker had followed the bewildered and heart-broken old man into the drawing-room, and holding out a handful of things, including his watch and some money, he asked him if he would take care of them. The squire angrily refused. He then took two bundles of her letters out of his pocket—all that was left of their miserable love story.

"Will you take care of these?" said he. "You may read them, burn them, do what you like with them. I don't wish them to be brought into court."

The grandfather took the letters and they were duly burned.

And now the doctor and the policeman, the twin attendants upon violence, came hurrying down the avenue. Poor Mary was dead upon the kitchen table, with three great wounds upon her throat. How, with a severed carotid, she could have come so far or lived so long is one of the marvels of the case. As to the policeman, he had no trouble in looking for his prisoner. As he entered the room Parker walked towards

"He knows and I know," said Parker, gloomily. "I am the man who has done this, and I shall be hanged for it. I have done it, and there is no question about that at all."

These replies never seem to have brought insult or invective upon his head, for everyone appears to have been silenced by the overwhelming tragedy of the situation.

"I am dying!" gasped poor Mary, and they were the last words which she ever said. Inside the hall-gates they met the poor old squire running wildly up on some vague

him and said that he wished to give himself up for murdering a young lady. When asked if he were aware of the nature of the charge he said, "Yes, quite so, and I will go with you quietly, only let me see her first."

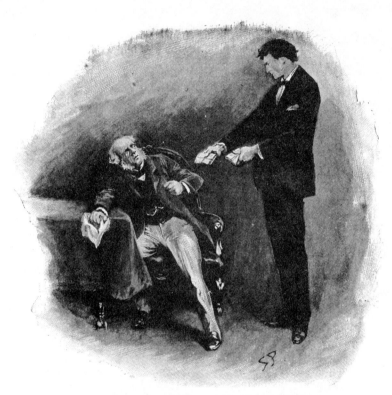

" ' WILL YOU TAKE CARE OF THESE,' SAID HE."

"What have you done with the knife?" asked the policeman.

Parker produced it from his pocket, a very ordinary one with a clasp blade. It is remarkable that two other penknives were afterwards found upon him. They took him into the kitchen and he looked at his victim.

"I am far happier now that I have done it than before, and I hope that she is," said he.

This is the record of the murder of Mary Groves by Vincent Parker, a crime characterized by all that inconsequence and grim artlessness which distinguish fact from fiction. In fiction we make people say and do what we should conceive them to be likely to say or do, but in fact they say and do what no one would ever conceive to be likely. That those letters should be a prelude to a murder, or that after a murder the criminal should endeavour to stanch the wounds of his victim, or hold such a conversation as that described with the old squire, is what no human invention would hazard. One finds it very difficult on reading all the letters and weighing the facts to suppose that Vincent Parker came out that day with the preformed intention of killing his former sweetheart. But whether the dreadful idea was always there, or whether it came in some mad flash of passion provoked by their conversation, is what we shall never know. It is certain that she could not have seen anything dangerous in him up to the very instant of the crime, or she would certainly have appealed to the labourer who passed them in the lane.

The case, which excited the utmost interest through the length and breadth of England, was tried before Baron Martin at the next assizes. There was no need to prove the guilt of the prisoner, since he openly gloried in it, but the whole question turned upon his sanity, and led to some curious complications which have caused the whole law upon the point to be reformed. His rela-

"HIS MOTHER APPEARED IN THE WITNESS-BOX."

tions were called to show that madness was rampant in the family, and that out of ten cousins five were insane. His mother appeared in the witness-box contending with dreadful vehemence that her son was mad, and that her own marriage had been objected to on the ground of the madness latent in her blood. All the witnesses agreed that the prisoner was not an ill-tempered man, but sensitive, gentle, and accomplished, with a tendency to melancholy. The prison chaplain affirmed that he had held conversations with Parker, and that his moral perception seemed to be so entirely wanting that he hardly knew right from wrong. Two specialists in lunacy examined him, and said that they were of opinion that he was of unsound mind. The opinion was based upon the fact that the prisoner declared that he could not see that he had done any wrong.

"Miss Groves was promised to me," said he, "and therefore she was mine. I could do what I liked with her. Nothing short of a miracle will alter my convictions."

The doctor attempted to argue with him. "Suppose anyone took a picture from you, what steps would you take to recover it?" he asked.

"I should demand restitution," said he; "if not, I should take the thief's life without compunction."

The doctor pointed out that the law was there to be appealed to, but Parker answered that he had been born into the world without being consulted, and therefore he recognised the right of no man to judge him. The doctor's conclusion was that his moral sense was more vitiated than any case that he had seen. That this constitutes madness would, however, be a dangerous doctrine to urge, since it means that if a man were only wicked enough he would be screened from the punishment of his wickedness.

Baron Martin summed up in a common-sense manner. He declared that the world was full of eccentric people, and that to grant them all the immunity of madness would be a public danger. To be mad within the meaning of the law a criminal should be in such a state as not to know that he has committed crime or incurred punishment. Now, it was clear that Parker did know this, since he had talked of being hanged. The Baron accordingly accepted the jury's finding of "Guilty," and sentenced the prisoner to death.

There the matter might very well have ended were it not for Baron Martin's conscientious scruples. His own ruling had been admirable, but the testimony of the mad doctors weighed heavily upon him, and his conscience was uneasy at the mere possibility that a man who was really not answerable for his actions should lose his life through his decision. It is probable that the thought kept him awake that night, for next morning he wrote to the Secretary of State, and told him that he shrank from the decision of such a case.

The Secretary of State, having carefully read the evidence and the judge's remarks, was about to confirm the decision of the latter, when, upon the very eve of the execution, there came a report from the gaol visitors—perfectly untrained observers—that Parker was showing undoubted signs of madness. This being so the Secretary of State had no choice but to postpone the execution, and to appoint a commission of four eminent alienists to report upon the condition of the prisoner. These four reported unanimously that he was perfectly sane. It is an unwritten law, however, that a prisoner once reprieved is never executed, so Vincent Parker's sentence was commuted to penal servitude for life—a decision which satisfied, upon the whole, the conscience of the public.

Strange Studies from Life.

BY A. CONAN DOYLE.

[The cases dealt with in this series of studies of criminal psychology—studies of which the moral is more full of warning than that of many sermons—are taken from the actual history of crime, though occasionally names have been changed where their retention might cause pain to surviving relatives.]

III.—THE DEBATABLE CASE OF MRS. EMSLEY.

N the fierce popular indigna-tion which is excited by a sanguinary crime there is a tendency, in which judges and juries share, to brush aside or to treat as irrelevant those doubts the benefit of which is sup-posed to be one of the privileges of the accused. Lord Tenterden has whittled down the theory of doubt by declaring that a jury is justified in giving its verdict upon such evidence as it would accept to be final in any of the issues of life. But when one looks back and remembers how often one has been very sure and yet has erred in the issues of life, how often what has seemed certain has failed us, and that which appeared impossible has come to pass, we feel that if the criminal law has been conducted upon such principles it is probably itself the giant murderer of England. Far wiser is the contention that it is better that ninety-nine guilty should escape than that one innocent man should suffer, and that, therefore, if it can be claimed that there is one chance in a hun-dred in favour of the prisoner he is entitled to his acquittal. It cannot be doubted that if the Scotch verdict of "Not proven," which neither condemns nor acquits, had been permissible in England it would have been the outcome of many a case which, under our sterner law, has ended upon the scaffold. Such a ver-dict would, I fancy, have been hailed as a welcome compromise by the judge and the jury who investigated the singular circum-stances which attended the case of Mrs. Mary Emsley.

The stranger in London who wanders away from the beaten paths and strays into the quarters in which the workers dwell is astounded by their widespread monotony, by the endless rows of uniform brick houses broken only by the corner public-houses and more infrequent chapels which are scattered amongst them. The expansion of the great city has been largely caused by the covering of district after district with these long lines of humble dwellings, and the years between the end of the Crimean War and 1860 saw great activity in this direction. Many small builders by continually mortgaging what they had done, and using the capital thus acquired to start fresh works which were them-selves in turn mortgaged, contrived to erect street after street, and eventually on account of the general rise of property to make con-siderable fortunes. Amongst these astute speculators there was one John Emsley, who, dying, left his numerous houses and various interests to his widow Mary.

Mary Emsley, now an old woman, had

MRS. MARY EMSLEY.

"IT WAS THE FOOTPRINT OF A MAN DIMLY OUTLINED ON THE FLOOR."

lived too long in a humble fashion to change her way of life. She was childless, and all the activities of her nature were centred upon the economical management of her property, and the collection of the weekly rents from the humble tenants who occupied them. A grim, stern, eccentric woman, she was an object of mingled dislike and curiosity among the inhabitants of Grove Road, Stepney, in which her house was situated. Her possessions extended over Stratford, Bow, and Bethnal Green, and in spite of her age she made long journeys, collecting, evicting, and managing, always showing a great capacity for the driving of a hard bargain. One of her small economies was that when she needed help in managing these widespread properties she preferred to employ irregular agents to engaging a salaried representative. There were many who did odd jobs for her, and among them were two men whose names were destined to become familiar to the public. The one was John Emms, a cobbler; the other George Mullins, a plasterer.

Mary Emsley, in spite of her wealth, lived entirely alone, save that on Saturdays a charwoman called to clean up the house. She showed also that extreme timidity and caution which are often characteristic of those who afterwards perish by violence—as if there lies in human nature some vague instinctive power of prophecy. It was with reluctance that she ever opened her door, and each visitor who approached her was reconnoitred from the window of her area. Her fortune would have permitted her to indulge herself with every luxury, but the house was a small one, consisting of two stories and a basement, with a neglected back garden, and her mode of life was even simpler than her dwelling. It was a singular and most unnatural old age.

Mrs. Emsley was last seen alive upon the evening of Monday, August 13th, 1860. Upon that date, at seven o'clock, two neighbours perceived her sitting at her bedroom window. Next morning, shortly after ten, one of her irregular retainers called upon some matter of brass taps, but was unable to get any answer to his repeated knockings. During that Tuesday many visitors had the same experience, and the Wednesday and Thursday passed without any sign of life within the house. One would have thought that this would have aroused instant suspicions, but the neighbours were so accustomed to the widow's eccentricities that they were slow to be alarmed. It was only upon the Friday, when John Emms, the cobbler,

found the same sinister silence prevailing in the house, that a fear of foul play came suddenly upon him. He ran round to Mr. Rose, her attorney, and Mr. Faith, who was a distant relation, and the three men returned to the house. On their way they picked up Police-constable Dillon, who accompanied them.

The front door was fastened and the windows snibbed, so the party made their way over the garden wall and so reached the back entrance, which they seem to have opened without difficulty. John Emms led the way, for he was intimately acquainted with the house. On the ground floor there was no sign of the old woman. The creak of their boots and the subdued whisper of their voices were the only sounds which broke the silence. They ascended the stair with a feeling of reassurance. Perhaps it was all right after all. It was quite probable that the eccentric widow might have gone on a visit. And then as they came upon the landing John Emms stood staring, and the others, peering past him, saw that which struck the hope from their hearts.

It was the footprint of a man dimly outlined in blood upon the wooden floor. The door of the front room was nearly closed, and this dreadful portent lay in front of it with the toes pointing away. The police-constable pushed at the door, but something which lay behind it prevented it from opening. At last by their united efforts they effected an entrance. There lay the unfortunate old woman, her lank limbs all asprawl upon the floor, with two rolls of wall-paper under her arm and several others scattered in front of her. It was evident that the frightful blows which had crushed in her head had fallen upon her unforeseen, and had struck her senseless in an instant. She had none of that anticipation which is the only horror of death.

The news of the murder of so well known an inhabitant caused the utmost excitement in the neighbourhood, and every effort was made to detect the assassin. A Government reward of £100 was soon raised to £300, but without avail. A careful examination of the house failed to reveal anything which might serve as a reliable clue. It was difficult to determine the hour of the murder, for there was reason to think that the dead woman occasionally neglected to make her bed, so that the fact that the bed was unmade did not prove that it had been slept in. She was fully dressed, as she would be in the evening, and it was unlikely that she would be doing business with wall-papers in the early morning. On the whole, then, the evidence seemed to point to the crime having been committed upon the Monday evening some time after seven. There had been no forcing of doors or windows, and therefore the murderer had been admitted by Mrs. Emsley. It was not consistent with her habits that she should admit anyone whom she did not know at such an hour, and the presence of the wall-papers showed that it was someone with whom she had business to transact. So far the police could hardly go wrong. The murderer appeared to have gained little by his crime, for the only money in the house, £48, was found concealed in the cellar, and nothing was missing save a few articles of no value. For weeks the public waited impatiently for an arrest, and for weeks the police remained silent though not inactive. Then an arrest was at last effected, and in a curiously dramatic fashion.

Amongst the numerous people who made small sums of money by helping the murdered woman there was one respectable-looking man, named George Mullins —rather over fifty years of age, with the straight back of a man who has at some period been well drilled. As a matter of fact, he had served in the Irish Constabulary, and had undergone many other curious experiences before he had settled down as a plasterer in the East-end of London. This man it was who called upon Sergeant Tanner, of the police, and laid before him a statement which promised to solve the whole mystery.

According to this account, Mullins had from the first been suspicious of Emms, the cobbler, and had taken steps to verify his suspicions, impelled partly by his love of justice and even more by his hope of the reward. The £300 bulked largely

before his eyes. "If this only goes right I'll take care of you," said he, on his first interview with the police, and added, in allusion to his own former connection with the force, that he "was clever at these matters." So clever was he that his account of what he had seen and done gave the police an excellent clue upon which to act.

It appears that the cobbler dwelt in a small cottage at the edge of an old brickfield. On this brickfield, and about fifty yards from the cottage, there stood a crumbling outhouse which had been abandoned. Mullins, it seems, had for some time back been keeping a watchful eye upon Emms, and he had observed him carrying a paper parcel from his cottage and concealing it somewhere in the shed. "Very likely," said the astute Mullins, "he is concealing some of the plunder which he has stolen." To the police also the theory seemed not impossible, and so, on the following morning, three of them,

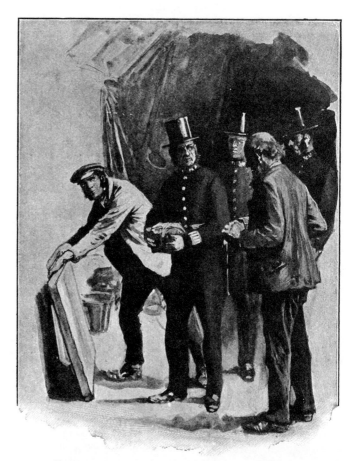

"THEY CAME ON A PAPER PARCEL OF A VERY CURIOUS NATURE."

with Mullins hanging at their heels, appeared at Emms's cottage, and searched both it and the shed. Their efforts, however, were in vain, and nothing was found.

This result was by no means satisfactory to the observant Mullins, who rated them soundly for not having half-searched the shed, and persuaded them to try again. They did so under his supervision, and this time with the best results. Behind a slab in the out-house they came on a paper parcel of a very curious nature. It was tied up with coarse tape, and when opened disclosed another parcel tied with waxed string. Within were found three small spoons and one large one, two lenses, and a cheque drawn in favour of Mrs. Emsley, and known to have been paid to her upon the day of the murder. There was no doubt that the other articles had also belonged to the dead woman. The discovery was of the first importance then, and the whole party set off for the police-station, Emms covered with confusion and dismay, while Mullins swelled with all the pride of the successful amateur detective. But his triumph did not last long. At the police-station the inspector charged him with being himself concerned in the death of Mrs. Emsley.

"Is this the way that I am treated after giving you information?" he cried.

"If you are innocent no harm will befall you," said the inspector, and he was duly committed for trial.

This dramatic turning of the tables caused the deepest public excitement, and the utmost abhorrence was everywhere expressed against the man who was charged not only with a very cold-blooded murder, but with a deliberate attempt to saddle another man with the guilt in the hope of receiving the reward. It was very soon seen that Emms at least was innocent, as he could prove the most convincing *alibi*. But if Emms was innocent who was guilty save the man who had placed the stolen articles in the outhouse—and who could this be save Mullins, who had informed the police that they were there? The case was prejudged by the public before ever the prisoner had appeared in the dock, and the evidence which the police had prepared against him was not such as to cause them to change their opinion. A damning series of facts were arraigned in proof of their theory of the case, and they were laid before the jury by Serjeant Parry at the Central Criminal Court upon the 25th of October, about ten weeks after the murder.

At first sight the case against Mullins appeared to be irresistible. An examination of his rooms immediately after his arrest enabled the police to discover some tape upon his mantelpiece which corresponded very closely with the tape with which the parcel had been secured. There were thirty-two strands in each. There was also found a piece of cobbler's wax, such as would be needed to wax the string of the inner parcel. Cobbler's wax was not a substance which Mullins needed in his business, so that the theory of the prosecution was that he had simply procured it in order to throw suspicion upon the unfortunate cobbler. A plasterer's hammer, which might have inflicted the injuries, was also discovered upon the premises, and so was a spoon which corresponded closely to the spoons which Mrs. Emsley had lost. It was shown also that Mrs. Mullins had recently sold a small gold pencil-case to a neighbouring barman, and two witnesses were found to swear that this pencil-case belonged to Mrs. Emsley and had been in her possession a short time before her death. There was also discovered a pair of boots, one of which appeared to fit the impression upon the floor, and medical evidence attested that there was some human hair upon the sole of it. The same medical evidence swore to a blood mark upon the gold pencil which had been sold by Mrs. Mullins. It was proved by the charwoman, who came upon Saturdays, that when she had been in the house two days before the murder Mullins had called, bringing with him some rolls of wall-paper, and that he had been directed by Mrs. Emsley to carry it up to the room in which the tragedy afterwards occurred. Now, it was clear that Mrs. Emsley had been discussing wall-papers at the time that she was struck down, and what more natural than that it should have been with the person who had originally brought them? Again, it had been shown that during the day Mrs. Emsley had handed to Mullins a certain key. This key was found lying in the same room as the dead body, and the prosecution asked how it could come there if Mullins did not bring it.

So far the police had undoubtedly a very strong case, and they endeavoured to make it more convincing still by producing evidence to show that Mullins had been seen both going to the crime and coming away from it. One, Raymond, was ready to swear that at eight o'clock that evening he had caught a glimpse of him in the street near Mrs. Emsley's. He was wearing a black billycock hat. A sailor was produced who testified that he had seen him at Stepney Green a little after five next morning. According to the sailor's account his attention was attracted by the nervous manner and excited appearance of the man whom he had met, and also by the fact that his pockets were very bulging. He was wearing a brown hat. When he heard of the murder he had of his own accord given information to the police, and he would swear that Mullins was the man whom he had seen.

This was the case as presented against the accused, and it was fortified by many smaller points of suspicion. One of them was that when he was giving the police information about Emms he had remarked that Emms was about the only man to whom Mrs. Emsley would open her door.

"Wouldn't she open it for you, Mullins?" asked the policeman.

"No," said he. "She would have called to me from the window of the area."

This answer of his—which was shown to be untrue—told very heavily against him at the trial.

It was a grave task which Mr. Best had to perform when he rose to answer this complicated and widely-reaching indictment. He first of all endeavoured to establish an *alibi* by calling Mullins's children, who were ready to testify that he came home particularly early upon that particular Monday. Their evidence, however, was not very conclusive, and was shaken by the laundress, who showed that they were confusing one day with another. As regards the

boot, the counsel pointed out that human hair was used by plasterers in their work, and he commented upon the failure of the prosecution to prove that there was blood upon the very boot which was supposed to have produced the blood-print. He also showed as regards the bloodstain upon the pencil-case that the barman upon buying the pencil had carefully cleaned and polished it, so that if there was any blood upon it it was certainly not that of Mrs. Emsley. He also commented upon the discrepancy of the evidence between Raymond, who saw the accused at eight in the evening in a black hat, and the sailor who met him at five in the morning in a brown one. If the theory of the prosecution was that the accused had spent the night in the house of the murdered woman, how came his hat to be changed? One or other or both the witnesses must be worthless. Besides, the sailor had met his mysterious stranger at Stepney Green, which was quite out of the line between the scene of the crime and Mullins's lodgings. As to the bulging pockets, only a few small articles had been taken from the house, and they would certainly not cause the robber's pockets to bulge. There was no evidence either from Raymond or from the sailor that the prisoner was carrying the plasterer's hammer with which the deed was supposed to have been done.

And now he produced two new and very important witnesses, whose evidence furnished another of those sudden surprises with which the case had abounded. Mrs. Barnes,

"HE HAD SEEN ONE ROWLAND, ALSO A BUILDER, COME OUT OF SOME HOUSE."

who lived in Grove Road, opposite to the scene of the murder, was prepared to swear that at twenty minutes to ten on Tuesday morning—twelve hours after the time of the commission of the crime according to the police theory—she saw someone moving paper-hangings in the top room, and that she also saw the right-hand window open a little way. Now, in either of these points she might be the victim of a delusion, but it is difficult to think that she was mistaken in them both. If there was really someone in the room at that hour, whether it was Mrs. Emsley or her assassin, in either case it proved the theory of the prosecution to be entirely mistaken.

The second piece of evidence was from Stephenson, a builder, who testified that upon that Tuesday morning he had seen one Rowland, also a builder, come out of some house with wall-papers in his hand. This was a little after ten o'clock. He could not swear to the house, but he thought that it was Mrs. Emsley's. Rowland was hurrying past him when he stopped him and asked him—they were acquaintances—whether he was in the paper line.

"Yes; didn't you know that?" said Rowland.

"No," said Stephenson, "else I should have given you a job or two."

"Oh, yes, I was bred up to it," said Rowland, and went on his way.

In answer to this Rowland appeared in the box and stated that he considered Stephenson to be half-witted. He acknowledged the meeting and the conversation, but asserted that it was several days before. As a matter of fact, he was engaged in papering the house next to Mrs. Emsley's, and it was from that that he had emerged.

So stood the issues when the Chief Baron entered upon the difficult task of summing up. Some of the evidence upon which the police had principally relied was brushed aside by him very lightly. As to the tape, most tape consisted of thirty-two strands, and it appeared to him that the two pieces were not exactly of one sort. Cobbler's wax was not an uncommon substance, and a plasterer could not be blamed for possessing a plasterer's hammer. The boot, too, was not so exactly like the blood-print that any conclusions could be drawn from it. The weak point of the defence was that it was almost certain that Mullins hid the things in the shed. If he did not commit the crime, why did he not volunteer a statement as to how the things came into his posses-

sion? His remark that Mrs. Emsley would not open the door to him, when it was certain that she would do so, was very much against him. On the other hand, the conflicting evidence of the sailor and of the other man who had seen Mullins near the scene of the crime was not very convincing, nor did he consider the incident of the key to be at all conclusive, since the key might have been returned in the course of the day. On the whole, everything might be got round except the hiding of the parcel in the shed, and that was so exceedingly damning that, even without anything else, it amounted to a formidable case.

The jury deliberated for three hours and then brought in a verdict of "Guilty," in which the judge concurred. Some of his words, however, in passing sentence were such as to show that his mind was by no means convinced upon the point.

"If you can even now make it manifest that you are innocent of the charge," said he, "I do not doubt that every attention will be paid to any cogent proof laid before those with whom it rests to carry out the finding of the law."

To allude to the possibility of a man's innocence and at the same time to condemn him to be hanged strikes the lay mind as being a rather barbarous and illogical proceeding. It is true that the cumulative force of the evidence against Mullins was very strong, and that investigation proved the man's antecedents to have been of the worst. But still, circumstantial evidence, even when it all points one way and there is nothing to be urged upon the other side, cannot be received with too great caution, for it is nearly always possible to twist it to some other meaning.

In this case, even allowing that the evidence for an *alibi* furnished by Mullins's children was worthless, and allowing also that Mr. Stephenson's evidence may be set aside, there remains the positive and absolutely disinterested testimony of Mrs. Barnes, which would seem to show that even if Mullins did the crime he did it in an entirely different way to that which the police imagined. Besides, is it not on the face of it most improbable that a man should commit a murder at eight o'clock or so in the evening, should remain all night in the house with the body of his victim, that he should do this in the dark—for a light moving about the house would have been certainly remarked by the neighbours—that he should not escape during the darkness, but that he should wait for the full sunlight of an August morning before he emerged?

After reading the evidence one is left with an irresistible impression that, though

" A VERDICT OF 'GUILTY.'"

ing one that universal prejudice was excited against the accused. Mullins was hanged on the 19th of November, and he left a statement behind him reaffirming his own

Mullins was very likely guilty, the police were never able to establish the details of the crime, and that there was a risk of a miscarriage of justice when the death sentence was carried out.

There was much discussion among the legal profession at the time as to the sufficiency of the evidence, but the general public was quite satisfied, for the crime was such a shocking one that universal prejudice was excited against the accused.

innocence. He never attempted to explain the circumstances which cost him his life, but he declared in his last hours that he believed Emms to be innocent of the murder, which some have taken to be a confession that he had himself placed the incriminating articles in the shed. Forty years have served to throw no fresh light upon the matter.

X

Professor van Dusen's Problems

JACQUES FUTRELLE

Cassell's Magazine

Professor Van Dusen's Problems.

By JACQUES FUTRELLE.

THE PROBLEM OF "DRESSING-ROOM A."

**Professor Van Dusen :
The Man.**

IT was absolutely impossible. Twenty-five chess masters from the world at large, foregathered in Boston for the annual championships, unanimously declared it impossible, and unanimity on any given point is an unusual mental condition for chess masters. Not one would concede for an instant that it was within the range of human achievement. Some grew red in the face as they argued it, others smiled loftily and were silent ; still others dismissed the matter in a word as wholly absurd.

A casual remark by the distinguished scientist and logician, Professor Van Dusen, provoked the discussion. He had, in the past, caused bitter disputes by chance remarks ; in fact, he had once been a sort of controversial centre of the sciences. It had been due to his modest announcement of a startling

PROFESSOR VAN DUSEN.

and unorthodox hypothesis that he had been asked to vacate the chair of Philosophy in a great university ; later that university had been honoured when he accepted its degree of LL.D.

For a score of years now educational and scientific institutions of the world had amused themselves by crowding degrees upon him. He had initials that stood for things he could not pronounce : degrees from England, Russia, Germany, Italy, Sweden, and Spain. These were expressed recognition of the fact that he was the foremost brain in science. The imprint of his crabbed personality lay heavily on half-a-dozen of its branches. Finally there came a time when argument was respectfully silent in the face of one of his conclusions.

The remark which had arrayed the chess masters of the world in so formidable and unanimous a dissent was made by

Professor Van Dusen in the presence of three other gentlemen of standing. One of these, Dr. Charles Elbert, happened to be a chess enthusiast.

"Chess is a shameless perversion of the functions of the brain," was Professor Van Dusen's declaration in his perpetually irritated voice. "It is a sheer waste of effort, greater because it is possibly the most difficult of all fixed abstract prob-lems. Of course logic will solve it. Logic will solve any problem—not *most* of them, but *any* problem. A thorough understanding of its rules would enable anyone to defeat your greatest chess players. It would be inevitable, just as inevitable as that two and two make four, not sometimes, but always. I don't know chess, because I never do useless things; but I could take a few hours of competent instruction and defeat a man who has devoted his life to it. His mind is cramped—bound down to the logic of chess. Mine is not; mine employs logic in its widest scope."

Dr. Elbert shook his head vigorously. "It is impossible," he asserted.

"Nothing is impossible," snapped the scientist. "The human mind can do anything. It is all we have to lift us above the brute creation. For Heaven's sake leave us that."

"Do you know the purposes of chess— its countless combinations?" asked Dr. Elbert.

"No," was the crabbed reply. "I know nothing whatever of the game beyond the general purpose which, I understand, is to move certain pieces in certain directions to stop an opponent from moving his King. Is that correct?"

"Yes," said Dr. Elbert, slowly, "but I never heard it stated just that way before."

"Then, if that is correct, I maintain that the true logician can defeat the chess expert by the pure mechanical rule of logic. I'll take a few hours some time, acquaint myself with the moves of the pieces, and defeat you to convince you."

Professor Van Dusen glared savagely into the eyes of Dr. Elbert.

"Not me," said Dr. Elbert. "You say anyone; you, for instance, might defeat the greatest chess player. Would you be willing to meet the greatest chess player after you 'acquaint' yourself with the game?"

"Certainly," said the scientist. "I have frequently found it necessary to make a fool of myself to convince people. I'll do it again."

This, then, was the acrimonious beginning of the discussion which aroused chess masters and brought open dissent from eminent men who had not dared for years to dispute any assertion by the distinguished Professor Van Dusen. It was arranged that at the conclusion of the championships Professor Van Dusen should meet the winner. This happened to be Tschaikowsky, the Russian, who had been chess champion for half a dozen years.

After this expected result of the tournament, Hillsbury, a noted American master, spent a morning with Professor Van Dusen in the latter's modest apartments on Beacon Hill. He left there with a sadly puzzled face. That afternoon Professor Van Dusen met the Russian champion. The newspapers had said a great deal about the affair, and hundreds were present to witness the game.

There was a little murmur of astonishment when Professor Van Dusen appeared. He was slight, to the point of childishness, and his thin shoulders seemed to droop beneath the weight of his enormous head. He wore a No. 8 hat. His brow rose straight and dome-like, and a heavy shock of long yellow hair gave him almost a grotesque appearance. The eyes were narrow slits of blue squinting eternally through thick glasses; the face was small, clean shaven, and white, with the pallor of the student; his lips made a perfectly straight line; his hands were remarkable for their whiteness, their flexibility, and for the length of the slender fingers. One glance showed that physical development had never entered into the schedule of the scientist's fifty years of life.

The Russian smiled at he sat down at the chess table. He felt that he was humouring a crank. The other masters were grouped near by, curiously expectant. Professor Van Dusen began the game, opening with a Queen's gambit. At his fifth move, made without the slightest hesitation, the smile left the Russian's face. At the tenth the masters grew tensely eager. The Russian champion was playing for honour now. Professor Van Dusen's fourteenth move was King's castle to Queen's four.

"Check," he announced.

After a long study of the board the Russian protected his King with a knight. Professor Van Dusen noted the play, then leaned back in his chair with finger tips pressed together. His eyes left the board, and dreamily studied the ceiling. For at least fifteen minutes there was no sound, no movement, then :

"PROFESSOR VAN DUSEN LEANED BACK, WITH FINGER TIPS PRESSED TOGETHER."

"Mate in fifteen moves," he said quietly.

There was a quick gasp of astonishment. It took the practised eyes of the masters several minutes to verify the announce-ment. But the Russian champion saw, and leaned back in his chair a little white and dazed. He was not astonished ; he was helplessly floundering in a maze of incomprehensible things. Suddenly he arose and grasped the slender hand of his conqueror.

"You have never played chess before ? " he asked.

"Never."

"Mon Dieu ! You are not a man ; you are a brain—a machine—a thinking machine."

"It is a child's game," said the scientist abruptly. There was no note of exultation in his voice ; it was still the irritable, impersonal tone which was habitual.

This, then, was Professor Van Dusen. This is how he came to be known to the world at large as The Thinking Machine. The Russian's phrase had been applied to the scientist as a title by a newspaper reporter, Hutchinson Hatch. It had stuck.

THE FIRST PROBLEM.

THAT strange, seemingly inexplicable chain of circumstances which had to do with the mysterious disappearance of a famous actress, Miss Irene Wallack, from her dressing-room in a Springfield theatre during a performance, while the echo of tumultuous appreciation still rang in her ears, was perhaps the first problem not purely scientific that The Thinking Machine was ever asked to solve. The scientist's aid was enlisted in this baffling case by Hutchinson Hatch, reporter.

"But I am a scientist, a logician," The Thinking Machine had protested. "I know nothing whatever of crime."

"No one knows that a crime has been committed," the reporter hastened to say. "There is something far beyond the ordinary in this affair. A woman has disappeared, evaporated into thin air in the hearing, almost in sight, of her friends. The police can make nothing of it. It is a problem for a greater mind than theirs."

Professor Van Dusen waved the newspaper man to a seat, and himself sank back into a great cushioned chair in which his diminutive figure seemed even more child-like than it really was.

"Tell me the story," he said petulantly. "All of it."

"Miss Wallack is thirty years old, and beautiful," the reporter began. "As an actress she has won recognition not only in this country, but in England. You may have read something of her in the daily papers, and if——"

"I never read the papers," the other interrupted curtly. "Go on."

"She is unmarried, and so far as anyone knows, had no immediate intention of changing her condition," Hatch resumed, staring curiously at the thin face of the scientist. "I presume she had admirers— most beautiful women of the stage have— but she is one whose life has been perfectly good, whose record is an open book. I tell you this because it might have a bearing on your conclusion as to a possible reason for her disappearance.

"Now for the actual circumstances of that disappearance. Miss Wallack has been playing in Shakespearean repertoire. Last week she was in Springfield. On Saturday night, which concluded her engagement there, she appeared as Rosalind in *As You Like It*. The house was crowded. She played the first two acts amid great enthusiasm, and this despite the fact that she was suffering intensely from headache, to which she was subject at times. After

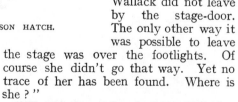

MR. HUTCHINSON HATCH.

the second act she returned to her dressing-room, and just before the curtain went up for the third the stage-manager called her. She replied that she would be out immediately. There seems no possible shadow of a doubt but that it was her voice.

"Rosalind does not appear in the third act until the curtain has been up for six minutes. When Miss Wallack's cue came she did not answer it. The stage-manager rushed to her door and again called her. There was no answer. Then, fearing that she might have fainted, he went in. She was not there. A hurried search was made without result, and the stage-manager finally was compelled to announce to the audience that the sudden illness of the star would make it impossible to finish the performance.

"The curtain was lowered, and the search resumed. Every nook and corner back of the footlights was gone over. The stage-door keeper, William Meegan, had seen no one go out. He and a policeman had been standing at the stage-door talking for at least twenty minutes. It is, therefore, conclusive that Miss Wallack did not leave by the stage-door. The only other way it was possible to leave the stage was over the footlights. Of course she didn't go that way. Yet no trace of her has been found. Where is she?"

"The windows?" asked The Thinking Machine.

"The stage is below the street level," Hatch explained. "The window of her dressing-room, room A, is small, and barred with iron. It opens into an air shaft that goes straight up for ten feet, and that is covered with an iron grating fixed in the granite. The other windows on the stage are not only inaccessible, but are also barred with iron. She could not have approached either of these windows without being seen by other members of the company or the stage hands."

"Under the stage?" suggested the scientist.

"Nothing," the reporter went on. "It is a large cemented basement, which was vacant. It was searched, because there was, of course, a chance that Miss Wallack might have become temporarily unbalanced, and wandered down there. There was even a search made of the 'flies'—that is, the galleries over the stage, where the men who work the drop-curtains are stationed."

"How was Miss Wallack dressed at the time of her disappearance?"

"In doublet and hose—that is, tights," the newspaper man responded. "She

"MISS WALLACK TAKING A 'CALL.'"

wears that costume from the second act until practically the end of the play."

"Was all her street clothing in her room?"

"Yes, everything, spread across an unopened trunk of costumes. It was all as if she had left the room to answer her cue—all in order, even to an open box of chocolate-cream on her table."

"No sign of a struggle, nor any noise heard?"

"No."

"Nor trace of blood?"

"Nothing."

"Her maid? Did she have one?"

"Oh, yes. I neglected to tell you that the maid, Gertrude Manning, had gone home immediately after the first act. She grew suddenly ill, and was excused."

The Thinking Machine turned his squint eyes on the reporter for the first time.

"Ill?" he repeated. "What was the matter?"

"That I can't say," replied the reporter.

"Where is she now?"

"I don't know. Everyone forgot all about her in the excitement about Miss Wallack."

"What kind of chocolate-cream was it?"

"I'm afraid I don't know that either."

"Where was it bought?"

The reporter shrugged his shoulders; that was something else he didn't know. The Thinking Machine shot out the questions aggressively, staring meanwhile steadily at Hatch, who squirmed uncomfortably.

"Where is the chocolate now?" demanded the scientist; and again Hatch shrugged his shoulders.

"How much did Miss Wallack weigh?"

The reporter was willing to guess at this. He had seen her half a dozen times. "Between a hundred and thirty and a hundred and forty," he ventured.

"Does there happen to be a hypnotist connected with the company?"

"I don't know," Hatch replied.

The Thinking Machine waved his slender hands impatiently; he was annoyed.

"It is perfectly absurd, Mr. Hatch," he expostulated, "to come to me with only a few facts, and ask advice. If you had *all* the facts I might be able to do something, but this——"

The newspaper man was nettled. In his own profession he was accredited a man of discernment and acumen. He resented the tone, the manner, even the seemingly trivial questions which the other asked.

"I don't see," he began, "that the chocolate, even if it had been poisoned, as I imagine you think possible, or a hypnotist, could have had anything to do with Miss Wallack's disappearance. Certainly neither poison nor hypnotism would have made her invisible."

"Of course you don't see," blazed The Thinking Machine. "If you did you wouldn't have come to me. When did this thing happen?"

"Saturday night, as I said," the reporter informed him a little more humbly. "It closed the engagement in Springfield. Miss Wallack was to have appeared here in Boston to-night."

"When did she disappear—by the clock, I mean?"

"Oh," said the reporter. "The stage-manager's time-slip shows that the curtain for the third act went up at 9.41—he spoke to her, say, one minute before, or at 9.40. The action of the play before she appears in the third act takes six minutes, therefore——"

"In precisely seven minutes a woman, weighing more than 130 pounds, certainly not dressed for the street, disappeared completely from her dressing-room. It is now 5.18 Monday afternoon. I think we may solve this crime within a few hours."

"Crime?" Hatch repeated eagerly. "Do you imagine there is a crime then?"

Professor Van Dusen did not heed the question. Instead he rose and paced back and forth across the reception-room half a dozen times, his hands behind his back, and his eyes cast down. At last he stopped and faced the reporter, who had also risen.

"Miss Wallack's company, I presume, with the baggage, is now in Boston," he said. "See every male member of the company, talk to them, and particularly *study their eyes*. Don't overlook anyone, however humble. Also find out what

became of the box of chocolate, and if possible how many pieces are out of it. Then report here to me. Miss Wallack's safety may depend upon your speed and accuracy."

Hatch was frankly startled.

"How——" he began.

"Don't stop to talk—hurry," commanded The Thinking Machine. "I will have a cab waiting when you come back. We must get to Springfield."

The newspaper man rushed away to obey orders. He did not understand them at all. Studying men's eyes was not in his line, but he obeyed nevertheless. An hour and a half later he returned, to be thrust unceremoniously into a waiting cab by The Thinking Machine. The cab rattled away toward South Station, where the two men caught a train, just about to move out for Springfield. Once settled in their seats, the scientist turned to Hatch, who was nearly suffocating with suppressed information.

"Well?" he asked.

"I found out several things," the reporter burst out. "First, Miss Wallack's leading man, Langdon Mason, who has been in love with her for three years, bought the chocolate at Schuyler's in Springfield, early Saturday evening, before he went to the theatre. He told me so himself, rather reluctantly, but I—I made him say it."

"Ah!" exclaimed The Thinking Machine. It was a most unequivocal ejaculation. "How many pieces are out of the box?"

"Only three," explained Hatch. "Miss Wallack's things were packed into the open trunk in her dressing-room, the chocolate with them. I induced the manager——"

"Yes, yes, yes," interrupted The Thinking Machine impatiently. "What sort of eyes has Mason? What colour?"

"Blue, frank in expression, nothing unusual at all," said the reporter.

"And the others?"

"I didn't quite know what you meant by studying their eyes, so I got a set of photographs. I thought perhaps they might help."

"Excellent! Excellent!" commented The Thinking Machine. He shuffled the pictures through his fingers, stopping now and then to study one and to read the name printed below.

" Is that the leading man ? " he asked at last, and handed one to Hatch.

" Yes."

Professor Van Dusen did not speak again. The train pulled up at Springfield at 9.20. Hatch followed the scientist out of the station and, without a word, into a cab.

" Schuyler's shop," commanded The Thinking Machine. " Hurry."

The cab rushed off through the night. Ten minutes later it stopped before a brilliantly lighted confectionery shop. The Thinking Machine led the way inside, and approached the girl behind the chocolate counter.

" Will you please tell me if you remember this man's face ? " he asked as he produced Mason's photograph.

" Oh, yes, I remember him," the girl replied. "He's an actor."

" Did he buy a small box of chocolates of you early on Saturday evening ? " was the next question.

" Yes. I recall it because he seemed to be in a hurry—in fact, I believe he said he was anxious to get to the theatre to pack."

" And do you recall that this man ever bought chocolates here ? " asked the scientist. He produced another photograph, and handed it to the girl. She studied it a moment, while Hatch craned his neck, vainly, to see.

" I don't recall that he ever did," the girl answered finally.

The Thinking Machine turned away abruptly and disappeared into a public telephone booth. He remained there for five minutes, then rushed out to the cab again, with Hatch following closely.

" City Hospital," he commanded.

Again the cab dashed away. Hatch was dumb ; there seemed to be nothing

THE GIRL IN THE SHOP.

to say. The Thinking Machine was plainly pursuing some definite line of inquiry, yet the reporter did not know what. The case was getting kaleidoscopic. This impression was strengthened when he found himself standing beside The Thinking Machine in City Hospital conversing with the House Surgeon, Dr. Carlton.

" Is there a Miss Gertrude Manning here ? " was the scientist's first question.

" Yes," replied the surgeon. " She was brought here Saturday night suffering from——"

" Strychnine poisoning, yes, I know," interrupted the other. " Picked up in the street, probably. I am a physician. If she is well enough I should like to ask her a couple of questions."

Dr. Carlton agreed, and Professor Van Dusen, still followed faithfully by Hatch, was ushered into the ward where Miss Wallack's maid lay pallid and weak. The Thinking Machine picked up her hand, and his slender finger rested for a minute on her pulse. He nodded as if satisfied.

" Miss Manning, can you understand me ? " he asked.

The girl nodded weakly.

" How many pieces of chocolate did you eat ? "

" Two," she replied. She stared into the face above her with dull eyes.

" Did Miss Wallack eat any of it up to the time you left the theatre ? "

" No."

If The Thinking Machine had been in a hurry previously he was racing now. Hatch trailed on dutifully behind, down the stairs and into the cab, whence Professor Van Dusen shouted a word of thanks to Dr. Carlton. This time their destination was the stage-door of the theatre from which Miss Wallack had disappeared.

The reporter was muddled. He did not know anything very clearly except that three pieces of chocolate were missing from the box. Of these the maid had eaten only two. She had been poisoned. Therefore it seemed reasonable to suppose that if Miss Wallack had eaten the third piece she also would be poisoned. But poison would not make her invisible. At this point the reporter shook his head hopelessly.

William Meegan, the stage-door keeper, was easily found.

"Can you inform me, please," began The Thinking Machine, "if Mr. Mason left a box of chocolate with you last Saturday night for Miss Wallack?"

"Yes," Meegan replied good-naturedly. He was amused at the little man. "Miss Wallack hadn't arrived. Mason brought a box of chocolates for her nearly every night, and usually left it here. I put the one Saturday night on the shelf here."

"Did Mr. Mason come to the theatre before or after the others on Saturday night?"

"Before," replied Meegan. "He was unusually early, presumably to pack."

"And the other members of the company coming in stop here, I imagine, to get their letters?" and the scientist squinted up at the correspondence box above the shelf.

"Always."

The Thinking Machine drew a long breath. Up to this time there had been little perplexed wrinkles in his brow. Now they disappeared.

"Now, please," he went on, "was any package or box *of any kind* taken from the stage on Saturday night between nine and eleven o'clock?"

"No," said Meegan, positively. "Nothing at all until the company's baggage was removed at midnight."

"Miss Wallack had two trunks in her dressing-room?"

"Yes. Two whacking big ones, too."

"How do you know?"

"Because I helped put 'em in, and helped take 'em out," replied Meegan sharply. "What's it to you?"

Suddenly The Thinking Machine turned and ran out to the cab, with Hatch, his shadow, close behind.

"Drive, drive as fast as you know how to the nearest long distance telephone," the scientist instructed the cabby. "A woman's life is at stake."

*   *   *   *   *

Half an hour later Professor Van Dusen and Hutchinson Hatch were on a train rushing back to Boston. The Thinking Machine had been in the telephone booth for fifteen minutes. When he came out Hatch had asked several questions, to which the scientist vouchsafed no answer. They were perhaps thirty minutes out of Springfield before the scientist showed any disposition to talk. Then he began, without preliminary, much as if he were resuming a former conversation.

"Of course if Miss Wallack didn't leave the stage of the theatre she was there," he said. "We will admit that she did not become invisible. The problem therefore was to find her on the stage. The fact that no violence was used against her was conclusively proven by half a dozen instances. No one heard her scream, there was no struggle, no trace of blood. Ergo, we assume in the beginning that she must have consented to the first steps which led to her disappearance. Remember her attire was wholly unsuited to the street.

"Now let's shape a hypothesis which will fit all the circumstances. Miss Wallack has a severe headache. Hypnotic influence will cure headaches. Was there a hypnotist to whom Miss Wallack would have submitted herself? Assume there was. Then would that hypnotist take advantage of his control to place her in a cataleptic condition? Assume a motive, and he would. Then, how would he dispose of her?

"From this point questions radiate in all directions. We will confine ourselves to the probable, granting for the moment that this hypothesis—the only one which fits all the circumstances—is correct. Obviously a hypnotist would not have attempted to get her out of the dressing-room. What remains? One of the two trunks in her room."

Hatch gasped.

"You mean you think it possible that

she was hypnotised and placed in that second trunk, the one that was strapped and locked?" he asked.

"It's the only thing that *could* have happened," said The Thinking Machine emphatically, "therefore that is just what *did* happen."

"Why, it's horrible," exclaimed Hatch. "A live woman in a trunk for forty-eight hours? Even if she were alive then, she must be dead now."

The reporter shuddered a little, and gazed curiously at the inscrutable face of his companion. He saw no pity, no horror there; there was merely the reflection of brain workings.

"It does not necessarily follow that she is dead," explained The Thinking Machine. "If she ate that third piece of chocolate *before* she was hypnotised she is probably dead. If it were placed in her mouth after she was in a cataleptic condition the chances are that she is not dead. The chocolate would not melt, and her system could not absorb the poison."

"But she would be suffocated—her bones would be broken by the rough handling of the trunk—there are a hundred possibilities," the reporter suggested.

"A person in a cataleptic condition is singularly impervious to injury," replied the scientist. "There is, of course, a chance of suffocation, but a great deal of air may enter a trunk."

"And the chocolate?" Hatch asked.

"Yes, the chocolate. We know that two pieces of chocolate nearly killed the maid. Yet Mr. Mason admitted having

DETECTIVE MALLORY.

bought it. This admission indicated that this poisoned chocolate is not the chocolate he bought. Is Mr. Mason a hypnotist? No. He hasn't the eyes. His picture tells me that. We know that Mr. Mason did buy chocolate for Miss Wallack on several occasions. We know that sometimes he left it with the stage-door keeper. We know that members of the company stopped there for their letters. We instantly see that it was possible for one to take away that box and substitute poisoned chocolate.

"Madness and the cunning of madness lie at the back of all this. It was a deliberate attempt to murder Miss Wallack, due, perhaps, to unrequited or hopeless infatuation. It began with the poisoned chocolate, and that failing, went to a point immediately following the moment when the stage-manager last spoke to the actress. The hypnotist was probably in her room then."

"Is Miss Wallack still in the trunk?" Hatch asked at last.

"No," replied The Thinking Machine. "She is out now, dead or alive — I am inclined to believe alive."

"And the man?"

"I will turn him over to the police in half an hour after we reach Boston."

From South Station the scientist and Hatch were driven immediately to the police headquarters. Detective Mallory, whom Hatch knew well, received them.

"We got your 'phone from Springfield," he began.

"Was she dead?" interrupted the scientist.

" 'YES; HE'S A HYPNOTIST.' "

"No," Mallory replied. "She was unconscious when we took her out of the trunk, but no bones are broken. She is badly bruised. The doctor says she's hypnotised."

"Was the piece of chocolate taken from her mouth?"

"Yes, a chocolate-cream. It hadn't melted."

"I'll come back here in a few minutes and awake her," said The Thinking Machine. "Come with us now, and get the man."

Wonderingly the detective entered the cab, and the three were driven to a big hotel a dozen streets away. Before they entered The Thinking Machine handed a photograph to Mallory, who studied it under an electric light.

"That man is upstairs with several others," explained the scientist. "Pick him out, and get behind him when we enter the room. He may attempt to shoot. Don't touch him until I say so."

In a large room on the fifth floor manager Stanfeld had assembled the Irene Wallack company. There were no preliminaries when Professor Van Dusen entered. He squinted comprehensively about him, then went straight to Langdon Mason, staring deeply into his eyes for a moment.

"Were you on the stage in the third act of your play before Miss Wallack was to appear—I mean the play last Saturday night?" he asked.

"I was," Mason replied, "for at least three minutes."

"Mr. Stanfeld, is that correct?"

"Yes," replied the manager.

There was a long tense silence, broken only by the steps of Mallory as he walked toward a distant corner of the room. A faint flush crept into Mason's face as he realised that the questions were almost an accusation. He started to speak, but the steady, impassive voice of The Thinking Machine stopped him.

"Mr. Mallory, take your prisoner," it said.

Instantly there was a fierce, frantic struggle, and those present turned to see Detective Mallory with his great arms locked about Stanley Wightman, the melancholy Jacques of *As You Like It*. By a sudden movement Mallory threw Wightman and manacled his hands, then looked up to find The Thinking Machine peering over his shoulder into the eyes of the prostrate man.

"Yes; he's a hypnotist," the scientist remarked in self-satisfied conclusion. "It always tells in the pupils of the eyes."

Miss Wallack was aroused, told a story almost identical with that of The Thinking Machine, and three months later resumed her tour. And meanwhile Stanley Wightman, whose brooding over a hopeless love for her made a maniac of him, raves and shrieks the lines of Jacques in the seclusion of a padded cell. Mental experts pronounce him incurable.

Professor Van Dusen's Problems.

By JACQUES FUTRELLE.

II.—THE MISSING NECKLACE.

DECIDEDLY Mr. Bradlee Cunnyngham Leighton was clever. His most ardent enemies admitted that. Scotland Yard, for instance, not only admitted it, but insisted on it. It was not any half-hearted insistence either, for in the words of Herbert Conway, one of the Yard's chief operators, he was smooth—" so smooth that he made ice feel like sandpaper." Whether or not Mr. Leighton was aware of this delicate compliment does not appear. It was perfectly possible that he was, although he had never mentioned it. He was a well-bred gentleman, and aware of many things that he never mentioned.

In his person Mr. Leighton had the distinguished honour of closely resembling the immaculate villain of melodrama. In his mental attainments, however, Scotland Yard gave him credit for being a genius—far beyond the cigarette-smoking mummer of crime, who is always transparent and is inevitably caught. Mr. Leighton has never been caught. Perhaps that was why Scotland Yard insisted on his cleverness, and was prepared to argue the point.

Mr. Leighton went everywhere. At those gatherings where the highest in the social world met, there was Mr. Leighton. He was on every matron's selected list of guests, a charming addition to any assembly. Scotland Yard knew this. Of course, it may have been only the merest chance that he was always present at those gatherings where valuable jewels had been " lost " or " mislaid." Yet Scotland Yard did not regard it as chance. That it did not was another compliment to Mr. Leighton.

From deep down in its innermost conscience Scotland Yard looked up to Mr. Leighton as the master mind, if not the actual vital instrument, in a long series of baffling jewel robberies. There was a finesse and delicacy—not to mention regularity—about these robberies that annoyed Scotland Yard. Yet, believing all this, Scotland Yard had never been so indiscreet as to mention the matter to Mr. Leighton. As a matter of fact Scotland Yard had never seen its way clear to mentioning it to anyone.

Conway had some ideas of his own about Mr. Leighton, whom he exalted to a position that would have surprised if not flattered him. Conway, perhaps, more nearly expressed the opinion of Scotland Yard in a few brief remarks than I could at greater length.

" He's a crook, and the cleverest in the world," he said of Mr. Leighton, almost enthusiastically. " He's got the Hemingway jewels, the Cheltenham bracelet, and the Quex shiners all right. I *know* he got them. But that doesn't do any good —merely knowing it. I can't put a finger on him because he's too smooth. I think I've got him and then—I haven't."

This was *before* the Varron necklace affair. When that remarkable episode came to be known to Scotland Yard, Conway's admiration for Mr. Leighton increased immeasurably. He *knew* that Leighton was the responsible one—he knew it in his own head and heart—but that was all. He gnawed his scrubby moustache fiercely, and set to work to prove it, feeling beforehand that it was a vain task.

The absolute simplicity of the thing— and in this it was like the others—was its most puzzling feature. Lady Varron had given a reception to the United States Ambassador at her London house. She had gathered about her a most distinguished company. There were representatives of England, France, and Russia ; there were some of the most beautiful women of the Continent ; there were two American duchesses ; there were a chosen few of the American colony— and Mr. Leighton. It may be well to repeat that he went everywhere.

163

Lady Varron on this occasion wore tne famous Varron necklace. Its intrinsic value was said to be £40,000 ; associations made it priceless. She was dancing with the American Ambassador when she slipped on the smooth floor and fell, dragging him down with her. It was an undignified, unromantic thing, but it happened. Mr. Leighton chanced to be one of those nearest, and rushed to her assistance. In an instant Lady Varron and the Ambassador were the centre of a little group. It was Mr. Leighton who helped Lady Varron to her feet.

"It's nothing," she assured him, smiling uncertainly. "I was a little awkward, that's all."

Mr. Leighton turned to assist the Ambassador, but found him standing again and puffing inordinately, then turned back to Lady Varron.

"You dropped your necklace," he remarked blandly.

"My necklace ? "

Lady Varron's white hand flew to her bare throat, and she paled a little as Mr. Leighton and others of the group stood back to look for the jewel. It was not to be seen. Lady Varron controlled herself admirably.

"It must have fallen somewhere," she said finally.

"Are you sure you had it on ? " asked another guest solicitously.

"Oh, yes," she replied positively, "but I may have dropped it somewhere else."

"I noticed it just before you—we—fell," said the Ambassador. "It must be here."

But it was not. In that respect—that is, visible non-existence—it resembled the Cheltenham bracelet. Mr. Leighton had, on that occasion, strolled out on the lawn at night with the Honourable Miss Cheltenham, and she had dropped the bracelet. That was all. It was never found.

In this Varron affair it would be useless to go into details of what immediately followed the loss of the necklace. It is sufficient to say that it was not found ; that men and women stared at each other in bewildered embarrassment and mutual suspicion, and that finally Mr. Leighton, who still stood beside Lady Varron, intimated courteously, tactfully, that a personal search of her guests would not be amiss. He did not say it in so many words, but the others understood.

Mr. Leighton was seconded heartily by the American Ambassador, a democratic individual with honest ideas which were foremost when a question of personal integrity was involved. But the search was not made, and the reception proceeded. Lady Varron bore her loss marvellously well.

"She's a brick," was the audible compliment of one of the American duchesses, whose father owned £47,000,000 worth of soap somewhere in vague America.

It was not until next day that Scotland Yard was notified of Lady Varron's loss.

"Leighton there ? " was Conway's first question.

"Yes."

"Then he got it," Conway asserted positively. "I'll get him this time or know why."

Yet at the end of a month he neither had him, nor did he know why. He had intercepted messengers, he had opened letters, telegrams, cable despatches ; he had questioned servants ; he had taken advantage of the absence of both Mr. Leighton and his valet to search his exquisite apartments. He had done all these things and more—all that a severely conscientious man of his profession could do, and had gnawed his scrubby moustache down to a disreputable ragged line. But of the necklace there was no clue, no mention, no trace, nothing.

Then Conway heard that Mr. Leighton was going to the United States for a few months.

"To take the necklace and dispose of it," he declared, out of the vexation of his own heart. "If he ever gets aboard ship with it I've got him—either I've got him or the United States Customs officials will have him."

Conway could not bring himself to believe that Leighton, with all his cleverness, would dare try to dispose of the pearls in England, and he flattered himself that he could not have sent them elsewhere—too close a watch had been kept.

It transpired naturally that when the Boston bound liner *Romanic* sailed from Liverpool four days later, not only was Mr. Leighton aboard but Conway was

"IT WAS MR. LEIGHTON WHO HELPED HER TO HER FEET,"

there. He knew Leighton, but was secure in the thought that Leighton did not know him.

On the second day out he was disabused on this point. He was beginning to think that it might not be a bad idea to know Leighton casually, so when he noticed that immaculate gentleman alone, leaning on the rail, smoking, he sauntered up and joined him in contemplation of the infinite ocean.

"Beautiful weather," Conway remarked after a long time.

"Yes," replied Leighton as he glanced around and smiled. "I should think you Scotland Yard men would enjoy a junket like this?"

Conway did not do any such foolish thing as start or show show astonishment, whatever he might have felt. Instead he smiled pleasantly.

"I've been working pretty hard on that Varron affair," he said frankly. "And now I'm taking a little vacation."

"Oh, that thing at Lady Varron's?" inquired Leighton lazily. "Indeed? I happened to be the one to notice that the necklace was gone."

"Yes, I know it," responded Conway grimly.

The conversation drifted to other things. Conway found Leighton an agreeable companion and a democratic one. They smoked together, walked together, and played shuffle-board together. That evening Leighton took a hand at bridge in the smoking-room. For hours Conway stared at the phosphorescent points in the sinister green waters, and smoked.

"If he did it," he remarked at last, "he's the cleverest scoundrel on earth, and if he did not I'm the biggest fool."

Six bells—eleven o'clock—struck. The deck was deserted. Conway stumbled along through the dark toward the smoking-room. Inside he saw Leighton still at play. As he paused at the open door he heard Leighton's voice.

"I'll play until two o'clock, not later," it said.

Conway made up his mind instantly. He turned, retraced his steps along the deck to Leighton's room, where he stopped. He knew Leighton had not burdened himself with a valet, and thought he knew why, so without hesitation he drew

out several keys and fumbled at the lock. It yielded at last, and he stepped inside the state-room, closing the door. His purpose was instantly apparent. It was to search.

Now Conway had his own ideas of just how a search should be conducted. First he took out all of Leighton's wearing apparel, and patted and pinched it inch by inch; he squeezed up neckties, unrolled handkerchiefs, examined shirts and crumpled up silken hosiery. Then he took the shoes—half a dozen pairs. He had been suspicious of shoes since he once found a dozen diamonds concealed in false heels. But these heels were not false.

Next, still without haste or apparent disappointment, he turned his attention to the handbag and the steamer trunk, both of which he had emptied. Such things had been known to have false bottoms and secret compartments. These had none. He satisfied himself absolutely on this point by every method known to his art.

In due time his examination came down to the room itself. He unmade the bed, and closely felt and scrutinised the mattress, sheets, blankets, pillows, and coverlid. He took the three drawers from the dressing cabinet, and looked behind them. He turned over several newspapers and shook them one by one. He peered into the water jug, and fumbled around the plumbing in the tiny bath-room adjoining. He examined the carpet to see if anything had been hidden beneath it. Finally he climbed on a chair and from his elevated position looked for a crack or crevice where a necklace or unset pearls could be hidden.

"There are still three possibilities," he told himself at the end, as he carefully restored the room to its previous condition. "He might have left them in a package in the ship's safe, but that's improbable—too risky; he might have left them in a trunk in the hold, which is still more improbable; or he might have them on his person, that is more than likely."

So Conway went out, extinguishing the light, and locking the door behind him. He stepped into his own state-room a moment, and took a mouthful of whisky, which he spat out again. But it must have had some deep, potent effect, for a few minutes later when he appeared in the smoking-room he was in a lamentable state of intoxication, and exhaled whisky noticeably. His was a maudlin, thick-tongued condition. Leighton glanced up at him with well-bred reproach.

It may have been only accident that Conway stumbled over Leighton's feet and noted that he wore flat-soled, loose slippers *without heels*, and also accident that he embraced him with exaggerated affection as he struggled to recover his equilibrium.

Be those things as they may, Leighton excused himself good-naturedly from the bridge party, and urged Conway to bed. Conway would only agree on condition that Leighton would assist him. Leighton consented cheerfully, and they left the smoking-room together, Conway clinging to him as the vine to the oak.

Half-way down the deck Conway stumbled and fell, despite the friendly supporting arm, and in his effort to save himself his hands slid all the way down Leighton's shapely legs. Then he was deposited in his state-room, and Leighton returned to his cards smiling.

"And he hasn't got them on him," declared Conway enigmatically to the bare walls. He was not intoxicated now.

It was an easy matter next day for him to learn that Leighton had left nothing in the ship's safe, and that his four trunks in the hold were inaccessible, being buried under hundreds of others. Whereupon Conway sat down to wait and learn what new and original ideas of searching Uncle Sam's Customs officers had invented.

At last came a morning when the wireless telegraph operator aboard picked up a signal from shore and announced that the *Romanic* was less than a hundred miles from Boston light. Later Conway found Leighton leaning on the rail, smoking and gazing shoreward.

It was three hours or so after that that several passengers noticed a motor boat coming toward them. Leighton watched it with idle interest. Finally it circled widely, and it became apparent that it was coming alongside the now slow-moving liner. When it was only a

hundred feet off and the liner was barely creeping along, Leighton grew suddenly interested.

"By Jove!" he exclaimed, then shouted: "Hello, Harry!"

"Hello, Leighton," came an answering shout. "Heard you were aboard and came out to meet you."

There was a rapid fire of uninteresting pleasantries as the motor boat slid in under the *Romanic's* lee, and bobbed up and down in her wash. The man aboard stood up with a package of newspapers in his hand.

"Here are some American papers for you," he called.

He flung the bundle, and Leighton caught it, left the rail, and passed into his state-room. He returned after a moment with a bundle of English newspapers—those Conway had previously seen.

"Catch," he called. "There's something in these that will interest you."

The man in the small boat caught the package and dropped it carelessly on a seat.

Then, suddenly, Conway awoke.

"There goes the necklace," he told himself with a start. A quick grasping movement of his hands attracted the attention of Leighton, who smiled inscrutably, daringly, into the blazing eyes of the Scotland Yard man. The motor boat, with a parting shout of "I'll meet you on the wharf," sped away.

Thoughts began to flow rapidly through Conway's fertile brain. Five minutes later he burst in on the wireless operator, and sent a long despatch to officials ashore. Then from the bow rail he watched the motor boat speeding away in the direction of Boston. It drew off about two miles, and remained relatively in that position for nearly all the forty miles into Boston Harbour.

It spoke no other craft, passed near none, in fact, while in Conway's sight, which was until it disappeared in the harbour.

An hour later the *Romanic* was warped in and tied up. Conway was the first man off. He went straight to a man who seemed to be waiting for him.

"Did you search the motor boat?" he demanded.

"Yes," was the reply. "We nearly

tore it to pieces, even took it out of the water. We also searched the man on her, Harry Cheshire. You must have been mistaken."

"Are you sure she spoke no one or got rid of the jewels to another vessel?"

"She didn't go near another vessel," was the reply. "I met her in my launch at the harbour mouth and came in with her."

For an instant Conway's face showed disappointment, then came animation again. He was just beginning to get really interested in the affair.

"Do you know the Customs officer in charge?" he asked.

"Yes."

"Introduce me."

There was an introduction, and the three men spoke aside for several minutes. The result of it was that when Leighton sauntered down the gang plank he was invited into a private office. He went smilingly, and submitted to a search of his person without anger or the slightest trace of uneasiness. As he came out Conway was standing at the door.

"Are you satisfied?" Leighton asked.

"No," blazed Conway savagely.

"What? Not after searching me *twice*, and my state-room once?"

Conway did not answer. He did not dare to at the moment, but he stood by when Leighton's four trunks were taken from the hold, and he saw that they were searched with the same minute care that he had given to the state-room. At the fruitless end of it he sat down on one of the trunks and stared at Leighton in a sort of admiration.

Leighton stared back for a moment, smiled, nodded pleasantly, and strolled up the dock, chatting carelessly with Harry Cheshire. Conway made no attempt to follow them. It was not worth while —nothing was worth while any more.

"But he *did* get them, and he's got them now," he told himself savagely, "or he has disposed of them in some way that I can't find."

The Thinking Machine—Professor Van Dusen—did not seem to regard the problem as at all difficult, when it came to his attention a couple of days later. Hutchinson Hatch, reporter, brought it to him.

Hatch had some good friends in the Customs Office, where Conway had told his story. He learned from them that that office had refused to have anything to do with the case, insisting that the Scotland Yard man must be mistaken.

Crushed in spirit, mangled in reputation, and taunted by Leighton's final words, Conway took a desolate view of life. Momentarily he lost even that bulldog tenacity which had never before faltered —lost it all except in so far as he still believed that Leighton was *the* man. It was about this time Hatch met him. Would he talk? He was burning to talk; caution was a senseless thing anyway. Then Hatch took him gently by the hand and led him to the Thinking Machine.

Conway unburdened himself at length and with vitriolic emphasis. For an hour he went on, while the scientist leaned back in his chair, with his great yellow head pillowed on a cushion, and squinted aggressively at the ceiling. At the end of the hour the Thinking Machine knew as much of the Varron problem as Conway knew, and knew as much of Leighton as any man knew, except Leighton.

"How many stones were in the necklace?" the scientist asked.

"One hundred and seventy-two," replied Conway.

"Was the man in the motor boat— Harry Cheshire you call him—an Englishman?"

"Yes, in speech, manner, and appearance."

For a long time the Thinking Machine twiddled his fingers, while Conway and the reporter sat staring at him impatiently. Hatch knew, from the past, that something tangible, something that led somewhere, would come from that wonderful analytical brain; Conway, not knowing, was only hopefully curious. But like most men of his profession he wanted action; sitting down and thinking did not seem to be any good.

"You see, Mr. Conway," said the scientist at last, "you haven't proven anything. Your investigations, as a matter of fact, indicate that Leighton did *not* take the pearls, therefore did not bring them with him. There is only one thing

" ' CATCH,' HE CALLED. ' THERE'S SOMETHING IN THESE THAT WILL INTEREST
YOU ' "

that indicates he might have. That is the throwing of the newspapers into the motor boat. That one act seems to have been a senseless one, unless——"

"Unless the pearls were concealed in the bundle," interrupted the Scotland Yard man.

"Or unless he was amusing himself at your expense, and is perfectly innocent," added the Thinking Machine. "It is perfectly possible that, if he were innocent, and discovered that you suspected him, he has merely made a fool of you. If we take any other view of it we must base it on an assumption which has no known fact to support it. We shall have to dispose of every other person who might have stolen the necklace, and pin it down to Leighton. Further, we shall have to assume out of hand that he brought the jewels to this country."

The Scotland Yard man was getting interested.

"That is not good logic, yet when we assume all this for our present purposes the problem is a simple one. And by assuming it we prove that your search of the state-room was not thorough. Did you, for instance, happen to look on the *under side* of the slats in the berth ? Do you *know* that the necklace, or its unset pearls, did not hang down in the drain pipe from the water bowl ? "

Conway snapped his fingers in annoyance. These were two things he had not done.

"There are other possibilities, of course," resumed the Thinking Machine, "therefore the search for the necklace was useless. Now we must take for granted that, if they came to this country at all, they came in one of those places and you overlooked them. Obviously Mr. Leighton would not have left them in the trunks in the hold. Therefore we must assume further that he hid them in his state-room, and threw them into the motor boat.

"In that event they were in the motor boat when it left the *Romanic*, and we must believe they were not in it when it docked. Yet the motor boat neither spoke nor approached any other vessel. The jewels were *not* thrown into the water. The man Cheshire could not have swallowed one hundred and seventy-two pearls—or any

great part of them—therefore, what have we ? "

"Nothing," promptly responded Conway. "That's what's the matter. I've had to give it all up."

"Instead of nothing we have the answer," replied the Thinking Machine tartly. "Let's see. Perhaps I can give you the name and address of the man who has the jewels now, assuming of course that Leighton brought them."

He arose suddenly and passed into the adjoining room. Conway turned and stared at Hatch inquiringly, with a queer expression on his face.

"Is he anything of a joker ? " he asked.

"No, but he's a good deal of a wonder," replied Hatch.

"Do you mean to say that I have been working on this thing for months and months without learning anything about it, and all he's got to do is to go in there and get the name and address of the man who has the necklace ? " demanded Conway in bewilderment.

"If he went into that room and said he'd bring back the Pacific Ocean in a teacup I'd believe him," said the reporter. "I *know* him."

They were interrupted by the tinkling of the telephone bell in the next room, then for a long time they heard the subdued hum of the scientist's irritable voice as he talked into the instrument. It was twenty-five or thirty minutes before he appeared in the door again. He paused there and scribbled something on a card which he handed to Hatch. The reporter read : " Henry C. H. Manderling, Scituate, Mass."

"There is the name and address of the man who probably has the jewels now," said the Thinking Machine quite as a matter of fact. "Mr. Hatch, you accompany Mr. Conway, let him see the surroundings, and act as his judgment dictates. You must search this man's house. I don't think you'll have much trouble. The pearls will be unset, and you will find them possibly in small oil-silk bags, not so large as your little finger. When you find them, take steps to apprehend both this man and Leighton. Call Detective Mallory when you get them, and bring them here."

" But—but——" stammered Conway.

" Come on," commanded Hatch.

And Conway went.

The sleepy little old town of Scituate sprawls along two or three miles of Massachusetts coast, facing the sea boldly in a series of cliffs which rise up and sink away with the utmost suddenness. The town was settled two or three hundred years ago, and nothing has ever happened there since. It was here, on the top of one of the cliffs, that Henry C. H. Manderling had lived alone for two or three months. He had gone there in the spring with other city folk who dream their summers away, and occupied a queer little dwelling through which the salt breezes wandered at will. A tiny barn was attached to the house.

Hutchinson Hatch and the Scotland Yard man found the house without difficulty, and entered it without hesitation. There was no one at hand to stop them, or to interfere with the search they made. The simple lock on the door was no obstacle. In less than half an hour the skilful hands of the Scotland Yard man had turned out a score or more small oil-silk bags, no larger than his little finger. He tore one open and six pearls fell into his hand.

" They're the Varron pearls all right," he exclaimed triumphantly after an examination. He dropped them all into his pocket.

" Sh-h-h-h ! " warned Hatch suddenly.

He had heard a step at the door, then two voices, as someone inserted a key in the lock. After a moment the door opened, and, crouching back in the shadow, they heard two men enter. It was just at that psychological moment that Conway stepped out and faced them.

" I want you, Leighton," he said calmly.

Hatch could not see beyond the Scotland Yard man, but he heard a shot, and a bullet whistled uncomfortably close to his head. Conway leaped forward ; Hatch saw his arm swing, and one of the men fell. Then came another shot. Conway staggered a little, took another step forward and again swung his great right arm. There was a scurrying of feet, the clatter of a revolver on the floor, and the front door slammed.

" Tie up that chap there," commanded Conway.

He opened the door, and Hatch heard him run along the verandah and leap off. He turned his attention to the senseless man on the floor. It was Harry Cheshire. A blow on the point of the chin had rendered him unconscious. Hatch bound him hand and foot where he lay, and ran out.

Conway was racing down the cliff to where a motor boat lay. Hatch saw a man climb into the boat, and an instant later it shot out into the water. Conway ran on to where it had been ; it was now fifty yards out.

" Not *this* time, Mr. Conway," came Leighton's voice as the boat sped on.

The Scotland Yard man stared after it a minute or more, then returned to Hatch. The reporter saw that he was pale, very pale.

" Did you bind him ? " Conway asked.

" Yes," Hatch responded. " Are you wounded ? "

" Yes," replied the Scotland Yard man. " He hit me in the fleshy part of the left arm. I never knew him to carry a revolver before. It's lucky for me those two shots were all he had."

The Thinking Machine put the finishing touches on the binding of Conway's wound—it was trivial—then turned to his other visitors. These were Harry Cheshire, or Manderling, and Detective Mallory, to whom he had been delivered a prisoner on the arrival of Hatch and Conway in Boston. A general alarm had been sent out for Leighton.

Conway apparently did not care anything about the wound, but he had a frank curiosity as to just what the Thinking Machine had done, and how those things which had happened had been brought to pass.

" It was all ridiculously simple," began the scientist at last in explanation. " It came down to this ; how could one hundred and seventy-two pearls be transferred from a boat forty miles at sea to a safe place ashore ? The motor boat did not speak or approach any other vessel ; obviously one could not *throw* them ashore, and I have never heard of such a thing as a trained fish which might have brought them in. Now what is the only other way they *could* have reached shore with comparative safety ? "

He looked from one to another inquiringly. Each in turn shook his head. Manderling, or Cheshire, was silent.

"There is only one possible answer," said the scientist at last. "That is—birds—homing pigeons."

"By Jove ! " exclaimed Conway, and he stared at Manderling. "And I did notice dozens of them about the place at Scituate."

"The jewels *were* on the ship as you suspected," resumed the scientist, "unset, and probably suspended in a long oil-silk bag in the drain pipe I mentioned. They *were* thrown into the motor boat, wrapped in the newspapers. Two miles away from the *Romanic* they were fastened to homing pigeons, and one by one the pigeons were released. You, Mr. Conway, could see the boat clearly at that distance, but you could not possibly see a bird rise from it. The birds went to their home, Mr. Manderling's place at Scituate. Homing pigeons are generally kept in automatically closing compartments, and each pigeon was locked in as it arrived. Mr. Manderling here and Mr. Leighton removed the pearls at their leisure.

"Of course, with homing pigeons as a clue we could get somewhere," the Thinking Machine went on after a moment. "There are numerous homing pigeon associations and fanciers, and it was possible that one of these would know an Englishman who had, say, twenty-five or fifty birds, and presumably lived somewhere near Boston. One *did* know. He gave me the name of Henry C. H. Manderling. Harry is a corruption of Henry, and Henry C is Henry Cheshire, or Harry Cheshire—the name Mr. Manderling gave when he was searched at the wharf."

"Can you explain how Leighton was able to get the necklace in the first place ? " asked Conway curiously.

"Just as he got the other things," replied the Thinking Machine, "by boldness and cleverness. Suppose, when Lady Varron fell, Leighton had had a stout elastic fastened high up, at the shoulder, say, inside his coat sleeve, and the end of this elastic, with a clamp of some sort, was drawn down until the elastic was taut, and fastened to his cuff ? Remember that this man was always waiting for an opportunity, and was always prepared to take advantage of it. Of course he did not plan the thing as it happened.

"Suppose that the necklace dropped off as he leaned over to help Lady Varron. In the momentary excitement he could, as he leaned over to help Lady Varron, under their very noses, have fastened the clamp to the necklace. Instantly the jewels would have disappeared up his sleeve, and he could have submitted to any sort of perfunctory search of his pockets as he suggested."

"That's a trick professional gamblers have to get rid of cards," remarked Detective Mallory.

"Oh, it isn't new, then ? " asked the Thinking Machine. "Immediately he left the ball-room he hid this necklace as he had hidden other jewels, and before you, Mr. Conway, knew of the theft, wrote and mailed full directions to Mr. Manderling here what to do. You did not intercept any letters, of course, until after you knew of this theft. Leighton had perhaps had other dealings with Mr. Manderling in other parts of the world, when he was not so closely watched as in this particular instance. I dare say, however, he had them all planned carefully for fear the very thing that did happen in this case would happen."

Half an hour later Conway shook hands with the Thinking Machine, thanked him heartily, and the little party dispersed.

"I had given it up," Conway confessed as he was going out.

"You see," remarked the Thinking Machine, "gentlemen of your profession use too little common sense. Remember that two and two always make four—not sometimes, but all the time."

Leighton has not yet been caught ; Manderling made a model prisoner.

Professor Van Dusen's Problems.

By JACQUES FUTRELLE.

III.—THE GREEN-EYED MONSTER.

WITH coffee-cup daintily poised in one hand, Mrs. Lingard van Safford lifted wistful, bewitching eyes towards her husband, who sat across the breakfast-table partially immersed in the morning papers.

"Are you going out this morning?" she asked.

Mr. van Safford grunted inarticulately.

"May I inquire," she went on placidly, and a dimple snuggled at a corner of her mouth, "if that particular grunt means that you are or are not?"

Mr. van Safford lowered his newspaper and glanced at his wife's pretty face. She smiled charmingly.

"Really, I beg your pardon," he apologised. "I hardly think I shall go out. I feel rather listless, and I must write some letters. Why?"

"Oh, nothing particularly," she responded.

She took a last sip of her coffee, brushed two or three tiny crumbs from her lap, laid her serviette aside, and arose. Once she turned and glanced back; Mr. van Safford was reading again.

After a while he finished the papers and stood looking out of window, yawning prodigiously at the prospect of letters to be written. His wife entered and picked up a handkerchief which had fallen beside her chair. He merely glanced around. She was dressed for the street—immaculately gowned as only a young and beautiful woman can gown herself.

"Where are you going, my dear?" he inquired, languidly.

"Out!" she responded archly.

She passed through the door. He heard her step and the rustle of her skirts in the hall, then he heard the front door open and close. For some reason, not quite clear even to himself, it surprised him; she had never done a thing like that before. He walked to the front window and looked out. His wife went straight down the street and turned the first corner. After a time he wandered

away to the library to nurse an emotion he had never felt before. It was curiosity.

Mrs. van Safford did not return home for luncheon, so he sat down alone. Afterwards he wandered restlessly about the house for an hour or so, then he went down town. He appeared at home again just in time to dress for dinner.

"Has Mrs. van Safford returned?" was his first question of Baxter, who opened the door.

"Yes, sir, half an hour ago," responded Baxter. "She's dressing."

Mr. van Safford ran up the stairs to his own apartments. At dinner his wife was radiant, rosily radiant. The flush of perfect health was in her cheeks, and her eyes sparkled beneath their long lashes. She smiled brilliantly upon her husband. To him it was all as if some great thing had been taken out of his life, leaving it desolate, then as suddenly returned. Unnamed emotions struggled within him, prompted by that curiosity of the morning, and a dozen questions hammered insistently for expression. But he repressed them gallantly, and for this he was duly rewarded.

"I had such a delightful time to-day!" his wife exclaimed, after the soup. "I called for Mrs. Blacklock immediately after I left here, and we were together all day shopping. We had luncheon down town."

"Oh! That was it!" Mr. van Safford laughed outright from a vague sense of relief which he could not have called by name, and toasted his wife silently by lifting his glass. Her eyes sparkled at the compliment. The glass drained, he snapped the slender stem in his fingers, laughed again and laid it aside. Mrs. van Safford dimpled with sheer delight.

"Oh, Van, you silly boy!" she reproved softly, and she stroked the hand which was prosaically reaching for the salt.

It was only a little while after dinner that Mr. van Safford excused himself and started for the club, as usual. His wife followed him demurely to the door, and there, under the goggling eyes of Baxter, he caught her in his arms and kissed her impetuously, fiercely even. It was the sudden outbreak of an impulsive nature—the sort of thing that makes a woman know she is loved. She thrilled at his touch and reached two white hands forward pleadingly. Then the door closed, and she stood staring down at the tip of her tiny boot with lowered lids and a little melancholy droop at the corners of her mouth.

It was after ten o'clock when Mr. van Safford awoke on the following morning. He had been at his club late—until after two—and now drowsily permitted himself to be overcome again by the languid listlessness which is the heritage of late hours. At ten minutes past eleven he appeared in the breakfast-room.

"Mrs. van Safford has been down, I suppose ? " he asked of a maid.

"Oh yes, sir," she replied. "She's gone out."

Mr. van Safford lifted his brows inquiringly.

"She was down a few minutes after eight o'clock, sir," the maid explained, " and hurried through her breakfast."

"Did she leave any word ? "

"No, sir."

"Be back to luncheon ? "

"She didn't say, sir."

Mr. van Safford finished his breakfast silently and thoughtfully. About noon he, too, went out. One of the first persons he met down town was Mrs. Black-lock, and she rushed toward him with outstretched hand.

"I'm so glad to see you," she bubbled, for Mrs. Blacklock was of that rare type which can bubble becomingly. "But where, in the name of goodness, is your wife ? I haven't seen her for weeks and weeks ! "

"Haven't seen her for——" Mr. van Safford repeated, slowly.

"No," Mrs. Blacklock assured him. "I can't imagine where she is keeping herself."

Mr. van Safford gazed at her in dumb bewilderment for a moment, and the lines about his mouth hardened a

little, despite his efforts to control himself.

"I had an impression," he said deliberately, "that you saw her yesterday—that you went shopping together ? "

"Goodness, no. It must be three weeks since I saw her."

Mr. van Safford's fingers closed slowly, fiercely, but his face relaxed a little, masking, with a slight smile, a turbulent rush of mingled emotions.

"She mentioned your name," he said at last, calmly. "Perhaps she said she was going to call on you. I misunderstood her."

He didn't remember the remainder of the conversation, but it was of no consequence at the moment. He had not misunderstood her, and he knew he had not. At last he found himself at his club, and there idle guesses and conjectures flowed through his brain in an unending stream. Finally he arose, grimly.

"I suppose I'm an ass," he mused. "It doesn't amount to anything, of course, but——"

And he sought to rid himself of distracting thoughts over a game of billiards ; instead he only subjected himself to open derision for glaringly inaccurate play. Finally he flung down the cue in disgust, strode away to the 'phone and called up his home.

"Is Mrs. van Safford there ? " he inquired of Baxter.

"No, sir. She hasn't returned yet."

Mr. van Safford banged the telephone viciously as he hung up the receiver. At six o'clock he returned home. His wife was still out. At half-past eight he sat down to dinner, alone. He did not enjoy it ; indeed, hardly tasted it. Then, just as he finished, she came in with a rush of skirts and a lilt of laughter. He drew a long breath and set his teeth.

"You poor, deserted dear," she sympathised, laughingly.

He started to say something, but two soft, clinging arms were about his neck, and a velvety cheek rested against his own, so—so he kissed her instead. And really he was not at all to be blamed. She sighed happily, and laid aside her hat and gloves.

"I simply couldn't get here any sooner,"

she explained poutingly as she glanced into his accusing eyes. "I was out with Nell Blakesley in her big, new touring car, and it broke down and we had to send for a man to repair it, so——"

He did not hear the rest; he was staring into her eyes, steadily, inquiringly. Truth shone triumphant there; he could only believe her. Yet—yet—that other thing! She had not told him the truth! In her face, at last, he read uneasiness as he continued to stare, and for a moment there was silence.

"What's the matter, Van?" she inquired solicitously. "Don't you feel well?"

He pulled himself together with a start, and for a time they chatted of inconsequential things as she ate. He watched her until she pushed her dessert plate aside, then casually, quite casually:

"I believe you said you were going to call on Mrs. Blacklock to-morrow?"

She looked up quickly.

"Oh no," she replied. "I was with her all day yesterday, shopping. I said I *had* called on her."

Mr. van Safford arose suddenly, stood glaring down at her for an instant, then turning abruptly left the house. Involuntarily she had started up, then she sat down again and wept softly over her coffee. Mr. van Safford seemed to have a very definite purpose, for when he reached the club he went straight to a telephone booth and called Miss Blakesley over the wire.

"My wife said something about—something about——" he stammered lamely, "something about calling on you to-morrow. Will you be in?"

"Yes, and I'll be so glad to see her," came the reply. "I'm dreadfully tired of staying cooped up here in the house, and really I was beginning to think all my friends had deserted me."

"Cooped up in the house?" Mr van Safford repeated. "Are you ill?"

"I have been," came the reply, "I'm better now, but I haven't been out of the house for more than a week."

"Indeed," remarked Mr. van Safford, sympathetically. "I'm awfully sorry, I assure you. Then you haven't had a chance to try your—your—'big, new touring car?'"

"Why, I haven't any new touring car," said Miss Blakesley. "I haven't any sort of a car. Where did you get that idea?"

Mr. van Safford did not answer her; rudely enough he hung up the telephone and left the club with a face like marble. When finally he stopped walking he was opposite his own house. For a minute he stood looking at it much as if he had never seen it before, then he turned and went back to the club. There was something of fright, of horror even, in his white face when he entered.

As Mr. van Safford did not go to bed that night it was not surprising that his wife should find him in the breakfast-room when she came down about eight o'clock. She smiled. He stared at her after a curt "Good-morning!" Then came an ominous silence. She finished her breakfast, arose and left the house without a word. He watched her from a window until she disappeared around the corner, just four doors below, then, overcome by fears, suspicions, hideous possibilities, he ran after her.

She had not been out of his sight more than half a minute when he reached the corner, yet now—now she was gone. He looked on both sides of the street, up and down, but there was no sign of her—not a woman in sight. He knew that she would not have had time to reach the next street below, and in that case there were two obvious possibilities. One was that she had stepped into a waiting cab and been driven away at full speed; another that she had entered some house near by. If so, which house? Whom did she know in this street? He turned the problem over in his mind several times, and then he was convinced that she had hurried away in a waiting cab. That emotion which had begun as curiosity was now a raging, turbulent torrent.

On the following morning Mrs. van Safford came down to breakfast at fifteen minutes to eight. She seemed a little tired, and there was a trace of tears about her eyes. Baxter looked at her curiously.

"Has Mr. van Safford been down yet?" she asked.

"No, madam," he replied.

"Did he come in at all last night?"

"TWO SOFT, CLINGING ARMS WERE ABOUT HIS NECK, AND A VELVETY CHEEK RESTED
AGAINST HIS OWN"

"Yes, madam. About half-past two. I let him in. He had forgotten his key."

Now as a matter of fact, at that particular moment Mr. van Safford was standing just around the corner, four doors down, waiting for his wife. Just what he intended to do when she appeared was not quite clear in his mind, but the affair had gone to a point where he felt that he must do something. So he waited impatiently, and smoked innumerable cigars. Two hours passed. He glanced around the corner. No one in sight. He strolled back to the house and met Baxter in the hall.

"Has Mrs. van Safford come down?" he asked of the servant.

"Yes, sir," was the reply. "She went out more than an hour ago."

* * * * *

Martha opened the door.

"Please, sir," she said, "there's a young gentleman having a fit in the reception-room."

Professor van Dusen—The Thinking Machine—turned away from his laboratory table and squinted at her aggressively. Her eyes were distended with nervous excitement, and her wrinkled hands twisted the apron she wore.

"Having a fit?" snapped the scientist.

"Yes, sir," she gasped.

"Dear me! Dear me! How annoying!" expostulated the man of achievement, petulantly. "Just what sort of a fit is it—epileptic, apoplectic, or merely a fit of laughter?"

"Lord, sir, I don't know," Martha confessed helplessly. "He's just a-walking and a-talking and a-pulling his hair, sir."

"What name?"

"I—I forgot to ask, sir," apologised the aged servant. "It surprised me so to see a gentleman a-wiggling like that. He said, though, he'd been to police headquarters and Detective Mallory sent him."

The eminent logician dried his hands and started for the reception-room. At the door he paused and peered in. With no knowledge of just what style of fit his visitor had chosen to have, he felt the necessity of this caution. What he saw was not alarming—merely a good-looking young man pacing back and forth across the room with quick, savage stride. His eyes were blazing, and his face was flushed with anger. It was Mr. van Safford.

At sight of the diminutive figure of The Thinking Machine, topped by the enormous yellow head, the young man paused and his anger-distorted features relaxed into something closely approaching surprise.

"Well?" demanded the Professor, querulously.

"I beg your pardon," said Mr. van Safford with a slight start. "I—I had expected to find a—a—rather a different sort of person."

"Yes, I know," said The Thinking Machine grumpily. "A man with a black moustache and big feet. Sit down."

Mr. van Safford sat down rather suddenly. It never occurred to anyone to do other than obey when the crabbed little scientist spoke. Then, with an incoherence which was thoroughly convincing, Mr. van Safford laid before The Thinking Machine in detail those singular happenings which had so disturbed him. The Professor leaned back in his chair, with finger tips pressed together, and listened to the end.

"My mental condition—my suffering —was such," explained Mr. van Safford in conclusion, "that when I proved to my own satisfaction that she had twice misrepresented the facts to me, wilfully, I—I could have strangled her."

"That would have been a nice thing to do," remarked the scientist, crustily. "You believe then, that there may be another——"

"Don't say it," burst out the young man passionately. He arose. His face was dead white. "Don't say it," he repeated, menacingly.

The Thinking Machine was silent a moment, then glanced up in the blazing eyes and cleared his throat.

"She never did such a thing before?" he asked.

"No, never."

"Does she—did she—ever speculate?" Mr. van Safford sat down again.

"Never," he responded, positively. "She wouldn't know one stock from another."

"Has her own bank account?"

"Yes—nearly four hundred thousand dollars. This was her father's gift at our wedding. It was deposited in her name, and has remained so. My own income is more than enough for our uses."

"You are rich, then?"

"My father left me nearly two million dollars," was the reply. "But all this doesn't matter. What I want——"

"Wait a minute," interrupted The Thinking Machine, testily. There was a long pause. "You have never quarrelled seriously?"

"Never one cross word," was the reply.

"Remarkable," commented The Thinking Machine ambiguously. "How long have you been married?"

"Two years—last June."

"*Most* remarkable," supplemented the scientist. Mr. van Safford stared. "How old are you?"

"Thirty."

"How long have you been thirty?"

"Six months—since last May."

There was a long pause. Mr. van Safford plainly did not see the trend of the questioning.

"How old is your wife?" demanded the scientist.

"Twenty-two, in January."

"She has never had any mental trouble of any sort?"

"No, no."

"Have you any brothers or sisters?"

"No."

"Has she?"

"No."

The Thinking Machine shot out the questions crustily, and Mr. van Safford answered briefly. There was another pause, and the young man arose and paced back and forth with nervous energy. From time to time he glanced inquiringly at the pale, wizened face of the scientist. Several thin lines had appeared in the dome-like brow, and he was apparently oblivious of the other's presence.

"It's a most intangible, elusive affair," he commented at last, and the wrinkles deepened. "It is, I may say, a problem without a given quantity. Perfectly extraordinary."

Mr. van Safford seemed a little relieved to find someone express his own thoughts so accurately.

"You don't believe, of course," continued the scientist, "that there is anything criminal in——"

"Certainly not," the young man exploded, violently.

"Yet, the moment we pursue this to a logical conclusion," pursued the other, "we are more than likely to uncover something which is, to put it mildly, not pleasant."

Mr. van Safford's face was perfectly white; his hands were clenched desperately. Then the loyalty to the woman he loved flooded his heart.

"It's nothing of that kind," he exclaimed, and yet his own heart misgave him. "My wife is the dearest, noblest, sweetest woman in the world. And yet——"

"Yet you are jealous of her," interrupted The Thinking Machine. "If you are so sure of her, why annoy me with your troubles?"

The young man read, perhaps, a deeper meaning than The Thinking Machine had intended, for he started forward impulsively. The Professor continued to squint at him impersonally, but did not change his position.

"All young men are fools," he went on, blandly, "and I may add that most of the old ones are, too. But now the question is: What purpose can your wife have in acting as she has, and in misrepresenting those acts to you? Of course we must spy upon her to find out, and the answer may be one that will wreck your future happiness. It *may* be, I say. I don't know. Do you still want the answer?"

"I want to know—I want to know," burst out Mr. van Safford, harshly. "I shall go mad unless I do know."

The Thinking Machine continued to squint at him with almost a gleam of pity in his eyes—almost, but not quite. And the habitually irritated voice was in no way softened when he gave some explicit and definite instructions.

"Go on about your affairs," he commanded. "Let things go as they are. Don't quarrel with your wife; continue to ask your questions, because if you don't, she'll suspect that you suspect;

report to me any change in her conduct. It's a very singular problem. Certainly I have never had another like it."

The Thinking Machine accompanied him to the door and closed it behind him.

"I have never seen a man in love," he mused, "who wasn't in trouble."

And with this broad, philosophical conclusion he went to the 'phone. Half an hour later Hutchinson Hatch, reporter, entered the laboratory where the scientist sat in deep thought.

"Mr. Hatch," he began, without preliminary, "did you ever happen to hear of Mr. and Mrs. van Safford ? "

"Well, rather," responded the reporter with quick interest. "He's a well-known clubman, worth millions, high in society and all that ; and she's one of the most beautiful women I ever saw. She was a Miss Potter before marriage."

"It's wonderful the memories you newspaper men have," observed the scientist. "You know her personally ? "

Hatch shook his head.

"You must find someone who knows her well," commanded The Thinking Machine ; "a girl friend, for instance— one who might be in her confidence. Learn from her why Mrs. van Safford leaves her house every morning at eight o'clock, then tells her husband she has been with someone that we know she hasn't seen. She has done this every day for four days. Your assiduity in this may prevent a divorce."

Hatch pricked up his ears.

"Also find out just what sort of an illness Miss Nell Blakesley has recently suffered. That's all."

An hour later Hutchinson Hatch, reporter, called on Miss Gladys Beekman, a young society woman who was an intimate of Mrs. van Safford's before the latter's marriage. Without feeling that he was dallying with the truth Hatch informed her that he called on behalf of Mr. van Safford. She began to smile. He laid the case before her emphatically, earnestly, and with great detail. The more he explained the more pleasantly she smiled. It made him uncomfortable, but he struggled on to the end.

"I'm glad she did it," exclaimed Miss Beekman. "But I—I couldn't believe she would."

Then came a sudden gust of laughter which left Hutchinson Hatch, reporter, with the feeling that he was being imposed upon. It continued for a full minute—a hearty, rippling, musical laugh. Hatch grinned sheepishly. Then, without an excuse, Miss Beekman arose and left the room. In the hall there came a fresh burst, and Hatch heard it dying away in the distance.

"Well," he muttered grimly, "I'm glad I was able to amuse her."

Then he called upon a Mrs. Francis, a young matron whom he had cause to believe was also favoured with Mrs. van Safford's friendship. He laid the case before *her*, and *she* laughed ! Then Hutchinson Hatch, reporter, began to get mule-headed about it. He visited eight other women who were known to be on friendly terms with Mrs. van Safford. Six of them intimated that he was an impertinent, prying, inquisitive person, and—the other two laughed ! Hatch paused and stroked his fevered brow.

"Here's a corking good joke on somebody," he told himself, "and I'm beginning to think it's me."

Whereupon he took his troubles to Professor van Dusen. That distinguished gentleman listened in pained surprise to the simple recital of what Hatch had not been able to learn, and spidery wrinkles on his forehead assumed the relative importance of the canals on Mars.

"It's astonishing," he declared raspily.

"Yes, it so struck me," agreed the reporter.

The Thinking Machine was silent for a long time ; the watery blue eyes were turned upward, and the slender white fingers pressed tip to tip. Finally he made up his mind as to the next step.

"There seems only one thing to do," he said. "And I won't ask you to do that."

"What is it ? " demanded the reporter.

"To watch Mrs. van Safford and see where she goes."

"I wouldn't have done it before, but I will now," Hatch responded promptly.

The bull-dog in him was aroused. "I want to see what the joke is."

It was ten o'clock next evening when Hatch called to make a report. He seemed a little weary and tremendously disgusted.

"I've been right behind her all day," he explained, "from eight o'clock this morning until twenty minutes past nine to-night, when she reached home. And if the Lord'll forgive me——"

"What did she do?" interrupted Professor van Dusen, impatiently.

"Well," and Hatch grinned as he drew out a note-book, "she walked eastward from her house to the first corner, turned, walked another block, took a down-town car, and went straight to the Public Library. There she read a Henry James book until fifteen minutes to one, and then she went to luncheon in a restaurant. I also had luncheon. Then she went to the North-end on a car. After she got there she wandered around aimlessly all afternoon, nearly. At ten minutes to four she gave a quarter to a crippled boy. He bit it to see if it was good, found it was, then bought cigarettes with it. At half-past four she left the North-end and went into a big department store. If there's anything there she didn't price I can't remember it. She *bought* a pair of shoe-laces. The store closed at six, so she went to dinner in another restaurant. I also had dinner. We left there at half-past seven o'clock and went back to the Public Library. She read until nine o'clock, and then went home. Phew!" he concluded.

The Thinking Machine had listened with growing and obvious disappointment on his face. He seemed so cast down by the recital that Hatch began to feel guilty.

"I couldn't help it, you know," said the reporter by way of apology. "That's what she did."

"She didn't speak to anyone?"

"Not a soul but clerks, waiters, and library attendants."

"She didn't give a note to anyone or receive a note?"

"No."

"Did she seem to have any purpose at all in anything she did?"

"No. The impression she gave me was that she was killing time."

Professor van Dusen was silent for several minutes. "I think, perhaps——" he began.

But what he thought Hatch did not learn, for he was sent away with additional instructions. Next morning found him watching the front of the van Safford house again. Mrs. van Safford came out at seven minutes past eight o'clock, and walked rapidly eastward. She turned the first corner and went on, still rapidly, to the corner of an alley. There she paused, cast a quick look behind her, and went in. Hatch was some distance back and ran forward just in time to see her skirts trailing into a door.

"Ah, here's something, anyhow," he told himself, with grim satisfaction.

He walked down the alley to the door. It was like the other doors along in that it led into the back hall of a house, and was intended for the use of delivery waggons. When he examined the door he scratched his chin thoughtfully; then came utter bewilderment, an amazing sense of hopeless inanity. For there, staring at him from a door-plate, was the name: "van Safford." She had merely come out of the front door and gone in at the back.

Hatch started to rap and ask some questions, then changed his mind and walked around to the front again, and up the steps.

"Is Mrs. van Safford in?" he inquired of Baxter, who opened the door.

"No, sir," was the reply. "She went out a few minutes ago."

Hatch stared at him coldly a minute, and walked away.

"Now this is a particularly savoury kettle of fish," he soliloquised. "She has either gone back into the house without his knowledge, or else he has been bribed, and then——"

And then he took the story to Professor van Dusen. That imperturbable man of science listened to the end, then arose and said "Oh!" three times. Which was interesting to Hatch in that it showed the end was in sight, but it was not illuminating. He was still floundering.

The Thinking Machine started into an adjoining room, then turned back.

"By the way, Mr. Hatch," he asked, "did you happen to find out what was the matter with Miss Blakesley?"

"By George, I forgot it," returned the reporter, ruefully.

"Never mind, I'll find out."

At eleven o'clock Hutchinson Hatch and The Thinking Machine called at the van Safford home. Mr. van Safford in person received them; there was a gleam of hope in his face at sight of the diminutive scientist. Hatch was introduced, then:

"You don't know of any other van Safford family in this block?" began the scientist.

"There's not another family in the city," was the reply. "Why?"

"Is your wife in now?"

"No. She went out this morning, as usual."

"Now, Mr. van Safford, I'll tell you how you may bring this matter to an end, and understand it all at once. Go upstairs to your wife's apartments—they are probably locked—and call her. She won't answer, but she'll hear you. Then tell her you understand it all, and that you're sorry. She'll hear that, as that alone is what she has been waiting to hear for some time. When she comes out bring her downstairs. Believe me, I should be delighted to meet so clever a woman."

Mr. van Safford was looking at him as if he doubted his sanity.

"Really," he said coldly, "what sort of child's play is this?"

"It's the only way you'll ever coax her out of that room," snapped Professor van Dusen belligerently, "and you'd better do it gracefully."

"Are you serious?" demanded the other.

"Perfectly serious," was the crabbed rejoinder. "She has taught you a lesson that you'll remember for some time. She has been merely going out the front door every day and coming in the back, of necessity with the full knowledge of the cook and her maid. That is what she did the day you ran after her and she disappeared."

Mr. van Safford listened in amazement.

"Why did she do it?" he asked.

"Why?" retorted Professor van Dusen. "That's for you to answer. A little less of your time at the club of evenings, and a little less of selfish amusement, so that you can pay attention to a beautiful woman who has, previous to her marriage at least, been accustomed to constant attention, would solve this little domestic problem. You've spent every evening at your club for months, and she was here alone probably a great part of that time. In your own selfishness you had never a thought of her, so she gave you a *reason* to think of her."

Suddenly Mr. van Safford turned and ran out of the room. They heard him as he took the stairs, two at a time.

"By George!" remarked Hatch. "That's a silly ending to a cracking good mystery, isn't it?"

Ten minutes later Mr. and Mrs. van Safford entered the room. Her pretty face was suffused with colour; he was frankly, outrageously happy. There were mutual introductions.

"It was perfectly dreadful of Mr. van Safford to call you gentlemen into this affair," Mrs. van Safford apologised, charmingly. "Really, I feel very much ashamed of myself for——"

"It's of no consequence, madam," Professor van Dusen assured her. "It's the first opportunity I have ever had of studying a woman's mind. It was not at all logical, but it was very—very instructive. I may add that it was effective, too."

He bowed low and, turning, picked up his hat.

"But your fee?" suggested Mr. van Safford.

Professor van Dusen squinted at him sourly. "Oh, yes, my fee," he mused. "It will be just five thousand dollars."

"Five thousand—what?" exclaimed Mr. van Safford.

"Five thousand dollars," repeated the scientist.

"Why, man, it's perfectly absurd to talk——"

Mrs. van Safford laid one white hand on her husband's arm. He glanced at her and she smiled radiantly.

"Don't you think I'm worth it, Van?" she asked, archly.

He wrote the cheque. The Professor inscribed his name across the back in a crabbed little hand, and passed it on to Hatch.

"Please hand that to some charitable organisation," he directed. "It was an excellent lesson, Mrs. van Safford. Good-day."

Professor van Dusen, scientist, and Hutchinson Hatch, reporter, walked along side by side for two blocks, without speaking. The reporter broke the silence.

"Why did you want to know what was the matter with Miss Blakesley?" he asked.

"Her name was mentioned, and I wanted to know if she really had been ill, or was merely attempting to mislead Mr. van Safford," was the reply. "She had a touch of grippe. I got that by 'phone. I also learned of Mr. van Safford's club habits by 'phone from his club."

"And those women who laughed—what was the joke?"

"The fact that they laughed made me see that the affair was not a serious one. They were intimate friends with whom the wife had evidently discussed doing just what she did do. All sorts of possibilities were suggested to me, but, everything considered, in this case the facts could only have been as logic developed them. I imagined the true state of affairs from your report of Mrs. van Safford's day of wandering; when I knew she went in the back door of her own house, I saw the solution. I saw it, Mr. Hatch," and the scientist paused and shook a long finger in the reporter's face, "because two and two *always* make four—not *some*times, but *all* the time."

Professor Van Dusen's Problems.

By JACQUES FUTRELLE.

IV.—THE PHANTOM MOTOR CAR.

TWO dazzling white eyes bulged suddenly through the night, as a motor-car swept round a curve in the wide road, and laid a smooth, glaring pathway ahead. Even at the distance the rhythmical crackling-chug informed Special Constable Baker that it was a gasoline car, and the headlong swoop of the unblinking lights toward him made him instantly aware of the fact that the speed ordinance of Yarborough County was being a little more than broken—it was being obliterated.

Now the County of Yarborough was one wide expanse of summer estates and superbly kept roads, level as a floor, and offered distracting temptations to the dangerous pastime of racing. But against this was the fact that the County was particular about its speed laws, so particular, in fact, that it had stationed half a hundred men on its highways to abate the nuisance. Incidentally it had found that keeping record of infractions of the law was an excellent source of income.

"Forty miles an hour if an inch," remarked Baker to himself.

He rose from a camp stool where he was wont to make himself comfortable on watch from six o'clock until midnight, picked up his lantern, turned up the light and stepped down to the edge of the road. He always remained on watch at the same place—at one end of a long stretch which motorists had unanimously dubbed "The Trap." The Trap was singularly tempting—a perfectly macadamised road bed lying between two tall stone walls with only enough of a sinuous twist in it to make each end invisible from the centre. Another man, Special Constable Bowman, was stationed at the other end of The Trap, and there was telephonic communication between the points, enabling the two to check each other and incidentally, if one failed to stop a car or get its number, the other would. That at least was the theory.

So now, with the utmost confidence, Baker waited beside the road. The approaching lights were only a couple of hundred yards away. At the proper instant he would raise his lantern, the car would stop, its occupants would protest, and then the county would add a mite to its general fund for making the roads even better and more tempting to motorists. Or sometimes the cars did not stop. In that event it was part of the Special Constable's duty to get the number as it flew past, and reference to the monthly motor car register gave the name of the owner. An extra fine was always imposed in such cases.

Without the slightest diminution of speed the car came hurtling on towards him and swung wide so as to take the straight path of The Trap at full speed. At the psychological instant Baker stepped out into the road and waved his lantern.

"Stop!" he commanded.

The crackling-chug came on, heedless of the cry. The car was almost on him before he leaped out of the road—a feat at which he was particularly expert—then it flashed by and plunged into The Trap. Baker was, at the instant, so busily engaged in getting out of the way that he could not read the number, but he was not disconcerted because he knew there was no escape from The Trap. On the one side a solid stone wall eight feet high marked the eastern boundary of the John Phelps Stocker country estate, and on the other side a stone fence nine feet high marked the western boundary of the Thomas Q. Rogers country estate. There was no turn out, no place, no possible way for an auto to get out of The Trap except at one of the two ends guarded by the special constables. So Baker, perfectly confident of results, seized the 'phone.

"Car coming through sixty miles an hour," he bawled. "It won't stop. I missed the number. Look out!"

"All right, answered Special Constable Bowman.

For ten, fifteen, twenty minutes Baker waited expecting a call from Bowman at the other end. It did not come and finally he picked up the 'phone again. No answer. He rang several times, battered the box and did some tricks with the receiver. Still no answer. Finally he began to feel worried. He remembered that at the same post one Special Constable had been badly hurt by a reckless chauffeur who refused to stop or turn his car when the officer stepped out into the road. In his mind's eye he saw Bowman now lying helpless, perhaps badly injured. If the car held the pace at which it passed him it would be certain death to whoever might be unlucky enough to get in its path.

With these thoughts running through his head, and with genuine solicitude for Bowman, Baker at last walked on along the road of The Trap toward the other end. The feeble rays of his lantern showed the unbroken line of the cold stone walls on each side. There was no shrubbery of any sort, only a narrow strip of grass close to the wall. The more Baker considered the matter the more anxious he became, and he increased his pace a little. As he turned a gentle curve he saw a lantern in the distance coming slowly toward him. It was evidently being carried by some one who was looking carefully along each side of the road.

"Hello!" called Baker, when the lantern came within distance. "That you, Bowman?"

"Yes," came the halloed response.

The lanterns moved on and met. Baker's solicitude for the other constable was quickly changed to curiosity.

"What're you looking for?" he asked.

"That motor," replied Bowman. "It didn't come through my end, and I thought perhaps there had been an accident, so I walked along looking for it. Haven't seen anything."

"Didn't come through your end?" repeated Baker in amazement. "Why it must have. It didn't come back my way and I haven't passed it, so it must have gone through."

"Well, it didn't," declared Bowman

conclusively. "I was on the look-out for it, too, standing beside the road. There hasn't been a car through my end in an hour."

Special Constable Baker raised his lantern until the rays fell full on the face of Special Constable Bowman, and for an instant they stared each at the other. Suspicion glowed from the keen, avaricious eyes of Baker.

"How much did they give you to let 'em by?" he asked.

"Give me?" exclaimed Bowman, in righteous indignation. "Give me? Nothing. I haven't seen a car."

A slight sneer curled the lips of Special Constable Baker.

"Of course that's all right to report at headquarters," he said, "but I happen to know that the motor came in here, that it didn't go back my way, that it couldn't get out except at the ends, therefore it went your way." He was silent for a moment. "And whatever you got, Jim, seems to me I ought to get half."

Then the worm—i.e., Bowman—turned. A polite curl appeared about his lips and was permitted to show through the grizzled moustache.

"I guess," he said deliberately, "you think because you do that, everybody else does. I haven't seen any motors."

"Don't I always give you half, Jim?" Baker demanded, almost pleadingly.

"Well I haven't seen any car, and that's all there is to it. If it didn't go back your way there wasn't any car." There was a pause; Bowman was framing up something particularly unpleasant. "You're seeing things, that's what's the matter."

So was sown discord between two officers of the County of Yarborough. After a while they separated with mutual sneers and open derision, and went back to their respective posts. Each was thoughtful in his own way. At five minutes of midnight, just before they went off duty, Baker called Bowman on the 'phone again.

"I've been thinking this thing over, Jim, and I guess it would be just as well if we didn't report it or say anything about it when we go in," said Baker slowly. "It seems foolish, and if we did say anything about it it would give the boys the laugh on us."

"Just as you say," responded Bowman.

Relations between Special Constable Baker and Special Constable Bowman were strained on the morrow. But they walked along side by side to their respective posts. Baker stopped at his end of The Trap; Bowman did not even look around.

"You'd better keep your eyes open to-night, Jim," Baker called as a last word.

"I had 'em open last night," was the disgusted retort.

Seven, eight o'clock passed. Two or three cars had gone through The Trap at moderate speed and one had been warned by Baker. At a few minutes past nine he was staring down the road which led into The Trap when he saw something that brought him quickly to his feet. It was a pair of dazzling white eyes, far away. He recognised them—the mysterious car of the night before.

"I'll get her this time," he muttered grimly, between closed teeth.

Then, when the onrushing car was a full two hundred yards away, Baker planted himself in the middle of the road and began to swing the lantern. The car seemed, if anything, to be travelling even faster than on the previous night. At a hundred yards Baker began to shout. Still the car did not lessen speed, merely rushed on. Again at the psychological instant Baker jumped. The car whisked by as the chauffeur gave it a dexterous twist to prevent running down the Special Constable.

Safely out of its way Baker turned and stared after it, trying to read the number. He could see there was a number because a white board swung from the tail axle, but he could not make out the figures. Dust and a swaying car conspired to defeat him. And he did see, too, that there were four persons in the car dimly silhouetted against the light reflected from the road. It was useless, of course, to conjecture as to sex, for even as he looked the fast-receding car swerved around the turn and was lost to sight.

Again he rushed to the telephone; Bowman responded promptly.

"That car's gone in again," Baker called. "Ninety miles an hour. Look out!"

"I'm looking," responded Bowman.

"Let me know what happens," Baker shouted.

With the receiver at his ear he stood for ten or fifteen minutes, then Bowman halloed from the other end.

"Well?" Baker responded. "Get 'em?"

"No car passed through and there's none in sight," said Bowman.

"But it went in," insisted Baker.

"Well, it didn't come out here," declared Bowman. "Walk along the road till I meet you and look out for it."

Then was repeated the search of the night before. When the two men met in the middle of The Trap their faces were blank—blank as the high stone walls which stared at them from each side.

"Nothing!" said Bowman.

"Nothing!" echoed Baker.

Special Constable Bowman perched his head on one side and scratched his grizzly chin.

"You're not trying to put up a job on me?" he inquired coldly. "You did see a car?"

"I certainly did," declared Baker, and a belligerent tone underlay his manner. "I certainly saw it, Jim, and if it didn't come out your end, why—why——"

He paused and glanced quickly behind him. The action inspired a sudden similar one on Bowman's part.

"Maybe—maybe——" said Bowman after a minute, "maybe it's a—a spook car?"

"Well it must be," mused Baker. "You know as well as I do that no car can get out of this Trap except at the ends. That car came in here, it isn't here now, and it didn't go out your end. Now where is it?"

Bowman stared at him a minute, picked up his lantern, shook his head solemnly and wandered along the road back to his post. On his way he glanced around quickly, apprehensively, three times—Baker did the same thing four times.

On the third night the phantom car appeared and disappeared precisely as it had done previously. Again Baker and Bowman met half way between posts and talked it over.

"I'll tell you what, Baker," said Bowman in conclusion, "maybe you're just imagining that you see a car. Maybe if I was at your end I couldn't see it."

Special Constable Baker was distinctly hurt at the insinuation.

"All right, Jim," he said at last, "if you think that way about it we'll swop posts to-morrow night. We won't have to say anything about it when we report."

"Now that's the talk," exclaimed Bowman with an air approaching enthusiasm. "I'll bet *I* don't see it."

On the following night Special Constable Bowman made himself comfortable on Special Constable Baker's campstool. And *he* saw the phantom car. It came upon him with a rush and a crackling-chug of engine, and then sped on, leaving him nerveless. He called Baker over the wire and Baker watched half an hour for the phantom. It did not appear.

Ultimately all things reach the newspapers. So with the story of the phantom motor-car Hutchinson Hatch, reporter, smiled incredulously when his city editor laid aside an inevitable cigar and tersely stated the known facts. The known facts in this instance were meagre almost to the disappearing point. They consisted merely of a corroborated statement that a motor-car, solid and tangible enough to all appearances, had rushed into The Trap each night and totally disappeared.

But there was enough of the bizarre about it to pique the curiosity, to make one wonder, so Hatch journeyed down to Yarborough County, an hour's ride from the city, met and talked to Baker and Bowman and then, in broad daylight strolled along The Trap twice. It was a leisurely, thorough investigation with the end in view of finding out how an automobile, once inside, might get out again without going out either end.

On the first trip through Hatch paid particular attention to the Thomas Q. Rogers side of the road. The wall, nine feet high, was an unbroken line of stone with not the slightest indication of a secret way through it anywhere. Secret way! Hatch smiled at the phrase. But when he reached the other end—Bowman's end—of The Trap he was perfectly convinced of one thing—that no motor-car had left the hard, macadamised road to go over, under, or through the Thomas Q. Rogers wall. Returning, still leisurely, he paid strict attention to the John Phelps Stocker side, and when he reached the other end—Baker's end——he was convinced of another thing—that no motor-car had left the road to go over, under, or through the John Phelps Stocker wall.

Hatch saw no shrubbery along the road, nothing but a strip of scrupulously cared-for grass, therefore the phantom car could not be hidden any time, night or day. Hatch failed, too, to find any holes in the road, so the car did not go down through the earth. At this point he involuntarily glanced up at the blue sky. Perhaps, he thought whimsically, the automobile was a strange sort of bird, or—or—and he stopped suddenly.

"By George!" he exclaimed. "I wonder if——"

And the remainder of the afternoon he spent systematically making inquiries. He went from house to house, the Stocker house, the Rogers house, both of which were at the time unoccupied, then to cottage, cabin and hut in turn. But he did not seem overladen with information when he joined Special Constable Baker at his end of The Trap that evening about seven o'clock.

Together they rehearsed the strange points of the mystery as the shadows grew about them, until finally the darkness was so dense that Baker's lantern was the only bright spot in sight. As the chill of evening closed in a certain awed tone crept into their voices. Occasionally a motor-car bowled along, and each time as it hove in sight Hatch glanced at Baker questioningly. And each time Baker shook his head. And each time, too, he called Bowman, in this manner accounting for every car that went into The Trap.

"It'll come all right," said Baker after a long silence, "and I'll know it the minute it rounds the curve coming toward us. I'd know its two lights in a thousand."

They sat still and smoked. After

(*Drawn by Stephen Spurrier*).

"THE PHANTOM CAR CAME UPON HIM WITH A RUSH, AND THEN SPED ON, LEAVING HIM NERVELESS."

awhile two dazzling white lights burst into view far down the road and Baker, in excitement, dropped his pipe.

"That's her!" he declared. "Look at her coming!"

And Hatch did look at her coming. The speed of the mysterious car was such as to make one look. Like the eyes of a giant the two lights came on toward them, and Baker perfunctorily went through the motions of attempting to stop it. The car fairly whizzed past them and the rush of air which tugged at their coats was convincing enough proof of its solidity. Hatch strained his eyes to read the number as the motor flashed by. But it was hopeless. The tail of the car was lost in an eddying whirl of dust.

"She certainly does travel," commented Baker, softly.

"She does," Hatch assented.

Then, for the benefit of the newspaper man, Baker called Bowman on the wire.

"Car's coming again," he shouted. "Look out and let me know!"

Bowman, at his end, waited twenty minutes, then made the usual report— the car had not passed. Hutchinson Hatch was a calm, cold, dispassionate young man, but now a queer, creepy sensation stole along his spinal column. He lighted a cigarette and pulled himself together with a jerk.

"There's one way to find out where it goes," he declared at last, emphatically, "and that's to place a man in the middle just beyond the bend of The Trap and let him wait and see. If the car goes up, down, and even evaporates he'll see and can tell us."

Baker looked at him curiously.

"I'd hate to be the man in the middle," he declared. There was something of uneasiness in his manner.

"I rather think I would, too," responded Hatch.

On the following evening, consequent on the appearance of the story of the phantom motor in Hatch's paper, there were twelve other reporters on hand. Most of them were openly, flagrantly sceptical; they even insinuated that no one had seen a car. Hatch smiled wisely.

"Wait!" he advised with deep conviction.

So when the darkness fell that evening the newspaper men of a great city had entered into a conspiracy to capture the phantom car. Thirteen of them, making a total of fifteen men with Baker and Bowman, were on hand, and they agreed to a suggestion for all to take positions along the road of The Trap from Baker's post to Bowman's, watch for the car, see what happened to it, and compare notes afterwards. So they scattered themselves along, a few hundred feet apart, and waited. That night the phantom did not appear at all and twelve reporters jeered at Hutchinson Hatch, and told him to light his pipe with the story. And next night when Hatch and Baker and Bowman alone were watching the phantom motor re-appeared.

Whereupon, like a child with a troublesome problem, Hatch took the entire matter and laid it before Professor van Dusen, the master brain which had, at various times, untangled facts from a score or more intricate affairs for his benefit. The Thinking Machine, with squint eyes turned steadily upward, and long, slender fingers pressed tip to tip, listened to the end.

"Now I know, of course, that motorcars don't fly," Hatch burst out savagely, in conclusion, "and if this one doesn't fly there is no earthly way for it to get out of The Trap, as they call it. I went over the thing carefully—I even went so far as to examine the ground and the tops of the walls to see if a runaway had been let down for the auto to go over."

The Thinking Machine squinted at him inquiringly.

"Are you sure you saw a motor-car?" he demanded irritably.

"Certainly I saw it," blurted the reporter. "I not only saw it—I smelt it. Just to convince myself that it was real I tossed my cane in front of the thing and it smashed it to tooth-picks."

"Perhaps, then, if everything is as you say, the car actually *has* wings," remarked the scientist.

The reporter stared into the calm, inscrutable face of The Thinking Machine, fearing first that he had not heard aright. Then he concluded that he had.

" You mean," he inquired eagerly, " that the phantom may be a motor-aëroplane affair, and that it actually does fly ? "

" It's not at all impossible," commented the scientist.

" I had an idea something like that myself," Hatch explained, " and questioned every soul within a mile or so, but I didn't get anything."

" The perfect stretch of road there might be the very place for some daring experimenter to get up sufficient speed to soar a short distance in a light machine," continued the scientist.

" Light machine ? " Hatch repeated " Didn't I tell you that this car had four people in it ? "

" Four people ! " exclaimed the scientist. " Dear me ! Dear me ! That makes it very different. Of course four people would be too great a lift for an——"

For ten minutes he sat silent, and tiny, cobwebby lines appeared in his dome-like brow. Then he arose and passed into the adjoining room. After a moment Hatch heard the telephone bell jingle. Five minutes later The Thinking Machine appeared, and scowled upon him unpleasantly.

" I suppose what you really want to learn is if the car is a—a material one, and to whom it belongs ? " he queried.

" That's it," agreed the reporter, " and, of course, why it does what it does, and how it gets out of The Trap."

" Do you happen to know a fast, long-distance bicycle rider ? " demanded the scientist abruptly.

" A dozen of them," replied the reporter promptly. " I think I see the idea, but——"

" You haven't the faintest inkling of the idea," declared The Thinking Machine positively. " If you can arrange with a fast rider who can go a distance—it might be thirty, forty, fifty miles—we may end this little affair without difficulty."

In these circumstances Professor van Dusen, scientist and logician, met the famous Jimmie Thalhauer, the world's champion long-distance bicyclist. He held every record from five miles up to and including six hours, had twice won the

six-day race and was, altogether, a master in his field. He came in chewing a tooth-pick. There were introductions.

" You ride the bicycle ? " inquired the crusty little scientist.

" Well, *some*," confessed the champion modestly with a wink at Hatch.

" Can you keep up with a motor-car for a distance of, say, thirty or forty miles ? "

" I can keep up with anything that ain't got wings," was the response.

" Well, to tell you the truth," volunteered Professor Van Dusen, " there is a growing belief that this particular car has wings. However, if you can keep up with it——"

" Ah, quit your kiddin'," said the champion, easily. " I can ride rings round anything on wheels. I'll start behind it and beat it where it's going."

Professor Van Dusen examined the champion, Jimmie Thalhauer, as a curiosity. In the seclusion of his laboratory he had never had an opportunity of meeting just such another worldly young person.

" How fast *can* you ride, Mr. Thalhauer ? " he asked at last.

" I'm ashamed to tell you," confided the champion in a hushed voice. " I can ride so fast that I scare myself." He paused a moment. " But it seems to me," he said, " if there's thirty or forty miles to do I ought to do it on a motor-cycle ? "

" Now that's just the point," explained Professor Van Dusen. " A motor-cycle makes noise, and if anything of that sort could have been used we should have hired a fast motor-cycle. The proposition, briefly, is : I want you to ride, without lights, behind a motor-car, which may also run without lights, and find out where it goes. No occupant of the car must suspect that it is followed."

" Without lights ? " repeated the champion. " Gee ! Rubber shoe, eh ? "

The Thinking Machine looked his bewilderment.

" Yes, that's it," Hatch answered for him.

" I guess it's good for a four-column head ? " inquired the champion. " Special pictures posed by the champion ? Eh ? "

" Yes," Hatch replied.

" ' Tracked on a Bicycle ' sounds good to me. Eh ? "

Hatch nodded.

So arrangements were concluded, and then and there Professor Van Dusen gave definite and conclusive instructions to the champion. While these apparently bore broadly on the problem in hand they conveyed absolutely no inkling of his plan to the reporter. At the end the champion arose to go.

" You're a most extraordinary young man, Mr. Thalhauer," commented the scientist, not without admiration for the sturdy, powerful figure.

And as Hatch accompanied the champion out of the room and down the steps, Jimmie smiled with easy grace " Nutty old guy, ain't he ? "

*   *   *   *   *

Night ! Utter blackness, relieved only by a white, ribbon-like road which winds away mistily under a starless sky. Shadowy hedges line either side, and occasionally a tree thrusts itself upward out of the sombreness. The murmur of human voices in the shadows, then the crackling-chug of an engine and a motor-car moves slowly, without lights, into the road. There is the sudden clatter of an engine at high speed, and the car rushes away.

From the hedge comes the faint rustle of leaves as of wind stirring, then a figure moves impalpably. A moment and it becomes a separate entity ; a quick movement and the creak of a leather bicycle saddle. Silently the single figure, bent low over the handle bars, moves after the car with ever-increasing momentum.

Then a long, desperate race. For mile after mile, mile after mile the car goes on. The silent cyclist has crept up almost to the rear axle and hangs there doggedly as a racer to his pacer. On and on they rush together through the darkness, the chauffeur moving with a perfect knowledge of his road, the single rider behind clinging on grimly with set teeth. The powerful piston-like legs move up and down to the beat of the engine.

At last, with dust-dry throat and stinging, aching eyes the cyclist feels the pace slacken and instantly he drops back out of sight. It is only by sound that he follows now. The car stops ; the cyclist is lost in the shadows.

For two or three hours the car stands deserted and silent. At last the voices are heard again, the car stirs, moves away, and the cyclist drops in behind. Another race, which leads off in another direction. Finally, from a knoll, the lights of a city are seen. Ten minutes elapse, the motor-car stops, the head lights flare up, and more leisurely it proceeds on its way.

*   *   *   *   *

On the following evening Professor Van Dusen and Hutchinson Hatch called upon Fielding Stanwood, President of the Fordyce National Bank. Mr. Stanwood locked at them with interrogative eyes.

" We called to inform you, Mr. Stanwood," explained Professor Van Dusen " that a box of securities, probably United States bonds, is missing from your bank."

" What ? " exclaimed Mr. Stanwood, and his face paled. " Robbery ? "

" I only know the bonds were taken out of the vault to-night by Joseph Marsh, your assistant cashier," said the scientist, " and that he, together with three other men, left the bank with the box and are now at—a place I can name."

Mr. Stanwood was staring at him in amazement.

" You know where they are ? " he demanded.

" I said I did," replied the scientist, shortly.

" Then we must inform the police at once, and——"

" I don't know that there has been an actual crime," interrupted the scientist. " I do know that every night for a week these bonds have been taken out, through the connivance of your watchman, and in each instance have been returned, intact, before morning. They will be returned to-night. Therefore I would advise, if you act, not to do so until the four men return with the bonds."

It was a singular party which met in the private office of President Stanwood at the bank just after midnight. Marsh and three companions, formally under arrest, were present, as were President Stanwood, Professor Van Dusen, and

Hutchinson Hatch, besides detectives. Marsh had the bonds under his arms when he was taken. He talked freely when questioned.

"I will admit," he said without hesitation, "that I have acted beyond my rights in removing the bonds from the vault here, but there is no ground for prosecution. I am a responsible officer of this bank and have violated no trust. Nothing is missing, nothing is stolen. Every bond that went out of the bank is here."

"But why—why did you take the bonds?" demanded Mr. Stanwood.

Marsh shrugged his shoulders.

"It's what has been called a 'get-rich-quick' scheme," said Professor Van Dusen. "Mr. Hatch and I made some investigations to-day. Mr. Marsh and these other three are interested in a business venture which is ethically dishonest but which is within the law. They have sought backing for the scheme amounting to about a million dollars. Those four or five men of means with whom they have discussed the matter have called each night for a week at Marsh's country place. It was necessary to make them believe that there was already a million or so in the scheme, so these bonds were borrowed and represented to be owned by themselves. They were taken to and fro between the bank and his home in a kind of motor-car. This is really what happened, based on knowledge which Mr. Hatch has gathered, and what I myself developed by the use of a little logic."

And his statement of the affair proved to be correct. Marsh and the others admitted it. It was while Professor Van Dusen was homeward bound that he explained the phantom car affair to Hatch.

"The phantom car, as you call it," he said, "is the vehicle in which the bonds were moved about. The phantom idea came merely by chance. On the night the vehicle was first noticed it was rushing along—we'll say to reach Marsh's house in time for an appointment. A road map will show you that the most direct line from the bank to Marsh's was through The Trap. If an automobile should go half way through there, then cut across the Stocker estate to the other road the distance would be lessened by a good five miles. This saving at first was, of course, valuable, so the car in which they rushed into The Trap was merely taken across the Stocker estate to the road in front. Of course they always returned to the bank by another route.

"But how?" demanded Hatch. "There's no road there."

"I learned by 'phone from Mr. Stocker that there is a narrow walk from a very narrow foot-gate in Stocker's wall on The Trap leading through the grounds to the other road. The phantom car wasn't really a motor at all—it was merely two motor cycles arranged with seats and a steering apparatus. The French Army has been experimenting with them. The motor cycles are, of course, separate machines, and as such it was easy to trundle them through a narrow gate and across to the other road. The seats are light; they can be carried under the arm. I knew instantly what the 'phantom' must be when I knew there was no road through the wall—only a gateway."

"Oh!" exclaimed Hatch suddenly, then after a minute: "But what did Jimmie Thalhauer do for you?"

"He waited in the road at the other end of the footpath—the opposite end from The Trap," the scientist explained. "When the auto was brought through and put together he followed it to Marsh's home and from there to the bank. The rest of it you and I worked out to-day. It's merely logic, Mr. Hatch, logic."

There was a pause.

"That Mr. Thalhauer is really a marvellous young man, Mr. Hatch, don't you think?"

Professor Van Dusen's Problems.

By JACQUES FUTRELLE.

V.—THE PROBLEM OF THE MOTOR-BOAT.

CAPTAIN HANK BARBER, master mariner, gripped the bow-rail of the *Liddy Ann* and peered off through the semi-fog of the early morning at a dark streak slashing along through the gray-green waters. It was a motor-boat of long, graceful lines ; and a single figure, that of a man, sat upright at her helm, staring uncompromisingly ahead. She nosed through a roller, staggered a little, righted herself, and sped on as a sheet of spray swept over her. The helmsman sat motionless, heedless of the stinging splash of wind-driven water in his face.

"She sure is a-goin' some," remarked Captain Hank reflectively. "By ginger ! if she keeps it up into Boston Harbour she won't stop this side o' the Public Gardens."

Captain Hank watched the boat curiously until she was swallowed up, lost, in the mist, then turned to his own affairs. He was a couple of miles out of Boston Harbour, going in ; it was six o'clock of a gray morning. A few minutes after the disappearance of the motor-boat, Captain Hank's attention was attracted by the hoarse shriek of a whistle two hundred yards away. He dimly traced through the mist the gigantic lines of a great vessel—it seemed to be a ship of war.

It was only a few minutes after Captain Hank lost sight of the motor-boat that she was again sighted—this time as she flashed into Boston Harbour at full speed. She fled past, almost under, the prow of a pilot-boat bound out, and was hailed. At the mess-table later the pilot's man on watch made a remark about her :

"Goin' ! Well, wasn't she, though ! Never saw one thing pass so close to another in my life without scrubbin' the paint offen it. She was so close up I could touch her, and when I spoke her the feller didn't even look up—just kept a-goin'. I told *him* a few things that was good for his soul."

Inside Boston Harbour the motor-boat performed a miracle. Pursuing a course which was singularly erratic and at a speed more than dangerous, she reeled on through the surge of the sea, regardless alike of fog, the proximity of other vessels, and the heavy wash from larger craft. Here she narrowly missed a tug ; there she skimmed by a slow-moving tramp, and a warning shout was raised ; a fisherman swore at her as only a fisherman can. And finally, when she passed into a clear space, headed for a dock at top speed, she was the most unanimously condemned craft that ever came into Boston Harbour.

"Guess that's a through boat," remarked an aged salt facetiously, as he gazed at her from a dock. "If that fool don't take some o' the speed offen her she'll go through all right—wharf an' all."

Still, the man in the boat made no motion ; the whizz of her motor, plainly heard in a sudden silence, was undiminished. Suddenly the tumult of warning was renewed. Only a chance would prevent a smash. Then big John Dawson appeared on the string piece of the dock. Big John had a voice that was noted from Newfoundland to Norfolk for its depth and width, and possessed objurgatory powers which were at once awe and admiration of the fishing fleet.

"You ijit !" he bellowed at the impassive helmsman. "Shut off that power and throw yer hellum !"

There was no response ; the boat came on directly toward the dock where Big John and his fellows were gathered. The fishermen and loungers saw that a crash was coming, and scattered from the string piece.

"The stupid fool !" said Big John, resignedly.

Then came the crash, the rending of timbers, and silence save for the grinding whirr of the motor. Big John ran to the end of the wharf and peered down. The speed of the motor had driven the boat half-way up on a float, which careened perilously. The man had been thrown forward, and lay huddled up, face downward and motionless, on the float. The dirty water lapped at him greedily.

Big John shinned down to the float, crept cautiously to the huddled figure, and turned it face upward. He gazed for an instant into wide-staring eyes, then turned to the curious ones peering down from the dock.

"No wonder he didn't stop," he said, in an awed tone. "The fool is dead!"

Willing hands gave aid, and after a minute the lifeless figure lay on the dock. It was that of a man in uniform—apparently the uniform of a foreign navy. He seemed about forty-five years old, large and powerful of frame, with the sun-browned face of a seaman. The jet black of moustache and goatee was startling against the dead colour of the face. The hair was tinged with grey; and on the back of the left hand was a single letter "D" tattooed in blue.

"He's French," said Big John, authoritatively, "an' that's the uniform of a French naval captain." He looked puzzled a moment as he stared at the figure. "An' ther' ain't been a French man-o'-war in Boston Harbour for six months."

After a while the police came, and with them Detective Mallory, the big man of the Bureau of Criminal Investigation; and finally Dr. Clough, Medical Examiner. While the detective questioned the fishermen and those who had witnessed the crash, Dr. Clough examined the body.

"An autopsy will be necessary," he announced as he arose.

"How long has he been dead?" asked the detective.

"Eight or ten hours, I should say. The cause of death doesn't appear. There is no shot or knife wound, so far as I can see."

Detective Mallory closely examined the dead man's clothing. There was no name or tailor mark; the linen was new; the name of the maker of the shoes had been cut out with a knife. There was nothing in the pockets, not a piece of paper nor even a vagrant coin.

Then Detective Mallory turned his attention to the boat. Both hull and motor were of French manufacture. Long, deep scratches on each side showed how the name had been removed. Inside the boat the detective saw something white and picked it up. It was a handkerchief —a lady's handkerchief—with the initials "E. M. B." in a corner.

"Ah, a woman's in it," soliloquised the detective.

Then the body was removed and carefully secluded from the prying eyes of the Press. Thus no picture of the dead man appeared. Hutchinson Hatch, reporter, and others asked many questions. Detective Mallory hinted vaguely at international questions. The dead man was a French officer, he said, and there might be something back of it.

"I can't tell you all of it," he said wisely; "but my theory is complete. It is murder. The victim was captain of a French man-o'-war. His body was placed in a motor-boat, possibly a part of the fittings of the war-ship, and the boat set adrift. I can say no more."

"Your theory is complete, then," Hatch remarked casually, "except the name of the man, the manner of death, the motive, the name of his ship, the presence of the handkerchief, and the precise reason why the body should be disposed of in this fashion instead of being cast into the sea?"

The detective snorted. Hatch went away to make some inquiries on his own account. Within half a dozen hours he had satisfied himself by telegraph that no French war-craft had been within five hundred miles of Boston for six months. Thus the mystery grew deeper. A thousand questions to which there seemed no answer arose.

It was at this point, the day following the events related, that the problem of the motor-boat came to the attention of Professor Van Dusen, the world's foremost analytical brain. The scientist listened interestedly, but petulantly, to the story Hatch told.

"Has there been an autopsy yet?" he asked at last.

"It is set for eleven o'clock to-day," replied the reporter; "it is now after ten."

"I shall attend it," said the scientist.

Medical Examiner Clough welcomed the eminent Professor Van Dusen's proffer of assistance in his capacity of M.D., while Hatch and other reporters im-

"THE MAN HAD BEEN THROWN FORWARD, AND LAY HUDDLED UP."

patiently cooled their toes on the kerb. In two hours the autopsy had been completed. Professor Van Dusen amused himself by studying the insignia on the dead man's uniform, leaving it to Dr. Clough to make a startling statement to the Press. The man had not been murdered ; he had died of heart-failure. There was no poison in the stomach, nor was there a knife or pistol wound.

Then the inquisitive Press poured in a flood of questions. Who had scratched off the name of the boat ? Dr. Clough didn't know. Why had it been scratched off ? Still he didn't know. How did it happen that the name of the maker of the shoes had been cut out ? He shrugged his shoulders. What did the handkerchief have to do with it ? Really, he couldn't conjecture. Was there any inkling of the dead man's identity ? Not so far as he knew. Any scar on the body which might lead to identification ? No.

Hatch made a few mental comments on officials in general, and skilfully steered the Professor away from the other reporters.

" Did that man die of heart-failure ? " he asked flatly.

" He did not," was the curt reply ; " it was poison."

" But the Medical Examiner specifically stated that there was no poison in the stomach ? " persisted the reporter.

The scientist did not reply. Hatch struggled with, and suppressed, a desire to ask more questions. On reaching home the Professor's first act was to consult an encyclopædia. After several minutes he turned to the reporter.

" Of course, the idea of a natural death in this case is absurd," he said shortly. " Every fact is against it. Now, Mr. Hatch, please get for me all the local and New York newspapers of the day the body was found—not the day after. Send or bring them to me, then come again at five this afternoon."

" But—but—— " Hatch blurted.

" I can say nothing until I know all the facts," interrupted Van Dusen.

Hatch personally delivered the specified newspapers into the hands of the Professor—this man who never read newspapers—and went away. It was an afternoon of agony, an agony of impatience.

Promptly at five o'clock he was ushered into Professor Van Dusen's laboratory. He sat half-smothered in newspapers, and popped up out of the heap aggressively.

" It was murder, Mr. Hatch," he exclaimed suddenly. " Murder — by an extraordinary method."

" Who—who is the man ? How was he killed ? " asked Hatch.

" His name is—— " the scientist began, then paused. " I presume your office has the book, ' Who's Who in America ' ? Please 'phone and ask them to give you the record of Langham Dudley."

" Is he the dead man ? " Hatch demanded quickly.

" I don't know," was the reply.

Hatch went to the telephone. Ten minutes later he returned, to find the Professor dressed to go out.

" Langham Dudley is a shipowner, fifty-one years old," the reporter read from notes he had taken. " He was once a sailor before the mast, and later became a shipowner in a small way. He was successful in his small undertakings, and for fifteen years has been a millionaire. He has a certain social position, partly by the aid of his wife, whom he married a year ago. She was Edith Marston Belding, a daughter of the famous Belding family. He has an estate on the North Shore."

" Very good," commented the scientist. " Now we will find out something about how this man was killed."

At North Station they took train for a small place on the North Shore, thirty-five miles from Boston. There Professor Van Dusen made some inquiries, and finally they entered a lumbersome vehicle and drove off. After a drive of half an hour through the dark they saw the lights of what seemed to be a pretentious country place. Somewhere off to the right Hatch heard the roar of the restless ocean.

" Wait for us," commanded Van Dusen.

He ascended the steps, followed by Hatch, and rang. After a minute or so the door was opened and the light flooded out. Standing before them was a Japanese—a man of indeterminate age with the graven face of his race.

" Is Mr. Dudley in ? " asked The Thinking Machine.

" He has not that pleasure," replied

the Japanese; and Hatch smiled at the queerly turned phrase.

"Mrs. Dudley?" asked the scientist.

"Mrs. Dudley is attiring herself in clothing," replied the Japanese. "If you will be pleased to enter."

Professor Van Dusen handed him a card and was shown into a reception-room. The Japanese placed chairs for them with courteous precision, and disappeared. After a short pause there was the rustle of silken skirts on the stairs, and a woman —Mrs. Dudley—entered.

She was not pretty. She was stunning, rather—tall, of superb figure, and crowned with a glory of black hair.

"Mr. Van Dusen?" she asked, as she glanced at the card.

The Professor bowed low, albeit awkwardly. Mrs. Dudley sank down on a couch, and the two men resumed their seats. There was a little pause. Mrs. Dudley broke the silence at last.

"Well, Mr. Van Dusen, if you——" she began.

"You have not seen a newspaper for several days?" asked the Professor abruptly.

"No," she replied, wonderingly, almost smiling. "Why?"

"Can you tell me just where your husband is?"

He squinted at her in that aggressive way which was habitual. A quick flush crept into her face, and grew deeper at the sharp scrutiny. Inquiry lay in her eyes.

"I don't know," she replied at last. "In Boston, I presume."

"You haven't seen him since the night of the ball?"

"No; I think it was half-past one o'clock that night."

"Is his motor-boat here?"

"Really I don't know. I presume it is. May I ask the purpose of this questioning?"

The Professor continued to squint at her for half a minute. Hatch was uncomfortable, half-resentful even, at the sharp, cold tone of his companion.

"On the night of the ball," the scientist went on, passing the question, "Mr. Dudley cut his left arm just above the wrist. It was only a slight wound. A piece of court-plaster was put on it. Do

you know if he put it on himself? If not, who did?"

"I put it on," replied Mrs. Dudley, unhesitatingly, wonderingly.

"And whose court-plaster was it?"

"Mine—some I had in my dressing-room. Why?"

The scientist arose and paced across the floor, glancing once out of the hall-door. Mrs. Dudley looked at Hatch inquiringly, and was about to speak when the Professor stopped beside her and placed his slim fingers on her wrist. She did not resent the action; was only curious, if one might judge from her eyes.

"Are you prepared for a shock?" the scientist asked.

"What is it?" she demanded in sudden terror. "This suspense——"

"Your husband is dead—murdered— poisoned," said the scientist, with sudden brutality. His fingers still lay on her pulse. "The court-plaster which you put on his arm, and which came from your room, was covered with a virulent poison which was instantly transfused into his blood."

Mrs. Dudley did not start or scream. Instead, she stared up at the Professor a moment, her face became pallid, a little shiver passed over her. Then she fell back on the couch in a dead faint.

"Good!" remarked Van Dusen, complacently; and then, as Hatch started up suddenly, "Shut that door."

The reporter did so. When he turned back his companion was leaning over the unconscious woman. After a moment he left her and went to a window, where he stood looking out. As Hatch watched, he saw the colour coming back into Mrs. Dudley's face. At last she opened her eyes.

"Don't get hysterical," Professor Van Dusen directed calmly. "I know you had nothing whatever to do with your husband's death. I want only a little assistance to find out who killed him."

"Oh, my God!" exclaimed Mrs. Dudley. "Dead! Dead!"

Suddenly tears leapt from her eyes, and for several minutes the two men respected her grief. When at last she raised her face her eyes were red, but there was a rigid expression about the mouth.

"If I can be of any service——" she began.

"Is this the boat-house I see from this window?" asked the Professor, irrelevantly; "that long low building, with a light over the door?"

"Yes," replied Mrs. Dudley.

"You say you don't know if the motor-boat is there now?"

"No, I don't."

"Will you ask your Japanese servant, and, if he doesn't know, let him go and see, please."

Mrs. Dudley arose and touched an electric button. After a moment the Japanese appeared at the door.

"Osaka, do you know if Mr. Dudley's motor-boat is in the boat-house?" she asked.

"No, honourable lady."

"Will you find out, please? Go yourself and see."

Osaka bowed low and left the room, closing the door gently behind him. The Professor again crossed to the window and sat down, staring out into the night. Mrs. Dudley asked questions, scores of them, and he answered them in order until she knew the details of the finding of her husband's body—that is, the details the public knew. She was interrupted by the reappearance of Osaka.

"I do not find the motor-boat in the house, honourable lady."

"That is all," said the scientist.

Again Osaka bowed, and retired.

"Now, Mrs. Dudley," resumed the Professor, almost gently, "we know your husband wore a French naval costume at the masked ball. May I ask what you wore?"

"It was a Queen Elizabeth costume," replied Mrs. Dudley, "very heavy, with a long train."

"And if you could let me see a photograph of Mr. Dudley?"

Mrs. Dudley left the room, returning immediately with a cabinet photograph. Hatch and the scientist looked at it together; it was unmistakably the man in the motor-boat.

"You can do nothing yourself," said the Professor at last, and he moved as if to go. "Within a few hours we shall have the guilty person. You may rest assured that your name will be in

no way brought into the matter unpleasantly."

Hatch glanced at his companion; he thought he detected a sinister note in the soothing voice, but the face expressed nothing. Mrs. Dudley ushered them into the hall. Osaka stood at the front door. They passed out, and the door closed behind them.

Hatch started down the steps, but the Professor stopped at the door and tramped up and down. The reporter turned back in astonishment. In the dim reflected light he saw the scientist's finger raised enjoining silence, then saw him lean forward suddenly with his ear pressed to the door. After a little he rapped gently. The door was opened by Osaka, who obeyed a beckoning motion of the scientist's hand and came out. Silently he was led off the verandah into the yard; he appeared in no way surprised.

"Your master, Mr. Dudley, has been murdered," said the Professor quietly to Osaka. "We know that Mrs. Dudley killed him," he went on, and Hatch stared at him in sudden amazement; "but I have told her she is not suspected. We are not officers, and cannot arrest her. Can you go with us to Boston, without the knowledge of anyone here, and tell what you know of the quarrel between husband and wife to the police?"

Osaka looked placidly into the eager face.

"I had the honour to believe that the circumstances would not be recognised," he said finally. "Since you know, I will go."

"We will drive down a little way and wait for you."

The Japanese disappeared into the house again. Hatch was too astounded to speak, but followed the Professor into the car. It drove away a hundred yards and stopped. After a few minutes an impalpable shadow came toward them through the night. The scientist peered out as it came up.

"Osaka?" he asked softly.

"Yes."

An hour later the three men were on a train, Boston-bound. Once comfortably settled, the scientist turned to the Japanese.

"Now, if you will, please tell me just

what happened on the night of the ball," he asked, " and the incidents leading up to the disagreement between Mr. and Mrs. Dudley."

" He drank elaborately," Osaka explained reluctantly, in his quaint English, " and when drinking he was brutal to the honourable lady. Twice with my own eyes I saw him strike her—once in Japan, where I entered his service while they were on their wedding journey, and once here. On the night of the ball he was immeasurably intoxicated, and when he danced he fell down to the floor. The honourable lady was chagrined and angry —she had been angry before. There was some quarrel which I am not comprehensive of. They had been widely divergent for several months. It was, of course, not prominent in the presence of others."

" And the cut on his arm where the court-plaster was applied ? " asked the scientist. " Just how did he get that ? "

" It was when he fell down," continued the Japanese. " He reached to embrace a carved chair, and the carved wood cut his arm. I assisted him to his feet, and the honourable lady sent me to her room to get court-plaster. I acquired it from her dressing-table, and she placed it on the cut."

" That makes the evidence against her absolutely conclusive," remarked the Professor, as if finally. There was a little pause, and then, " Do you happen to know just how Mrs. Dudley placed the body in the boat ? "

" I have not the honour of knowing how she did it," said Osaka. " Indeed, I am not comprehensive of anything that happened after the court-plaster was put on, except that Mr. Dudley was affected some way and went out of the house. Mrs. Dudley, too, was not in the ball-room for many minutes or so afterwards."

Hutchinson Hatch stared frankly into the face of the Professor. There was nothing to be read there. Still deeply thoughtful, Hatch heard the brakeman bawl " Boston ! " and mechanically followed the scientist and Osaka out of the station into a cab. They were driven immediately to police headquarters. Detective Mallory was just about to go home when they entered his office.

" It may enlighten you, Mr. Mallory," announced the scientist coldly, " to know that the man in the motor-boat was not a French naval officer who died of natural causes—he was Langham Dudley, a millionaire shipowner. He was murdered. It just happens that I know the person who did it."

The detective arose in astonishment and stared at the slight figure before him inquiringly ; he knew the man too well to dispute any assertion he might make.

" Who is the murderer ? " he asked.

The Professor closed the door, and the spring-lock clicked.

" That man there," he said calmly, turning on Osaka.

For one brief instant there was a pause and silence ; then the detective advanced upon the Japanese with hand outstretched. The agile Osaka leapt suddenly, as a snake strikes ; there was a quick, fierce struggle, and Detective Mallory sprawled on the floor. There had been just a twist of the wrist—a trick of jiu-jitsu—and Osaka had flung himself at the locked door. As he fumbled there, Hatch, deliberately and without compunction, raised a chair and brought it down on his head. Osaka sank down without a sound.

It was an hour before they brought him around. Meanwhile, the detective had patted and petted half-a-dozen suddenly acquired bruises, and had then searched Osaka. He found nothing to interest him save a small bottle. He uncorked it and started to smell it, when the Professor snatched it away.

" You fool ! that'll kill you," he exclaimed.

* * * * *

Osaka sat, lashed hand and foot to a chair, in Detective Mallory's office—so placed by the detective for safe keeping. His face was no longer expressionless ; there were fear and treachery and cunning there. So he listened perforce to the statement of the case by the Professor, who leaned back in his chair, squinting steadily upward, and with his long, slender fingers pressed together.

" Two and two make four, not sometimes but *all* the time," he began at last, as if disputing some previous assertion. " As the figure two, wholly disconnected from any other, gives small indication of a result, so is an isolated fact of little consequence. Yet that fact, added to another, and the resulting fact added to a third, and so on, will give a final result. That result, if every fact is considered, *must* be correct. Thus any problem may be solved by logic ; logic is inevitable. In this case the facts, considered singly, might have been compatible with either a natural death, suicide, or murder ; considered together, they proved murder. The climax of this proof was the removal of the maker's name from the dead man's shoes, and a fact strongly contributory was the attempt to destroy the identity of the boat. A subtle mind lay back of it all."

" I so regarded it," said Detective Mallory. " I was confident of murder until the Medical Examiner——"

" We prove a murder," the Professor went on serenely. " The method ? I was with Dr. Clough at the autopsy. There was no shot or knife wound, no poison in the stomach. Knowing there was murder, I sought further. Then I found the method in a slight, jagged wound on the left arm. It had been covered with court-plaster. The heart showed constriction without apparent cause, and while Dr. Clough examined it I took off this court-plaster. Its odour—an unusual one—told me that poison had been transfused in the blood through the wound. So two and two had made four.

" Then—what poison ? A knowledge of botany aided me. I recognised faintly the trace of an odour of a herb which is not only indigenous to, but grows exclusively, in Japan—thus a Japanese poison. Analysis later in my laboratory proved it *was* a Japanese poison, virulent, but necessarily slow to act in this case because it was not placed directly in an artery. The poison on the court-plaster and that you took from Osaka are identical."

The scientist uncorked the bottle and permitted a single drop of a green liquid to fall on his handkerchief. He allowed a minute or more for evaporation ; then handed it to Detective Mallory, who sniffed at it from a respectful distance. Then the Professor produced the bit of court-plaster he had taken from the dead man's arm, and again the detective sniffed.

" The same," the scientist resumed, as he touched a lighted match to the handkerchief and watched it crumble to ashes ; " and so powerful that in its pure state mere inhalation is fatal. I permitted Dr. Clough to make public his opinion —heart-failure—after the autopsy for obvious reasons. It would reassure the murderer, for instance, if he saw it printed, and, besides, Dudley did die from heart-failure—the poison caused it.

" Next came identification. Mr. Hatch learned that no French warship had been within hundreds of miles of Boston for months. The one seen by Captain Barber might have been one of our own. This man was supposed to be a French naval officer, and had been dead less than eight hours. Obviously he did not come from a ship of his own country. Then from where ?

" I know nothing of uniforms, yet I examined the insignia on the arms and shoulders closely, after which I consulted my encyclopædia. I learned that, while the uniform was more French than anything else, it was really the uniform of *no country*, because it was not correct. The insignia were mixed.

" Then what ? There were several possibilities. A fancy-dress ball seemed probable. Absolute accuracy would not be essential there. Where had there been a fancy-dress ball ? I trusted to the newspapers to tell me that. They did. A short dispatch from a place on the North Shore showed that on the night before the man was found dead there had been a fancy-dress ball at the Langham Dudley estate.

" Now, it is as necessary to remember *every* fact in solving a problem as it is to consider every figure in arithmetic. Dudley ! Here was the ' D ' tattooed on the dead man's hand. ' Who's Who ' showed that Langham Dudley married Edith Marston Belding. Here was the " E. M. B." on the handkerchief in the boat. Langham Dudley was a shipowner, had been a sailor, was a millionaire. Possibly this was his own boat, built in France."

Detective Mallory was staring into the eyes of the Professor in frank admiration. Osaka, to whom the narrative had thus far been impersonal, gazed— gazed as if fascinated. Hutchinson

"THERE HAD BEEN JUST A TWIST OF THE WRIST—A TRICK OF JIU-JITSU—AND OSAKA
HAD FLUNG HIMSELF AT THE LOCKED DOOR"

Hatch, reporter, was drinking in every word greedily.

"We went to the Dudley place," the scientist resumed after a moment. "This Japanese opened the door. Japanese poison! Two and two were still making four. But I was first interested in Mrs. Dudley. She showed no agitation, and told me frankly that she placed the court-plaster on her husband's arm, and that it came from her room. There was instantly a doubt as to her connection with the murder; her immediate frankness aroused it.

"Finally, with my hand on her pulse, which was normal, I told her as brutally as I could that her husband had been murdered. Her pulse jumped frightfully, and as I related the cause of death it wavered, weakened, and she fainted. Now, if she had *known* her husband was dead—even if she had killed him—a mere statement that he was dead would not have caused that pulse. Further, I doubt if she could have disposed of her husband's body in the motor-boat. He was a large man, and she is not a powerful woman; and the manner of her dress even was against this. Therefore we presume her innocent.

"And then? The Japanese Osaka here. I could see the door of the boat-house from the room where we were. Mrs. Dudley asked Osaka if Mr. Dudley's boat were in the house. He said he didn't know. Then she sent him to see. He returned and said the boat was not there, *yet he had not gone to the boat-house at all.* Ergo, he knew the boat was not there. He may have learned it from another servant, still it was a point against him."

Again the scientist paused and squinted at the Japanese. For a moment Osaka withstood the gaze, then his beady eyes shifted and he moved uncomfortably.

"I tricked Osaka into coming here by a ludicrously simple expedient," the Professor went on steadily. "On the train I asked if he knew just how Mrs. Dudley got the body of her husband into the boat. Remember, at this point he was not supposed to know that the body had been in a boat at all. He said he didn't know, and *by that very answer* admitted that he knew the body had been placed in the boat. He knew because he put it there in the

himself; he put the poison on the court-plaster when he went to get it. He didn't throw the body into the water, because he had sense enough to know if the tide didn't take it out it would rise.

"After the slight injury, Mr. Dudley evidently wandered out toward the boat-house. The poison was working, and perhaps he fell. Then this man removed all identifying marks, even to the name in the shoes, put the body in the boat, and turned on full power. He had a right to assume that the boat would be lost, or that the dead man would be thrown out. Wind and tide and a loose rudder brought it into Boston Harbour. I do not attempt to account for the presence of Mrs. Dudley's handkerchief in the boat. It might have gotten there in any one of a hundred ways."

"How did you know husband and wife had quarrelled?" asked Hatch.

"Surmise, to account for her not knowing where he was," replied the Professor. "If they had had a violent disagreement it was possible that he would have gone away without telling her, and she would not have been particularly worried—at least, up to the time we saw her. As it was, she presumed he was in Boston; perhaps Osaka here gave her that impression?"

The Professor stared at the Japanese curiously.

"Is that correct?" he asked.

Osaka did not answer.

"And the motive?" asked Detective Mallory, at last.

"Will you tell us just *why* you killed Mr. Dudley?" asked the Professor of the Japanese.

"I will not," exclaimed Osaka suddenly. It was the first time he had spoken.

"It probably had to do with a girl in Japan," explained the Professor, easily. "The murder had been a long-cherished project, such a one as revenge through love would have inspired."

It was a day or so later that Hutchinson Hatch called to inform Professor Van Dusen that Osaka had confessed, and had given his motive for the murder. It was not a nice story.

"One of the most astonishing things

to me," Hatch added, "is the complete case of circumstantial evidence against Mrs. Dudley, beginning with the quarrel and leading to the application of the poison with her own hands. I believe she could have been convicted on the actual circumstantial evidence had you not shown conclusively that Osaka did it."

"Circumstantial fiddlesticks!" snapped the Professor. "I wouldn't convict a yellow dog of stealing jam on circumstantial evidence alone, even if he had jam all over his nose." He squinted truculently at Hatch for a moment. "In the first place, well-behaved dogs don't eat jam," he added, more mildly.

Professor Van Dusen's Problems.

By JACQUES FUTRELLE.

VI.—THE STOLEN BANK-NOTES.

THERE was no mystery whatever about the identity of the man who, alone and unaided, robbed the Thirteenth National Bank of $109,437 in cash and $1.29 in postage stamps. It was "Mort" Dolan, an expert safe-cracker, albeit a young one, and he had made a clean sweep. Nor yet was there any mystery as to his whereabouts. He was safely in a cell at Police Head-quarters, having been captured within less than twelve hours after the robbery was discovered.

Dolan had offered no resistance to the officers when he was cornered, and had attempted no denial when questioned by Detective Mallory. He knew he had been caught fairly and squarely, and no argument was possible, so he confessed with a glow of pride at a job well done. It was four or five days after his arrest that the matter came to the attention of Professor van Dusen. Then the problem was——

But perhaps it were better to begin at the beginning.

* * * * *

Despite the fact that he was considerably less than thirty years old, "Mort" Dolan was a man for whom the police had a wholesome respect. He had a record, for he had started early. This robbery of the Thirteenth National was his "big" job, and was to have been his last. With the proceeds he had intended to take his wife, and quietly disappear beneath a full beard and an alias, in some place far removed from former haunts. But the mutability of human events is a matter of proverb. While the robbery as a robbery was a thoroughly artistic piece of work, and in full accordance with plans which had been worked out to the minutest detail months before, he had made one mistake. This was leaving behind him in the bank the can in which the nitro-glycerine had been bought. Through this carelessness he had been traced.

Dolan and his wife occupied three poor rooms in a poor tenement house. From the moment the police got a description of the person who bought the explosive they were confident, for they knew their man. Therefore four clever detectives were on watch about the poor tenement. Neither Dolan nor his wife was there when they arrived, but from the condition of things in the rooms the police believed that they intended to return, so they took up their positions hopefully.

Unsuspecting enough, for his one mistake in the robbery had not recurred to him, Dolan came along just about dusk and started up the five steps to the front door of the tenement. It just happened that he glanced back and saw a head drawn suddenly behind a projecting pillar. But the electric light glared strongly there, and Dolan recognised Detective Downey, one of many men who revolved around Detective Mallory within a limited orbit. Now Dolan did not start nor do anything foolish; he paused a moment and rolled a cigarette while he thought it over. Perhaps, instead of entering, it would be best to stroll on down the street, turn a corner and make a dash for it! But just at that moment he spied another head in the direction of contemplated flight. That was Detective Blanton.

Deeply thoughtful Dolan smoked half the cigarette and stared blankly in front of him. He knew of a back door opening on an alley. Perhaps the detectives had not thought to guard that! He tossed his cigarette away, entered the house with affected unconcern and closed the door. Running lightly through the long, unclean hall which extended the full length of the building, he flung open the back door. He turned back instantly— just outside he had seen and recognised Detective Cunningham.

Then he had an inspiration! The roof! The building was four storeys. He ran up the four flights lightly but rapidly, and was half way up the last, which led to the opening in the roof, when he stopped. From above he caught the whiff of a bad cigar, then the measured tread of heavy boots. Another detective! With a sickening depression at his heart Dolan came softly down the stairs again, opened the door of his flat with a latch-key and entered.

Then and there he sat down to figure it all out. There seemed no escape for him. Every way out was blocked, and it was only a question of time before they would close in on him. He imagined now they were only waiting for his wife's return. He could fight for his freedom, of course—even kill one, per-haps two, of the detectives who were waiting for him. But that would only mean his own death. If he tried to run for it past either of the detectives he would get a shot in the back. And, besides, murder was repugnant to Dolan's artistic soul. It did not do any good. But could he warn Isabel, his wife? He feared she would walk into the trap as he had done, and she had had no con-nection of any sort with the affair.

Then, from a fear that his wife would return, there swiftly came a fear that she would not. He suddenly remembered that it was necessary for him to see her. The police could not connect her with the robbery in any way; they could only hold her for a time, and then would be com-pelled to free her, for her innocence of this particular crime was beyond question. And if he were taken before she returned she would be left penniless; and that was a thing which Dolan dreaded to con-template. There was a spark of human tenderness in his heart, and in prison it would be comforting to know that she was well cared for. If she would only come now he would tell her where the money—— !

For ten minutes Dolan considered the question in all possible lights. A letter telling her where the money was? No. It would inevitably fall into the hands of the police. A cipher? She would never get it. How? How? How? Every moment he expected a clamour at the door which would mean that the police had come for him. They knew he was cornered. Whatever he did must be done quickly. Dolan took a long breath, and started to roll another cigarette. With the thin white paper held in his left hand, and tobacco pouch raised in the other, he had an inspiration.

For a little more than an hour after that he was left alone. Finally his quick ear caught the shuffle of stealthy feet in the hall, then came an imperative rap on the door. The police had evidently feared to wait longer. Dolan was leaning over a sewing machine when the summons came. Instinctively his hand closed on his revolver, then he tossed it aside and walked to the door.

" Well ? " he demanded.

" Let us in, Dolan," came the reply.

" That you, Downey ? " Dolan in-quired.

" Yes. Now don't make any mistakes, Mort. There are three of us here, and Cunningham is in the alley watching your windows. There's no way out."

For one instant—only an instant—Dolan hesitated. It was not that he was repentant ; it was not that he feared prison—it was regret at being caught. He had planned it all so differently, and the little woman would be heart-broken. Finally, with a quick backward glance at the sewing machine, he opened the door. Three revolvers were thrust into his face with a unanimity that spoke well for the police opinion of the man. Dolan promptly raised his hands over his head.

" Oh, put down your guns," he ex-postulated. " I'm not crazy. My gun is over on the couch there."

Detective Downey, by a personal search, corroborated this statement, then the revolvers were lowered.

" The chief wants you," he said. " It's about that Thirteenth National Bank robbery."

" All right," said Dolan, calmly, and he held out his hands for the steel nippers.

" Now, Mort," said Downey, ingratia-tingly, " you can save us a lot of trouble by telling us where the money is."

" Doubtless I could," was the am-biguous response.

Detective Downey looked at him and understood. Cunningham was called in from the alley. He and Downey re-mained in the apartment, and the other two men led Dolan away. In the natural course of events the prisoner appeared before Detective Mallory at Police Headquarters. They were well acquainted, professionally.

Dolan told everything frankly from the inception of the plan to the actual completion of the crime. The detective sat with his feet on his desk listen'ng. At the end he leaned forward towards the prisoner.

"And where is the money?" he asked.

Dolan paused long enough to roll a cigarette.

"That's my business," he responded, pleasantly.

"You might just as well tell us," insisted Detective Mallory. "We shall find it, of course, and it will save us trouble."

"I'll just bet you a hat you don't find it," replied Dolan, and there was a glitter of triumph in his eyes. "On the level, between man and man now, I will bet you a hat that you never find that money."

"You're on," replied Detective Mallory. He looked keenly at his prisoner, and his prisoner stared back without a quiver. "Did your wife get away with it?"

From the question Dolan surmised that she had not been arrested.

"No," he answered.

"Is it in your flat?"

"Downey and Cunningham are searching now," was the rejoinder. "They will report what they find."

There was silence for several minutes

"'THAT YOU, DOWNEY?' DOLAN INQUIRED"
(p. 619).

as the two men—officer and prisoner—stared each at the other. When a thief takes refuge in a refusal to answer questions he becomes a difficult subject to handle. There was the "third degree," of course, but Dolan was the kind of man who would only laugh at that; the kind of man from whom anything less than physical torture could not bring a statement if he did not choose to make it. Detective Mallory was perfectly aware of this dogged trait in the man's character.

"It's this way, chief," explained Dolan at last. "I robbed the bank, I got the money, and it's now where you will never find it. I did it by myself, and am willing to take my medicine. Nobody helped me. My wife—I knew your men waited for her before they took me—my wife knows nothing on earth about it. She had no connection with the thing at all, and she can prove it. That's all I'm going to say. You might just as well make up your mind to it."

Detective Mallory's eyes snapped.

"You will tell where that money is," he blustered, "or—or I'll see that you get——"

"Twenty years is the absolute limit," interrupted Dolan quietly. "I expect to get twenty years—that's the worst you can do for me."

The detective stared at him hard.

"And besides," Dolan went on, "I won't be lonesome when I get where you're going to send me. I've got lots of friends there—been there before. One of the jailors is the best bridge player I ever met."

Like most men who find themselves balked at the outset Detective Mallory sought to appease his indignation by heaping invective upon the prisoner, by threats, by promises, by wheedling, by bluster. It was all the same. Dolan remained silent. Finally he was led away and locked up.

A few minutes later Downey and Cunningham appeared. One glance told their chief that they could not enlighten him as to the whereabouts of the stolen money.

"Have you any idea where it is ? " he demanded.

"No, but I have a very definite idea where it *isn't*," replied Downey grimly. " It isn't in that flat. There's not one square inch of it that we didn't go over—not one object there that we didn't tear to pieces looking. It simply isn't there. He hid it somewhere before we got him."

"Well, take all the men you want and keep at it," instructed Detective Mallory. " One of you, by the way, had better bring in Dolan's wife. I am fairly certain that she had nothing to do with it, but she might know something, and I can bluff a woman." Detective Mallory announced that accomplishment as if it were a thing to be proud of. " There's nothing to do now but get the money. Meanwhile I'll see that Dolan isn't permitted to communicate with anybody."

"There is always the chance," suggested Downey, " that a man as clever as Dolan could in a cipher letter, or by some seemingly innocent remark, inform her where the money is if we assume she doesn't know, and that should be guarded against."

"It will be guarded against," declared Detective Mallory emphatically. " Dolan will not be permitted to see or talk to anyone for the present—not even a lawyer. He may weaken later on."

But day succeeded day and Dolan showed no signs of weakening. His wife, meanwhile, had been apprehended and subjected to the " third degree." When this ordeal was over the net result was that Detective Mallory was convinced that she had had nothing whatever

to do with the robbery, and had not the faintest idea where the money was. Half a dozen times Dolan asked permission to see her or to write to her. Each time the request was curtly refused.

Newspaper men, with and without inspiration, had sought the money vainly ; and the police were now seeking to trace the movements of " Mort " Dolan from the moment of the robbery until the moment of his appearance on the steps of the house where he lived. In this way they hoped to get an inkling of where the money had been hidden, for the idea of the money being in the flat had been abandoned. Dolan simply would not say anything. Finally, one day, Hutchinson Hatch, reporter, made an exhaustive search of Dolan's flat for the fourth time, then went over to Police Headquarters to talk it over with Mallory. While there President Ashe and two directors of the victimised bank appeared. They were worried.

"Is there any trace of the money ? " asked Mr. Ashe.

"Not yet," responded Detective Mallory.

" Well, could we talk to Dolan a few minutes ? "

" If we didn't get anything out of him you won't," said the detective. " But it won't do any harm. Come along."

Dolan did not seem particularly glad to see them. He came to the bars of his cell and peered through. It was only when Mr. Ashe was introduced to him as the President of the Thirteenth National Bank that he seemed to take any interest in his visitors. This interest took the form of a grin. Mr. Ashe evidently had something of importance on his mind, and was seeking the happiest method of expression. Once or twice he spoke aside to his companions, and Dolan watched them curiously. At last he turned to the prisoner.

" You admit that you robbed the bank ? " he asked.

" There's no need of denying it," replied Dolan.

" Well," and Mr. Ashe hesitated a moment, " the Board of Directors held a meeting this morning, and speaking on their behalf I want to say something. If you will inform us of the whereabouts of the money we will, upon its recovery, exert every effort within our power to have your sentence cut in half. In other words, as I understand it, you have given the police no trouble, you have confessed the crime, and this, with the return of the money, would weigh for you when sentence is pronounced. Say the maximum is twenty years, we might be able to get you off with ten if we get the money."

Detective Mallory looked doubtful. He realised, perhaps, the futility of such a promise, yet he was silent. The proposition might draw out something on which to proceed.

"Can't see it," said Dolan at last. "It's this way. I'm twenty-seven years old. I'll get twenty years. About two of that'll come off for good behaviour, so I'll really get eighteen years. At the end of that time I'll come out with one hundred and nine thousand dollars odd—rich for life and able to retire at forty-five years. In other words, while in prison I'll be working for a good, stiff salary—something really worth while. Very few men are able to retire at forty-five."

Mr. Ashe readily realised the truth of this statement. It was the point of view of a man to whom mere prison has few terrors—a man content to remain immured for twenty years for a consideration. He turned and spoke aside to the two directors again.

"But I'll tell you what I will do," said Dolan, after a pause. "If you'll fix it so that I get only two years, say, I'd give you half the money."

There was silence. Detective Mallory strolled along the corridor beyond the view of the prisoner and summoned President Ashe to his side by a jerk of his head.

"Agree to that," he said. "Perhaps he'll really give up."

"But it wouldn't be possible to arrange it, would it?" asked Mr. Ashe.

"Certainly not," said the detective, "but agree to it. Get your money, if you can, and then we'll nail him anyhow."

Mr. Ashe stared at him a moment, vaguely indignant at the treachery of the thing; then greed triumphed. He walked back to the cell.

"We'll agree to that, Mr. Dolan," he said briskly. "Fix a two years' sentence for you in return for half the money."

Dolan smiled a little.

"All right, go ahead," he said. "When sentence of two years is pronounced, and a first-class lawyer arranges it for me so that the matter can never be reopened, I'll tell you where you can get your half."

"But of course you must tell us that now," said Mr. Ashe.

Dolan smiled cheerfully. It was a taunting, insinuating, accusing sort of smile, and it informed the bank president that the duplicity contemplated was discovered. Mr. Ashe was silent for a moment, then blushed.

"Nothing doing," said Dolan, and he retired into a recess of his cell as if his interest in the matter were at an end.

"But—but we need the money now," stammered Mr. Ashe. "It was a large sum, and the theft has crippled us considerably."

"All right," said Dolan carelessly. "The sooner I get two years the sooner you get it."

"How could it be—be fixed?"

"I'll leave that to you."

That was all. The bank president and the two directors went out fuming impotently. Mr. Ashe paused in Detective Mallory's office long enough for a final word.

"Of course, it was brilliant work on the part of the police to capture Dolan," he said caustically, "but it isn't doing us a particle of good. All I see now is that we lose a hundred and nine thousand dollars."

"It looks very much like it," assented the detective, "unless we find it."

"Well, why *don't* you find it?"

Detective Mallory had to give it up.

"What did Dolan do with the money?" Hutchinson Hatch was asking of Professor van Dusen. The distinguished scientist and logician was sitting with his head pillowed on a cushion, and with squint eyes turned upward. "It isn't in the flat. Everything indicates that it was hidden somewhere else."

"And Dolan's wife?" inquired the Professor in his perpetually irritated

(Drawn by STEVEN SPURRIER.)

"'WE'LL AGREE TO THAT, MR. DOLAN,' HE SAID BRISKLY. 'FIX A TWO-YEARS' SENTENCE FOR YOU IN RETURN FOR HALF THE MONEY.'"

voice. " It seems conclusive that she has no idea where it is ? "

" She has been put through the ' third degree,' " explained the reporter, " and if she had known she would probably have told."

" Is she living in the flat now ? "

" No ! She is staying with her sister. The flat is under lock and key—Mallory has the key. He has shown the utmost care in everything he has done. Dolan has not been permitted to write to or see his wife for fear he would let her know someway where the money is ; he has not been permitted to communicate with anybody at all, not even a lawyer. He did see President Ashe and two directors of the bank, but naturally he wouldn't give them a message for his wife."

The Professor was silent. For five, ten, twenty minutes he sat with long, slender fingers pressed tip to tip, squinting unblinkingly at the ceiling. Hatch waited patiently.

" Of course," said the scientist at last, " one hundred and nine thousand dollars, even in large bills, would make a considerable bundle, and would be extremely difficult to hide in a place that has been gone over so often. We may suppose, therefore, that it isn't in the flat. What have the detectives learned as to Dolan's whereabouts after the robbery, and before he was taken ? "

" Nothing," replied Hatch, " nothing, absolutely. He seemed to disappear off the earth for a time. That time, I suppose, was when he was disposing of the money. His plans were evidently well laid."

" It would be possible, of course, by the simple rules of logic, to sit still here and ultimately locate the money," remarked the Professor musingly, " but it would take a long time. We might begin, for instance, with the idea that he contemplated flight. When ? By rail or steamer ? The answers to those questions would, in a way, enlighten us as to the probable location of the money, because, remember it would have to be placed where it was readily accessible in case of flight. But the process would be a long one. Perhaps it would be best to make Dolan tell us where he hid it."

" It would if he would tell," agreed the reporter, " but he is reticent to a degree that is maddening when the money is mentioned."

" Naturally," remarked the scientist. " That really doesn't matter. I have no doubt he will inform me."

So Hatch and the Professor called upon Detective Mallory. They found him in deep abstraction. He glanced up at the intrusion with an appearance, almost, of relief. He knew intuitively what it was.

" If you can find out where that money is, Professor," he declared emphatically, " I'll—I'll—well, you can't."

The Professor squinted into the official eyes thoughtfully, and the corners of his straight mouth were drawn down disapprovingly.

" I think perhaps there has been a little too much caution here, Mr. Mallory," he said. " I have no doubt Dolan will inform me as to where the money is. As I understand it his wife is practically without means ? "

" Yes," was the reply. " She is living with her sister."

" And he has asked several times to be permitted to write to or see her ? "

" Yes, dozens of times."

" Well, now suppose you *do* let him see her ? " suggested the Professor.

" Lord, that's just what he wants," blurted the detective. " If he ever sees her I know he will, in some way, by something he says, by a gesture or a look, inform her where the money is. As it is now I know she does not know where it is."

" Well, if he informs her won't he also inform us ? " demanded the Professor tartly. " If Dolan wants to convey knowledge of the whereabouts of the money to his wife let him talk to her— let him give her the information. I dare say if she is clever enough to interpret a spoken word as a clue to where the money is, I am too."

The detective thought that over. He knew of old this crabbed little scientist with the enormous head ; and he knew, too, some of the amazing results he had achieved by methods wholly unlike those known to the police. But in this case he was frankly in doubt.

" This way," the Professor continued. " Get the wife here, let her pass Dolan's cell and speak to him so that he will know that it is she, then let her carry on a conversation with him while she is beyond his sight. Have a stenographer, without the knowledge of either, take down just what is said, word for word. Give me a transcript of the conversation, and hold the wife on some pretext until I can study it a little. If he gives her a clue I'll get the money."

There was not the slightest trace of egotism in the irritable tone. It seemed merely a statement of fact. Detective Mallory, looking at the wizened face of the logician, was doubtfully hopeful, and at last he consented to the experiment. The wife was sent for and came eagerly, a stenographer was placed in the cell adjoining Dolan's, and Mrs. Dolan was led along the corridor. As she paused in front of Dolan's cell he started toward her with an exclamation. Then she was led on a little way out of his sight.

With face pressed close against the bars Dolan glowered out upon Detective Mallory and Hatch. An expression of awful ferocity leapt into his eyes.

"What're you doing with her?" he demanded.

"Mort, Mort," she called.

"Bell, is it you?" he asked in turn.

"They told me you wanted to talk to me," she explained. She was panting fiercely as she struggled to shake off the hands which held her beyond his sight.

"What sort of a game is this, Mallory?" demanded the prisoner.

"You've wanted to talk to her," Mallory replied, "now go ahead. You may talk, but you must not see her."

"Oh, that's it, eh?" snarled Dolan. "What did you bring her here for then? Is she under arrest?"

"Mort, Mort," came his wife's voice again. "They won't let me come where I can see you."

There was utter silence for a moment. Hatch was overpowered by a feeling that he was intruding on a family tragedy, and tiptoed beyond reach of Dolan's roving eyes to where the Professor was sitting on a stool, twiddling his fingers. After a moment the detective joined them.

"Bell?" called Dolan again. It was almost a whisper.

"Don't say anything, Mort," she panted. "Cunningham and Blanton are holding me—the others are listening."

"I don't want to say anything," said Dolan easily. "I did want to see you. I want to know if you are getting along all right. Are you still at the flat?"

"No, at my sister's," was the reply. "I have no money—I can't stay at the flat."

"You know they're going to send me away?"

"Yes," and there was almost a sob in the voice. "I—I know it."

"That I'll get the limit — twenty years?"

"Yes."

"Can you—get along?" asked Dolan solicitously. "Is there anything you can do for yourself?"

"I will do something," was the reply. "Oh, Mort, Mort, why——"

"Oh, never mind that," he interrupted impatiently. "It doesn't do any good to regret things. It isn't what I planned, little girl, but it's here, so—so I'll meet it. I'll get the good behaviour allowance—that'll save two years, and then——"

There was a menace in the tone which was not lost upon the listeners.

"Eighteen years," he heard her moan.

For one instant Dolan's lips were pressed tightly together, and in that instant he had a regret—regret that he had not killed Blanton and Cunningham rather than submit to capture. He shook off his anger with an effort.

"I don't know if they'll permit me ever to see you," he said, desperately, "as long as I refuse to tell where the money is hidden, and I know they'll never permit me to write to you for fear I'll tell you where it is. So I suppose the good-bye 'll be like this. I'm sorry, little girl."

He heard her weeping and hurled himself against the bars in a passion. It passed after a moment. He must not forget that she was penniless, and the money—that vast fortune——!

"There's one thing you must do for me, Bell," he said, more calmly. "This sort of thing doesn't do any good. Brace up, little girl, and wait—wait for me. Eighteen years is not for ever; we're both young, and—but never mind that.

I wish you would please go up to the flat and—do you remember my heavy, brown coat ? "

" Yes, the old one ? " she asked.

" That's it," he answered. " It's cold here in this cell. Will you please go up to the flat when they let you loose and sew up that tear under the right arm and send it to me here ? It's probably the last favour I'll ask of you for a long time, so will you do it this afternoon ? "

" Yes," she answered, tearfully.

" The tear is under the right arm, and be certain to sew it up," said Dolan again. " Perhaps, when I am tried, I shall have a chance to see you and——"

The Professor arose and stretched himself a little.

" That's all that's necessary, Mr. Mallory," he said. " Have her held until I tell you to release her."

Mallory made a motion to Cunningham and Blanton, and the woman was led away, screaming. Hatch shuddered a little, and Dolan, not understanding, flung himself against the bars of his cell like a caged animal.

" Clever, aren't you ? " he snarled as he caught sight of Detective Mallory. " Thought I'd try to tell her where it was, but I didn't, and you never will know where it is—not in a thousand years."

Accompanied by the Professor and Hatch the detective went back to his private office. All were silent, but the detective glanced from time to time into the eyes of the scientist.

" Now, Mr. Hatch, we have the whereabouts of the money settled," said the Professor, quietly. " Please go at once to the flat and bring the brown coat Dolan mentioned. I dare say the secret of the hidden money is somewhere in that coat."

" But two of my men have already searched that coat," protested the detective.

" That doesn't make the least difference," snapped the scientist.

The reporter went out without a word. Half an hour later he returned with the brown coat. It was a commonplace looking garment, badly worn and in sad need of repair, not only in the tear under the arm but in other places. When he saw it the Professor nodded his head

abruptly, as if it were just what he had expected.

" The money can't be in that, and I'll bet my head on it," declared Detective Mallory, flatly. " There isn't room for it."

The Thinking Machine gave him a glance in which there was a touch of pity.

" We know," he said, " that the money isn't in this coat. But can't you see that it is perfectly possible that a slip of paper on which Dolan has written down the hiding place of the money can be hidden in it somewhere ? Can't you see that he asked for this coat—which is not as good a one as the coat he is wearing now—in order to attract his wife's attention to it ? Can't you see it is the one definite thing that he mentioned when he knew that in all probability he would not be permitted to see his wife again, at least for a long time ? "

Then, seam by seam, the brown coat was taken to pieces. Each piece in turn was submitted to the sharpest scrutiny. Nothing resulted. Detective Mallory frankly regarded it all as wasted effort, and when there remained nothing of the coat save strips of cloth and lining he was inclined to be triumphant. The Professor was merely thoughtful.

" It went further back than that," the scientist mused, and tiny wrinkles appeared in the dome-like brow. " Ah ! Mr. Hatch, please go back to the flat, look in the sewing machine drawers, or work basket, and you will find a spool of brown thread. Bring it to me."

" How do you know there's a spool of brown thread there ? " said the detective.

" I know it because Mr. Hatch will bring it back to me," snapped the Professor. " I know it by the simplest, most rudimentary rules of logic."

Hatch went out again. In half an hour he returned with a spool of brown thread. Professor van Dusen's white fingers closed on it eagerly, and his watery squint eyes examined it. A portion of it had been used—the spool was only half gone. But he noted—and as he did his eyes reflected a glitter of triumph— he noted that the paper cap on each end was still in place.

" Now, Mr. Mallory," he said, " I'll

demonstrate to you that in Dolan the police are dealing with a man far beyond the ordinary bank thief. In his way he is a genius. Look here!"

With a penknife he ripped off the paper caps and then looked through the hole of the spool. For an instant his face showed blank amazement. Then he put the spool down on the table and squinted at it for a moment in absolute silence.

"It must be here," he said at last. "It must be, else why did he—of course!"

With quick fingers he began to unwind the thread. Yard after yard it rolled off in his hand, and finally in the mass of brown on the spool appeared a white strip. In another instant the Thinking Machine held in his hand a tiny, thin sheet of paper—a cigarette paper. It had been wound around the spool and the thread wound over it so smoothly that it was impossible to see that it had ever been removed.

The detective and Hatch were leaning over his shoulder watching him curiously. The tiny paper unfolded—something was written on it. Slowly the Professor deciphered it.

"47, Causeway Street, basement, tenth flagstone from north-east corner."

And there the money was found— $109,437. The house was unoccupied, and within easy reach of a wharf from which a European-bound steamer sailed. Within half an hour of sailing time it would have been an easy matter for Dolan to recover it all, and that without in the least exciting the suspicion of those who might be watching him. For a saloon next door opened into an alley behind, and a broken window in the basement gave quick access to the treasure.

"Dolan reasoned," the Professor explained, "that even if he was never permitted to see his wife she would probably use that thread and in time find the directions for recovering the money. Further, he argued that the police would never suspect that a spool contained the secret for which they sought so long. His conversation with his wife, to-day, was merely to draw her attention to something which would require her to use the spool of brown thread. The brown coat was all that he could think of. And that's all, I think."

Dolan was a sadly surprised man when news of the recovery of the money was broken to him. But a certain quaint philosophy did not desert him. He gazed at Detective Mallory incredulously as the story was told, and at the end went over and sat down on his cell cot.

"Well, chief," he said, "I didn't think it was in you That makes me owe you a hat."

XI

I.D.B. Being Tales of the Diamond Fields

GEORGE GRIFFITH

BEING TALES OF THE DIAMOND FIELDS.

<small>RE-TOLD BY GEORGE GRIFFITH.</small>

FIVE HUNDRED CARATS.

(A Complete Story.)

IT was several months after the brilliant if somewhat mysterious recovery of the £15,000 parcel from the notorious but now vanished Seth Salter that I had the pleasure, and I think I may fairly add the privilege, of making the acquaintance of Inspector Lipinzki.

I can say without hesitation that in the course of wanderings which have led me over a considerable portion of the lands and seas of the world I have never met a more interesting man than he was. I say "was," poor fellow, for he is now no longer anything but a memory of bitterness to the I.D.B.—but that is a yarn with another twist.

There is no need of further explanation of the all too brief intimacy which followed our introduction, than the statement of the fact that the greatest South African detective of his day was after all a man as well as a detective, and hence not only justifiably proud of the many brilliant achievements which illustrated his career, but also by no means loth that some day the story of them should, with all due and proper precautions and reservations, be told to a wider and possibly less prejudiced audience than the motley and migratory population of the Camp as it was in his day.

I had not been five minutes in the cosy, tastily-furnished sanctum of his low, broad-roofed bungalow in New De Beers Road before I saw it was a museum as well as a study. Specimens of all sorts of queer apparatus employed by the I.D.B.'s for smuggling diamonds were scattered over the tables and mantelpiece.

There were massive, handsomely-carved briar and meerschaum pipes which seemed to hold wonderfully little tobacco for their size; rough sticks of firewood ingeniously hollowed out, which must have been worth a good round sum in their time; hollow handles of travelling trunks; ladies' boot heels of the fashion affected on a memorable occasion by Mrs. Michael Mosenstein; and novels, hymn-books, church-services, and bibles, with cavities cut out of the centre of their leaves which had once held thousands of pounds' worth of illicit stones on their unsuspected passage through the book-post.

But none of these interested, or, indeed, puzzled me so much as did a couple of curiously-assorted articles which lay under a little glass case on a wall bracket. One was an ordinary piece of heavy lead tubing, about three inches long and an inch in diameter, sealed by fusing at both ends, and having a little brass tap fused into one end. The other was a small ragged piece of dirty red sheet-indiarubber, very thin—in fact almost transparent—and, roughly speaking, four or five inches square.

I was looking at these things, wondering what on earth could be the connection between them, and what manner of strange story might be connected with them, when the Inspector came in.

"Good-evening. Glad to see you!" he said, in his quiet and almost gentle voice, and without a trace of foreign accent, as we shook hands. "Well, what do you think of my museum? I daresay you've guessed already that if some of these things could speak they could keep your readers entertained for some little time, eh?"

"Well, there is no reason why their owner shouldn't speak for them," I said, making the obvious reply, "provided always, of course, that it wouldn't be giving away too many secrets of state."

"My dear sir," he said, with a smile which curled up the ends of his little, black, carefully-trimmed moustache ever so slightly, "I should not have made you the promise I did at the club the other night if I had not been prepared to rely absolutely on your discretion—and my own. Now, there's whisky-and-soda or brandy; which do you prefer? You smoke, of course, and I think you'll find these pretty good, and that chair I can recommend. I have unravelled many a knotty problem in it, I can tell you."

"And now," he went on when we were at last comfortably settled, "may I ask which of my relics has most aroused your professional curiosity?"

It was already on the tip of my tongue to ask for the story of the gas-pipe and piece of india-rubber, but the Inspector forestalled me by saying:

"But perhaps that is hardly a fair question, as they will all probably seem pretty strange to you. Now, for instance, I saw you looking at two of my curios when I came in. You would hardly expect them to be associated, and very intimately too, with about the most daring and skilfully planned diamond robbery that ever took place on the Fields, or off them, for the matter of that, would you?"

"Hardly," I said. "And yet I think I have learned enough of the devious ways of the I.D.B. to be prepared for a perfectly logical explanation of the fact."

"As logical as I think I may fairly say romantic," replied the Inspector as he set his glass down. "In one sense it was the most ticklish problem that I've ever had to tackle. Of course you've heard some version or other of the disappearance of the Great De Beers' Diamond?"

"I should rather think I had!" I said, with a decided thrill of pleasurable anticipation, for I felt sure that now, if ever, I was going to get to the bottom of the great mystery. "Everybody in Camp seems to have a different version of it, and, of course, everyone seems to think that if he had only had the management of the case the mystery would have been solved long ago."

"It is invariably the case," said the Inspector, with another of his quiet, pleasant smiles, "that everyone can do work better than those whose reputation depends upon the doing of it. We are not altogether fools at the Department, and yet I have to confess that I myself was in ignorance as to just how that diamond disappeared, or where it got to, until twelve hours ago.

"Now, I am going to tell you the facts exactly as they are, but under the condition

"Good evening. Glad to see you!" he said.

that you will alter all the names except, if you choose, my own, and that you will not publish the story for at least twelve months to come. There are personal and private reasons for this which you will probably understand without my stating them. Of course it will, in time, leak out into the papers, although there has been, and will be, no prosecution; but anything in the newspapers will of necessity be garbled and incorrect, and—well, I may as well confess that I am sufficiently vain to wish that my share in the transaction shall not be left altogether to the tender mercies of the imaginative penny-a-liner."

I acknowledged the compliment with a bow as graceful as the easiness of the Inspector's chair would allow me to make, but I said nothing, as I wanted to get to the story.

" I had better begin at the beginning," the Inspector went on, as he meditatively snipped the end of a fresh cigar. " As I suppose you already know, the largest and most valuable diamond ever found on these fields was a really magnificent stone, a perfect octahedron, pure white, without a flaw, and weighing close on 500 carats. There's a photograph of it there on the mantelpiece. I've got another one by me; I'll give it you before you leave Kimberley.

" Well, this stone was found about six months ago in one of the drives on the 800-foot level of the Kimberley Mine. It was taken by the overseer straight to the De Beers' offices and placed on the Secretary's desk—you know where he sits, on the right hand side as you go into the Board Room through the green baize doors. There were several of the Directors present at the time, and, as you may imagine, they were pretty well pleased at the find, for the stone, without any exaggeration, was worth a prince's ransom.

" Of course, I needn't tell you that the value per carat of a diamond which is perfect and of a good colour increases in a sort of geometrical progression with the size. I dare say that stone was worth anywhere between one and two millions, according to the depth of the purchaser's purse. It was worthy to adorn the proudest crown in the world instead of—but there, you'll think me a very poor story-teller if I anticipate.

" Well, the diamond, after being duly admired, was taken upstairs to the Diamond Room by the Secretary himself, accompanied by two of the Directors. Of course, you have been through the new offices of De Beers, but still, perhaps I had better just run over the ground, as the locality is rather important.

" You know that when you get upstairs and turn to the right on the landing from the top of the staircase there is a door with a little grille in it. You knock, a trap-door is raised, and, if you are recognised and your business warrants it, you are admitted. Then you go along a little passage out of which a room opens on the left, and in front of you is another door leading into the Diamond Rooms themselves.

· " You know, too, that in the main room fronting Stockdale Street and Jones Street the diamond tables run round the two sides under the windows, and are railed off from the rest of the room by a single light wooden rail. There is a table in the middle of the room, and on your right hand as you go in there is a big safe standing against the wall. You will remember, too, that in the corner exactly facing the door stands the glass case containing the diamond scales. I want you particularly to recall the fact that these scales stand diagonally across the corner by the window. The secondary room, as you know, opens out on to the left, but that is not of much consequence."

I signified my remembrance of these details and the Inspector went on.

" The diamond was first put in the scale and weighed in the presence of the Secretary and the two Directors by one of the higher officials, a licensed diamond broker and a most trusted employé of De Beers, whom you may call Phillip Marsden when you come to write the story. The weight, as I told you, in round figures was 500 carats. The stone was then photographed, partly for purposes of identification and partly as a reminder of the biggest stone ever found in Kimberley in its rough state.

" The gem was then handed over to Mr. Marsden's care pending the departure of the Diamond Post to Vryburg on the following Monday—this was a Tuesday. The Secretary saw it locked up in the big safe by Mr. Marsden, who, as usual, was accompanied by another official, a younger man than himself, whom you can call Henry Lomas, a connection of his, and also one of the most trusted members of the staff.

"Every day, and sometimes two or three times a day, either the Secretary or one or other of the Directors came up and had a look at the big stone, either for their own satisfaction or to show it to some of their more intimate friends. I ought, perhaps, to have told you before that the whole Diamond Room staff were practically sworn to secrecy on the subject, because, as you will readily understand, it was not considered desirable for such an exceedingly valuable find to be made public property in a place like this. When Saturday came it was decided not to send it down to Cape Town, for some reasons connected with the state of the market. When the safe was opened on Monday morning the stone was gone.

"I needn't attempt to describe the absolute panic which followed. It had been seen two or three times in the safe on the Saturday, and the Secretary himself was positive that it was there at closing time, because he saw it just as the safe was being locked for the night. In fact, he actually saw it put in, for it had been taken out to show to a friend of his a few minutes before.

"The safe had not been tampered with, nor could it have been unlocked, because when it is closed for the night it cannot be opened again unless either the Secretary or the Managing Director is present, as they have each a master-key without which the key used during the day is of no use.

"Of course I was sent for immediately, and I admit that I was fairly staggered. If the Secretary had not been so positive that the stone was locked up when he saw the safe closed on the Saturday I should have worked upon the theory—the only possible one, as it seemed—that the stone had been abstracted from the safe during the day, concealed in the room, and somehow or other smuggled out, although even that would have been almost impossible in consequence of the strictness of the searching system and the almost certain discovery which must have followed an attempt to get it out of the town.

"Both the rooms were searched in every

"When the safe was opened on Monday morning the stone was gone."

nook and cranny. The whole staff, naturally feeling that every one of them must be suspected, immediately volunteered to submit to any process of search that I might think satisfactory, and I can assure you the search was a very thorough one.

"Nothing was found, and when we had done there wasn't a scintilla of evidence to warrant us in suspecting anybody. It is true that the diamond was last actually seen by the Secretary in charge of Mr. Marsden and Mr. Lomas. Mr. Marsden opened the safe, Mr.

Lomas put the tray containing the big stone and several other fine ones into its usual compartment, and the safe door was locked. Therefore that fact went for nothing.

" You know, I suppose, that one of the Diamond Room staff always remains all night in the room; there is at least one night-watchman on every landing; and the frontages are patrolled all night by armed men of the special police. Lomas was on duty on the Saturday night. He was searched as usual when he came off duty on Sunday morning. Nothing was found, and I recognised that it was absolutely impossible that he could have brought the diamond out of the room or passed it to any confederate in the street without being discovered. Therefore, though at first sight suspicion might have pointed to him as being the one who was apparently last in the room with the diamond, there was absolutely no reason to connect that fact with its disappearance."

" I must say that that is a great deal plainer and more matter-of-fact than any of the other stories that I have heard of the mysterious disappearance," I said, as the Inspector paused to re-fill his glass and ask me to do likewise.

"Yes," he said drily, " the truth *is* more commonplace up to a certain point than the sort of stories that a stranger will find floating about Kimberley, but still I daresay you have found in your own profession that it sometimes has a way of—to put it in sporting language — giving Fiction a seven-pound handicap and beating it in a canter."

" For my own part," I answered with an affirmative nod, "my money would go on Fact every time. Therefore it would go on now if I were betting. At any rate, I may say that none of the fiction that I have so far heard has offered even a reasonable explanation of the disappearance of that diamond, given the conditions which you have just stated, and, as far as I can see, I admit that I couldn't give the remotest guess at the solution of the mystery."

" That's exactly what I said to myself after I had been worrying day and night for more than a week over it," said the Inspector. "And then," he went on, suddenly getting up from his seat and beginning to walk up

and down the room with quick, irregular strides, "all of a sudden in the middle of a very much smaller puzzle, just one of the common I.D.B. cases we have almost every week, the whole of the work that I was engaged upon vanished from my mind, leaving it for the moment a perfect blank. Then, like a lightning flash out of a black cloud, there came a momentary ray of light which showed me the clue to the mystery. That was the idea. These," he said, stopping in front of the mantelpiece and putting his finger on the glass case which covered the two relics that had started the story, "these were the materialisation of it."

" And yet, my dear Inspector," I ventured to interrupt, " you will perhaps pardon me for saying that your ray of light leaves me just as much in the dark as ever."

" But your darkness shall be made day all in good course," he said with a smile. I could see that he had an eye for dramatic effect, and so I thought it was better to let him tell the story uninterrupted and in his own way, so I simply assured him of my ever-increasing interest and waited for him to go on. He took a couple of turns up and down the room in silence, as though he were considering in what form he should spring the solution of the mystery upon me, then he stopped and said abruptly :

" I didn't tell you that the next morning— that is to say, Sunday—Mr. Marsden went out on horseback, shooting in the veld up towards that range of hills which lies over yonder to the north-westward between here and Barkly West. I can see by your face that you are already asking yourself what that has got to do with spiriting a million or so's worth of crystallised carbon out of the safe at De Beers'. Well, a little patience, and you shall see.

" Early that same Sunday morning, I was walking down Stockdale Street, in front of the De Beers' offices, smoking a cigar, and, of course, worrying my brains about the diamond. I took a long draw at my weed, and quite involuntarily put my head back and blew it up into the air—there, just like that—and the cloud drifted diagonally across the street dead in the direction of the hills on which Mr. Philip Marsden would just then be hunting buck. At the same instant the revelation which had scattered my thoughts about the other little case that I mentioned just now came back to me. I saw, with my mind's eye, of course—well, now, what do you think I saw?"

"If it wouldn't spoil an incomparable detective," I said, somewhat irrelevantly, "I should say that you would make an excellent story-teller. Never mind what I think. I'm in the plastic condition just now. I am receiving impressions, not making them. Now, what did you see?"

"I saw the Great De Beers' Diamond—say from ten to fifteen hundred thousand pounds' worth of concentrated capital—floating from the upper storey of the De Beers' Consolidated Mines, rising over the housetops, and drifting down the wind to Mr. Philip Marsden's hunting-ground."

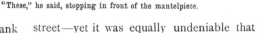

"These," he said, stopping in front of the mantelpiece.

To say that I stared in the silence of blank amazement at the Inspector, who made this astounding assertion with a dramatic gesture and inflection which naturally cannot be reproduced in print, would be to utter the merest commonplace. He seemed to take my stare for one of incredulity rather than wonder, for he said almost sharply:

"Ah, I see you are beginning to think that I am talking fiction now; but never mind, we will see about that later on. You have followed me, I have no doubt, closely enough to understand that, having exhausted all the resources of my experience and such native wit as the Fates have given me, and having made the most minute analysis of the circumstances of the case, I had come to the fixed conclusion that the great diamond had not been carried out of the room on the person of a human being, nor had it been dropped or thrown from the windows to the street—yet it was equally undeniable that it had got out of the safe and out of the room."

"And therefore it flew out, I suppose!" I could not help interrupting, nor, I am afraid, could I quite avoid a suggestion of incredulity in my tone.

"Yes, my dear sir!" replied the Inspector, with an emphasis which he increased by slapping the four fingers of his right hand on the palm of his left. "Yes, it flew out. It flew some seventeen or eighteen miles before it returned to the earth in which it was born, if we may accept the theory of the terrestrial origin of diamonds. So far, as the event proved, I was absolutely correct, wild and all as you may naturally think my hypothesis to have been.

"But," he continued, stopping in his walk and making an eloquent gesture of apology, "being only human, I almost instantly deviated from truth into error. In fact, I freely confess to you that there and then I made what I consider to be the greatest and most fatal mistake of my career.

"Absolutely certain as I was that the diamond had been conveyed through the air to the Barkly Hills, and that Mr. Philip Marsden's shooting expedition had been undertaken with the object of recovering it, I had all the approaches to the town watched till he came back. He came in by the Old Transvaal Road about an hour after dark. I had him arrested, took him into the house of one of my men who happened to live out that way, searched him, as I might say, from the roots of his hair to the soles of his feet, and found—nothing.

"Of course he was indignant, and of course I looked a very considerable fool. In fact, nothing would pacify him but that I should meet him the next morning in the Board Room at De Beers', and, in the presence of the Secretary and at least three

"I had him arrested."

directors, apologise to him for my unfounded suspicions and the outrage that they had led me to make upon him. I was, of course, as you might say, between the devil and the deep sea. I had to do it, and I did it; but my convictions and my suspicions remained exactly what they were before.

"Then there began a very strange, and, although you may think the term curious, a very pathetic, waiting game between us. He knew that in spite of his temporary victory I had really solved the mystery and was on the right track. I knew that the great diamond was out yonder somewhere among the hills or on the veld, and I knew, too, that he was only waiting for my vigilance to relax to go out and get it.

"Day after day, week after week, and month after month the game went on in silence. We met almost every day. His credit had been completely restored at De Beers'. Lomas, his connection and, as I firmly believed, his confederate, had been, through his influence, sent on a mission to England, and when he went I confess to you that I thought the game was up—that Marsden had somehow managed to recover the diamond, and that Lomas had taken it beyond our reach.

"Still I watched and waited, and as time went on I saw that my fears were groundless and that the gem was still on the veld or in the hills. He kept up bravely for weeks, but at last the strain began to tell upon him. Picture to yourself the pitiable position of a man of good family in the Old Country, of expensive tastes and very considerable ambition, living here in Kimberley on a salary of some £12 a week, worth about £5 in England, and knowing that within a few miles of him, in a spot that he alone knew of, there lay a concrete fortune of say, fifteen hundred thousand pounds, which was his for the picking up if he only dared to go and take it, and yet he dared not do so.

"Yes, it is a pitiless trade this of ours, and professional thief-catchers can't afford to have much to do with mercy, and yet I tell you that as I watcl d that man day after day, with the fever growing hotter in his blood and the unbearable anxiety tearing ever harder and harder at his nerves, I pitied him —yes, I pitied him so much that I even found myself growing impatient for the end to come. Fancy that, a detective, a thief-catcher getting impatient to see his victim out of his misery!

"Well, I had to wait six months—that is to say, I had to wait until five o'clock this morning— for the end. Soon after four one of my men came and knocked me up; he brought a note into my bed-room and I read it in bed. It was from Philip Marsden asking me to go and see him at once and alone. I went, as you may be sure, with as little delay as possible. I found him in his sitting-room. The lights were burning. He was fully dressed, and had evidently been up all night.

"Even I, who have seen the despair that comes of crime in most of its worst forms, was shocked at the look of him. Still he greeted me politely and with perfect composure. He affected not to see the hand that I held out to him, but asked me quite kindly to sit down and have a chat with him. I sat down, and when I looked up I saw him standing in front of me, covering me with a brace of revolvers. My life, of course, was absolutely at his mercy, and whatever I might have thought of myself or the situation,

"I saw him standing in front of me, covering me with a brace of revolvers."

there was obviously nothing to do but to sit still and wait for developments.

"He began very quietly to tell me why he had sent for me. He said: 'I wanted to see you, Mr. Lipinzki, to clear up this matter about the big diamond. I have seen for a long time—in fact from that Sunday night— that you had worked out a pretty correct notion as to the way that diamond vanished. You are quite right; it did fly across the veld to the Barkly Hills. I am a bit of a chemist you know, and when I had once made up my mind to steal it—for there is no use in mincing words now—I saw that it would be perfectly absurd to attempt to smuggle such a stone out by any of the ordinary methods.

"'I daresay you wonder what these revolvers are for. They are to keep you there in that chair till I've done, for one thing. If you attempt to get out of it or utter a sound I shall shoot you. If you hear me out you will not be injured, so you may as well sit still and keep your ears open.

"'To have any chance of success I must have had a confederate, and I made young Lomas one. If you look on that little table beside your chair you will see a bit of closed lead piping with a tap in it and a piece of thin sheet india-rubber. That is the remains of the apparatus that I used. I make them a present to you; you may like to add them to your collection.

"'Lomas, when he went on duty that Saturday night, took the bit of tube charged with compressed hydrogen and an empty child's toy balloon with him. You will remember that that night was very dark, and that the wind had been blowing very steadily all day towards the Barkly Hills. Well, when everything was quiet he filled the balloon with gas, tied the diamond——'

"'But how did he get the diamond out of the safe? The Secretary saw it locked up that evening!' I exclaimed, my curiosity getting the better of my prudence.

"'It was not locked up in the safe

"The other—well. I can spare you the details."

at all that night,' he answered, smiling with a sort of ghastly satisfaction. 'Lomas and I, as you know, took the tray of diamonds to the safe, and, as far as the Secretary could see, put them in, but as he put the tray into its compartment he palmed the big diamond as I had taught him to do in a good many lessons before. At the moment that I shut the safe and locked it, the diamond was in his pocket.

"'The Secretary and his friends left the room, Lomas and I went back to the tables, and I told him to clean the scales as I wanted to test them. While he was doing

so he slipped the diamond behind the box, and there it lay between the box and the corner of the wall until it was wanted.

"'We all left the room as usual, and, as you know, we were searched. When Lomas went on night-duty there was the diamond ready for its balloon voyage. He filled the balloon just so that it lifted the diamond and no more. The lead pipe he just put where the diamond had been — the only place you never looked in. When the row was over on the Monday I locked it up in the safe. We were all searched that day; the next I brought it away and now you may have it.

"'Two of the windows were open on account of the heat. He watched his opportunity, and committed it to the air about two hours before dawn. You know what a sudden fall there is in the temperature here just before daybreak. I calculated upon that to contract the volume of the gas sufficiently to destroy the balance and bring the balloon to the ground, and I knew that, if Lomas had obeyed my instructions, it would fall either on the veld or on this side of the hills.

"'The balloon was a bright red, and, to make a long story short, I started out before daybreak that morning, as you know, to look for buck. When I got outside the camp I took compass bearings and rode straight down the wind towards the hills. By good luck or good calculation, or both, I must have followed the course of the balloon almost exactly, for in three hours after I left the camp I saw the little red speck ahead of me up among the stones on the hillside.

"'I dodged about for a bit as though I were really after buck, in case anybody was watching me. I worked round to the red spot, put my foot on the balloon, and burst it. I folded the india-rubber up, as I didn't like to leave it there, and put it in my pocket-book. You remember that when you searched me you didn't open my pocket-book, as, of course, it was perfectly flat, and the diamond couldn't possibly have been in it. That's how you missed your clue, though I don't suppose it would have been much use to you as you'd already guessed it. However, there it is at your service now.'

"'And the diamond?'

"As I said these three words his whole manner suddenly changed. So far he had spoken quietly and deliberately, and without even a trace of anger in his voice, but now his white, sunken cheeks suddenly flushed a bright fever red and his eyes literally blazed at me. His voice sank to a low, hissing tone that was really horrible to hear.

"'The diamond!' he said. 'Yes, curse it, and curse you, Mr. Inspector Lipinzki—for it and you have been a curse to me! Day and night I have seen the spot where I buried it, and day and night you have kept your nets spread about my feet so that I could not move a step to go and take it. I can bear the suspense no longer. Between you—you and that infernal stone—you have wrecked my health and driven me mad. If I had all the wealth of De Beers' now it wouldn't be any use to me, and to-night a new fear came to me—that if this goes on much longer I shall go mad, really mad, and in my delirium rob myself of my revenge on you by letting out where I hid it.

"'Now listen. Lomas has gone. He is beyond your reach. He has changed his name—his very identity. I have sent him by different posts, and to different names and addresses, two letters. One is a plan and the other is a key to it. With those two pieces of paper he can find the diamond. Without them you can hunt for a century and never go near it.

"'And now that you know that—that your incomparable stone, which should have been mine, is out yonder somewhere where you can never find it, you and the De Beers' people will be able to guess at the tortures of Tantalus that you have made me endure. That is all you have got by your smartness. That is my legacy to you—curse you! If I had my way I would send you all out there to hunt for it without food or drink till you died of hunger and thirst of body, as you have made me die a living death of hunger and thirst of mind.'

"As he said this, he covered me with one revolver, and put the muzzle of the other into his mouth. With an ungovernable impulse, I sprang to my feet. He pulled both triggers at once. One bullet passed between my arm and my body, ripping a piece out of my coat sleeve; the other—well, I can spare you the details. He dropped dead instantly."

"And the diamond?" I said.

"The reward is £20,000, and it is at your service," replied the Inspector, in his suavest manner, "provided that you can find the stone — or Mr. Lomas and his plans."

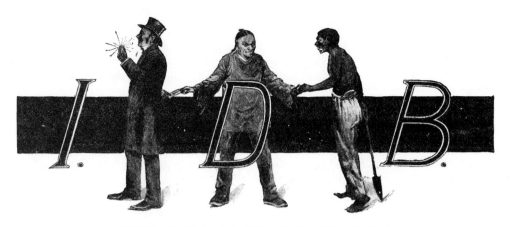

BEING TALES OF THE DIAMOND FIELDS.

RE-TOLD BY GEORGE GRIFFITH.

THE BORDER GANG.

(A Complete Story.)

"EH, mon, you're no tellin' me! It's the domdest, barefacedest robbery! It's dog eatin' dog—just cannibalism in beesness, that's what it is."

"It vas true, though, Sandy, s'welp me, may I never see the glint of a goniva again if it isn't. There vas three thousand pounds worth of the klips in poor little Tommy's insides, as you know. The tecs pulls me up near the border. In the dark Tommy slips out of the cart as usual, and makes for the clump of gums on the other side of the drift without bein' seen. The tecs find nothing, of course, and I drives on, thinking what sort of a lawsuit we shall have this time against Lipinzki and his people, crosses the drift, and pulls up by the trees. I whistles, and Tommy, like a good obedient little tyke what knows his bizness, jumps in and——"

"Oh, Lord, to think ye'd got such a beautiful lot so far only to—aweel, go on, Ike, and let's have the rest of it."

"As I says, the dog jumps in, and I drives off again. 'Bout a hundred yards farther on both my horses comes to the ground with a crash, and I goes after them on to my head. When I comes to myself and picks myself up, there was half-a-dozen fellows on horseback round the cart. One jumps down, and before I can so much as shout he has a cloth over my head and ties me up so tight I can neither see nor speak. Then he knocks with his knuckles on

my head, and tells me if I don't want a bullet in it I'll keep quiet and be good. Of course I vas good as they make 'em."

"But the dog, mon, why didn't he mak' a bolt for't when he saw there was trouble? He's been vera weel trained. I'd 'a thocht he might 'a got awa' in the scrimmage."

"He didn't have a chance. I hears him give a smothered-up yelp and squeal, and from that I knows that he is like my head—in a bag. That tells me that they had tumbled to the lay, or that there was someone there that knew it. Well, they bundles me and the dog into the cart, and drives away somewhere for about half-an-hour. Then they pulls up, hauls me out, hustles me into a house of some sort, and takes the bag off my head. When I looks about me I was in a bit of a small room, and there was four fellows there, all with masks on."

"Kidnappers an midnight robbers—maybe murderers as weel!" groaned the Scotchman. "Ike, mon, I'm thinkin' ye had a narrow escape. That Free State's a dom'd sight too free if it's comin' to this. It's naethin' better nor a savage land wi'out law nor order in't. What did they do till ye then?"

"They asked me how many klips I'd got, and where they were, and of course I says I have none, and they can search me if they like, and they does—a good bit worse than

225

the tecs did, I can tell you. Of course they finds nothin', and then they laughs and says if I haven't got them the dog has. So they turns poor Tommy out of the sack and— s'welp me, old pal, I doesn't like to tell you what happened then. I'd educated that dog perfect, and I loved the little fellow, and, besides, he was worth a lot of money with all he knew!"

Sandy Fraser's little Hebrew accomplice quite broke down here for a moment or two, and Sandy himself gave a sympathetic sniff, for they had both lost, not only a lot of money, but also a guiltless accomplice whom it would be very hard to replace.

"They murdered him, Sandy, right before my eyes in a big tin footbath, and, of course, they found the klips. Then they offered to sell them back to me for two thousand, and told me they'd have made it five hundred more if they hadn't had to kill the dog."

"Eh, sakes, what a murderous price!

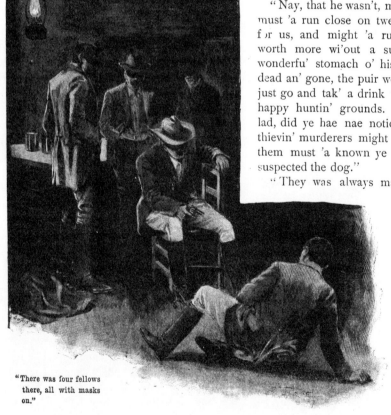

"There was four fellows there, all with masks on."

Blank robbery! Why they cost us three hundred straight from the kaffirs. An' ye paid?"

"Well, they was worth three thousand trade price, and the thieves knew it, so I did. I gave them a draft on the bank here, and they kept me there till one of them got the cash and brought it back, and then they ties my head up again, puts me into the cart, and drives me away with the klips in my pocket. When they took the bag off it was night, and I was in a little kloof. They showed me the way to Freetown, and rode off. I got into Freetown by the morning, and found Sandheim there wondering if I was dead or gone to the Breakwater for change of air.

"Well, I told him the story, and got three thousand three hundred out of him for the klips on the strength of it. Then I drives back, breaking my heart about poor little Tommy, and wondering where we shall get another dog like that. That Chinaman's dog that he fooled Löwenthal so sweetly with wasn't in it with poor Tommy."

"Nay, that he wasn't, mon. Why, Tommy must 'a run close on twenty thousand worth for us, and might 'a run twenty thousand worth more wi'out a suspeecion, wi' that wonderfu' stomach o' his. But, there, he's dead an' gone, the puir wee martyr, and we'll just go and tak' a drink till his future in the happy huntin' grounds. But tell me, Ike, lad, did ye hae nae notion wha ony o' they thievin' murderers might 'a been? Some o' them must 'a known ye or they'd never 'a suspected the dog."

"They was always masked when I saw any of them, but, Sandy, if I wasn't sure as death that Lipinzki and his chaps did for Seth Salter that night he ran the big parcel and they got it back, I could swear that the boss of 'em had just his Yankee twang, and his build wasn't unlike, neither," replied

Ike, whose English was of the Oriental order, and whose tenses changed with the variations of his mental temperature. "Now, where was we going to? Let's go to the Queen's,—that's Lipinzki's place. Let's see if he's there, and if he's heard anything about this gang over the line."

When they entered the bar-room they found Mr. Inspector Lipinzki, the famous detective, not only there, but the central figure of the somewhat motley crowd that was wont to foregather there for their evening limejuice, to use a conveniently generic term.

He was standing, as usual the most nattily dressed man in the place, with one elbow resting on the bar counter, and a glass half full of whisky and soda beside him. Opposite to him stood no less a personage than Mr. Michael Mosenstein—the events herein to be described happened some two months after Jossey Mo's vicarious conviction—and there seemed to be a discussion of some little heat going on between them. Just as they went in he slapped his glass down on the mahogany, and said in a loud, angry tone:

"Of course you fellows never take any responsibility, unless it's a case of searching private houses and annoying innocent people. But what I say is that this is just as much your affair as the Free State police's. Why don't you combine, instead of everlastingly bickering and letting criminals slip through your fingers? If there's been a robbery on their side of the line to-night, there'll be one on your side to-morrow, or the night after. As for saying that the parcel was illicit, that's all rot, and neither here nor there. Max Sandheim is a perfectly respectable man. Why, I've done business with him myself scores of times."

"I've no doubt you have, Mr. Mosenstein. I wish I'd been there at the time," replied the Inspector with a snap of malice in his tone which sent a chuckling laugh round the crowd and brought out a red spot between Mickey's eyebrows. Before he had his retort ready Ike pushed his way through the half-circle about them, and said with ill-advised anxiety:

"Wha-at was that? What has happened to Max Sandheim, and when did it happen? Was he robbed?"

"Aw, the blighted eediot!" murmured his partner, but he didn't shout it like a stage aside, and so it wasn't heard. He went to the far end of the counter and ordered a drink, hoping that no one had seen him come in with Ike.

The Inspector pulled himself up straight and, as he could do on occasions, suddenly assumed an air of authority which kept even the angry Mickey quiet while he answered:

"Ah, Mr. Cohen, good evening! So you've got back all safe, but you're a bit anxious about your friend Sandheim. Very natural, of course. Well, I'm sure you'll be sorry to hear that a few hours after you left him, say about ten o'clock last night, he was held up on the road between Freetown and Boshoff by four armed and masked men and robbed of a parcel of stones which he valued at four thousand pounds. I dare say you'll know about how near that is to the truth. He rode into Boshoff and reported, and we have just had the news here by telegraph. By the way, how's that dog of yours?"

The crowd noticed unanimously that this was the first time since the story of the Diamond Dog had become common property in Camp that the Inspector had mentioned one of its species publicly, and they closed up a little, thinking there was something coming. Mr. Mosenstein, for reasons of his own, paid his apparently exclusive attention to his drink, while Sandy Fraser cursed all Jews and dogs in silence and kept his ears anxiously open.

Now Ikey Cohen, though not a strong man, nor yet one of conspicuous pluck, was one of those peculiarly constituted individuals who gain a sort of secondary courage through stress of circumstances, somewhat as runners get their second wind. From what the Inspector had said, he saw that he knew a good deal more about his late adventure "on the other side" than he thought he did. Suspicions are sometimes as good as knowledge. He stuck his hands deep down into his pockets, looked the Inspector squarely in the face, and said:

"If you want me to sell you a pup, Mr. Lipinzki, I'll be happy to oblige you. I can't sell you that one, because it's dead. But I think I could tell you the name of the man who ordered it to be killed. Anyhow—I—guess—you'd—'a—recog-nised—his voice—as I calcerlate—I—did."

Ikey didn't do the Yankee drawl at all badly, and the shot went right home. For the first and the last time in his life, Inspector Lipinzki lost his self-command in public. But his start was only momentary, and the flush that came into his cheeks died out again in an instant.

"What do you mean by that, sir?" he asked in a tone as calm as

He walked to the door, followed by his official satellite.

usual, but with a distinctly threatening ring in it.

"Just about what he says, I reckon," drawled Mickey Mosenstein, who was about as good a mimic as he was a juggler. "If you don't recognise that twang, I do. That was well done, Ikey boy. What'll you take? The next's with me."

What might have happened after this no one will ever know, for just at that moment one of the Inspector's men entered hurriedly and handed him a note. He opened it, glanced at it, folded it up in his hand, and said:

"Gentlemen, I'm sorry, but, so far as I'm concerned, this entertainment will have to be postponed. Another man wants to see me very urgently about a dog."

With this he drank off the remains of his whisky and soda and turned and walked to the door, followed by his official satellite, not a little pleased at such an opportunely good "get out" from a situation which was bidding fair to become embarrassing.

It pleased the Fates to draw out the tragedy which thus began with the inhuman butchery of poor little Tommy—one of many a like innocent martyr to the unholy cause of I.D.B.—into more scenes than could be reproduced here. The present narrative is,

however, only concerned with the last of them, or perhaps it would be more correct to say the last but one, and that which brought the curtain down.

As week after week went by, the outrages committed by the mysterious Border Gang, as the unknown desperadoes who had so suddenly invaded the hitherto comparatively peaceful frontiers of the Free State and Griqualand West very soon came to be called, seemed to increase in number and daring.

It was quite a curious situation—such an one as the student of human crime had never had the chance of studying before, and may never have again. It was a sort of three-cornered contest between underhand roguery, open violence, and the forces which worked for law and order. The old struggle between the police and the I.D.B. fraternity went on as before, but with an added terror for the evildoer, who, if he eluded the clutches of the law, might the next hour fall into the no more merciful grasp of the gang. The honest and lawful trader still hated the I.D.B.

as his worst enemy, but the Gang robbed both with an impartiality worthy of a more honourable calling.

The police naturally had anything but a happy time of it. If they devoted an adequate amount of time and force to hunting for the Gang—which was never where it was expected or wanted—the occupation of the I.D.B. became comparatively pleasant and easy; while, if they did their proper work thoroughly, the Gang promptly went on the war-path with renewed vigour and extended scope, and raked in the plunder with both hands from the honest and the dishonest alike.

It will be readily understood that no state of affairs could possibly be more distasteful to Mr. Inspector Lipinzki than this. Not only was his professional credit at stake, but men like Mickey Mosenstein, Ikey Cohen, Sandy Fraser, and Alexander Macadam, whom he absolutely knew either to be or to have been involved in extensive I.D.B. transactions, but who were now getting rich, and therefore men of influence in a town where the faculty of making money anyhow was the only one that "got a man on," were making sarcastic comparisons between Hounslow Heath a hundred years ago and the Diamond Fields of to-day, and were asking ugly questions about the efficiency—nay, even the incorruptibility— of the police force in general and the Detective Department in particular.

It was this last suspicion that touched the puzzled and harassed Inspector most keenly. As a practical man he had no belief in miraculous escapes or the possibility of people being in two different places at once, and gradually the conviction forced itself upon him that the immunity of the Gang from capture and its evasion of trap after trap that he had laid for it with all the skill and cunning at his command could only be due to the connivance of some of his own men and the Free State Police, which he knew to be anything but immaculate.

This conviction led him at last to the resolve to risk, not only reputation and position, but life itself on the attempt to personally break up the Gang, or at least to penetrate the mystery which shrouded its doings and shielded it from justice. This resolve once made, it did not take a man of

his character very long to translate it into action.

He caused certain information to leak out through some of the underground channels which were always at his service, to the effect that, in consequence of strong suspicions that the Diamond Mail to Vryburg was going to be held up by the Border Gang on a certain night when it would be carrying an exceptionally valuable consignment of gems, the stones would be run the night before, as though they were an illicit parcel, over the border to Freetown, and thence conveyed in the usual way to Port Elizabeth instead of Cape Town. The Diamond Mail of the following day was to take no consignment at all, but was to be accompanied by a double guard.

On the appointed night the Inspector had a score of his best and most trusted men, armed to the teeth, posted along the border within hail of the point where the road to Freetown crosses it. On the other side a detachment of the Free State Police were, by arrangement with the District Chief, to be lying in wait ready to act in concert with them, and to catch the Gang between the two forces at the moment of attack.

When Inspector Lipinzki set out that night to take his part in the working out of his scheme, he took an even more than usually affectionate leave of his daughter—a pretty, graceful girl of between sixteen and seventeen, who was the incarnation of the one romance in his life, the daughter of the only woman he had ever looked upon to love and long for, and the one rose that he had saved out of the paradise which he had once dwelt in.

He went to his office, and changed his usual attire for a suit of clothes that he had never been seen in, a sort of semi-sporting rig that he had had up specially from Cape Town, put his favourite Smith-Wesson in his right-hand coat pocket, and then started out to walk to Beaconsfield. On the way he overtook his kaffir groom, leading his best horse. He mounted, saw that the pair of heavy Colts in the holsters were ready for immediate use, and then cantered off towards the border, which he had timed himself to reach a little before one in the morning.

Then came a jerk that nearly broke his neck.

It had been arranged that two of his own men should hail him just before he got to it, and that then the game was to begin. News had reached him that the Gang had got wind of the big parcel he was supposed to be carrying, and had vowed to have him and it at any price. If his men only did their duty, and the Free State police kept faith with him, the new terror of the border would be a thing of the past by morning.

Two mounted figures loomed out of the darkness ahead of him, and pulled up on either side of the road. A gruff hail came growling down the wind.

"Is that you, Davies, Mays? All right! I suppose the others are ready. Open a bit and let me through, then chase for all you're worth. You needn't be afraid of catching me."

As he said this he touched his horse with the spur, and the easy canter broke into a gallop. The two men pulled their animals aside. As he came up, the moon broke through a rift in the clouds, and he saw that they were both masked. It was too late to stop. He ducked his head and dived for his Smith-Wesson, but the next instant a rein, or plaited rope of raw hide, stretched taut across the road, passed over his horse's head and took him under the chin. Then came a jerk that nearly broke his neck, a thump against the hard mud of the road, a mist of dancing stars before his eyes, and then darkness.

When he came to himself he was half sitting, half lying in a hammock deck-chair in the same little hut in which Ikey Cohen had witnessed the murder of poor little Tommy. There was a burning taste of raw brandy in his mouth and throat, and his head was aching terribly. He looked up and saw a man with a black cloth mask over the upper part of his face sitting astride a wooden chair in front of him, with his arms across the back, looking at him through the eye-holes of his mask. Even in the first moments of returning consciousness he seemed to recognise something familiar in him, and the seeming soon became certainty.

" Evenin', Inspector. Comin' round a bit? That's right. Been waitin' quite a time to have a bit of a chat with you. Feel

The Inspector staggered to his feet.

up to it now? Have another nip? "

There was no mistaking the drawling tone, or the clip of the word-ends. The Inspector's rallying thoughts went back to that night at Freetown, nearly eighteen months ago now, when, for the sake of personal pique and a threatened reputation, he had sanctioned—in fact, assisted in the doing of—a deed of treachery and violence, the one unlawful and unmanly act of his life, with which the worst of the offences laid to the charge of the Gang would compare only too favourably.

Now he felt instinctively that he was in the presence and at the mercy of the chief of this band of outlaws, against which he had declared war to the death—a man who owed him a grudge that life would hardly pay. Still he had deliberately staked his life on this very venture, and he was not the man to take his stakes off the table when the game was going against him. He looked in silence at the masked man for a few moments to let his thoughts get into something like order. Then he said quietly :

" Well, Mr. Salter, I confess I never expected to see you in the flesh again, but, since you have manifestly resurrected, I don't quite see the point of that mask of yours—at least not in private life."

" Resurrected ! By thunder, sonny, you've hit it in once. Say, did you ever see anything more like a last year's corpse than me ? "

He tore the mask from his face as he uttered the last word. The Inspector staggered to his feet and dropped back into the chair with a gasp of amazement and a groan of horror mingled in the same breath. What had been Seth Salter's not uncomely face was now a one-eyed, noseless mass of pits and seams and scars too hideous to imagine.

" Ya-as, looks sorter pretty, don't it? Don't seem to think much of it. Waal, p'raps not, 'tain't likely ; but if you an' your chaps didn't exactly do it, them as you was kind enough to leave me to out yonder in the kloof did. Yes, sir, that's vultures' work. I'd a bullet of yours through my right arm, one through the chest from one of your slouches, and a crack over the head with a carbine stock that'd 'a knocked the gruel outer some people's skulls ; so, you see, I hadn't much chance agin the critturs. But I thought I'd fight to a finish, and I should hev done if a Cape lad hadn't come through the kloof before I was all gone and toted what was left of me to his hut, and fetched an old kaffir medicine man to patch me up.

"No, you needn't trouble to make any remarks; you're weak yet, and I'm on deck just now. It'll make things shorter and pleasanter if you just make yourself comfortable an' hear me out. I shan't worry you with what happened to me just after. I got better, and I'd one eye and a mouth left, as you see, and the eye had to look around for something to put in the mouth.

"Waal, after considerable ups and downs, I met your Lootenant Mays way down in Natal. I told him who I was, or had been— for you can bet he didn't recognise me—and we put our heads together, and worked out this Border Gang scheme. I found the requisite hard cases for the actual work, and he got round your chaps, or kept 'em off the scent, as the case might be. The game worked like an angelic picnic. We robbed thieves, and the thieves darn't split. Then, as the organisation got better, we extended things, and by about three months ago we'd half your chaps and nearly all the slops on this side in our pay.

"Waal, we've made tons of money, and we're just thinking about retiring into respectable society, but, Mr. Lipinzki, there's just two things I want to do before I do that."

"And those are—revenge on me, and— what else, may I ask?"

"Guess you're nervy, little man, and you may ask. Ya-as, one of 'em's to square up things with you, and the other is to clean out the mail when it takes that big consignment that you tried to fool us over to-night on board, which, I take it, 'll be the day after to-morrow, or, I should say, to-day, for it's morning now. We've got you safe, and all the guard but two are chippin' in with us, so that's as good as done."

"And may I ask again what you intend to do in the way of squaring things up with me? Something with vultures in it, I suppose. I can't growl under the circumstances, though, for the sake of my own conscience, I'd like to tell you that we honestly thought you were dead before we left you. I can't think how you stood all we gave you. What a thousand pities you didn't give the stones up quietly!"

"I guess it is—for you. Why didn't you let me keep 'em, after I'd played the game an' run 'em fair and honourable? But that's nowhere. If I didn't think you a white man and grit all through, I wouldn't give yer a chance. I'd have your livin' bones, so to speak, picked clean by to-morrow night, as I mighty near had mine. But I believe you did think me dead, and so I'll give you a square show. But I'm goin' to give you half-an-hour's hell first, just to even things up for what I had when I was fighting them vultures."

"And that?"

"I'm goin' to make you play me Chicago, best seven games out of thirteen. If I win, I shall plug you fatally, and go and clean the mail out. If you win, I'll give you back your shooter, and back my one eye agin your two at shootin' on the drop. I'll set the alarum of that clock to go off two minutes after we've taken our places. Then when it goes, we'll go—one or both of us. That's about as fair as I can afford to be. What do you think?"

"I don't see much hell in that, to tell you the truth."

"No, because you seem to have forgotten that Miss Radna's goin' down with the mail that day. You know I've admired her a lot. How d'you think she'd like to have some of the stones we shall get if I had 'em cut for her as a weddin' present? I shouldn't take the dead gems and leave the livin' and the best of 'em all behind, *you* bet."

"That'll do, curse you; get out the dice."

"Waal, that's bizness, anyhow, if it ain't over grateful or polite. Take a drink first, just to steady your hand? No? Then I will. Here's the dice. We'll shake for first throw."

Now, for the instruction of the unsophisticated, the game of Chicago is played with dice in this wise: Five dice are thrown. Aces count a hundred, the first six thrown sixty, others six. From five down to two spots are counted. One bone must be left on the table after each throw, hence there are five throws, and the highest possible is five aces, counting five hundred.

The two played in silence. People usually do when the stakes are so big that if they lose they can never play again. The Fates must have been looking over their shoulders, and enjoying the deadly game, for they drew it out to its utmost length. After the tenth game Salter was two ahead, and the Inspector won the eleventh by six and the twelfth by seven.

"Six and seven's thirteen, and we've the thirteenth game to play," said Salter, shaping the first actual sentence that had been spoken since the play began. "Shouldn't wonder if I lost now. That's right, help yourself. Whisky's good for shootin'. My throw, I reckon."

He shook the dice up, canted the box gently over, and the dice trickled out in a little white rattling stream. When they settled there were two aces, a six, a four, and a two.

"Two hundred and sixty's not a bad start, but I guess I'll give the aces another chance."

He shook up the three dice. They came out an ace and two sixes. His score was now three hundred and sixty, with two more throws, but he had the option of leaving the six or including it in the next throw, on the chance of getting an ace instead of it. He left it, and threw the two. They came up six and four, making his total four hundred and twenty-four with one more throw. He tossed the four into the box and sent it rolling along the table. When it stopped it was a three.

"I've seen better," he said, as he gathered the dice into the box and pushed it over to the Inspector; "but anythin' over four hundred takes figures to beat it."

Lipinzki's first throw was a poor one. Six, five, two threes, and a two! The second throw three aces came up together, making

"An ace! By thunder, I thought so!"

his score three hundred and sixty. The other was a four. He picked it up, threw, and made a three of it. He tried again, and made it a six. He was now four hundred and twenty—four behind.

"Tough luck, but I guess you've got to try again, pard."

The hand of the man was firm though the heart of the father was shaking as the Inspector turned the box over for the last time.

"An ace! By thunder, I thought so! Waal, if that ain't the luck of hell tell me. There's your gun!"

By every law save that of the unwritten code of gamblers' honour, Inspector Lipinzki would have been justified in covering Salter as he went to set the alarum, and he had another very strong motive for doing it, but he didn't. He knew the game, and he played it. They took their places in opposite corners of the hut, about eight paces apart. The little Ansonia clock seemed to think itself a boiler factory for the time being, so loudly did it tick the fatal seconds away.

W-h-irrrr—bang—bang—bang—ting-a-ling-a-ling —bang — bang — ting —bang— surrr-up.

It was as strange a chorus as mortal ears ever heard, and the little clock seemed to think so, and did its best to keep its end up. When it was over, Inspector Lipinzki pulled himself up on to his hands, and, looking across the hut through a mist of blood and a fog of smoke, saw Seth Salter's one eye glaring at him over the barrel of a revolver which was swaying to and fro about a foot or so from the floor.

Then he remembered that his Smith-Wesson had only five chambers. Salter's Colt probably had six. He saw the flame leap from the muzzle, and at the same instant Salter's head dropped with a thump on the floor. A red-hot knife seemed to pierce his shoulder, and then he dropped too, just too soon to hear angry shouts and the stamping of horses' hoofs outside.

The Free State Police didn't mind winking, for satisfactory considerations, at I.D.B., or even at a peaceable form of robbery under arms, but they had neither the stomach nor the heart for a share of blood-guiltiness, and so, when one of the Inspector's traitors dropped a hint as to the real purpose for which he had been taken to the hut, their righteously indignant commandant ordered an immediate raid on it.

He got there three minutes too late. Salter was unconscious, and bleeding to death with five bullet holes in him. The Inspector was insensible too, but he revived and lived long enough to give the true story of what had happened. The Dutch policeman wisely concluded that a process of whitewashing would be good for his soul, so he had the Inspector's body conveyed with all honour across the border, and delivered it to the British authorities with such an account of the night's doings as fully insured their being the last of the exploits of the Border Gang.

"Yes," said the gentleman who had given me the main points of the foregoing narrative as we sat under the verandah in the garden of the Central one night after dinner; "yes; Lipinski was a good sort, a very good sort, and so was Salter. I knew them both and liked them both. It's a pity that two such men should have been started off plugging each other with lead just because they had different ideas about the diamond trade. And it all went for nothing too. There were I.D.B.'s then and there are I.D.B.'s now—only they work differently. These infernal stones are too tempting, and as long as diamonds are diamonds there'll be I.D.B.'s of some sort."

W-h-ir-rr—bang—bang—bang.

XII

The Stolen Cigar-Case

BRETT HARTE

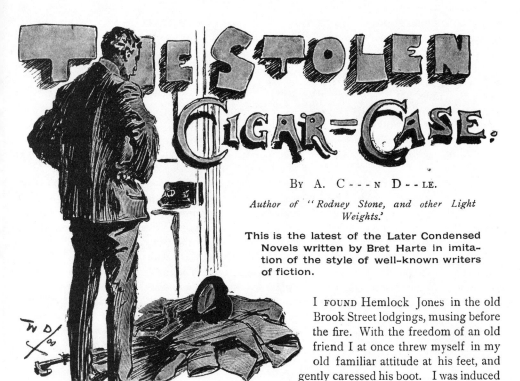

THE STOLEN CIGAR-CASE.

By A. C - - - n D - - le.

Author of "Rodney Stone, and other Light Weights."

This is the latest of the Later Condensed Novels written by Bret Harte in imitation of the style of well-known writers of fiction.

I FOUND Hemlock Jones in the old Brook Street lodgings, musing before the fire. With the freedom of an old friend I at once threw myself in my old familiar attitude at his feet, and gently caressed his boot. I was induced to do this for two reasons; one that it enabled me to get a good look at his bent, concentrated face, and the other that it seemed to indicate my reverence for his superhuman insight. So absorbed was he, even then, in tracking some mysterious clue, that he did not seem to notice me. But therein I was wrong—as I always was in my attempt to understand that powerful intellect.

" It is raining," he said, without lifting his head.

" You have been out then ? " I said quickly.

" No. But I see that your umbrella is wet, and that your overcoat, which you threw off on entering, has drops of water on it."

I sat aghast at his penetration. After a pause he said carelessly, as if dismissing the subject : " Besides, I hear the rain on the window. Listen."

I listened. I could scarcely credit my ears, but there was the soft pattering of drops on the pane. It was evident, there was no deceiving this man !

" Have you been busy lately ? " I asked, changing the subject. " What new problem—given up by Scotland Yard as inscrutable—has occupied that gigantic intellect ? "

He drew back his foot slightly, and seemed to hesitate ere he returned it to its original position. Then he answered wearily : " Mere trifles—nothing to speak of. The Prince Kopoli has been here to get my advice regarding the disappearance of certain rubies from the Kremlin ; the Rajah of Pootibad, after vainly beheading his entire bodyguard, has been obliged to seek my assistance to recover a jewelled sword. The Grand Duchess of Pretzel-Brauntswig is desirous of discovering where her husband was on the night of the 14th of February, and last night"—he lowered his voice slightly—" a lodger in this very house, meeting me on the stairs, wanted to know ' Why they don't answer his bell.' "

I could not help smiling—until I saw a frown gathering on his inscrutable forehead.

" Pray to remember," he said coldly, " that it was through such an apparently trivial question that I found out, ' Why Paul Ferroll killed his Wife,' and ' What happened to Jones !' "

I became dumb at once. He paused for a moment, and then suddenly changing back to his usual pitiless, analytical style, he said : " When I say these are trifles—they are so in comparison to an affair that is now before me. A crime has been committed, and, singularly enough, against myself. You start," he said ; " you wonder who would have dared to attempt it ! So did I ; nevertheless, it has been done. *I* have been *robbed !* "

" *You* robbed—you, Hemlock Jones, the Terror of Peculators ! " I gasped in amazement, rising and gripping the table as I faced him.

" Yes ; listen. I would confess it to no other. But *you* who have followed my career, who know my methods ; yea, for whom I have partly lifted the veil that conceals my plans from ordinary humanity ; you, who have for years rapturously accepted my confidences, passionately admired my inductions and inferences, placed yourself at my beck and call, become my slave, grovelled at my feet, given up your practice except those few unremunerative and rapidly-decreasing patients to whom, in moments of abstraction over *my* problems, you have administered strychnine for quinine and arsenic for Epsom salts ; you, who have sacrificed everything and everybody to me—*you* I make my confidant ! "

I rose and embraced him warmly, yet he was already so engrossed in thought that at the same moment he mechanically placed his hand upon his watch chain as if to consult the time. " Sit down," he said ; " have a cigar ? "

" I have given up cigar smoking," I said.

" Why ? " he asked.

I hesitated, and perhaps coloured. I had really given it up because, with my diminished practice, it was too expensive. I could only afford a pipe. " I prefer a pipe," I said laughingly. " But tell me of this robbery. What have you lost ? "

He rose, and planting himself before the fire with his hands under his coat tails, looked down upon me reflectively for a moment. " Do you remember the cigar-case presented to me by the Turkish Ambassador for discovering the missing favourite of th Grand Vizier in the fifth chorus girl at the Hilarity Theatre ? It was that one. It was incrusted with diamonds. I mean the cigar-case."

" And the largest one had been supplanted by paste," I said.

" Ah," he said with a reflective smile, " you know that ? "

" You told me yourself. I remember considering it a proof of your extraordinary perception. But, by Jove, you don't mean to say you have lost it."

He was silent for a moment. " No ; it has been stolen, it is true, but I shall still find it. And by myself alone ! In your profession, my dear fellow, when a member is severely ill he does not prescribe for himself, but calls in a brother doctor. Therein we differ. I shall take this matter in my own hands."

" And where could you find better ? " I said enthusiastically. " I should say the cigarcase is as good as recovered already."

" I shall remind you of that again," he said lightly. " And now, to show you my confidence in your judgment, in spite of my determination to pursue this alone, I am willing to listen to any suggestions from you."

He drew a memorandum book from his pocket, and, with a grave smile, took up his pencil.

I could scarcely believe my reason. He, the great Hemlock Jones ! accepting suggestions from a humble individual like myself ! I kissed his hand reverently, and began in a joyous tone :

" First I should advertise, offering a reward ; I should give the same intimation in handbills, distributed at the ' pubs ' and the pastrycooks. I should next visit the different pawnbrokers ; I should give notice at the police station. I should examine the servants. I should thoroughly search the house and my own pockets. I speak relatively," I added with a laugh, " of course, I mean *your* own."

He gravely made an entry of these details.

" Perhaps," I added, " you have already done this ? "

" Perhaps," he returned enigmatically. " Now, my dear friend," he continued, putting the note-book in his pocket, and rising—" would you excuse me for a few moments? Make yourself perfectly at home until I return; there may be some things," he added with a sweep of his hand towards his heterogeneously filled shelves, " that may interest you, and while away the time. There are pipes and tobacco in that corner and whiskey on the table." And nodding to me with the same inscrutable face, he left the room. I was too well accustomed to his methods to think much of his unceremonious withdrawal, and made no doubt he was off to investigate some clue which had suddenly occurred to his active intelligence.

Left to myself, I cast a cursory glance over his shelves. There were a number of small glass jars, containing earthy substances labeled "Pavement and road sweepings," from the principal thoroughfares and suburbs of London, with the sub-directions "For identifying foot tracks." There were several other jars labeled "Fluff from omnibus and road-car seats," "Cocoanut fibre and rope strands from mattings in public places," "Cigarette stumps and match ends from floor of Palace Theatre, Row A, 1 to 50." Everywhere were evidences of this wonderful man's system and perspicacity.

He was a rough-looking man, with a shabby overcoat.

I was thus engaged when I heard the slight creaking of a door, and I looked up as a stranger entered. He was a rough-looking man, with a shabby overcoat, a still more disreputable muffler round his throat, and a cap on his head. Considerably annoyed at his intrusion I turned upon him rather sharply, when, with a mumbled, growling apology for mistaking the room, he shuffled out again and closed the door. I followed him quickly to the landing and saw that he disappeared down the stairs.

With my mind full of the robbery, the incident made a singular impression on me. I knew my friend's habits of hasty absences from his room in his moments of deep inspiration; it was only too probable that with his powerful intellect and magnificent perceptive genius concentrated on one subject, he should be careless of his own belongings, and, no doubt, even forget to take the ordinary precaution of locking up his drawers. I tried one or two and found that I was right — although for some reason I was unable to open one to its fullest extent. The handles were sticky, as if someone had opened them with dirty fingers. Knowing Hemlock's fastidious cleanliness, I resolved to inform him of this circumstance, but I forgot it, alas! until—but I am anticipating my story.

His absence was strangely prolonged. I at last seated myself by the fire, and lulled by warmth and the patter of the rain on the window, I fell asleep. I may have dreamt, for during my sleep I had a vague semi-consciousness as of hands being softly pressed on my pockets—no doubt induced by the story of the robbery. When I came fully to my senses, I found Hemlock Jones sitting on the other side of the hearth, his deeply concentrated gaze fixed on the fire.

" I found you so comfortably asleep that I could not bear to waken you," he said with a smile.

I rubbed my eyes. " And what news? " I asked. " How have you succeeded? "

" Better than I expected," he said, "and I think," he added, tapping his note-book—" I owe much to *you*."

Deeply gratified, I awaited more. But in vain. I ought to have remembered that in his moods Hemlock Jones was reticence itself. I told him simply of the strange intrusion, but he only laughed.

Later, when I rose to go, he looked at me playfully. " If you were a married man," he said, "I would advise you not to go home until you had brushed your sleeve. There are a few short, brown seal-skin hairs on the inner side of the fore-arm—just where they would have adhered if your arm had encircled a seal-skin sacque with some pressure! "

" For once you are at fault," I said triumphantly, " the hair is my own as you will perceive; I have just had it cut at the hair-dressers, and no doubt this arm projected beyond the apron."

He frowned slightly, yet nevertheless, on my turning to go he embraced me warmly—a rare exhibition in that man of ice. He even helped me on with my overcoat and pulled out and smoothed down the flaps of my pockets. He was particular, too, in fitting my arm in my overcoat 'sleeve, shaking the sleeve down from the armhole to the cuff with his deft fingers. " Come again soon! " he said, clapping me on the back.

" At any and all times," I said enthusiastically. " I only ask ten minutes twice a day to eat a crust at my office and four hours' sleep at night, and the rest of my time is devoted to you always—as you know."

" It is, indeed," he said, with his impenetrable smile.

Nevertheless I did not find him at home when I next called. One afternoon, when nearing my own home I met him in one of his favourite disguises—a long, blue, swallow-tailed coat, striped cotton trousers, large turn-over collar, blacked face, and white hat, carrying a tambourine. Of course to others the disguise was perfect, although it was known to myself, and I passed him—according to an old understanding between us—without the slightest recognition, trusting to a later explanation. At another time, as I was making a professional visit to the wife of a publican at the East End, I saw him in the disguise of a broken-down artisan looking into the window of an adjacent pawnshop. I was delighted to see that he was evidently following my suggestions, and in my joy I ventured to tip him a wink; it was abstractedly returned.

Two days later I received a note appointing a meeting at his lodgings that night. That meeting, alas! was the one memorable occurrence of my life, and the last meeting I ever had with Hemlock Jones! I will try to set it down calmly, though my pulses still throb with the recollection of it.

I found him standing before the fire with that look upon his face which I had seen only once or twice in our acquaintance—a look which I may call an absolute concatenation of inductive and deductive ratiocination—from which all that was human, tender, or sympathetic, was absolutely discharged. He was simply an icy, algebraic symbol! Indeed his whole being was concentrated to that extent that his clothes fitted loosely, and his head was absolutely so much reduced in size by his mental compression that his hat tipped back from his forehead and literally hung on his massive ears.

After I had entered, he locked the doors, fastened the windows, and even placed a chair before the chimney. As I watched those significant precautions with absorbing interest, he suddenly drew a revolver and presenting it to my temple, said in low, icy tones :

." Hand over that cigar-case ! "

Even in my bewilderment, my reply was truthful, spontaneous, and involuntary. " I haven't got it," I said.

He smiled bitterly, and threw down his revolver. " I expected that reply ! Then let me now confront you with something more awful, more deadly, more relentless and convincing than that mere lethal weapon— the damning inductive and deductive proofs of your guilt ! " He drew from his pocket a roll of paper and a note-book.

" But surely," I gasped, " you are joking ! You could not for a moment believe——"

" Silence ! " he roared. " Sit down ! " I obeyed.

" You have condemned yourself," he went on pitilessly. " Condemned yourself on my processes—processes familiar to you, applauded by you, accepted by you for years ! We will go back to the time when you first saw the cigar-case. Your expressions," he said in cold, deliberate tones, consulting his paper, " were : ' How beautiful ! I wish it were mine.' This was your first step in crime —and my first indication. From ' I *wish* it were mine ' to ' I *will* have it mine,' and the mere detail, ' How *can* I make it mine,' the advance was obvious. Silence ! But as in my methods, it was necessary that there should be an overwhelming inducement to the crime, that unholy admiration of yours for the mere trinket itself was not enough. You are a smoker of cigars."

" But," I burst out passionately, " I told you I had given up smoking cigars."

" Fool ! " he said coldly, " that is the *second* time you have committed yourself. Of course, you *told* me ! what more natural than for you to blazon forth that prepared and unsolicited statement to *prevent* accusation. Yet, as I said before, even that wretched attempt to cover up your tracks was not enough. I still had to find that overwhelming, impelling motive necessary to affect a man like you. That motive I found in *passion*, the strongest of all impulses—love, I suppose you would

" Hand over that cigar-case ! "

call it," he added bitterly ; " that night you called ! You had brought the damning proofs of it in your sleeve."

" But," I almost screamed.

" Silence," he thundered. " I know what you would say. You would say that even if you had embraced some young person in a sealskin sacque what had that to do with the robbery. Let me tell you then, that that sealskin sacque represented the quality and character of your fatal entanglement ! If you are at all conversant with light sporting literature you would know that a sealskin sacque indicates a love induced by sordid mercenary interests. You bartered your honour for it— that stolen cigar-case was the purchaser of the sealskin sacque ! Without money, with a decreasing practice, it was the only way you could insure your passion being returned by that young person, whom, for your sake, I have not even pursued. Silence! Having thoroughly established your motive, I now proceed to the commission of the crime itself. Ordinary people would have begun with that—with an attempt to discover the whereabouts of the missing object. These are not my methods."

So overpowering was his penetration, that although I knew myself innocent, I licked my lips with avidity to hear the further details of this lucid exposition of my crime.

"You committed that theft the night I showed you the cigar-case and after I had carelessly thrown it in that drawer. You were sitting in that chair, and I had risen to take something from that shelf. In that instant you secured your booty without rising. Silence! Do you remember when I helped you on with your overcoat the other night? I was particular about fitting your arm in. While doing so I measured your arm with a spring tape measure from the shoulder to the cuff. A later visit to your tailor confirmed that measurement. It proved to be *the exact distance between your chair and that drawer!*"

I sat stunned.

"The rest are mere corroborative details! You were again tampering with the drawer when I discovered you doing so. Do not start! The stranger that blundered into the room with the muffler on—was myself. More, I had placed a little soap on the drawer handles when I purposely left you alone. The soap was on your hand when I shook it at parting. I softly felt your pockets when you were asleep for further developments. I embraced you when you left—that I might feel if you had the cigar-case, or any other articles, hidden on your body. This confirmed me in the belief that you had already disposed of it in the manner and for the purpose I have shown you. As I still believed you capable of remorse and confession, I allowed you to see I was on your track twice, once in the garb of an itinerant negro minstrel, and the second time as a workman looking in the window of the pawnshop where you pledged your booty."

"But," I burst out, "if you had asked the pawnbroker you would have seen how unjust—— "

"Fool!" he hissed; "that was one of *your* suggestions to search the pawnshops. Do you suppose I followed any of your suggestions—the suggestions of the thief? On the contrary, they told me what to avoid."

"And I suppose," I said bitterly, "you have not even searched your drawer."

"No," he said calmly.

I was for the first time really vexed. I went to the nearest drawer and pulled it out sharply. It stuck as it had before, leaving a part of the drawer unopened. By working it, however, I discovered that it was impeded by some obstacle that had slipped to the upper part of the drawer, and held it firmly fast. Inserting my hand, I pulled out the impeding object. It was the missing cigar-case. I turned to him with a cry of joy.

But I was appalled at his expression. A look of contempt was now added to his acute, penetrating gaze. "I have been mistaken," he said slowly. "I had not allowed for your weakness and cowardice. I thought too highly of you even in your guilt; but I see now why you tampered with that drawer the other night. By some incredible means—possibly another theft—you took the cigar-case out of pawn, and like a whipped hound restored it to me in this feeble, clumsy fashion. You thought to deceive me, Hemlock Jones: more, you thought to destroy my infallibility. Go! I give you your liberty. I shall not summon the three policemen who wait in the adjoining room—but out of my sight for ever."

As I stood once more dazed and petrified, he took me firmly by the ear and led me into the hall, closing the door behind him. This re-opened presently wide enough to permit him to thrust out my hat, overcoat, umbrella and overshoes, and then closed against me for ever!

I never saw him again. I am bound to say, however, that thereafter my business increased—I recovered much of my old practice—and a few of my patients recovered also. I became rich. I had a brougham and a house in the West End. But I often wondered, pondering on that wonderful man's penetration and insight, if, in some lapse of consciousness, I had not really stolen his cigar-case!

XIII

At The Pistol's Point

E.W. HORNUNG

At the Pistol's Point.

By E. W. Hornung.

HE church bells were ringing for evensong, croaking across the snow with short, harsh strokes, as though the frost had eaten into the metal and made it hoarse. Outside, the scene had all the cheery sparkle, all the peaceful glamour, of an old-fashioned Christmas card. There was the snow-covered village, there the church-spire coated all down one side, the chancel windows standing out like oil-paintings, the silver sickle of a moon, the ideal thatched cottage with the warm, red light breaking from the open door, and the peace of Heaven seemingly pervading and enveloping all. Yet on earth we know that this peace is not; and the door of the ideal cottage had been opened and was shut by a crushed woman, whose husband had but now refused her pennies for the plate, with a curse which followed her into the snow. And the odour prevailing beneath the thatched roof was one of hot brandy-and-water, mingled with the fumes of some rank tobacco.

Old Fitch was over sixty years of age, and the woman on her way to church was his third wife; she had borne him no child, nor had Fitch son or daughter living who would set foot inside his house. He was a singular old man, selfish and sly and dissolute, yet not greatly disliked beyond his own door, and withal a miracle of health and energy for his years. He drank to his heart's content, but he was never drunk, nor was Sunday's bottle ever known to lose him the soft side of Monday's bargain. By trade he was game-dealer, corn-factor, money-lender, and mortgagee of half the village; in appearance, a man of medium height, with bow-legs and immense round shoulders, a hard mouth, shrewd eyes, and wiry hair as white as the snow outside.

The bells ceased, and for a moment there was no sound in the cottage but the song of the kettle on the hob. Then Fitch reached for the brandy-bottle, and brewed himself another steaming bumper. As he watched the sugar dissolve, a few notes from the organ reached his ears, and the old man smiled cynically as he sipped and smacked his lips. At his elbow his tobacco-pipe and the weekly newspaper were ranged with the brandy-bottle, and he was soon in enjoyment of all three. Over the paper Fitch had already fallen asleep after a particularly hearty mid-day meal, but he had not so much as glanced at the most entertaining pages, and he found them now more entertaining than usual. There was a scandal in high life running to several columns, and sub-divided into paragraphs labelled with the most pregnant head-lines; the old man's mouth watered as he determined to leave this item to the last. It was not the only one of interest; there were several suicides, an admirable execution, a burglary, and—what? Fitch frowned as his quick eye came tumbling down a paragraph; then all at once he gasped out an oath and sat very still. The pipe in his mouth went out, the brandy-and-water was cooling in his glass; you might have heard them singing the psalms in the church hard by; but the old man heard nothing, saw nothing, thought of nothing but the brief paragraph before his eyes.

ESCAPE FROM PORTLAND.
ONE CONVICT KILLED, ANOTHER WOUNDED, BUT A THIRD GETS CLEAN AWAY.

The greatest excitement was caused at Weymouth yesterday morning on the report being circulated that several convicts had effected their escape from the grounds of the Portland convict establishment. There appears to have been a regularly concerted plan on the part of the prisoners working in one of the outdoor gangs to attempt to regain their liberty, as yesterday morning three convicts bolted simultaneously from their party. They were instantly challenged to stop, but as the order was not complied with, the warders fired several shots. One of the runaways fell dead, and another was so badly wounded that he was immediately recaptured, and is now lying in a precarious condition. The third man, named Henry Cattermole, continued his course despite a succession of shots, and was soon beyond range of the rifles. He was pursued for some distance, but was ultimately lost to view in the thick fog which prevailed. A hue and cry was raised, and search parties continued to scour the neighbourhood long after dark, but up to a late hour his recapture had not been effected. Cattermole will be remembered as the man who was sentenced to death some years ago for the murder of Lord Wolborough's game-keeper, near Bury St. Edmund's, but who afterwards received the benefit of the doubt involved in the production of a wad which did not fit the convict's gun. In spite of the successful efforts then made on his behalf, however, the authorities at Portland describe Cattermole as a most daring criminal, and one who is only too likely to prove a danger to the community as long as he remains at large.

Fitch stared stupidly at the words for several minutes after he had read them through; it was the last sentence which at length fell into focus with his seeing eye. Henry Cattermole at large! How long had he been at large? It was a Sunday paper, but the Saturday edition, and this was among the latest news. But it said "yesterday morning," and that meant Friday morning last. So Henry Cattermole had been at large since

"HE WAS PURSUED FOR SOME DISTANCE."

then, and this was the Sunday evening, and that made nearly three days altogether. Another question now forced itself upon the old man's mind: how far was it from Portland prison—to—this—room?

Like most rustics of his generation, old Fitch had no spare knowledge of geography: he knew his own country-side and the road to London, but that was all. Portland he knew to be on the other side of London; it might be ten miles, might be two hundred; but this he felt in his shuddering heart and shaking bones, that near or far, deep snow or no snow, Henry Cattermole was either recaptured or else on his way to that cottage at that moment.

The feeling sucked the blood from the old man's vessels, even as his lips drained the tumbler he had filled with so light a heart. Then for a little he had spurious courage. He leant back in his chair and laughed aloud, but it sounded strangely in the empty cottage; he looked up at the bell-mouthed gun above the chimney-piece, and that gave him greater confidence, for he kept it loaded. He got up and began to whistle, but stopped in the middle of a bar.

"Curse him!" he said aloud, "they should ha' hanged him, and then I never should ha' been held like this. That'll be a good job if they take an' hang him now, for I fare to feel afraid, I do, as long as Harry Cattermole's alive."

Old Fitch opened his door a moment, saw the thin moon shining on the snow, but no living soul abroad, and for once he was in want of a companion; however, the voices of the choir sounded nearer than ever in the frosty air, and heartened him a little as he shut the door again, turned the heavy key, and shot both bolts well home. He was still stooping over the bottom one, when his eyes fell upon a ragged trouser-leg and a stout stocking planted close behind him. It was instantly joined by another ragged leg and another stout stocking. Neither made a sound, for there were no shoes to the cat-like feet; and the stockings were remarkable for a most conspicuous stripe.

Then old Fitch knew that his enemy had found him out, and he could not stir. He was waiting for a knife to plunge into the centre of his broad, round back; and when a hand slapped him there instead, he thought for a moment he was stabbed indeed. When he knew that he was not, he turned round, still stooping, in a pitiable attitude, and a new shock greeted him. Could this be Henry Cattermole?

The poacher had been stout and thick-set; the convict was gaunt and lean. The one had been florid and youthful; the other was yellow as parchment, and the stubble on the cropped head and on the fleshless jaw was of a leaden grey.

"That—that ain't Harry Cattermole?" the old man whimpered.

"No, that ain't; but 'twas once, and means to be again! Lead the way in beside the fire. I wish you'd sometimes use that front parlour of yours! I've had it to myself this half-hour, and that's cold."

Old Fitch led the way without a word, walked innocently up to the fire, and suddenly sprang for his gun. He never reached it. The barrel of a revolver, screwed round in his ear, drove him reeling across the floor.

"Silly old fool!" hissed Cattermole. "Did you think I'd come to you unarmed? Sit down on that chair before I blow your brains out."

Fitch obeyed.

"I—I can't make out," he stuttered, "why you fare to come to me at all!"

"O' course you can't," said Cattermole, ironically.

"OLD FITCH SUDDENLY SPRANG FOR HIS GUN."

"If I'd been you, I'd ha' run anywhere but where I was known so well."

"You would, would you? Then you knew I'd got out, eh, old man?"

"Just been a-reading about it in this here paper."

"I see—I see. I caught a bit o' what you was a-saying to yourself, just as I was thinking it was a safe thing to come out o' that cold parlour o' yours. So that was me you was locking out, was it? Yet you pretend you don't know why I come! You know well enough. You know—you know!"

The convict had seated himself on the kitchen table, and was glaring down on the trembling old man in the chair. He wore a long overcoat, and under it some pitiful rags. The cropped head and the legs swinging in the striped stockings were the only incriminating features, and old Fitch was glancing from the one to the other, wondering why neither had saved him from this horrible interview. Cattermole read his thoughts, and his eyes gleamed.

"So you think I've come all the way in these here, do you?" he cried, tapping one shin. "I tell you I've walked and walked till my bare legs were frozen, and then sat behind a hedge and slipped these on and rubbed them to life again! Where do you think I got these rotten old duds? Off of a scare-crow in a field, I did! I wasn't going to break into no houses and leave my tracks all along the line. But yesterday I got a long lift in a goods train, or I shouldn't be here now; and last night I did crack a crib for this here overcoat and a bit o' supper, and another for the shooter. That didn't so much matter then. I was within twenty mile of you! Of *you*, you old devil —do you hear?"

Fitch nodded with an ashen face.

"And now do you know why I've come?"

Fitch moistened his blue lips. "To—to murder me!" he whispered, like a dying man.

"That rests with you," said the convict, fondling his weapon.

"What do you want me to do?"

"Confess!"

"Confess what?" whispered Fitch.

"That you swore me away at the trial."

The old man had been holding his breath; he now expelled it with a deep sigh, and taking out a huge red handkerchief, wiped the moisture from his face. Meanwhile, the convict had descried writing-materials on a chiffonnier, and placed them on the table beside the brandy-bottle and the tobacco-jar.

"Turn your chair round for writing."

Fitch did so.

"Now take up your pen and write what I tell you. Don't cock your head and look at me! I hear the psalm-singing as well as you do; they've only just got started, and nobody'll come near us for another hour. Pity you didn't go too, isn't it? Now write what I tell you, word for word, or, so help me, you're a stiff 'un!"

Fitch dipped his pen in the ink. After all, what he was about to write would be written under dire intimidation, and nobody would attach any importance to statements so obtained. He squared his elbows to the task.

"'I, Samuel Fitch,'" began Cattermole, "'do hereby swear' and declare before God Almighty'—before God Almighty, have you got that down?—'that I, Samuel Fitch, did bear false witness against my neighbour, Henry Cattermole, at his trial at Bury Assizes, November 29th, 1887. It is true that I saw both Henry Cattermole and James Savage, his lordship's gamekeeper, in the wood at Wolborough on the night of

September 9th in the same year. It is true that I was there by appointment with Savage, as his wife stated in her evidence. It is *not* true that I heard a shot and heard Savage sing out, "Harry Cattermole!" as I came up and before ever I had a word with him. That statement was a deliberate fabrication on my part. The real truth is——' but hold on ! I'm likely going too fast for you—I've had it in my head that long ! How much have you got down, eh ? "

" ' Fabrication on my part,' " repeated old Fitch, in a trembling voice, as he waited for more.

" Good ! Now pull yourself together," said Cattermole, suddenly cocking his revolver. " ' *The real truth is that I, Samuel Fitch, shot James Savage with my own hand !* ' "

Fitch threw down his pen.

" That's a lie," he gasped. " I never did ! I won't write it."

The cocked revolver covered him.

" Prefer to die in your chair, eh ? "

" Yes."

" I'll give you one minute by your own watch."

Still covering his man, the convict held out

all at once the watch was ticking like an eight-day clock.

Fitch rolled his head from side to side.

" Fifteen seconds," said Cattermole.

The old man's brow was white and spangled like the snow outside.

" Half-time," said Cattermole.

Five, ten, fifteen, twenty seconds passed ; then Fitch caught up the pen. " Go on ! " he groaned. " I'll write any lie you like ; that'll do you no good ; no one will believe a word of it." Yet the perspiration was streaming down his face ; it splashed upon the paper as he proceeded to write, in trembling characters, at Cattermole's dictation.

" ' The real truth is that I, Samuel Fitch, shot James Savage with my own hand. The circumstances that led to my shooting him I will confess and explain hereafter. When he had fallen I heard a shout and someone running up. I got behind a tree, but I saw Harry Cattermole, the poacher, trip clean over the body. His gun went off in the air, and when he tried to get up again, I saw he couldn't because he'd twisted his ankle. He never saw me ; I slipped away and gave my false evidence, and Harry Cattermole caught escaping from the wood on his hands and knees, with blood upon his hands and clothes, and an empty gun. I gave evidence against him to stop him giving evidence against me. But this is the whole truth, and nothing but the truth, so help me God ! ' "

"I'LL GIVE YOU ONE MINUTE."

Cattermole paused, Fitch finished writing ; again the eyes of the two men met ; and those of the elder gleamed with a cunning curiosity.

" How—how did you know ? " he asked, lowering his voice and leaning forward as he spoke.

his other hand for the watch, and had momentary contact with a cold, damp one as it dropped into his palm. Cattermole placed the watch upon the table where both could see the dial.

" Your minute begins now," said he ; and

" Two and two," was the reply. " I put 'em together as soon as ever I saw you in the box."

" That'll never be believed—got like this."

" Will it not ? Wait a bit ; you've not done yet. ' As a proof of what I say '—do you hear me?—'as a proof of what I say, the gun which the wad will fit, that saved Henry Cattermole's life, will be found——' "

Cattermole waited until the old man had caught him up.

"Now," said he, "you finish the sentence for yourself!"

"What?" cried Fitch.

"Write where that gun's to be found—you know—I don't—and then sign your name!"

"But I *don't* know——"

"You do."

"I sold it!"

"You wouldn't dare. You've got that somewhere, I see it in your face. Write down where, and then show me the place; and if you've told a lie——"

The revolver was within a foot of the old man's head, which had fallen forward between his hands. The pen lay blotting the wet paper. Cattermole took the brandy-bottle, poured out a stiff dram, and pushed it under the other's nose.

"Drink!" he cried. "Then write the truth, and sign your name. Maybe they won't hang an old man like you; but, by God, I sha'n't think twice about shooting you if you don't write the truth!"

Fitch gulped down the brandy, took up the pen once more, and was near the end of his own death-warrant, when the convict sprang lightly from the table and stood listening in the centre of the room. Fitch saw him, and listened too. In the church they were singing another hymn; the old man saw by his watch, still lying on the table, that it must be the last hymn, and in a few minutes his wife would be back. But that was not all. There was another sound —a nearer sound —the sound of voices outside the door. The handle was turned—the door pushed—but Fitch himself had locked and bolted it. More whispers; then a loud rat-tat.

"Who is it?" cried Fitch, trembling with excitement, as he started to his feet.

"The police! Let us in, or we break in your door!"

There was no answer. Cattermole was watching the door; suddenly he turned, and there was Fitch in the act of dropping his written confession into the fire. The convict seized it before it caught, and with the other hand hurled the old man back into his chair.

"Finish it," he said below his breath, "or you're a dead man! One or other of us is going to swing! Now, then, under the floor of what room did you hide the gun? Let them hammer, the door is strong. What room was it? Ah, your bedroom! Now sign your name."

A deafening crash; the lock had given; only the bolt held firm.

"Sign!" shrieked Cattermole. A cold ring pressed the old man's temple. He signed his name, and fell forward on the table in a dead faint.

Cattermole blotted the confession, folded it up, strode over to the door, and smilingly flung it open to his pursuers.

"HE FLUNG IT OPEN TO HIS PURSUERS."

XIV

In the Chains of Crime

E.W. HORNUNG

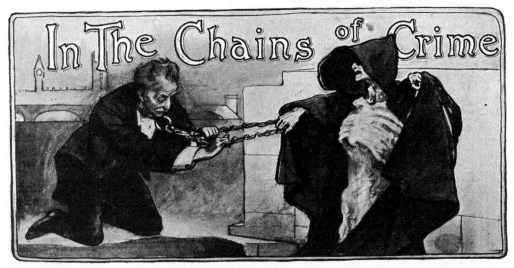

Being the Confessions of a late Prisoner of the Crown, and sometime accomplice of the more notorious A. J. Raffles, Cricketer and Criminal, whose fate is unknown.

BY E. W. HORNUNG.

I.—THE IDES OF MARCH.

IT was about half-past twelve when I returned to the Albany as a last desperate resort. Little had changed there while my heart had been turning grey. The baccarat counters still strewed the table, with the empty glasses and the loaded ash-trays. A window had been opened to let the smoke out, and was letting in the fog instead. Raffles himself had merely changed his dining jacket for one of his many blazers, yet he arched his eye-brows as though I had dragged him from his bed.

"Forgotten something?" said he, when he saw me on his mat.

"No," said I, pushing past him without ceremony, and leading the way into his room with an impudence amazing to myself.

"Not come back for your revenge, have you? Because I'm afraid I can't give it you single-handed. I was sorry myself that the others——"

We were face to face by his fireside, and I cut him short.

"Raffles," said I, "you may well be surprised at my coming back in this way and at this hour. I hardly know you. I was never in your rooms before to-night. But I was your fag at school, and you said you remembered me. Of course that's no excuse; but will you listen to me—for two minutes?"

In my emotion I had at first to struggle for every word; but his face reassured me as I went on, and I was not mistaken in its expression.

"Certainly, my dear man," said he; "as many minutes as you like. Have a Sullivan and sit down." And he handed me his silver cigarette case.

"No," said I, finding a full voice as I shook my head; "no, I won't smoke, and I won't sit down, thank you. Nor will you ask me to do either when you've heard what I have to say."

"Really?" said he, lighting his own cigarette with one clear blue eye upon me. "How do you know?"

"Because you'll probably show me the door," I cried bitterly; "and you'll be justified in doing it! But let me get it over, for God's sake! You know I dropped over two hundred just now?"

He nodded.

"I hadn't the money in my pocket."

"I remember."

"But I had my cheque-book, and I wrote each of you a cheque at that desk."

"THE BARREL TOUCHED MY TEMPLE, AND MY THUMB THE TRIGGER."

" Well ? "

" Not one of them was worth the paper it was written on, Raffles. I am overdrawn already at my bank ! "

" Surely only for the moment ? "

" No. I have spent everything."

" But somebody told me you were so well off. I heard you had come in for money ? "

" So I did. Three years ago. It has been my curse ; now it's all gone—every penny ! Yes, I've been a fool ; there never was nor will be such a fool as I've been. . . . Isn't this enough for you ? Why don't you turn me out ? " He was walking up and down with a very grave face instead.

" Couldn't your people do anything ? " he asked at length.

" My people ! I have none ; thank God there were no hearts to break ! I was an only son—that's where the mischief began. This was my poor father's money ; he worked hard for it ; thank God he is gone and will never know."

I cast myself into a chair and hid my face. Raffles continued to pace the rich carpet that was of a piece with everything else in his rooms. There was no variation in his soft and even foot-falls.

" You have a flat somewhere ? " he said at last.

" Yes, in Mount Street."

" What about the furniture ? "

I laughed aloud in my misery. " There's been a bill of sale on every stick for months ! "

Raffles stood quite still, with raised eyebrows and stern eyes that I could meet the better now that he knew the worst ; then, with a shrug, he resumed his walk, and for some minutes neither of us spoke. But in his handsome unmoved face I read my fate and death-warrant ; and with every breath I cursed my folly and my cowardice in coming to him at all. Because he had been kind to me at school, when he was captain of the eleven, and I his fag, I had dared to look for kindness from him now ; because I was ruined, and he rich enough to play cricket all the summer, and do nothing for the rest of the year, I had fatuously counted on his mercy, his sympathy, his help ! Yes, I had relied on him in my heart, for all my outward diffidence and humility ; and I was rightly served. There was little mercy and less sympathy in that curling nostril, that rigid jaw, that cold blue eye which never glanced my way. I caught up my hat. I blundered to my feet. I would have gone without a word ; but Raffles stood between me and the door.

" Where are you going ? " said he.

" That's my business," I replied. " I won't trouble you any more."

" Then how am I to help you ? "

" I didn't ask your help."

" Then why come to me ? "

" God knows ! " I exclaimed. " Will you let me pass ? "

" Not until you tell me where you are going, and what you mean to do."

" Can't you guess ? " I cried. And for many seconds we stood staring in each other's eyes.

" Have you got the pluck ? " said he, breaking the spell in a tone so cynical that it brought my last drop of blood to the boil.

" You shall see," said I, as I stepped back and whipped the pistol from my overcoat pocket. " Now, will you let me pass, or shall I do it here ? "

The barrel touched my temple, and my thumb the trigger. Mad with excitement as I was, ruined, dishonoured, and now finally determined to make an end of my mis-spent life, my only surprise to this day is that I did not do it then and there. The despicable satisfaction of involving another in one's destruction added its miserable appeal to my baser egoism ; and had fear or horror flown to my companion's face, I shudder to think I might have died diabolically happy with that look for my last impious consolation. It was the look that came instead which held my hand. Neither fear nor horror were in it ; only wonder, admiration, and such a measure of pleased expectancy as caused me after all to pocket my revolver with an oath.

" You devil ! " I said. " I believe you wanted me to do it ! "

" Not quite," was the reply, made with a little start, and a change of colour that came too late. " To tell you the truth, though, I half thought you meant it, and was never more fascinated in my life. I never dreamt you had such stuff in you, Bunny ! No, I'm hanged if I let you go now. And you'd better not try that game again, for you won't catch me stand and look on a second time. We must think of some way out of the mess. I had no idea that you were a chap of that sort ! There, let me have the gun."

With that, one of his hands fell kindly on my shoulder, while the other slipped into the pocket of my overcoat, and I suffered him to deprive me of my weapon without a murmur. Nor was this simply because Raffles had the subtle power of making himself irresistible at will. He was beyond comparison the most masterful man whom I have ever known ; yet my acquiescence was due to more than the mere subjection of the weaker nature to the stronger. The forlorn hope which had brought me to the Albany was turned as by magic into an almost staggering sense of safety. Raffles would help me after all! Raffles would be my friend! It was as though all the world had come round suddenly to my side; so far, therefore, from resisting his action, I caught and clasped his hand with a fervour as uncontrollable as the frenzy which had preceded it.

"God bless you!" I cried. "Forgive me for everything. I will tell you the truth. I *did* think you might perhaps help me in my extremity, though I well knew that I had no claim upon you. Still—for the old school's sake—the sake of old times—I thought you might give me another chance. If you wouldn't, I meant to blow out my brains—and will still if you change your mind!"

In truth, I feared that it was changing, with his expression, even as I spoke; in spite of his kindly tone, and his kindlier use of my old school nickname. His next words showed me my mistake.

"What a boy it is for jumping to conclusions! I have my vices, Bunny, but backing and filling is not one of them. Sit down, my good fellow, and have a cigarette to soothe your nerves. I insist. Whisky? The worst thing for you; here's some coffee that I was brewing when you came in. Now listen to me. You speak of 'another chance.' What do you mean by that? Another chance at baccarat? Not if I know it! You think the luck must turn; suppose it didn't? We should only have made bad worse. No, my dear chap, you've plunged enough. Do you put yourself in my hands or do you not? Very well, then you plunge no more, and I undertake not to present my cheque. Unfortunately there are the other men; and still more unfortunately, Bunny, I'm as hard up at this moment as you are yourself!"

It was my turn to stare at Raffles. "You?" I vociferated. "You hard up? How am I to sit here and believe that?"

"Did I refuse to believe it of you?" he returned, smiling. "And, with your own experience, do you think that because a man has rooms in this place, and belongs to a club or two, and plays a little cricket, he must necessarily have a balance at the bank? I

tell you, my dear man, that at this moment I'm as hard up as you ever were. I have nothing but my wits to live on—absolutely nothing else—it was as necessary for me to win some money this evening as it was for you. We're in the same boat, Bunny; we'd better pull together."

"Together!" I echoed, eagerly. "I'll do anything in this world for you, Raffles, if you really mean that you won't give me away. Think of anything you like, and I'll do it! I was a desperate man when I came here, and

"HE HAD TURNED AND FLASHED A TINY LANTERN IN MY FACE"

I'm just as desperate now. I don't mind what I do if only I can get out of this without a scandal."

Again I see him, leaning back in one of the luxurious chairs with which his room was furnished. I see his indolent, athletic figure; his pale, sharp, clean-shaven features; his curly black hair; his strong, unscrupulous mouth. And again I feel the clear beam of his wonderful eye, cold and luminous as a star, shining into my brain—sifting the very secrets of my heart.

"I wonder if you would!" he said at length. "You would in your present mood ; but who can back your mood to last ? Still, there's hope when a chap takes that tone. Now I think of it, too, you were a plucky little devil at school ; you once did me rather a good turn, I recollect. Remember it, Bunny ? Well, wait a bit, and perhaps I'll be able to do you a better one. Give me time to think."

He got up, lit a fresh cigarette, and fell to pacing the room once more, but with a slower and more thoughtful step, and for a much longer period than before. Twice he stopped at my chair as though on the point of speaking, but each time he checked himself and resumed his stride in silence. Once he threw up the window, which he had shut some time since, and stood for some moments leaning out into the fog which filled the Albany courtyard. Meanwhile a clock on the chimney-piece struck one, and one again for the half-hour, without a word between us.

Yet I not only kept my chair with patience, but I acquired an incongruous equanimity in that half-hour. Insensibly I had shifted my burden to the broad shoulders of this splendid friend, and my thoughts wandered with my eyes as the minutes passed. The room was the good-sized square one, with the folding doors, the marble mantel-piece, and the gloomy, old-fashioned distinction peculiar to the Albany. It was charmingly furnished and arranged, with the right amount of negligence and the right amount of taste. What struck me most, however, was the absence of the usual insignia of a cricketer's den. Instead of the conventional rack of war-worn bats, a carved oak book-case, with every shelf in a litter, filled the better part of one wall ; and where I looked for cricketing groups, I found reproductions of such works as "Love and Death" and "The Blessed Damozel," in dusty frames and different parallels. The man might have been a minor poet instead of an athlete of the first water. Yet there had always been a fine streak of æstheticism in his complex composition ; some of these very pictures I had myself dusted in his study at school ; and they set me thinking of yet another of his many sides—and of the little incident to which he had just referred.

Everybody knows how largely the tone of a public school depends on that of the eleven, and on the character of the captain of cricket in particular ; and I have never heard it denied that in Raffles's time our tone was good, or

that such influence as he troubled to exert was on the side of the angels. Yet it was whispered in the school that he was in the habit of parading the town at night in loud checks and a false beard. It was whispered, and disbelieved. I alone knew it for a fact ; for night after night had I pulled the rope up after him when the rest of the dormitory were asleep, and kept awake by the hour to let it down again on a given signal. Well, one night he was over-bold, and within an ace of ignominious expulsion in the hey-day of his fame. Consummate daring and extra-ordinary nerve on his part, aided, doubtless, by some little presence of mind on mine, averted that untoward result ; and no more need be said of a discreditable incident. But I cannot pretend to have forgotten it in throwing myself on this man's mercy in my desperation. And I was wondering how much of his leniency was owing to the fact that Raffles had not forgotten it either, when he stopped and stood over my chair once more.

"I've been thinking of that night we had the narrow squeak," he began. "Why do you start ? "

"I was thinking of it, too."

He smiled, as though he had read my thoughts.

"Well, you were the right sort of little beggar then, Bunny ; you didn't talk and you didn't flinch. You asked no questions and you told no tales. I wonder if you're like that now ? "

"I don't know," said I, slightly puzzled by his tone. "I've made such a mess of my own affairs that I trust myself about as little as I'm likely to be trusted by anybody else. Yet I never in my life went back on a friend. I will say that ; otherwise perhaps I mightn't be in such a hole to-night."

"Exactly," said Raffles, nodding to himself, as though in assent to some hidden train of thought. "Exactly what I remember of you, and I'll bet it's as true now as it was ten years ago. We don't alter, Bunny. We only develop. I suppose neither you nor I are really altered since you used to let down that rope and I used to come up it hand over hand. You would still stick at nothing for a pal—what ? "

"At nothing in this world," I was pleased to cry.

"Not even at crime ? " said Raffles, smiling.

I stopped to think, for his tone had changed, and I felt sure he was chaffing me. Yet his eye seemed as much in earnest as ever, and for my part I was in no mood for reservations.

"No, not even at that," I cried ; "name your crime, and I'm your man."

He looked at me one moment in wonder, and another moment in doubt ; then turned the matter off, with a shake of his head, and the little cynical laugh that was all his own.

"You're a nice chap, Bunny! A real desperate character. What? Suicide one moment, and any crime I like the next! What you want is a drag, my boy, and you did well to come to a decent law-abiding citizen with a reputation to lose. None the less we must have that money to-night—by hook or crook."

"To-night, Raffles?"

"The sooner the better. Every hour after ten o'clock to-morrow morning is an hour of risk. Let one of those cheques be presented at your own bank, and you and it are dishonoured together. No, we must raise the wind to-night. And I rather think I know where it can be raised."

"At two o'clock in the morning?"

"Yes."

"But how—where—at such an hour?"

"From a friend of mine here in Bond Street."

"He must be a very intimate friend!"

"Intimate's not the word. I have the run of his place and a latch-key all to myself."

"You would knock him up at this hour of the night?"

"If he's in bed."

"And it's essential that I should go in with you?"

"Absolutely."

"Then I must ; but I'm bound to say I don't like the idea, Raffles."

"Do you prefer the alternative?" asked my companion with a sneer. "No, hang it, that's unfair!" he cried apologetically in the same breath. "I quite understand. It's a beastly ordeal. But it would never do for you to stay outside. I tell you what, you shall have a peg before we start—just one. There's the whisky, here's a syphon, and I'll be putting on an overcoat while you help yourself."

Well, I dare say I did so with some freedom, for this plan of his was not the less distasteful to me from its apparent inevitability. I must own, however, that it possessed fewer terrors before my glass was empty. Meanwhile Raffles rejoined me, with a covert-coat over his blazer, and a soft felt hat set carelessly on the curly head he shook with a smile as I passed him the decanter.

"When we come back," said he. "Work first, play afterwards. Do you see what day it is?" he added, tearing a leaflet from a Shakespearian calendar, as I drained my glass. "March 15th. 'The Ides of March, the Ides

of March, remember.' Eh, Bunny, my boy? You won't forget them, will you?"

And, with a laugh, he threw some coals on the fire before turning down the gas like a careful householder. So we went out together as the clock on the chimney-piece was striking two.

II.

PICCADILLY was a trench of raw white fog, rimmed with blurred street-lamps, and lined with a thin coating of adhesive mud. We met no other wayfarers on the deserted flag-stones, and were ourselves favoured with a very hard stare from the constable of the beat, who, however, touched his helmet on recognising my companion.

"You see, I'm known to the police," laughed Raffles as we passed on. "Poor devils, they've got to keep their weather-eye open on a night like this! A fog may be a bore to you and me, Bunny, but it's a perfect godsend to the criminal classes, especially so late in their season. Here we are, though, and I'm hanged if the beggar isn't in bed and asleep after all!"

We had turned into Bond Street, and had halted on the curb a few yards down on the right. Raffles was gazing up at some windows across the road, windows barely discernible through the mist, and without the glimmer of a light to throw them out. They were over a jeweller's shop, as I could see by the peep-hole in the shop-door, and the bright light burning within. But the entire "upper part," with the private street-door next the shop, was black and blank as the sky itself.

"Better give it up for to-night," I urged. "Surely the morning will be time enough!"

"Not a bit of it," said Raffles. "I have his key. We'll surprise him. Come along."

And seizing my right arm, he hurried me across the road, opened the door with his latch-key, and in another moment had shut it swiftly but softly behind us. We stood together in the dark. Outside, a measured step was approaching ; we had heard it through the fog as we crossed the street ; now, as it drew nearer, my companion's fingers tightened on my arm.

"It may be the chap himself," he whispered. "He's the devil of a night-bird. Not a sound, Bunny! We'll startle the life out of him. Ah!"

The measured step had passed without a pause. Raffles drew a deep breath, and his singular grip of me slowly relaxed.

"But still, not a sound," he continued in the same whisper. "We'll take a rise out of him, wherever he is! Slip off your shoes and follow me."

Well, you may wonder at my doing so; but you can never have met A. J. Raffles. Half his power lay in a conciliating trick of sinking the commander in the leader. And it was impossible not to follow one who led with such a zest. You might question, but you followed first. So now, when I heard

"AND THERE I STOOD, SHINING MY LIGHT AND HOLDING MY OIL-BOTTLE"

him kick off his own shoes, I did the same, and was on the stairs at his heels before I realised what an extraordinary way was this of approaching a stranger for money in the dead of night. But obviously Raffles and he were on exceptional terms of intimacy, and I could not but infer that they were in the habit of playing practical jokes upon each other.

We groped our way so slowly upstairs that I had time to make more than one note before we reached the top. The stair was uncarpeted. The spread fingers of my right hand encountered nothing on the damp wall; those of my left trailed through a dust that could be felt on the banisters. An eerie sensation had been upon me since we entered the house. It increased with every step we climbed. What hermit were we going to startle in his cell?

We came to a landing. The banisters led us to the left, and to the left again. Four steps more, and we were on another and a longer landing, and suddenly a match blazed from the black. I never heard it struck. Its flash was blinding. When my eyes became accustomed to the light, there was Raffles holding up the match with one hand, and shading it with the other, between bare boards, stripped walls, and the open doors of empty rooms.

"Where have you brought me?" I cried. "The house is unoccupied!"

"Hush! Wait!" he whispered, and he led the way into one of the empty rooms. His match went out as we crossed the threshold, and he struck another without the slightest noise. Then he stood with his back to me, fumbling with something that I could not see. But, when he threw the second match away, there was some other light in its stead, and a slight smell of oil. I stepped forward to look over his shoulder, but before I could do so he had turned and flashed a tiny lantern in my face.

"What's this?" I gasped. "What devil's trick are you going to play?"

"It's played," he answered, with his quiet laugh.

"On me?"

"I'm afraid so."

"Is there no one in the house, then?"

"No one but ourselves."

"So it was mere chaff about your friend in Bond Street, who could let us have that money?"

"Not altogether. It's quite true that Danby is a friend of mine."

"Danby?"

"The jeweller underneath."

"What do you mean?" I whispered, trembling like a leaf as his meaning dawned upon me. "Are we to get the money from the jeweller?"

"Well, not exactly."

"What then?"

"The equivalent—from his shop!"

There was no need for another question. I understood everything but my own density. He had given me a dozen hints, and I had taken none. And there I stood staring at him, in that empty room; and there he stood with his dark lantern, laughing at me.

"A burglar!" I gasped. "You! you!"

"I told you I lived by my wits."

"Why couldn't you tell me what you were going to do? Why couldn't you trust me? Why must you lie?" I demanded, piqued to the quick for all my horror.

"I wished to tell you," said he. "I was on the point of telling you more than once. You may remember how I sounded you about crime, though you have probably forgotten what you said yourself. I didn't think you meant it at the time, but I thought I'd put you to the test. Now I see you didn't, and I don't blame you. I only am to blame. Get out of it, my dear boy, as quick as you can; leave it to me. You won't give me away, whatever else you do!"

Oh, his cleverness! His cursed cleverness! Had he fallen back on threats, coercion, sneers, all might have been different even yet. But he set me free to leave him in the lurch. He would not blame me. He did not even bind me to secrecy. He trusted me. He knew my weakness and my strength, and was playing on both with his master's touch.

"Not so fast," said I. "Did I put this into your head, or were you going to do it in any case?"

"Not in any case," said Raffles. "It's true I've had the key for days, but when I won to-night I thought of chucking it; for, as a matter of fact, it's not a one-man job."

"That settles it. I'm your man."

"You mean it?"

"Yes—for to-night!"

"Good old Bunny!" he murmured, holding the lantern for one moment to my face; the next he was explaining his plans, and I was nodding, as though we had been fellow-cracksmen all our days.

"I know the shop," he whispered, "because I've got a few things there. I know this upper part, too; it's been to let for a month, and I got an order to view it, and took a cast of the key before using it. The one thing I don't know is how to make a connection between the two; at present there's none. We may make it up here, though I rather fancy the basement myself. If you wait a minute I'll tell you."

He set his lantern on the floor, crept to a back window, and opened it with scarcely a sound—only to return shaking his head, after shutting the window with the same care.

"That was our one chance," said he. "A back window above a back window; but it's too dark to see anything, and we daren't show an outside light. Come down after me to the basement; and remember, though there's not a soul on the premises, you can't make too little noise. There—there—listen to that!"

It was the measured tread that we had heard before on the flag-stones outside. Raffles darkened his lantern, and again we stood motionless till it had passed.

"Either a policeman," he muttered, "or a watchman that all these jewellers run between them. The watchman's the man for us to watch; he's simply paid to spot this kind of game."

We crept very gingerly down the stairs, which creaked a bit in spite of us, and we picked up our shoes in the passage; then down some narrow stone steps, at the foot of which Raffles showed his light, and put on his shoes once more, bidding me do the same in a rather louder tone than he had permitted himself to employ overhead. We were now considerably below the level of the street, in a small space with as many doors as it had sides. Three were ajar, and we saw through them into empty cellars; but in the fourth a key was turned and a bolt drawn; and it let us out presently into the bottom of a deep, square well of fog. A similar door faced it across this area, and Raffles had the lantern close against it, and was hiding the light with his body, when a short and sudden crash made my heart stand still. Next moment I saw the door wide open, and Raffles standing within and beckoning me with a jemmy.

"Door number one," he whispered. "Deuce knows how many more there'll be, but I know of two at least. We won't have to make much noise over them, either; down here there's less risk."

We were now at the bottom of the exact fellow to the narrow stone stair which we had just descended; the yard, or well, being the one thing common to both the private and the business premises. But this flight led to no open passage; instead, a singularly solid mahogany door confronted us at the top.

"I thought so," muttered Raffles, handing me the lantern, and pocketing a bunch of skeleton keys, after tampering for a few minutes with the lock. "It'll be an hour's work to get through that!"

"Can't you pick it?"

"No. I know these locks. It's no use trying. We must cut it out, and it'll take us an hour."

It took us forty-seven minutes by my

watch ; or, rather, it took Raffles ; and never in my life have I seen anything more deliberately done. My part was simply to stand by with the dark lantern in one hand, and a small bottle of rock-oil in the other. Raffles had produced a pretty embroidered case, intended obviously for his razors, but filled instead with the tools of his secret trade, including the rock oil. Then he took off his covert-coat and his blazer, spread them neatly on the top step—knelt on them—turned up his shirt-cuffs—and went to work with brace-and-bit near the key-hole. But first he oiled the bit to minimise the noise, and this he did invariably before beginning a fresh hole, and often in the middle. It took thirty-two separate borings to cut round the lock.

I noticed that through the first circular orifice Raffles thrust a forefinger ; then, as the circle became an ever-lengthening oval, he got his hand through up to the thumb ; and I heard him swear softly to himself.

" I was afraid of it ! "

" What is it ? "

" An iron gate on the other side ! "

" How on earth are we to get through that ? " I asked in dismay.

" Pick the lock. But there may be two. In that case we shall have to make two fresh holes, as the door opens inwards. It won't open two inches as it is."

I confess I did not feel sanguine about the lock-picking, seeing that one lock had baffled us already ; and my disappointment and impatience must have been a revelation to me had I stopped to think. My moral sense and my sense of fear were stricken by a common paralysis. And there I stood, shining my light and holding my oil-bottle with a keener interest than I had ever brought to any honest avocation. And there knelt Raffles, with his black hair tumbled, and the same watchful, quiet, determined half-smile with which I have seen him send down over after over in a county match !

At last the chain of holes was complete, the lock wrenched out bodily, and a splendid bare arm plunged up to the shoulder through the aperture, and through the bars of the iron gate beyond.

" Now," whispered Raffles, " if there's only one lock it'll be in the middle. Joy ! Here it is ! Only let me pick it, and we're through at last."

He withdrew his arm, a skeleton key was selected from the bunch, and then back went his arm to the shoulder. It was a breathless moment. I heard the heart throbbing in my body, the very watch ticking in my pocket, and ever and anon the tinkle-tinkle of the skeleton key. Then—at last—there came a single unmistakable click. In another minute the mahogany door and the iron gate yawned behind us ; and Raffles was sitting on an office table, wiping his face, with the lantern throwing a steady beam by his side.

We were now in a bare and roomy lobby behind the shop, but separated therefrom by an iron curtain, the very sight of which filled me with despair. Raffles, however, did not appear in the least depressed, but hung up his coat and hat on some pegs in the lobby before examining this curtain with his lantern.

" That's nothing," said he, after a minute's inspection ; " we'll be through that in no time, but there's a door on the other side which may give us trouble."

" Another door ! " I groaned. " And how do you mean to tackle this thing ? "

" Prise it up with the jemmy. The weak point of these iron curtains is the leverage you can get from below. But it makes a noise, and this is where you're coming in, Bunny ; this is where I couldn't do without you. I must have you overhead to knock through when the street's clear. I'll come with you and show a light."

Well, you may imagine how little I liked the prospect of this lonely vigil ; and yet there was something very stimulating in the vital responsibility which it involved. Hitherto I had been a mere spectator. Now I was to take part in the game. And the fresh excitement made me more than ever insensible to those considerations of conscience and of safety which were already as dead nerves in my breast.

So I took my post without a murmur in the front room above the shop. The fixtures had been left for the refusal of the incoming tenant, and fortunately for us they included Venetian blinds which were already down. It was the simplest matter in the world to stand peeping through the laths into the street, to beat twice with my foot when anybody was approaching, and once when all was clear again. The noises that even I could hear below, with the exception of one metallic crash at the beginning, were indeed incredibly slight ; but they ceased altogether at each double rap from my toe ; and a policeman passed quite half a dozen times beneath my eyes, and the man whom I took to be the jeweller's watchman oftener still, during the better part of an hour that I spent at the window. Once, indeed, my heart was in my mouth, but only once. It was when the watchman stopped and peered through the peep hole into the lighted shop. I waited for his whistle—I waited for the gallows or the gaol ! But my signals had been studiously obeyed, and the man passed on in undisturbed serenity. In the end I had a signal in my turn, and retraced my steps with lighted matches, down the broad stairs, down the narrow ones, across the area, and up into the lobby where Raffles awaited me with an outstretched hand.

"Well done, my boy !" said he. "You're the same good man in a pinch, and you shall have your reward. I've got a thousand pounds' worth if I've got a penn'oth. It's all in my pockets. And here's something else I found in this locker ; very decent port and some cigars, meant for Danby's business friends. Take a pull, and you shall light up presently. I've found a lavatory, too, and we must have a wash and brush up before we go, for I'm as black as a sweep."

The iron curtain was down, but he insisted on raising it until I could peep through the glass door on the other side and see his handiwork in the shop beyond. Here two electric lights were left burning all night long, and in their cold white rays I could at first see nothing amiss. I looked along an orderly lane, an empty glass counter on my left, glass cupboards of untouched silver on my right, and facing me the filmy black eye of the peephole that shone like a stage moon on the street. The counter had not been emptied by Raffles ; its contents were in the Chubb's safe, which he had given up at a glance ; nor had he looked at the silver, except to choose a cigarette-case for me. He had confined himself entirely to the shop window. This was in three compartments, each secured for the night by removable panels with separate locks. Raffles had removed them a few hours before their time, and the electric light shone on a corrugated shutter bare as the ribs of an empty carcase. Every article of value was gone from the one place which was invisible from the little window in the door ; elsewhere all was as it had been left over night. And but for a train of mangled doors behind the iron curtain, a bottle of wine and a cigar-box with which liberties had been taken, a rather

"I CAN SEE HIM PICK OUT THE CARTRIDGES"

black towel in the lavatory, a burnt match here and there and our finger-marks on the dusty banisters, not a trace of our visit did we leave.

"Had it in my head for long ? " said Raffles, as we strolled through the streets towards dawn, for all the world as though we were returning from a dance. " No, Bunny, I never thought of it till I saw the upper part empty about a month ago, and bought a few things in the shop to get the lie of the land. That reminds me that I never paid for them ; but, by Jove, I will to-morrow, and if that isn't poetic justice, what is ? One visit showed me the possibilities of the place, but a second convinced me of its impossibilities without a pal. So I had practically given up the idea, when you came along on the very night and in the very plight for it ! But here we are at the Albany, and I hope there's some fire left ; for I don't know how you feel, Bunny, but for my part I'm as cold as Keats's owl."

He could think of Keats on his way from a felony! He could hanker for his fireside like another! Floodgates were loosed within me, and the plain English of our adventure rushed over me like an icy torrent. Raffles was a burglar. I had helped him to commit one burglary, therefore I was a burglar too. Yet I could stand and warm myself by his fire, and watch him empty his pockets, as though we had done nothing wonderful or wicked!

I saw that he was emptying his pockets; the table sparkled with their hoard. Rings by the dozen, diamonds by the score; bracelets, pendants, aigrettes, necklaces; pearls, rubies, amethysts, sapphires, and diamonds always, diamonds in everything; flashing bayonets of light, dazzling me—blinding me—making me disbelieve because I could no longer forget. Last of all came no gem, indeed, but my own revolver from an inner pocket. And that struck a chord. I suppose I said something—my hand flew out. I can see Raffles now, as he looked at me once more with a high arch over each clear eye. I can see him pick out the cartridges with his quiet, cynical smile, before he would give me my pistol back again.

"You mayn't believe it, Bunny," said he, "but I never carried a loaded one before. On the whole, I think it gives one confidence. Yet it would be very awkward if anything went wrong; one might use it, and that's not the game at all, though I have often thought that the murderer who has just done the trick must have great sensations before things get too hot for him. Don't look so distressed, my dear chap. I've never had those sensations, and I don't suppose I ever shall."

"But this much you have done before?" said I hoarsely.

"Before? My dear Bunny, you offend me! Did it look like a first attempt? Of course I have done it before."

"Often?"

"Well—no! Not often enough to destroy the charm, at all events; never, as a matter of fact, unless I'm cursedly hard up. Did you hear about the Thimbleby diamonds? Well, that was the last time—and a poor lot of paste they were! Then there was the little business of the Dormer house-boat at Henley. That was mine also—such as it was."

"How came you to begin?" I asked, as curiosity overcame mere wonder, and a fascination for his career gradually wove itself into my fascination for the man.

"Ah! that's a long story," said Raffles. "It was in the Colonies, when I was out there playing cricket. It's too long a story to tell you now, but I was in much the same fix that you were in to-night, and it was my only way out. I never meant it for anything more; but I'd tasted blood, and it was all over with me. Why settle down to some humdrum uncongenial billet, when excitement, romance, danger and a decent living were all going begging together? Of course, it's very wrong, but we can't all be moralists, and the distribution of wealth is very wrong to begin with. Besides, you're not at it all the time. I only wonder if you'll like the life as much as I do?"

"Like it?" I cried out. "Not I! It's no life for me. Once is enough!"

"You wouldn't give me a hand another time?"

"Don't ask me, Raffles. Don't ask me, for God's sake!"

"Yet you said you would do anything for me! You asked me to name my crime! But I knew at the time you didn't mean it; you didn't go back on me to-night, and that ought to satisfy me, goodness knows! I suppose I'm ungrateful, and unreasonable, and all that. I ought to let it end at this. But you're the very man for me, Bunny, the—very—man! Just think how we got through to-night. Not a scratch—not a hitch! There's nothing very terrible in it, you see; there never would be, while we worked together!"

He was standing in front of me with a hand on either shoulder; he was smiling as he knew so well how to smile. I turned on my heel, planted my elbows on the chimney-piece, and my burning head between my hands. Next instant a still heartier hand had fallen on my back.

"All right, my boy! You are quite right, and I'm worse than wrong. I'll never ask it again. Go, if you want to, and come again about mid-day for the cash. There was no bargain; but, of course, I'll get you out of your scrape—especially after the way you've stood by me to-night."

I was round again with my blood on fire.

"I'll do it again," I said, through my teeth. He shook his head. "Not you," he said, smiling quite good-humouredly on my insane enthusiasm.

"I will," I cried with an oath. "I'll lend you a hand as often as you like! What does it matter now? I've been in it once. I'll be in it again. I've gone to the devil anyhow. I can't go back, and wouldn't if I could. Perhaps I'm bitten with it just as you were; perhaps I meant what I said when you promised to help me, and perhaps I mean it still. What does it matter? When you want me I'm your man!"

And that is how Raffles and I joined felonious forces on the Ides of March.

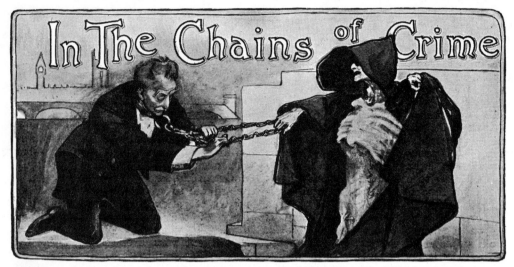

In The Chains of Crime

Being the Confessions of a late Prisoner of the Crown, and sometime accomplice of the more notorious A. J. Raffles, Cricketer and Criminal, whose fate is unknown.

BY E. W. HORNUNG.

II.—A COSTUME PIECE.

LONDON was just then talking of one whose name is already a name and nothing more. Reuben Rosenthall had made his millions on the diamond fields of South Africa, and had come home to enjoy them according to his lights ; how he went to work will scarcely be forgotten by any reader of the halfpenny evening papers, which revelled in endless anecdotes of his original indigence and present prodigality, varied with interesting particulars of the extraordinary establishment which the millionaire set up in St. John's Wood. Here he kept a retinue of Kaffirs, who were literally his slaves ; and hence he would sally, with enormous diamonds in his shirt and on his finger, in the convoy of a prize-fighter of heinous repute, who was not, however, by any means the worst element in the Rosenthall *ménage*. So said common gossip ; but the fact was sufficiently established by the interference of the police on at least one occasion, followed by certain magisterial proceedings which were reported with justifiable gusto and huge headlines in the newspapers aforesaid. And this was all my knowledge of Reuben Rosenthall up to the time when the Old Bohemian Club, having fallen on evil days, found it worth its while to organise a great dinner in honour of so wealthy an exponent of the club's principles.

I was not at the banquet myself, but a member took Raffles, who told me all about it that very night.

"Most extraordinary show I ever went to in my life," said he. "As for the man himself—well, I was prepared for something grotesque, but the fellow fairly took my breath away. To begin with, he's the most astounding brute to look at, well over six feet, with a chest like a barrel, and a great hook-nose, and the reddest hair and whiskers you ever saw. Drank like a fish, but only got muddled enough to make us a speech that I wouldn't have missed for ten pounds. I'm only sorry you weren't there too, Bunny, old chap."

I began to be sorry myself, for Raffles was anything but an excitable person, and never had I seen him so excited before. Had he been following Rosenthall's example ? His coming to my rooms at midnight merely to tell me about his dinner was in itself so extraordinary as to excuse a suspicion which was certainly at variance with my knowledge of the man.

"What did he say ?" I inquired mechanically, divining some subtler explanation of this visit, and wondering what in the world it could be.

"Say ?" cried Raffles. "What did he not say ! He boasted of his rise, he bragged of his riches, and he blackguarded society for taking him up for his money and dropping him out of sheer pique and jealousy because he had so much. He mentioned names, too, with the most charming freedom, and swore he was as good a man as the Old Country had to show—*pace* the Old Bohemians. To prove it, he pointed to a great diamond in the middle of his shirt-front with a little finger loaded with another just like it—and which of our bloated princes could show a pair like that? As a matter of fact, they seemed quite wonderful stones, with a curious purple gleam to them that must mean a pot of money. But old Rosenthall swore he wouldn't take fifty thousand pounds for the two, and wanted to know where the other man was who went about with twenty-five thousand in his shirt-front and another twenty-five on his little finger. He didn't exist. If he did, he wouldn't have the pluck to wear them. But *he* had—he'd tell us why. And before you could say Jack Robinson he had whipped out a whacking great revolver."

"Not at the table?"

"At the table! In the middle of his speech! But it was nothing to what he wanted to do. He actually wanted us to let him write his name in bullets on the opposite wall to show us why he wasn't afraid to go about in all his diamonds! That brute Purvis, the prize-fighter, who is his paid bully, had to bully his master before he could be persuaded out of it. There was quite a panic for the moment; one fellow who was queer got under the table, and the waiters bolted to a man."

"What a grotesque scene!"

"Grotesque enough, but I rather wish they had let him do the thing and blaze away. He was as keen as knives to show us how he could take care of his purple diamonds; and do you know, Bunny, *I* was as keen as knives to see."

And Raffles leant towards me with a sly, slow smile that made the hidden meaning of his visit only too plain to me at last.

"So you think of having a try for his diamonds yourself?"

He shrugged his shoulders.

"It is horridly obvious, I admit. But—yes, I have set my heart upon them! To be quite frank, I have had them on my conscience for some time; one couldn't hear so much of the man and his prize-fighter and his diamonds without feeling it a kind of duty to have a go for them; but when it comes to brandishing a revolver and practically challenging the world, the thing becomes inevitable. It is simply thrust upon one. I was fated to hear that challenge, Bunny, and I, for one, must

take it up. I was only sorry I couldn't get on my hind legs and say so then and there."

"Well," I said, "I don't see the necessity as things are with us; but, of course, I'm your man."

My tone may have been half-hearted. I did my best to make it otherwise. But it was barely a month since our Bond Street exploit, and we certainly could afford to behave ourselves for several months to come. I thought we ought to know when we were well off, and could see no point in our running fresh risks before we were obliged. On the other hand, I was anxious not to show the least disposition to break the pledge that I had given a month ago. But it was not on my manifest faint-heartedness that Raffles fastened.

"Necessity, my dear Bunny? Does the writer only write when the wolf is at the door? Does the painter paint for bread alone? Must you and I be *driven* to crime like Tom of Bow and Dick of Whitechapel? You pain me, my dear chap; you needn't laugh, because you do. Art for art's sake is a vile catchword, but I confess it appeals to me. In this case my motives are absolutely pure, for I doubt if we shall ever be able to dispose of such peculiar stones. But if I don't have a try for them—after to-night—I shall never be able to hold up my head again."

His eye twinkled, but it glittered too.

"We shall have our work cut out," was all I said.

"And do you suppose I should be keen on it if we hadn't?" cried Raffles. "My dear fellow, I would rob a millionaire if I could, but I could no more scoop a till when the shopwalker wasn't looking than I could bag the apples out of an old woman's basket. Even that little business last month was a sordid affair, but it was necessary, and I think its strategy redeemed it to some extent. Now there's some credit, and more sport, in going where they boast they're on their guard against you. The Bank of England, for example, is the ideal crib; but that would need half a dozen of us, with years to give to the job; and meanwhile Reuben Rosenthall is high enough game for you and me. We know he's armed. We know how Billy Purvis can fight. It'll be no soft thing, I grant you. But what of that, my good Bunny —what of that? A man's reach must exceed his grasp, dear boy, or what the deuce is an ambition for?"

"I would rather we didn't gratify ours just yet," I answered laughing, for his spirit was irresistible, and the plan was growing upon me, despite my qualms.

"Trust me for that," was his reply; "I'll see you through. After all, I expect to find that the difficulties are nearly all on the surface. These fellows both drink like the deuce, and that should simplify matters considerably. But we shall see, and we must take our time. There will probably turn out to be a dozen different ways in which the thing might be done, and we shall have to choose between them. It will mean watching the house for at least a week in any case; it may mean lots of other things that will take much longer; but give me a week, and I will tell you more. That's to say if you're really on?"

"Of course I am," I replied indignantly. "But why should I give you a week? Why shouldn't we watch the house together?"

you. You shall have your share of the fun, never fear, and a purple diamond all to yourself—if we're lucky."

On the whole, however, this conversation left me less than lukewarm, and I still remember the depression which came upon me when Raffles was gone. I saw the folly of the enterprise to which I had committed myself — the sheer, gratuitous, unnecessary folly of it. And the paradoxes in which Raffles revelled, and the frivolous casuistry which was nevertheless half sincere, and which his mere personality rendered wholly plausible at the moment of utterance, appealed very little to me when recalled in cold blood. I admired the spirit of pure mischief in which he seemed prepared to risk his liberty and

"'HE ACTUALLY WANTED US TO LET HIM WRITE HIS NAME IN BULLETS ON THE OPPOSITE WALL'"

"Because two eyes are as good as four—and take up less room. Never hunt in couples, unless you're obliged. But don't you look offended, Bunny; there'll be plenty for you to do when the time comes, that I promise

his life, but I did not find it an infectious spirit on calm reflection. Yet the thought of withdrawal was not to be entertained for a moment. On the contrary, I was impatient of the delay ordained by Raffles;

and, perhaps, no small part of my secret disaffection came of his galling determination to do without me until the last moment.

It made it no better that this was characteristic of the man and of his attitude towards me. For a month we had been, I suppose, the thickest thieves in all London, and yet our intimacy was curiously incomplete. With all his charming frankness, there was in Raffles a vein of capricious reserve which was perceptible enough to be very irritating. He had the instinctive secretiveness of the inveterate criminal. I said nothing about it, but it rankled every day, and never more than in the week that succeeded the Rosenthall dinner. When I met Raffles at the club he would tell me nothing; when I went to his rooms he was out, or pretended to be. One day he told me he was getting on well, but slowly; it was a more ticklish game than he had thought; but when I began to ask questions he would say no more. Then and there, in my annoyance, I took my own decision. Since he would tell me nothing of the result of his vigils, I determined to keep one on my own account, and that very evening found my way to the millionaire's front gates.

The house he was occupying is, I believe, quite the largest in the St. John's Wood district. It stands in the angle formed by two broad thoroughfares, neither of which, as it happens, is a 'bus route, and I doubt if many quieter spots exist within the four-mile radius. Quiet also was the great square house, in its garden of grass plots and shrubs; the lights were low, the millionaire and his friends obviously spending their evening elsewhere. The garden walls were only a few feet high. In one there was a side door opening into a glass passage; in the other two five-barred, grained-and-varnished gates, one at either end of the little semi-circular drive, and both wide open. So still was the place that I had a great mind to walk boldly in and, learn something of the premises; in fact, I was on the point of doing so when I heard a quick, shuffling step on the pavement behind me. I turned round and faced the dark scowl and the dirty clenched fists of a dilapidated tramp.

"You fool!" said he. "You utter idiot!"

"Raffles!"

"That's it," he whispered savagely; "tell all the neighbourhood—give me away at the top of your voice!"

With that he turned his back upon me and shambled down the road, shrugging his shoulders and muttering to himself as though I had refused him alms. A few moments I stood astounded, indignant, at a loss; then I followed him. His feet trailed, his knees gave, his back was bowed, his head kept nodding; it was the gait of a man eighty years of age. Presently he waited for me midway between two lamp-posts. As I came up he was lighting rank tobacco in a cutty-pipe with an evil-smelling match, and the flame showed me the suspicion of a smile.

"You must forgive my heat, Bunny, but it really was very foolish of you. Here am I trying every dodge—begging at the door one night—hiding in the shrubs the next—doing every mortal thing but stand and stare at the house as you went and did. It's a costume piece, and in you rush in your ordinary clothes! I tell you they're on the look-out for us night and day. It's the toughest nut I ever tackled!"

"Well," said I, "if you had told me so before I shouldn't have come. You told me nothing."

He looked hard at me from under the broken brim of a battered billycock.

"You're right," he said at length. "I've been too close. It's become second nature with me when I've anything on. But here's an end of it, Bunny, so far as you're concerned. I'm going home now, and I want you to follow me; but for heaven's sake keep your distance, and don't speak to me again till I speak to you. There—give me a start." And he was off again, a decrepit vagabond, with his hands in his pockets, his elbows squared, and frayed coat-tails swinging raggedly from side to side.

I followed him to the Finchley Road. There he took an Atlas omnibus, and I sat some rows behind him on the top, but not far enough to escape the pest of his vile tobacco. That he could carry his character-sketch to such a pitch—he who would only smoke one brand of cigarettes! It was the last, least touch of the insatiable artist, and it charmed away what mortification there still remained in my spirit. I felt once more the fascination of a comrade who was for ever dazzling one with a fresh and unsuspected facet of his character.

As we neared Piccadilly I wondered what he would do. Surely he was not going into the Albany like that? No, he took another omnibus to Sloane Street, I sitting behind him as before. At Sloane Street we changed again, and were presently in the long lean artery of the King's Road. I was now all agog to know our destination, nor was I kept many more minutes in doubt. Raffles got down. I followed. He crossed the road and disappeared up a dark turning. I pressed after him, and was in time to see his coat-tails as he plunged into a still darker flagged alley to the right. He was holding himself up and stepping out like a young man once more; also, in some subtle way, he already looked less disreputable. But I alone was there to see him, the alley was absolutely deserted, and desperately dark. At the further end he opened a door with a latch-key, and it was darker yet within.

Instinctively I drew back and heard him chuckle. We could no longer see each other.

"All right, Bunny! There's no hanky-panky this time. These are studios, my friend, and I'm one of the lawful tenants."

Indeed, in another minute we were in a lofty room with skylight, easels, dressing-cupboard, platform, and every other adjunct, save the signs of actual labour. The first thing I saw, as Raffles lit the gas, was its reflection in his top hat on the pegs beside the rest of his normal garments.

"Looking for the works of art?" continued Raffles, lighting a cigarette and beginning to divest himself of his rags. "I'm afraid you won't find any, but there's the canvas I'm always going to make a start upon. I tell them I'm looking high and low for my ideal model. I have the stove lit on principle twice a week, and look in and leave a newspaper and a smell of Sullivans —how good they are after shag! Meanwhile I pay my rent and am a good tenant in every way; and it's a very useful little *pied-à-terre*—there's no saying how useful it might be at a pinch. As it is, the billycock comes in and the topper goes out, and nobody takes the slightest notice of either; at this time of night the chances are that there's not a soul in the building except ourselves."

"You never told me you went in for disguises," said I, watching him as he cleansed the grime from his face and hands.

"No, Bunny; I've treated you very shabbily all round. There was really no reason why I shouldn't have shown you this place a month ago, and yet there was no point in my doing so, and circumstances are just conceivable in which it would have suited us both for you to be in genuine ignorance of my whereabouts. I have something to sleep on, as you perceive, in case of need, and, of course, my name is not Raffles in the King's Road. So you will see that one might bolt further and fare worse."

"Meanwhile you use the place as a dressing-room?"

"It's my private pavilion," said Raffles. "Disguises? In some cases they're half the battle, and it's always pleasant to feel that, if the worst comes to the worst, you needn't necessarily be convicted under your own name. Then they're indispensable in dealing with the fences. I drive all my bargains in the tongue and raiment of Shoreditch. If I didn't, there'd be the very devil to pay in blackmail. Now, this cupboard's full of all sorts of toggery. I tell the woman who cleans the room that it's for my models when I find 'em. By the way, I only hope I've got something that'll fit you, for you'll want a rig for to-morrow night."

"To-morrow night!" I exclaimed. "Why, what do you mean to do?"

"The trick," said Raffles. "I intended writing to you as soon as I got back to my chambers, to ask you to look me up to-morrow afternoon; then I was going to unfold my plan of campaign, and take you straight into action then and there. There's nothing like putting the nervous players in first; it's the sitting with their pads on that upsets their applecart; that was another of my reasons for being so confoundedly close. You must try to forgive me. I remembered how well you played up last trip, without any time to weaken on it beforehand. All I want is for you to be as cool and smart to-morrow night as you were then; though, by Jove, there's no comparison between the two cases!"

"I thought you would find it so."

"You were right: I have. Mind you, I don't say this will be the tougher job all round; we shall probably get in without any difficulty at all; it's the getting out again that may flummox us. That's the worst of an irregular household!" cried Raffles, with quite a burst of virtuous indignation. "I assure you, Bunny, I spent the whole of Monday night in the shrubbery of the garden next door looking over the wall, and, if you'll believe me, somebody was about all night long! I don't mean the Kaffirs. I don't believe they ever get to bed at all—poor devils! No, I mean Rosenthall himself, and that pasty-faced beast Purvis. They were up and drinking from midnight, when they came in, to broad daylight, when I cleared out. Even then I left them sober enough to slang each other. By the way, they very nearly came to blows in the garden, within a few yards of me, and I heard something that might come in useful and make Rosenthall shoot crooked at a critical moment. You know what an I. D. B. is?"

"Illicit Diamond Buyer?"

"Exactly. Well, it seems that Rosenthall was one. He must have let it out to Purvis in his cups. Anyhow, I heard Purvis taunting him with it, and threatening him with the breakwater at Capetown; and I begin to think our friends are friend and foe. But about to-morrow night: there's nothing subtle in my plan. It's simply to get in while these fellows are out on the loose, and to lie low till they come back, and longer. If possible we must doctor the whisky. That would simplify the whole thing, though it's not a very sporting game to play; still, we must remember Rosenthall's revolver; we don't want him to sign his name on *us*. With all those Kaffirs about, however, it's ten to one on the whisky, and a hundred to one against us if we go looking for it. A brush with the heathen would spoil everything, if it did no more. Besides, there are the ladies——"

"The deuce there are!"

"His relations, the very voices for raising Cain. I fear, I fear the clamour! It would be fatal to us. *Au contraire*, if we can manage to stow ourselves away unbeknown, half the battle will be won. If Rosenthall turns in queer, it's a purple diamond apiece. If he sits up sober, it may be a bullet instead. We will hope not, Bunny; and all the firing wouldn't be on one side; but it's on the knees of the gods."

And so we left it when we shook hands in Piccadilly—not by any means as much later as I could have wished. Raffles would not ask me to his rooms that night. He said he made it a rule to have a long night before playing cricket and—other games. His final word to me was framed on the same principle.

"Mind, take care of yourself to-night, Bunny. Take care of yourself — as you value your life—and mine!"

I remember my abject obedience, and the endless, sleepless night it gave me, and the roofs of the houses opposite standing out at last against the blue-grey London dawn. I wondered whether I should ever see another, and was very hard on myself for that little expedition which I had made on my own wilful account.

It was between eight and nine o'clock in the evening when we took up our position in the garden adjoining that of Reuben Rosenthall; the house itself was shut up, thanks to the outrageous libertine next door,

"I TURNED ROUND AND FACED THE DARK SCOWL . . . OF A DILAPIDATED TRAMP"

who, by driving away the neighbours, had gone far towards delivering himself into our hands.

Practically secure from surprise on that side, we could watch our house from the safe side of a wall just high enough to see over, while a fair margin of shrubs in either garden afforded us additional protection. Thus entrenched, we had stood an hour, watching a pair of lighted bow windows, with vague shadows flitting continually across the drawn blinds, and listening to the drawing of corks, the clink of glasses, and a gradual crescendo of coarse voices within. Our luck seemed to have deserted us: the owner of the purple diamonds was dining at home and dining at undue length. I thought it was a dinner-party. Raffles differed; in the end he proved right. Wheels grated in the drive, a carriage and pair stood at the steps; there was a stampede from the dining-room, and the loud voices died away, to burst forth presently from the porch.

Let me make our position perfectly clear. We were over the wall, at the side of the house, but a few feet from the dining-room windows. On our right, one angle of the building cut the back lawn in two diagonally ; on our left, another angle just permitted us to see the jutting steps and the waiting carriage. We saw Rosenthall come out—saw the glimmer of his diamonds before anything. Then came the pugilist ; then a lady with a head of hair like a bath sponge ; then another, and the party was complete.

Raffles ducked and pulled me down in great excitement.

"The ladies are going with them," he whispered. "This is great ! "

"That's better still."

"The Gardenia ! " the millionaire had bawled.

"And that's best of all," said Raffles, standing upright as hoofs and wheels crunched through the gates and rattled off at a fine speed.

"Now what ? " I whispered, trembling with excitement.

"They'll be clearing away. Yes, here come their shadows. The drawing-room windows open on the lawn. Bunny, it's the psychological moment. Where's that mask ? "

I produced it with a hand whose trembling I tried in vain to still, and could have died for Raffles when he made no comment on what he could not fail to notice. His own hands were firm and cool as he adjusted my mask for me, and then his own.

" By Jove, old boy," he whispered cheerily, "you look about the greatest ruffian I ever saw ! These masks alone will down a horse, if we meet one. But I'm glad I remembered to tell you not to shave. You'll pass for Whitechapel if the worst comes to the worst, and don't you forget to talk the lingo. Better sulk like a mule if you're not sure of it, and leave the lip to me ; but, please our stars, there will be no need. Now, are you ready ? "

" Quite."

" Got your gag ? "

" Yes."

" Shooter ? "

" Yes."

" Then follow me."

In an instant we were over the wall, in another on the lawn behind the house. There was no moon. The very stars in their courses had veiled themselves for our benefit. I crept at my leader's heels to some French windows opening upon a shallow verandah. He pushed. They yielded.

" Luck again," he whispered ; "nothing *but* luck ! Now for a light."

And the light came !

A good score of electric burners glowed red for the fraction of a second, then rained merciless white beams into our blinded eyes. When we found our sight four revolvers covered us, and between two of them the colossal frame of Reuben Rosenthall shook with a wheezy laughter from head to foot.

": Good - evening, boys," he hiccoughed. " Glad· to see ye, by James ! Shift foot or finger, you on the left, though, and you're a dead boy. I mean you, you beggar ! " he roared out at Raffles. " I know you. I've been waitin' for you. I've been *watching* you all this week ! Plucky smart you thought yerself, didn't you ? One day beggin', next time shammin' ill, and next one o' them old pals from Kimberley what never come when I'm in. But you left the same tracks every day, you buggins, an' the same tracks every night all round the blessed premises."

" All right, guv'nor," drawled Raffles ; " don't excite yourself. It's a fair do. We don't want to know 'ow you brung it orf. On'y don't you go for to shoot, 'cos we 'int awmed, s'help me."

" Ah, you're a knowing one," said Rosenthall, fingering his triggers. " But you've struck a knowinger."

" Ho, yuss, we know all abaht thet ! Set a thief to ketch a thief—ho, yuss."

My eyes had torn themselves from the round black muzzles, from the accursed diamonds that had been our snare, the pasty pig-face of the over-fed pugilist, and the flaming cheeks and hook nose of Rosenthall himself. I was looking beyond them at the doorway filled with quivering silk and plush, black faces, white eye-balls, woolly pates. But a sudden silence recalled my attention to the millionaire. And only his nose retained its colour.

" What d'ye mean ? " he whispered with a hoarse oath. " Spit it out, or I shall have to drill you ! "

" Whort price thet brikewater ? " drawled Raffles coolly.

" Eh ? "

Rosenthall's revolvers were describing widening orbits.

" Whort price thet brikewater — old *I. D. B.* ? "

" Where did you get that from ? " asked Rosenthall with a rattle in his thick neck, meant for mirth.

" You may well arst," said Raffles. " It's all over the plice w'ere *I* come from."

" Who can have spread such rot ? "

"WHORT PRICE THET BRIKEWATER?" DRAWLED RAFFLES COOLLY."

"I dunno," says Raffles; "arst the gen'leman on yer left; p'r'aps 'e knows."

The gentleman on his left had turned livid with emotion. Guilty conscience never declared itself in plainer terms. For a moment his small eyes bulged as if they would leave his head; the next, he had pocketed his pistols on a professional instinct, and was upon us with his fists.

"Out o' the light—out o' the light!" yelled Rosenthall in a frenzy.

He was too late. No sooner had the burly pugilist obstructed his fire than Raffles was through the window at a bound; while I, for standing still and saying nothing, was scientifically felled to the floor.

I cannot have been many moments without my senses. When I recovered them there was a great to-do in the garden, but I had the drawing-room to myself. I sat up. Rosenthall and Purvis were rushing about outside, cursing the Kaffirs and nagging at each other.

"Over *that* wall, I tell you!"

"I tell you it was this one. Can't you whistle for the police?"

"Police be hanged! I've had enough of the blessed police."

"Then we'd better get back and make sure of the other bounder."

"Oh, make sure o' your skin. That's what you'd better do. Jala, you black hog, if I catch *you* skulking . . . ."

I never heard the threat. I was creeping from the drawing-room on my hands and knees, my own revolver swinging by its steel ring from my teeth.

For an instant I thought that the hall also was deserted. I was wrong, and I crept upon a Kaffir on all fours. Poor beggar, I could not bring myself to deal him a base blow, but I threatened him most hideously with my revolver, and left the white teeth chattering in his black head as I took the stairs three at a time. Why I went upstairs in that decisive fashion as though it were my only course I cannot explain. But garden and ground floor seemed alive with men, and I might have done worse.

I turned into the first room I came to on the first floor. It was a bedroom—empty, though lit up; and never shall I forget how I started as I entered, on encountering the awful villain that was myself at full length in a pier-glass! Masked, armed, and ragged, I was indeed fit carrion for a bullet or the hangman, and to one or the other I made up my mind. Nevertheless, I hid myself in the wardrobe behind the mirror; and there I stood shivering and cursing my fate, my folly, and Raffles most of all—Raffles first

and last—for I dare say half an hour. Then the wardrobe door was flung suddenly open; they had stolen into the room without a sound, and I was hauled downstairs, an ignominious captive.

Gross scenes followed in the hall; the ladies were now upon the stage, and at sight of the desperate criminal they screamed with one accord.

Purvis and the ladies were for calling the police in and giving me in charge without delay. Rosenthall would not hear of it. He swore that he would shoot man or woman who left his sight. He had had enough of the police. He was not going to have them coming there to spoil sport; he was going to deal with me in his own way. With that he dragged me from all other hands, flung me against a door, and sent a bullet crashing though the wood within an inch of my ear.

"You drunken fool! It'll be murder!" shouted Purvis, getting in the way a second time.

"Murder it is then! He's armed, isn't he? I shot him in self-defence. It'll be a warning to others. Will you stand aside, or do you want it yourself?"

"You idiot," said Purvis, still between us. "I saw you take a neat tumblerful since you come in, and it's made you a perfect fool. Pull yourself together. You ain't a-going to do what you'll be sorry for."

"Then I won't shoot at him, I'll only shoot roun' an' roun' the beggar. You're quite right, ole feller. Wouldn't hurt him. Great mistake. Roun' an' roun'. There — like that!"

His freckled paw shot up over Purvis's shoulder, mauve lightning came from his ring, a red flash from his revolver, and shrieks from the women as the reverberations died away. Some splinters fell upon my hair.

Next instant the prize-fighter disarmed him; and I was safe from the man, but finally doomed to the deep sea. A policeman was in our midst. He had entered through the drawing-room window; he was an officer of few words and creditable promptitude. In a twinkling he had the handcuffs on my wrists, while the pugilist explained the situation, and his patron reviled the force and its representative with impotent malignity. A fine watch they kept; a lot of good they did; coming in when all was over, and the whole household might have been murdered while in bed. The officer only deigned to notice him as he marched me off.

"We know all about *you*, sir," said he contemptuously, and he refused the sovereign Purvis proffered. "You will be seeing me again, sir, at Marylebone."

" Shall I come now ? "

" As you please, sir. I rather think the other gentleman requires you more, and I don't fancy this young man means to give much trouble."

" Oh, I'm coming quietly," I said.

And I went.

In silence we traversed perhaps a hundred yards. It must have been midnight. We did not meet a soul. At last I whispered :

" How on earth did you manage it ? "

" Purely by luck," said Raffles. " I had the luck to get clear away through knowing every brick of those back-garden walls, and the double luck to have these togs with the rest over at Chelsea. The helmet is one of a collection I made up at Oxford ; here it goes over this wall, and we'd better carry the coat and belt before we meet a real officer. I got them once for a fancy ball— ostensibly — and thereby hangs a yarn. I always thought they might come in useful a second time. My chief crux to-night was getting rid of the hansom that brought me back. I sent him off to Scotland Yard with ten bob and a special message to good old Mackenzie. The whole detective department will be at Rosenthall's in about half an hour. Of course, I speculated on our gentleman's hatred of the police — another huge slice of luck. If you'd got away, well and good ; if not I felt he was the man to play with his mouse as long as possible. Yes, Bunny, it's been more of a costume piece than I intended, and we've come out of it with a good deal less credit. But, by Jove, we're jolly lucky to have come out of it at all ! "

" NEXT INSTANT THE PRIZE-FIGHTER DISARMED HIM."

In The Chains of Crime

Being the Confessions of a late Prisoner of the Crown, and sometime accomplice of the more notorious A. J. Raffles, Cricketer and Criminal, whose fate is unknown.

BY E. W. HORNUNG.

III.—GENTLEMEN AND PLAYERS.

OLD RAFFLES may or may not have been an exceptional criminal, but as a cricketer I dare swear he was unique. Himself a dangerous bat, a brilliant field, and perhaps the very finest slow bowler of his decade, he took incredibly little interest in the game at large. He never went up to Lord's without his cricket-bag, or showed the slightest interest in the result of a match in which he was not himself engaged. Nor was this mere hateful egotism on his part. He professed to have lost all enthusiasm for the game, and to keep it up only from the very lowest motives.

"Cricket," said Raffles, "like everything else, is good enough sport until you discover a better. As a source of excitement it isn't in it with other things you wot of, Bunny, and the involuntary comparison becomes a bore. What's the satisfaction of taking a man's wicket when you want his spoons? Still, if you can bowl a bit, your low cunning won't get rusty, and always looking for the weak spot's just the kind of mental exercise one wants. Yes, perhaps there's some affinity between the two things after all. But I'd chuck up cricket to-morrow, Bunny, if it wasn't for the glorious protection it affords a person of my proclivities."

"How so?" said I. "It brings you before the public, I should have thought, far more than is either safe or wise."

"My dear Bunny, that's exactly where you make a mistake. To follow Crime with reasonable impunity you simply *must* have a parallel, ostensible career—the more public the better. The principle is obvious. Mr. Peace, of pious memory, disarmed suspicion by acquiring a local reputation for playing the fiddle and taming animals; and it's my profound conviction that Jack the Ripper was a really eminent public man, whose speeches were very likely reported alongside his atrocities. Fill the bill in some prominent part, and you'll never be suspected of doubling it with another of equal prominence. That's why I want you to cultivate journalism, my boy, and sign all you can. And it's the one and only reason why I don't burn my bats for firewood."

Nevertheless, when he did play there was no keener performer on the field, nor one more anxious to do well for his side. I remember how he went to the nets, before the first match of the season, with his pocket full of sovereigns, which he put on the stumps instead of bails. It was a sight to see the professionals bowling like demons for the hard cash; for whenever a stump was hit a pound was tossed to the bowler and another balanced in its stead, while one man took £3 with a ball that spread-eagled the wicket. Raffles's practice cost him either eight or nine sovereigns; but he had absolutely first-class bowling all the time; and he made fifty-seven runs next day.

It became my pleasure to accompany him to all his matches, to watch every ball he bowled, or played, or fielded, and to sit chatting with him in the pavilion when he was doing none of these three things. You might have seen us there, side by side, during the greater part of the Gentlemen's first innings against the Players (who had lost the toss) on the second Monday in July. We were to be seen, but not heard, for Raffles had failed to score, and was uncommonly cross for a player who cared so little for the game. Merely taciturn with me, he was positively rude to more than one member who wanted to know how it had happened, or who ventured to commiserate him on his luck; there he sat, with a Zingari straw hat tilted over his nose and a cigarette stuck between lips that curled disagreeably at every advance. I was therefore much surprised when a young fellow of the exquisite type came and squeezed himself in between us, and met with a perfectly civil reception despite the liberty. I did not know the boy by sight, nor did Raffles introduce us; but their conversation proclaimed at once a slightness of acquaintanceship and a licence on the lad's part which combined to puzzle me. Mystification reached its height when Raffles was informed that the other's father was anxious to meet him, and he instantly consented to gratify that whim.

"He's in the Ladies' Enclosure. Will you come round now?"

"With pleasure," says Raffles. "Keep a place for me, Bunny."

And they were gone.

"Young Crowley," said some voice further back. "Last year's Harrow eleven."

"I remember him. Worst man in the team."

"Keen cricketer, however. Stopped till he was twenty to get his colours. Governor made him. Keen breed. Oh, pretty, sir! Very pretty!"

The game was boring me. I only came to see old Raffles perform. Soon I was looking wistfully for his return, and at length I saw him beckoning me from the palings to the right.

"Want to introduce you to old Amersteth," he whispered when I joined him. "They've a cricket week next month, when this boy Crowley comes of age, and we've both got to go down and play."

"Both!" I echoed. "Both? But I'm no cricketer!"

"Shut up," says Raffles. "Leave that to

me. I've been lying for all I'm worth," he added sepulchrally as we reached the bottom of the steps. "I trust to you not to give the show away."

There was the gleam in his eye that I knew well enough elsewhere, but was unprepared for in those healthy, sane surroundings; and it was with very definite misgivings and surmises that I followed the Zingari blazer through the vast flower-bed of hats and bonnets that bloomed beneath the ladies' awning.

Lord Amersteth was a fine-looking man with a short moustache and a double chin. He received me with much dry courtesy, through which, however, it was not difficult to read a less flattering tale. I was accepted as the inevitable appendage of the invaluable Raffles, with whom I felt deeply incensed as I made my bow.

"I have been bold enough," said Lord Amersteth, "to ask one of the Gentlemen of England to come down and play some rustic cricket for us next month. He is kind enough to say that he would have liked nothing better, but for this little fishing expedition of yours, Mr. ——, Mr. ——" and Lord Amersteth succeeded in remembering my name.

It was, of course, the first I had ever heard of that fishing expedition, but I made haste to say that it could easily, and should certainly, be put off. Raffles gleamed approval through his eyelashes. Lord Amersteth bowed and shrugged.

"You're very good, I'm sure," said he. "But I understand you're a cricketer yourself?"

"He was one at school," said Raffles, with infamous readiness.

"Not a real cricketer," I was stammering meanwhile.

"In the eleven?" asked Lord Amersteth.

"I'm afraid not," said I.

"But only just out of it," declared Raffles, to my horror.

"Well, well, we can't all be Gentlemen of England," said Lord Amersteth slyly. "My son Crowley only just scraped into the eleven at Harrow, and he's going to play. I may even come in myself at a pinch; so you won't be the only duffer, if you are one, and I shall be very glad if you will come down and help us too. You shall flog a stream before breakfast and after dinner, if you like."

"I should be very proud," I was beginning, as the mere prelude to resolute excuses; but the eye of Raffles opened wide upon me; and I hesitated weakly, and was lost.

"Then that's settled," said Lord Amersteth, with the slightest suspicion of grimness.

"It's to be a little week, you know, when my son comes of age. We play the Free Foresters, the Dorsetshire Gentlemen, and probably some local lot as well. But Mr. Raffles will tell you all about it, and Crowley shall write. Another wicket! By Jove, they're all out! Then I rely on you both." And, with a little nod, Lord Amersteth rose and sidled to the gangway.

Raffles rose also, but I caught the sleeve of his blazer.

"What are you thinking of?" I whispered savagely. "I was nowhere near the eleven. I'm no sort of cricketer. I shall have to get out of this!"

ashamed to say that it revolted me much less than the notion of making a public fool of myself on a cricket-field. My gorge rose at this as it no longer rose at crime, and it was in no tranquil humour that I strolled about the ground while Raffles disappeared in the pavilion. Nor was my annoyance lessened by a little meeting I witnessed between young Crowley and his father, who shrugged as he stopped and stooped to convey some information which made the young man look a little blank. It may have been pure self-consciousness on my part, but I could have sworn that the trouble was their inability to secure the great Raffles without his insignificant friend.

"THERE HE SAT, WITH A ZINGARI STRAW HAT TILTED OVER HIS NOSE."

"Not you," he whispered back. "You needn't play, but come you must. If you wait for me after half-past six, I'll tell you why."

But I could guess the reason; and I am

Then the bell rang, and I climbed to the top of the pavilion to watch Raffles bowl. No subtleties are lost up there; and if ever a bowler was full of them, it was A. J. Raffles on this day, as, indeed, all the cricket world remembers. One had not to be a cricketer one's self to appreciate his perfect command of pitch and break, his beautifully easy action, which never varied with the varying pace, his great ball on the leg-stump—his dropping head-ball—in a word, the infinite ingenuity of that versatile attack. It was no mere exhibition of athletic prowess, it was an intellectual treat, and one with a special significance in my eyes. I saw the "affinity between the two things," saw it in that afternoon's tireless warfare against the flower of professional cricket. It was not that Raffles took many wickets for few runs; he was too fine a bowler to mind being hit; and time was short, and the wicket good. What I admired, and what I remember, was the combination of resource and cunning, of patience and precision, of head-work and handiwork, which made every over an artistic whole. It was all so characteristic of that other Raffles whom I alone knew!

"I felt like bowling this afternoon," he told me later in the hansom. "With a pitch to help me, I'd have done something big; as it is, three for thirty-eight, out of the four that fell, isn't so bad for a slow bowler on a plumb wicket against those fellows. But I felt venomous! Nothing riles me more than being asked about for my cricket as though I were a pro. myself."

"Then why on earth go?"

"To punish them, and—because we shall be jolly hard up, Bunny, before the season's over."

"Ah!" said I. "I thought it was that."

"Of course, it was! It seems they're going to have the very dickens of a week of it—balls—dinner-parties—swagger house-party—general junketings—and obviously a houseful of diamonds as well. Diamonds galore! As a general rule, nothing would induce me to abuse my position as a guest. I've never done it, Bunny. But in this case we're engaged like the waiters and the band, and by heaven we'll take our toll! Let's have a quiet dinner somewhere and talk it over."

"It seems rather a vulgar sort of theft," I remarked. And to this, my single protest, Raffles instantly assented.

"It *is* a vulgar sort," said he; "but I can't help that. We're getting vulgarly hard up again, and there's an end on 't. Besides, these people deserve it, and can afford it. And don't you run away with the idea that all will be plain sailing; nothing will be easier than getting some stuff, and nothing harder than avoiding all suspicion, as, of course, we must. We may come away with no more than a good working plan of the premises. Who knows? In any case there's weeks of thinking in it for you and me."

But with those weeks I will not weary you further than by remarking that the "thinking" was done entirely by Raffles, who did not always trouble to communicate his thoughts to me. His reticence, however, was no longer an irritant. I began to accept it as a necessary convention of these little enterprises. And, after our last adventure of the kind, more especially after its *dénouement*, my trust in Raffles was much too solid to be shaken by a want of trust in me, which I still believe to have been more the instinct of the criminal than the judgment of the man.

It was on Monday, the tenth of August, that we were due at Milchester Abbey, Dorset; and the beginning of the month found us cruising about that very county, with fly-rods actually in our hands. The idea was that we should acquire at once a local reputation as decent fishermen and some knowledge of the countryside, with a view to further and more deliberate operations in the event of an unprofitable week. There was another idea which Raffles kept to himself until he had got me down there. Then one day he produced a cricket-ball in a meadow we were crossing, and threw me catches for an hour together. More hours he spent in bowling to me on the nearest green; and, if I was never a cricketer, at least I came nearer to being one, by the end of that week, than ever before or since.

Incident began early on the Monday. We had sallied forth from a desolate little junction within quite a few miles of Milchester, had been caught in a shower, had run for shelter to a wayside inn. A florid, overdressed man was drinking in the parlour, and I could have sworn it was at the sight of him that Raffles recoiled on the threshold, and afterwards insisted on returning to the station through the rain. He assured me, however, that the odour of stale ale had almost knocked him down. And I had to make what I could of his speculative, downcast eyes and knitted brows.

Milchester Abbey is a grey, quadrangular pile, deep-set in rich wooded country, and twinkling with triple rows of quaint windows, every one of which seemed alight as we drove up just in time to dress for dinner. The carriage had whirled us under I know not how many triumphal arches in process of construction, and past the tents and flag-poles of a juicy-looking cricket-field, on which Raffles undertook to bowl up to his reputation. But the chief signs of festival were within, where we found an enormous house-party assembled, including more persons of pomp, majesty, and dominion than I had ever encountered in one room before. I confess I felt overpowered. Our errand and my own pretences combined to rob me of an address on which I have sometimes plumed myself ; and I have a grim recollection of

interested me ; but a great deal that followed did not ; and, obviously to recapture my unworthy attention, Miss Melhuish suddenly asked me, in a sensational whisper, whether I could keep a secret.

I said I thought I might, whereupon another

"BURGLARS ! I WAS ROUSED AT LAST."

my nervous relief when dinner was at last announced. I little knew what an ordeal it was to prove !

I had taken in a much less formidable young lady than might have fallen to my lot. Indeed, I began by blessing my good fortune in this respect. Miss Melhuish was merely the rector's daughter, and she had only been asked to make an even number. She informed me of both facts before the soup reached us, and her subsequent conversation was characterised by the same engaging candour. It exposed what was little short of a mania for imparting information. I had simply to listen, to nod, and to be thankful. When I confessed to knowing very few of those present, even by sight, my entertaining companion proceeded to tell me who everybody was, beginning on my left and working conscientiously round to her right. This lasted quite a long time, and really

question followed, in a still lower and more sensational tone :

"Are you afraid of burglars ?"

Burglars ! I was roused at last. The word stabbed me. I repeated it in horrified query.

"So I've found something to interest you at last !" said Miss Melhuish, in naïve triumph. "Yes—burglars ! But don't speak so loud. It's supposed to be kept a great secret. I really oughtn't to tell you at all !"

"But what is there to tell ?" I whispered with satisfactory impatience.

"You promise not to speak of it ?"

"Of course !"

"Well, then, there are burglars in the neighbourhood."

"Have they committed any robberies ?"

"Not yet."

"Then how do you know ?"

"They've been seen. In the district. Two well-known London thieves !"

Two! I looked at Raffles. I had looked at him often during the evening, envying him his high spirits, his iron nerve, his buoyant wit, his perfect ease and self-possession. But now I pitied him; through all my own terror and consternation, I pitied him as he sat eating and drinking, and laughing and talking, without a cloud of fear or of embarrassment on his handsome, charming, dare-devil face. I caught up my champagne and emptied the glass.

"Who has seen them?" I then asked calmly.

"A detective. They were traced down from town a few days ago. They are believed to have designs on the Abbey!"

"But why aren't they run in?"

"Exactly what I asked papa on the way here this evening; he says there is no warrant out against the men at present, and all that can be done is to watch their movements."

"Oh! so they are being watched?"

"Yes, by a detective who is down here on purpose. And I heard Lord Amersteth tell papa that they had been seen this afternoon at Warbeck Junction!"

The very place where Raffles and I had been caught in the rain! Our stampede from the inn was now explained; on the other hand, I was no longer to be taken by surprise by anything that my companion might have to tell me; and I succeeded in looking her in the face with a smile.

"This is really quite exciting, Miss Melhuish," said I. "May I ask how you come to know so much of such a thrilling business?"

"It's papa," was the confidential reply. "Lord Amersteth consulted him, and he consulted me. But, for heaven's sake, don't let it get about! I can't think *what* tempted me to tell you!"

"You may trust me, Miss Melhuish. But—aren't you frightened?"

Miss Melhuish giggled.

"Not a bit! They won't come to the rectory. There's nothing for them there. But look round the table: look at the diamonds: look at old Lady Melrose's necklace alone!"

The Dowager-Marchioness of Melrose was one of the few persons whom it had been unnecessary to point out to me. She sat on Lord Amersteth's right, flourishing her ear-trumpet, and drinking champagne with her usual notorious freedom, as dissipated and kindly a dame as the world has ever seen. It was a necklace of diamonds and sapphires that rose and fell about her ample neck.

"They say it's worth five thousand pounds at least," continued my companion. "Lady Margaret told me so this morning (that's Lady Margaret Amersteth next your Mr. Raffles, you know); and the old dear *will* wear them every night. Think what a haul they would be! No; we don't feel in immediate danger at the rectory."

When the ladies rose, Miss Melhuish bound me to fresh vows of secrecy; and left me, I should think, with some remorse for her indiscretion, but more satisfaction at the importance which it had undoubtedly given her in my eyes. The opinion may smack of vanity, though, in reality, the very springs of conversation reside in that same human, universal itch to thrill the auditor. The peculiarity of Miss Melhuish was that she must be thrilling at all costs. And thrilling she had surely been.

I spare you my feelings of the next two hours. I tried hard to get a word with Raffles, but again and again I failed. In the dining-room he and Crowley lit their cigarettes with the same match, and had their heads together all the time. In the drawing-room I had the mortification of hearing him talk interminable nonsense into the ear-trumpet of Lady Melrose, whom he knew in town. Lastly, in the billiard-room, they had a great and lengthy pool, while I sat aloof and chafed more than ever in the company of a very serious Scotchman, who had arrived since dinner, and who would talk of nothing but the recent improvements in instantaneous photography. He had not come to play in the matches (he told me), but to obtain for Lord Amersteth such a series of cricket photographs as had never been taken before; whether as an amateur or a professional photographer I was unable to determine. I remember, however, seeking distraction in little bursts of resolute attention to the conversation of this bore. And so at last the long ordeal ended; glasses were emptied, men said good-night, and I followed Raffles to his room.

"It's all up!" I gasped, as he turned up the gas and I shut the door. "We're being watched. We've been followed down from town. There's a detective here on the spot!"

"How do *you* know?" asked Raffles, turning upon me quite sharply, but without the least dismay. And I told him how I knew.

"Of course," I added, "it was the fellow we saw in the inn this afternoon."

"The detective?" cried Raffles. "Do you mean to say you don't know a detective when you see one, Bunny?"

"If that wasn't the fellow, which is?"

Raffles shook his head.

"To think that you've been talking to him for the last hour in the billiard-room, and couldn't spot what he was!"

"That Scotch photographer——"

I paused aghast.

"Scotch he is," said Raffles, "and photographer he may be. He is also Inspector Mackenzie of Scotland Yard—the very man I sent the message to that night last April. And you couldn't spot who he was in a whole hour! O Bunny, Bunny, you were never built for Crime!"

"But," said I, "if that was Mackenzie, who was the fellow you bolted from at Warbeck?"

"The man he's watching."

"But he's watching us!"

Raffles looked at me with a pitying eye, and shook his head again before handing me his open cigarette-case.

"I don't know whether smoking's forbidden in one's bedroom, but you'd better take one of these and stand tight, Bunny, because I'm going to say something offensive."

I helped myself with a laugh.

"Say what you like, my dear fellow, if it really isn't you and I that Mackenzie's after."

"Well, then, it isn't, and it couldn't be, and nobody but a born Bunny would suppose for a moment that it was! Do you seriously think he would sit there and knowingly watch his man playing pool under his nose? Well, he might; he's a cool hand, Mackenzie; but I'm not cool enough to win a pool under such conditions. At least, I don't think I am; it would be interesting to see. The situation wasn't free from strain as it was, though I knew he wasn't thinking of us. Crowley told me all about it after dinner, you see, and then I'd seen one of the men for myself this afternoon. You thought it was a detective that made me turn tail in the afternoon. I really don't know why I didn't tell you at the time, but it was just the opposite. That loud, red-faced brute is one of the cleverest thieves in London, and I once had a drink with him and our mutual 'fence.' I was an East-ender from tongue to toe at the moment, but you will understand that I don't run unnecessary risks of recognition by a brute like that."

"He's not alone, I hear."

"By no means; there's at least one other man with him; and it's suggested that there may be an accomplice here in the house."

"Did Lord Crowley tell you so?"

"Crowley and the champagne between them. In confidence, of course, just as your girl told you; but even in confidence he never let on about Mackenzie. He told me there was a detective in the background, but that was all. Putting him up as a guest is evidently their big secret, to be kept from the other guests because it might offend them, but more particularly from the servants whom

it's doubtless his billet to watch. That's my reading of the situation, Bunny, and you will agree with me that it's infinitely more interesting than we could have imagined it would prove."

"But infinitely more difficult for us," said I, with a sigh of pusillanimous relief. "Our hands are tied for this week, at all events."

"Not necessarily, my dear Bunny, though I admit that the chances are against us. Yet I'm not so sure of that either. There are all sorts of possibilities in these three-cornered combinations. Set A to watch B, and he won't have an eye left for C. That's the obvious theory, but then Mackenzie's a very big A. I should be sorry to have any boodle about me with that man in the house. Yet it would be great to nip in between A and B and score off them both at once! It would be worth a risk, Bunny, to do that; it would be worth risking something merely to take on old hands like B and his men at their own old game! Eh, Bunny? That would be something like a match. Gentlemen and Players at single wicket, by Jove!"

His eyes were brighter than I had known them for many a day. They shone with the perverted enthusiasm which was roused in him only by the contemplation of some new audacity. He kicked off his shoes and began pacing his room with noiseless rapidity; not since the night of the Old Bohemian dinner to Reuben Rosenthall had Raffles exhibited such excitement in my presence; and I was not sorry at the moment to be reminded of the fiasco to which that banquet had been the prelude.

"My dear Raffles," said I in his very own tone, "you're far too fond of the uphill game; you will eventually fall a victim to the sporting spirit and nothing else. Take a lesson from our last escape, and fly lower as you value our skins. Study the house as much as you like, but do—not—go and shove your head into Mackenzie's mouth!"

My wealth of metaphor brought him to a standstill, with his cigarette between his fingers and a grin beneath his shining eyes.

"You're quite right, Bunny. I won't. I really won't. Yet—you saw old Lady Melrose's necklace? I've been wanting it for years! But I'm not going to play the fool; honour bright, I'm not; yet—by Jove!—to get to windward of the professors and Mackenzie too! It would be a great game, Bunny, it would be a great game!"

"Well, you mustn't play it this week."

"No, no, I won't. But I wonder how the professors think of going to work? That's what one wants to know. I wonder if they've really got an accomplice in the house? How

I wish I knew their game! But it's all right, Bunny ; don't you be jealous ; it shall be as you wish."

And with that assurance I went off to my own room, and so to bed with an incredibly light heart. I had still enough of the honest man in me to welcome the postponement of

" HE OPENED HIS FIST, TO SHUT IT NEXT INSTANT ON THE BUNCH OF DIAMONDS AND OF SAPPHIRES "

our actual felonies, to dread their performance, to deplore their necessity : which is merely another way of stating the too patent fact that I was an incomparably weaker man than Raffles, while every whit as wicked. I had, however, one rather strong point. I possessed the gift of dismissing unpleasant considerations, not intimately connected with the passing moment, entirely from my mind. Through the exercise of this faculty I had lately been living my frivolous life in town with as much ignoble enjoyment as I had derived from it the year before ; and similarly, here at Milchester, in the long-dreaded

cricket week, I had after all a quite excellent time.

It is true that there were other factors in this pleasing disappointment. In the first place, *mirabile dictu*, there were one or two even greater duffers than I on the Abbey cricket field. Indeed, quite early in the week, when it was of most value to me, I gained considerable kudos for a lucky catch ; a ball, of which I had merely heard the hum, stuck fast in my hand, which Lord Amersteth himself grasped in public congratulation. This happy accident was not to be undone even by me, and, as nothing succeeds like success, and the constant encouragement of the one great cricketer on the field was in itself an immense stimulus, I actually made a run or two in my very next innings. Miss Melhuish said pretty things to me that night at the great ball in honour of Viscount Crowley's majority ; she also told me that was the night on which the robbers would assuredly make their raid, and was full of arch tremors when we sat out in the garden, though the entire premises were illuminated all night long. Meanwhile, the quiet Scotchman took countless photographs by day, which he developed at night in a dark room admirably situated in the servants' part of the house ; and it is my firm belief that only two of his fellow-guests knew Mr. Clephane of Dundee for Inspector Mackenzie of Scotland Yard.

The week was to end with a trumpery match on the Saturday, which two or three of us intended abandoning early in order to return to town that night. The match, however, was never played. In the small hours of the Saturday morning a tragedy took place at Milchester Abbey.

Let me tell of the thing as I saw and heard it. My room opened upon the central gallery, and was not even on the same floor as that on which Raffles—and I think all the other men—were quartered. I had been put, in fact, into the dressing-room of one of the grand suites, and my too near neighbours were old Lady Melrose and my host and hostess. Now, by the Friday evening the actual festivities were at an end, and, for the first time that week, I must have been sound asleep since midnight, when all at once I found myself sitting up breathless. A heavy thud had come against my door, and now I heard hard breathing and the dull stamp of muffled feet.

"I've got ye," muttered a voice. "It's no use struggling."

It was the Scotch detective, and a new fear turned me cold. There was no reply, but the hard breathing grew harder still, and the muffled feet beat the floor to a quicker measure. In sudden panic I sprang out of bed and flung open my door. A light burnt low on the landing, and by it I could see Mackenzie swaying and staggering in a silent tussle with some powerful adversary.

"Hold this man!" he cried, as I appeared. "Hold the rascal!"

But I stood like a fool until the pair of them backed into me, when, with a deep breath, I flung myself on the fellow, whose face I had seen at last. He was one of the footmen who waited at table; and no sooner had I pinned him than the detective loosed his hold.

"Hang on to him," he cried. "There's more of 'em below!"

And he went leaping down the stairs, as other doors opened and Lord Amersteth and his son appeared simultaneously in their pyjamas. At that my man ceased struggling; but I was still holding him when Crowley turned up the gas.

"What the dickens is all this?" asked Lord Amersteth, blinking. "Who was that ran downstairs?"

"Mac—Clephane!" said I hastily.

"Aha!" said he, turning to the footman. "So you're the scoundrel, are you? Well done! Well done! Where was he caught?"

I had no idea.

"Here's Lady Melrose's door open," said Crowley. "Lady Melrose! Lady Melrose!"

"You forget she's deaf," said Lord Amersteth. "Ah! that'll be her maid."

An inner door had opened; next instant there was a little shriek, and a white figure gesticulated on the threshold.

"Où donc est l'écrin de Madame la Marquise? La fenêtre est ouverte. Il a disparu!"

"Window open and jewel-case gone, by Jove!" exclaimed Lord Amersteth. "Et Madame la Marquise? Va-t-elle bien?"

"Oui, milor. Elle dort."

"Sleeps through it all," said my lord. "She's the only one, then!"

"What made Mackenzie — Clephane — bolt?" young Crowley asked me.

"Said there were more of them below."

"Why the deuce couldn't you tell us so before?" he cried, and went leaping downstairs in his turn.

He was followed by nearly all the cricketers, who now burst upon the scene in a body, only to desert it for the chase. Raffles was one of them, and I would gladly have been another, had not the footman chosen this moment to hurl me from him, and to make a dash in the direction from which they had come. Lord Amersteth had him in an instant; but the fellow fought desperately, and it took the two of us to drag him downstairs, amid a terrified chorus from half-open doors. Eventually we handed him over to two other footmen who appeared with their nightshirts tucked into their trousers, and my host was good enough to compliment me as he led the way outside.

"I thought I heard a shot," he added. "Didn't you?"

"I thought I heard three."

And out we dashed into the darkness.

I remember how the gravel pricked my feet, how the wet grass numbed them as we made for the sound of voices on an outlying lawn. So dark was the night that we were in the cricketers' midst before we saw the shimmer of their pyjamas; and then Lord Amersteth almost trod on Mackenzie as he lay prostrate in the dew.

"Who's this?" he cried. "My God! What's happened?"

"It's Clephane," said a man who knelt over him. "He's got a bullet in him somewhere."

"Is he alive?"

"Barely."

"Good heavens! Where's Crowley?"

"Here I am," called a breathless voice. "It's no good, you fellows. There's nothing to show which way they've gone. Here's Raffles; he's chucked it, too." And they ran up panting.

"Well, we've got one of them, at all events," muttered Lord Amersteth. "The next thing is to get this poor fellow indoors. Take his shoulders, somebody. Now his middle. Join hands under him. All together, now; that's the way. Poor fellow! Poor fellow! His name isn't Clephane at all. He's a Scotland Yard detective, down here for these very villains!"

Raffles was the first to express surprise; but he had also been the first to raise the wounded man. Nor had any of them a stronger or more tender hand in the slow procession to the house. In a little while we had the senseless man stretched on a sofa in the library. And there, with ice on his wound and brandy in his throat, his eyes opened and his lips moved.

Lord Amersteth bent down to catch the words.

"Yes, yes," said he; "we've got one of them safe and sound. The brute you collared upstairs." Lord Amersteth bent lower. "By Jove! Lowered the jewel-case out of the window, did he? And they've got clean away with it! Well, well! I only hope we'll be able to pull this good fellow through. He's off again."

An hour passed : the sun was rising.

It found a dozen young fellows on the settees in the billiard room, drinking whisky and soda-water in their overcoats and pyjamas, and still talking excitedly in one breath. A time-table was being passed from hand to hand : the doctor was still in the library. At last the door opened, and Lord Amersteth put in his head. .

"It isn't hopeless," said he, "but it's bad enough. There'll be no cricket to-day."

Another hour, and most of us were on our way to catch the early train ; between us we filled a compartment almost to suffocation. And still we talked all together of the night's event ; and still I was a little hero in my way, for having kept my hold of the one ruffian who had been taken ; and my gratification was subtle and intense. Raffles watched me under lowered lids. Not a word had we had together ; not a word did we have until we had left the others at Paddington, and were skimming through the familiar, crowded streets in a hansom with noiseless tires and a tinkling bell.

"Well, Bunny," said Raffles, "so the professors have it, eh ? "

"Yes," said I. " And I'm jolly glad ! "

"That poor Mackenzie has a ball in his chest ? '

"That you and I have been on the decent side for once."

He shrugged his shoulders.

"You're hopeless, Bunny, quite hopeless ! I take it you wouldn't have refused your share if the boodle had fallen to us ? Yet you positively enjoy coming off second best —for the second time running ! I confess,

however, that the professors' methods were full of interest to me. I, for one, have probably gained as much in experience as I have lost in other things. That lowering the jewel-case out of the window was a very simple and effective expedient ; two of them had been waiting below for it for hours."

"How do you know ? " I asked.

"I saw them from my own window, which was just above the dear old lady's. I was fretting for that necklace, in particular, when I went up to turn in for our last night—and I happened to look out of my window. In point of fact, I wanted to see whether the one below was open, and whether there was the slightest chance of working the oracle with my sheet for a rope. Of course I took the precaution of turning my light off first, and it was a lucky thing I did. I saw the pros. right down below, and they never saw me. I saw a little tiny luminous disc just for an instant, and then again for an instant a few minutes later. Of course I knew what it was, for I have my own watch-dial daubed with luminous paint ; it makes a lantern of a sort when you can get no better. But these fellows were not using theirs as a lantern. They were under the old lady's window. They were watching the time. The whole thing was arranged with their accomplice inside. Set a thief to catch a thief : in a minute I had guessed what the whole thing proved to be."

"And you did nothing ! " I exclaimed.

"On the contrary, I went downstairs and straight into Lady Melrose's room——"

"You did ? "

"Without a moment's hesitation. To save her jewels. And I was prepared to yell as much into her ear-trumpet for all the house to hear. But the dear lady is too deaf and too fond of her dinner to wake easily."

"Well ? "

"She didn't stir."

"And yet you allowed the professors, as you call them, to take her jewels, case and all ! "

"All but this," said Raffles, thrusting his fist into my lap. "I would have shown it you before, but really, old fellow, your face all day has been worth a fortune to the firm ! "

And he opened his fist, to shut it next instant on the bunch of diamonds and of sapphires that I had last seen encircling the neck of Lady Melrose.

In The Chains of Crime

Being the Confessions of a late Prisoner of the Crown, and sometime accomplice of the more notorious A. J. Raffles, Cricketer and Criminal, whose fate is unknown.

BY E. W. HORNUNG.

IV.—NINE POINTS OF THE LAW.

"WELL," said Raffles, "what do you make of it?"

I read the advertisement once more before replying. It was in the last column of the *Daily Telegraph*, and it ran:—

TWO THOUSAND POUNDS REWARD.—The above sum may be earned by anyone qualified to undertake delicate mission and prepared to run certain risk.—Apply by telegram, Security, London.

"I think," said I, "it's the most extraordinary advertisement that ever got into print!"

Raffles smiled.

"Not quite all that, Bunny; still, extraordinary enough, I grant you."

"Look at the figure!"

"It is certainly large."

"And the mission—and the risk!"

"Yes; the combination is frank, to say the least of it. But the really original point is requiring applications by telegram to a telegraphic address! There's something in the fellow who thought of that, and something in his game; with one word he chokes off the million who answer an advertisement every day—when they can raise the stamp. My answer cost me five bob; but then I prepaid another."

"You don't mean to say that you've applied?"

"Rather," said Raffles. "I want two thousand pounds as much as any man."

"Put your own name?"

"Well—no, Bunny, I didn't. In point of fact, I smell something interesting and illegal, and you know what a cautious chap I am. I signed myself Saumarez, care of Hickey, 28, Conduit Street; that's my tailor, and after sending the wire I went round and told him what to expect. He promised to send the reply along the moment it came—and, by Jove, that'll be it!"

And he was gone before a double-knock on the outer door had done ringing through the rooms, to return next minute with an open telegram and a face full of news.

"What do you think?" said he. "Security's that fellow Addenbrooke, the police-court lawyer, and he wants to see me *instanter*!"

"And you're going to him now?"

"This minute," said Raffles, brushing his hat; "and so are you."

"But I came in to drag you out to lunch."

"You shall lunch with me when we've seen this fellow. Come on, Bunny, and we'll choose your name on the way. Mine's Saumarez, and don't you forget it."

Mr. Bennett Addenbrooke occupied substantial offices in Wellington Street, Strand, and was out when we arrived; but he had only just gone "over the way to the court;"

and five minutes sufficed to produce a brisk, fresh-coloured, resolute-looking man, with a very confident, rather festive air, and black eyes that opened wide at the sight of Raffles.

"Mr.—Saumarez?" exclaimed the lawyer.

"My name," said Raffles, with dry effrontery.

"Not up at Lord's, however!" said the other, slyly. "My dear sir, I have seen you take far too many wickets to make any mistake!"

For a moment Raffles looked venomous; then he shrugged and smiled, and the smile grew into a little cynical chuckle.

"So you have bowled me out in my turn?" said he. "Well, I don't think there's anything to explain. I am harder up than I wished to admit under my own name, that's all, and I want that thousand pounds reward."

"Two thousand," said the solicitor. "And the man who is not above an *alias* happens to be just the sort of man I want; so don't let that worry you, my dear sir. The matter, however, is of a strictly private and confidential character." And he looked very hard at me.

"Quite so," said Raffles. "But there was something about a risk?"

"A certain risk is involved."

"Then surely three heads will be better than two. I said I wanted that thousand pounds; my friend here wants the other. Must you have his name too? Bunny, give him your card."

Mr. Addenbrooke raised his eyebrows over my name, address, and club; then he drummed on my card with his finger-nail, and his embarrassment expressed itself in a puzzled smile.

"The fact is, I find myself in a difficulty," he confessed at last. "Yours is the first reply I have received; people who can afford to send long telegrams don't rush to the advertisements in the *Daily Telegraph;* but, on the other hand, I was not quite prepared to hear from men like yourselves. Candidly, and on consideration, I am not sure that you *are* the stamp of men for me—men who belong to good clubs! I rather intended to appeal to the—er—adventurous classes."

"We are adventurers," said Raffles gravely.

"But you respect the law?"

The black eyes gleamed shrewdly.

"We are not professional rogues, if that's what you mean," said Raffles calmly. "But on our beam-ends we are; we would do a good deal for a thousand pounds apiece."

"Anything," I murmured.

The solicitor rapped his desk.

"I'll tell you what I want you to do. You can but refuse. It's illegal, but it's illegality

in a good cause; that's the risk, and my client is prepared to pay for it. He will pay for the attempt, in case of failure; the money is as good as yours once you consent to run the risk. My client is Sir Bernard Debenham, of Broom Hall, Esher."

"I know his son," I remarked.

"Then," said the solicitor, "you have the privilege of knowing one of the most complete young blackguards about town, and the *fons et origo* of the whole trouble. As you know the son, you may know the father also—at all events, by reputation; and in that case I needn't tell you that he is a very peculiar man. He lives alone in a storehouse of treasures which no eyes but his ever behold. He is said to have the finest collection of pictures in the south of England, though nobody ever sees them to judge; pictures, fiddles, and furniture are his hobby, and he is undoubtedly very eccentric. Nor can one deny that there has been considerable eccentricity in his treatment of his son. For years Sir Bernard paid his debts, and the other day, without the slightest warning, not only refused to do so any more, but absolutely stopped the lad's allowance. Well, I'll tell you what has happened. But, first of all, you must know, or you may remember, that I appeared for young Debenham in a little scrape he got into a year or two ago. I got him off all right, and Sir Bernard paid me handsomely on the nail. And no more did I hear or see of either of them until one day last week."

The lawyer drew his chair nearer ours, and leant forward with a hand on either knee.

"On Tuesday of last week I had a telegram from Sir Bernard; I was to go to him at once. I found him waiting for me in the drive; without a word he led me to the picture-gallery, which was locked and darkened, drew up a blind, and stood simply pointing to an empty picture-frame. It was a long time before I could get a word out of him. Then at last he told me that that frame had contained one of the rarest and most valuable pictures in England—in the world—an original Velasquez. I have checked this," said the lawyer, "and it seems literally true; the picture was a portrait of the Infanta Maria Teresa, said to be one of the artist's greatest works, and second only to his portrait of one of the Popes in Rome—so they told me at the National Gallery, where they had its history by heart. They say there that the picture is practically priceless. And young Debenham has sold it for five thousand pounds!"

"The deuce he has!" said Raffles.

I inquired who had bought it.

"A Queensland legislator of the name of

Craggs—the Hon. John Montagu Craggs, M.L.C., to give him his full title. Not that we knew anything about him on Tuesday last; we didn't even know for certain that young Debenham had stolen the picture. But he had gone down for money on the Monday evening, had been refused, and it was plain enough that he had helped himself in this way; he had threatened revenge, and this was obviously it. Indeed, when I hunted him up in town on the Tuesday night, he confessed as much in the most brazen manner imaginable. But he wouldn't tell me who was the purchaser, and finding out that took the rest of the week; but find it out I did, and a nice time I've had of it ever since! Backwards and forwards between Esher and the Métropole, where the Queenslander is staying, sometimes twice a day; threats, offers, prayers, entreaties, not one of them a bit of good!"

"But," said Raffles, "surely it's a clear case? The sale was illegal; you can pay him back his money and force him to give the picture up."

"Exactly; but not without an action and a public scandal, and that my client declines to face. He would rather lose even his picture than have the whole thing get into the papers; he has disowned his son, but he will not disgrace him; yet his picture he must have by hook or crook, and there's the rub! I am to get it back by fair means or foul. He gives me *carte blanche* in the matter, and, I verily believe, would throw in a blank cheque if asked. He offered one to the Queenslander, but Craggs simply tore it in two; the one old boy is as much a character as the other, and between the two of them I'm at my wits' end."

"So you put that advertisement in the paper?" said Raffles, in the dry tones he had adopted throughout the interview.

"As a last resort. I did."

"And you wish us to *steal* this picture?"

It was magnificently said; the lawyer flushed from his hair to his collar.

"I knew you were not the men!" he groaned. "I never thought of men of your stamp! But it's *not* stealing," he exclaimed heatedly; "it's recovering stolen property. Besides, Sir Bernard will pay him his five thousand as soon as he has the picture; and, you'll see, old Craggs will be just as loth to let it come out as Sir Bernard himself. No, no—it's an enterprise, an adventure, if you like—but not stealing."

"You yourself mentioned the law," murmured Raffles.

"And the risk," I added.

"We pay for that," he said once more.

"But not enough," said Raffles, shaking his head. "My good sir, consider what it means to us. You spoke of those clubs; we should not only get kicked out of them, but put in prison like common burglars. It's true we're hard up, but it simply isn't worth it at the price—double your stakes, and I for one am your man."

Addenbrooke wavered.

"Do you think you could bring it off?"

"We could try."

"But you have no——"

"Experience? No; not as thieves."

"And you would really run the risk for four thousand pounds?"

Raffles looked at me. I nodded.

"We would," said he, "and blow the odds!"

"It's more than I can ask my client to pay," said Addenbrooke, growing firm.

"Then it's more than you can expect us to risk."

"You are in earnest?"

"God wot!"

"Say three thousand if you succeed!"

"No, four."

"Then nothing if you fail——"

"Double or quits?" said Raffles. "Well, that's sporting. Done!"

Addenbrooke opened his lips, half rose, then sat back in his chair, and looked long and shrewdly at Raffles—never once at me.

"I know your bowling," said he reflectively. "I go up to Lord's whenever I want an hour's real rest, and I've seen you bowl again and again—yes, and take the best wickets in England on a plumb pitch. I don't forget the last Gentlemen and Players; I was there. You're up to every trick—every one . . . I'm inclined to think you would bowl out this old Australian if anybody can. Why! I believe you're my very man!" . . .

The bargain was clinched at the Café Royal, where Bennett Addenbrooke insisted on playing host at an extravagant luncheon. I remember that he took his whack of champagne with the nervous freedom of a man at high pressure, and have no doubt I kept him in countenance by an equal indulgence; but Raffles, ever an exemplar in such matters, was more abstemious even than his wont, and very poor company to boot. I can see him now, his eyes in his plate—thinking—thinking. I can see the solicitor glancing from him to me in an apprehension of which I did my best to disabuse him by reassuring looks. At the close Raffles apologised for his preoccupation, called for an A B C time-table, and announced his intention of catching the 3.2 to Esher.

"You must excuse me, Mr. Addenbrooke," said he, "but I have my own idea, and for the moment I should much prefer to keep it to myself. It may end in fizzle, so I would rather not speak about it to either of you just yet. But speak to Sir Bernard I must, so will you write me one line to him on your card ? Of course, if you wish, you must come down with me and hear what I say ; but I really don't see the point."

And, as usual, Raffles had his way, though

furiously in a hansom, and jumped out without a word to the man. I met him next minute at the lift gates, and he fairly pushed me back into my rooms.

"Five minutes, Bunny !" he cried. "Not a second more."

And he tore off his coat before flinging himself into the nearest chair.

"I'm fairly on the rush," he panted ;

"MR. ADDENBROOKE DRUMMED ON MY CARD WITH HIS FINGER-NAIL"

Bennett Addenbrooke was visibly provoked, and I myself shared his annoyance to no small extent. I could only tell him that it was in the nature of Raffles to be self-willed and secretive, but that no man of my acquaintance had half his audacity and determination—that I, for my part would trust him through and through, and let him gang his own gait every time. More I dared not say, even to remove those chill misgivings with which I knew that the lawyer went his way.

That day I saw no more of Raffles, but a telegram reached me when I was dressing for dinner :—

" Be in your rooms to-morrow from noon and keep rest of day clear.—RAFFLES."

It had been sent off from Waterloo at 6.42.

So Raffles was back in town ; at an earlier stage of our relations I should have hunted him up then and there, but now I knew better. His telegram meant that he had no desire for my society that night or the following forenoon ; that when he wanted me I should see him soon enough.

And see him I did, towards one o'clock next day. I was watching for him from my window in Mount Street, when he drove up

"having the very dickens of a time ! Not a word till I tell you all I've done. I settled my plan of campaign yesterday at lunch. The first thing was to get in with this man Craggs ; you can't break into a place like the Métropole—it's got to be done from the inside. Problem one, How to get at the fellow. Only one sort of pretext would do—it must be something to do with this blessed picture, so that I might see where he'd got it, and all that. Well, I couldn't go and ask to see it out of curiosity, and I couldn't go as a second representative of the other old chap, and it was thinking how I could go that made me such a bear at lunch. But I saw my way before we got up. If I could only lay hold of a copy of the picture I might ask leave to go and compare it with the original. So down I went to Esher to find out if there was a copy in existence, and was at Broom Hall for one hour and a half yesterday afternoon. There was no copy there, but they must exist, for Sir Bernard himself (such a rum old boy !) has allowed a couple to be made since the picture has been in his possession. He hunted up the painters' addresses, and the rest of the evening I spent in hunting up the painters themselves ; but their work had been done on commission— one copy had gone out of the country, and I'm still on the track of the other."

" Then you haven't seen Craggs yet ? "

" Oh yes, I have seen him and made friends with him, and if possible he's the funnier old cuss of the two. I took the bull by the horns this morning, went in and lied like Ananias, and it was just as well I did—the old ruffian sails for Australia by to-morrow's boat. I told him a man wanted to sell me a copy of the celebrated Infanta Maria Teresa of Velasquez, that I'd been down to the supposed owner of the picture, only to find that he had just sold it to him. You should have seen his face when I told him that ! He grinned all round his wicked old head. 'Did *old* Debenham admit it ? ' says he ; and when I said he had, he chuckled to himself for about five minutes. He was so pleased that he did just what I hoped he would do ; he showed me the great picture—luckily it isn't by any means a large one—and took a special pride in showing me the case he's got it in. It's an iron map-case in which he brought over the plans of his land in Brisbane ; he wants to know who would suspect it of containing an Old Master, too ? But he's had it fitted with a new Chubb's lock, and I managed to take an interest in the key while he was gloating over the canvas. I had the wax in the palm of my hand, and I shall make my duplicate this afternoon."

Raffles looked at his watch and jumped up, saying he had given me a minute too much.

" By the way," he added, " you've got to dine with him at the Métropole to-night ! "

" I ? "

" Yes ; don't look so scared. Both of us are invited—I swore you were dining with me ; but I shan't be there."

His clear eye was upon me, bright with meaning and with mischief. I implored him to tell me what his meaning was.

" You will dine in his private sitting-room," said Raffles ; " it adjoins his bedroom. You must keep him sitting as long as possible, Bunny, and talking all the time ! "

In a flash I saw his plan.

" ' THOUGHT I HEARD A DOOR GO,' HE SAID "

" You're going for the picture while we're at dinner ? "

" Exactly."

" If he hears you ! "

" He shan't."

" But if he did ! "

And I fairly trembled at the thought.

" If he did," said Raffles, " there would be a collision, that's all. You had better take your revolver. I shall certainly take mine."

" But it's ghastly ! " I cried. " To sit and talk to an utter stranger and know that you're at work in the next room ! "

" Two thousand apiece,' said Raffles, quietly.

" Upon my soul I believe I shall give it away ! "

" Not you, Bunny. I know you better than you know yourself."

He put on his coat and his hat.

" What time have I to be there ? " I asked him with a groan.

" Quarter to eight. There will be a tele-gram from me saying I can't turn up. He's a terror to talk, you'll have no difficulty in keeping the ball rolling ; but head him off his picture for all you're worth. If he offers to show it you, say you must go. He locked up the case elaborately this afternoon, and there's no earthly reason why he should unlock it again in this hemisphere."

" Where shall I find you when I get away ? "

" I shall be down at Esher. I hope to catch the 9.55."

" But surely I can see you again this after-noon ? " I cried in a ferment, for his hand was on the door. " I'm not half coached up yet ! I know I shall make a mess of it ! "

" Not you," he said again, " but *I* shall if I waste any more time. I've got a deuce of a lot of rushing about to do yet. You won't find me at my rooms. Why not come down to Esher yourself by the last train ? That's it—down you come with the latest news. I'll tell old Debenham to expect you ; he shall give us both a bed. By Jove ! he won't be able to do us too well if he's got his picture ! "

" If ! " I groaned, as he nodded his adieu ; and he left me limp with apprehension, sick with fear, in a perfectly pitiable condition of pure stage-fright.

For, after all, I had only to act my part ; unless Raffles failed where he never did fail, unless Raffles the neat and noiseless was for once clumsy and inept, all I had to do was indeed to " smile and smile and be a villain." I practised that smile half the afternoon. I rehearsed putative parts in hypothetical conversations. I got up stories. I dipped in a book on Queensland at the club. And at last it was 7.45 and I was making my bow to

a somewhat elderly man with a small bald head and a retreating brow.

" So you're Mr. Raffles's friend ? " said he, overhauling me rather rudely with his light small eyes. " Have you seen anything of him ? I expected him early to show me something, but he's never come."

No more, evidently, had his telegram, and my troubles were beginning early. I said I had not seen Raffles since one o'clock, telling the truth with unction while I could ; even as we spoke there came a knock at the door, it was the telegram at last, and, after reading it himself, the Queenslander handed it to me.

" Called out of town ! " he grumbled " Sudden illness of near relative ! Wha near relatives has he got ? "

Now, Raffles had none, and for an instant I quailed before the perils of invention ; then I replied that I had never met any of his people, and again felt fortified by my veracity.

" Thought you were bosom pals ? " said he, with (as I imagined) a gleam of suspicion in his crafty little eyes.

" Only in town," said I. " I've never been to his place."

" Well," he growled, " I suppose it can't be helped. Don't know why he couldn't come and have his dinner first. Like to see the death-bed that *I'd* go to without *my* dinner ; it's a full-skin billet, if you ask me. Well, we must just dine without him, and he'll have to buy his pig in a poke after all. Mind touching that bell ? Suppose you know what he came to see me about ? Sorry I shan't see him again, for his own sake. I liked Raffles—took to him amazingly. He's a cynic. I like cynics. I'm one myself. Rank bad form of his mother or his aunt to go and kick the bucket to-day."

I connect these specimens of his conversa-tion, though they were doubtless detached at the time, and interspersed with remarks of mine here and there. They filled the inter-val until dinner was served, and they gave me an impression of the man which his every subsequent utterance confirmed. It was an impression which did away with all remorse for my treacherous presence at his table. He was that terrible type, the Silly Cynic, his aim a caustic commentary on all things and all men, his achievement mere vulgar irre-verence and unintelligent scorn. Ill-bred and ill-informed, he had (on his own showing) fluked into fortune on a rise in land ; yet cunning he possessed, as well as malice, and he chuckled till he choked over the mis-fortunes of less astute speculators in the same boom. Even now I cannot feel much com-punction for my behaviour to the Hon. J. M. Craggs, M.L.C.

But never shall I forget the private agonies of the situation, the listening to my host with one ear and for Raffles with the other! Once I heard him—though the rooms were divided by the old-fashioned folding-doors, and though the dividing door was not only shut but richly curtained, I could have sworn I heard him once. I spilt my wine and laughed at the top of my voice at some coarse sally of my host's. And I heard nothing more, though my ears were on the strain. But later, to my horror, when the waiter had finally withdrawn, Craggs himself sprang up and rushed to his bedroom without a word. I sat like stone till he returned.

"Thought I heard a door go," he said. "Must have been mistaken . . . imagination . . . gave me quite a turn. Raffles tell you priceless treasure I got in there?"

It was the picture at last; up to this point I had kept him to Queensland and the making of his pile. I tried to get him back there now, but in vain. He was reminded of his great ill-gotten possession. I said that Raffles had just mentioned it, and that set him off. With the confidential garrulity of a man who has been drinking freely he plunged into his darling topic, and I looked past him at the clock. It was only a quarter to ten.

In common decency I could not go yet. So there I sat (we were still at port) and learnt what had originally fired my host's ambition to possess what he was pleased to call a "real, genuine, twin-screw, double-funnelled, copper-bottomed Old Master"; it was to "go one better" than some rival legislator of pictorial proclivities. But even an epitome of his monologue would be so much weariness; suffice it that it ended inevitably in the invitation I had dreaded all the evening.

"But you must see it. Next room. This way."

"Isn't it packed up?" I inquired hastily.

"Lock and key. That's all."

"Pray don't trouble," I urged.

"Trouble be hanged!" said he. "Come along."

And all at once I saw that to resist him further would be to heap suspicion upon myself against the moment of impending discovery. I therefore followed him into his bedroom without further protest, and suffered him first to show me the iron map-case which stood in one corner; and he took a crafty pride in this receptacle, and I thought he would never cease descanting on its innocent appearance and its Chubb's lock. It seemed an interminable age before the key was in the latter. Then the ward clicked, and my pulse stood still.

"By Jove!" I cried next instant.

The canvas was in its place among the maps!

"Thought it would knock you," said Craggs, drawing it out and unrolling it for my benefit. "Grand thing, ain't it? Wouldn't think it had been painted two hundred and thirty years? But it has, *my* word! Old Johnson's face will be a treat when he sees it; won't go bragging about *his* pictures much more. Why, this one's worth all the pictures in Colony o' Queensland put together. Worth fifty thousand pounds, my boy—and I got it for five!"

He dug me in the ribs, and seemed in the mood for further confidences. My appearance checked him, and he rubbed his hands.

"If you take it like that," he chuckled, "how will old Johnson take it? Go out and hang himself to his own picture-rods, I hope!"

Heaven knows what I contrived to say at last. Struck speechless first by my relief, I continued silent from a very different cause. A new tangle of emotions tied my tongue. Raffles had failed—Raffles had failed! Could I not succeed? Was it too late? Was there no way?

"So long," he said, taking a last look at the canvas before he rolled it up—"so long till we get to Brisbane."

The flutter I was in as he closed the case!

"For the last time," he went on, as his keys jingled back into his pocket. "It goes straight into the strong-room on board."

For the last time! If I could but send him out to Australia with only its legitimate contents in his precious map-case! If I could but succeed where Raffles had failed!

We returned to the other room. I have no notion how long he talked, or what about. Whisky and soda-water became the order of the hour. I scarcely touched it, but he drank copiously, and before eleven I left him incoherent. And the last train for Esher was the 11.50 out of Waterloo.

I took a hansom to my rooms. I was back at the hotel in thirteen minutes. I walked upstairs. The corridor was empty; I stood an instant on the sitting-room threshold, heard a snore within, and admitted myself softly with my master-key.

Craggs never moved; he was stretched on the sofa fast asleep. But not fast enough for me. I saturated my handkerchief with the chloroform I had brought, and I laid it gently over his mouth. Two or three stertorous breaths, and the man was a log.

I removed the handkerchief; I extracted the keys from his pocket. In less than five minutes I put them back, after winding the

"IT'S A COPY!' I CRIED"

picture about my body beneath my Inverness cape. I took some whisky and soda-water before I went.

The train was easily caught—so easily that I trembled for ten minutes in my first-class smoking carriage, in terror of every footstep on the platform, in unreasonable terror till the end. Then at last I sat back and lit a cigarette, and the lights of Waterloo reeled out behind.

Some men were returning from the theatre. I can recall their conversation even now. They were disappointed with the piece they had seen. It was one of the later Savoy operas, and they spoke wistfully of the days of *Pinafore* and *Patience*. One of them hummed a stave, and there was an argument as to whether the air was out of *Patience* or the *Mikado*. They all got out at Surbiton, and I was alone with my triumph for a few intoxicating minutes. To think that I had succeeded where Raffles had failed! Of all our adventures, this was the first in which I had played a commanding part; and, of them all, this was infinitely the least discreditable. It left me without a conscientious qualm; I had but robbed a robber, when all was said. And I had done it myself, single-handed—*ipse egomet!*

I pictured Raffles, his surprise, his delight. He would think a little more of me in future. And that future, it should be different. We had two thousand pounds apiece—surely enough to start afresh as honest men—and all through me!

In a glow I sprang out at Esher, and took the one belated cab that was waiting under the bridge. In a perfect fever I beheld Broom Hall, with the lower storey still lit up, and saw the front door open as I climbed the steps.

"Thought it was you," said Raffles cheerily. "It's all right. There's a bed for you. Sir Bernard's sitting up to shake your hand."

His good spirits disappointed me. But I knew the man—he was one of those who wear their brightest smile in the blackest hour. I knew him too well by this time to be deceived.

"I've got it!" I cried in his ear—"I've got it!"

"Got what?" he asked me, stepping back.

"The picture!"

"*What?*"

"The picture. He showed it me. You had to go without it; I saw that. So I determined to have it. And here it is."

"Let's see," said Raffles grimly.

I threw off my cape and unwound the canvas from about my body. While I was doing so an untidy old gentleman made his appearance in the hall, and stood looking on with raised eyebrows.

"Looks pretty fresh for an Old Master, doesn't it?" said Raffles.

His tone was strange. I could only suppose that he was jealous of my success.

"So Craggs said. I hardly looked at it myself."

"Well, look now—look closely. By Jove, I must have faked it better than I thought!"

"It's a copy!" I cried.

"It's *the* copy," he answered. "It's the copy I've been tearing all over the country to procure. It's the copy I faked back and front, so that, on your own showing, it imposed upon Craggs, and might have made him happy for life. And you go and rob him of that!"

I could not speak.

"How did you manage it?" inquired Sir Bernard Debenham.

"Have you killed him?" asked Raffles sardonically.

I did not look at him; I turned to Sir Bernard Debenham, and to him I told my story, hoarsely, excitedly, for it was all that I could do to keep from breaking down. But as I spoke I became calmer, and I finished in mere bitterness, with the remark that another time Raffles might tell me what he meant to do.

"Another time!" he cried instantly. "My dear Bunny, you speak as though we were going to turn burglars for a living!"

"I trust you won't," said Sir Bernard, smiling, "for you are certainly two very daring young men. Let us hope our friend from Queensland will do as he said, and not open the case till he gets back there. He will find my cheque awaiting him, and I shall be very much surprised if he troubles any of us again."

Raffles and I did not speak till I was in the room which had been prepared for me. Nor was I anxious to do so then. But he followed me and took my hand.

"Bunny," said he, "don't you be hard on a fellow! I was in the deuce of a hurry, and didn't know that I should ever get what I wanted in time, and that's a fact. But it serves me right that you should have gone and undone one of the best things I ever did. As for *your* handiwork, old chap, you won't mind my saying that I didn't think you had it in you? In future——"

"For God's sake, don't talk about the future!" I cried. "I hate the whole thing; I'm going to give it up!"

"So shall I," said Raffles, "when I've made my pile."

In The Chains of Crime

Being the Confessions of a late Prisoner of the Crown, and sometime accomplice of the more notorious A. J. Raffles, Cricketer and Criminal, whose fate is unknown.

BY E. W. HORNUNG.

V.—THE RETURN MATCH.

 HAD turned into Piccadilly, one thick evening in the following November, when my guilty heart stood still at the sudden grip of a hand upon my arm. I thought — I was always thinking—that my inevitable hour was come at last. It was only Raffles, however, who stood smiling at me through the fog.

" Well met ! " said he. " I've been looking for you at the club."

"I was just on my way there," I returned, with an attempt to hide my tremors. It was an ineffectual attempt, as I saw from his broader smile and the little deprecatory shake of his head.

" Come up to my place instead," said he. " I've something amusing to tell you."

I made excuses, for his tone foretold the kind of amusement, and it was a kind against which I had successfully set my face for months. I have stated before, however, and I can but reiterate, that to me, at all events, there was never anybody in the world so irresistible as Raffles when his mind was made up. That we had both been independent of crime since our little service to Sir Bernard Debenham—that there had been no occasion for that masterful mind to be made up in any such direction for many a day—was the undeniable basis of a longer spell of honesty than I had hitherto enjoyed during the term of our mutual intimacy. Be sure I would deny it if I could ; the very thing I am to tell you would discredit such a boast. I made my excuses, as I have said. But his arm slid through mine, with his little laugh of light-hearted mastery. And even while I argued we were on his staircase in the Albany.

His fire had fallen low. He poked and replenished it after lighting the gas. As for me, I stood by sullenly in my overcoat until he dragged it off my back.

" What a chap you are ! " said Raffles playfully. " One would really think I had proposed to crack another crib this blessed night ! Well, it isn't that, Bunny ; so get into that chair, and take one of these Sullivans and sit tight."

He held the match to my cigarette ; he brought me a whisky and soda. Then he went out into the lobby, and, just as I was beginning to feel happy, I heard a bolt shot home. It cost me an effort to remain in that chair ; next moment he was straddling another and gloating over my discomfiture across his folded arms.

" You remember Milchester, Bunny, my boy ? "

His tone was as bland as mine was grim when I answered that I did.

" We had a little match there that wasn't

down on the card. Gentlemen and Players, if you recollect?"

"I don't forget it."

"Seeing that you never got an innings, so to speak, I thought you might. Well, the Gentlemen romped in winners, and the Players went presently to quod——"

"Poor beggars!"

"Don't be too sure. You remember the fellow we saw in the inn? The florid, over-dressed chap who, I told you, was one of the cleverest thieves in town?"

"I remember him. Crawshay his name turned out to be."

"Well, it was certainly the name he was convicted under, so Crawshay let it be. You needn't waste any pity on *him*, old chap; he escaped from Dartmoor yesterday afternoon."

"Well done!"

Raffles smiled, but his eyebrows had gone up, and his shoulders followed suit.

"You are perfectly right; it was very well done indeed. I wonder you didn't see it in the paper. In a dense fog on the moor yesterday good old Crawshay made a bolt for it, and got away without a scratch under heavy fire. All honour to him, I agree; a fellow with that much grit deserves his liberty. But Crawshay has a good deal more. They hunted him all night long; couldn't find him for nuts; and that was all you missed in the morning papers."

He unfolded a *Pall Mall*, which he had brought in with him.

"But listen to this; here's an account of the escape, with just the addition which puts the whole thing on a higher level. 'The fugitive has been traced to Totnes, where he appears to have committed a peculiarly daring outrage in the early hours of this morning. He is reported to have entered the lodgings of the Rev. A. H. Ellingworth, curate of the parish, who missed his clothes on rising at the usual hour; later in the morning those of the convict were discovered neatly folded at the bottom of a drawer. Meanwhile Crawshay had made good his second escape, though it is believed that so distinctive a disguise will lead to his re-capture during the day.' What do you think of that, Bunny?"

"He is certainly a sportsman," said I, reaching for the paper.

"He's more," said Raffles; "he's an artist, and I envy him. The curate, of all men! Beautiful — beautiful! But that's not all. I saw just now on the board at the club that there's been an outrage on the line near Dawlish. Parson found insensible in the six-foot way. Our friend again! The

telegram doesn't say so, but it's obvious; he's simply knocked some other fellow out, changed clothes again, and come on gaily to town. Isn't it great? I do believe it's the best thing of the kind that's ever been done!"

"But why should he come to town?"

In an instant the enthusiasm faded from Raffles's face; clearly I had reminded him of some prime anxiety, forgotten in his impersonal joy over the exploit of a fellow criminal. He looked over his shoulder towards the lobby before replying.

"I believe," said he, "that the beggar's on *my* tracks!"

And as he spoke he was himself again — quietly amused — cynically unperturbed — characteristically enjoying the situation and my surprise.

"But look here, what do you mean?" said I. "What does Crawshay know about you?"

"Not much; but he suspects."

"Why should he?"

"Because, in his way, he's very nearly as good a man as I am; because, my dear Bunny, with eyes in his head and brains behind them, he couldn't help suspecting. He saw me once in town with old Baird. He must have seen me that day in the pub. on the way to Milchester, as well as afterwards on the cricket field. As a matter of fact, I know he did, for he wrote and told me so before his trial."

"He wrote to you! And you never told me!"

The old shrug answered the old grievance.

"What was the good, my dear fellow? It would only have worried you."

"Well; what did he say?"

"That he was sorry he had been run in before getting back to town, as he had proposed doing himself the honour of paying me a call; however, he trusted it was only a pleasure deferred, and he begged me not to go and get lagged myself before he came out. Of course, he knew the Melrose necklace was gone, though he hadn't got it; and he said that the man who could take that and leave the rest was a man after his own heart. And so on, with certain little proposals for the far future, which I fear may be the very near future indeed! I'm only surprised he hasn't turned up yet."

He looked again towards the lobby which he had left in darkness, with the inner door shut as carefully as the outer one. I asked him what he meant to do.

"Let him knock — if he gets so far. The porter is to say I'm out of town; it will be true, too, in another hour or so."

"You're going off to-night?"

"By the 7.15 from Liverpool Street. I don't say much about my people, Bunny, but I have the best of sisters married to a country parson in the eastern counties. They always make me welcome, and let me read the lessons for the sake of getting me to church. I'm sorry you won't be there to hear me on Sunday, Bunny. I've figured out some of

bowed to us until his bullet head presented an unbroken disc of short red hair.

Brief as was my survey of this astounding apparition, the interval was long enough for Raffles to recover his composure; his hands were in his pockets, and a smile on his face, when my eyes flew back to him.

"Let me introduce you, Bunny," said he,

"BOWED TO US UNTIL HIS BULLET HEAD PRESENTED AN UNBROKEN DISC OF SHORT RED HAIR."

my best schemes in that parish, and I know of no better port in a storm. But I must pack. I thought I'd just let you know where I was going, and why, in case you cared to follow my example."

He flung the stump of his cigarette into the fire, stretched himself as he rose, and remained so long in that inelegant attitude that my eyes mounted from his body to his face; a second later they had followed his across the room, and I also was on my legs. On the threshold of the folding doors that divided bedroom and sitting-room, a well-built man stood in ill-fitting broadcloth, and

"to our distinguished colleague, Mr. Reginald Crawshay."

The bullet head bobbed up, and there was a wrinkled brow above the coarse, shaven face that was crimson, I remember, from the grip of a collar several sizes too small. But I noted nothing consciously at the time. I had jumped to my own conclusion, and I turned on Raffles with an oath.

"It's a trick!" I cried. "It's another of your cursed tricks! You got him here, and then you got me. You want me to join you, I suppose? I'll see you hanged!"

So cold was the stare which met this

outburst that I became ashamed of my words while they were yet upon my lips.

"Really, Bunny!" said Raffles, and turned his shoulder with a shrug.

"Lord love yer," cried Crawshay, "'e knew nothin'. 'E didn't expect me; 'e's all right. And you're the cool canary, *you* are," he went on to Raffles. "I knoo you were, but, do me proud, you're one after my own kidney!" And he thrust out a shaggy hand.

"After that," said Raffles, taking it, "what am I to say? But you must have heard my opinion of you. I am proud to make your acquaintance. How the deuce did you get in?"

"Never you mind," said Crawshay, loosening his collar; "let's talk about how I'm to get out. Lord love yer, but that's better!" There was a livid ring round his bull-neck, that he fingered tenderly. "Didn't know how much longer I might have to play the gent," he explained; "didn't know who you'd bring in."

"Drink whisky and soda?" inquired Raffles, when the convict was in the chair from which I had leapt.

"No, I drink it neat," replied Crawshay, "but I talk business first. You don't get over me like that, Lor' love yer!"

"Well, then, what can I do for you?"

"You know without me tellin' you."

"Give it a name."

"Clean heels, then; that's what I want to show, and I leave the way to you. We're brothers in arms, though I ain't armed this time. It ain't necessary. You've too much sense. But brothers we are, and you'll see a brother through. Let's put it at that. You'll see me through in yer own way. I leave it all to you."

His tone was rich with conciliation and concession; he bent over and tore a pair of button boots from his bare feet, which he stretched towards the fire, painfully uncurling his toes.

"I hope you take a larger size than them," he said. "I'd have had a see if you'd given me time. I wasn't in long afore you."

"And you won't tell me how you got in?"

"Wot's the use? I can't teach *you* nothin'. Besides, I want out. I want out of London, an' England, an' bloomin' Europe too. That's all I want of you, mister. I don't arst how *you* go on the job. You know w'ere I come from, 'cos I 'eard you say; you know w'ere I want to 'ead for, 'cos I've just told yer; the details I leave entirely to you."

"Well," said Raffles, "we must see what can be done."

"We must," said Mr. Crawshay, and leaned back comfortably, and began twirling his stubby thumbs.

Raffles turned to me with a twinkle in his eye; but his forehead was scored with thought, and resolve mingled with resignation in the lines of his mouth. And he spoke exactly as though he and I were alone in the room.

"You seize the situation, Bunny? If our friend here is 'copped,' to speak his language, he means to 'blow the gaff' on you and me. He is too considerate to say so in so many words, but it's plain enough, and natural enough for that matter. I would do the same in his place. We had the bulge before; he has it now; it's perfectly fair. We must take on this job; we aren't in a position to refuse it; even if we were, I should take it on! Our friend is a great sportsman; he has got clear away from Dartmoor; it would be a thousand pities to let him go back. Nor shall he; not if I can think of a way of getting him abroad."

"Any way you like," murmured Crawshay, with his eyes shut. "I leave it all to you."

"But you'll have to wake up and tell us things."

"All right, mister; but I'm fair on the rocks for a sleep!"

And he stood up, blinking.

"Think you were traced to town?"

"Must have been."

"And here?"

"Not in this fog—with any luck."

Raffles went into the bedroom, lit the gas there, and returned next minute.

"So you got in by the window?"

"That's about it."

"It was devilish smart of you to know which one; it beats me how you brought it off in daylight, fog or no fog! But let that pass. You don't think you were seen?"

"I don't think it, sir."

"Well, let's hope you are right. I shall reconnoitre and soon find out. And you'd better come too, Bunny, and have something to eat and talk it over."

As Raffles looked at me, I looked at Crawshay, anticipating trouble; and trouble brewed in his blank, fierce face, in the glitter of his startled eyes, in the sudden closing of his fists.

"And what's to become of me?" he cried out with an oath.

"You wait here."

"No, you don't!" he roared, and at a bound had his back to the door. "You don't get round me like that, you cuckoos!"

Raffles turned to me with a twitch of the shoulders.

"That's the worst of these professors," said he; "they will not use their heads. They see the pegs, and they mean to hit 'em; but that's all they do see and mean, and they think we're the same. No wonder we licked them last time!"

"Don't talk through yer neck," snarled the convict. "Talk out straight, curse you!"

"Right!" said Raffles. "I'll talk as straight as you like. You say you put yourself in my hands—you leave it all to me—yet you don't trust me an inch! I know what's to happen if I fail. I accept the risk. I take this thing on. Yet you think I'm going straight out to give you away and make you give me away in turn. You're a fool, Mr. Crawshay, though you have broken Dartmoor; you've got to listen to a better man, and obey him. I see you through in my own way, or not at all. I come and go as I like, and with whom I like, without your interference; you stay here and lie just as low as you know how, be as wise as your word, and leave the whole thing to me. If you won't—if you're fool enough not to trust me—there's the door. Go out and say what you like, and be hanged to you!"

Crawshay slapped his thigh.

"That's talking!" said he. "Lord love yer, I know where I am when you talk like that. I'll trust yer. I know a man when he gets his tongue between his teeth; you're all right. I don't say so much about this other gent, though I saw him along with you on the job that time in the provinces; but if he's a pal of yours, Mr. Raffles, he'll be all right too. I only hope you gents ain't too stony——"

And he touched his pockets with a rueful face.

"I only went for their togs," said he. "You never struck two such stony-broke cusses in yer life!"

"That's all right," said Raffles. "We'll see you through properly. Leave it to us, and you sit tight."

"Rightum!" said Crawshay. "And I'll have a sleep time you're gone. But no sperrits—no, thank'ee—not yet. Once let me loose on the drink, and, Lord love yer, I'm a gone coon!"

Raffles got his overcoat, a long, light driving-coat, I remember, and even as he put it on our fugitive was dozing in the chair; we left him murmuring incoherently, with the gas out, and his bare feet toasting.

"Not such a bad chap, that professor," said Raffles on the stairs; "a real genius in his way, too, though his methods are a little elementary for my taste. But technique isn't everything; to get out of Dartmoor and into the Albany in the same twenty-fours is a whole that justifies its parts. Good Lord!"

We had passed a man in the foggy court-yard, and Raffles had nipped my arm.

"Who was it?"

"The last man we want to see! I hope to heaven he didn't hear me!"

"But who is he, Raffles?"

"Our old friend Mackenzie, from the Yard!"

I stood still with horror.

"Do you think he's on Crawshay's track?"

"I'll find out."

And before I could remonstrate he had wheeled me round; when I found my voice he merely laughed, and whispered that the bold course was the safe one every time.

"But it's madness——"

"Not it. Shut up. Is that *you*, Mr. Mackenzie?"

The detective turned about and scrutinised us keenly; and through the gaslit mist I noticed that his hair was grizzled at the temples, and his face still cadaverous, from the wound that had nearly been his death.

"I don't know ye, sirs," said he.

"I hope you're fit again," said my companion. "My name is Raffles, and we met at Milchester last year."

"Is that a fact?" cried the Scotsman with quite a start. "Yes, now I remember your face, and yours too, sir. Ay, yon was a bad business, but it ended vera well, an' that's the main thing."

His native caution had returned to him. Raffles pinched my arm.

"Yes, it ended splendidly, but for you," said he. "But what about this escape of the leader of the gang, that fellow Crawshay? What do you think of that, eh?"

"I havena the parteeculars," replied the Scot.

"Good!" cried Raffles. "I was only afraid you might be on his tracks once more!"

Mackenzie shook his head with a dry smile, and wished us good-evening as an invisible window was thrown up, and a whistle blown softly through the fog.

"We must see this out," whispered Raffles. "Nothing more natural than a little curiosity on our part. After him quick!"

And we followed the detective into another entrance on the same side as that from which we had emerged, the left-hand side on one's way to Piccadilly; quite openly we followed him, and at the foot of the stairs met one of the porters of the place. Raffles stopped him and asked what was wrong.

"Nothing, sir," said the fellow glibly.

"Rot!" said Raffles. "That was Mackenzie, the detective. I've just been speaking to him. What's he here for? Come on, my good fellow ; we won't give you away, if you've instructions not to tell."

The man looked quaintly wistful, the temptation of an audience hot upon him ; a door shut upstairs, and he fell.

"It's like this," he whispered. " This afternoon a gen'leman comes after rooms, and I sent him to the orfice ; one of the clerks, 'e goes round with 'im an' shows 'im the empties, an' the gen'leman's partic'ly struck on the set the coppers is up in now. So he sends the clerk to fetch the manager, as there was one or two things he wished to speak about ; an' when they come back, blowed if the gent isn't gone. Beg yer pardon, sir, but he's clean disappeared off the face o' the premises ! " And the porter looked at us with shining eyes.

" Well ? " said Raffles.

" Well, sir, they looked about, an' looked about, an' at larst they give 'im up for a bad job ; thought he'd changed his mind an' didn't want to tip the clerk ; so they shut up the place an' come away. An' that's all till about 'alf an hour ago, when I takes the manager his extry speshul *Staw ;* in about ten minutes he comes running out with a note, an' sends me with it to Scotland Yard in a hansom. An' that's all I know, sir—straight. The coppers is up there now, and the 'tec,' and the manager, and they think their gent is about the place somewhere still. Least, I reckon that's their idea ; but who he is, or what they want him for, I dunno."

" Jolly interesting ! " said Raffles. " I'm going up to inquire. Come on, Bunny ; there should be some fun."

" Beg yer pardon, Mr. Raffles, but you won't say nothing about me ? "

" Not I ; you're a good fellow. I won't forget it if this leads to sport. Sport ! " he whispered as we reached the landing. " It looks like precious poor sport for you and me, Bunny ! "

" What are you going to do ? "

" I don't know. There's no time to think. This, to start with."

And he thundered on the shut door ; a policeman opened it. Raffles strode past him with the air of a chief commissioner, and I followed before the man had recovered from his astonishment. The bare boards rang under us ; in the bedroom we found a knot of officers stooping over the window-ledge with a constable's lantern. Mackenzie was the first to stand upright, and he greeted us with a glare.

" May I ask what you gentlemen want ? " said he severely.

" We want to lend a hand," said Raffles briskly. " We lent one once before, and it was my friend here who took over from you the fellow who split on all the rest, and held him tight. Surely that entitles him, at all events, to see any fun that's going ? As for myself, well, it's true I only helped to carry you to the house ; but for old acquaintance sake I do hope, my dear Mackenzie, that you will permit us to share such sport as there may be. I myself can only stop a few minutes, in any case."

" Then you won't see much," growled the detective, " for he's not up here. Constable, go you and stand at the foot of the stairs, and let no other body come up on any conseederation ; these gentlemen may be able to help us, after all."

" That's kind of you, Mackenzie ! " cried Raffles warmly. " But what is it all ? I questioned one of the porters, but could get nothing out of him, except that somebody had been to see these rooms and not since been seen himself."

" He's a man we want," said Mackenzie. " He's concealed himself somewhere about these premises, or I'm vera much mistaken. Do you reside in the Albany, Mr. Raffles ? "

" I do."

" Will your rooms be near these ? "

" On the next staircase but one."

" Have you just left them ? "

" Just."

" Been in all the afternoon, perhaps ? "

" No."

" Then I may have to search your rooms, sir. I am prepared to search every room in the Albany ! Our man seems to have gone for the leads ; but unless he's left more marks outside than in, or we find him up there, I shall have the entire building to ransack."

" I will leave you my key," said Raffles at once. " I am dining out, but I'll leave it with the officer down below."

I caught my breath in mute amazement. What was the meaning of this insane promise ? It was wilful, gratuitous, suicidal ; it made me pluck at his sleeve in open horror and disgust ; but, with a word of thanks, Mackenzie had returned to his window-sill, and we sauntered unwatched through the folding doors into the adjoining room. Here the window looked down into the courtyard ; it was still open ; and as we gazed out in apparent idleness, Raffles reassured me.

" It's all right, Bunny ; you do what I tell you and leave the rest to me. It's a tight corner, but I don't despair. What you've got to do is to stick to these chaps, especially if they search my rooms ; they mustn't poke about more than necessary, and they won't if you're there."

"But where will you be? You're never going to leave me to be landed alone?"

"If I do, it will be to turn up trumps at the right moment. Besides, there are such things as windows, and Crawshay's the man to take his risks. You must trust me, Bunny; you've known me long enough."

"And you're going now?"

"There's no time to lose. Stick to them, old chap; don't let them suspect *you*, whatever else you do."

His hand lay an instant on my shoulder; then he left me at the window, and recrossed the room.

"I've got to go now," I heard him say; "but my friend will stay and see this through, and I'll leave the gas on in my rooms and my key with the constable downstairs. Good luck, Mackenzie; only wish I could stay."

"Good-night, sir," came in a preoccupied voice, "and many thanks."

Mackenzie was still busy at his window, and I remained at mine, a prey to mingled fear and wrath, for all my knowledge of Raffles and of his infinite resource. By this time I felt that I knew more or less what he would do in any given emergency; at least I could conjecture a characteristic course of equal cunning and audacity. He would return to his rooms, put Crawshay on his guard, and—stow him away? No—there were such things as windows. Then why was Raffles going to desert us all? I thought of many things— lastly of a cab. These bedroom windows looked into a narrow side-street; they were not very high; from them a man might drop on to the roof of a cab—even as it passed— and be driven away—even under the noses of the police! I pictured Raffles driving that cab, unrecognisable in the foggy night; the vision came to me as he passed under the window, tucking up the collar of his great driving-coat on the way to his rooms; it was still with me when he passed again on his way back, and stopped to hand the constable his key.

" 'MAY I ASK WHAT YOU GENTLEMEN WANT?' SAID HE SEVERELY."

"We're on his track," said a voice behind me. "He's got up on the leads, sure enough, though how he's managed it from yon window is a myst'ry to me. We're going to lock up here and try from the attics. So you'd better come with us if you've a mind."

The top floor at the Albany, as elsewhere, is devoted to the servants — congeries of little kitchens and cubicles, used by many as lumber-rooms—by Raffles among the many. The annex in this case was, of course, empty as the rooms below; and that was lucky, for we filled it, what with the manager, who now joined us, and another tenant whom he brought with him, to Mackenzie's undisguised annoyance.

"Better let in Piccadilly at a crown a head," said he. "Here, my man, out you go on the roof to make one less, and have that truncheon ready."

"'DO YOU KNOW WHO YOU'VE LET SLIP, BUTTER-FINGERS?'"

We crowded to the little window, which Mackenzie took care to fill; and a minute yielded no sound but the crunch and slither of constabulary boots upon sooty slates. Then came a shout.

"What is it?" cried Mackenzie.

"A rope," we heard, "hanging from the spout by a hook!"

"Sirs," cried Mackenzie, "that's how he got up from below! He would just sling it up till it caught, an' I never thocht o't! How long a rope, my lad?"

"Quite short. I've got it."

"Did it hang over a window? Ask him that!" cried the manager. "He can see by leaning over the parapet."

The question was repeated by Mackenzie; a pause, then "Yes, it did."

"Ask him how many windows along!" shouted the manager in high excitement.

"Six, he says," said Mackenzie next minute; and he drew in his head and shoulders. "I should just like to see those rooms, six windows along."

"Mr. Raffles's," announced the manager after a mental calculation.

"Is that a fact?" cried Mackenzie. "Then we shall have no difficulty at all. He's left me his key down below."

The words had a dry, speculative intonation, which even then I found time to dislike; it was as though the coincidence had already struck the Scotsman as something more.

"Where is Mr. Raffles?" asked the manager, as we all filed downstairs.

"He's gone out to his dinner," said Mackenzie.

"Are you sure?"

"I saw him go," said I. My heart was beating horribly. I would not trust myself to speak again. But I wound my way to a front place in the little procession, and was, in fact, the second man to cross the threshold that had been the Rubicon of my life. As I did so I uttered a cry of pain, for Mackenzie had trod back heavily on my toes; in another second I saw the reason, and saw it with another cry.

A man was lying at full length before the fire on his back, with a little wound in the white forehead, and the blood running into his eyes. And the man was Raffles himself.

"Suicide," said Mackenzie calmly. "No—here's the poker—looks more like murder." He went on his knees, and shook his head

quite cheerfully. "An' it's not even murder," said he with a shade of disgust in his matter-of-fact voice; "yon's no more than a flesh-wound, and I have my doubts whether it felled him; but, sirs, he just stinks o' chlory-form!"

He got up and fixed his keen grey eyes upon me; my own were full of tears, but they faced him unashamed.

"I understood you to say you saw him go out?" said he sternly.

"I saw that long driving-coat; of course, I thought he was inside it."

"And I could ha' sworn it was the same gent when he give me the key!"

It was the disconsolate voice of the constable in the background; on him turned Mackenzie, white to the lips.

"You'd think anything, some of you policemen," said he. "What's your number, you rotter? P 34? You'll be hearing more of this, Mr. P 34! If that gentleman was dead—instead of coming to himself while I'm talking—do you know what you'd be? Guilty of his manslaughter, you stuck pig in buttons! Do you know who you've let slip, butter-fingers? Crawshay—no less—him that broke Dartmoor yesterday. By the God that made you, P 34, if I lose him I'll hound you from the force!"

Working face—shaking fist—a calm man on fire. It was a new side of Mackenzie, and one to remember. Next moment he had dashed from our midst.

"Difficult thing to break your own head," said Raffles later; "infinitely easier to cut your own throat. Chloroform's another matter; when you've used it on others, you know the dose to a nicety. So you thought I was really gone! Poor old Bunny! But I hope Mackenzie saw your face?"

"He did," said I. I would not tell him all Mackenzie had seen, however.

"That's all right. I wouldn't have had him miss it for the world; and you mustn't think me a brute, old boy, for I fear that man, and, you know, we sink or swim together."

"And now we sink or swim with Crawshay too," said I dolefully.

"Not we!" said Raffles with conviction. "Old Crawshay's a true sportsman, and he'll do by us as we've done by him; besides, this makes us quits; and I don't think, Bunny, that we'll take on the professors again!"

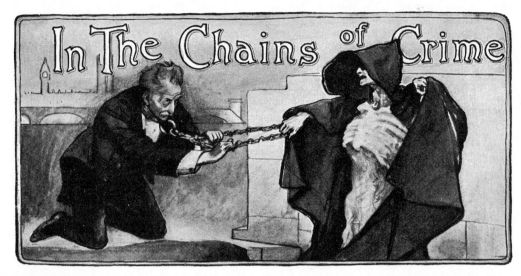

In The Chains of Crime

Being the Confessions of a late Prisoner of the Crown, and sometime accomplice of the more notorious A. J. Raffles, Cricketer and Criminal, whose fate is unknown.

BY E. W. HORNUNG.

VI.—THE GIFT OF THE EMPEROR.

I.

WHEN the King of the Cannibal Islands made faces at Queen Victoria, and his European counterpart set the cables tingling with his compliments on the exploit, the indignation in England was not less than the surprise, for the thing was not so common as it has since become. But when it transpired that a gift of peculiar significance was to follow the congratulations, to give them weight, the inference prevailed that the white potentate and the black had taken simultaneous leave of their fourteen senses. For the gift was a pearl of price unparalleled, picked aforetime by British cutlasses from a Polynesian setting, and presented by British royalty to the monarch who seized this opportunity of restoring it to its original possessor.

The incident would have been a godsend to the Press a few weeks later. Even in June there were leaders, letters, large headlines, leaded type; the *Daily Chronicle* devoting half its literary page to a charming drawing of the island capital which the new *Pall Mall*, in a leading article, headed by a pun, advised the Government to blow to flinders. I was myself driving a poor but honest pen at the time, and the topic of the hour goaded me into satiric verse which obtained a better place than anything I had yet turned out. I had let my flat in town, and taken inexpensive quarters at Thames Ditton, on the plea of a disinterested passion for the river.

"First-rate, old boy!" said Raffles (who must needs come and see me there), lying back in the boat while I sculled and steered. "I suppose they pay you pretty well for these, eh?"

"Not a penny."

"Nonsense, Bunny! I thought they paid so well? Give them time, and you'll get your cheque."

"No, I shan't," said I gloomily. "I've got to be content with the honour of getting in ; the editor wrote to say so, in so many words," I added. But I gave the gentleman his distinguished name.

"You don't mean to say you've written for payment already?"

No ; it was the last thing I had intended to admit. But I had done it. The murder was out ; there was no sense in further concealment. I had written for my money because I really needed it ; if he must know, I was cursedly hard up. Raffles nodded as though he knew already. I warmed to my woes. It was no easy matter to keep your end up as a raw free-lance of letters ; for my part, I was afraid I wrote neither well enough nor ill enough for success. I suffered from

302

a persistent ineffectual feeling after style. Verse I could manage ; but it did not pay. To personal paragraphs and the baser journalism I could not, and I would not, stoop.

Raffles nodded again, this time with a smile that stayed in his eyes as he leant back watching me. I knew that he was thinking of other things I had stooped to, and I thought I knew what he was going to say. He had said it before so often ; he was sure to say it again. I had my answer ready, but evidently he was tired of asking the same question. His lids fell, he took up the paper he had dropped, and I sculled the length of the old red wall of Hampton Court before he spoke again.

"And they gave you nothing for these ! My dear Bunny, they're capital, not only *quâ* verses, but for crystallising your subject and putting it in a nutshell. Certainly you've taught *me* more about it than I knew before. But is it really worth fifty thousand pounds—a single pearl ? "

"A hundred, I believe ; but that wouldn't scan."

"A hundred thousand pounds ! " said Raffles, with his eyes shut. And again I made certain what was coming, but again I was mistaken. "If it's worth all that," he cried at last, "there would be no getting rid of it at all ; it's not like a diamond that you can subdivide. But I beg your pardon, Bunny. I was forgetting ! "

And we said no more about the emperor's gift ; for pride thrives on an empty pocket, and no privation would have drawn from me the proposal which I had expected Raffles to make. My expectation had been half a hope, though I only knew it now. And neither did we touch again on what Raffles professed to have forgotten—my "apostasy," my "lapse into virtue," as he had been pleased to call it. We were both a little silent, a little constrained, each preoccupied with his own thoughts. It was months since we had met, and, as I saw him off towards eleven o'clock that Sunday night, I fancied it was for more months that we were saying good-bye.

But as we waited for the train I remarked those clear eyes peering at me under the station lamps, and when I met their glance Raffles shook his head.

"You don't look well on it, Bunny," said he. "I never did believe in this Thames Valley. You want a change of air."

I wished I might get it.

"What you really want is a sea voyage."

"And a winter at St. Moritz, or do you recommend Cannes or Cairo ? It's all very well, old chap, but you forget what I told you about my funds."

"I forget nothing. I merely don't want to hurt your feelings. But, look here, a sea voyage you shall have. I want one myself, and you shall come with me as my guest. We'll spend July in the Mediterranean."

"But you're playing cricket——"

"Hang the cricket ! "

"Well, if I thought you meant it——"

"Of course I mean it. Will you come ? "

"Like a shot—if you go."

And I shook his hand, and waved mine in farewell, with the perfectly good-humoured conviction that I should hear no more of the matter. It was a passing thought—no more, no less. I soon wished it were more ; that week found me wishing myself out of England for good and all. I was making nothing. I could but subsist on the difference between the rent I paid for my flat and the rent at which I had sublet it, furnished, for the season. And the season was near its end, and creditors awaited me in town. Was it possible to be entirely honest ? I had run no bills when I had money in my pocket, and the more downright dishonesty seemed to me the less ignoble.

But from Raffles, of course, I heard nothing more ; a week went by, and half another week ; then, late on the second Wednesday night, I found a telegram from him at my lodgings, after seeking him vainly in town and dining with desperation at the solitary club to which I still belonged.

"Arrange to leave Waterloo by North German Lloyd special," he wired, " 9.25 a.m. Monday next, will meet you Southampton aboard *Uhlan* with tickets am writing."

And write he did, a light-hearted letter enough, but full of serious solicitude for me and my health and prospects ; a letter that touched me the more in the light of our past relations, in the twilight of their complete rupture. He said that he had booked two berths to Naples, that we were bound for Capri, which was clearly the Island of the Lotos-eaters, that we would bask there together, "and for a while forget." It was a charming letter. I had never seen Italy ; the privilege of initiation should be his. No mistake was greater than to deem it an impossible country for the summer. The Bay of Naples was never so divine, and he wrote of "faëry lands forlorn," as though the poetry sprang unbidden to his pen. To come back to earth and prose, I might think it unpatriotic of him to choose a German boat, but on no other line did you receive such attention and accommodation for your money. There was a hint of better reasons. Raffles wrote, as he had telegraphed, from Bremen ; and I gathered that the personal use of some little influence with the authorities there had resulted in a material reduction in our fares.

Imagine my excitement and delight! I managed to pay what I owed at Thames Ditton, to squeeze a small editor for a very small cheque, and my tailors for one more flannel suit. I remember that I broke my last sovereign to get a box of Sullivan's cigarettes for Raffles to smoke on the voyage. But my heart was as light as my purse on the Monday morning, the fairest morning of an unfair summer, when the special whirled me through the sunshine to the sea.

A tender awaited us at Southampton. Raffles was not on board, nor did I really look for him till we reached the liner's side. And then I looked in vain. His face was not among the many that fringed the rail; his hand was not of the few that waved to friends. I climbed aboard in a sudden heaviness. I had no ticket, nor the money to pay for one. I did not even know the number of my room. My heart was in my mouth as I waylaid a steward and asked if a Mr. Raffles was on board. Thank heaven—he was! But where? The man did not know, was plainly on some other errand, and a-hunting I had to go. But there was no sign of him on the promenade deck, and none below in the saloon; the smoking-room was empty but for a little German with a red moustache twisted into his eyes; nor was the fellow in his own cabin, whither I inquired my way in desperation, and where the sight of his own name on the baggage was certainly a further reassurance. Why he himself kept in the background, however, I could not conceive, and only sinister reasons would suggest themselves in explanation.

"So there you are! I've been looking for you all over the ship!"

Despite the graven prohibition I had tried the bridge as a last resort, and there, indeed, was A. J. Raffles, seated on a skylight, and leaning over one of the officers' long chairs, in which reclined a girl in a white drill coat and skirt, a slim girl with a pale skin, dark hair, and rather remarkable eyes. So much I noted as he rose and quickly turned; thereupon I could think of nothing but the swift grimace which preceded a start of well-feigned astonishment.

"Why——*Bunny?*" cried Raffles. "Is it really *you?*"

I stammered something as he pinched my hand.

"And are you coming in this ship? And to Naples, too? Well, upon my word! Miss Werner, may I introduce him?"

And he did so without a blush, describing me as an old schoolfellow whom he had not seen for months, with wilful circumstance and gratuitous detail that filled me at once with confusion, suspicion, and revolt. I felt myself blushing for us both, and I did not care. My address utterly deserted me, and I made no effort to recover it, to carry the thing off. All I would do was to mumble such words as Raffles actually put into my mouth, and that I doubt not with a thoroughly evil grace.

"So you saw my name in the list of passengers and came in search of me? Good old Bunny! I say, though, I wish you'd share my cabin? I've got a beauty on the promenade deck, but they wouldn't promise to keep me by myself. We ought to see about it before they shove in some alien. In any case we shall have to get out of this."

For a quartermaster had entered the wheel-house, and even while we had been speaking the pilot had taken possession of the bridge; as we descended, the tender left us with flying handkerchiefs and shrill good-byes; and as we bowed to Miss Werner on the promenade deck, there came a deep slow throbbing under foot, and our voyage had begun.

It did not begin pleasantly between Raffles and me. On deck he had overborne my stubborn perplexity by dint of a forced though forceful joviality; in his cabin the gloves were off.

"You idiot," he snarled, "you've given me away again!"

"How have I given you away?"

I ignored the fresh insult in his last word.

"How? I should have thought any clod could see that I meant us to meet by chance!"

"After taking both tickets yourself?"

"They know nothing about that on board; besides, I hadn't decided when I took the tickets."

"Then you should have let me know when you did decide. You lay your plans, and never say a word, and expect me to tumble to them by light of Nature. How was I to know you had anything on?"

I had turned the tables with some effect. Raffles almost hung his head.

"The fact is, Bunny, I didn't mean you to know. You—you've grown such a pious rabbit in your old age!"

My nickname and his tone went far to mollify me, other things went farther, but I had much to forgive him still.

"If you were afraid of writing," I pursued, "it was your business to give me the tip the moment I set foot on board. I would have taken it all right. I am not so virtuous as all that!"

Was it my imagination, or did Raffles look slightly ashamed? If so, it was for the first and last time in all the years I knew him; nor can I swear to it even now.

"That," said he, "was the very thing I meant to do—to lie in wait in my room and get you as you passed. But——"

"You were better engaged?"

"Say otherwise."

"Confound you!" he said, and, though he was laughing, I thought it was a point at which the subject might be changed.

"Well," I said, "it wasn't for Miss Werner you wanted us to play strangers, was it? You have some deeper game than that, eh?"

"'WHY——*BUNNY?*' CRIED RAFFLES. 'IS IT REALLY *YOU?*'"

"The charming Miss Werner?"

"She is quite charming."

"Most Australian girls are," said I, dryly.

"How did you know she was one?" he cried.

"I heard her speak."

"Brute!" said Raffles, laughing, "she has no more twang than you have. Her people are German, she has been to school in Dresden, and is on her way out alone."

"Money?" I inquired.

"I suppose I have."

"Then hadn't you better tell me what it is?"

Raffles treated me to the old cautious scrutiny that I knew so well; the very familiarity of it, after all these months, set me smiling in a way that might have reassured him; for dimly already I divined his enterprise.

"It won't send you off in the pilot's boat, Bunny?"

"Not quite."

"Then—you remember the pearl you wrote the——"

I did not wait for him to finish his sentence.

"You've got it!" I cried, my face on fire, for I caught sight of it that moment in the state-room mirror.

Raffles seemed taken aback.

"Not yet," said he; "but I mean to have it before we get to Naples."

"Is it on board?"

"Yes."

"But how—where—who's got it?"

"A little German officer, a whipper-snapper with perpendicular moustaches."

"I saw him in the smoke-room."

"That's the chap; he's always there. Herr Capitain Wilhelm von Heumann, if you look in the list. Well, he's the special envoy of the emperor, and he's taking the pearl out with him!"

"You found this out in Bremen?"

"No, in Berlin, from a newspaper man I know there. I'm ashamed to tell you, Bunny, that I went there on purpose!"

I burst out laughing.

"You needn't be ashamed. You are doing the very thing I was rather hoping you were going to propose the other day on the river."

"You were *hoping* it?" said Raffles, with his eyes wide open. Indeed, it was his turn to show surprise, and mine to be much more ashamed than I felt.

"Yes," I answered, "I was quite keen on the idea, but I wasn't going to propose it."

"Yet you would have listened to me the other day?"

Certainly I would, and I told him so without reserve; not brazenly, you understand; not even now with the gusto of a man who likes such an adventure for its own sake, but doggedly, defiantly, through my teeth, as one who had tried to live honestly and failed. And, while I was about it, I told him much more. Eloquently enough, I dare say, I gave him chapter and verse of my hopeless struggle, my inevitable defeat; for hopeless and inevitable they were to a man with my record, even though that record was written only in one's own soul. It was the old story of the thief trying to turn honest man; the thing was against Nature, and there was an end of it.

Raffles entirely disagreed with me. He shook his head over my conventional view. Human nature was a board of chequers; why not submit one's self to alternate black and white? Why desire to be all one thing or all the other, like our forefathers on the stage or in the old-fashioned fiction? For his part, he enjoyed himself on all squares of the board, and liked the light the better for the shade. My conclusion he considered absurd.

"But you err in good company, Bunny, for all the cheap moralists preach the same twaddle—old Virgil was the first and worst offender of you all. I back myself to climb out of Avernus any day I like, and sooner or later I shall climb out for good. I suppose I can't very well turn myself into a Limited Liability Company. But I could retire and settle down and live blamelessly ever after. I'm not sure that it couldn't be done on this pearl alone!"

"Then you don't still think it too remarkable to sell?"

"We might take a fishery and haul it up with smaller fry. It would come after months of ill luck, just as we were going to sell the schooner; by Jove, it would be the talk of the Pacific!"

"Well, we've got to get it first. Is this von Heumann a formidable cuss?"

"More so than he looks; and he has the cheek of the devil!"

As he spoke, a white drill skirt fluttered past the open state-room door, and I caught a glimpse of an upturned moustache beyond.

"But is he the chap we have to deal with? Won't the pearl be in the purser's keeping?"

Raffles stood at the door, frowning out upon the Solent, but for an instant he turned to me with a sniff.

"My good fellow, do you suppose the whole ship's company knows there's a gem like that aboard? You said that it was worth a hundred thousand pounds; in Berlin they say it's priceless. I doubt if the skipper himself knows that von Heumann has it on him."

"And he has?"

"Must have."

"Then we have only him to deal with?"

He answered me without a word; something white was fluttering past once more, and Raffles, stepping forth, made the promenaders three.

II.

I DO not ask to set foot aboard a finer steamship than the *Uhlan* of the Norddeutscher Lloyd, to meet a kindlier gentleman than her then commander, or better fellows than his officers. This much at least let me have the grace to admit. I hated the voyage. It was no fault of anybody connected with the ship; it was no fault of the weather, which was monotonously ideal. Not even in my own heart did the reason reside; conscience and I were divorced at last, and the decree made absolute. With my scruples had fled all fear, and I was ready to revel between bright skies and sparkling sea with the light-hearted detachment of Raffles himself. It was Raffles himself who prevented me, but not Raffles alone. It was Raffles and that Colonial minx on her way home from school.

What he could see in her—but that begs the question. Of course, he saw no more than I did, but to annoy me, or perhaps to punish me for my long defection, he must turn his back on me and devote himself to this chit from Southampton to the Mediterranean. They were always together. It was too absurd. After breakfast they would begin, and go on until eleven or twelve at night; there was no intervening hour at which you might not hear her nasal laugh, or his quiet voice talking soft nonsense into her ear. Of course it was nonsense! Is it conceivable that a man like Raffles, with his knowledge of the world, and his experience of women (a side of his character upon which I have purposely never touched, for it deserves another volume) ; is it credible, I ask, that such a man could find anything but nonsense to talk by the day together to a giddy young schoolgirl? I would not be unfair for the world. I think I have admitted that the young person had points. Her eyes, I suppose, were really fine, and certainly the shape of the little brown face was charming, so far as mere contour can charm. I admit also more audacity than I cared about, with enviable health, mettle, and vitality. I may not have occasion to report any of this young lady's speeches (they would scarcely bear it), and am, therefore, the more anxious to describe her without injustice. I confess to some little prejudice against her. I resented her success with Raffles, of whom in consequence I saw less and less each day. It is a mean thing to have to confess, but there must have been something very like jealousy rankling within me.

Jealousy there was in another quarter— crude, rampant, undignified jealousy. Captain von Heumann would twirl his moustaches into twin spires, shoot his white cuffs over his rings, and stare at me insolently through his rimless eyeglasses ; we ought to have consoled each other, but we never exchanged a syllable. The captain had a murderous scar across one of his cheeks, a present from Heidelberg, and I used to think how he must long to have Raffles there to be served the same. It was not as though von Heumann never had his innings. Raffles let him go in several times a day, for the malicious pleasure of bowling him out as he was "getting set" ; those were his words when I taxed him disingenuously with obnoxious conduct towards a German on a German boat.

"You'll make yourself disliked on board ! "

"By von Heumann merely."

"But is that wise when he's the man we've got to diddle ? "

"The wisest thing I ever did. To have chummed up with him would have been fatal —the common dodge."

I was consoled, encouraged, almost reconciled. I had feared Raffles was neglecting things, and I told him so in a burst. Here we were near Gibraltar, and not a word since the Solent. He shook his head with a smile.

"Plenty of time, Bunny, plenty of time. We can do nothing before we get to Genoa, and that won't be till Sunday night. The voyage is still young, and so are we ; let's make the most of things while we can."

It was after dinner on the promenade deck, and, as Raffles spoke, he glanced sharply fore and aft, leaving me next moment with a step full of purpose. I retired to the smoking-room, to smoke and read in a corner, and to watch von Heumann, who soon came to drink beer and to sulk in another.

Few travellers tempt the Red Sea at midsummer ; the *Uhlan* was very empty indeed. She had, however, but a limited supply of cabins on the promenade deck, and there was just that excuse for my sharing Raffles's room. I could have had one to myself downstairs, but I must be up above. Raffles had urged that I should insist on the point. So we were together, I think, without suspicion, and most certainly without any object that I could see.

On the Sunday afternoon I was asleep in my berth, the lower one, when the curtains were shaken by Raffles, who was in his shirt-sleeves on the settee.

"Achilles—sulking in his tent as usual ! "

"What else is there to do ? " I asked him as I stretched and yawned. I noted, however, the good-humour of his tone, and did my best to catch it.

"I have found something else, Bunny."

"I dare say ! "

"You misunderstand me. The whipper-snapper's making his century this afternoon. I've had other fish to fry."

I swung my legs over the side of my berth and sat forward, as he was sitting, all attention. The inner door, a grating, was shut and bolted, and curtained like the open port-hole.

"We shall be at Genoa before sunset," continued Raffles. "It's the place where the deed's got to be done."

"So you still mean to do it."

"Did I ever say I didn't ? "

"You have said so little either way."

"Advisedly so, my dear Bunny ; why spoil a pleasure trip by talking unnecessary shop ?

But now the time has come. It must be done at Genoa or not at all."

"On land?"

"No, on board, to-morrow night. To-night would do, but to-morrow is better, in case of mishap. If we were forced to use violence we could get away by the earliest train, and nothing be known till the ship was sailing and von Heumann found dead or drugged—"

"Not dead!" I exclaimed.

"Of course not," assented Raffles, "or there would be no need for us to bolt ; but if we should have to bolt, Tuesday morning is our time, when this ship has got to sail, whatever happens. But I don't anticipate any violence. Violence is a confession of terrible incompetence. In all these years how many blows have you known me strike? Not one, I believe ; but I have been quite ready to kill my man every time, if the worst came to the worst."

I asked him how he proposed to enter von Heumann's state-room unobserved, and even through the curtained gloom of ours his face lighted up.

"Climb up into my bunk, Bunny, and you shall see."

I did so, but could see nothing. Raffles reached across me and tapped the ventilator, a sort of trap-door in the wall above his bed, some eighteen inches long and half that height, and opening outwards into the ventilating shaft.

"That," said he, "is our door to fortune. Open it if you like ; you won't see much, because it doesn't open far, but loosening a couple of screws will set that all right. The shaft, as you may see, is more or less bottomless ; you pass under it whenever you go to your bath, and the top is a skylight on the bridge. That's why this thing has to be done while we're at Genoa, because they keep no watch on the bridge in port. The ventilator opposite ours is von Heumann's. It again will only mean a couple of screws, and there's a beam to stand on while you work."

"But if anybody should look up from below?"

"It's extremely unlikely that anybody will be astir below, so unlikely that we can afford to chance it. No, I can't have you there to make sure. The great point is that neither of us should be seen from the time we turn in. A couple of ship's boys do sentry-go on these decks, and they will be our witnesses ; by Jove, it'll be the biggest mystery that ever was made!"

"If von Heumann doesn't resist."

"Resist! He won't get the chance. He drinks too much beer to sleep light, and nothing is so easy as to chloroform a heavy

sleeper ; you've even done it yourself on an occasion of which it's perhaps unfair to remind you. Von Heumann will be past sensation almost as soon as I get my hand through his ventilator. I shall crawl in over his body, Bunny, my boy!"

"And I?"

"You will hand me what I want, and hold the fort in case of accidents, and generally lend me the moral support you've made me require. It's a luxury, Bunny, but I found it uncommon difficult to do without it after you turned pi!"

He said that von Heumann was certain to sleep with a bolted door, which he. of course, would leave unbolted, and spoke of other ways of laying a false scent while rifling the cabin. Not that Raffles anticipated a tiresome search. The pearl would be about von Heumann's person ; in fact, Raffles knew exactly where and in what he kept it. Naturally, I asked how he could have come by such knowledge, and his answer led up to a momentary unpleasantness.

"It's a very old story, Bunny. I really forget in what Book it comes. I'm only sure of the Testament. But Samson was the unlucky hero, and one Delilah the heroine."

And he looked so knowing that I could not be in a moment's doubt as to his meaning.

"So the fair Australian has been playing Delilah?" said I.

"In a very harmless, innocent sort of way."

"She got his mission out of him?"

"Yes, I've forced him to score all the points he could, and that was his great stroke, as I hoped it would be. He has even shown Amy the pearl."

"Amy, eh! and she promptly told you?"

"Nothing of the kind. What makes you think so? I had the greatest trouble in getting it out of her."

His tone should have been a sufficient warning to me. I had not the tact to take it as such. At last I knew the meaning of his furious flirtation, and stood wagging my head and shaking my finger, blinded to his frowns by my own enlightenment.

"Wily dog!" said I. "Now I see through it all ; how dense I've been!"

"Sure you're not still?"

"No ; now I understand what has beaten me all the week. I simply couldn't fathom what you saw in that little girl. I never dreamt it was part of the game."

"So you think it was that and nothing more?"

"You deep old rascal—of course I do!"

"You didn't know she was the daughter of a wealthy squatter?"

"There are wealthy women by the dozen who would marry you tomorrow."

"It doesn't occur to you that I might like to draw stumps, start clean, and live happily ever after—in the bush?"

"With Amy Werner? It certainly does not!"

"Bunny!" he cried so fiercely, that I braced myself for a blow.

But no more followed.

"Do you think you would live happily?" I made bold to ask him.

"God knows!" he answered. And with that he left me, to marvel at his look and tone, and, more than ever, at the insufficiently exciting cause.

" 'THAT,' SAID HE, 'IS OUR DOOR TO FORTUNE.' "

III.

OF all the mere feats of cracksmanship which I have seen Raffles perform, at once the most delicate and most difficult was that which he accomplished between one and two on the Tuesday morning, aboard the North German steamer *Uhlan*, lying at anchor in Genoa harbour.

Not a hitch occurred. Everything had been foreseen; everything happened as I had been assured everything must. Nobody was about below, only the ship's boys on deck, and nobody on the bridge. It was twenty-five minutes past one when Raffles, without a stitch of clothing on his body, but with a glass phial, corked with cotton-wool, between his teeth, and a tiny screw-driver behind his ear, squirmed feet first through the ventilator over his berth; and it was nineteen minutes to two when he returned, head first, with the phial still between his teeth, and the cotton-wool rammed home to still the rattling of that which lay like a great grey bean within. He had taken screws out and put them in again; he had unfastened von Heumann's ventilator and had left it fast as he had found it—fast as he instantly proceeded to make his own. As for von Heumann, it had been enough to place the drenched wad first on his moustache, and then to hold it between his gaping lips; thereafter the intruder had climbed both ways across his shins without eliciting a groan.

And here was the prize—this pearl as large as a filbert—with a pale pink tinge like a lady's finger-nail—this spoil of a filibustering age—this gift from a European emperor to a South Sea chief. We gloated over it when all was snug. We toasted it in whisky and soda-water laid in over night in view of the great moment. But the moment was greater, more triumphant, than our most sanguine dreams. All we had now to do was to secrete the gem (which Raffles had prised from its setting, replacing the latter) so that we could stand the strictest search and yet take it ashore with us at Naples; and this Raffles was doing when I turned in. I myself would have gone incontinently ashore and bolted with the spoil; he would not hear of it, and for a dozen good reasons which will be obvious.

On the whole I do not think that anything was discovered or suspected before we weighed anchor; but I cannot be sure. It is difficult to believe that a man could be chloroformed in his sleep and feel no tell-tale effects, sniff no suspicious odour, in the morning. Nevertheless, von Heumann reappeared as though nothing had happened to him, his German cap over his eyes and his moustaches brushing the peak. And by ten o'clock we were quit of Genoa ; the last lean, blue-chinned official had left our decks ; the last fruitseller had been beaten off with bucketfuls of water and left cursing us from his boat ; the last passenger had come aboard at the last moment—a fussy greybeard who kept the big ship waiting while he haggled with his boatman over half a lira. But at length we were off, the tug was shed, the lighthouse passed, and Raffles and I leaned together over the rail, watching our shadows on the pale green, liquid, veined marble that again washed the vessel's side.

Von Heumann was having his innings once more ; it was part of the design that he should remain in all day and so postpone the inevitable hour ; and, though the lady looked bored, and was for ever glancing in our direction, he seemed only too willing to avail himself of his opportunities. But Raffles was moody and ill-at-ease. He had not the air of a successful man. I could but opine that the impending parting at Naples sat heavily on his spirit.

He would neither talk to me, nor would he let me go.

"Stop where you are, Bunny. I've things to tell you. Can you swim ? "

" A bit."

" Ten miles ? "

" Ten ? " I burst out laughing. " Not one ! Why do you ask ? "

" We shall be within a ten miles' swim of the shore most of the day."

" What on earth are you driving at, Raffles ? "

" Nothing ; only I shall swim for it if the worst comes to the worst. I suppose you can't swim under water at all ? "

I did not answer his question. I scarcely heard it : cold beads were bursting through my skin.

" Why should the worst come to the worst ? " I whispered. " We aren't found out, are we ? "

" No."

" Then why speak as though we were ? "

" We may be ; an old enemy of ours is on board."

" An old enemy ? "

" Mackenzie."

" Never ! "

" The man with the beard who came aboard last."

" Are you sure ? "

" Sure ! I was only surprised you didn't recognise him too."

I took my handkerchief to my face ; now that I thought of it, there had been something familiar in the old man's gait, as well as something very youthful for his apparent years ; his very beard seemed unconvincing, now that I recalled it in the light of this horrible revelation. I looked up and down the deck, but the old man was nowhere to be seen.

" That's the worst of it," said Raffles. " I saw him go into the Captain's cabin twenty minutes ago."

" But what can have brought him ? " I cried miserably. " Can it be a coincidence—is it somebody else he's after ? "

Raffles shook his head.

" Hardly this time."

" Then you think he's after you ? "

" I've been afraid of it for some weeks."

" Yet there you stand ! "

" What am I to do ? I don't want to swim for it before I must. I begin to wish I'd taken your advice, Bunny, and left the ship at Genoa. But I've not the smallest doubt that Mac was watching both ship and station till the last moment. That's why he ran it so fine."

He took a cigarette and handed me the case, but I shook my head impatiently.

" I still don't understand," said I. " Why should he be after you ? He couldn't come all this way about a jewel which was perfectly safe for all he knew. What's your own theory ? "

" Simply that he's been on my track for some time, probably ever since friend Crawshay slipped clean through his fingers last November. There have been other indications. I am really not unprepared for this. But it can only be pure suspicion. I'll defy him to bring anything home, and I'll defy him to find the pearl ! Theory, my dear Bunny ? I know how he's got here as well as though I had been inside that Scotsman's skin, and I know what he'll do next. He found out I'd gone abroad, and looked for a motive ; he found out about von Heumann and his mission, and there was his motive cut-and-dried. Great chance—to nab me on a new job altogether. But he won't do it, Bunny ; mark my words, he'll search the ship and search us all, when the loss is known ; but he'll search in vain. And there's the skipper beckoning the whipper-snapper to his cabin : the fat will be in the fire in five minutes ! "

Yet there was no conflagration, no fuss, no searching of the passengers, no whisper of what had happened in the air ; instead of a stir there was portentous peace ; and it was clear to me that Raffles was not a little disturbed at the falsification of all his predictions.

There was something sinister in silence under such a loss, and the silence was sustained for hours during which Mackenzie never reappeared. But he was abroad during the luncheon-hour—he was in our cabin! I had left my book in Raffles's berth, and in taking it after lunch I touched the quilt. It was warm from the recent pressure of flesh and blood, and on an instinct I sprang to the ventilator; as I opened it the ventilator opposite was closed with a snap.

I waylaid Raffles. "All right! Let him find the pearl."

"Have you dumped it overboard?"

"That's a question I shan't condescend to answer."

He turned on his heel, and at subsequent intervals I saw him making the most of his last afternoon with the inevitable Miss Werner. I remember that she looked both cool and smart in quite a simple affair of brown holland, which toned well with her complexion, and was cleverly relieved with touches of scarlet. I quite admired her that afternoon, for her eyes were really fine, and so were her teeth, yet I had never admired her more directly in my own despite. For I passed them again and again in order to get a word with Raffles, to tell him I knew there was danger in the wind; but he would not so much as catch my eye. So at last I gave it up. And I saw him next in the Captain's cabin.

They had summoned him first; he had gone in smiling; and smiling I found him when they summoned me. The state-room was spacious, as befitted that of a commander. Mackenzie sat on the settee, his beard in front of him on the polished table; but a revolver lay in front of the Captain; and, when I had entered, the chief officer, who had summoned me, shut the door and put his back to it. Von Heumann completed the party, his fingers busy with his moustache.

Raffles greeted me.

"This is a great joke!" he cried. "You remember the pearl you were so keen about, Bunny, the Emperor's pearl, the pearl money wouldn't buy? It seems it was entrusted to our little friend here, to take out to Canoodle Dum, and the poor little chap's gone and lost it; ergo, as we're Britishers, they think we've got it!"

"But I know ye have," put in Mackenzie, nodding to his beard.

"You will recognise that loyal and patriotic voice," said Raffles. "Mon, 'tis our auld acquaintance Mackenzie, o' Scoteland Yarrd an' Scoteland itsel'!"

"Dat is enough," cried the Captain. "Have

you submid to be searge, or do I vorce you?"

"What you will," said Raffles, "but it will do you no harm to give us fair play first. You accuse us of breaking into Captain von Heumann's state-room during the small hours of this morning and abstracting from it this confounded pearl. Well, I can prove that I was in my own room all night long, and I have no doubt my friend can prove the same."

"Most certainly I can," said I, indignantly. "The ship's boys can bear witness to that."

Mackenzie laughed and shook his head at his reflection in the polished mahogany.

"That was very clever," said he, "and like enough it would ha' served ye had I not stepped aboard. But I've just had a look at they ventilators, and I think I know how ye worrked it. Anyway, Captain, it makes no matter. I'll just be clappin' the darbies on these young sparrks, an' then—"

"By what right?" roared Raffles, in a ringing voice, and I never saw his face in such a blaze. "Search us if you like; search every scrap and stitch we possess; but you dare to lay a finger on us without a warrant!"

"I wouldna' dare," said Mackenzie, gravely, as he fumbled in his breast pocket, and Raffles dived a hand into his own. "Haud his wrist!" shouted the Scotsman; and the huge Colt that had been with us many a night, but had never been fired in my hearing, clattered on the table and was raked in by the Captain.

"All right," said Raffles savagely to the mate. "You can let go now. I won't try it again. Now, Mackenzie, let's see your warrant!"

"Ye'll no mishandle it?"

"What good would that do me? Let me see it," said Raffles, peremptorily, and the detective obeyed. Raffles raised his eyebrows as he perused the document; his mouth hardened, but suddenly relaxed; and it was with a smile and a shrug that he returned the paper.

"Will that do for ye?" inquired Mackenzie.

"It may. I congratulate you, Mackenzie; it's a strong hand, at any rate. Two burglaries and the Melrose necklace, Bunny!" And he turned to me with a rueful smile.

"An' all easy to prove," said the Scotsman, pocketing the warrant. "I've one o' these for you," he added, nodding to me, "only not such a long one."

"To thingk," said the Captain, reproachfully, "that my shib should be made a den of thiefs! It shall be a very disagreeable madder. I have been obliged to pud you both in irons until we ged to Nables."

"Surely not!" exclaimed Raffles. "Mackenzie, intercede with him; don't give your countrymen away before all hands! Captain, we can't escape; surely you could hush it up for the night? Look here, here's everything I have in my pockets; you empty yours too, Bunny, and they shall strip us stark if they suspect we've weapons up our sleeves. All I

our watches, pocket-books, pencils, penknives, cigarette cases—lay on the shiny table along with the revolvers already mentioned.

"Ye're humbuggin' us," said Mackenzie. "What's the use?"

"I'm doing nothing of the sort," laughed Raffles. "I'm testing you. Where's the harm?"

"It's here, joke apart?"

"On that table, by all my gods."

"RAFFLES GREETED ME. 'THIS IS A GREAT JOKE!' HE CRIED"

ask is that we are allowed to get out of this without gyves upon our wrists!"

"Webbons you may not have," said the Captain; "but wad about der bearl dat you were sdealing?"

"You shall have it!" cried Raffles. "You shall have it this minute if you guarantee no public indignity on board!"

"That I'll see to," said Mackenzie, "as long as you behave yourselves. There now, where is it?"

"On the table under your nose."

My eyes fell with the rest, but no pearl was there; only the contents of our pockets—

Mackenzie opened the cigarette cases and shook each particular cigarette. Thereupon Raffles prayed to be allowed to smoke one, and, when his prayer was heard, observed that the pearl had been on the table much longer than the cigarettes. Mackenzie promptly caught up the Colt and opened the chamber in the butt.

"Not there, not there," said Raffles; "but you're getting hot. Try the cartridges."

Mackenzie emptied them into his palm, and shook each one at his ear without result.

"Oh, give them to me!"

And, in an instant, Raffles had found the

right one, had bitten out the bullet, and placed the Emperor's pearl with a flourish in the centre of the table.

"After that you will perhaps show me such little consideration as is in your power. Captain, I have been a bit of a villain, as you see, and as such I am ready and willing to lie in irons all night if you deem it requisite for the safety of the ship. All I ask is that you do me one favour first."

"That shall debend on wad der vafour has been."

"Captain, I've done a worse thing aboard your ship than any of you know. I have become engaged to be married, and I want to say good-bye!"

I suppose we were all equally amazed; but the only one to express his amazement was von Heumann, whose deep-chested German oath was almost his first contribution to the proceedings. He was not slow to follow it, however, with a vigorous protest against the proposed farewell; but he was overruled, and the masterful prisoner had his way. He was to have five minutes with the girl, while the Captain and Mackenzie stood within range (but not earshot), with their revolvers behind their backs. As we were moving from the cabin, in a body, he stopped and gripped my hand.

"So I've let you in at last, Bunny, at last and after all! If you knew how sorry I am. . . . But you won't get much—I don't see why you should get anything at all. Can you forgive me? This may be for years, and it may be for ever, you know! You were a good pal always when it came to the scratch; some day or other you mayn't be so sorry to remember you were a good pal at the last!"

There was a meaning in his eye that I understood; and my teeth were set, and my nerves strung ready, as I wrung that strong and cunning hand for the last time in my life.

How that last scene stays with me, and will stay to my death! How I see every detail, every shadow on the sunlit deck! We were among the islands that dot the course from Genoa to Naples; that was Elba falling back on our starboard quarter, that purple patch with the hot sun setting over it. The Captain's cabin opened to starboard, and the starboard promenade deck, sheeted with sunshine and scored with shadow, was deserted but for the group of which I was one, and for the pale, slim, brown figure further aft with Raffles. Engaged? I could not believe it, cannot to this day. Yet there they stood together, and we did not hear a word; there they stood out against the sunset, and the

long, dazzling highway of sunlit sea that sparkled from Elba to the *Uhlan's* plates; and their shadows reached almost to our feet.

Suddenly—an instant—and the thing was done—a thing I have never known whether to admire or to detest. He caught her—he kissed her before us all—then flung her from him so that she almost fell. It was that action which foretold the next. The mate sprang after him, and I sprang after the mate. Raffles was on the rail, but only just.

"Hold him, Bunny!" he cried. "Hold him tight!"

And, as I obeyed that last behest with all my might, without a thought of what I was doing, save that he bade me do it, I saw his hands shoot up and his head bob down, and his lithe, spare body cut the sunset as cleanly and precisely as though he had plunged at his leisure from a diver's board!

*   *   *   *   *

Of what followed on deck I can tell you nothing, for I was not there. Nor can my final punishment, my long imprisonment, my everlasting disgrace, concern or profit you, beyond the interest and advantage to be gleaned from the knowledge that I at least had my deserts. But one thing I must set down, believe it who will—one more thing only and I am done.

It was into a second-class cabin, on the starboard side, that I was promptly thrust in irons, and the door locked upon me as though I were another Raffles. Meanwhile a boat was lowered, and the sea scoured to no purpose, as is doubtless on record elsewhere. But either the setting sun, flashing over the waves, must have blinded all eyes, or else mine were victims of a strange illusion.

For the boat was back, the screw throbbing, and the prisoner peering through his porthole across the sunlit waters that he believed had closed for ever over his comrade's head. Suddenly the sun sank behind the Island of Elba, the lane of dancing sunlight was instantaneously quenched and swallowed in the trackless waste, and in the middle distance, already miles astern, either my sight deceived me or a black speck bobbed amid the grey. The bugle had blown for dinner: it may well be that all save myself had ceased to strain an eye. And now I lost what I had found, now it rose, now it sank, and now I gave it up utterly. Yet anon it would rise again, a mere mote dancing in the dim grey distance, drifting towards a purple island, beneath a fading western sky, streaked with dead gold and cerise. And night fell before I knew whether it was a human head or not.

XV

The Tragedy of a Third Smoker

CUTCLIFFE HYNE

THE TRAGEDY OF A THIRD SMOKER.

A STORY OF THE METROPOLITAN RAILWAY.

By Cutcliffe Hyne.

Illustrated by J. Finnemore, R.B.A.

"I ABOMINATE detective stories," said the Q.C., laying down his cue along the corner of the billiard-table and going across to the shelf where the cigar-boxes stood. "You see, when a man makes a detective story to write down on paper, he begins at the butt-end and works backwards. He notes his points and manufactures his clues to suit 'em, so it's all bound to work out right. In real life it's very different,"—he chose a Partaga, looking at it through his glasses thoughtfully—"and I ought to know; I've been studying the criminal mind for half my working life."

"But," said O'Malley, "a defending counsel is a different class of animal from the common detective."

"Oh, is he?" said the Q.C.; "that's all you know about it." He dragged one of the big chairs up into the deep chimney corner and settled himself in it, after many luxurious shruggings; then he spoke on, between whiffs at the Partaga.

"Now I'll just state you a case, and you'll see for yourself how we sometimes have to ravel out things. The solicitor who put the brief in my hands was, as solicitors go, a smart chap. He had built up a big business out of nothing, but criminal work was slightly out of his line. He had only taken up this case to oblige an old client, and I must say he made an uncommonly poor show of it. I never had such a thin brief given me in my life.

"The prisoner was to be tried on the capital charge; and if murder really had been committed, it was one of a most cold-blooded nature. Hanging would follow conviction as surely as night comes on the heels of day; and a client who gets the noose given him always damages his counsel's reputation, whether that counsel deserves it or not.

"As my brief put it, the case fined down to this:

"Two men got into an empty third-class smoking compartment at Addison Road. One of them, Guide, was a drain contractor; the other, Walker, was a foreman in Guide's employ. The train took them past the Shepherd's Bush and Grove Road Hammersmith stations without anything being reported; but at Shaftesbury Road Walker was found on the floor, stone dead, with a wound in the skull, and on the seat of the carriage was a small miner's pickaxe with one of its points smeared with blood.

"It was proved that Guide had been seen to leave the Shaftesbury Road station. He was dishevelled and agitated at the time, and this made the ticket collector notice him specially amongst the crowd of out-going passengers. After it was found out who he was, inquiries were made at his home. His wife stated that she had not seen him since Monday—the morning of Walker's death. She also let out that Walker had been causing him some annoyance of late, but she did not know about what. Subsequently—on the Friday, four days later—Guide was arrested at the West India Dock. He was trying to obtain employ as coal trimmer on an Australian steamer, obviously to escape from the country. On being charged he surrendered quietly, remarking that he supposed it was all up with him.

"That was the gist of my case, and the solicitor suggested that I should enter a plea of insanity.

317

"THE TICKET COLLECTOR SPECIALLY NOTICED HIM."

"Now, when I'd conned the evidence over—additional evidence to what I've told you, but all tending to the same end—I came to the conclusion that Guide was as sane as any of us are, and that, as a defence, insanity wouldn't have a leg to stand upon. 'The fellow,' I said, 'had much better enter a plea of guilty and let me pile up a long list of extenuating circumstances. A jury will always listen to those, and feeling grateful for being excused a long and wearisome trial, recommend to mercy out of sheer gratitude.' I wrote a note to this effect. On its receipt the solicitor came to see me—by the way, he was Barnes, a man of my own year at Cambridge.

"'My dear Grayson,' said he, 'I'm not altogether a fool. I know as well as you do that Guide would have the best chance if he pleaded guilty; but the difficult part of it is that he flatly refuses to do any such thing. He says he no more killed this fellow Walker than you or I did. I pointed out to him that the man couldn't very conveniently have slain himself, as the wound was well over at the top of his head, and had obviously been the result of a most terrific blow. At the P.M. it was shown that Walker's skull was of abnormal thickness, and the force required to drive through it even a heavy, sharp-pointed instrument like the pickaxe, must have been something tremendous.

"'I tell you, Grayson, I impressed upon the fellow that the case was as black as ink against him, and that he'd only irritate the jury by holding out; but I couldn't move him. He held doggedly to his tale—he had not killed Andrew Walker.'

"'He's not the first man who's stuck to an unlikely lie like that,' I remarked.

"'The curious part of it is,' said Barnes, 'I'm convinced that the man believes himself to be telling the absolute truth.'

"'Then what explanation has he to offer?'

"'None worth listening to. He owns that he and Walker had a fierce quarrel over money matters, which culminated in a personal struggle. He knows that he had one blow on the head which dazed him, and fancies that he must have had a second which reduced him to unconsciousness. When next he knew what was happening, he saw Walker lying on the floor, stone dead, though he was still warm and supple. On the floor was the pickaxe, with one of its points slimy with blood. How it came to be so he couldn't tell. He picked it up and laid it on a seat. Then in an instant the thought flashed across him how terribly black things looked against himself. He saw absolutely no chance of disproving them, and with the

"GUIDE WAS ARRESTED AT THE WEST INDIA DOCK."

usual impulse of crude minds resolved at once to quit the country. With that idea he got out at the Shaftesbury Road Station, and being an ignorant man and without money, made his way down to the Ratcliff Highway—beg its pardon, St. George's High Street. Using that as a centre, he smelt about the docks at Limehouse and Millwall trying for a job in the stokehold; but as that neighbourhood is one of the best watched spots on earth, it is not a matter for surprise that he was very soon captured. That's about all I can tell you.'

" ' I'm afraid it doesn't lighten matters up very much.'

" ' I never said it would. The gist of this is down in your brief, Grayson. I only came round to chambers because of your letter.'

" ' Still,' I persisted, ' you threw out a hint that Guide had offered some explanation.'

" ' Oh, yes; but such a flimsy, improbable theory that no sane man could entertain it for a minute. In fact, he knew it to be absurd himself. After pressing him again and again to suggest how Walker could have been killed (with the view of extorting a confession), he said, in his slow, heavy way, "Why, I suppose, Mr. Barnes, someone else must ha' done it. Don't you think as a man could ha' got into the carriage whilst I was lying there stupid, and hit Walker with the pick and got out again afore I come to? Would that do, sir?"

" ' I didn't think,' added Barnes, drily, ' that it was worth following that theory any deeper. What do you say?'

" I thought for a minute and then spoke up. ' Look here, Barnes; if in the face of this cock-and-bull story Guide persists in his innocence, there may be something in it after all; and if by any thousand-to-one chance we could bring him clear, it would be a red feather in the caps of both of us. Do you object to my seeing the man personally?'

" ' It's a bit irregular,' said Barnes, doubtfully.

" ' I know it is bang in the teeth of etiquette. But suppose we compromise, and you come with me?'

" ' No, I won't do that. My time's busy just now; and besides, I don't want to run up the costs of this case higher than necessary. But if you choose to shove your other work aside and waste a couple of hours, just go and interview him by yourself, and we'll waive ceremony. I'll get the necessary prison order, and send it round to you to-morrow.'

" Next afternoon I went down to see Guide in the waiting-room at the Old Bailey. He was a middle-aged man,

"THEY HAD A FIERCE QUARREL OVER MONEY MATTERS."

heavy-faced, and evidently knocked half stupid by the situation in which he found himself. He was perhaps as great a fool to his own interests as one might often meet with. There was no getting the simplest tale out of him except by regular question-and-answer cross-examination. What little he did tell seemed rather to confirm his guilt than otherwise; though, strange to say, I was beginning to believe him when he kept on assuring me between every other sentence that he did not commit the murder. Perhaps it was the stolid earnestness of the fellow in denying the crime which convinced me. One gets to read a good deal from facial expression when a man has watched what goes on in the criminal dock as long as I have done;

and one can usually spot guilt under any mask.

"'But tell me,' I said, 'what did you quarrel about in the first instance?'

"'Money,' said Guide, moodily.

"'That's vague. Tell me more. Did he owe you money?'

"'No, sir, it was t'other way on.'

"'Wages in arrear?'

"'No, it was money he had advanced

"HE KEPT ON ASSURING ME THAT HE DIDN'T COMMIT THE MURDER."

me for the working of my business. You see Walker had always been a hard man, and he'd saved. He said he wanted his money back, he knowing that I was pinched a bit just then and couldn't pay. Then he tried to thrust himself into partnership with me in the business, which was a thing I didn't want. I'd good contracts on hand which I expected would bring me in a matter of nine thousand pounds, and I didn't want to share it with any man, least of all him. I told him so, and that's how the trouble began. But it was him that hit me first.'

"'Still, you returned the blow?'

"Guide passed a hand wearily over his forehead. 'I may have struck him back, sir—I was dazed, and I don't rightly remember. But before God I'll swear that I never lifted that pick to Andrew Walker—it was his pick.'

"'But,' I persisted, 'Walker couldn't very conveniently have murdered himself.'

"'No, sir, no—no, he couldn't. I thought of that myself since I been in here, and I said to Mr. Barnes that perhaps somebody come into the carriage when I was knocked silly, and killed him; but

Mr. Barnes he said that was absurd. Besides, who could have done it?'

"'Don't you know anybody, then, who would have wished for Walker's death?'

"'There was them that didn't like him,' said Guide, drearily.

"That was all I could get out of him, and I went away from the prison feeling very dissatisfied. I was stronger than ever in the belief that Guide was in no degree guilty, and yet for the life of me I did not see how to prove his innocence. He had not been a man of any strong character to begin with, and the shock of what he had gone through had utterly dazed him. It was hopeless to expect any reasonable explanation from him; he had resigned himself to puzzlement. If he had gone melancholy mad before he came up to trial, I should not have been one whit surprised.

"I brooded over the matter for a couple of days, putting all the rest of my practice out of thought, but I didn't get any forwarder with it. I hate to give anything up as a bad job, and in this case I felt that there was on my shoulders a huge load of responsibility. Guide, I had thoroughly persuaded myself, had not murdered Andrew Walker; as sure as the case went into court, on its present grounding, the man would be hanged out of hand; and I persuaded myself that then I, and I alone, should be responsible for an innocent man's death.

"At the end of those two days only one course seemed open to me. It was foreign to the brief I held, but the only method left to bring in my client's innocence.

"I must find out who did really murder the man. I must try to implicate some third actor in the tragedy.

"To begin with, there was the railway carriage; but a little thought showed me that nothing was to be done there. The compartment would have been inspected by the police, and then swept and cleaned and garnished, and coupled on to its train once more, and used by unconscious passengers for weeks since the uproar occurred in it.

"All that I had got to go upon were the notes and relics held at Scotland Yard.

"The police authorities were very good. Of course, they were keen enough to bring off the prosecution with professional *éclat;* but they were not exactly anxious to hand over a poor wretch to the hangman if he was not thoroughly deserving of a dance on nothing. They placed at my disposal every scrap of their evidence, and said that they thought the reading of it all was plain beyond dispute. I thought so, too, at first. They sent an inspector to my chambers as their envoy.

"On one point, though, after a lot of thought, I did not quite agree with them. I held a grisly relic in my hand, gazing at it fixedly. It was a portion of Walker's skull—a disc of dry bone with a splintered aperture in the middle.

"'And so you think the pickaxe made that hole,' I said to the inspector.

"'I don't think there can be any doubt about it, Mr Grayson. Nothing else could have done it, and the point of the pick was smeared with blood.'

"'But would there be room to swing such a weapon in a third-class Metropolitan railway carriage?'

"'We thought of that, and at first it seemed a poser. The roof is low, and both Guide and Walker are tall men; but if Guide had gripped the shaft by the end, so, with his right hand pretty near against the head, so, he'd have had heaps of room to drive it with a sideways swing. I tried the thing for myself; it acted perfectly. Here's the pickaxe: you can see for yourself.'

"I did see, and I wasn't satisfied; but I didn't tell the inspector what I thought. It was clearer to me than ever that Guide had not committed the murder. What I asked the inspector was this: 'Had either of the men got any luggage in the carriage?'

"The inspector answered, with a laugh, 'Not quite, Mr. Grayson, or you would see it here.'

"Then I took on paper a rough outline

of that fragment of bone, and an accurate sketch of exact size of the gash in it, and the inspector went away. One thing his visit had shown me. Andrew Walker was not slain by a blow from behind by the pickaxe.

"I met Barnes whilst I was nibbling lunch, and told him this. He heard me doubtfully. 'You may be right,' said he, 'but I'm bothered if I see what you have to go upon.'

"'You know what a pickaxe is like?' I said.

"'Certainly.'

"'A cross-section of one of the blades would be what?'

"'Square—or perhaps oblong.'

"'Quite so. Rectangular. What I want to get at is this: it wouldn't even be diamond shape, with the angles obtuse and acute alternately.'

"'Certainly not. The angles would be clean right-angles.'

"'Very good. Now look at this sketch of the hole in the skull, and tell me what you see.'

"Barnes put on his glasses, and gazed attentively for a minute or so, and then looked up. 'The pick point has crashed through without leaving any marks of its edges whatever.'

"'That is to say, there are none of your right-angles showing.'

"'None. But that does not go to prove anything.'

"'YOU THINK THE PICKAXE MADE THAT HOLE,' I SAID TO THE INSPECTOR."

"'No. It's only about a tenth of my proof. It gives the vague initial idea. It made me look more carefully, and I saw this'—I pointed with my pencil to a corner of the sketch.

"Barnes whistled. 'A clean arc of a circle,' said he, 'cut in the bone as though a knife had done it. You saw that pickaxe. Was it much worn? Were the angles much rounded near the point?'

"'They were not. On the contrary, the pick, though an old one, had just been through the blacksmith's shop to be re-sharpened, and had not been used since. There was not a trace of wear upon it: of that I am certain.'

"Barnes whistled again in much perplexity. At length said he, 'It's an absolutely certain thing that Walker was not killed in the way they imagine. But I don't think this will get Guide off scot-free. There's too much other circumstantial evidence against him. Of course you'll do your best, but——'

"'It would be more than a toss up if I could avoid a conviction. Quite so. We must find out more. The question is, how was this wound made? Was there a third man in it?'

"'Guide may have jobbed him from behind with some other instrument, and afterwards thrown it out of window.'

"'Yes,' said I, 'but that is going on the assumption that Guide did the trick, which I don't for a moment think is the case. Besides, if he did

"LOOK AT THIS SKETCH OF THE HOLE IN THE SKULL."

throw anything out of window, it would most assuredly have been found. They keep the permanent way very thoroughly inspected upon the Metropolitan. No, Barnes. There is some other agent in this case, animate or inanimate, which so far we have overlooked completely; and an innocent man's life depends upon our ravelling it out.'

"Barnes lifted his shoulders helplessly, and took another sandwich. 'I don't see what we can do.'

"'Nor I, very clearly. But we must start from the commencement, and go over the ground inch by inch.'

"So wrapped up was I in the case by this time, that I could not fix my mind to anything else. Then and there I went out and set about my inquiries.

"With some trouble I found the compartment in which the tragedy had taken place, but learnt nothing new from it. The station and the railway people at Addison Road, Kensington, were similarly drawn blank. The ticket inspector at Shaftesbury Road, who distinctly remembered Guide's passage, at first seemed inclined to tell me nothing new, till I dragged it out of him by a regular emetic of questioning.

"Then he did remember that Guide had been carrying in his hand a carpenter's straw bass, as he passed through the wicket. He did not recollect whether he had mentioned this to the police: didn't see that it mattered.

"I thought differently, and with a new vague hope in my heart, posted back to the prison. I had heard no word of this

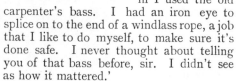

hand-baggage from Guide. It remained to be seen what he had done with it.

"They remembered me from my previous visit, and let me in to the prisoner without much demur. Guide owned up to the basket at once. 'Yes,' he said, 'I had some few odd tools to carry from home, and as I couldn't find anything else handy to put them in I used the old carpenter's bass. I had an iron eye to splice on to the end of a windlass rope, a job that I like to do myself, to make sure it's done safe. I never thought about telling you of that bass before, sir. I didn't see as how it mattered.'

"'Where is the bass now?'

"'In the Left Luggage Office at Shaftesbury Road Station. Name of Hopkins. I've lost the ticket.'

"'Where did you put your basket on entering the carriage at Addison Road?'

"'On the seat, sir, in the corner by the window.'

"And with that I left him.

"'Now,' thought I, 'I believe I can find out whether you murdered Walker or not,' and drove back to Hammersmith.

"I inquired at the cloak-room. Yes,

"A DISCOLORATION WHICH I KNEW TO BE DRIED HUMAN BLOOD."

the carpenter's bass was there, beneath a dusty heap of other unclaimed luggage. There was demurrage to pay on it, which I offered promptly to hand over, but as I could produce no counterfoil bearing the name of Hopkins, the clerk, with a smile, said that he could not let me have it. However, when he heard what I wanted, he made no objection to my having an overhaul.

"The two lugs of the bass were threaded together with a hammer. I took this away, and opened the sides. Within was a ball of marline, another of spun-yarn, a grease-pot, and several large iron eyes. Also a large marline-spike. It was this last that fixed my attention. It was brand new, with a bone handle and a bright brass ferrule. Most of the iron also was bright, but three inches of the point were stained with a faint dark brown. From a casual inspection I should have put this down to the marline-spike having been last used to make a splice on tarred rope; but now my suspicions made me think of something else.

"I raised the stained point to my nose. There was no smell of tar whatever. On the bright part there was the indefinable odour of iron; at the tip, that thin coat of dark brown varnish had blotted this scent completely away.

"I think my fingers trembled when I turned to the bass again.

"Yes, there, opposite to where the point

of the marline-spike had been lying—it was tilted up over the ball of spun-yarn—was a closed-up gash in the side of the bass. The spike had passed through there, and then been withdrawn. Round the gash was a dim discoloration which I knew to be dried human blood.

"In my mind's eye I saw the whole ghastly accident clearly enough now. The two men had been standing up, struggling. Guide had gone down under a blow, knocked senseless, and Walker had stumbled over him. Pitching forward, face downwards, on to the seat before he could recover, his head had dashed violently against the carpenter's bass. The sharp marline-spike inside, with its heel resting against the solid wall of the carriage, had entered the top of his skull like a bayonet. No human hand had been raised against him, and yet he had been killed.

"I kept my own particular ramblings in this case remarkably quiet, and in court led up to my facts through ordinary cross-examination.

"At the proper psychological moment I called attention to the shape of the puncture in Walker's skull, and then dramatically sprang the bass and the marline-spike upon them unawares. After that, as the papers put it, 'there was applause in court, which was instantly suppressed.'"

"Oh, the conceit of the man," said O'Malley, laughing.

Grayson laughed too. "Well," he said, "I was younger then, and I suppose I was a trifle conceited. The Crown didn't throw up. But the jury chucked us a 'Not guilty' without leaving the box, and then leading counsel for the other side came across and congratulated me on having saved Guide from the gallows. 'Now I'd have bet anything on hanging that man,' said he."

"I'D HAVE BET ANYTHING ON HANGING THAT MAN."

XVI

The Count's Chauffeur

WILLIAM LE QUEUX

THE COUNT'S CHAUFFEUR.

A SERIES OF COMPLETE STORIES BY WILLIAM LE QUEUX.

No. I.—A MOVE ON THE " FORTY."

IN Paris, in Rome, in Florence, in Berlin, in Vienna—in fact, over half the face of Europe, from the Pyrenees to the Russian frontier—I am now known as " The Count's Chauffeur."

An Englishman, as my name, George Ewart, denotes, I am of cosmopolitan birth and education, my early youth being spent on the Continent, where my father was agent for a London firm. When I was fourteen, my father, having prospered, came to London, and established himself as an agent in Wood Street, City, representing a great firm of silk manufacturers in Lyons. At twenty I tried City life, but an office with a high stool, a dusty ledger, and sandwich lunches, had no attraction for me. I had always had a turn for mechanics, but was never allowed to adopt engineering as a profession, my father's one idea being that I should follow in his footsteps—a delusive hope entertained by many a fond parent.

Six months of office life sufficed me. One day I went home to Teddington and refused to return again to Wood Street. This resulted in an open quarrel between my father and myself, with the result that a week later I was on my way to Canada. In a year I was back again, and, after some months of semi-starvation in London, I managed to obtain a job in a motor factory. I was then entirely in my element. During two years I learned the mechanism of the various petrol-driven cars, until I became classed as an expert driver and engineer.

Where I was employed there was manufactured one of the best and most expensive makes of English car, and, being at length placed on the testing staff, it was my duty to take out each new chassis for its trial-run before being delivered to a customer.

Upon my certificate each chassis was declared in perfect running order, and was then handed over to the body-makers indicated by the purchaser.

Being an expert driver, my firm sent me to drive in the Tourist Trophy races in the Isle of Man, and I likewise did the Ardennes Circuit and came in fourth in the Brescia race for the Florio Cup, my successes, of course, adding glory and advertisement to the car I drove.

Racing, however, aroused within me, as it does in every motorist, an ardent desire to travel long distances. The testing of those chassis in Regent's Park, and an occasional run with some wealthy customer out on the Great North road or on the Bath or Brighton roads, became too quiet a life for me. I was now seized by a desire to tour and see Europe. True, in my capacity of tester, I met all classes of men. In the seat beside me have sat Cabinet Ministers, Dukes, Indian Rajahs, Members of Parliament, and merchant princes, customers or prospective purchasers, all of whom chatted with me, mostly displaying their ignorance of the first principles of mechanics. It was all pleasant enough—a merry life and good pay. Yet I hated London, and the height of my ambition was a good car to drive abroad.

After some months of waiting, the opportunity came, and I seized it.

By appointment, at the Automobile Club one grey December morning, I met Count Bindo di Ferraris, a young Italian aristocrat, whose aspect, however, was the reverse of a Southerner. About thirty, he was tall, lithe, and well dressed in a dark brown lounge suit. His complexion, his chestnut hair, his erect, rather soldierly bearing, his clean-shaven face, and his open countenance gave him every appearance of an English gentleman. Indeed, I took him at first for an Englishman, for he spoke English perfectly.

When he had examined my testimonials and made a number of inquiries, he asked :

" You speak French ? "

" Yes," was my reply ; " a little Italian, and a little German."

327

"Italian ! " he exclaimed in surprise. "Excellent ! "

Then while we sat alone, with no one within hearing, he told me the terms upon which he was willing to engage me to drive on the Continent, and added :

"Your salary will be doubled—providing I find you entirely loyal to me. That is to say, you must know how to keep your mouth closed—understand ? "

And he regarded me rather curiously, I thought.

"No," I answered ; "I don't quite understand."

"Well, well, there are matters—private family matters — of which you will probably become cognisant. Truth to tell, I want help—the help of a good careful driver who isn't afraid, and who is always discreet. I may as well tell you that before I wrote to you I made certain secret inquiries regarding you, and I feel confident that you can serve me very much to our mutual advantage."

This puzzled me, and my curiosity was further aroused when he added :

"To be plain, there is a certain young lady in very high society in the case. I need not tell you more, need I ? You will be discreet, eh ? "

I smiled and promised. What did it all mean ? I wondered. My employer was mysterious ; but in due course I should, as he prophesied, obtain knowledge of this secret — a secret love affair, no doubt.

The Count's private affairs did not, after all, concern me. My duty was to drive on the Continent, and for what he was to pay me I was to serve him loyally, and see that his tyre and petrol bills were not too exorbitant.

He went to the writing-table and wrote out a short agreement which he copied, and we both signed it—a rather curiously worded agreement by which I was to serve him for three years, and during that

"I SCRIBBLED MY NAME."

time our interests were " to be mutual." That last phrase caused me to wonder, but I scribbled my name and refrained from comment, for the payment was already double that which I was receiving from the firm.

"My car is outside," he remarked, as he folded his copy of the agreement and placed it in his pocket. " Did you notice it ? "

I had not, so we went out into Piccadilly together, and there, standing at the kerb, I saw a car that caused my heart to bound with delight—a magnificent six-cylinder forty horse-power " Napier," of the very latest model. The car was upon the market. I lifted the long bonnet, looked around the engine, and saw those six cylinders in a row—the latest invention of a celebrated inventor.

"Splendid!" I ejaculated. "There's nothing yet to beat this car. By Jove! we can get a move on a good road!"

"Yes," smiled the Count. "My man Mario could make her travel, but he's a fool and has left me in a fit of temper. He was an Italian, and we Italians are,

"I SAW THAT HE EXCHANGED A MEANING GLANCE WITH SIR CHARLES."

open, with side entrance, a dark green body with coronet and cipher on the panels, upholstered in red, with glass removable screen to the splash-board—a splendid, workmanlike car just suitable for long tours and fast runs. Of all the cars and of all the makes, that was the only one which it was my ambition to drive.

I walked around it in admiration, and saw that every accessory was the best and very latest that money could buy—even to the newly invented gas-generator which had only a few weeks ago been placed

alas! hot-headed," and he laughed again. " Would you like to try her ? "

I assented with delight, and, while he returned inside the Club to get his fur coat, I started the engine and got in at the steering-wheel. A few moments later he seated himself beside me, and we glided down Piccadilly on our way to Regent's Park—the ground where, day after day, it had been my habit to go testing. The car ran perfectly, the engines sounding a splendid rhythm through the Regent Street traffic into broad Portland Place, and on into the Park, where I was afforded some scope to see what she could do. The Count declared that he was in no hurry, therefore we went up through Hampstead to Highgate Station, and then on the Great North Road, through East End, Whetstone, Barnet, and Hatfield, to Hitchin —thirty-five miles of road which was as well known to me as the Strand.

The morning was dry and cold, the roads in excellent condition bar a few patches of new metal between Codicote and Chapelfoot, and the sharp east wind compelled us to goggle. Fortunately, I had on my leather-lined frieze coat, and was therefore fully equipped. The North Road between London and Hitchin is really of little use for trying the speed of a car, for there are so many corners, it is mostly narrow, and it abounds in police-traps. That twenty miles of flat, straight road, with perfect surface, from Lincoln to New Holland, opposite Hull, is one of the best places in England to see what a car is worth.

Nevertheless, the run to Hitchin satisfied me perfectly that the car was not a "roundabout," as so many are, but a car well "within the meaning of the Act."

"And, what is your opinion of her, Ewart?" asked the Count, as we sat down to cold beef and pickles in the long, old-fashioned upstairs room of the Sun Inn at Hitchin.

"Couldn't be better," I declared. "The brake would do with re-lining, but that's about all. When do we start for the Continent?"

"The day after to-morrow. I'm staying just now at the Cecil. We'll run the car down to Folkestone, ship her across, and then go by Paris and Aix to Monte Carlo first; afterwards we'll decide upon our itinerary. Ever been to Monty?"

I replied in the negative. The prospect of going on the Riviera sounded delightful.

After our late luncheon we ran back from Hitchin to London, but, not arriving before lighting-up time, we had to turn on the head-lights beyond Barnet. We drove straight to the fine garage on the Embankment beneath the Cecil, and after I had put things square and received orders for ten o'clock next day, I was preparing to go to my lodgings in Bloomsbury to look through my kit in preparation for the journey, when my employer suddenly exclaimed:

"Come up to the smoking-room a moment. I want to write a letter for you to take to Boodle's in St. James's Street, for me, if you will."

I followed him upstairs to the great tiled smoking-room overlooking the Embankment, and as we entered, two well-dressed men—Englishmen, of aristocratic bearing—rose from a table and shook him warmly by the hand.

I noticed their quick, apprehensive look as they glanced at me as though in inquiry, but my employer exclaimed:

"This is my new chauffeur, Ewart, an expert. Ewart, these are my friends— Sir Charles Blythe," indicating the elder man, "and Mr. Henderson. These gentlemen will perhaps be with us sometimes, so you had better know them."

The pair looked me up and down and smiled pleasantly. Sir Charles was narrow-faced, about fifty, with a dark beard turning grey; his companion was under thirty, a fair-haired, rather foppishly-dressed young fellow, in a fashionable suit and a light fancy vest.

Then, as the Count went to the table to write, Sir Charles inquired where we had been, and whether I had driven much on the Continent.

When the Count handed me the letter, I saw that he exchanged a meaning glance with Sir Charles, but what it was intended to convey I could not guess. I only know that, for a few seconds, I felt some vague distrust of my new friends, and yet they treated me more as an equal than as a mere chauffeur.

The Count's friends were certainly a merry, easy-going pair, yet somehow I instinctively held them in suspicion. Whether it was on account of the covert glance which Sir Charles shot across at my employer, or whether there was something unusual about their manner, I cannot tell. I am only aware that when I left the hotel I went on my way in wonder.

Next day, at ten punctually, I ran the car from the Strand into the courtyard of the hotel and pulled up at the restaurant entrance, so as to be out of the way of the continuous cab traffic. The Count, however, did not make his appearance until nearly half an hour later, and when he did arrive he superintended the dispatch by cab of a quantity of luggage which he told me he was sending forward by *grande vitesse* to Monte Carlo.

After the four-wheeler had moved off, the hall-porter helped him on with his big fur coat, and he, getting up beside me, told me to drive to Piccadilly.

As we were crossing Trafalgar Square into Pall Mall, he turned to me, saying :

" Remember, Ewart, your promise yesterday. If my actions—I mean, if you think I am a little peculiar sometimes, don't trouble your head about it. You are paid to drive—and paid well, I think. My affairs don't concern you, do they ? "

" Not in the least," I answered, nevertheless puzzled.

He descended at a tobacconist's in Bond Street, and bought a couple of boxes of cigars, and then made several calls at shops, also visiting two jewellers to obtain, he remarked, a silver photograph frame of a certain size.

At Gilling's—the third shop he tried—he remained inside some little time—quite twenty minutes, I should think. As you know, it is in the narrowest part of Bond Street, and the traffic was congested owing to the road at the Piccadilly end being partially up.

As I sat in my place staring idly before me, and reflecting that I should be so soon travelling due south over the broad, well-kept French roads, and out of the gloom and dreariness of the English winter, I suddenly became conscious of a familiar face in the crowd of hurrying foot-passengers.

I glanced up quickly as a man bustled past. Was I mistaken ? I probably had been, but the thin, keen, bearded countenance was very much like that of Sir Charles Blythe. But no. When I looked back after him I saw that his figure was much more bent and his appearance was not half so smart and well-groomed as the Count's friend.

At one moment I felt absolutely positive that the man had really been watching me, and was now endeavouring to escape recognition, yet at the next I saw the absurdity of such a thought. Sir Charles's face had, I suppose, been impressed upon my memory on the previous evening, and the passer-by merely bore some slight resemblance.

And so I dismissed it from my mind.

A few moments later a man in a frock-coat, probably the jeweller's manager, opened the door, looked up and down the street for a few moments, shot an inquisitive glance at me, and then disappeared within.

I found that the clock on the splash-board required winding, and was in the act of doing this when my eyes fell upon a second person who was equally a mystery. This time I felt convinced that I was not mistaken. The fair-moustached young man Henderson went by, but without recognising me.

Did either of the pair recognise the car ? If so, what object had they in not acknowledging me ?

My suspicions were again aroused. I did not like either of the two men. Were they following my master with some evil intent ? In London, and especially in certain cosmopolitan circles, one cannot be too cautious regarding one's acquaintances. They had been slightly too over-dressed and too familiar with the Count to suit me, and I had resolved that if I had ever to drive either of them I would land them in some out-of-the-world hole with a pretended break-down. The non-motorist is always at the mercy of the chauffeur, and the so-called " break-downs " are frequently due to the vengeance of the driver, who gets his throttle stuck, or some trouble which sounds equally serious, but which is remedied in one, two, three, or four hours, according to how long the chauffeur decides to detain his victim by the roadside.

I wondered, as I sat ruminating, whether these two men were really " crooks ; " and so deep-rooted were my suspicions that I decided, when the Count returned, to drop him a hint that we were being watched.

I am not nervous by any means, and, moreover, I always carry for my own protection a handy little revolver. Yet I admit that at that moment I felt a decidedly uncomfortable feeling creeping over me.

A Move on the "Forty."

"'WE WANT TO ASK YOU A QUESTION OR TWO'"

mind the police ; if they say anything, tell them I'll be back in ten minutes."

The lad, eager to earn a trifle, at once consented, and descending, I entered the shop, the door of which was being still held open for me, while the Count hailed a hansom and drove away.

The shop is one of the finest in Bond Street, as you know. At that moment there were, however, no other customers. The manager politely invited me to be seated, saying :

"His lordship will only be a short time," and then, standing with his hands behind his back, he commenced to chat with me.

"That's a very fine car of yours," he said. "You ought to be able to travel pretty fast, eh ?"

"Well, we do, as a matter of fact," I replied.

Then he went to the door, and looking over the panes of frosted glass, asked what horse-power it was, and a number of other questions with which non-motorists always plague the chauffeur.

Then, returning to me, he remarked what a very nice gentleman his lordship was, adding that he had been a customer on several occasions.

"Have you been long in his service ?" he inquired.

Those men meant mischief. I had detected it in their eyes on the previous night. By some kind of mysterious intuition I became aware that we were in peril.

Almost at the moment the shop-door was opened by the manager, and the Count, emerging, crossed to me and said :

"Go into the shop, Ewart, and wait there till I return. I'm just going round to get some money," and seeing a boy passing, he called him, saying, "Just mind this car for ten minutes, my boy, and I'll give you half-a-crown. Never

"Oh, yes," I replied, determined not to be thought a new hand. "Quite a long time. As you say, he is a very charming man."

"He's very wealthy, according to report. I read something about him in the papers the other day—a gift of some thousands to the Hospital Fund."

·This rather surprised me. I never remembered having seen the name of Count Bindo di Ferraris in the papers.

Presently I got up, and wandering about the shop, inspected some of the beautiful jewels in the fine show-cases, many of them ornaments of enormous value. The manager, a pleasant, elderly man, took me round and showed me some of the most beautiful jewellery I had ever seen. Then, excusing himself, he retired to the office beyond the shop, and left me to chat with one of the assistants.

I looked at the clock, and saw that nearly half an hour had elapsed since the Count had left. A constable had looked in and inquired about the car, but I had assured him that in a few minutes we should be off, and begged, as a favour, that it might be allowed to remain until my master's return.

Another quarter of an hour elapsed, when the door opened, and there entered two respectably-dressed men in dark overcoats, one wearing a soft brown felt hat and the other a "bowler."

They asked to see the manager, and the assistant who had been chatting to me conducted them through the shop to the office beyond. Both men were of middle age and well set up, and as they entered, I saw that a third man, much younger, was with them. He, however, did not come in, but stood in the doorway, idly glancing up and down Bond Street.

Within the office I distinctly heard the manager utter an exclamation of surprise, and then one of the men, in a deep, low voice, seemed to enter into a long explanation.

Then the elder of the two strangers walked along the shop to the door, and going outside, spoke some words to the man who had accompanied them. On re-entering, he passed me, giving me a sharp glance, and then disappeared again into the office, where, for five minutes or so, he remained closeted with the manager.

Presently the last-named came out, and as he approached me I noticed an entire change in his manner. He was pale, almost to the lips.

"Will you step into my office for one moment?" he asked. "There's—well, a little matter upon which I want to speak to you."

This surprised me. What could he mean?

Nevertheless, I consented, and in a few moments found myself in a large, well-lit office with the manager and the two strangers.

The man in the brown felt hat was the first to speak.

"We want to ask you a question or two?" he said. "Do you recognise this?" and he produced a small square photograph of a man upon whose coat was a white ticket bearing a bold number. I started when my eyes fell upon it.

"My master!" I ejaculated.

The portrait was a police photograph! The men were detectives!

The inspector, for such he was, turned to the jeweller's manager, and regarded him with a significant look.

"It's a good job we've arrested him with the stuff on him," he remarked, "otherwise you'd never have seen the colour of it again. He's worked the same dodge in Rome and Berlin, and both times got clear away. I suppose he became a small customer, in order to inspire confidence—eh?"

"Well, he came in this morning, saying that he wished to give his wife a tiara for the anniversary of her wedding, and asked that he might have two on approval, as he was undecided which to choose, and wished her to pick for herself. He left his car and chauffeur here till his return, and took away two worth five thousand pounds each. I, of course, had not the slightest suspicion. Lord Ixwell — the name by which we know him—is reputed everywhere to be one of the richest peers in the kingdom."

"Yes. But, you see, Detective-Sergeant Rodwell here chanced to see him come out of the shop, and, recognising him as the jewel-thief we've wanted for months past, followed his cab down to Charing Cross Station, and there arrested him and brought him to Bow Street."

I stood utterly dumbfounded at this sudden ending of what I believed would be an ideal engagement.

"What's your name?" inquired the inspector.

"George Ewart," was my answer. "I only entered the Count's service yesterday."

"And yet you told me you had been his chauffeur for a long time!" exclaimed the jeweller's manager.

"Well," said the elder of the detectives, "we shall arrest you, at any rate. You must come round to Bow Street, and I warn you that any statement you may make will be taken down and used as evidence against you."

"Arrest me!" I cried. "Why, I haven't done anything! I'm perfectly innocent. I had no idea that——"

"Well, you have more than an idea now, haven't you?" laughed the detective. "But come along; we have no time to lose," and he asked the manager to order a four-wheeled cab.

I remonstrated in indignation, but to no avail.

"What about the car?" I asked anxiously as we went outside together and stepped into the cab, the third police-officer, who had been on guard outside, holding open the door, while the constable who had been worrying me about the car stood looking on.

"Diplock, you can drive a motor-car," exclaimed the inspector, turning to the detective at the cab door. "Just bring that round to Bow Street as quick as you can."

The constable took in the situation at a glance. He saw that I had been arrested, and asked the detectives if they needed any assistance. But the reply was negative, and with the inspector at my side and the sergeant opposite, we moved off towards Piccadilly, the jeweller's manager having been requested to

"I STARTED AWAY TOWARDS LORDSHIP LANE"

attend at Bow Street Police Station in an hour, in order to identify the stolen property. By that time the charge would be made out, and we should, the inspector said, be up before the magistrate for a remand before the Court rose.

As we drove along Piccadilly, my heart fell within me. All my dreams of those splendid, well-kept roads in the sunny south, of touring to all the gayest places on the Continent, and seeing all that was to be seen, had been shattered at a single blow. And what a blow!

I had awakened to find myself under arrest as the accomplice of one of the most expert jewel thieves in Europe!

My companions were not communicative. Why should they have been?

Suddenly I became aware of the fact that we had driven a considerable distance. In my agitated state of mind I had taken no notice of our route, and my captors had, it seemed, endeavoured to take my attention off the direction we had taken.

Collecting my scattered senses, however, I recollected that we had crossed one of the bridges over the Thames, and looking out of the window, I found that we were in a long, open road of private houses, each with a short strip of railed-off garden in front—a South London thoroughfare evidently.

"This isn't the way to Bow Street!" I exclaimed in wonder.

"Well, not exactly the straight way," grinned the inspector. "A roundabout route, let's call it."

I was puzzled. The more so when I recognised a few minutes later that we had come down the Camberwell New Road, and were passing Camberwell Green.

We continued up Denmark Hill until, at the corner where Champion Hill branches off, the inspector called to the cabman to stop, and we all descended, the detective-sergeant paying the fare.

Where were they taking me? I wondered. I asked, but they only laughed, and would vouchsafe no reply.

Together we walked up the quiet, semi-rural Champion Hill, until we reached Green Lane, when at the sharp right angle of the road, as we turned, I saw before me an object which caused me to hold my breath in utter amazement.

The car was standing there, right before me in the lonely suburban road, and in it, seated at the wheel, a man whom I next second recognised as the Count himself! He was evidently awaiting me.

He was wearing a different motor-coat, the car bore a different number, and as I approached I noticed that the coronet and cipher had been obliterated by a dab of green paint!

"Come on, Ewart!" cried the Count, jumping down to allow me to take his place at the steering.

I turned to my captors in wonder.

"Yes, away you go, Ewart," the inspector said, "and good luck to you!"

Without another second's delay, I sprang upon the car, and while the Count, as he jumped up at my side, shouted good-bye to my captors, I started away towards Lordship Lane and the open country of Surrey.

"Where shall we go?" I inquired breathlessly, utterly amazed at our extraordinary escape.

"Straight on through Sydenham, and then I'll tell you. The sooner we're out of this, the better. We'll run along to Winchester, where I have a little house at Kingsworthy, just outside the city, and where we can lie low comfortably for a bit."

"But shan't we be followed by those men?" I asked apprehensively.

"Followed—by them? Oh, dear no!" he laughed. "Of course, you don't understand, Ewart. They all three belong to us. We've played a smartish game upon the jeweller, haven't we? They had to frighten you, of course, because it added a real good touch of truth to the scheme. We ought to be able to slip away across the Channel in a week's time, at latest. They'll leave to-night—in search of me!" and he laughed lightly to himself.

"Then they were not detectives?" I exclaimed, utterly staggered by the marvellous ingenuity of the robbery.

"No more than you are, Ewart," was his reply. "But don't bother your head about them now. All you've got to look after is your driving. Let's get across to Winchester as quickly as possible. Just here!—sharp to the right and the first to the left takes us into the Guildford road. Then we can move."

THE COUNT'S CHAUFFEUR.

A SERIES OF COMPLETE STORIES BY WILLIAM LE QUEUX.

No. 2.—A SENTIMENTAL SWINDLE.

COUNT BINDO'S retreat near Winchester proved to be a small, rather isolated house near Kingsworthy. It stood in its own grounds, surrounded by a high wall, and at the rear was a very fair garage, that had been specially constructed, with inspection-pit and the various appliances.

The house was rather well furnished, but the only servant was a man, who turned out to be none other than the yellow-haired young fellow who had been introduced to me at the Cecil as "Mr. Henderson."

He no longer wore the light fancy vest and smartly-cut clothes, but was in a somewhat shabby suit of black. He smiled grimly as I recognised him, while his master said:

"Got back all right, Henderson—eh?"

"I arrived only ten minutes ago, sir. All was quiet, wasn't it?"

"Absolutely," replied the Count, who then went upstairs, and I saw him no more that evening.

For nearly a fortnight the car remained in the garage. It now bore a different identification-plate, and to kill time I idled about, wondering when we should start again. It was a strange *ménage*. Count Bindo was a very easy-going cosmopolitan, who treated both Henderson and myself as intimates, inasmuch as we ate at table with him, and smoked together each evening.

We were simply waiting. The papers were, of course, full of the clever theft from Gilling's, and the police, it appeared, were doing their utmost to track the tricksters—but in vain. The Count, under the name of Mr. Claude Fielding, seemed to be very popular in the neighbourhood, though he discouraged visitors. Indeed, no one came there. He dined, however, at several houses during the second week of his concealment, and seemed to be quite confident of his safety.

At last we left, but not, however, before

Sir Charles Blythe had stayed one night with us and made some confidential report to his friend. It being apparent that all was clear, some further alteration was made both in the appearance of the car and in the personal aspect of Count Bindo and myself, after which we started for the Continent by way of Southampton.

We crossed and ran up to Paris, where we stayed at the Ritz. The Count proved a devil-may-care fellow with plenty of friends in the French capital. When with the latter he treated me as a servant; when alone as a friend.

Whatever the result of the clever piece of trickery in Bond Street, it was quite clear that my employer was in funds, for he spent freely, dined and supped at the expensive restaurants, and thoroughly enjoyed himself with his chums.

We left Paris and went on the broad good road to Lyons and to Monte Carlo. It was just before Christmas, and the season had, of course, not yet commenced. We stayed at the Hotel de Paris—the hotel where most men *en garçon* put up— and the car I put into the Garage Meunier.

It was the first time I had seen "Monty," and it attracted me as it does every man and woman. Here, too, Bindo di Ferraris seemed to have hosts of friends. He dined at the Grand, the Métropole, or the Riviera Palace, and supped each night at Ciro's, indulging in a little mild play in the Rooms in the interval between the two meals.

He did not often go out in the car, but frequently went to Nice and Cannes by train. About a fortnight after our arrival, however, we ran, one bright morning, along the lower road by Beaulieu to Nice—bad, by the way, on account of the sharp corners and electric trams—and called at a small hotel in the Boulevard Gambetta.

The Count apparently had an appointment with a tall, dark-haired, extremely good-looking young French girl, with whom he lunched at a small restaurant, and afterwards he walked for an hour on the Promenade, talking with her very earnestly.

She was not more than nineteen—a smart, very *chic* little Parisienne, quietly dressed in black, but in clothes that bore unmistakably the *cachet* of a first-class dressmaker. They took a turn on the Jetée Promenade, and presently returned to the hotel, when the Count told her to go and get a close hat and thick coat, and he would wait for her.

Then, when she had gone, he told me that we were about to take her over to the Bristol at Beaulieu, that great white hotel that lies so sheltered in the most delightful bay of the whole Riviera.

It was a clear, bright December afternoon. The roads were perfect, though dusty as the Corniche always is, and very soon, with the Count and his lady friend, I swung into the curved drive before the hotel.

"You can go to the garage for an hour or so, Ewart," my employer said, after they had descended. Therefore I turned the car and went to the huge garage at the rear of the hotel—the garage which every motorist on the Riviera knows so well.

After an hour I re-entered the hotel to look for the Count and receive orders, when I saw, in the great red-carpeted lounge, my employer and the little Parisienne seated with the man whom I knew as Sir Charles Blythe, but who really was one of Count Bindo's confederates.

We exchanged glances, and his was a meaning one. That some deep and ingenious game was in progress I felt certain, but what it was I had no idea.

Blythe was smartly dressed in a grey flannel suit and white shoes—the costume *de rigueur* on the Riviera—and as he smoked his cigar, easily reclining in the wicker lounge-chair, he presented the complete picture of the English aristocrat " putting in " a month or two for sunshine.

Both men were talking earnestly in French with the dark-eyed little lady, who now and then laughed, or, raising her shoulders, looked from one to the other and protruded her chin in a gesture of uncertainty.

I retired and watched closely. It was quite plain in a few moments that the young lady was entirely devoted to the handsome Bindo. Both manner and glances betrayed it. I saw him look at Blythe, and knew that they were working in accord towards some pre-arranged end.

Presently a noisy party of American girls who had just returned from " Monty " entered and sat close to them, calling for tea. Therefore the trio rose and went out into the evening dusk. They wished, it seemed, to talk in private, and they did so until, half an hour later, I received orders to bring round the car, and drove them all three back to Nice, which we reached in plenty of time for dinner.

" Now, you will not forget, Gabrielle, you're sure ? " said Bindo in French as he handed her out of the car and shook her hand as he bared his head.

" I have promised, m'sieur," was her reply in a low, rather musical voice. " I shall not forget."

And then she bowed to Blythe, ascended the steps, and disappeared into the hotel.

Her quietness and neatness of dress were, to me, attractive. She was a dainty little thing, and yet her plain black dress, so well cut, was really very severe. She had the manner of a lady, sweet and demure. The air of the woman-of-the-world was, somehow, entirely absent.

Well, to confess it, I found myself admiring her very much. She was, I thought, delightful—one of the prettiest, sweetest girls I had ever seen.

Evidently our run to Beaulieu and back was her first experience of motoring, for she laughed with girlish delight when, on an open piece of road here and there, I put on a " move." And as she disappeared into the hotel she turned and waved her tiny black-gloved hand back at the handsome Bindo.

" Done, my dear chap ! " chuckled Blythe in a low voice to his companion as the neat figure disappeared behind the glass swing-doors. " The rest is easy— if we keep up pluck."

" It's a big thing, of course ; but I'm sanguine enough," declared my employer. " That little girl is a perfect brick. She's entirely unsuspicious. Flatter and court a woman, and if she falls in love with you she'll go any length to serve you ! "

"You're a splendid lover!" declared Sir Charles as he mounted into the car beside the Count, while the latter, laughing lightly, bent to me saying:

"Back to Monte Carlo, as quick as we can get."

I slipped along out of Nice, through

myself from a leather-coated chauffeur into a Monte Carlo lounger, and just before ten o'clock met the Count going across the flower-scented Place to the Rooms.

He was alone, and, recognising me, crossed and said:

"Ewart, let's walk up through the

"'NOW YOU WILL NOT FORGET, GABRIELLE?'"

Villefranche, round Beaulieu, slowing up for the corners, but travelling sharply on the open road, and we were soon back at the Paris.

Having put the car into the garage, I walked round to the hotel, transformed

gardens. I want to have a word with you."

I turned on my heel, and strolled with him.

"You know what we've done to-day—eh? You stand in, so you can just shut your eyes to anything that isn't exactly in order—understand ? There's a big thing before us—a very big thing—a thing that's simply dropped from the clouds. You want money, so do I. We all want money. Just keep a still tongue, and obey my orders, and you'll see that we'll bring off the biggest *coup* that the Riviera has yet known."

" I know how to be silent," I said, though I did not at all like the aspect of affairs.

" Yes, you do. I give you credit for that. One word of this and I go to durance vile. Silence, and the whole of us profit and get the wherewithal to live. I often think, Ewart, that the public, as they call it—the British public—are an extraordinary people. They are so confoundedly honest. But, nowadays, there surely isn't any honesty in life— at least, I've never found any. Why, your honest business man who goes to church or chapel each Sunday, and is a model of all the virtues, is, in the City, the very man who'll drive a hard bargain, pay a starvation wage, and button his pockets against the widow ! Who are your successful men in business ? Why, for the most part, the men who, by dint of sharp practice or unscrupulousness, have been able to get in front of their competitors. Therefore, after all, am I very much worse than the successful City man ? I live on my brains—and I'm happy to say I've lived very well—up to the present. But enough of this philosophy," laughed the easy-going young scoundrel. " I want to give you instructions. You stand in with us, Ewart. Your share of the Gilling affair is to your credit, and you'll have it before long. At present, we have another little matter in hand—one which requires extremely delicate handling, but will be successful providing Mademoiselle Gabrielle doesn't change her mind. But women are so often fickle, and the morning brings prudence far too frequently. You'll see some strange happenings to-morrow or the next day. Keep your eyes and ears closed ; that's all you have to do. You understand—eh ? "

" Perfectly," was my reply, for my curiosity was now thoroughly whetted.

There was a desperate project in the air,

and the spirit of adventure had now entered thoroughly into me.

Early next morning I drove the Count back to Nice where, at a quiet spot beyond the Magnan, he met the pretty Gabrielle clandestinely.

When we drew up to where she was apparently awaiting us, I saw that she was annoyed at my presence.

" Ewart, my chauffeur," he explained, introducing me, " will say nothing about this meeting. He knows how to be discreet."

I raised my peaked motor-cap, as our eyes met. I thought I detected a curiously timid glance in them, for in an instant she dropped her gaze.

That she was an intimate friend of the Count was shown by the instructions he gave her.

" You two walk along the Promenade des Anglais, and I'll meet you at the other end by the Hotel Suisse. I'll take the car myself on to the garage."

This meant that I was to walk with her a full three-quarters of an hour along the whole of the beautiful sea-front of Nice. Why, I wondered ?

" But, Bindo, can't you come ? "

" I'll meet you outside the Suisse. It's better to do that," was his answer. " Go along ; you'll find Ewart a clever fellow. He'll tell you how to drive a motor-car."

She laughed lightly, and then, as Bindo mounted into the car again and turned away, we strolled together on the broad asphalte back towards the town.

The morning was delightful, with bright sunshine and blue sea. The sweet-smelling wallflowers were already out, and the big palms waved lazily in the soft breeze.

I quickly found my companion most charming, and envied the Count his acquaintanceship. Was she marked down as a victim ? Or was she an accomplice ? I could not grasp the motive for being sent to walk the whole length of the promenade with her. But the Count and his companions were, they admitted, working a " big thing," and this was part of it, I supposed.

" This is the first time you have been in Nice, eh ? " she asked in her pretty broken English as she stopped a moment to open her sunshade.

Yes," I answered ; " but the Count is an old *habitué*, I believe ? "

" Oh, yes," she laughed ; " he knows everybody. Last year he was on the Fêtes Committee and one of the judges at the Battle of Flowers."

And so we gossiped on, walking leisurely, and passing many who, like ourselves, were idling in the winter sunshine.

There was an air of refined ingenuousness about her that was particularly attractive. She walked well, holding her skirt tightly about her as only a true Parisienne can, and displaying a pair of extremely neat ankles. She inquired about me—how long had I been in the Count's service, how I liked him, and such like ; while I, by careful questioning, discovered that her name was Gabrielle Deleuse, and that she came to the Côté d'Azur each season.

Just as we were opposite the white façade of the Hotel Westminster we encountered a short, rather stout, middle-aged lady, accompanied by a tall, thin, white-haired gentleman. They were well-dressed, the lady wearing splendid sables.

She started when she recognised them, instantly lowering her sunshade in order to hide her face. Whether the pair noticed her I cannot say. I only know that, as soon as ever they passed, she exclaimed, in annoyance :

" I can't think why Bindo sent you along here with me."

" I regret, mademoiselle, that my companionship should be distasteful to you," I replied, mystified.

" No, no, not that, m'sieur," she cried anxiously. " I do not mean that. You do not know—how can you know what I mean ? "

" You probably mean that you ought not to be seen walking here, on the Promenade des Anglais, with a common chauffeur."

" If you are a chauffeur, m'sieur, you are also a gentleman," she said, looking straight into my face.

" I thank mademoiselle for her high compliment," I said, bowing, for really I was in no way averse to a little mild flirtation with such a delightful companion. And yet what, I wondered, was my *rôle* in this latest piece of complicated trickery ?

She quickened her pace, glancing anxiously at everyone we met, as though wishing to arrive at the end of our walk.

I was sorry our little chat was drawing to a close. I would like to have had her at my side for a day's run on the car, and I told her so.

" Perhaps you will take me for a long trip one day—who knows ? " she laughed. " Yesterday it was perfect."

A few moments later we arrived before the Suisse, and from a seat on the Promenade Count Bindo rose to greet us. He had left his motor-coat and cap in the car, and stood before us in his grey flannels and white soft felt hat—a smart, handsome figure, such as women mostly admire. Indeed, Bindo was essentially a lady's man, for he seemed to have a bowing acquaintance with hundreds of the fair sex.

" Well, Gabrielle, and has Ewart been saying lots of pretty things to you—eh ? "

" How unkind of you ! " she protested, blushing slightly. " You really ought not to say such things."

" Well, well, forgive me, won't you ? " said the Count quickly, and together we strolled into the town, where we had an *aperatif* at the gay Café de l'Opera, opposite the public gardens.

Here, however, a curious *contretemps* occurred.

She accidentally upset her glass of " Dubonnet " over her left hand, saturating her white glove so that she was compelled to take it off.

" Why ! " ejaculated the Count in sudden amazement, pointing to her uncovered hand. " What does that mean ? "

She wore upon her finger a wedding ring !

Her face went crimson. For a moment the pretty girl was too confused to speak.

" Ah ! " she cried in a low, earnest tone, as she bent towards him. " Forgive me, Bindo. I—I did not tell you. How could I ? "

" You should have told me. It was your duty to tell me. Remember, we are old friends. How long have you been married ? "

" Only three weeks. This is my honeymoon."

" And your husband ? "

" Four days ago business took him to Genoa. He is still absent."

"And, in the meanwhile, you meet me, and are the merry little Gabrielle of the olden days—eh?" remarked Bindo, placing both elbows upon the marble-topped table and looking straight into her face.

bleau. Do you still remember them?" Her eyelids trembled.

I saw that, though married, she still regarded the handsome Bindo with a good deal of affection.

"I don't blame you," was his soft reply. "I suppose it is what anybody else would have done in the circumstances. Do I remember those days, you ask? Why, of course I do. Those picnics in the forest

"'WHY!' EJACULATED THE COUNT IN SUDDEN AMAZEMENT, POINTING TO HER UNCOVERED HAND. 'WHAT DOES THAT MEAN?'"

"Do you blame me, then?" she asked. "I admit that I deceived you, but it was imperative. Our encounter has brought back all the past—those summer days of two years ago when we met at Fontaine-

with you, your mother, and your sister Julie were delightful days—days never to return, alas! And so you are really married! Well, you must tell me all about it later. Let's lunch together at the London House." Then he added, reflectively, "Well, this really *is* a discovery—

my little Gabrielle actually married! I had no idea of it."

She laughed, blushing again.

" No; I don't suppose you had. I was very, very foolish to take off my glove, yet if I had kept up the deception any longer I might perhaps have compromised myself."

" Was it not—well, a little risky of you to go to Beaulieu with me yesterday?"

" Yes. I was foolish—very foolish, Bindo. I ought not to have met you to-day. I ought not to have told you the truth from the very first."

" Not at all. Even if your husband is away, there is surely no reason why you should not speak to an old friend like myself, is there?"

" Yes; I'm known in Nice, as you are well aware."

" Known as the prettiest woman who comes on the Riviera," he declared, taking her hand and examining the wedding-ring and the fine circle of diamonds above it. Bindo de Ferraris was an expert in gems.

" Don't be a flatterer," she protested, with a light laugh. " You've said that, you know, hundreds of times before."

" I've said only what's the truth, and I'm sure Ewart will bear me out."

" I do, most certainly. Madame is most charming," I asserted; and it was undoubtedly my honest opinion. I was, however, disappointed equally with the Count, to discover that my dainty divinity

in black was married. She was certainly not more than nineteen, and had none of the self-possessed air of the matron about her.

Twice during that conversation I had risen to go, but the Count bade me stay, saying with a laugh:

" There is nothing in this that you may not hear. Madame has deceived us both."

He treated the situation as a huge joke, yet I detected that the deception had annoyed him. Had the plans he had laid been upset by this unexpected discovery of the marriage? From his demeanour of suppressed chagrin I felt sure they had been.

Suddenly he glanced at his watch, and

" ON WE FLEW, AS FAST AS THE SHARP CORNERS WOULD ALLOW "

then taking from his pocket an envelope containing some small square hard object, about two inches long by one inch broad, he said :

"Go to the station and meet the 12.15 from Beaulieu to Cannes. You'll find Sir Charles Blythe in the train. Give him this from me, and say that I'll meet him at the Beau Site at Cannes at four o'clock. Have the car ready at two. I'll come to the garage. You haven't much time to spare, so take a cab."

I rose, raised my hat to the dark-eyed little woman, who bowed gracefully, and then, mounting into a *fiacre*, drove rapidly up the Avenue de la Gare.

The situation was decidedly interesting. My ideal of that sunny morning had been shattered. Gabrielle of the luminous eyes was already a wife.

I met the train, and discovered Sir Charles looking out for me. I handed him the packet, and gave him the Count's message. I noticed that he had some light luggage with him, and presumed that he was moving from Beaulieu to Cannes—to the tea-and-tennis Beau Site.

Then, when the train had moved off, I wandered across to a small restaurant opposite the station, and lunched alone, thinking and wondering about the dainty little girl-wife who had so completely fascinated me.

That she was still in love with Bindo was quite clear, yet he, on his part, was distinctly annoyed at being deceived.

At two o'clock, almost punctually, he entered the garage, flung his hat into the car, put on his cap, goggles, and motor-coat, and without a word I drew the 40 "Napier" out into the road.

"To Cannes—quick!" he snapped. "Round to the right into the Rue Magnan, then straight along. You saw Blythe?"

"Yes, I gave him the packet and the message."

"Good! then we haven't any time to lose. Get a move on her whenever you can."

On we flew, as fast as the sharp corners would allow, until presently we slipped down the long hill into Cannes, and passing through the town, pulled up at the Beau Site, where we found Sir Charles awaiting us.

The latter had changed his clothes, and

was now in a smart blue serge suit, and was idly smoking a cigar as we swept round to the entrance.

The two men met enthusiastically, some words were exchanged in an undertone, and both burst out laughing—a laugh of triumph. Was it at the expense of poor little Gabrielle ?

I was left outside to mind the car, and waited for fully an hour and a half. The wind blew bitterly cold at sundown, as it always does on the Riviera in December, and I was glad of my big fur coat.

Whatever was the subject of discussion it was evidently a weighty one. Both men had gone to Blythe's room and were closeted there.

A little after five Blythe came out, hailed a cab, and drove away into the town ; while the Count, whose appearance was so entirely changed that I scarcely knew him, sauntered slowly down the hall after his friend. Blythe had evidently brought him some fresh clothes from Monte Carlo, and he had used his room as a dressing-room. He looked very much older, and the dark brown suit he now wore was out of shape and ill-fitting. His hair showed grey over the ears, and he wore gold spectacles.

Instantly I saw that the adventurous scheme was still in progress, so I descended and lit the big head-lights. About a dozen idlers were in the vicinity of the car, and in sight of them all, he struggled into his big motor-coat, and entering, gave me orders to drive into the centre of the town. Then, after we had got clear of the hotel, he said :

"Stop at the station ; we have to pick up Blythe."

Directed by him, we were soon at the spot where Sir Charles awaited us.

"I've got it!" he exclaimed in a low voice as he took out a big coat, motor-cap, and goggles, "Quick work, wasn't it ?"

"Excellent!" declared the Count, and then, bending to me, he added, "Round there to the left. The high road is a little further on—to Marseilles!"

"To Marseilles!" I echoed, surprised that we were going so far as a hundred odd miles, but at that moment I saw the wide highway and turned into it, and with our big search-lights throwing a white radiance on the road, I set the car westward through St. Raphael and Les Arcs. It commenced to rain, with a biting wind, and turned out a very disagreeable night ; but, urged on by both men, I went forward at as quick a pace as I dared go on that road, over which I had never before travelled.

At Toulon we pulled up for a drink —for by that time we were all three chilled to the bone, notwithstanding our heavy leather-lined coats, and then we set out again for Marseilles, which we reached just after one o'clock in the morning, drawing up at the Louvre et Paix, which every visitor to the capital of southern France knows so well. Here we had a good hearty meal of cold meat and bock. Prior, however, to entering Marseilles, we had halted, changed our identification-plate, and made certain alterations, in order more thoroughly to disguise the car.

After supper we all got in again, and Bindo directed me up and down several long streets until we were once more in the suburbs. In a quiet, unfrequented road we pulled up, where from beneath the dark shadow of a wall a man silently approached us.

I could not distinguish his face in the darkness, but from his voice I knew it was none other than Henderson, the servant from Kingsworthy.

"Wait here for half an hour. Then run the car back to that church I pointed out to you as we came along. The one at the top of the Cannebière. Wait for us there. We shall be perhaps an hour, perhaps a little more," said the Count, taking a stick from the car, and then the trio disappeared into the darkness.

Fully an hour elapsed, until at length, along in the shadow the three crept cautiously, each bearing a heavy bundle, wrapped in black cloth, which they deposited in the car. The contents of the bundles chinked as they were placed upon the floor. What their booty was I knew not.

Next instant, however, all three were in, the door was closed, and I drew off into the dark open road straight before me—out into the driving rain.

The Count, who was at my side, seemed panting and agitated.

"We've brought it off all right, Ewart," he whispered, bending to me a few minutes later. "In behind there's over twenty thousand pounds' worth of jewellery for us to divide later on. We must get into Valence for breakfast, and thence Henderson will take the stuff away by train into Holland ! "

"But how—what have you done ? " I asked, puzzled.

"I'll explain in the morning, when we've got rid of it all."

He did explain. Blythe and Henderson both left us at Valence with the booty, while Bindo and myself, in the morning sunshine, went forward at an easy pace along the Lyons road.

"The affair wanted just a little bit of delicate manœuvring," he explained. "It was an affair of the heart, you see. We knew that the pretty little Gabrielle had married old Lemaire, the well-known jeweller in the Cannebière, in Marseilles, and that she had gone to spend her honeymoon at Nice. Unknown to either, I took a room next theirs at the hotel, and, thanks to the communicating doors they have in foreign hotels, overheard her husband explain that he must go to Genoa on pressing business. He also left her his safe-keys—the duplicates of those held by his manager in Marseilles—with injunctions to keep them locked in her trunk. I allowed him to be absent a couple of days, then, quite unexpectedly, I met her on the Promenade, pretending, of course, that I was entirely unaware of her marriage with old Lemaire. In case of accident, however, it was necessary that the little woman should be compromised with somebody, and as you were so discreet, I sent you both yesterday morning to idle along the whole length of the promenade. In the meantime, I nipped back to the hotel, entered Gabrielle's room, obtained the two safe-keys, and took impressions of them in wax. These I put into a tin matchbox and sent them by you to Blythe at the station. Blythe, with his usual foresight, had already engaged a locksmith in Cannes, telling him a little fairy-story of how he had lost his safe-keys, and how his manager in London, who had duplicates, had sent him out impressions. The keys were made to time ; Blythe took a cab from the hotel, and got them, rejoined us at Cannes station, and then we went on to Marseilles. There the affair became easier, but more risky. Henderson had already been reconnoitring the shop for a week,

stock. I'm rather sorry to have treated little Gabrielle so—but, after all, it really doesn't hurt her, for old Lemaire is very rich, and he won't miss twenty thousand pounds as much as we're in need of it.

"THE THREE CREPT CAUTIOUSLY, EACH BEARING A HEAVY BUNDLE"

and had conceived a clever plan by which we got in from the rear, quickly opened the two big safes with the copied keys, and cleared out all old Lemaire's best

The loving husband is still in Genoa, and poor little Gabrielle is no doubt thinking herself a fool to have so prematurely shown her wedding-ring."

THE COUNT'S CHAUFFEUR.

A SERIES OF COMPLETE STORIES BY WILLIAM LE QUEUX.

No. 3.—THE STORY OF A SECRET.

THE story of the secret was not without its humorous side.

Before entering Paris, after our quick run up from Marseilles after the affair of the jeweller's shop, we had stopped at Melun, beyond Fontainebleau. There, a well-known carriage-builder had been ordered to repaint the car pale blue, with a dead white band. Upon the panels, my employer, the impudent Bindo, had ordered a count's coronet, with the cipher " G. B." beneath, all to be done in the best style and regardless of expense. Then, that same evening, we took the express to the Gare de Lyon, and put up, as before, at the Ritz.

For three weeks, without the car, we had a pleasant time. Usually Count Bindo di Ferraris spent his time with his gay friends, lounging in the evening at Maxim's, or giving costly suppers at the Americain. One lady with whom I often saw him walking in the streets, or sitting in cafés, was, I discovered, known as " Valentine of the Beautiful Eyes," for I recognised her one night on the stage of a music-hall in the Boulevard de Clichy, where she was evidently a great favourite. She was young—not more than twenty, I think—with wonderful big coal-black eyes, a wealth of dark hair worn with a *bandeau*, and a face that was perfectly charming.

She seemed known to Blythe, too, for one evening I saw her sitting with him in the Brasserie Universelle, in the Avenue de l'Opéra—that place where one dines so well and cheaply. She was laughing, and had a *demi-blonde* raised to her lips. So essentially a Parisienne, she was also something of a mystery, for though she often frequented cafés, and went to the Folies Bergères and Olympia, sang at the Marigny, and mixed with a Bohemian crowd of champagne-drinkers, she seemed nevertheless a most decorous little lady. In fact, though I had not spoken to her, she had won my admiration. She was

very beautiful, and I—well, I was only a man, and human.

One bright morning, when the car came to Paris, I called for her, at Bindo's orders, at her flat in the Avenue Kléber, where she lived, it appeared, with a prim, sharp-nosed old aunt, of angular appearance, peculiarly French. She soon appeared, dressed in the very latest motor clothes, with her veil properly fixed, in a manner which showed me instantly that she was a motorist. Besides, she would not enter the car, but got up beside me, wrapped a rug about her skirts in a business-like manner, and gave me the order to move.

" Where to, Mademoiselle ? " I asked.

" Did not the Count give you instructions ? " she asked in her pretty broken English, turning her great dark eyes upon me in surprise. " Why, to Brussels, of course."

" To Brussels ! " I ejaculated, for I thought the run was to be only about Paris—to meet Bindo, perhaps.

" Yes. Are you surprised ? " she laughed. " It is not far—two hundred kilometres, or so. Surely that is nothing for you ? "

" Not at all. Only the Count is at the Ritz. Shall we not call there first ? "

" The Count left for Belgium by the seven-fifty train this morning," was her reply. " He has taken our baggage with his, and you will take me by road alone."

I was, of course, nothing loth to spend a few hours with such a charming companion as La Valentine ; therefore in the Avenue des Champs Elysées I pulled up, and consulting my road-book, decided to go by way of Arras, Douai, St. Amand, and Ath. Quickly we ran out beyond the fortifications ; while, driving in silence, I wondered what this latest manœuvre was to be. This sudden flight from Paris was more than mysterious. It caused me considerable apprehension, for when I had seen the Count in his room at midnight he had made no mention of his intention to leave so early.

At last, out upon the straight high road that ran between lines of high bare poplars, I put on speed, and quickly the

journey in comfort in such weather one must be wind-proof.

"You are cold, Mademoiselle," I remarked. "Will you not put on my leather jacket? You'll feel the benefit of it, even though it may not appear very smart." And I pulled up.

With a light merry laugh she consented, and I got out the garment in question, helped her into it over her coat, and though a trifle tight across the chest, she at once declared that it was a most excellent idea. She was, indeed, a merry child of Paris, and allowed me to button the coat, smiling the while at my masculine clumsiness.

Then we continued on our way, and a few moments later were going for all we were worth over the dry, well-kept, level road eastward, towards the Belgian frontier. She laughed and chatted as the hours went by. She had been in London last spring, she told me, and had

"TEARING IT OPEN IN SURPRISE, I READ THE HASTILY PENCILLED LINES."

cloud of white dust rose behind us. The northerly wind that grey day was biting, and threatened snow; therefore my pretty companion very soon began to feel the cold. I saw her turning up the collar of her cloth motor-coat, and guessed that she had no leather beneath. To do a day's

stayed at the Savoy. The English were so droll, and lacked *cachet*, though the hotel was smart—especially at supper.

"We pass Douai," she remarked presently, after we had run rapidly through many villages and small towns. "I must call for a telegram." And then, somehow, she settled down into a thought-ful silence.

At Arras I pulled up, and got her a glass of hot milk. Then on again, for she declared that she was not hungry, and preferred to get to Brussels than to linger on the road. On the broad highway to Douai we went at the greatest speed that I could get out of the fine six-cylinder, the engines beating beautiful time, and the car running as smoothly as a watch. The clouds of whirling dust became very bad, however, and I was compelled to goggle, while the tall-fronted veil adequately protected my sweet-faced travelling companion.

At Douai she descended and entered the post-office herself, returning with a tele-gram and a letter. The latter she handed to me, and I found it was addressed in my name, and had been sent to the Poste-restante.

Tearing it open in surprise I read the hastily pencilled lines it contained—in-structions in the Count's handwriting which were extremely puzzling, not to say disconcerting. The words I read were :—

"After crossing the frontier you will assume the name of Count de Bourbriac, and Valentine will pass as the Countess. A suitable suite of rooms have been taken for you at the Grand Hotel, Brussels, where you will find your luggage on your arrival. Mademoiselle will supply you with funds. I shall be in Brussels, but shall not approach you.—B. di F."

The pretty Valentine who was to be my *pseudo*-wife crushed the blue telegram into her coat-pocket, mounted into her seat, wrapped her rug around her, and ordered me to proceed.

I glanced at her, but she was to all appearances quite unconscious of the extraordinary contents of the Count's letter.

We had run fully twenty miles in silence when at last, on ascending a steep hill, I turned to her and said :

"The Count has sent me some very extraordinary instructions, Mademoiselle. I am, after passing the frontier, to become Count de Bourbriac, and you are to pass as the Countess ! "

"Well ? " she asked, arching her well-marked eyebrows. " Is that so very difficult, m'sieur ? Are you disinclined to allow me to pass as your wife ? "

"Not at all," I replied smiling. "Only —well—it is somewhat—er—unconven-tional, is it not ? "

"Rather an amusing adventure than otherwise," she laughed. " I shall call you *mon cher* Gaston, and you—well, you will call me your *petite* Liane—Liane de Bourbriac will sound well, will it not ? "

"Yes. But why this masquerade ? " I inquired. " I confess, Mademoiselle, I don't understand it at all."

"Dear Bindo does. Ask him." Then, after a brief pause, she added : " This is really a rather novel experience," and she laughed gleefully, as though thoroughly enjoying the adventure.

Without slackening speed I drove on through the short winter afternoon. The faint yellow sunset slowly disappeared behind us, and darkness crept on. With the fading day the cold became intense, and when I stopped to light the head-lamps I got out my cashmere muffler and wrapped it around her throat.

At last we reached the small frontier village, where we pulled up before the Belgian Custom House, paid the deposit upon the car, and obtained the leaden seal. Then, after a liqueur-glass of cognac each at a little café in the vicinity, we set out again upon that long wide road that leads through Ath to Brussels.

A puncture at a place called Leuze caused us a little delay, but the *pseudo* Countess descended and assisted me, even helping me to blow up the new tube, declaring that the exercise would warm her.

For what reason the pretty Valentine was to pass as my wife was, to me, entirely mysterious. That Bindo was engaged in some fresh scheme of fraud was certain, but what it was I racked my brains in vain to discover.

Near Enghien we had several other tyre troubles, for the road had been newly metalled for miles. As every motorist knows, misfortunes never come singly, and in consequence it was already seven o'clock next morning before we entered Brussels by the Porte de Hal, and ran along the fine Boulevard d'Anspach, to the Grand Hotel.

The gilt-laced hall-porter, who was evidently awaiting us, rushed out cap in hand, and I, quickly assuming my *rôle* as Count, helped out the "Countess" and gave the car over to one of the employés of the hotel garage.

By the manager we were ushered into a fine suite of six rooms on the first floor, overlooking the Boulevard, and treated with all the deference due to persons of highest standing.

At that moment Valentine showed her cleverness by remarking that she had not brought Elise, her maid, as she was to follow by train, and that I would employ the services of one of the hotel valets for the time being. Indeed, so cleverly did she assume the part that she might really have been one of the ancient nobility of France.

I spoke in English. On the Continent just now it is considered rather smart to talk English. One often hears two German or Italian women speaking atrocious English together, in order to air their superior knowledge before strangers. Therefore that I spoke English was not remarked by the manager, who explained that our courier had given him all instructions, and had brought the baggage, in advance. The courier was, I could only suppose, the audacious Bindo himself.

That day passed quite merrily. We lunched together, took a drive in the pretty Bois de la Cambre, and after dining, went to the Monnaie to see *Madame Butterfly*. On our return to the hotel I found a note from Bindo, and saying good-night to Valentine I went forth again to keep the appointment he had made in a café in the quiet Chausée de Charleroi, on the opposite side of the city.

When I entered the little place I found the Count seated at a table with Blythe and Henderson. The two latter were dressed shabbily, while the Count himself was in dark grey, with a soft felt hat—the perfect counterfeit of the foreign courier.

With enthusiasm I was welcomed into the corner.

"Well?" asked Bindo with a laugh, "And how do you like your new wife, Ewart?" and the others smiled.

"Charming," I replied. "But I don't see exactly where the joke comes in."

"I don't suppose you ao, just yet."

"It's a risky proceeding, isn't it?" I queried.

"Risky! What risk is there in gulling hotel people?" he asked. "If you don't intend to pay the bill it would be quite another matter."

"But why is the lady to pass as my wife? Why am I the Count de Bourbriac? Why, indeed, are we here at all?"

"That's our business, my dear Ewart. Leave matters to us. All you've got to do is to just play your part well. Appear to be very devoted to La Comtesse, and it'll be several hundreds into your pocket—perhaps a level thou'—who knows?"

"A thou' each—quite," declared Blythe, a cool, audacious international swindler of the most refined and cunning type.

"But what risk is there?" I inquired, for my companions seemed to be angling after big fish this time, whoever they were.

"None, as far as you are concerned. Be advised by Valentine. She's as clever a girl as there is in all Europe. She has her eyes and ears open all the time. A lover will come on the scene before long, and you must be jealous—devilish jealous—you understand?"

"A lover? Who? I don't understand."

"You'll see, soon enough. Go back to the hotel—or stay with us to-night, if you prefer it. Only don't worry yourself over risks. We never take any. Only fools do that. Whatever we do is always a dead certainty before we embark upon the job."

"Then I'm to understand that some fellow is making love to Valentine—eh?"

"Exactly. To-morrow night you are both invited to a ball at the Belle Vue, in aid of the Hospital St. Jean. You will go, and there the lover will appear. You will withdraw, and allow the little flirtation to proceed. Valentine herself will give you further instructions as the occasion warrants."

"I confess I don't half like it. I'm working too much in the dark," I protested.

"That's just what we intend. If you knew too much you might betray yourself, for the people we've got to deal with have eyes in the backs of their heads," declared Bindo.

It was five o'clock next morning before I returned to the Grand, but during the hours we smoked together, at various obscure cafés, the trio told me nothing further, though they chaffed me regarding the beauty of the girl who had consented to act the part of my wife, and who, I could only suppose, "stood in" with us.

At noon, surely enough, came a special invitation to the "Comte et Comtesse de Bourbriac" for the great ball that evening at the Hotel Belle Vue, and at ten o'clock that night Valentine entered our private salon splendidly dressed in a low-cut gown of smoke-grey chiffon covered with sequins. Her hair had been dressed by a maid of the first order, and as she stood pulling on her long gloves she looked superb.

"How do you find me, my dear M'sieur Ewart? Do I look like a Comtesse?" she asked laughing.

"You look perfectly charming, Mademoiselle."

"Liane, if you please," she said reprovingly, holding up her slim forefinger. "Liane, Comtesse de Bourbriac, Château de Bourbriac, Côtes du Nord!" and her pretty lips parted, showing her even pearly teeth.

When, half an hour later, we entered the ball-room we found all smart Brussels assembled around a royal prince and his wife who had given their patronage in the cause of charity. The affair was, I saw at a glance, a distinctly society function, for many men from the Ministries were present, and several of the Ambassadors in uniform, together with their staffs, who, wearing their crosses and ribbons, made a brave show, as they do in every ball-room.

We had not been there ten minutes before a tall good-looking young man in a German cavalry uniform strode up in recognition, and bowing low over Valentine's outstretched hand, said in French:

"My dear Countess! How very delighted we are to have you here with us to-night. You will spare me a dance, will you not? May I be introduced to the Count?"

"My husband—Captain von Stolberg, of the German Embassy."

And we shook hands. Was this fellow the lover, I wondered?

"I met the Countess at Vichy last autumn," explained the Captain in very good English. "She spoke very often of you. You were away in Scotland, shooting the grouse," he said.

"Yes—yes," I replied for want of something better to say.

We both chatted with the young attaché for a few minutes, and then, as a waltz struck up, he begged a dance of my "wife," and they both whirled down the room. Valentine was a splendid dancer, and as I watched them I wondered what could be the nature of the plot in progress.

I did not come across my pretty fellow-traveller for half-an-hour, and then I found that the captain had half filled her programme. Therefore I "laid low," danced once or twice with uninteresting Belgian matrons, and spent the remainder of the night in the *fumoir*, until I found my "wife" ready to return to the Grand.

When we were back in the salon at the hotel she asked:

"How do you like the Captain, M'sieur Ewart? Is he not—what you call in English—a duck?"

"An overdressed, swaggering young idiot, I call him," was my prompt reply.

"And there you are right—quite right, my dear M'sieur Ewart. But you see we all have an eye to business in this affair. He will call to-morrow, because he is extremely fond of me. Oh! if you had heard all his pretty love phrases! I suppose he has learnt them out of a book. They couldn't be his own. Germans are not romantic—how can they be? But he—ah! he is Adonis in the flesh—with corsets!" And we laughed merrily together.

"He thinks you are fond of him—eh?"

"Why, of course. He made violent love to me at Vichy. But he was not attaché then."

"And how am I to treat him when he calls to-morrow?"

"As your bosom friend. Give him confidence—the most perfect confidence. Don't play the jealous husband yet. That will come afterwards. *Bon soir, m'sieur,*" and when I had bowed over her soft little hand she turned, and swept out of the room with a loud *frou-frou* of her silken train.

That night I sat before the fire smoking for a long time. My companions were evidently playing some deep game upon this young German, a game in which neither trouble nor expense was being spared—a game in which the prize was a level thousand pounds apiece all round. I quite appreciated that I had now become an adventurer, but I had done so out of pure love of adventure.

About four o'clock next afternoon the Captain came to take " fif-o'-clock," as he called it. He clicked his heels together as he bowed over Valentine's hand, and she smiled upon him even more sweetly than she had smiled at me when I had helped her into my leather motor-coat. She wore a beautiful toilette, one of the latest of Doeillet's she had explained to me, and really presented a delightfully dainty figure as she sat there pouring out tea, and chatting with the infatuated Captain of Cuirassiers.

I saw quickly that I was not wanted ; therefore I excused myself, and went for a stroll along to the Café Métropole, afterwards taking a turn up the Montagne de la Cour. All day I had been on the look-out to see either Bindo or his companions, but they were evidently in hiding.

When I returned, just in time to dress for dinner, I asked Valentine what progress her lover was making, but she merely replied :

" Slow—very slow. But in things of this magnitude one must have patience. We are invited to the Embassy ball in honour of the Crown Prince of Saxony to-morrow night. It will be amusing."

Next night she dressed in a gown of pale rose chiffon, and we went to the Embassy, where one of the most brilliant balls of the season was in progress, King Leopold himself being present to honour the young Crown Prince. Captain Stolberg soon discovered the woman who held him beneath her spell, and I found myself dancing attendance upon the snub-nosed little daughter of a Burgomaster, with whom I waltzed the greater part of the evening.

On our return my " wife " told me with a laugh that matters were progressing well. " Otto," she added, " is such a fool. Men in love will believe any fiction a woman tells them. Isn't it really extraordinary ? "

" Perhaps I'm one of those men, Mademoiselle," I said looking straight into her beautiful eyes, for I own she had in a measure fascinated me, even though I knew her to be an adventuress.

She burst out laughing in my face.

" Don't be absurd, M'sieur Ewart." she cried. " Fancy you ! But you certainly wouldn't fall in love with me. We are only friends—in the same swim, as I believe you term it in English."

I was a fool. I admit it. But when one is thrown into the society of a pretty woman even a chauffeur may make speeches he regrets.

So the subject dropped, and with a mock curtsey, and a saucy wave of the hand, she went to her room.

On the following day she went out alone at eleven, not returning until six. She offered no explanation of where she had been, and of course it was not for me to question her. As we sat at dinner in our private salle-à-manger an hour later she laughed at me across the table, and declared that I was sitting as soberly as though I really were her dutiful husband. And next day she was absent again the whole day, while I amused myself in visiting the Law Courts, the picture galleries, and the general sights of the little capital of which Messieurs the brave Belgians are so proud. On her return she seemed thoughtful, even *triste*. She had been on an excursion somewhere with Otto, but she did not enlighten me regarding its details. I wondered that I had had no word from Bindo. Yet he had told me to obey Valentine's instructions, and I was now doing so. At dinner she once clenched her little hand involuntarily, and drew a deep breath, showing me that she was indignant at something.

The following morning, as she mentioned that she should be absent all day, I took a run on the car as far as the quaint little town of Dinant, up the Meuse, getting back to dinner.

In the salon she met me, already in her dinner-gown, and told me that she had invited Otto to dine.

" To-night you must show your jealousy. You must leave us together here, in the salon, after dinner, and then a quarter of an hour later return suddenly. I will compromise him. Then you will quarrel violently, order him to leave the hotel, and thus part bad friends."

I hardly liked to be a party to such a trick, yet the whole plot interested me. I could not see to what material end all this tended.

Well, the gay Captain duly arrived, and we dined together merrily. His eyes were fixed admiringly upon Valentine the whole time and his conversation was mainly reminiscent of the days at Vichy. The meal over, we passed into the salon, and there I left them. But on re-entering shortly afterwards I found him standing behind the couch,

the pair with my fists clenched in jealous anger. What I said I scarcely remember. All I know is that I let forth a torrent of reproaches and condemnations, and ended by practically kicking the fellow out of the room, while my " wife " sank upon her knees and implored my forgiveness which I flatly refused.

" SHE HAD HER ARMS CLASPED AROUND HIS NECK."

bending over and kissing her. She had her arms clasped around his neck so tightly that he could not disengage himself.

In pretended fury I dashed across to

The Captain took his kicking in silence, but in his glance was murder, as he turned once and faced me ere he left the room.

"Well, Valentine," I asked, when he was safely out of hearing, and when she had raised herself from her knees laughing. "And what now?"

"The whole affair is now plain sailing. To-morrow you will take the car to Liège, and there await me outside the cathedral at midnight on the following night. You will easily find the place. Wait until two o'clock, and if I am not there go on to Cologne, and put up at the Hotel du Nord."

"Without baggage?"

"Without baggage. Don't trouble about anything. Simply go there and wait."

At midday on the following day the pretty Valentine dressed herself carefully, and went out. Then, an hour later, pretending that I was only going for a short run, I mounted into the car and set out for Liège, wondering what was now to happen.

Next day I idled away, and at a quarter to twelve that night, after a run around the town, I pulled up in the shadow before the cathedral and stopped the engines. The old square was quite quiet, for the good Liègois retire early, and the only sound was the musical carillon of the bells.

In impatience I waited. The silent night was clear, bright, and frosty, with a myriad shining stars above. Time after time the great clock above me chimed the quarters, until just before two o'clock, there came a dark female figure round the corner, walking quickly. In an instant I recognised Valentine, who was dressed in a long travelling coat with fur collar, and a sealskin toque. She was carrying something beneath her coat.

"Quick!" she said breathlessly. "Let us get away. Get ready. Count Bindo is following me!" And ere I could start the engines, my employer, in a long dark overcoat and felt hat, hurriedly approached us, saying:

"Come, let's be off, Ewart. We've a long journey to-night to Cassel. We must go through Aix, and pick up Blythe, and then on by way of Cologne, Arnsburg, and the Hoppeke-Tal."

Quickly they both put on the extra wraps from the car, entered, and wrapped the rugs about them, while two minutes later, with our big head-lamps shedding a broad white light before us, we turned out upon the wide high road to Verviers.

"It's all right!" cried Bindo, leaning over to me when we had covered about five miles or so. "Everything went off perfectly."

"And M'sieur made a most model 'husband,' I assure you," declared the pretty Valentine, with a musical laugh.

"But what have you done?" I inquired half turning, but afraid to take my eyes from the road.

"Be patient. We'll explain everything when we get to Cassel," responded Valentine. And with that I had to be content.

At the station at Aix we found Blythe awaiting us, and when he had taken the seat beside me we set out by way of Duren to Cologne, and on to Cassel, a long and bitterly cold journey.

It was not until we were dining together late the following night in the comfortable old König von Preussen, at Cassel, that Valentine revealed the truth to me.

"When I met the German at Vichy I was passing as Countess de Bourbriac, and pretending that my husband was in Scotland. At first I avoided him," she said. "But later on I was told, in confidence, that he was a spy in the service of the War Office in Berlin. Then I wrote to Count Bindo, and he advised me to pretend to reciprocate the fellow's affections, and to keep a watchful eye for the main chance. I have done so—that's all."

"But what was this 'main chance'?" I asked.

"Why, don't you see, Ewart," exclaimed the Count, who was standing by, smoking a cigarette. "The fact that he was in the Intelligence Department in Berlin, and that he had been suddenly appointed military attaché at Brussels, made it plain that he was carrying out some important secret-service work in Belgium. On making inquiries I heard that he was constantly travelling in the country, and, speaking French so well, he was passing himself off as a Belgian. Blythe, in the guise of an English tourist, met him in Boxtel two months ago, and satisfied himself as to the character of the task he had undertaken, a risky but most important one. Then we all agreed that, when completed, the secrets he had possessed himself of should become ours, for the Intelligence Department of either France or England would be certain to purchase them for almost any sum we liked to name, so important were they. About two months we waited for the unsuspecting Otto to complete his work, and then suddenly the Countess reappears, accompanied by her husband. And—well, Valentine, you can best tell Ewart the remainder of the story," added the audacious scoundrel, replacing his cigarette in his mouth.

"As M'sieur Ewart knows, Captain Stolberg was in love with me, and I pretended to be infatuated with him. The other night he kissed me, and my dear 'Gaston' saw it, and in just indignation and jealousy promptly kicked him out. Next day I met him, told him that my husband was a perfect hog, and urged him to take me from him. At first he would not sacrifice his official position as attaché, for he was a poor man. Then we talked money matters, and I suggested that he surely possessed something which he could turn into money sufficient to keep us for a year or two, as I had a small income though not absolutely sufficient for our wants. In fact, I offered, now that he had compromised me in the eyes of my husband, to elope with him. We walked in the Bois de la Cambre for two solid hours that afternoon, until I was footsore, and yet he did not catch on. Then I played another game, declaring that he did not love me sufficiently to make such a sacrifice, and at last taking a dramatic farewell of him. He allowed me to get almost to the gates of the Bois, when he suddenly ran after me, and told me that he had a packet of documents for which he could obtain a large sum abroad. He would take them, and myself, to Berlin by that night's mail, and then we would go on to St. Petersburg, where he could easily dispose of the mysterious papers. So we met at the station at midnight, and by the same train travelled Bindo and M'sieurs Blythe and Henderson. In the carriage he told me where the precious papers were—in a small leathern hand-bag—and this fact I whispered to Blythe when he brushed past me in the corridor. At Pepinster, the junction for Spa, we both descended to obtain some

refreshment, and when we returned to our carriage the Captain glanced reassuringly at his bag. Bindo passed along the corridor, and I knew the truth. Then on arrival at Liège I left the Captain smoking, and strolled to the back end of the carriage, waiting for the train to move off. Just as it did so I sprang out upon the platform, and had the satisfaction of seeing, a moment later, the red tail-lights of the Berlin express disappear. I fancy I saw the Captain's head out of the window and heard him shout, but next instant he was lost in the darkness."

"As soon as you had both got out at Pepinster Blythe slipped into the compartment, broke the lock of the bag with a special tool we call 'the snipper,' and had the papers in a moment. These he passed on to me, and travelled past Liège on to Aix."

"Here are the precious plans," remarked the Count, producing a voluminous packet in a big blue envelope, the seal of which had been broken.

And on opening this he displayed to me a quantity of carefully drawn plans of the whole canal system, and secret defences between the Rhine and the Meuse, the waterway, he explained, which one day Germany, in time of war with England, will require to use in order to get her troops through the port of Antwerp, and the Belgian coast—the first complete and reliable plans ever obtained of the chain of formidable defences that Belgium keeps a profound secret.

What sum was paid to the pretty Valentine by the French Intelligence Department for them I am not aware. I only know that she one day sent me a beautiful gold cigarette-case inscribed with the words "From Liane de Bourbriac," and inside it was a draft on the London branch of the Crédit Lyonnais for eight hundred and fifty pounds.

Captain Otto Stolberg has, I hear, been transferred as attaché to another European capital. No doubt his first thoughts were of revenge, but on mature consideration he deemed it best to keep his mouth closed, or he would have betrayed himself as a spy. The Count had, no doubt, foreseen that. As for Valentine, she actually declares that, after all, she merely rendered a service to her country!

THE COUNT'S CHAUFFEUR.

By WILLIAM LE QUEUX.

No. 4.—A RUN WITH ROSALIE.

SEVERAL months had elapsed since my adventure with " Valentine of the Beautiful Eyes."

From Germany Count Bindo di Ferraris had sent me with the car right across Europe to Florence, where, at Nenci's, the builders of motor-bodies, I, in obedience to orders, had it repainted a bright yellow—almost the colour of mustard.

When, a fortnight later, it came out of the Nenci works, I hardly recognised it. At Bindo's orders I had had a second body built, one made of wicker, and lined inside with glazed white leather, which, when fixed upon the chassis, completely transformed it. This second body I sent by rail down to Leghorn, and then drove the car along the Arno valley, down to the sea-shore.

My orders were to go to the Palace Hotel at Leghorn, and there await my master. The hotel in question was, I found, one of the best in Italy, filled by the smartest crowd of men and women, mostly of the Italian aristocracy, who went there for the magnificent sea-bathing. It was a huge white building, with many balconies, and striped awnings, facing the blue Mediterranean.

Valentine had travelled with me as far as Milan, while he had taken train, I believe, to Berlin. At Milan, my pretty companion had wished me adieu, and a month later I had taken up my residence in Leghorn, and there led an idle life, wondering when I was to hear next from Bindo. Before we parted he gave me a fairly large sum of money, and told me to remain at Leghorn until he joined me.

Weeks passed. Leghorn in summer is the Brighton of Italy, and everything there was delightfully gay. In the garage of the hotel were many cars, but not one so good as our 40-h.p " Napier." The Italians all admired it, and on several occasions I took motoring enthusiasts of both sexes out for short runs along the old Maremma sea-road.

The life I led was one of idleness, punctuated by little flirtations, for by Bindo's order I was staying at the Palace as owner of the car, and not as a mere chauffeur. The daughters of Italian countesses and marchionesses, though brought up so strictly, are always eager for flirtation, and so as I sat alone at my table in the big *salle-à-manger* I caught many a glance from black eyes that danced with merry mischievousness.

Valentine, when she left me in Milan, had said, laughingly :

" I may rejoin you again ere long, M'sieur Ewart, but not as your pretended wife, as at Brussels."

" I hope not, Mademoiselle," I had answered quite frankly. " That game is a little too dangerous. I might really fall in love with you."

" With me ? " she cried, holding up her small hands in a quick gesture. " What an idea ! Oh ! la la ! *Jamais.*"

I smiled. Mademoiselle was extremely beautiful. No woman I had ever met possessed such wonderful eyes as hers.

" *Au revoir, mon cher,*" she said. " And a pleasant time to you till we meet again." Then as I mounted on the car and traversed the big Piazza del Duomo, before the Cathedral, she waved her hand to me in farewell.

It was, therefore, without surprise that, sitting in the hall of the hotel about five o'clock one afternoon I watched her in an elegant white gown descending the stairs, followed by a neat French maid in black.

Quickly I sprang up, bowed, and greeted her in French before a dozen or so of the idling guests.

As we walked across to Pancaldi's baths she told her new maid to go on in front, and in a few quick words explained.

" I arrived direct from Paris this morning. Here, I am the Princess Helen of Dornbach-Laxenburg of the Ringstrasse, in Vienna, the Schloss Kirchbüchl, on the

Drave, and Avenue des Champs Elysées, Paris, a Frenchwoman married to an Austrian. My husband, a man much older than myself, will arrive here in a few days."

"And the maid ?"

"She knows nothing to the contrary. She has been with me only a fortnight. Now you must speak of me in the hotel. Say that you knew me well at Monte Carlo, Rome, Carlsbad, and Aix; that you have stayed at Kirchbüchl, and have dined at our house in Paris. Talk of our enormous wealth, and all that, and to-morrow invite me for a run on the car."

"Very well—Princess," I laughed. "But what's the new scheme—eh ?"

"At present nothing has been definitely settled. I expect Bindo in a few days, but he will appear to us as a stranger—a complete stranger. At present all I wish to do is to create a sensation, you understand. A foreign princess is always popular at once, and I believe my arrival is already known all over the hotel. But it is you who will help me, M'sieur Ewart. You are the wealthy Englishman who is here with his motor-car, and who is one of my intimate friends —you understand?"

"Well," I said with some hesitation. "Don't you think that all this kind of thing is very risky ? Candidly, I expect before very long we shall all find ourselves under arrest."

She laughed heartily at my fears.

"But, in any case, you would not suffer. You are simply Ewart, the Count's chauffeur."

"I know. But at this moment I'm posing here as the owner of the car, and

"IN AN ELEGANT WHITE GOWN DESCENDING THE STAIRS, FOLLOWED BY A NEAT FRENCH MAID.'

living upon part of the proceeds of that little transaction in the train between Brussels and the German frontier."

"Ah, *mon cher !* Never recall the past. It is such a very bad habit. Live for the future; and let the past take care of itself. Just remain perfectly confident that you run no risk in this present affair."

" What's your maid's name ? "

" Rosalie Barlet."

" And she knows nothing ? "

" Absolutely nothing."

I watched the neat-waisted figure in black walking a little distance ahead of us. She was typically Parisienne, with Louis XV. shoes, and a glimpse of smart *lingerie* as she lifted her skirt daintily. Rather good-looking she was, too, but with a face as bony as most of the women of Paris, and a complexion slightly sallow.

By this time we had arrived at the entrance to the baths, where, on the asphalte promenade, built out into the clear crystal Mediterranean, all smart Leghorn was sitting in chairs, and gossiping beneath the awnings, as Italians love to do.

Pancaldi's is essentially Italian. English, French, or German visitors are rarely if ever seen, therefore the advent of the Princess, news of whose arrival had spread from mouth to mouth but an hour ago, caused a perceptible flutter among the lounging idlers of both sexes.

My companion was, I saw, admired on every hand, while surprise was being expressed that I should turn out to be a friend of so very distinguished a person.

In the brilliant sundown, with just a refreshing breath of air coming across the glassy sea, we sat watching the antics of the swimmers and the general merriment in the water. I lit a cigarette and gossiped with her in French, ostentatiously emphasising the words " your Highness " when I addressed her, for the benefit of those passing and re-passing behind us.

For an hour she remained, and then returning to the hotel, dressed, and dined.

As she sat with me at table that night in the handsome restaurant, she looked superb, in pale turquoise chiffon, with a single row of diamonds around her throat. Paste they were, of course, but none of the women who sat with their eyes upon her even dreamed that they were anything but the family jewels of the princely house of Dornbach-Laxenburg. Her manner and bearing were distinctly that

of a patrician, and I saw that all in the hotel were dying to know her.

Yes. Her Highness was already a great success.

About ten o'clock she put on a wrap, and, as is usual with the guests at the Palace at Leghorn, we went for a brief stroll along the promenade.

As soon as we were entirely alone she said:

" To-morrow you will take me for a run on the car, and the next day you will introduce me to one or two of the best people. I will discover who are the proper persons for me to know. I shall say that you are George Ewart, eldest son of a member of the English Parliament, and well known in London—eh ? "

As we were walking in the shadow, through the small leafy public garden lying between the roadway and the sea, we suddenly encountered the figure of a young woman who, in passing, saluted my companion with deep respect. It was Rosalie.

" She's wandering here alone, and watching for me to re-enter the hotel," remarked Valentine. " But she need not follow me like this, I think."

" No," I said. " Somehow, I don't like that girl."

" Why not ? She's all right. What more natural than that she should be on the spot to receive me when I come in ? "

" But you don't want to be spied upon like this, surely ! " I said resentfully. " Have you done anything to arouse her suspicions that you are not—well, not exactly what you pretend yourself to be ? "

" Nothing whatever; I have been a model of discretion. She never even went to the Avenue Kléber. I was staying for two nights at the Grand— under my present title—and after engaging her I told her that the house in the Avenue des Champs Elysées was in the hands of decorators."

" Well, I don't half like her following us. She may have overheard something of what we've just been saying—who knows ? "

" Rubbish ! Ah ! *mon cher ami*, you are always scenting danger where there is none."

I merely shrugged my shoulders, but

my opinion remained. There was something mysterious about Rosalie—what it was I could not make out.

At ten o'clock next morning her Highness met me in the big marble hall of the hotel, dressed in the smartest motor-clothes, with a silk dust-coat and the latest invention in veils—pale blue with long ends twisted several times around her throat. Even in that costume she looked dainty and extremely charming.

I, too, was altered in a manner that certainly disguised my true calling; and when I brought the car round to the front steps, quite a crowd of visitors gathered to see her climb to the seat beside me, wrap the rug around her skirts, and start away.

With a deep blast on the horn I swept out of the hotel grounds to the left, and a few moments later we were heading away along the broad sea-road through the pretty villages of Ardenza and Antignano, out into that wild open country that lies between Leghorn and the wide deadly marshes of the fever-stricken Maremma. The road we were travelling was the old road to Rome, for two hundred miles along it—a desolate, dreary and uninhabited way—lay the Eternal City. Over that self-same road on the top of the brown rocks the conquering Roman legions marched to Gaul, and war-chariots once ran where now sped motor-cars. Out there in those great solitudes through which we were passing nothing has changed since the days of Nero and of the Cæsars.

Twenty-five miles into the country we ran, and then pulled up to smoke and chat. She was fond of a cigarette, and joined me, laughing merrily at the manner in which we were so completely deceiving the gay world of Leghorn. The local papers that morning had announced that her Highness the Princess Helen of Dornbach-Laxenburg, one of the most beautiful women in Europe, had "descended" at the Palace Hotel, and had been seen at Pancaldi's later in the afternoon.

"As soon as I came down this morning I was pounced upon for information," I explained. "A young Italian Marquis, who has hitherto snubbed me, begged that I would tell him something concerning her Highness. He is deeply smitten with your beauty, that's very evident," I laughed.

"My beauty! You are really incorrigible, M'sieur Ewart," she answered reprovingly, as she blew the tobacco-smoke from her lips. "And what, pray, is the name of this admirer?"

"The Marquis of Rapallo—the usual hard-up but well-dressed elegant, you know. He wears two fresh suits of white linen a day, with socks to match his ties. Last night he sat at the table next to us, and couldn't keep his eyes off you—a rather short fellow with a little black moustache turned upwards."

"Ah, yes, I recollect," she replied, and then I thought that her countenance changed. "And so he's been inquiring about me? Well, let's run back to déjeuner—or collazione, as they call it here in Italy, I believe."

An hour later we drew up again at the hotel, and her Highness disappeared within. Then, after I had taken the car to the garage in the rear, and entered the hotel myself, I quickly became surrounded by people who wanted introductions to my charming acquaintance, and to whom I romanced about her wealth, her position, and her home surroundings.

On the following day Valentine allowed me to introduce her to four persons—an Italian marchioness who moved in the most exclusive Roman set, the wife of a Sicilian Duke, the wife of Jacobi, the wealthy Jew banker of Turin, and a Captain of Bersaglieri.

One night a lonely but well-dressed stranger entered the restaurant and seated himself in a corner almost unnoticed, save by Valentine and myself. The newcomer was the audacious Bindo, passing as Mr. Bellingham, an Englishman, but he gave us no sign of recognition. Indeed, the days went on, but he never approached either of us. He simply idled about the hotel, or across at Pancaldi's, having picked up one or two acquaintances, kindred spirits in the art of graceful idling. He never even wrote me a note.

Some deep game was in progress, but its nature I was entirely unable to gather.

Now, truth to tell, I experienced a growing uneasiness concerning Rosalie.

To me, she was always the modest maid devoted to her Highness, and yet I thought I once detected a glance of mischief in her dark eyes. Determined to discover all I could, I at once commenced a violent flirtation with her, unknown, of course, to Valentine.

Mademoiselle seemed flattered by the attentions of one whom she believed to be an English gentleman. Therefore I met her out one evening and took her for a long walk, pretending to be deeply smitten by her charms. From the first moment I began to talk with her I saw that she was not the shallow giddy girl I had believed her to be. She, no doubt, appreciated my attentions, for I took her to a *café* on the opposite side of the town where we should not be recognised, and there we sat a long time chatting. She seemed extremely curious to know who I really was, yet the queries she put to me were just a trifle blundering. They betrayed an earnest desire to know more than I intended that she should know.

" I wish her Highness would go back to Aix-les-Bains, or to Vichy, or to Luchon. I'm tired of this wretched hole where I know nobody," she complained presently. " I had quite sufficient of Italy when I was with the Duchess of Pandolfini. I did not know we were coming here, otherwise I should not have accepted the engagement, and yet—well, the Princess is very kind and considerate."

" She certainly is to her friends, and I hope the same to her servants," I said ; and then we rose to walk back, for it was nearly eleven, and her Highness, who had gone to the Opera with two of the ladies to whom I had introduced her, would soon be due back, and the dainty Rosalie must be there to receive her.

On our walk across the town I flattered her, pretending to be her devoted admirer, but when I left her I felt more convinced than ever upon three points—namely, that she was much older than twenty-two, as she had declared ; that she was unduly inquisitive ; and that she certainly was no fool.

That night I sent my master a note to his room warning him to be wary of her, and on the following morning I told her Highness my suspicions.

From that moment I made it my object in life to keep a watchful eye upon the new French maid. Each evening after her services were no longer required she went forth alone and wandered idly up and down the esplanade. Sometimes she walked out to Ardenza, a village a mile and a half distant, halted always at the same stone seat in the little public garden, and then strolled back again, in blissful ignorance of being so closely watched.

If Rosalie had any suspicion that Valentine was not the Princess Helen, then there was, I foresaw, a grave and constant danger. And I, for one, did not intend to run any further risk.

Her Highness had been in Leghorn just over three weeks, and had become intensely popular everywhere, being invited to the houses of many of the principal residents, when one night an incident occurred which afforded me grave food for reflection.

Just after ten o'clock at night I had followed Rosalie along by the sea to Ardenza, where she was sitting alone upon her usual seat in a secluded spot, at the edge of the public garden on a kind of small promontory that ran in a semicircle out to the sea. Behind her was a dark thicket of azaleas, and in front the calm moonlit Mediterranean.

I was standing back in the shadow at a spot where I had often stood before, when, after about five minutes, I saw the tall dark figure of a man in a grey deerstalker hat join her, and sit down unceremoniously at her side.

As soon as they met she began to tell him some long story, to which the stranger listened without comment. Then he seemed to question her closely, and they remained together fully a quarter of an hour, until at last they rose and parted, she walking calmly back to the hotel.

Was it possible that the dainty Rosalie was a spy ?

When I got half way back to the Palace I regretted deeply that I had not followed the stranger and ascertained whom he might be. Next day I told Valentine, but she merely smiled, saying that Rosalie could know nothing, and the fellow was probably some secret lover. The next night, and the next, I watched, until, on the third evening, they met again at the same time and place, and on that occasion

I followed the mysterious stranger. He was a thin, cadaverous-looking Frenchman, hollow-cheeked, rather shabbily dressed, and wore pince-nez. I watched him back into the town and lingered near him in a *café* until nearly one o'clock, when he entered his quarters at an uninviting, unfashionable and animating hotel, the "Falcon," in the Via Vittorio. From the manner he had treated her I judged him to be a relation, probably her uncle. Yet why she should meet him clandestinely was an utter mystery.

In order still to keep watch upon the maid I made a fervent protest of affection, and frequently met her between the dinner hour and midnight. Through all this time, however, Bindo never gave a sign, even in secret, that he was acquainted with Valentine or myself, and this very fact in itself aroused my suspicions that he knew our movements were being closely watched.

Meanwhile, Princess Helen, who had become the most popular figure in Leghorn, and had given her patronage to

"I SAW THE TALL DARK FIGURE OF A MAN IN A GREY DEERSTALKER HAT JOIN HER, AND SIT DOWN UNCEREMONIOUSLY AT HER SIDE."

several functions in the cause of charity, went out a great deal, and I accompanied her very frequently to the best houses.

"Poor Bindo is having a pretty quiet time, I fear," she laughed to me one day in her easy irresponsible way. "He is lying low."

"Waiting for the *coup*—eh ? "

She smiled, but would, even then, tell me nothing.

Among the most devoted of her admirers was the Jew banker of Turin, named Jacobi, and his wife, a stout, vulgar, over-dressed person, who was constantly dancing attendance upon her "dear Princess," as she called her. Valentine rather liked her, or pretended to, for on several occasions she lent her Rosalie to dress her hair. Jacobi himself was, it seemed, on friendly terms with Bindo. Sometimes I saw the pair strolling together at Pancaldi's, and once the young Marquis of Rapallo was with them.

One hot, stifling night, a brilliant ball was held, arranged at the Princess's instigation, in the cause of charity. All the smart world attended, and dancing was almost at an end when Bindo met me alone out upon one of the balconies.

"Go and change at once," he whispered. "Take the car out of the town beyond the railway-station, a little way on the Pisa road. There wait, but attract no attention." And the next instant he had re-entered the ball-room, and was making his most elegant bow over a lady's hand.

Wondering what was the nature of the *coup*, I presently slipped away to my room, but as I walked along the corridor I felt almost certain that I saw Rosalie's black skirts flouncing round the corner. It was as though I had discovered her on the wrong floor, and that she had tried to escape me. The movements of that girl were so constantly suspicious.

I threw off my evening-clothes, and putting on a rough suit, an overcoat, and motor cap, went down the back staircase and along to the garage, where, amid the coming and going of the cars, of departing guests, I was able to run out without being noticed.

Ten minutes later I was outside the town, and drawing up in the dark lonely road that leads across the plain for fifteen miles to quaint old Pisa, I got down and examined my tyres, pretending I had a puncture should anyone become too inquisitive. Glancing at my watch I found it was already twenty minutes to two. The moon was overcast, and the atmosphere stifling and oppressive, pre-cursory of a thunderstorm.

Each minute seemed an hour. Indeed, I grew so nervous that I felt half-inclined to escape upon the car. Yet if I left that spot I might leave my audacious friend in the lurch, and in peril of arrest most likely.

It was close upon half-past two, as nearly as I could judge, when I heard a quick footstep in the road. I took off one of the acetylene head-lamps of the car and turned it in that direction in order to ascertain who was coming along.

A woman in a dark stiff dress, and wear-ing a veil approached quickly. A mo-ment later, to my mingled surprise and dismay, I saw it was none other than the dainty Rosalie herself, in a very admirable disguise, which gave her an appearance of being double her age.

"Ah ! Monsieur ! " she gasped, quite out of breath from walking so rapidly. "Drive me at once to Pisa. Don't lose a single instant. The Paris express passes at four minutes past three, and I must catch it. The last train left here three hours ago."

"You—alone ? "

"Yes. I go alone."

"But—well, let us speak quite frankly. Is no one else coming ? " I inquired.

"*Non, M'sieur*. You will take me to Pisa at once, please," she said impatiently.

So perforce I had to mount into the car, and when she had settled herself beside me, I drew off upon the dark and execrable road to the city she had indicated in order to catch the Rome-Paris express.

Was it all a trap, I wondered ? What had occurred ? I dared not ask her any-thing, while, she, on her part, preserved an absolute silence. Her only fear seemed lest she lost her train. That something had occurred was very evident, but of its nature I still remained in entire ignorance, even when, a short distance from the great echoing station, I dropped the *chic* little maid with whom I had for the past three weeks pretended to be so violently in love.

On getting down she told me to await her. She would be only a few minutes. This surprised me, as I thought she was leaving for Paris.

She hurried away, and as I watched her going down the road towards the station I saw the dark figure of a man emerge from the shadow and join her. For a moment he became silhouetted against the station lights, and I recognised that it was her mysterious friend.

Five minutes later she rejoined me. Then, on turning back, I was forced to remain at the level-crossing until the Paris express, with its long *wagon-lit*, had roared past, and afterwards I put on a move, and we were soon back in Leghorn. She did not return to the hotel with me, but at her request I dropped her just before we entered the town.

Morning revealed the startling truth. Three women, occupying adjacent rooms, had lost the greater part of their valuable jewels which they had had sent from home on purpose to wear at the ball. The police were ferreting about the hotel questioning everybody. There was commotion everywhere, and loud among those expressing amazement at the audaciousness of the thief were both Bindo and her Highness, the latter declaring herself lucky that no attempt had been made to secure any of her own valuable jewels.

At noon I took her for a run on the car, in order to have an opportunity to chat. When we were alone on the road she said—

"You entertained a foolish but quite reasonable suspicion of Rosalie. She and Kampf, the man you saw her with, always work together. They indeed suggested this present little affair, for they knew that Italian women bring lots of jewellery here, in order to show it off. Besides, hotels are their speciality. So there seemed to Bindo no reason why we should not have a little of the best of it. The diamond necklace of the Signora Jacobi is well known to be one of the finest in all Italy; therefore, on several occasions, I lent her Rosalie for hairdressing, and she, clever girl, very soon discovered where all the best of the stuff was kept. Bindo, in the meantime, was keeping his keen eye open in other quarters. Last night, when the Jewess went up to her room, she found her own maid had gone to bed very unwell, and the faithful Rosalie had, at my orders, taken her place. 'How kind it was of the dear Princess,' she said! When Rosalie left the room she carried with her the necklace, together with several other trifles which she had pretended to lock in the jewel-case. Ten minutes later Bindo also slipped into her hands all that he had obtained in a swift raid in two other rooms during the dance, and she left the hotel carrying away gems worth roughly, we believe, about sixteen thousand pounds sterling. Kampf was awaiting her in Pisa, and by this time is already well on his way to the frontier at Modane, with the precious packet in his pocket."

"And there is really no suspicion upon us?" I asked apprehensively.

"Certainly not. Not a soul knows that Rosalie left the hotel last night. She re-entered by a window Bindo left open."

"But the garage people know that I was out," I said.

"Well, and what of that? You have had no hand in it, have you, *mon cher?* No. We shall remain here another week. It is quite pleasant here—and quite safe. To leave might arouse suspicion."

"Have not the police questioned Rosalie?"

"Certainly. But they have no suspicion of the maid of Princess Helen of Dornbach-Laxenburg. How could they? Especially as the Prefect and his wife were my guests at dinner last night!"

"Well," I declared, "the way the whole affair has been managed is perfectly artistic."

"Of course," she said. "We do not blunder. Only poor people and fools do that."

THE COUNT'S CHAUFFEUR.

By WILLIAM LE QUEUX.

No. 5.--THE SIX NEW NOVELS.

THE car had again undergone a transformation.

With a new racing-body, built in Northampton, and painted in white picked out with gilt, no one would have recognised it as the car which had carried away the clever jewel-thief from Bond Street.

Since the adventure at Leghorn I had seen nothing of La Belle Valentine. With Bindo, however, I had driven the car across from Rome to Calais by way of Ventimiglia and Marseilles, and, after crossing the Channel I had gone alone to Northampton, and there awaited the making of the smart new racing-body.

Count Bindo di Ferraris, who seemed ever on the move with an eye open for " a good thing," wrote me from Ilfracombe, Southampton, Manchester, Perth, Aberdeen, and other places, remitting me the necessary money, and urging me to push on the work, as he wanted the car again immediately.

At last, when it was finished, I drove it to a garage I knew at the back of Regent Street, and that same evening met him at the Automobile Club. At his request, I dressed smartly and gave no outward appearance of the chauffeur; therefore he invited me to dine, and afterwards, while we sat alone in a corner of the smoking-room, he began to unfold a series of plans for the future. They were, however, hazy, and only conveyed to me an idea that we were going on a long tour in England.

I ventured to remark that to be in England, after the little affair in Bond Street, might be somewhat dangerous. He replied, however, with his usual nonchalant air :

" My dear Ewart, there's not the slightest fear. Act as I bid, and trust in me. To-morrow, at eleven, we go north together — into Yorkshire. You will be my servant again after to-night. You understand—eh ? "

" Perfectly. Shall we start from here ? "

" Yes. But before we set out I can only warn you that you'll want all your wits about you this time. If we have luck, we shall bring off a big thing—a very big thing."

" And if we have no luck ? "

" Well—well, we shan't bring it off—that's all," he laughed.

" Where are we going ? "

" Yorkshire. To spend a week at the seaside. It will do us both good. I've decided that the Scarborough air will be extremely beneficial to us. One of our friends is already there—at the Grand."

" Sir Charles ? "

" Exactly. He's very fond of Scarborough—likes the church parade on Sundays, the music on the Spa, and all that kind of thing. So we'll join him. I wonder if we shall get through in a day ? "

" We ought to—with luck," was my response, and then, after urging me to leave everything in his hands, he told me that I'd better get early to bed, and thoroughly overhaul the car early next morning before starting.

So next day at ten he took his seat by my side outside the club in Piccadilly, and we drove away into the traffic towards Regent's Park on our way to that much overrated highway, the Great North Road. The day was warm and dusty, and as it was a Saturday there were police traps out everywhere. Therefore progress was slow, for I was forced at every few miles to slow down to escape a ten-pound fine.

Leafy Hatfield, crooked Hitchin, quaint old Stamford, we passed until we swung into the yard of " The Angel," that antique and comfortable hotel well known to all motorists at Grantham, where we had a hasty meal.

Then out again in the sunset, we headed

through Doncaster to York, and in the darkness, with our big head-lamps shining, we tore through Malton and slipped down the hill into Scarborough. The run had been a long and dusty one, the last fifty miles in darkness and at a high speed, therefore when we pulled up before the Grand I leaned heavily upon the steering-wheel, weary and fagged.

It was about eleven o'clock at night, and Sir Charles, who had evidently been expecting our arrival in the big hall of the hotel, rushed out and greeted Bindo effusively. Then, directed by a page-boy, who sat in the Count's seat, I took the car round to Hutton's garage, close by.

With Sir Charles I noticed another man, young, with very fair hair—a mere boy, he seemed—in evening clothes of the latest cut. When I returned to the hotel I saw them all seated in the big hall over whiskies and sodas, laughing merrily together. It was late, and all the other guests had retired.

Next day Bindo took the young man, whose name I discovered to be Paul Clayton, for a run on the car to Bridlington. Bindo drove, and I sat upon the step. The racing-body gave the "forty" a rakish appearance, and each time we went up and down the Esplanade, or across the Valley Bridge, we created considerable interest. After lunch we went on to Hornsea, and returned to Scarborough at tea-time.

That same evening, after dinner, I saw Bindo's new friend walking on the Esplanade with a fair-haired, well-dressed young girl. They were deep in conversation, and it struck me that she was warning him regarding something.

Days passed—warm, idle August days. Scarborough was full of visitors. The Grand was overrun by a smartly-dressed crowd, and the Spa was a picturesque sight during the morning promenade. The beautiful "Belvedere" grounds were a blaze of roses, and, being private property, were regarded with envy by thousands who trod the asphalte of the Esplanade. Almost daily Bindo took Paul for a run on the car. To York, to Castle Howard, to Driffield, and to Whitby we went—the road to the last-named place, by the way, being execrable. Evidently Bindo's present object was to

ingratiate himself with young Clayton, but with what ulterior motive I could not conceive.

Sir Charles remained constantly in the background. Well-dressed and highly respectable, he presented a rather superior air, and walked on the Spa at certain hours, establishing a kind of custom from which he did not depart. He had now changed his name to Sinclair, while Bindo Ferraris went under the less foreign cognomen of Albert Cornforth. I alone kept my own name, George Ewart.

As day succeeded day, I kept wondering what was really in the wind. Why were they so friendly with Paul Clayton ? Of one fact I felt assured, and it was that jewels were not the object of the manœuvre on this occasion. That Bindo and his friends had laid some deep plot was, of course, quite certain, but the Count never took me into his confidence until the last moment, when the *coup* was made. Therefore, try how I would, I could not discover the intentions of the gang.

From Leghorn to Scarborough is a far cry. At least we were safe from detection for all our little business affairs, save that of the Bond Street jewellers. Continually I reflected that our description had been circulated by the police, and that some enterprising constable or detective might pick upon us on the off-chance of being correct.

Count Bindo—or Albert Cornforth, as he now chose to be known—was having a most excellent time. He soon grew to know many people in the hotel, and being so essentially a ladies' man was greatly in request at the dances. Continually he apologised to the ladies for being unable to take them motoring, but, as he explained, the space on a racing-car is limited.

Thus a fortnight passed. Round at the garage were a number of cars from London, Manchester, and elsewhere, and I soon grew friendly with several expert chauffeurs, two of whom were old friends.

One day Bindo and I had been to Harrogate, dined at the Majestic, and returned. After taking the car to the garage I went out for a turn along the Esplanade, in order to stretch my legs. It was midnight, brightly starlit, and silent save for the low soughing of the waves upon the shore. I had lit my pipe and walked nearly to the Holbeck Gardens at the extreme end of the South of their faces. One was Paul Clayton and the other the pretty, fair-haired young woman I had seen him with before. They were sitting in the attitude

"SHE SEEMED CONSTANTLY ALARMED LEST I SHOULD FALL OFF"

Cliff when, in the darkness, I discerned two figures sitting upon a seat in the shadow. One was a man, and the other a woman in a light evening dress, with a wrap thrown over her head and shoulders. As I passed I managed to get a glimpse of lovers. He held her hand and, I believe, had just raised it to his lips.

I hurried on, annoyed with myself for being so inquisitive. But the beautiful face of the girl became impressed upon my memory.

Count Bindo, the nonchalant, audacious cosmopolitan, who spent money so freely, was a veritable marvel of cleverness and cunning in all matters of chicanery and fraud. He was evidently a man who, though still young, had a pretty dark record. But what it really was he carefully concealed from me. I can only admit that I had now become an adventurer like the others, for in each case I had received a certain portion of the profits of the *coups* which we had assisted each other in effecting. True, we lived a life full of excitement and change, but it was a life I liked, for at heart I was nothing if not a wanderer and adventurer. I liked adventure for adventure's sake, and cared nothing for the constant peril of detection. Strange how easily one can be enticed from a life of honesty into one of fraud, especially if the inducements held out are an adequate recompense for any qualm of conscience.

The actions of our friend, Sir Charles Blythe, were also rather puzzling. He seemed to be taking no part in whatever scheme was in progress. If I met him in public on the Esplanade, or elsewhere, I saluted him as a chauffeur should, but when we met unobserved I was his equal, and on several occasions I made inquiries which he refused to satisfy.

We had been nearly three weeks in Scarborough when, after dinner, one evening in the big hall of the hotel I saw the audacious Bindo seated drinking coffee with a little queer, wizen-faced but rather over-dressed old lady, towards whom he seemed to be particularly polite. She was evidently one of those wrinkled, yellow-toothed old tabbies who still believe themselves to be attractive, for, as I watched covertly, I saw how she assumed various poses for the benefit of those seated in her vicinity. Though so strikingly dressed, in a gown trimmed with beautiful old lace, she wore no jewellery, save her wedding-ring. Her airs and mannerisms were, however, amusing, and quickly made it apparent that she moved in a good set.

From the hall-porter I presently learned that she was a Mrs. Clayton, of St. Mellions Hall, near Peterborough, the widow of a wealthy Oldham cotton-spinner, who generally spent a month at that hotel each year.

"She's a quaint old girl," he informed me in confidence. "Thinks no end of herself, and always trying to hang on to some woman with a title, even if she's only a knight's wife. Some ill-natured woman has nicknamed her the Chameleon —because she changes her dresses so often and is so fond of bright colours. But she's a good old sort," he added. "Always pretty free with her tips. Her son is here, too."

Whoever or whatever she was, it was evident that Bindo was busily engaged ingratiating himself with her, having previously established a firm friendship with her son, who, by the way, had left Scarborough on the previous day.

I happened to have a friend who was chauffeur to a doctor in Peterborough, therefore I wrote to him that evening, making inquiries regarding St. Mellions and its owner. Three days later a reply came to the effect that the Hall was about ten miles from Peterborough, and one of the finest country seats in Northamptonshire. It had been the property of a well-known Earl who, having become impoverished by gambling, had sold it, together with the great estate, to old Joshua Clayton, the Lancashire millionaire. "She keeps a couple of cars," my friend concluded. "One is a Humber voiturette, and the other a twenty-four Mercedes. You know her chauffeur— Saunders—from the Napier works."

Of course I knew Saunders. He was once a very intimate friend of mine, but for the past couple of years I had lost sight of him.

Why, I wondered, was Bindo so intensely interested in the over-dressed old crone? He walked with her constantly on the Spa or along the Esplanade; he lounged at her side when she sat to watch the parading summer girls and their flirtations, and he idled at coffee with her every evening. After a few days Sir Charles Blythe, alias Sinclair, was introduced. By pre-arrangement the bogus baronet chanced to be standing by the railings looking over the Spa grounds one morning when Bindo and his companion strolled by. The men saluted each other, and Bindo asked

Mrs. Clayton's leave to introduce his friend. The instant the magic title was spoken the old lady became full of smiles and graces, and the trio walking together passed along in the direction of Holbeck.

Two days later Henderson appeared on the scene quite suddenly. I was walking along Westborough late one evening when somebody accosted me, and, turning, I found it was our friend—whom I believed to be still on the Continent. He was dressed as foppishly as usual, and certainly betrayed no evidence that he was a "crook."

"Well, Ewart?" he asked. "And how goes things? Who's this old crone we've got in tow? A soft thing, Bindo says."

I told him all I knew concerning her, and he appeared to be reassured. He had taken a room at the Grand, he told me, and I afterwards found that on the following morning Bindo pretended to discover him at the hotel and introduced him to the unsuspecting old lady as young Lord Kelham. Mrs. Clayton was delighted at thus extending her acquaintanceship with England's bluest blood.

That same afternoon the old lady, who seemed to be of a rather sporting turn of mind, expressed a desire to ride upon a racing-car; therefore I brought round the forty, and Bindo drove her over to Malton, where we had tea, and a quick run back in the evening. There are no police-traps on the road between Scarborough and York, therefore we were able to put on a move, and the old lady expressed the keenest delight at going so fast. As I sat upon the step at her feet, she seemed constantly alarmed lest I should fall off.

"My own cars never go so quickly," she declared. "My man drives at snail's pace."

"Probably because you have traps in Northamptonshire," Bindo replied. "There are always lurking constables along the Great North Road and the highways leading into it. But you must let me come and take your driver's place for a little while. If the cars are worth anything at all I'll get the last mile out of them."

"I only wish you would come and pay me a visit, Mr. Cornforth. I should be so very delighted. Do you shoot?"

"A little," Bindo answered. "My friend, Sir Charles Sinclair, is said to be one of the best shots in England. But I'm not much of a shot myself."

"Then can't you persuade him to come with you?"

"Well, I'll ask him," my employer replied. "He has very many engagements, however. He's so well known, you see."

"He'll come if you persuade him, I'm sure," the old lady said, with what she believed to be a winning smile. "You can drive my Mercedes, and he can shoot. I always have a house-party through September, so you both must join it. I'll make you as comfortable as I can in my humble house. Paul will be at home."

"Humble, Mrs. Clayton? Why, I have years ago heard St. Mellions spoken of as one of the show-houses of the Midlands."

"Then you've heard an exaggeration, my dear Mr. Cornforth," was her response, as she laughed lightly. "Remember, I shall expect you, and you can bring your own car if you like. Our roads are fairly good, you'll find."

Bindo accepted with profuse thanks, and shot me a glance by which I knew that he had advanced one step further towards the consummation of his secret intentions—whatever they were. Sir Charles would, no doubt, go with us. What, I wondered, was intended?

Three weeks later we arrived one evening at St. Mellions, and found it a magnificent old Tudor mansion, in the centre of a lordly domain, and approached from the high road by a great beech avenue nearly a mile in length. The older wing of the house—part of an ancient Gothic abbey—was ivy-covered, while in front of the place was a great lake, originally the fish-pond of the Carmelite monks.

It wanted an hour before dinner when we arrived, and at sound of our horn nearly a dozen men and women of the house-party came forth to greet us.

"They seem a pretty smart crowd," remarked Bindo under his breath to Sir Charles, seated beside him.

"Yes, but we'll want all our wits

about us," replied the other. "I hear that the wife of Gilling, the jeweller in Bond Street, is here with her daughter. Suppose her husband takes it into his head to run down here for the week-end—eh ? "

"We won't suppose anything of the sort, my dear fellow. I always hate supposing. It's a bad habit when you've got your living to earn, as we have."

And with those words he ran along to the main entrance, and pulled up sharply, being greeted by our hostess herself, who, in a cream serge dress, stood upon the steps and shouted us a warm welcome.

My two friends were quickly introduced by Paul to the assembled party, while several of the men came around the car to admire it, one of them questioning me as to its horse-power, its make, and other details, inquiries which showed his ignorance. Round in the garage I found my friend Saunders, and later on he took me over the splendid old place, filled as it was with the relics of the noble but now decadent English family.

My eyes and ears were open everywhere. The house-party, numbering eighteen, consisted mostly of the parvenu set, people who having made money by trade were attempting to pass as county families. The men possessed for the most part the air of " the City " and the womenkind were painfully "smart" without the good breeding necessary to carry it off.

After dinner, under the guidance of Saunders, I managed to get a glimpse of the great hall, where the party had assembled for coffee. It was a fine, lofty, oak-panelled old place, once the refectory of the monks, with great Gothic windows of stained glass, antique cabinets, and stands of armour. Against the dark oak, from floor to ceiling, the dresses of the women showed well, and, amid the laughter and chatter, I saw the gay, careless Bindo—a well set-up, manly figure in his evening clothes—standing beside his hostess, chatting and laughing with her, while Sir Charles was bending over the chair of a pretty fair-haired girl in turquoise, whom I recognised as the same girl I had seen with Paul at Scarborough. Her name was Ethel

Gilling, Saunders said, and told me that young Clayton was, in secret, deeply in love with her. Would her father arrive and put a premature end to our conspiracy ? I feared that he might.

Saunders asked me a good deal about my berth and position, and I fancy he envied me. He did not know that I had become a " crook " like my master, but believed me to be a mere chauffeur whose duties took him hither and thither across Europe. No chauffeur can bear private service with a cheap car in a circumscribed area. Every man who drives a motor-car—whether master or servant—longs for wide touring and a high-power car.

Contrary to Bindo's declaration, he proved to be a very good shot, while Sir Charles provoked the admiration of all the men when, next morning, they went forth in search of birds. That same afternoon Bindo drove the Mercedes containing Mrs. Clayton and three ladies, of the party, while I drove one of the men—a Captain Halliday—in our own car, and we all went over to the ruins of Crowland Abbey. Saunders had told me that he had never driven the Mercedes to her full power, as his mistress was so nervous. But, with Bindo driving, the old lady now seemed to want to go faster and faster. Our car was, of course, the more powerful, and ere we had gone ten miles I put on full speed, and passed my master with ease, arriving at Crowland fully twenty minutes before him.

It was, however, very apparent that Bindo, the good-looking adventurer, had wormed himself entirely into the Chameleon's good graces. Both he and Halliday escorted the ladies over the ruins, and after tea at the old-fashioned " George " we made a quick and enjoyable run home in the sunset by way of Eye, Peterborough, Castor, and Wansford.

The autumn days went by, and, amid such pleasant surroundings, our visit was proving a most merry one. Yet, try how I would, I could not see what Bindo and his friend intended.

The girl in turquoise who flirted so outrageously with young Clayton was, I discovered, also very friendly with Sir Charles. Then I saw that his partiality towards her was with a distinct object—

namely, in order to be aware of her father's movements.

Truly, Bindo and Blythe were past-masters in the art of genteel scoundrelism. Adventurers of the very first water, they seldom, if ever, let me into their secrets until their plans were actually matured. Their reason for this reticence was that they believed I might show the white feather. They could not yet rely upon my audacity or courage.

Within a week Bindo was the most popular man in the house-party, the humorist of the dinner-table, and an expert in practical jokes, of which many were being played, one half the party being pitted against the other half, as is so often the case.

In the servants' hall we were also having a pretty merry time. Medhurst, the maid of Mrs. Clayton, was a particularly prepossessing young woman, and I had many chats and a few walks with her. From her, at Bindo's instigation, I learned a good deal regarding her mistress's habits and tastes, all of which I, in due course, reported to my master. A shrewd girl was Medhurst, however, and I was compelled to exercise a good deal of judicious tact in putting my questions to her.

One evening, however, while sitting alone in the park smoking, just before going to bed, I saw Bindo himself strolling at her side. She was speaking softly, but what about I could not make out. They were in a part of the park into which the guests never went, and it seemed as though she had kept a secret tryst. Not wishing to disturb them, I slipped away unobserved.

Next morning Paul Clayton went up to London in order to see his mother's solicitors, and that same afternoon, about four o'clock, Mrs. Clayton received a very urgent telegram to come at once, as her lawyers desired some instructions immediately. The message she received evidently caused her very great anxiety, for she took Medhurst, and drove in the Mercedes to Peterborough station, where she caught the up-express at seven o'clock.

She had apologised to her house-party for her absence, explained the urgency of her presence in London, and promised to be back in time for dinner on the morrow.

She left the Hall at half-past six. At seven Bindo called me out of the servants' hall and whispered :

" Hold yourself in readiness. Go to my room at nine punctually, and you'll find on the table half-a-dozen novels done up in a strap. Just take them carefully, put them in the car, and then get away, first to Northampton to change the body, and then to Harwich. Wait for me there at the Great Eastern Hotel, in the name of Parker. Take great care of the books. I shall give you other instructions before people presently, but take no notice of them. I'll join you as soon as it's safe."

And with that he turned upon his heel and left me.

The dressing-gong was just sounding as I walked across to the garage in order to look through the car and charge the lamps, prior to my night journey. I was wondering what was about to happen. That some *coup* was to be made that night was very evident. I spent half-an-hour on the car, and had all in order, when a servant came to say that my master wanted me.

I found Bindo in the hall, laughing gaily with some ladies, prior to going in to dinner.

" Oh, Ewart," he said, when I entered, cap in hand. " I want you to run the car over to Birmingham to-night, and bring Colonel Fielding here to-morrow. You know where he lives—at Welford Park. He's expecting you. The roads are all right, so you'll make good time. You'd better get a couple of outer covers too, when you're there. You'll bring the Colonel back in time for dinner to-morrow—you understand ! "

" Yes, sir," I replied, and, bowing, went out, while with the ladies he turned in the direction of the dining-room.

I idled about until the stable clock was just on the point of striking nine, when I made my way by the servants' staircase to my master's room. The corridor was in semi-darkness. I rapped, but there being no one there, I entered, switched on the light, and there upon the table found the small pile of new, cloth-bound six-shilling novels, held together with a strap of webbing, such as lawyers use to tie up their papers.

I took them up, switched off the light, and carried them downstairs to the car, which I had previously brought out into the stable-yard. My lamps were already lit, and I was in the act of putting on my frieze coat when Saunders, driving the Mercedes, passed me, going towards the main entrance of the Hall. He had a passenger—a guest from the station, judging from his dress.

As the stranger descended from the car the light over the steps revealed his face. I started. It was the jeweller I had spoken to in Bond Street—the man I had taken for the manager, but who was none other than Mr. Gilling himself!

I saw that all was lost. In a few moments he would come face to face with Bindo!

In an instant, however, I had made up my mind, and, re-entering the house, I made my way quickly through into the large hall. But Gilling was already there, kissing his wife and daughter. I glanced round, but was reassured to see both Bindo and Sir Charles were absentees. Did they know of Gilling's impending arrival?

I ran up to the rooms of both my friends, but could not find them. In Bindo's room a dress-coat had been thrown upon the bed. He had changed since I had been up there for the books. Alarmed by the news of the jeweller's arrival, they had, in all probability, changed hurriedly and slipped away. Therefore I ran down to the car, and, telling Saunders that I was off to Birmingham and should return on the morrow, I ran quietly down the long dark avenue.

From St. Mellions to Harwich, as the crow flies, is about one hundred and thirty miles. First, however, I went to Northampton, and put the previous body on the car. Then the road I took was by Huntingdon, Cambridge, Halstead, and Colchester—in all, about 170 miles. The night was dark, but the roads were in fairly good condition, therefore I went at as high a speed as I dare, full of wonder as to what had really happened.

Bindo's dress-coat on the bed showed that he had left, therefore I had every hope that he had not been recog- nised by the jeweller. After I had changed the body at the coachbuilder's at Northampton, the run to the Essex coast proved an exciting one, for I had one narrow escape at a level crossing. But to give details of the journey would serve no purpose. Suffice it to say that I duly arrived at the Great Eastern Hotel at Harwich next morning, and registered there in the name of Parker.

Then I waited in patience until, two days later, I received a note from Bindo, and met him at some distance from the hotel. His personal appearance was greatly altered, and he was shabbily dressed as a chauffeur.

"By Jove!" he said, when we were alone. "We've had a narrow squeak. We had no idea when Henderson sent the telegram from London calling the old crone up to town that Gilling had been invited. We only heard of his impending arrival at the very moment we were bringing off the *coup*. Then, instead of remaining there, becoming indignant, and assisting the police, we were compelled to fly, and thus give the whole game away. If we had stayed Gilling would have recognised us. By Jove! I never had such a tough quarter of an hour in all my life. Blythe has gone up to Scotland, and we shall ship the car across to Hamburg by to-night's boat from Parkeston. You've got those books all right. Don't lose them."

"I've left them in the car," I replied.

"Left them in the car!" he cried, glaring at me. "Are you mad?"

"Mad! Why?"

"Go and get them at once and lock them up in your bag. I'll show you something when we get an opportunity."

The opportunity came three days later, when we were alone together in a room in Höfer's Hotel, in the Bahnhofs-Platz in Hamburg. He took the books from me, undid the buckle, and, to my surprise, showed me that the centres of the popular books had been cleverly cut out, so that they were literally boxes formed by the paper leaves. And each book was filled with splendid jewels!

The haul was a huge one, for several of the diamond ornaments which had been taken from the Chameleon's safe were of enormous value. The old lady was passionately fond of jewellery, and spent huge sums with Mr. Gilling. We afterwards discovered that several of the finest pieces we had taken had actually been sent to her on approval by Gilling, so, curiously enough, we had touched his property on a second occasion.

"It was a difficult affair," Bindo declared. "I had to pretend to make love to Medhurst, or I should never have been able to get a cast of the safe-key. However, we've been able to take the best of the old lady's collection, and they'll fetch a good price in Amsterdam, or I'm a Dutchman myself. Of course, there's a big hue-and-cry after us, so we must lie very low over here for a bit. Fancy your leaving those novels kicking about in the car! Somebody might have wanted to read them!"

"HE UNDID THE BUCKLE, AND SHOWED ME THAT THE CENTRES OF THE POPULAR BOOKS HAD BEEN CLEVERLY CUT OUT."

XVII

Followed

L.T. MEADE and ROBERT EUSTACE

Followed.

By L. T. Meade and Robert Eustace.

AM David Ross's wife. I was married to him a month ago. I have lived through the peril and escaped the danger. What I have lived through, how it happened, and why it happened, this story tells.

My maiden name was Flower Dalrymple. I spent my early days on the Continent, travelling about from place to place and learning much of Bohemian life and Bohemian ways. When I was eighteen years of age my father got an appointment in London. We went to live there—my father, my mother, two brothers, a sister, and myself. Before I was twenty I was engaged to David Ross. David was a landed proprietor. He had good means, and was in my eyes the finest fellow in the world. In appearance he was stalwart and broad-shouldered, with a complexion as dark as a gipsy. He had a passionate and almost wild look in his eyes, and his wooing of me was very determined, and I might almost say stormy.

When first he proposed for me I refused him from a curious and unaccountable sense of fear, but that night I was miserable, and when two days after he repeated his offer, I accepted him, for I discovered that, whatever his character, he was the man I could alone love in all the world.

He told me something of his history. His father had died when he was a baby, and he had spent all the intervening years, except when at school and the University, with his mother. His mother's name was Lady Sarah Ross. On her own mother's side she was of Spanish extraction, but she was the daughter of Earl Reighley. She was a great recluse, and David gave me to understand that her character and ways of life were peculiar.

"You must be prepared for eccentricities in connection with my mother," he said. "I see her, perhaps, through rose-coloured spectacles, for she is to me the finest and the most interesting woman, with the exception of yourself, in the world. Her love for me is a very strange and a very deep passion. She has always opposed the idea of my marrying. Until I met you, I have yielded to her very marked wishes in this respect. I can do so no longer. All the same, I am almost afraid to tell her that we are engaged."

"Your account of your mother is rather alarming," I could not help saying. "Must I live with her after we are married, David?"

"Certainly not," he answered, with some abruptness. "You and I live at my place, Longmore; she goes to the Dower House."

"She will feel being deposed from her throne very acutely," I said.

"It will be our object in life, Flower, not to let her feel it," he answered. "I look forward with the deepest interest to your conquering her, to your winning her love. When you once win it, it is yours for ever."

All the time David was speaking I felt that he was hiding something. He was holding himself in check. With all his pluck and dash and daring, there was a weight on his mind, something which caused him, although he would not admit it, a curious sensation of uneasiness.

We had been engaged for a fortnight when he wrote to Lady Sarah apprising her of the fact. His letter received no answer. After a week, by his request, I wrote to her, but neither did she notice my letter.

At last, a month after our letters were written, I received a very cordial invitation from Lady Sarah. She invited me to spend Christmas with David and herself at Longmore. She apologized for her apparent rudeness in not writing sooner, but said she had not been well. She would give me, she said, a very hearty welcome, and hoped I would visit the old place in the second week in December and remain over Christmas.

"You will have a quiet time," she wrote, "not dull, for you will be with David; but if you are accustomed to London and the ways of society, you must not expect to find them at Longmore."

Of course I accepted her invitation. Our wedding was to take place on the 10th of January. My trousseau was well under way, and I started for Longmore on a certain snowy afternoon, determined to enjoy myself and to like Lady Sarah in spite of her eccentricities.

Longmore was a rambling old place situated on the borders of Salisbury Plain. The house was built in the form of a cross. The roof was turreted, and there was a tower at one end. The new rooms were in a distant wing. The centre of the cross, forming the body of the house, was very old, dating back many hundreds of years.

David came to meet me at Salisbury. He drove a mail phaeton, and I clambered up to my seat by his side. A pair of thoroughbred black horses were harnessed to the carriage. David touched the arched neck of one of his favourites with his whip, and we flew through the air.

It was a moonlight night, and I looked at David once or twice. I had never regarded him as faultless, but I now saw something in his appearance which surprised me. It was arbitrary and haughty. He had a fierce way of speaking to the man who sat behind. I could guess that his temper was overbearing.

"I NOW SAW SOMETHING IN HIS APPEARANCE WHICH SURPRISED ME."

Never mind! No girl could care for David Ross a little. She must love him with all her heart, and soul, and strength, or hate him. I cared for him all the more because of his faults. He was human, interesting, very tender when he chose, and he loved me with a great love.

We arrived at Longmore within an hour, and found Lady Sarah standing on the steps of the old house to welcome us. She was a tall and very stately woman, with black eyes and a swarthy complexion—a complexion unnaturally dark. Notwithstanding the grace of her appearance I noticed from the very first that there was something wild and uncanny about her. Her eyes were long and almond-shaped. Their usual expression was somewhat languid, but they had a habit of lighting up suddenly at the smallest provocation with a fierce and almost unholy fire. Her hair was abundant and white as snow, and her very black eyes, narrow-arched brows, and dark complexion were brought out into sharper contrast by this wealth of silvery hair.

She wore black velvet and some very fine Brussels lace, and as she came to meet me I saw the diamonds glittering on her fingers. Whatever her faults, few girls could desire a more picturesque mother-in-law.

Without uttering a word she held out both her hands and drew me into the great central hall. Then she turned me round and looked me all over in the firelight.

"Fair and *petite*," she said. "Blue eyes, lips indifferent red, rest of the features ordinary. An English girl by descent, by education, by appearance. Look me full in the face, Flower!"

I did what I was bid. She gazed from her superior height into my eyes. As my eyes met hers I was suddenly overpowered by the most extraordinary feeling which had ever visited me. All through my frame there ran a thrill of ghastly and overmastering fear. I shrank away from her, and I believe my face turned white. She drew me to her side again, stooped, and kissed me. Then she said, abruptly :—

"Don't be nervous "—and then she turned to her son.

"You have had a cold drive," she said. "I hope you have not taken a chill?"

"Dear me, no, mother. Why should I?" he replied, somewhat testily. "Flower and I enjoyed our rush through the air."

He was rubbing his hands and warming himself by the log fire as he spoke—now he came to me and drew me towards its genial blaze. Lady Sarah glanced at us both. I saw her lips quiver and her black brows meet across her forehead. A very strange expression narrowed her eyes, a vindictive look, from which I turned away.

She swept, rather than walked, across the hall and rang a bell. A neatly dressed, pleasant-looking girl appeared.

"Take Miss Dalrymple to her room, Jessie, and attend on her," said Lady Sarah.

I was conducted up some low stairs and down a passage to a pretty, modern-looking room.

"Longmore is very old, miss," said Jessie, "and some of it is even tumbling to pieces, but Lady Sarah is never one for repairs. You won't find anything old, however, in this room, miss, for it has not been built more than ten years. You will have a lovely view of Salisbury Plain from here in the morning. I am glad, very glad, Miss Dalrymple, that you are not put into one of the rooms in the other wing."

I did not ask Jessie the meaning of her words. I thought she looked at me in an expressive way, but I would not meet her glance.

When I was ready Jessie conducted me to the drawing-room, where I found David standing on the rug in front of a log fire.

"Where is your mother?" I asked.

"She will be down presently. I say, what a pretty little girl it is," he cried, and he opened his big arms and folded me in a close embrace.

Just at that moment I heard the rustle of a silk dress, and, turning, saw Lady Sarah.

She wore a rich ruby gown, which rustled and glistened every time she moved. I tore myself from David's arms and faced her. There was a flush on my cheeks, and my eyes, I am sure, were suspiciously bright. She called me to her side and began to talk in a gentle and pleasant way.

Suddenly she broke off.

"Dinner is late," she said. "Ring the bell, David."

David's summons was answered by a black servant : a man with the most peculiar and, I must add, forbidding face I had ever seen.

"Is dinner served, Sambo?" inquired his mistress.

"It is on the table, missis," he replied, in excellent English.

Lady Sarah got up.

"David," she said, "will you take Flower to her place at the dinner-table?"

David led the way with me ; Lady Sarah followed. David took the foot of the table, his mother the head. I sat at Lady Sarah's left hand.

During the meal which followed she seemed to forget all about me. She talked incessantly, on matters relating to the estate, to her son. I perceived that she was a first-rate business woman, and I noticed that David listened to her with respect and interest. Her eyes never raised themselves to meet his without a softened and extraordinary expression filling them. It was a look of devouring and overmastering love. His eyes, as he looked into hers, had very much the same expression. Even at me he had never looked quite like this. It was as if two kindred souls, absolutely kindred in all particulars, were holding converse one with the other, and as if I, David's affianced wife, only held the post of interloper.

Sambo, the black servant, stood behind Lady Sarah's chair. He made a striking figure. He was dressed in the long, soft, full trousers which Easterns wear. I learnt afterwards that Sambo was an aborigine from Australia, but Lady Sarah had a fancy to dress him as though he hailed from the Far East. The colour of his silken garments was a rich deep yellow. His short jacket was much embroidered in silver, and he had a yellow turban twisted round his swarthy head.

His waiting was the perfection of the art. He attended to your slightest wants, and never made any sound as he glided about the apartment. I did not like him, however; I felt nearly as uncomfortable in his presence as I did in that of Lady Sarah.

We lingered for some little time when the meal was over ; then Lady Sarah rose.

"SAMBO, THE BLACK SERVANT, STOOD BEHIND
LADY SARAH'S CHAIR."

"Come, Flower," she said.

She took my hand in one of hers.

"You will join us, David, when you have had your smoke," she continued, and she laid her shapely hand across her son's broad forehead.

He smiled at her.

"All right, madre," he said, "I shall not be long."

His black eyes fell from his mother's face to mine, and he smiled at me—a smile of such heart-whole devotion that my momentary depression vanished.

Lady Sarah took me into the drawing-room. There she made me seat myself in a low chair by her side, and began to talk.

"Has David never told you of my peculiar tastes, my peculiar recreations?"

"No," I replied; "all he has really told me about you, his mother, is that you love him with a very great love, and that he feared

our marriage would pain you."

"Tut!" she replied. "Do you imagine that a little creature like you can put a woman like me out? But we won't talk personal things to-night. I want you to see the great charm of my present life. You must know that I have for several years eschewed society. David has mingled with his kind, but I have stayed at home with my faithful servant Sambo and—my pets."

"Your pets!" I said; "dogs, horses?"

"Neither."

"Cats then, and perhaps birds?"

"I detest cats, and always poison any stray animals of that breed that come to Longmore. It is true I keep a few pigeons, but they are for a special use. I also keep rabbits for the same purpose."

"Then what kind of pets have you?" I asked.

"Reptiles," she said, shortly. "Would you like to see them?"

I longed to say to Lady Sarah that nothing would induce me to look at her horrible pets, but I was afraid. She gazed full at me, and I nodded my head. Her face was white, and her lips had taken on once more that hard, straight line which terrified me.

She rose from her seat, took my hand, and led me across the drawing-room into the hall. We crossed the hall to the left. Here she opened a baize door and motioned to me to follow her. We went down some stairs—they were narrow and winding. At the bottom of the stairs was a door. Lady Sarah took a key from her pocket, fitted it into the lock, and opened the door.

A blast of wintry air blew on my face, and some scattered, newly-fallen snow wetted my feet.

"I forgot about the snow," she said. "The reptile-house is only just across the yard. It is warm there ; but if you are afraid of wetting your feet, say so."

" I am not afraid," I replied.

" That is good. Then come with me."

She held up her ruby-coloured silk dress, and I caught a glimpse of her neat ankles and shapely feet.

At the other side of the stone yard was a building standing by itself and completely surrounded with a high fence of closely meshed wire netting. Lady Sarah opened a door in the fence with another key, then she locked it carefully behind her. With a third key she unfastened the door of the building itself. When she opened this door the air from within, hot and moist, struck on my face.

She pushed me in before her, and I stood just within the entrance while she lit a lantern. As the candle caught the flame I uttered a sudden cry, for against my arm, with only the glass between, I saw a huge mottled snake, which, startled by the sudden light, was coiling to and fro. Its black forked tongue flickered about its lips as if it were angry at being disturbed in its slumbers.

" WAKE UP, DARKEY ! "

I drew back from the glass quickly, and caught Lady Sarah's eyes fixed upon me with a strange smile.

" My pets are here," she said, " and this is one. I was a great traveller in my youth, as was my father before me. After my husband died I again went abroad. When David's education was finished he went with me. I inherit my father's taste for snakes and reptiles. I have lived for my pets for many long years now, and I fancy I possess the most superb private collection in the kingdom. Look for yourself, Flower. This is the *Vipera Nascicornis,* or in our English language the African nose-horned snake. Pray notice his flat head. He is a fine specimen, just nine feet long. I caught him myself on the Gold Coast, with my friend Jane Ashley."

" Is he—venomous ? " I asked. My lips trembled so that I could scarcely get out the words.

" Four hours for a man," was the laconic reply. " We count the degree of poison of a snake by the time a man lives after he is bitten. This fellow is, therefore, comparatively harmless. But see, here is the *Pseudechis Porphyriacus*—the black snake of Tasmania and Australia. His time is six minutes. Wake up, Darkey!" and she tapped the glass with her knuckles.

An enormous glistening coil, polished as ebony, moved, reared its head, and disappeared into the shadow of the wall.

I gave a visible shudder. Lady Sarah took no notice. She walked slowly between the cases, explaining various attributes and particulars with regard to her favourites.

" Here are puff adders," she said ; " here are ring snakes ; in this cage are whip snakes. Ah ! here is the dreaded moccasin from Florida—here are black vipers from the South African mountains and copper-heads from the Peruvian swamps. I have a pet name for each," she continued ; " they are as my younger children."

As she said the words it flashed across my

mind, for the first time, that, perhaps, Lady Sarah was not in her right senses. The next instant her calm and dignified voice dispelled my suspicions.

"I have shown you my treasures," she said; "I hope you think it a great honour. My father, the late Lord Reighley, had a passion for reptiles almost equal to my own. The one thing I regret about David is that he has not inherited it."

"But are you not afraid to keep your collection here?" I asked. "Do you not dread some of them escaping?"

"I take precautions," she said, shortly; "and as to any personal fear, I do not know the meaning of the word. My favourites know me, and after their fashion they love me."

As she spoke she slid back one of the iron doors and, reaching in her hand, took out a huge snake and deliberately whipped the creature round her neck.

"This is my dear old carpet snake," she said; "quite harmless. You can come close to him and touch him, if you like."

"No, thank you," I replied.

She put the snake back again and locked the door.

We returned to the drawing-room. I went and stood by the fire. I was trembling all over, but not altogether from the coldness of the atmosphere.

"You are nervous," said Lady Sarah. "I thought you brave a few minutes ago. The sight of my beauties has shocked you. Will you oblige me by not telling David to-night that I showed them to you?"

I bowed my head, and just at that moment David himself entered the room.

He went to the piano, and almost without prelude began to sing. He had a magnificent voice, like a great organ. Lady Sarah joined him. He and she sang together, the wildest, weirdest, most extraordinary songs I had ever listened to. They were mostly Spanish. Suddenly Lady Sarah took out her guitar and began to play—David accompanying her on the piano.

The music lasted for about an hour. Then Lady Sarah shut the piano.

"The little white English girl is very tired," she said. "Flower, you must go to bed immediately. Good-night."

When I reached my room I found Jessie waiting to attend on me. She asked me at once if I had seen the reptiles.

"Yes," I said.

"And aren't you nearly dead with terror of them, miss?"

"I am a little afraid of them," I said. "Is there any fear of their escaping?"

"Law, no, miss! Who would stay in the house if there were? You need not be frightened. But this is a queer house, very queer, all the same."

The next day after breakfast David asked me if I had seen his mother's pets.

"I have," I replied, "but she asked me not to mention the fact to you last night. David, I am afraid of them. Must they stay here when I come to live at Longmore?"

"The madre goes, and her darlings with her," he answered, and he gave a sigh, and a shadow crossed his face.

"You are sorry to part with your mother?" I said.

"I shall miss her," he replied. "Even you, Flower, cannot take the place my mother occupies in my heart. But I shall see her daily, and you are worth sacrificing something for, my little white English blossom."

"Why do you speak of me as if I were so essentially English?" I said.

"You look the part. You are very much like a flower of the field. Your pretty name, and your pretty ways, and your fair complexion foster the idea. Mother admires you; she thinks you very sweet to look at. Now come into the morning-room and talk to her."

That day, after lunch, it rained heavily. We were all in the morning-room, a somewhat dismal apartment, when David turned to his mother.

"By the way, madre," he said, "I want to have the jewels re-set for Flower."

"What do you say?" inquired his mother.

"I mean to have the diamonds and the other jewels re-set for my wife," he replied, slowly.

"I don't think it matters," said Lady Sarah.

"Matters!" cried David; "I don't understand you. Flower must have the jewels made up to suit her *petite* appearance. I should like her to see them. Will you give me the key of the safe and I will bring them into this room?"

"You can show them, of course," said Lady Sarah. She spoke in a careless tone.

He looked at her, shrugged his shoulders, and I was surprised to see an angry light leap into his eyes. He took the key without a word and left the room.

I sat down on the nearest window-ledge— a small, slight, very fair girl. No one could feel more uncomfortable and out of place.

David returned with several morocco cases. He put them on the table, then he opened them one by one. The treasures within were magnificent. There were necklets and bracelets and rings and tiaras innumerable. David fingered them, and Lady Sarah stood close by.

"This tiara is too heavy for you, Flower," said David, suddenly.

As he spoke, he picked up a magnificent circlet of flashing diamonds and laid them against my golden head. The next moment the ornament was rudely snatched away by Lady Sarah. She walked to a glass which stood between two windows and fitted the tiara over her own head.

"Too heavy for Flower, and it suits you, mother," said the young man, his eyes flashing with a sudden genuine admiration.

She laid the tiara on the table.

"Leave the things as they are for the present," she said. "It is not necessary to have them altered. You are marrying a flower, remember, and flowers of the field do not need this sort of adornment."

She tried to speak quietly, but her lips trembled and her words came in jerks.

"And I don't want to wear them," I cried. "I don't like them."

"That is speaking in a very childish way," said Lady Sarah.

"You must wear them when you are presented, dear," remarked David. "But there is time enough; I will put the things away for the present."

The jewels were returned to the safe, and I breathed a sigh of relief.

That night I was tired out and slept well, and as the next morning was a glorious one, more like spring than mid-winter, David proposed that he and I should spend the day driving about Salisbury Plain and seeing the celebrated stones.

He went to the stables to order the dog-

"HE LAID THEM AGAINST MY GOLDEN HEAD."

cart to be got ready, and I ran up to my room to put on my hat and warm jacket.

When I came back to the hall my future mother-in-law was standing there. Her face was calm and her expression mild and genial. She kissed me almost affectionately, and I went off with David in high spirits, my fears lulled to slumber.

He knew every inch of the famous Stonehenge, and told me many of the legends about its origin. There was one stone in particular which we spent some time in observing. It was inside the circle, a flat, broad stone, with a depression in the middle.

"This," said David, "is called the 'Slaughter Stone.' On this stone the Druids killed their victims."

"How interesting and how horrible!" I cried.

"THIS IS CALLED THE 'SLAUGHTER STONE.'"

Lady Sarah made no answer. After a pause, during which an expression of annoyance and displeasure visited her thin lips, she said :—

"An urgent telegram has arrived from our lawyers for David. He must go to town by the first train in the morning."

"I will come back to-morrow night, little girl," he said.

He patted me on my hand as he spoke, and I did not attempt to raise any objection. A moment later we went into the dining-room.

During the meal I was much disturbed by the persistent way in which Sambo watched me. Without exception, Sambo had the ugliest face I had ever seen. His eyes were far apart, and wildly staring out of his head. His features were twisted, he had very thick lips, and the whole of the lower part of his face was in undue prominence. But, ugly as he was in feature, there was a certain dignity about him. His very upright carriage, his very graceful movements, his very picturesque dress, could not but impress me, although, perhaps, in a measure they added to the uneasiness with which I regarded him. I tried to avoid his gaze, but whenever I raised my eyes I encountered his, and, in consequence, I had very little appetite for dinner.

The evening passed quickly, and again that night I slept well. When I awoke it was broad daylight, and Jessie was pouring hot water into a bath for me.

"Mr. Ross went off more than two hours ago, miss," she said. "He left a message that I was to be very attentive to you, so if you want anything I hope you will ask me."

"Certainly I will," I replied.

Jessie was a pretty girl, with a rosy face and bright, pleasant eyes. I saw her fix these eyes now upon my face—she came close to me.

"I am very glad you are going to marry

"It is true," he answered. "These stones, dating back into the ages of the past, have always had a queer fascination for me. I love them almost as much as my mother does. She often comes here when her nerves are not at their best and wanders about this magic circle for hours."

David told me many other legends. We lunched and had tea in the small town of Wilton, and did not return home until time for late dinner.

I went to my room, and saw nothing of Lady Sarah until I entered the drawing-room. I there found David and his mother in earnest conversation. His face looked full of annoyance.

"I am sorry," said Lady Sarah; "I am afraid, Flower, you will have to make up your mind to having a dull day alone with me to-morrow."

"But why dull?" interrupted David. "Flower will enjoy a day by herself with you, mother. She wants to know you, she wants to love you, as I trust you will soon love her."

Mr. Ross," she said, "and I am very glad that you will be mistress here, for if there was not to be a change soon, I could not stay."

"What do you mean?" I said.

She shrugged her shoulders significantly.

"This is a queer house," she said—"there are queer people in it, and there are queer things done in it, and—*there are the reptiles!*"

I gave an involuntary shiver.

"There are the reptiles," she repeated. "Lady Sarah and Sambo play tricks with them at times. Sambo has got a stuff that drives them nearly mad. When Lady Sarah is at her wildest he uses it. I have watched them when they didn't know I was looking: half-a-dozen of the snakes following Sambo as if they were demented, and Lady Sarah looking on and laughing! He puts the thing on his boots. I do not know what it is. They never hurt him. He flings the boots at them and they are quiet. Yes, it is a queer house, and I am afraid of the reptiles. By the way, miss, would you not like *me* to clean your boots for you?"

"Why so?" I asked. My face had turned white and my teeth were chattering. Her words unnerved me considerably.

"I will, if you like," she said. "Sambo sha'n't have them. Now, miss, I think you have everything you want."

She left me, and I dressed as quickly as I could. As I did so my eyes fell upon a little pair of brown boots, for which I had a special affection. They were polished up brightly; no boots could be more beautifully cleaned. What did Jessie mean? What did she mean, too, by speaking of Lady Sarah's wild fits?

I went downstairs, to find Lady Sarah in a genial humour. She was smiling and quite agreeable. Sambo did not wait at breakfast, and in consequence we had a pleasant meal. When it was over she took my hand and led me into her morning-room.

"Come here," she said, "I want to speak to you. So you are David's choice! Now listen. The aim and object of my life ever since I lost my husband has been to keep David single."

"What do you mean?" I asked.

"What I say. I love my son with a passion which you, you little white creature, cannot comprehend. I want him for myself *entirely*. You have dared to step in—you have dared to take him from me. But listen: even if you do marry him, you won't keep him long. You would like to know why—I will tell you. Because his love for you is only the passion which a man may experience

for a pair of blue eyes, and a white skin, and childish figure. It is as water unto wine compared to the love he feels for me. He will soon return to me. Be warned in time. Give him up."

"I cannot," I said.

"You won't be happy here. The life is not your life. The man is not the right sort of man for you. In some ways he is half a savage. He has been much in wild countries, in lands uninhabited by civilized people. He is not the man for you, nor am I the mother-in-law for you. Give him up. Here is paper and here is a pen. Write him a letter. Write it now, and the carriage shall be at the door and you will be taken to Wilton—from there you can get a train to London, and you will be safe, little girl, quite safe."

"You ask the impossible," I replied; "I love your son."

She had spoken with earnestness, the colour flaming into her cheeks, her eyes very bright. Now her face grew cold and almost leaden in hue.

"I have given you your choice and a way of escape," she said. "If you don't take the offer, it is not my fault." She walked out of the room.

What did she mean? I stayed where she had left me. I was trembling all over. Terrors of the most overmastering and unreasoning sort visited me. All I had lived through since I came to Longmore now flooded my imagination and made me weak with nervous fears. The reptile-house—Lady Sarah—Sambo's strange behaviour—Sambo's wicked glance—Jessie's words. Oh, why had I come? Why had David left me alone in this terrible place?

I got up, left the room, and strode into the grounds. The grounds were beautiful, but I could find no pleasure in them. Over and over the desire to run away visited me. I only restrained my nervous longing for David's sake. He would never forgive me if I left Longmore because I feared his mother.

The gong sounded for lunch, and I went into the house. Lady Sarah was seated at the table; Sambo was absent.

"I have had a busy morning," she said. "Darkey is ill."

"Darkey!" I exclaimed.

"Yes, the black snake whose bite kills in six minutes. Sambo is with him; he and I have been giving him some medicine. I trust he will be better soon. He is my favourite reptile—a magnificent creature."

I made no remark.

"I am afraid you must amuse yourself as best you can this afternoon," she continued, "for Sambo and I will be engaged with the snake. I am sorry I cannot offer to send you for a drive, but two of the horses are out and the bay mare is lame."

I said I would amuse myself, and that I should not require the use of any of the horses, and she left me.

I did not trouble to go on the Plain. I resumed my restless wanderings about the place. I wondered, as I did so, if Longmore could ever be a real home to me. As the moments flew past I looked at my watch, counting the hours to David's return. When he was back, surely the intangible danger which I could not but feel surrounded me would be over.

At four o'clock Sambo brought tea for one into the drawing-room. He laid it down, with a peculiar expression.

"You will be sorry to hear, missie," he said, "that Missah Ross not coming back to-night." The man spoke in a queer kind of broken English.

I sprang to my feet, my heart beating violently.

"Sorry, missie, business keep him—telegram to missis; not coming back till morning. Yah, missie, why you stay?"

"What do you mean?" I asked.

The man had a hazel wand in his hand. I had noticed it without curiosity up to the present. Now he took it and pointed it at me. As he did so he uttered the curious word "*Ullinka.*" The evil glitter in his eyes frightened me so much that I shrank up against the wall.

"What are you doing that for?" I cried. He snapped the stick in two and flung it behind him.

"Missie, you take Sambo's word and go right away to-night. Missis no well—Darkey no well — Sambo no well. No place for missie with blue eyes and fair hair. I say 'Ullinka,' and 'Ullinka' means *dead*—this fellah magic stick. Missie run to Wilton, take train from Wilton to London. Short track 'cross Plain—nissie go quick. Old Sambo open wicket-gate and let her go. Missie go soon."

"Do you mean it?" I said.

"*Yowi*—yes."

"I will go," I said. "You terrify me. Can I have a carriage?"

"No time, missie. Old missis find out. Old missis no wish it—missie go quick 'cross Plain short track to Wilton. Moon come up short time."

"I will go," I whispered.

"Missie take tea first and then get ready," he continued. "Sambo wait till missie come downstairs."

I did not want the tea, but the man brought me a cup ready poured out.

"One cup strengthen missie, then short track 'cross Plain straight ahead to Wilton. Moon in sky. Missie safe then from old missis, from Darkey, and from Sambo."

"HE UTTERED THE CURIOUS WORD 'ULLINKA.'"

I drank the tea, but did not touch the cake and bread and butter. I went to my room, fear at my heels. In my terror I forgot to remark, although I remembered it well afterwards, that for some extraordinary reason most of my boots and shoes had disappeared. My little favourite pair of brown boots alone was waiting for me. I put them on, buttoned them quickly, put on my fur coat and cap, and with my purse in my pocket ran downstairs. No matter what David thought of me now. There was something terrible in this house—an unknown and indescribable *fear*—I must get away from Longmore at any cost.

Sambo conducted me without a word down the garden and out on to the Plain through the wicket-gate.

"Quick, missie," he said, and then he vanished from view, shutting and locking the gate behind him.

It was a perfect evening, still and cold. The sun was near the horizon and would soon set, and a full moon was just rising. I determined to walk briskly. I was strong and active, and the distance between Longmore and Wilton did not frighten me. I could cross the Plain direct from Longmore, and within two hours at longest would reach Wilton. My walk would lead past Stonehenge.

The Plain looked weird in the moonlight. It looked unfathomable : it seemed to stretch into space as if it knew no ending. Walking fast, running at intervals, pausing now and then to take breath, I continued my fearful journey.

Was Lady Sarah mad, was Sambo mad, and what ailed Darkey, the awful black snake whose bite caused death in six minutes? As the thought of Darkey came to me, making my heart throb until I thought it would stop, I felt a strange and unknown sensation of fatigue creeping over me : my feet began to lag. I could not account for this. I took out my watch and looked at it. I felt so tired that to go on without a short rest was impossible. There was a stone near. I sat on it for a moment or two. While resting I tried to collect my scattered thoughts. I wondered what sort of story I should tell David : how I would appease his anger and satisfy him that I did right in flying like a runaway from the home which was soon to be my own. As these thoughts came to me I closed my eyes ; I felt my head nodding. Then all was lost in unconsciousness.

I awoke after what seemed a moment's sleep to find that I had been sitting on the stone for over half an hour. I felt refreshed by my slumber, and started now to continue my walk rapidly. I went lightly over the springy turf. I knew my bearings well, for David had explained everything to me on our long expedition yesterday.

I must have gone over a mile right on to the bare Plain when I began once again to experience that queer and unaccountable sensation of weakness. My pace slowed down and I longed again to rest. I resolved to resist the sensation and continued my way, but more slowly now and with a heavily beating heart. My heart laboured in a most unnatural way. I could not account for my own sensations.

Suddenly I paused and looked back. I fancied that I heard a noise, very slight and faint and different from that which the wind made as it sighed over the vast, billowy undulations of the Plain. Now, as I looked back, I saw something about fifty yards away, something which moved swiftly over the short grass. Whatever the thing was, it came towards me, and as it came it glistened now and then in the moonlight. What could it be? I raised my hand to shade my eyes from the bright light of the moon. I wondered if I was the subject of an hallucination. But, no ; whatever that was which was now approaching me, it was a reality, no dream. It was making straight in my direction. The next instant every fibre in my body was tingling with terror, for gliding towards me, in great curves, with head raised, was an enormous black snake !

For one moment I gazed, in sickened horror, and then I ran—ran as one runs in a nightmare, with thumping heart and clogged feet and knees that were turned to water. There could be no doubt of what had happened : the great black snake, Darkey, had escaped from Longmore and was following me. Why had it escaped? How had it escaped? Was its escape premeditated? Was it meant to follow me? Was I the victim of a pre-arranged and ghastly death? Was it—was it ?—my head reeled, my knees tottered. There was not a tree or a house in sight. The bare, open plain surrounded me for miles. As I reeled, however, to the crest of the rise I saw, lying in the moonlight, not a quarter of a mile away, the broken ring of Stonehenge. I reached it in time to clamber on to one of the stones. I might be saved. It was my only chance.

Summoning all my energies I made for the ruined temple. For the first hundred yards I felt that I was gaining on the brute, though I could hear, close on my track, its low,

"A LOUD REPORT RANG IN MY EARS."

"I GAZED IN SICKENED HORROR."

continuous
hiss. Then
the deadly
faintness for which I
could not account
once more seized me. I fancied
I heard someone calling me in
a dim voice, which sounded miles away.

Making a last frantic effort, I plunged
into the circle of stones and madly clambered on to the great "Slaughter Stone."
Once more there came a cry, a figure flashed
past me, a loud report rang in my ears, and
a great darkness came over me.

"Drink this, Flower."

I was lying on my back. Lady Sarah was
bending over me. The moonlight was
shining, and it dazzled my eyes when I first
opened them. In the moonlight I could see
that Lady Sarah's face was very white. There
was a peculiar expression about it. She put
her hand gently and deftly under my head,
and held something to my lips. I drank
a hot and fiery mixture, and was revived.

"Where am I—what has happened?" I
asked.

"You are on the great 'Slaughter Stone' on
Salisbury Plain. You have
had a narrow escape.
Don't speak. I am going
to take you home."

"Not back to Long-
more?"

"Yes, back to Long-
more, your future home.
Don't be silly."

"But the snake, Darkey,
the black snake?" I said.
I cowered, and pressed my
hand to my face. "He
followed me, he followed
me," I whispered.

"He is dead," she
answered; "I shot him
with my own hands. You
have nothing to fear from
me or from Darkey any
more. Come!"

I was too weak to resist
her. She did not look
unkind. There was no
madness in her eyes. At
that moment Sambo ap-
peared in view. Sambo
lifted me from the stone
and carried me to a dog-
cart which stood on the
Plain. Lady Sarah seated
herself by my side, took
the reins, and we drove
swiftly away.

Once again we entered
the house. Lady Sarah
took me to the morning-
room. She shut the door,
but did not lock it. There
was a basin of hot soup
on the table.

"Drink, and be quick,"
she said, in an imperious voice.

I obeyed her; I was afraid to do otherwise.

"Better?" she asked.

"Yes," I replied, in a semi-whisper.

"Then listen."

I tried to rise, but she motioned me to
stay seated.

"The peril is past," she said. "You have
lived through it. You are a plucky girl, and
I respect you. Now hear what I have to say."

I tried to do so and to keep down my
trembling. She fixed her eyes on me and
she spoke.

"Long ago I made a vow," she said. "I
solemnly vowed before Almighty God that as
long as I lived I would never allow my only

son to marry. He knew that I had made this vow, and for a long time he respected it, but he met you and became engaged to you in defiance of his mother's vow and his mother's wish. When I heard the tidings I lost my senses. I became wild with jealousy, rage, and real madness. I would not write to you nor would I write to him."

" Why did you write at last—why did you ask me here ? " I said then.

" Because the jealousy passed, as it always does, and for a time I was sane."

"Sane !" I cried.

"Yes, little girl; yes, *sane!* But listen. Some years ago, when on the coast of Guinea, I was the victim of a very severe sunstroke. From that time I have had fits of madness. Any shock, any excitement, brings them on.

" I had such a fit of madness when my son wrote to say that he was engaged to you. It passed, and I was myself again. You were not in the house an hour, however, before I felt it returning. There is only one person who can manage me at these times ; there is only one person whom I fear and respect—my black servant Sambo. Sambo manages me, and yet at the same time I manage him. He loves me after his blind and heathen fashion. He has no fear ; he has no conscience ; to commit a crime is nothing to him. He loves me, and he passionately loves the reptiles. To please me and to carry out my wishes are the sole objects of his life.

"With madness in my veins I watched you and David during the last two days, and the wild desire to crush you to the very earth came over me. David went to London, and I thought the opportunity had come. I spoke to Sambo about it, and Sambo made a suggestion. I listened to him. My brain was on fire. I agreed to do what he suggested. My snake Darkey was to be the weapon to take your life. I felt neither remorse nor pity. Sambo is a black from Australia, an aborigine from that distant country. He knows the secrets of the blacks. There is a certain substance extracted from a herb which the blacks know, and which, when applied to any part of the dress or the person of an enemy, will induce each snake which comes across his path to turn and follow him. The substance drives the snake mad, and he will follow and kill his victim. Sambo possessed the stuff, and from time to time, to amuse me, he has tried its power on my reptiles. He has put it on his own boots, but he himself has never been bitten, for he has flung the boots

to the snakes at the last moment. This afternoon he put it on the brown boots which you are now wearing. He then terrified you, and induced you to run away across Salisbury Plain. He put something into your tea to deprive you of strength, and when you were absent about three-quarters of an hour he let Darkey loose. Darkey followed you as a needle will follow a magnet. Sambo called me to the wicket-gate and showed me the glistening creature gliding over the Plain in your direction. As I looked, a veil fell from my eyes. The madness left me, and I became sane. I saw the awful thing that I had done. I repented with agony. In a flash I ordered the dog-cart, and with Sambo by my side I followed you. I was just in · time. I shot my favourite reptile. You were saved."

Lady Sarah wiped the drops of perspiration from her forehead.

" You are quite safe," she said, after a pause, " and I am sane. What I did, I did when I was not accountable. Are you going to tell David ? "

" How can I keep it from him ? "

" It seems hard to you now, but I ask you to do it. I promise not to oppose your marriage. I go meekly to the Dower House. I am tired of the reptiles—my favourite is dead, and the others are nothing to me. They shall be sent as a gift to the Zoological Gardens. Now will you tell David ? If you do, I shall shoot myself to-night. Think for an hour, then tell me your decision." She left the room.

How I endured that hour I do not know ! At the end of it I went to seek her. She was pacing up and down the great hall. I ran to her. I tried to take her hand, but she held her hands behind her.

" He will love you, he will worship you, and I, his old mother, will be nothing to him. What are you going to do ? " she said then.

" I will never tell him," I whispered.

She looked hard at me, and her great black eyes softened.

" You are worthy to be his wife," she said, in a hoarse voice, and she left me.

I am David's wife, and David does not know. He will never know. We are still on our honeymoon, but David is in trouble, for by the very last post news reached him of Lady Sarah's sudden death. He was absent from her when she breathed her last. He shall never know the worst. He shall always treasure her memory in his heart.

XVIII

The Secret of Emu Plain

L.T. MEADE and ROBERT EUSTACE

THE SECRET OF EMU PLAIN

BY L. T. MEADE AND ROBERT EUSTACE, AUTHORS OF "A MASTER OF MYSTERIES."

T so happened that business called me to Queensland in the late October of 1894, and hearing that my old friend, Rosamund Dale, was about to be married, I determined to present myself at Jim Macdonald's station on the Barcoo District in December, in order to be present at the ceremony. I had seen a good deal of Rosamund when she was a child, and it was an old promise of mine that, if possible, I was to be one of the guests at her wedding.

I arrived at Macdonald's a week before Christmas, and when a hot wind, or sirocco, was blowing in from the west. I little thought, as I did so, that the strangest and most terrible adventure of my life was about to take place in the Queensland bush. But so it was, and this is the story just as it happened.

I had been delayed on my journey, and on the evening of my arrival the wedding was to take place. Macdonald's property was about seven hundred and fifty square miles in extent, and was in the heart of the hills, which are the fountain-head of the countless creeks that run south, and join to form the Warrego, and eventually the Great Darling River, some four hundred miles away. It was good grazing country on the whole, but contained one enormous tract of arid sand, some forty square miles in extent, which went by the name of Emu Plain. Skirting one corner of this plain ran the coach road from Blackall to Charleville, along which ran Cobb & Co.'s coach once a fortnight. Almost in the middle of the plain stood in solitary grandeur the great Emu Rock, a grotesque, bare, perpendicular crag of limestone, rising a sheer three hundred feet from the ground.

Leaving my heavy luggage at Blackall, I had come with a valise by Cobb & Co.'s coach to the cross roads, and had then ridden over to Macdonald's house, a low wooden homestead of one storey, with a verandah running all round it. The sitting-rooms opened into the verandah. There was a garden at the back, enclosed by a fence. Macdonald met me with words of hearty welcome.

"But you are late, Bell," he exclaimed, " Rosamund has been waiting impatiently for your arrival all day. She never forgets how good you were to her when she was a child, and all alone in the old country. But let me take you to your room for a tub and brush up, for she would like to see you for a moment or two before the wedding."

Jim took me to my apartment in the left wing of the house, and half an hour later I joined Rosamund Dale on the balcony. She was a handsome dark-eyed girl, with a bright vivacious face and sparkling eyes. She had changed much in appearance since I had last seen her, as a small and somewhat awkward schoolgirl, but her affectionate heart and frank manners were still abundantly manifest. She made me seat myself in a deck chair, and began at once to talk about her bridegroom. Goodwin was the best man in the world, she loved him with all her heart and soul ; she liked the life in the bush, too. Notwithstanding its loneliness there was an element of excitement about it which quite suited her nature.

As she spoke to me I noticed that she looked anxiously out, and shading her eyes with her hand I saw them travel across the paddock, and up the road.

"What is the matter, Rosamund," I said at last; "and, by the way," I added, "won't you introduce me to Mr. Goodwin?"

"He has not come yet, and I cannot understand it," replied the girl; "he ought to have been here an hour ago. His station is about thirty miles from here, just across Emu Plain."

"What a hideous piece of desolation that Emu Plain is," I answered. "I skirted it on the coach, and never saw anything so repulsive in my life."

I noticed that Rosamund shuddered, and her face turned pale.

"It is an ugly place," she said at last, "and bears a bad name."

"What do you mean by that?" I interrupted.

"You will laugh at me, Mr. Bell," was her reply, "but people say the plain is haunted. Some most extraordinary disappearances have taken place there from time to time. If Frank came across the plain there is no saying, but "—she looked me full in the face.

"I am surely frightening myself about nothing," she said. "Will you excuse me a moment? I must just go into the drawing-room and ask if there is any news of Frank."

She rose, and I followed her into the room behind the verandah. I there, for the first time, made Mrs. Macdonald's acquaintance. She was a hearty, good-natured looking woman, with eyes like Rosamund's. She seemed devotedly attached to her niece, and now went up to the girl, and kissed her affectionately.

"Your uncle has just gone off to meet Frank," she said; "they are sure to be here in a few moments."

She spoke cheerfully, but I felt certain that I noticed a veiled anxiety in her eyes.

At that moment a man crossed the room, came up to Rosamund, and held out his hand.

"How do you do, Mr. Corry?" said the girl gravely. She had beautiful dark eyes, with magnificent lashes, and I observed, as Corry spoke to her, that she lowered them, and avoided looking at him. He was a thin, tall man, with red hair, and a slight cast in one eye. His lips were thin, the thinnest I had ever seen, and their expression, joined to the cast in the eye, gave him a sinister look. He was on good terms, however, with all the guests, and had the manners of a gentleman. Rosamund returned to the verandah, and I followed her.

"Are you really nervous about anything?" I said. "Is it possible that you apprehend that an accident has happened to Goodwin?"

"How can I tell?" she answered, and now a look of agony crossed her strong face. "He ought to be here before now; he has never failed before, and on his wedding evening, too! The Plain is haunted, you know, Mr. Bell. Don't

"A MAN CROSSED THE ROOM AND CAME UP TO ROSAMUND."

laugh at me when I say that I—I believe in the ghost of Emu Plain."

"You must tell me more," I answered. "You know," I continued with a smile, "that I am interested in ghosts."

She could not return my smile; her face grew whiter and whiter.

"Who is that man Corry?" I said, after a pause.

"Oh, never mind about him," she answered impatiently. "He has a selection about twenty miles from here, and is, I believe, an Englishman. I cannot think what is keeping Frank," she added. "Ah! thank God! I hear horses' hoofs at last."

She ran to the farther end of the verandah, and stood there, gazing up the road with the most longing, perplexed expression I had ever seen on human face. Alas! only one rider was returning, and that was Macdonald himself. He came in cheerfully, said that Frank might appear at any moment, and suggested we should all go to supper.

At that meal I noticed that Rosamund only played with her food. She was seated near Mr. Lee, the clergyman from the nearest township, who had come over to marry her. He talked to her in low tones, and she replied listlessly. It was evident that her thoughts were with her absent lover, and that she could think of nothing else. At last the miserable meal had dragged to an end, the evening passed away somehow, and the different guests retired to their rooms. By-and-by Macdonald and I found ourselves alone.

"Now, what is up?" I said, going up to him at once; "Jim, what is the meaning of this?"

"God only knows," was his reply; "I don't like it, Bell, and that's a fact. You noticed that big plain as you came along by the coach?"

"Emu Plain?" I replied.

Jim nodded.

"It bears an ugly reputation," he said. "There have been the most extraordinary disappearances there from time to time. The blacks say that the place is haunted by a ghost, which they call the Bunyip. Of course, I don't believe in anything of that sort; but it is a fact that you will scarcely get a black man to cross the plain after dark, and two or three of our settlers have entered that plain alone and never been heard of since. Whether the agency which causes them to disappear is ghostly or otherwise it is impossible for me to say."

"You surely do not believe in the Bunyip?" I said, with a slight laugh.

"Hush!" he answered. "The fact is this, Bell, old man; I cannot laugh over the matter.

If anything has happened to Goodwin I believe he——hollo! who can this be? Lie down boy," added Jim to Help, his big collie.

We went out into the paddock. As we did so a man rode quickly up, whom Jim recognised at once as one of the mounted police.

"What's up, Jack?" said Jim.

"A traveller riding alone from Blackall has got bushed on the ranges," was the man's reply. "I heard that Frank Goodwin had not turned up here, and it occurred to me that you ought to know at once. The man's horse, with an empty saddle, was found on your boundary fence. It is possible that he had an accident. Could you let me have Billy, your black tracker? The poor chap may be lying crippled and cannot move on some of the ranges. There is not a moment to lose."

"Good God! Then it must be Goodwin," exclaimed Jim. "We won't tell Rosamund yet. We will bring Billy and go with you at once, Jack," he continued. "You will come along, too, won't you, Bell?" he added briskly. "Anything is better than suspense. I'll get the horses up and we'll start in a moment, though we won't be able to do much before daylight."

In less than a quarter of an hour we set out. Billy, the black tracker, looked sulky, and also considerably alarmed, and Jim whispered to me that he had great difficulty in making him come at all.

"He believes in that Bunyip," he added, dropping his voice to a hoarse whisper.

Billy himself was an ill-favoured looking creature, but as a tracker he was possessed of almost superhuman powers, and was noted in all the district as one who could follow tracks of almost any kind. He had only one eye, the other having been knocked out in a scrimmage, but with that eye he could read the ground as a civilised man reads a book.

We started off slowly. Billy was presently induced to ride ahead. He sucked his pipe as if he took no interest in the affair.

"Goodwin must be somewhere on the ranges," said Macdonald emphatically. "But how he got off the track beats me, as he knows every yard of the place. There is foul play somewhere."

Just as he said the last words Billy turned in his saddle, and cocking his one eye round, said slowly:

"Baal boodgeree Emu Plain night time. Bunyip there."

"Nonsense, Billy," replied Macdonald almost angrily. "There is no such thing as the Bunyip, and you know that as well as I do."

" I see Bunyip once in Emu Plain, along rock," the black went on. " I make tracks, my word ! "

Just as the day broke our way led us out of the scrub, and the trees began to get more sparsely scattered, till we suddenly burst upon the borders of the great plain itself. A few moments afterwards Billy uttered a cry and picked up the tracks. With his one eye fixed on the ground he dismounted, and began to examine some bent grass and disturbed stones. To my unaccustomed vision the signs that guided him were absolutely invisible. It was an exhibition of instinct that no one would believe without seeing it.

On and on we went through the heat, silent and expectant ; now up, now down, over ridge and gully. Suddenly Billy uttered a sharp cry, and leaping from his horse gave me the reins, and walked round and round, peering about and grunting to himself. At last, looking up, he exclaimed—

" Man meet someone here."

" Meet someone," cried Macdonald. " Are you sure, Billy ? "

" Quite sure," was the answer. He took his tomahawk and cut a notch in one of the trees in order to mark the spot. We then remounted and rode on. In a moment Billy spoke again.

" More horses ! my word ! " he said. Look ! "

The marks were clear enough now, even to us. In a piece of soft ground were the hoof-marks of three horses. Billy said no more, but put his horse in a canter. We followed him. About a mile farther we pulled up at the edge of the scrub. We were now close to the great Emu Rock. I noticed at once that a number of crows were wheeling round its summit.

" It is strange," said Jim, speaking in a hoarse voice, " but I never come near this great rock that I don't see the crows whirling round the top. Ay, there they go, as usual," he added, clutching my arm. " My God ! whenever a man disappears there are marks of a struggle at the foot of the rock. Watch Billy now, he will know in a moment. Oh ! merciful heaven ! it is true then, and something has happened to Goodwin. Poor Rosamund ; this will break her heart. Yes, there are the marks, Billy notices them. Now Bell, you never had a greater mystery than this to solve. Marks at the foot of the rock, a man disappears, never found again. What does it mean, Bell ? Where does he go ? There must be devilry in the matter."

Billy had dismounted and was bending over the ground. Suddenly he uttered a sharp shrill cry.

" The marks ! the marks ! " he gasped. " Bunyip here, man here. Debil, debil take him. See ! see ! see ! "

His intense excitement communicated itself to us. He began to run about, peering down low over the ground.

" See ! see ! " he repeated. " They get off here. Go this way, that way. Ah ! a spur come off." His quick eye had caught the glitter. He picked up a long spur. " Yes, yes; it is as it always is: three men fight, two men go away; one man—where he go ? Debil take him." He pointed to the sky, gazing up and showing his white teeth in horror.

" Nonsense, Billy ! " said Macdonald, in a voice which he tried to render commonplace and assured.

I looked at him and saw that he was shaking from head to foot.

" Come away," he said to me. " Poor girl, poor Rosamund. Billy," he added abruptly, turning to the tracker, " we must pick up the tracks of these horses."

We mounted and followed the horse tracks again. We ran the tracks back to the coach road, and then lost them in the confusion of a mob of cattle that had passed during the morning.

" Well, this is a bad business," said Macdonald. " Goodwin is missing, and what took place on the plain by the rock, and how he has disappeared from the face of the earth, and who are the men who had a hand in it, are insoluble problems. It is not the first time, Bell, and that's the horror of the thing. I tell you, I don't like the business at all. It looks uncommonly like another of those queer disappearances."

" Tell me about them," I said suddenly.

He began to talk, lowering his voice to a whisper.

" A year ago a man was lost on Emu Plain ; he was a young fellow, an Englishman, and the heir to a big property. He was seen to cross the plain on horseback one afternoon, and was never heard of or seen again, and there were the marks of a struggle by the great rock, just as we saw them to-day, Bell. His people have spent thousands trying to discover the mystery, but all in vain. Since then the neighbourhood of the rock has been avoided, and the horror of the plain has grown in the minds of everybody. For this disappearance was not the first, others had preceded it. From time to time, at longer or shorter intervals, a man entered that desolate plain, and never, as far as human being could tell, left it again. What does the thing portend ? "

Billy kept on croaking " Bunyip ! Bunyip ! " At last Macdonald shouted to him that he

would break his head if he said
the word any more.

We returned to the station.
Rosamund, with a face like death,
came out to meet us.

"You must bear up, my dear,"
said her uncle.

"Any news?" she asked.

"Well, there are tracks of a
struggle on the plain," he said,
with evident reluctance, "but we
cannot follow them. A mob of
cattle passed up the road this
morning and have confused the
tracks."

"Where was the struggle?"
she said in a low voice.

Macdonald avoided her eyes.
She gave him a direct and piercing
glance.

"Come on to the verandah,
Uncle Jim, and you too, Mr. Bell,
and tell me everything," said the
girl. Her voice was quiet and
had a strange stillness about it.
We followed her without a word.
She drew deck chairs forward as
we entered the cool verandah, and
then kneeling by my side, laid her
hand on my shoulder.

"Now," she said, facing Macdonald, "tell me all. Where was
the struggle?"

"Rosamund, you must bear up;
it was in the old spot, at the foot
of the great rock. There, my
girl," he added hastily, rising as
he spoke, "I don't give up hope
yet. I will send off Jack immediately, and have the affair telegraphed all
round the country."

He left the verandah, walking slowly.
Rosamund turned to me.

"My fears are certainties," she said; "and
Frank has disappeared just as the other men
have disappeared; but oh, my God," she
added, rising hastily to her feet, "I will find
him, I will. If he is alive I will find him,
and you, Mr. Bell, must help me. You have
solved mysteries before, but never so great a
one as this. You will help me, will you not?"

"With all my heart, my child," I answered.

"Then there is not a moment to lose, let
us go at once."

"No, no, Rosamund, that would be madness,"
I said. "If Goodwin is alive the police will
get tidings of him, and if not——" my voice
fell; Rosamund looked at me intently.

"Do you think I can rest so?" she said. "If
you do not want to drive me mad something
must be done immediately."

"HE BEGAN TO RUN ABOUT, PEERING DOWN LOW OVER THE
GROUND."

"Then what do you propose?" I asked,
looking at her.

"To go back with you to the plain, to
examine those marks myself, to bring my
woman's wit and intuition to bear on the
matter. Where man may fail to discover any
cause a woman may succeed; you know I am
right."

"And I would take you with me gladly if it
were possible, but it is not."

"Do you think anything that is possible for
a man is impossible for a woman?" she said.
"We can take some food with us, and start at
once. We won't consult anyone. If we are
quick, we can reach the rock an hour or two
before sunset, and I know the whole of the
ghastly place so well that we can return in
the moonlight. Oh, don't oppose me," she
added, "for if you do I will start alone. Anything is better than inaction."

I did not say a word. She gave me a quick,
grateful glance, and left the verandah. Half

an-hour later she appeared in the paddock, equipped in a stout habit, and mounted on a splendid black horse ; she led another by the bridle for me. We started off at once, and reached the great rock by daylight. The sweltering sun beat down upon our heads, and the arid sand rose in clouds around us, but Rosamund neither faltered nor complained—a spirit burned within her which no obstacle could daunt. There were the marks of the struggle plainly visible. Rosamund knelt on the ground and examined them with as close and keen an eye as even Billy the black tracker himself. We walked round and round the rock, the crows whirled in circles over our heads, making hideous noises as they did so. But, search as we would, we could find no clue beyond the very manifest one, that where three had fought and struggled only two had gone away. What—what in the name of heaven had become of the third ?

Before sunset Rosamund put her hand in mine. "Take me home," she said faintly. I did so. We neither of us spoke on that desolate return journey.

Again the next day we visited the rock, and made a careful search, and the next day and the next, and meanwhile the country rang with the disappearance of Frank Goodwin, and with news of Rosamund's grief. But no clue could we obtain anywhere. We could not get the faintest tidings of the missing man. That it was Goodwin's horse which was found by the boundary fence was beyond doubt. He had started from his station in good time on that fatal morning, and in the best of health and spirits, but from that moment he had never been seen.

I stayed with the Macdonalds for over a fortnight, and then, loth as I was to leave Rosamund in her trouble, I had to take my departure, owing to some pressing business in Brisbane, but I promised to return again as soon as I could. My plan was to ride for my first stage to Corry's selection. Billy would come with me, and bring back the horse I was riding. I would then wait for the coach to pick me up.

I arrived at Corry's in good time, sent Billy back with my horse, and as there were still some hours before Cobb's coach would pass it suddenly occurred to me that I would go once again to the Emu Rock, and exert every faculty I possessed to discover the mystery. Corry and the two friends who lived with him, Englishmen of much his own build and make, were out. I told Corry's black servant that I was going to try and bag a plain turkey, and borrowed one of his guns for the purpose.

In about half an hour I reached the rock. The sun was already dipping low over the hills. Across the summit of the rock crows and eagle-hawks wheeled to and fro. I walked round and round it in despair. I longed to tear its ghastly secret out of the silent rock. What strange scene had it not, in all probability, recently witnessed ?

By-and-by I sat down at the base of the rock, and watched the shadow creeping across the plain as the sun sank lower and lower. I was just making up my mind to return to Corry's when suddenly, within a few yards of me, I saw something drop on the sand. It made no noise, but as it fell it caught my eye. Wondering vaguely what it might be I got up, and sauntered across to the place. I saw something on the ground, an odd-looking thing. I bent down to see what it was. As I did so my heart stood still. I was looking at a human finger. The flesh was nearly all picked from the bone. I took it in my hand and gazed at it—my pulses were throbbing, and a deadly fear seized me. Where had it come from ? What did it mean ? Then in an instant a wild thought struck me. I looked up. Still flying to and fro noisily were the crows and hawks. Could one of them have dropped the finger ? Was the body of Frank Goodwin at the top of the Emu Rock ? The idea was monstrous, and yet there was the finger, and the crows wheeling round and round above me. But how could I prove my ghastly suspicion ? By no earthly means would it be possible to scale three hundred feet of perpendicular rock. If the body of poor Goodwin was there, how in the name of all that was mysterious had it been put there ? One thing, at least, was certain, I must go back at once to Macdonald's station and report the horrible discovery I had made, and arrange for an investigation of the summit of the rock to take place immediately.

The sirocco was still blowing hard, and great eddies of sand were circling in the air. A sand-storm was evidently coming on, and there was nothing for me to do but to lie down and bury my face in the ground until it passed by. I did so, my pulses throbbing, the most nameless fear and depression stealing over me. The storm grew greater, it was upon me. I kept my eyes shut, and my face buried. All of a sudden, from what quarter I knew not, there came a dizzy pain ; lights danced before my eyes. I seemed to sink into nothingness, my terrors were lifted from me, I was enshadowed in an impregnable darkness, and remembered no more.

*   *   *   *   *

When I came to myself I was lying on my back, and gazing up at the stars. Everything around me was silent as the grave, except the noise of the wind through the scrub which, curiously enough, now sounded far below me. I was lying on hard rock, and every bone in my body ached. I managed to turn myself slowly round, and then gazed about me. Where in the name of heaven was I? I saw that I was lying in a sort of basin of rock, the edge of which was some ten feet above me, but what was this dark mass lying a little to my left? I managed to crawl towards it. Great Heavens! it was a human body. The moment I saw it memory returned. I knew what my last conscious thoughts had been. I was in the

that I must be the victim of some hideous nightmare.

The moon was riding high in the heavens; the sand-storm had completely passed; the stars were bright. In this subdued light I could see every object around me almost as vividly as if it were day. I gazed once again at the body of the man by my side. Suddenly my heart leapt with fresh fear, and I raised myself on my elbow. I thought I saw the body stir. Could it be still alive? No. Yet, as if poised above the shoulder, something was moving—a black, smooth object, which swayed gently to and fro with a horrible and

"ROSAMUND KNELT ON THE GROUND AND EXAMINED THEM."

midst of a sand-storm at the foot of the great Emu Rock. Darkness, joined to heavy pain, had overtaken me. When I came to myself I was at the top of the Emu Rock, and the body beside me was, doubtless, that of Frank Goodwin. By what supernatural agency had I been transported here? For a moment my brain reeled, and I thought

perfect regularity. The silence was suddenly broken by a long low hiss, and I now perceived that the coils of an enormous snake heaved and rolled, as the loathsome creature slowly unwound itself, and glided noiselessly up the side of the rock. Drops of sweat broke out upon my forehead, and for fully an hour I lay still, literally paralysed with fear. Then the mad courage of desperation seized me, and with a reckless disregard of danger from the reptile I sprang back to the edge of the rock ; but as I did so I knew all the time that a pair of glittering eyes was fixed upon me. Never for a moment did they blink, or withdraw their gaze. Single-handed and unharmed, in a prison from which escape was impossible, I was face to face with this deadly reptile. For all I knew there might be many others close beside me among the rocks.

The dawn began slowly to break. The light grew stronger every moment, as I crouched on one side of my prison, tense and motionless. I knew that if I stirred, the reptile would spring upon me. It was coiled up now on the rock exactly opposite the spot where the body of Frank Goodwin lay. Once I ventured to turn my eyes and look round. Three hundred feet below stretched the plain. Yes ; escape was impossible. Now I had to face either a quick death from the bite of this huge brown snake, or a lingering death from thirst and starvation. Just for a moment I nearly yielded to a sudden impulse that assailed me, to take one step back over the edge of the basin and end my sufferings instantaneously. But, sick and faint as I still was, I determined to have one last fight before I destroyed myself. Cautiously, and still keeping my eyes upon the brute, I loosened a large flat stone, weighing nearly a couple of pounds ; and gently and slowly—for all the while those eyes, which never blinked, were fixed upon me—I unfastened my leather belt and made a loop with one end through the buckle. Then slipping in the stone, I drew the strap tightly round the stone. Here was an improvised weapon, a good one if I chanced to have the first blow. Wrapping the end of the belt twice round my hand I crept slowly forward, across the body of the dead men. As I did so, the great snake moved to and fro, and, opening its jaws, hissed at me in fury. I knew now that in a moment he would spring. I held out my hand, keeping the strap with the stone at the end well behind me, and then with all my force swung it round over my shoulder at the brute. At the same instant, with incredible swiftness, it struck out sideways at me. The huge stone met it halfway, and it fell, with its back broken, at my feet, hissing and wriggling in hideous contortions. I sprang back and, once more swinging round the stone with all my force, crushed its head against the rock. In another moment I had flung it over, and was watching its great body whirling down through the air to the plain below.

This immediate danger passed, I now began as coolly as I could to calculate my own chances. It was impossible to say when the news of my disappearance might reach Jim Macdonald's station. Perhaps not for weeks. Meanwhile, what was to become of me ? If there were no more brown snakes lurking between the crevices of the rock, I must, at best, slowly die from thirst and starvation. Surely by superhuman agency had I been transported to this giddy eminence. But escape was absolutely impossible. Poor Rosamund ! I had at last succeeded in my quest, and Goodwin's mangled body lay close to me. Was I to share a similar fate ?

As the hopelessness of the situation came upon me I trembled. The sun was now well up, and I knew that my sufferings from heat and thirst were all too soon to begin. I removed my shirt, and tearing it into strips fastened them together and then attached the free end to a projection of rock. I then flung the body of poor Goodwin on to the plain below. As I did so the grim idea of ending my sufferings by suicide recurred to me once more. If no help came I would, when my pains became intolerable, fling myself also from the dizzy height. I sat down on a huge stone and looked out towards the coach road. The hours dragged wearily on, but no sign of human life did I see.

The blazing sun beat mercilessly upon my head, and by midday the pangs of thirst had almost arisen to torture, and hunger also now assailed me. I was faint and giddy too, and discovered that I was suffering from a severe blow on the head. Doubtless I had received this blow at the foot of the rock ; it had rendered me unconscious, and the mysterious agency which had lifted me to the height above was then brought into requisition. Were they indeed ghostly hands which had dealt me this blow ? Was the Bunyip a real devil ? Was Emu Plain haunted by a horror which admitted of no solution ?

From time to time I shouted insanely, in order to keep off the eagle-hawks and crows which swooped down and wheeled round me. More than once I rose and peered down over the edge of my awful prison. There was not the slightest ledge or projection from the smooth sides for more than a hundred feet. Escape was out of the question.

My weakness was increasing hour by hour, and I resolved that if relief did not come before the sun set to-morrow, I would take that desperate leap and end my sufferings. I dared not sleep lest I might miss the frail chance of anyone coming, and the whole long night I paced around, shouting at intervals, though my voice came hoarse and thick from

"WITH INCREDIBLE SWIFTNESS, IT STRUCK OUT SIDEWAYS."

my parched lips. As morning broke once more I was utterly exhausted, and lay down, now half delirious from raging fever. My head felt as if it would burst, and the great rock seemed to reel and totter beneath me. The hours went by I know not how ; time seemed nowhere ; reality had merged into a ghostly phantasmagoria, hunger and thirst grew greater and greater. Insensibly, and scarcely knowing why I did it, I crept to the edge of that terrible cup in the rock. I could stand my tortures no longer. Instantaneous death should end my sufferings. I gazed round with haggard eyes for my last look at earth. Suddenly a shrill shout rent the air. I reeled back and clung to the corner of the rock for support. Once again came the noise. I heard my name, followed immediately by the report of a gun. The next instant I saw lying across the cup of rock close beside me a thin piece of cord.

" Catch it and haul in," I heard in a drawling voice as through a telephone from below.

I leapt up, hope had returned. My delirium fell from me like a mantle. For the time I was myself once more. I obeyed the words from below, and began frantically to haul in the rope. Coil after coil came up thicker and thicker till presently I held in my hands a stout rope. I now mustered all my remaining strength and fastened the rope tightly round the neck of a piece of solid rock. After doing this I remembered nothing more.

They told me afterwards, long weeks afterwards, when my fever had left me, and weak as a child I submitted to Rosamund's ministrations—they told me then, in my room at Jim Macdonald's station, what had really occurred.

Rosamund had dreamt the strangest dream of her life. She had gone through overmastering terror ; horror beyond description had visited her. She had dreamt that I was on the top of the Emu Rock, and insisted on going there, accompanied by Jim and Billy the black tracker. At the base of this mighty rock evidence of the most terrible character met her eyes, but, brave girl that she was, she turned her attention to the rescue of the living. A cord was sent up to my dizzy eminence by means of a rocket gun, and when I had fastened the rope to the rock Billy himself had come up and brought me down.

Thus I was saved from the very jaws of death. But what the mystery was, and how Frank Goodwin's body had been hauled up to the top of the Emu Rock, and how I myself had got there, are insoluble mysteries. I have unearthed more than one ghost in my day, but the great Bunyip of Emu Plain has baffled my ingenuity. He has won in the fight, and I bow my head in silence, owning that he, in his unfathomable mystery, is stronger than I.

A Mystery Competition.

OPEN TO ALL READERS OF THE ABOVE STORY.

*T*HIS *exceedingly clever story is the sequel to the adventures of John Bell, the ghost exposer, related for us by Mrs. Meade last year, under the title of "*A Master of Mysteries.*" Some of our readers will remember that Mrs. Meade spoke then of one mystery which John Bell had not been able to fathom. The above story of Emu Plain is the mystery in question. That which John Bell could not explain is, however, known to the authors of the adventure. We suggest that our readers attempt to solve the mystery themselves, and we will award* **Ten Prizes** *of* **One Guinea** *each to the ten solutions which, in Mrs. Meade's opinion, are the best sent to us. These solutions, marked "*Story Prize,*" and addressed to the Editor of* Cassell's Magazine, *La Belle Sauvage, London, E.C., must reach us on or before February 15th. We shall publish Mrs. Meade's explanation of the mystery in our April Number. No person may send more than one solution of the story, and no solution must exceed 300 words in length.*

THE SECRET OF EMU PLAIN

BY L. T. MEADE AND ROBERT EUSTACE, AUTHORS OF "A MASTER OF MYSTERIES."

* The following is the authors' solution of the mystery which was left unexplained in our December number.

BEFORE leaving the old country for Australia, Corry, who was a clever mechanician, had been engaged for a long time in investigating the possible uses of kites for military operations, and had made a large number of very interesting experiments as to their lifting power. He found (and his results corresponded with those of other investigators) that in a fairly strong wind one square foot of kite surface would raise half a pound. He found, also, that to obviate the inconvenience of using a large and unwieldy kite for raising heavy weights, a series of small kites attached vertically one above the other answered the purpose equally well. And by this means he succeeded in raising weights up to 200 lb. by attaching them to the ground-rope about six feet from the lowest of the kites and employing a horse to draw the rope.

By means of a slip-rope arrangement an enormous explosive charge could be raised and dropped over an enemy's fortification with considerable accuracy, three kites, each ten feet square, raising eleven stone.

Hereditarily tainted with criminal instincts, coupled with a fantastic imagination, the peculiar construction of the Emu rock suggested to him that by means of kites the body of a man could be raised and deposited upon the top where it could never by any possibility be discovered. An opportunity for practically putting this diabolical scheme to the test soon occurred. So long as the sirocco was blowing, the feat was comparatively easy. The manner in which John Bell became one of his victims is already known.

AWARD OF THE PRIZES.

THE task of selecting the winners of the ten prizes, of one guinea each, offered in our December number for the best solutions of the mystery left unexplained by the authors of "The Secret of Emu Plain," has proved no light one. Of the three hundred and eighty-six competitors who essayed the solution of the problem, only four actually indicated the use of a kite, and one of these four, Mr. F. M. Holmes, being a contributor to CASSELL'S MAGAZINE, was *hors concours.*

Many competitors sent with their solutions letters which spoke of the interest which the unexplained problem had aroused, and attempts to solve it came from every country of Europe as well as from the Far West of the United States, the West Indies, Canada, India, and Australia. Even more diversified than the origin of the solutions was their nature. Nearly half the competitors found their way to the top of the rock by means of a fissure or tunnel in the limestone, whose existence was known only to Corry and his associates; and a very large number staked its chance of a prize on the suggestion that a whirlwind was the sole force by which the bodies were raised from the plain to the top of the crag. Not a few hazarded the suggestion that the rocket-gun, which played so important a part in the rescue of Mr. Bell, had a counterpart which was equally active in getting him "into the hole." The united efforts of crows and eagle-hawks, the snake, balloons—both captive and free—and even indigestion on the part of Mr. Bell, were all, in turn, offered as explanations of the mystery. Though so few of the solutions were absolutely in accord with that deposited by the authors, under seal, before a single competitor had entered the lists, and only opened after the most laggard of our competitors had shot his bolt, the ingenuity with which so many competitors defended most plausible keys to the mystery added to the difficulty of making an award. The names of the ten prize-winners are given in alphabetical order in the following list :—

AGNES CLANCHY, Sunville, Cork.

MISS CROSLAND, c/o Messrs. Homberger and Co., Stoney Street, Nottingham.

W. R. FOSTER, 73, Port Street, Bengeworth, Evesham.

SAM. H. GOOD, *Advertiser* Offices, Adelaide, S.A.

E. T. JONES, Potomas, Salto, Uruguay.

The Rev. J. MIREHOUSE, Colsterworth, Grantham.

MINNIE ROBERTSON, 12, Salisbury Square, Fleet Street, E.C.

THOS. V. STATON, Duddo, Norham-on-Tweed.

W. H. TWAMLEY, Trinolin Glebe, Ballyboro, co. Kildare, Ireland.

DORA M. WATTS, Carrholme, Stackhouse, Settle.

XIX

Skin O' My Tooth

BARONESS ORCZY

"SKIN O' MY TOOTH":

HIS MEMOIRS, BY HIS CONFIDENTIAL CLERK.

COMPILED AND EDITED BY

THE BARONESS ORCZY.

I.—THE MURDER IN SALTASHE WOODS.

E all called him "Skin o' my Tooth": his friends, who were few; his clients, who were many; and I, his confidential clerk, *solus*—and very proud I am to hold that position. I believe, as a matter of fact, that his enemies—and *their* name is legion—call him Patrick Mulligan; but to us all who know him as he is, "Skin o' my Tooth" he always was, from the day that he got a verdict of "Not guilty" out of the jury who tried James Tovey, "the Dartmouth murderer." Tovey hadn't many teeth, but it was by the skin of those few molars of his that he escaped the gallows; not thanks to the pleading of his counsel, but all thanks to the evidence collected by Patrick Mulligan, his lawyer.

Of course, Skin o' my Tooth is not popular among his colleagues; there is much prejudice and petty spite in all professions, and the Law is not exempt from this general rule.

Everyone knows that Skin o' my Tooth is totally unacquainted with the use of kid gloves. He works for the best of his client; let the other side look to themselves, I say.

Funny-looking man, too, old Skin o' my Tooth—fat and rosy and comfortable as an Irish pig, with a face as stodgy as a boiled currant dumpling. His hair, I believe, would be red if he gave it a chance at all, but he wears it cropped so close to his bulky head that he looks bald in some lights. Then, we all know that gentle smile of his, and that trick of casting down his eyes which gives him a look that is best described by the word "coy"; that trick is always a danger-signal to the other side.

Now, in the case of Edward Kelly, everyone will admit that that young man came nearer being hanged for murder than any of us would care for.

But this is how it all happened.

On Tuesday, September 3rd, Mary Mills and John Craddock—who were walking through the Saltashe Woods—came across the body of a man lying near the pond, in a pool of blood. Mary, of course, screamed, and would have fled; but John, manfully conquering the feeling of sickness which threatened to overcome him too, went up to the body to get a closer view of the face. To his horror he recognised Mr. Jeremiah Whadcoat, a well-known, respectable resident of Pashet. The unfortunate man seemed to John Craddock to be quite dead; still, he thought it best to despatch Mary at once for Doctor Howden, and also to the police-station; whilst he, with really commendable courage, elected to remain beside the body alone.

It appears that about half an hour after Mary had left him, John thought that he detected a slight movement in the rigid body, which he had propped up against his knee, and that the wounded man uttered a scarcely audible sigh and then murmured a few words. The young man bent forward eagerly, striving with all his might to catch what these words might be. According to his subsequent evidence before the coroner's jury, Mr. Whadcoat then opened his eyes, and murmured quite distinctly—

"The letter . . . Kelly . . . Edward . . . the other." After that all seemed over, for the face became more rigid and more ashen in colour than before.

It was past six o'clock before the doctor and the inspector, with two constables and a stretcher from Pashet police-station, appeared upon the scene and relieved John Craddock of his lonely watch. Mr. Whadcoat had not spoken again, and the doctor pronounced life to be extinct. The body

"Came across the body of a man in a pool of blood."

was quietly removed to Mr. Whadcoat's house in Pashet, Mary Mills having already volunteered for the painful task of breaking the news to Miss Amelia, Mr. Whadcoat's sister, who lived with him.

The unfortunate man was cashier to Messrs. Kelly and Co., the great wine merchants ; so Mr. Kelly, of Saltashe Park, also Mr. Edward Kelly, of Wood Cottage, were apprised of the sad event.

At this stage the tragic affair seemed wrapped up in the most profound mystery. Mr. Jeremiah Whadcoat was not known to possess a single enemy, and he certainly was not sufficiently endowed with worldly wealth to tempt the highway robber. So far the police had found nothing on the scene of the crime which could lead to a clue—footsteps of every shape and size leading in every direction, a few empty cartridges here and there ; all of which meant nothing, since Saltashe Woods are full of game, and both Mr. Kelly and Mr. Edward Kelly had had shooting parties within the last few days.

The public understood that permission had been obtained from Mr. Kelly to drag the pond, and, not knowing what to think or fear, it awaited the day of the inquest with eager excitement.

I believe that that inquest was one of the most memorable in the annals of a coroner's court. There was a large crowd, of course, for the little town of Pashet was a mass of seething curiosity.

The expert evidence of Dr. Howden, assisted by the divisional surgeon, was certainly very curious. Both learned gentlemen gave it as their opinion that deceased met his death through the discharge of small shot fired from a rifle at a distance of not more than a couple of yards. All the shot had lodged close together in the heart, and the flesh round the wound was slightly charred.

The police, on the other hand, had quite a tit-bit of sensation ready for the eager public. They had dragged the pond and had found the carcass of a dog. The beast had evidently been shot with the same rifle which had ended poor Mr. Whadcoat's days, the divisional surgeon, who had examined the carcass, having pronounced the wound— which was in the side – to be exactly similar in character. A final blow dealt on the animal's head with the butt-end of the rifle, however, had been the ultimate cause of its death. As the medical officer gave this sensational bit of evidence, a sudden and dead silence fell over all in that crowded

court, for it had leaked out earlier in the day that the dead dog found in the pond was "Rags," Mr. Edward Kelly's well-known black retriever.

In the midst of that silence, Miss Amelia Whadcoat—the sister of the deceased gentleman—stepped forward, dressed in deep black, and holding a letter, which she handed to the coroner.

"It came under cover, addressed to me," she explained, "on the Tuesday evening."

The coroner, half in hesitation, turned the square envelope between his fingers. At last he read aloud—

"To the Coroner and Jury at the inquest, should a fatal accident occur to me this (Tuesday) afternoon, in Saltashe Wood."

Then he tore open the envelope. Immediately everyone noticed the look of boundless astonishment which spread over his face. There was a moment of breathless, silent expectation among the crowd, while Miss Amelia stood quietly with her hands demurely folded over her gingham umbrella, and her swollen eyes fixed anxiously upon that letter.

At last the coroner, turning to the jury, said—

"Gentlemen, this letter is addressed to you as well as to myself. I am, therefore, bound to acquaint you of its contents ; but I must, of course, warn you not to allow your minds to be unduly influenced, however strange these few words may seem to you. The letter is dated from Ivy Lodge, Pashet, Tuesday, September 3rd, and signed 'Jeremiah Whadcoat.' It says : ' Mr. Coroner and Gentlemen of the Jury,—I beg to inform you that on this day, at 2.30 p.m., I am starting to walk to Saltashe, there to see Mr. Kerhoet and Mr. Kelly on important business. Mr. Edward Kelly has desired me to meet him by the pond in Saltashe Woods, on my way. He knows of the business which takes me to Saltashe. He and I had a violent quarrel at the office on the subject last night, and he has every reason for wishing that I should never speak of it to Mr. Kelly and to Mr. Kerhoet. Last night he threatened to knock me down. If any serious accident happen to me, let Mr. Edward Kelly account for his actions.'"

A deadly silence followed, and then a muttered curse from somewhere among the crowd.

"This is damnable !"

And Mr. Edward Kelly, young, good-looking, but, at this moment, as pale as death, pushed his way forward among the spectators.

He wanted to speak, but the coroner waved him aside in his most official manner, while Miss Amelia Whadcoat demurely concluded her evidence. Personally, she knew nothing of her brother's quarrel with Mr. Edward Kelly. She did not even know that he was going to Saltashe Woods on that fatal afternoon. Then she retired, and Mr. Edward Kelly was called.

Questioned by the coroner, he admitted the quarrel spoken of by the deceased, admitted meeting him by the pond in Saltashe Woods, but emphatically denied having the slightest ill-feeling against "Old Whadcoat," as he called him, and, above all, having the faintest desire for wishing to silence him for ever.

"The whole thing is a ghastly mistake or a weird joke," he declared firmly.

"But the quarrel?" persisted the coroner.

"I don't deny it," retorted the young man. "It was the result of a preposterous accusation old Whadcoat saw fit to level against me."

"But why should you meet him clandestinely in the Woods?"

"It was not a clandestine meeting. I knew that he intended walking to Saltashe from Pashet through the Woods; a road from my house cuts the direction which he would be bound to follow, exactly at right angles. I wished to speak to him, and it saved me a journey all the way to Pashet, or him one down to my house. I met him at half-past three. We had about fifteen minutes' talk; then I left him and went back home."

"What was he doing when you left him?" asked the coroner, with distinct sarcasm.

"He had sat down on a tree stump and was smoking his pipe."

"You had your gun with you, of course, on this expedition through the Woods?"

"I seldom go out without my gun this time of year."

"Quite so," assented the coroner grimly. "But what about your dog, who was found with its head battered in, close to the very spot where lay the body of the deceased?"

"Poor old 'Rags' strayed away that morning. I did not see him at all that day. He certainly was not with me when I went to meet old Whadcoat."

The rapidly spoken questions and answers had been listened to by the public and the jury with breathless interest. No one uttered a sound, but all were watching that handsome young man, who seemed, with every word he uttered, to incriminate himself more and more. The quarrel, the assignation, the gun he was carrying—he denied nothing; but he did protest his innocence with all his might.

One or two people had heard the report of a gun whilst walking on one or other of the roads that skirt Saltashe Woods, but their evidence as to the precise hour was unfortunately rather vague. Reports of guns in Saltashe Woods were very frequent, and no one had taken particular notice. On the other hand, the only witness who had seen Mr. Edward Kelly entering the wood was not ready to swear whether he had his dog with him or not.

Though it had been fully expected ever since Jeremiah Whadcoat's posthumous epistle had been read, the verdict of "Wilful murder against Edward St. John Kelly" found the whole population of Pashet positively aghast. Brother of Mr. Kelly, of Saltashe Park, the accused was one of the most popular figures in this part of Hertfordshire. When his subsequent arrest became generally known in London, as well as in his own county, horror, amazement, and incredulity were quite universal.

II.

THE day after that memorable inquest and sensational arrest—namely, on the Saturday, I arrived at our dingy old office in Finsbury Square at about twelve o'clock, after I had seen to some business at Somerset House for my esteemed employer.

I found Skin o' my Tooth curled up in his arm-chair before a small fire—as the day was wet and cold—just like a great fat and frowsy dog. He waited until I had given him a full report of what I had been doing, then he said to me—

"I have just had a visit from Mr. Kelly, of Saltashe Park."

I was not astonished. That case of murder in the Saltashe Woods was just one of those which inevitably drifted into the hands of Skin o' my Tooth. Though the whole aspect of it was remarkably clear, instinctively one scented a mystery somewhere.

"I suppose, sir, that it was on Mr. Edward Kelly's behalf?"

"Your penetration, Muggins, my boy, surpasses human understanding."

(My name is Alexander Stanislaus Mullins, but Skin o' my Tooth will have his little joke).

"You are going to undertake the case, sir?"

"I am going to get Edward Kelly out of the hole his own stupidity has placed him in."

"It will be by the skin of his teeth if you do, sir; the evidence against him is positively crushing," I muttered.

"A miss is as good as a mile, where the hangman's rope is concerned, Muggins. But you had better call a hansom; we can go down to Pashet this afternoon. Edward Kelly is out on bail, and Mr. Kelly tells me that I shall find him at Wood Cottage. I must get out of him the history of his quarrel with the murdered man."

"Mr. Kelly did not know it?"

"Well, anyway, he seemed to think it best that the accused should tell me his own version of it. In any case, both Mr. Kelly and his wife are devoured with anxiety about this brother, who seems to have been a bit of a scapegrace all his life."

There was no time to say more then, as we found that, by hurrying, we could catch the 1.5 p.m. train to Pashet. We found Mr. Edward Kelly at Wood Cottage, a pretty little house on the outskirts of Salt-ashe Woods. He had been told of our likely visit by his brother. He certainly looked terribly ill and like a man over-weighted by fate and circumstances.

But he did protest his innocence, loudly and emphatically.

"I am the victim of the most damnable circumstances, Mr. Mulligan," he said; "but I swear to you that I am incapable of such a horrible deed."

"I always take it for granted, Mr. Kelly," said Skin o' my Tooth blandly, "that my client is innocent. If the reverse is the case, I prefer not to know it. But you have to appear before the magistrate on Monday. I must get a certain amount of evidence on your behalf, in order to obtain the remand I want. So will you try and tell me, as concisely and as clearly as possible, what passed between you and Mr. Whadcoat the day before the murder? I understand that there was a quarrel."

"Old Whadcoat saw fit to accuse me of certain defalcations in the firm's banking account, of which I was totally innocent," began Mr. Edward Kelly quietly. "As you know, my brother and I are agents in England for M. de Kerhoet's champagne. Whadcoat was our cashier and book-keeper. Twice a year we pay over into M. de Kerhoet's bank in Paris the money derived from the sale of his wines, after deducting our commission. In the meanwhile, we have—jointly—the full control of the money—that is to

"'By Jove! I've got it, Muggins!'"

say, all cheques paid to the firm have to be endorsed by us both, and all cheques drawn on the firm must bear both our signatures.

"It was just a month before the half-yearly settlement of accounts. Whadcoat, it appears, went down to the bank, got the pass-book and cancelled cheques, and discovered that some £10,000, the whole of the credit balance due next month to M. de

Kerhoet, had been drawn out of the bank, the amounts not having been debited in the books.

"To my intense amazement, he showed me these cheques, and then and there accused me of having forged my brother's name and appropriated the firm's money to my own use. You see, he knew of certain unavowed extravagances of mine which had often landed me in financial difficulties more or less serious, and which are the real cause of my being forced to live in Wood Cottage whilst my brother can keep up a fine establishment at Saltashe Park. But the accusation was preposterous, and I was furious with him. I looked at the cheques. My signature certainly was perfectly imitated, that of my brother perhaps a little less so. They were 'bearer' cheques, made out in a replica of old Whadcoat's handwriting to 'E. de Kerhoet,' and endorsed at the back in a small, pointed, foreign hand.

"Old Whadcoat persisted in his accusations, and very high words ensued between us. I believe I did threaten to knock him down if he did not shut up. Anyway, he told me that he would go over the next afternoon to Saltashe Park to expose me before my brother and M. de Kerhoet, who was staying there on a visit to England for the shooting.

"I left him then, meaning to go myself that same evening to Saltashe Park and see my brother about it; but on my journey home, certain curious suspicions with regard to old Whadcoat himself crept up in my mind, and then and there I determined to try and see him again and to talk the matter over more dispassionately with him, in what I thought would be his own interests. My intention was to make, of course, my brother acquainted with the whole matter at once, but to leave M. de Kerhoet out of the question for the present; so I wired to Whadcoat in the morning to make the assignation which has proved such a terrible mistake."

Edward Kelly added that he left Jeremiah Whadcoat, after his interview with him by the pond, in as excited a frame of mind as before. Fearing that his own handwriting on the cheques might entail serious consequences to himself, nothing would do but M. de Kerhoet as well as Mr. Kelly must be told of the whole thing immediately.

"When I left him," concluded the young man, "he was sitting on a tree stump by the pond, smoking his pipe, and I walked away towards Wood Cottage."

"Do you know what became of the cheques?" asked Skin o' my Tooth.

"Old Whadcoat had them in his pocket when I left him. I conclude, as there has been no mention of them by the police, that they have not been found."

There was so much simplicity and straightforwardness in Edward Kelly's narrative that I, for one, was ready to believe every word of it. But Skin o' my Tooth's face was inscrutable. He sat in a low chair with his hands folded before him, his eyes shut, and a general air of polite imbecility about his whole unwieldy person. I could see that our client was viewing him with a certain amount of irritability.

"Well, Mr. Mulligan?" he said at last, with nervous impatience.

"Well, sir," replied Skin o' my Tooth, "it strikes me that what with your quarrel with the deceased, the assignation in the Woods, his posthumous denunciation of you as his assassin, and his dying words, we have about as complete a case as we could wish."

"Sir——"

"In all cases of this sort, my dear sir," continued Skin o' my Tooth quietly, "the great thing is to keep absolutely cool. If you are innocent—remember, I do not doubt it for a moment—then I will bring that crime home to its perpetrator. Justice never miscarries – at least, when I have the guidance of it in my hands."

It would be impossible to render the tone of supreme conceit with which Skin o' my Tooth made this last assertion; but it had the desired effect, for Edward Kelly brightened up visibly as he said—

"I have implicit faith in you, Mr. Mulligan. When shall I see you again?"

"On Monday, before the magistrate. I can get that remand for you, I think, and then we shall have a free hand. Now we had better get along; I want to have a quiet think over this affair."

III.

On the Monday, Edward Kelly was formally charged before the beak; and I must say that when I then heard the formidable array of circumstantial evidence which the police had collected against our client, I sadly began to fear that not even by the skin of his teeth would Edward Kelly escape from the awful hole in which he was literally wallowing. However, Skin o' my Tooth hammered away at the police evidence with regard to the dog. The prosecution made a great point of the fact that Mr. Whadcoat and "Rags" had been killed by the same rifle and at the same time and place, and the one point in Edward Kelly's favour was that neither his servants at Wood Cottage, nor the witness who saw him enter the wood, could swear that the dog was with him on that day. On the strength of that, and for the purpose of collecting further evidence with regard to the dog, Skin o' my Tooth finally succeeded in obtaining a remand until the following Friday.

Personally, I thought that there was quite sufficient evidence for hanging any man, without the testimony of the dead dog, but I am quite aware that my opinion counts for very little.

"Now, Muggins," said Skin o' my Tooth to me later in the day, "the fun is about to begin. You go down to Coutts's this afternoon and find out all about those cheques which caused the quarrel, and by whom they were presented. Don't mix the police up in our affairs, whatever you do. If there is anything you can't manage, get Fairburn to help you; he is discretion itself and hates the regular force. Beyond that, try and work alone."

I had done more difficult jobs than that before now, and Skin o' my Tooth knows he can rely on me. I left him curled up in an arm-chair with a French novel in his hand and started on my quest. I got to Coutts's just before closing time, saw the chief cashier and explained my errand and its importance to him, asking for his kind help in the matter. He was courteous in the extreme, and within a few moments I had ascertained from him that cheques on Kelly and Co.'s account, perfectly *en règle*, and made out to "E. de Kerhoet, or Bearer," had been cashed on certain dates which he gave me. They were in each instance presented by a commissionaire in uniform, who brought a card—"M. Edouard de Kerhoet," with "Please give bearer amount in £5 notes," scribbled in pencil in the same handwriting as the endorsement on the cheques.

"The amounts varied between £1,200 and £3,000," continued the cashier, still referring to his book. "Being 'bearer' cheques, and signed in the usual manner, we had no occasion to doubt them, and of course we cashed them. The first cheque was drawn on July 3rd, and the last on August 29th."

The cashier added one more detail which fairly staggered me—namely, that the com-

missionaire wore a cap with "Kelly and Co." embroidered upon it. If necessary, there were plenty of cashiers and clerks at the bank who could identify him. He was a tall man of marked foreign appearance, with heavy black hair, beard and moustache cut very trim. On one occasion when he left, he dropped a bit of paper which contained the name "Van Wort, Turf Commission Agent, Flushing, Holland."

I thanked the cashier and took my leave.

When I got back to the office, I found Skin o' my Tooth placidly sleeping in his big arm-chair. I had had a hard day and was dead tired, and for the moment when I saw him there, looking so fat, so pink, and so comfortable, well—I have a great respect for him, but I really felt quite angry.

However, I told him what I had done.

"Capital! capital, Muggins!" he ejaculated languidly. "But, by Jove! that's a clever rascal. That touch about the name on the cap is peculiarly happy and daring. It completely allayed the suspicions of the cashiers at Coutts's. Now, listen, Muggins," he added, with that sudden, quick-changing mood of his which in a moment transformed him from the lazy, apathetic Irish lawyer to the weird human bloodhound who scents the track. "That foreign commissionaire is a disguise, of course; the cap hides the edge of the wig and shades the brow, the black beard and moustache conceal the mouth and chin, the foreign accent disguises the voice. We may take it, therefore, that the thief and his ambassador are one and the same person —a man, moreover, well known at Coutts's, since disguise was necessary. Do you follow me, Muggins? And remember, the motive is there. The man who defrauded Kelly and Co. is the same who murdered Whadcoat later on. Whadcoat was effectually silenced, the tell-tale cheques have evidently been destroyed. There would have been silence and mystery over the whole scandal, until the defalcations could be made good, but for Whadcoat's letter to the coroner and his dying words: 'The letter . . . Kelly . . . Edward . . . the other . . . .'" He paused suddenly and seemed lost in thought, then he muttered—

"It's that confounded dog I can't quite make out! . . . Did Edward Kelly, after all . . ."

It was that great "after all!" which had puzzled me all along. "Was Edward Kelly guilty, after all?" I had asked myself that question a hundred times a day. Then, as I was silent — lost in conjectures over this extraordinary, seemingly impenetrable mystery—he suddenly jumped up and shouted—

"By Jove! I've got it, Muggins! 'The other.' What a fool I have been! Go to bed, my boy; I want a rest, too. To-

"'I did kill old Whadcoat in a moment of unreasoning fear.'"

morrow will be time enough to think about 'the other.'"

IV.

FROM that moment Skin o' my Tooth was a transformed being. He always is when he

has got a case "well in hand," as he calls it. He certainly possesses a weird faculty for following up the trail of blood. Once he holds what he believes to be a clue, his whole appearance changes; his great, fat body seems, as it were, to crouch together ready for a spring, and there is a weird quiver about his nostrils which palpably suggests the bloodhound; only his eyes remain inscrutably hidden beneath their thick and fleshy lids.

It was twelve o'clock the next day when our train steamed into Pashet station. We had a fly from there and drove down to Saltashe Park, the lordly country seat of Mr. Kelly.

At the door, Skin o' my Tooth asked for the master of the house; but hearing that he was out, he requested that his card might be taken in to Mrs. Kelly. The next moment we were ushered into a luxuriously furnished library, full of books and flowers, and with deep mullioned windows opening out upon a Queen Anne terrace.

The mistress of the house—an exceedingly beautiful woman, received us with every mark of eagerness and cordiality.

She welcomed us — or, rather, my esteemed employer — most effusively; and when we were all seated, she asked many questions about Mr. Edward Kelly, to which Skin o' my Tooth replied as often as she allowed him to get a word in.

"Oh, Mr. Mulligan," she said finally, "I

am *so* glad that you asked to see me. I have been positively ill and devoured with anxiety about my brother-in-law. My husband thinks that I upset myself and only get hopelessly wretched if I read about it all in the papers, so he won't allow me to see one now ; but, I assure you, the uncertainty is killing me, as I feel sure that Mr. Kelly is trying to comfort me and to make Edward's case appear more hopeful than it is."

Skin o' my Tooth gravely shook his head.

" It could not very well be more hopeless," he said.

" You can't mean that ? " she said, while tears gathered in her eyes. " He is innocent, Mr. Mulligan. I swear he is innocent. You don't know him. He never would do anything so vile."

" I quite believe that, my dear lady ; but unfortunately circumstances are terribly against him. Even his dead dog, ' Rags,' speaks in dumb eloquence in his master's condemnation."

" ' Rags ! ' she exclaimed in astonishment — " what can the poor doggie have to do with this awful tragedy ? Poor old thing ! it lost its way the very morning that the terrible catastrophe occurred. M. de Kerhoet was staying here that day, and I had taken him for a drive to Hitching before luncheon. On the way home I saw ' Rags ' in the road, looking very sorry for himself. I took him in the carriage with me and brought him home."

Skin o' my Tooth looked politely interested, but I hardly liked to breathe ; it seemed to me that a fellow creature's life was even now hanging in the balance.

" ' Rags ' knew us all here just as well as it did its own master," continued Mrs. Kelly ; " and when my husband went out with his gun in the afternoon, ' Rags ' followed him, whilst M. de Kerhoet and I went on to a garden-party."

" And what happened to ' Rags ' after that ? " asked Skin o' my Tooth.

" To tell you the truth, the awful tragedy I heard of that afternoon drove poor ' Rags ' out of my mind ; then the next day, I am thankful to say, M. de Kerhoet left us and went back to Paris. I did hear something about the poor dog being drowned in the pond ; he was a shocking rover, and really more trouble than pleasure to his master."

Mrs. Kelly was sitting with her back to the great mullioned windows ; she could not, therefore, see her husband, who seemed to have just walked across the terrace and to

have paused a moment, with his hand on the open window, before entering the room. Whether he had heard what his wife was saying, I did not know ; certain it is that his face looked very white and set.

" I remember now," continued Mrs. Kelly innocently, " seeing my husband put away ' Rags' ' collar the other day in his bureau. I dare say Edward will be glad to have it later on, when all this horrid business is over. You must tell him that we have got it quite safe."

I all but uttered an exclamation then. It seemed too horrible to hear this young wife so hopelessly and innocently denouncing her own husband with every word she uttered. I looked up at the motionlessly figure still standing in the window, Skin o' my Tooth, who sat immediately facing it, seemed to make an almost imperceptible sign of warning. Mr. Kelly then retired as silently as he had come.

Two minutes later he entered the room by the door. He seemed absolutely calm and collected, and held out his hand to Skin o' my Tooth, who took it without the slightest hesitation ; then Mr. Kelly turned to his wife and said quietly—

" You will forgive me, won't you, dear, if I take Mr. Mulligan into my study ? There are one or two points I want to discuss with him over a cigar."

" Oh ! I'll run away," she said gaily. " I must dress for luncheon. You'll stay, won't you, Mr. Mulligan ? No ? I am so sorry ! Well, good-bye ; and mind you bring better news next time."

She was gone, and we three men were left alone. I offered to leave the room, but Mr. Kelly motioned me to stay.

" The servants would wonder," he said icily, " and it really does not matter."

Then he turned to Skin o' my Tooth and said quietly—

" I suppose that you came here to-day for the express purpose of setting a trap for my wife ; and she fell into it, poor soul ! not knowing that she was damning her own husband. Of course, you did your duty by your client. Now, what is your next move ? "

" To place Mrs. Kelly in the witness-box on my client's behalf, and make her repeat the story she told us to-day," replied Skin o' my Tooth with equal calm.

" And after that ? "

" After that, you must look to yourself, Mr. Kelly. I am not a detective, and you know best whether you have anything to fear when once the attention of the police is directed upon yourself. I shall obtain Mr. Edward Kelly's discharge to-morrow, of course. Backed by Mrs. Kelly's testimony, and, if need be, that of Mr. Kerhoet, in Paris, I can now prove that the dog could not have been shot by my client, since it was following you on the afternoon that the murder was committed. Since the chief point in the theory of the prosecution lies in the fact that Mr. Whadcoat and the dog were shot on the same day and with the same rifle, and seeing that the animal's collar was known to be in your possession the day following the crime, my client is absolutely sure to obtain a full discharge and to be allowed to leave the court without a stain upon his character."

Mr. Kelly had listened to Skin o' my Tooth's quiet explanation without betraying the slightest emotion ; then he said—

"Thank you, Mr. Mulligan. I think I quite understand the situation. Personally, I feel that it is entirely for the best ; life under certain conditions becomes abominable torture, and I have no strength left with which to combat fate. I did kill old Whadcoat in a moment of unreasoning fear, just as I killed 'Rags' because he made too much noise ; but, by Heaven ! I had no intention to kill the old man, and I certainly would never have allowed my brother to suffer seriously under an unjust accusation. I firmly believed that justice could not miscarry ; and while I thought that you were sharp enough to save him, I also reckoned that I had been clever enough to shield myself from every side."

He paused a moment and then continued ; just like a man who for a long time has been burdened with a secret and is suddenly made almost happy by confiding it to a stranger.

"I had had many losses on the turf," he said, "and had made my losses good by defrauding our firm. It was a long and laborious plan, very carefully laid ; but I was always clever with my pen, and my brother's signature and Whadcoat's writing were easy enough to imitate. Then, one day, I found an old uniform in the cellar at the office— my father used to keep a commissionaire when he had the business. It was about my size and gave me the idea for the disguise. It all worked right, and I knew that I could make my defalcations good at the bank very soon. It was a positive thunderbolt to me when, on the Tuesday morning, I received a letter from old Whadcoat, telling me that he was coming over to Saltashe that afternoon to see M. de Kerhoet and myself about a terrible discovery which he had just made. I knew that he would walk through the Woods, and I found him sitting near the pond, smoking, alone. I only meant to persuade him to hold his tongue and say nothing to M. de Kerhoet for the present. But he was obstinate ; he guessed that I was guilty ; he threatened me with disclosure, like the fool he was, and I had to kill him . . . . in self-defence."

Somehow, although he undoubtedly was a great criminal, I could not help sympathising with this man. The beautiful house we were in, all the luxury and comfort with which he was outwardly surrounded, seemed such terrible mockery beside the moral tortures he must have endured. I was quite glad when he had finished speaking, and Skin o' my Tooth was able presently to take his leave.

Only a few hours later, the evening papers were full of the sensational suicide of Mr. Kelly in his library at Saltashe Park. Almost at the same time that this astonishing news was published in the Press, the authorities at Scotland Yard had received a written confession, signed by Mr. Kelly, in which he confessed to having caused the death of Mr. Jeremiah Whadcoat in Saltashe Woods, by the accidental discharge of his gun.

A little frightened at first of any complications that might arise, he had said nothing about the accident at the time ; then, when his own brother became implicated in the tragedy, and he felt how terrible his own position would be if he now made a tardy confession, the matter began to prey upon his mind until it became so unhinged that he sought, in death, solace from his mental agony.

"That man was a genius," was Skin o' my Tooth's comment upon this confession. "Strange that he should have lost his nerve at the last, for I feel sure that the crime would never have been brought absolutely home to him ; at any rate, *I* could always have got him off. What do you think, Muggins ? "

And I quite agreed with Skin o' my Tooth.

"SKIN O' MY TOOTH":

HIS MEMOIRS, BY HIS CONFIDENTIAL CLERK.

COMPILED AND EDITED BY

THE BARONESS ORCZY.

II.—THE CASE OF THE POLISH PRINCE.

I DOUBT whether full credit was given to Skin o' my Tooth for the solution of that mysterious incident in the Saltashe Woods, which he—and no one else—brought about. Personally, I firmly believe that Kelly, of Saltashe Park, would have allowed his brother to hang, sooner than confess, if Skin o' my Tooth had not succeeded in absolutely cornering him. Now, in the case of the Polish Prince, no one could deny—but perhaps I had better say how it all happened.

The Swanborough tragedy was filling all London and provincial papers with its gruesome mysteries. Early on Tuesday morning, March 18th, the body of a man, shockingly mutilated, was found on the level crossing, just below the Swanborough station of the London and North-Western Railway. It is always difficult to dwell on the grim details which are the usual accompaniment to this type of drama; sufficient to say, in this instance, that the body was found lying straight along the metals, so that the passing express had gone clean over the trunk and face. What mutilation the train had left unaccomplished had been completed by the sparks from the engine. The face was unrecognisable, the hair had been singed, the flesh on hands and neck had been charred. The peculiar position of the body, so carefully laid down, with the feet pointing towards Swanborough station, and the head towards Bletchley, disposed of any theory of accident that may at first have suggested itself. It was clearly either a case of murder—the unfortunate man having, presumably, been rendered unconscious and then placed on the metals—or one of deliberate suicide.

The grim tragedy immediately assumed the appearance of complete mystery. Though

Swanborough is but a tiny, straggling village, and this part of Buckinghamshire but scantily populated, no one seemed to have missed a relative or friend, or to recognise the clothes and sundry small articles of jewellery, etc., found upon the mutilated body. The police had published a description of these clothes and articles, and of the body, as far as this could be done. The unfortunate man seemed to be about thirty-five years of age, five feet nine inches in height, and of slight build. He was evidently in the habit of wearing a green silk shade over one eye, for one was found lying on the ground quite close to the head; the right forearm showed a very recent wound caused by the burning of some acid—probably vitriol.

The people of Swanborough, however, in spite of the horrible gruesomeness of the tragedy, seemed to take very little interest in the elucidation of its mysteries; perhaps, too, they had the average English yokel's horror of having anything to do with the police. Be that as it may, it was not until the following day that a more enlightened or more enterprising villager bethought himself of walking to the police-station and informing the inspector there that "maybe the murdered man was Mrs. Stockton's lodger."

It appears that Mrs. Stockton, who rented a small cottage not far from the railway, had had a lodger on and off for the past six months. No one in the village had ever seen him; if he ever went outside the cottage, he must have done so at nights; but young Stockton had sometimes talked to the neighbours about his mother's lodger. He was a foreigner, he said, and "no end of a swell," with a name no decent body could pronounce, as it was about half a yard long. He was certainly very odd in his ways, for he used to go away quite suddenly, and not come home for a week or so on end. Mrs.

Stockton never knew where he went to ; and then he would turn up again, mostly in the very early mornings.

Life in rural districts is wonderfully self-centred ; still, the police thought it odd that this tardy information did not come from Mrs. Stockton herself or from her son, if, indeed, her lodger were missing just now. The detective-inspector immediately went down to the cottage. Finding the door locked, and getting no answer to his repeated knocks, he forced his way in, followed by two constables. Parlour and kitchen were empty, but up on the floor above, in one of the three little bedrooms, the men found the unfortunate woman lying in bed with her throat cut. There was no sign or trace anywhere of young Stockton.

The mystery, of course, had deepened more and more. Nothing in the cottage seemed to have been touched ; there were even a couple of sovereigns and some silver lying in a money-box. So far, it appeared that two purposeless and shocking murders had been committed probably within a few moments of each other, as Mrs. Stockton had evidently been dead a good many hours. The detective-inspector instituted immediate inquiries in the neighbourhood on the subject of young Stockton, who certainly had unaccountably disappeared. It seems that he was a platelayer by trade, lately in the employ of the North-Western Railway, but recently dismissed owing to ill-conduct.

"'I was engaged to Prince Sierotka, who was murdered on the railway.'"

A description of the missing man was telegraphed to every police and railway station in the kingdom, but so far not a trace of him had been found. The theory of the police was that he had boarded the very train which had mangled the body of his victim, and then dropped off it again a good deal further down the line. Whether he had murdered the "foreign swell" for purposes of robbery, and killed his mother in order to get rid of an inconvenient witness, was, of course, a mere matter of conjecture ; certain it is that he had vanished, almost as if the earth had swallowed him up.

II.

FROM the first, Skin o' my Tooth was greatly interested in the Swanborough tragedy. The enigmatic personality of one of the victims, the veil of complete mystery which the murderer had succeeded in throwing over his crime, the "foreign swell" who lived in the English cottage, all appealed to my chief's love for what was dramatic and mysterious.

It was on the afternoon of the 20th, just after I had come in with the evening papers, that there was a timid rap at an outer office door. I went to open it, and, to my amazement, saw before me the daintiest vision that had ever graced our fusty old office in Finsbury Square.

It was a lovely young girl, scarcely out of her teens, beautifully dressed in deep black, who asked me if she could speak to

Mr. Mulligan immediately. It is such an unusual thing for us to receive the visits of charming young ladies that for the moment I quite forgot to ask for her name.

However, Skin o' my Tooth was quite ready to receive her, whoever she was, and the next moment I had shown the lady into the private office.

She walked up to my esteemed employer and held out a daintily gloved hand to him.

"My name is quite unknown to you, Mr. Mulligan," she began. "I am Miss Marion Calvert, and I would not have ventured to come like this to your office without any introduction, and all alone, but I want the best possible legal advice, and——"

"Yes ? "

"My friend, Miss Morton, who is engaged to Mr. Edward Kelly, of Saltashe Park, told me all about you once, a long time ago, and how much you had done for Mr. Kelly. I remember then making up my mind that if ever I were in trouble and wanted a lawyer, I would come to you ; and now——"

She had undone her furs and seated herself beside the desk. Skin o' my Tooth gave me a wink. I knew what that meant. I was to sit in my usual corner behind the wooden partition and take shorthand notes of everything the lady said.

"Mr. Mulligan," she resumed very abruptly, "I was engaged to Prince Sierotka, who was murdered the other day on the railway near Swanborough."

"Then, indeed, you are in trouble," said Skin o' my Tooth very gently, "and that is why you have come to consult me. Tell me what I can do for you."

"I am afraid that my story will seem a very foolish one to you. I was only a schoolgirl then. It was six months ago," she explained with touching *naïveté.* "I had just left school, and was going down to Buckinghamshire to stay with my guardian, Mr. Percival Lake and his wife, when I first met Prince Sierotka. It was in the train between Euston and Swanborough, and he was so kind and attentive, an l oh ! so interesting. He told me that he was a Pole, and he talked about his country, and the revolution, and the Polish martyrs who had suffered in the cause of freedom. He himself was an exile from the country he loved so well, because he had taken part in the revolution. He had large estates, but they were temporarily confiscated by the Czar ; so he had to come to England, which he loved, and he lived in a small cottage

amidst roses and lilies, and dreamt there of Poland and her liberty.

"You may imagine how delighted I was when he told me that this ideal cottage was in Swanborough, close to where my guardian lived, for I had hopes then that I should see him again. Well, Mr. Mulligan, I won't bore you with all the details of what was the happiest time of my life. Mrs. Lake was kindness itself, but she kept rather a strict eye over my movements. However, very soon I discovered that I could always slip out in the evenings, while she went to sleep over her game of 'patience,' and then I used to meet Constantine — Prince Sierotka—in the fields at the bottom of the garden. Very soon we had both realised that we loved one another passionately."

"But surely your guardian——" suggested Skin o' my Tooth.

"My guardian was away during the first fortnight of my stay in Swanborough. When he came, things were very much altered. Someone—one of the servants, perhaps—had evidently spied upon me and had told him of my meetings with Prince Sierotka, for he read me a long lecture on the subject of foreign adventurers and English girls with money, and forbade me ever to see this Polish Prince again. Of course, I was obliged to obey him then, as he kept a pretty sharp look-out over my movements, and I saw nothing of Constantine for a week ; but the moment Mr. Lake went back to town, we were able to resume our happy evening meetings in the fields.

"This went on for some time, during which my love for my future husband grew with every obstacle my guardian placed in my way. But Mr. Lake was often obliged to be absent from home on business, and you may be sure that Constantine and I made the most of these happy intervals. We had agreed that we should be married as soon as I was of age and free to do as I pleased.

"During all this time, Mr. Mulligan, I was in absolute ignorance of my future financial position, and Constantine, with a delicacy that was positively sublime, and which put to shame Mr. Lake's cynical insinuations, had never asked me any questions on the subject. I knew vaguely that my father had left me a considerable fortune, under the trusteeship of Mr. Lake, and I concluded that I should have the use of that fortune when I came of age.

"To my astonishment, however, on my eighteenth birthday, which was the ninth of this month, my guardian informed me that by the terms of my father's will, I was now to become sole mistress of the £40,000 he had left me. The next day Mr. Lake took me up to his office in London and rendered me an account of his guardianship; he then placed into my hands three large packets, which contained my £40,000 worth of securities, chiefly railway and mining shares, he said, and told me that I was free now to do with them what I pleased. It had been ostensibly arranged that I should stay in London a few days with some school friends of mine, but, secretly, Constantine and I had planned to spend long, happy days together. I took a room in Victoria Street, and he used to come up from Swanborough in the mornings sometimes, and we would go out to see the sights of London. We meant to get married almost immediately, and go and live abroad. I was rich now, and we could afford to live in the style befitting Prince Sierotka's rank."

She paused. It seemed as if she could not continue her narrative; so far it had been one of simple, delicate love romance, in which only the mysterious personality of the foreign adventurer appeared as a dim presage of coming evil; now, for the first time since the terrible tragedy occurred, the young girl —little more than a child—found herself forced to speak of it to a stranger, and her very nerves must have quivered at the ordeal. But Skin o' my Tooth did not speak. He sat in the shadow, watching the play of every emotion upon the delicately chiseled face before him.

"Last Monday, Mr. Mulligan," she resumed at last, with an effort at self-control, "Constantine went down to Swanborough in the afternoon, after having spent the day in town with me. He meant to settle what small accounts he had in the village, and stay in London until our marriage. I was sitting quietly at tea at a shop yesterday, when I heard someone close to me read aloud from a newspaper the account of the mysterious tragedy at Swanborough. A man had been found killed on the level crossing, his body and head shockingly mutilated. A description of his clothes followed—one or two articles found near the body. Oh! it was terrible, Mr. Mulligan! From those descriptions I knew that the murdered man must be my *fiancé*, Prince Sierotka."

There was a long silence in the fusty old office. Skin o' my Tooth was giving the young girl time to recover herself, when he said quietly: "It must indeed have been hard to bear in your peculiarly isolated position. But you have not yet told me how I can be of service to you."

"Oh! it's about the money, Mr. Mulligan— my whole fortune. Prince Sierotka had charge of it all, of course, and now I am penniless."

"You need have no fear; we can easily trace those securities for you; the thief won't be able to negotiate them."

"Oh, the securities!" she said naïvely, "they were all sold."

"Indeed?" was Skin o' my Tooth's very dry comment.

"Yes. At Constantine's suggestion, I instructed the brokers, Messrs. Furnival and Co., to sell my shares for me. They sent me a cheque for £38,000, which I endorsed, and Prince Sierotka cashed the cheque. He had all the money in notes, and he told me to write my name at the back of each. On the Monday we went round together to several foreign banks, where we changed our English notes into foreign money. You see, we intended to live in Russia, and meant to start for Paris almost immediately."

I wished then that I could have caught a glimpse of Skin o' my Tooth's face; as it is, I thought I heard the peculiar low whistle he usually gives when a point in a case particularly strikes his fancy.

"I see," he said at last. 'And that money? Did the Prince carry it about with him?"

"He gave me fifty pounds, as I meant to go shopping after he left me; the remainder he kept in his pocket-book."

"Hm! Life's strange ironies!"

But, fortunately for her many illusions, the young girl did not catch the drift of this last remark, for she said with great vehemence: "You see, now, Mr. Mulligan, that there could be no question of accident or suicide. Prince Sierotka was murdered and robbed, and I have come to you so that you may help me to track his murderer."

"I will do my best," said Skin o' my Tooth, with a smile; "and at the same time, we must hope to track your lost fortune for you. But I think that is all I need trouble you about this morning. Where are you staying?"

"I am still at 182, Victoria Street."

"Then I can easily communicate with you. I will see the detective-inspector in charge of the case, and, of course, let him know about the money, which should be found in the murderer's possession. Was the money French or Russian?"

She shook her head.

"Skin o' my Tooth was looking at the surroundings and at the ground before him."

"I really couldn't tell you. You see, Constantine saw to everything."

Skin o' my Tooth sighed. So much *naïveté* and blind confidence would be ridiculous were it not sublime.

Five minutes later I had shown the lady downstairs, and when I returned, I found Skin o' my Tooth lounging in his big arm-chair.

"It was a case of biter bit, with a vengeance, wasn't it, sir?" I said, with a laugh, whilst I carefully collected my notes. "This so-called Prince seems to have been as complete a scoundrel as the man who murdered him."

"Muggins, you're an ass!" was the only comment my esteemed employer made during the whole of the rest of that afternoon.

III.

In the meanwhile the evening papers had brought no further news of the Swanborough mystery. No trace of the missing platelayer had been found, and it was pretty clear that at the inquest, which was fixed for to-morrow (Friday), the police would have no important evidence to add to the scanty scraps already collected and published.

"The authorities at Scotland Yard will resent my interference in this case," said Skin o' my Tooth to me; "but I must chance that. If I leave them to blunder on, as they have done over this murder, I shall never get Miss Calvert's money for her, for the scoundrel will succeed in slipping through our fingers."

He sent me down to Scotland Yard the next morning, to make the necessary declaration with regard to Prince Sierotka's antecedents as related to us by Miss Calvert, and also to the missing quantity of foreign money. The detective-inspector who was looking after the case was greatly excited to hear my news.

"This gives us the motive for the crime," he said, "and the foreign money in the possession of an uneducated Buckinghamshire yokel like Stockton is sure to lead to his discovery and speedy arrest. At any rate, now that we have so much fresh data, I will send one of our men—Mason is very capable—down to Swanborough again. I will give him instructions to place himself at Mr. Mulligan's disposal should he require any local information."

When I went back to the office, I found a hansom at the door, and Skin o' my Tooth waiting for me with his hat on.

"Come down to Swanborough with me, Muggins," he said. "I have worked out

this case in my own mind, and I want to ascertain, by studying the geography of the place, whether I am right or wrong."

We went down to Swanborough, catching the 12.5 p.m. from Euston. It is a couple of hours' run on the North-Western line, but during the whole of the journey Skin o' my Tooth never spoke a word. He sat leaning back in his corner, with that funny little smile of his playing round the corners of his fat mouth, and the thick lids drooping as if in semi-somnolence. But every now and then I caught a flash, a steely, almost cruel look in his lazy blue eyes, and then his nostrils would quiver like those of a hound who has just found a scent. I knew those symptoms well. I had seen them in him whenever the sharp and astute lawyer was for the time being merged in the tracker of crime. Skin o' my Tooth had all the instincts of a bloodhound. Placed face to face with a murder, he would follow the trail of the assassin with almost superhuman cunning. He did not deduce, he seldom reasoned; he *felt* the criminal. I believe firmly that he scented him.

When we steamed into the small country station, a little after 2 p.m., we found that Mason, the detective, who was personally known to Skin o' my Tooth, had come down by the previous train. He was standing talking to the booking-clerk when my chief went up to speak to him.

I think that he was none too pleased to see a lawyer mixed up in a case which he no doubt considered strictly the business of the police; but Skin o' my Tooth seemed to have armed himself for the afternoon with a limitless fund of Irish urbanity.

"I won't detain you long, Mason," he said, with a bland smile. "I should presently like to have a look at the body, with you; and in the meanwhile, I daresay, while we walk through the village, you will put me *au fait* of the latest news in connection with this interesting case."

"There is very little news," said Mason, with marked impatience. "The case is a very troublesome one; and if it is meddled with, I don't believe we shall ever get at the rights of it."

"I see that you were having a chat with the young booking-clerk here," said Skin o' my Tooth, quietly ignoring the detective's rudeness. "I wonder what his impression was of the Polish Prince. So few people seem to have seen him; but, of course, at the railway-station they must have known him by sight."

"The porters and the booking-clerk only saw him once, and that was on the Monday, when he came down by an afternoon train, and one man saw him soon after eleven the same evening. It was just after the last slow train had gone through, and they were closing the booking-office; he was then walking along the line with young Stockton, towards the level crossing."

"What sort of a looking man was he?"

"Oh! a regular foreigner, it appears, with thick black hair falling back over his forehead, and a heavy black moustache. He had a huge scar right across the left side of his face—from a wound, I suppose. They say it looked like a sabre cut, and it seems to have injured his eye as well, for he wore a guard over the left one. Anyway, he is quite unrecognisable now," he added grimly.

Mason had led the way along the platform while he was talking, and we had followed him. He was now walking along the railway line, about two paces in front of us. On our left a tall and neat hedge fenced off a field, and some two hundred yards ahead was the level crossing, where a road cut the line at right angles.

About twenty yards from the level crossing there was a wide gap in the hedge. Mason pointed this out to us.

"It is supposed that Stockton enticed his victim into the field under some pretence or other, and rendered him unconscious there, then he dragged him on to the metals. This gap, Mr. Lake tells me, used to be quite a small one. It has obviously been broken and widened quite recently."

"Mr. Lake?" queried Skin o' my Tooth.

"Mr. Percival Lake. This field is his property; his house and grounds are at the opposite end of it."

"Oh! Ah, yes! I am glad to hear that, as I should like to call on Mr. Lake before I leave Swanborough to-day."

We had come to a standstill on the very spot where the awful and gruesome murder of the mysterious foreign prince had been perpetrated. Skin o' my Tooth was looking at the surroundings and at the ground before him, and every now and then I could hear him snorting, and caught sight of that weird and quick flash in his eyes which gave his jovial, fat face such a cruel look. Then, without word or warning, he suddenly darted through the gap in the hedge, into the field beyond. With an impatient shrug of the shoulders, Mason followed him, and I brought up the rear.

It was mid-December, and the ground was as hard as nails; a few patches of dead grass only showed here and there. We were in a field of about thirty acres, triangular in shape, with the same tall hedge surrounding it, and the house and grounds forming its apex. A road ran on either side of it, converging towards one another on the other side of the house.

The afternoon had rapidly drawn in. It was past three o'clock, and a thick mist had descended. Mason followed, with evident and unconcealed ill-humour, Skin o' my Tooth's peregrinations through that field. At first he had offered certain hints and volunteered some information, but at last he seemed to have resigned himself to the part of a bad-tempered man in charge of a lunatic.

We walked straight across the field to where the house and its thick shrubbery formed its extreme boundary. There, too, a small gate led to a cottage and tiny garden, which occupied a piece of ground that seemed to have been sliced out of Mr. Lake's property.

"It is Mrs. Stockton's cottage," explained Mason, in answer to Skin o' my Tooth's inquiry. Quite close to the gate there was a tool-shed, which seemed to interest Skin o' my Tooth immensely, for he lighted match after match in order to examine it inside and out. However, he expressed no desire to view the interior of the cottage, and at last, when I was quite numb with fatigue and cold, he turned to Mason and said quietly: "I am quite ready to go to the station now and have a look at the body."

For a moment I thought that Mason meant to go on strike; but evidently he had had his orders, or perhaps he, too, began to feel, as I had done so often, that curious magnetic influence of Skin o' my Tooth's personality, which commands obedience at strange moments and in strange places. Be that as it may, he refrained from making any remark, but passing through the gate and cottage garden, he went out into the road. About five minutes' brisk and silent walk brought us to the village, and then on to the little police-station. Still without a word, Mason led the way into an inner room. There upon a deal table, and covered over with a sheet, lay the body of the murdered man.

IV.

IT is not often—thank Heaven for that!—that I have to go through such unpleasant moments in my faithful adherence to my duty towards my employer. I shall never forget the terrible feeling and sickly horror which overcame me when Skin o' my Tooth so quietly lifted the sheet which covered the dead man. The whole scene is even now vividly impressed upon my mind—the small, low-raftered room, the oil-lamp hanging from the ceiling and throwing its feeble light upon the gruesome thing on which I dared not look, and upon the strange, bulky figure, so strangely impressive at this moment, of my chief. Mason stood close by in the shadow. I could see that even he did not care to cast too long a look at the hopelessly mutilated face of the murdered man. Skin o' my Tooth, however, was quite unmoved. He had dropped the sheet, and calmly, one by one, he took up each garment from the pile of clothes which lay neatly folded beside the body.

"These were found upon the deceased, I understand?" he asked. The detective nodded.

"All," he replied, "except the gloves, which were in the grip of the hand."

"And which this man could never have worn," commented Skin o' my Tooth drily, "though they are quite old; they are two sizes too small for the hand."

There was silence again for a few moments; then Skin o' my Tooth, having carefully examined each individual garment, put the last one down; then, placing his hand upon the pile, he said: "I hope for your sake, Mason—and for mine, too, for that matter, since it would save arguments—that you have arrived at the only possible and complete solution of the so-called mystery."

"The only mystery in this matter," retorted Mason gruffly, "is the real personality of the deceased. We know who murdered him all right enough, though we don't know where the murderer may be at the present moment."

"The personality of the deceased is no mystery to me. He was a young man named Stockton, a platelayer by trade, and an inhabitant of this village," said Skin o' my Tooth, making this extraordinary announcement as if he were stating the most obvious and commonplace fact.

Mason shrugged his shoulders and looked almost appealingly at me, as if he wanted me to take charge of this raving lunatic.

"The only thing that puzzles *me*," continued Skin o' my Tooth imperturbably, "is that it never struck any of you gentlemen in charge of this case how very badly some of these clothes must have fitted this man."

"People don't always have their clothes cut by a London tailor," muttered Mason sarcastically.

"Undoubtedly. But in this case the fit is so erratic; while the trousers would be at least three-quarters of an inch too long in the leg, the coat-sleeves would be at least an inch too short. This man could not have had these gloves on at all; and every time he wore these boots, which are not new, he must have endured positive tortures, yet he has no corns on his feet."

"The clothes might have been a scratch lot, bought at a second-hand clothes shop," suggested Mason.

"A man does not buy second-hand boots that are much too small for him."

"What is your idea, then?"

"That they are another man's clothes," said Skin o' my Tooth quietly.

"But——"

"Note one thing more. The suit of clothes are good, such as a gentleman might wear; boots, gloves, hat, all are of an expensive kind; but the underclothes are of the commonest and coarsest make."

"That often happens," muttered Mason obstinately.

"It certainly in itself would mean but little were it not for the fact that with almost superhuman cunning everything has been devised in order to completely destroy the identity of the victim. From the clothes, every tag and some buttons have been removed which might bear the tailor's name; on the forearm, vitriol was used, in order, obviously, to obliterate some mark—tattoo, perhaps—which might have made the body recognisable, whilst the same corrosive substance destroyed the finger-nails, which might have told a tale."

"The accepted theory is that deceased was engaged in some work which necessitated the use of sulphuric acid."

"That might account for the corroded finger-nails, if the man was particularly careless, but not for the wound on the forearm. Think of it all carefully, Mason, and then bear in mind the fact that the only person who might by chance have identified the body, in spite of its mutilation, was also murdered."

"You mean Mrs. Stockton?"

"The mother undoubtedly," replied Skin o' my Tooth quietly. "Surely you see for yourself now that the body we have here before us is that of Stockton, the platelayer, whereas it is this so-called Prince Sierotka, this arch-scoundrel, thief, liar, and assassin,

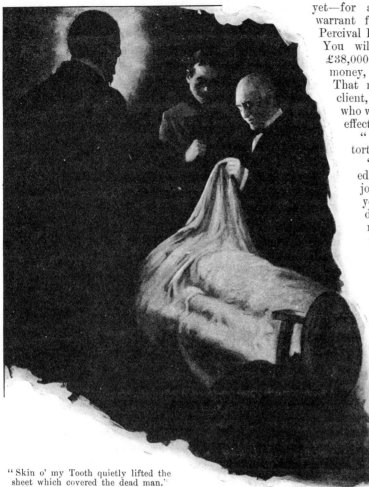

"Skin o' my Tooth quietly lifted the sheet which covered the dead man."

yet—for a search-warrant and warrant for the arrest of Mr. Percival Lake, of Swanborough. You will find most of the £38,000 there, in foreign money, Russian or French. That money belongs to my client, Miss Marion Calvert, who will file affidavits to this effect to-morrow."

"You are mad !" retorted Mason.

"Mad, am I ?" laughed Skin o' my Tooth jovially. "Why, man, you know as well as I do by now that I am right. Why, I guessed the trick the moment Miss Calvert told me her pathetic little history ; then I came down here, and I saw how admirably the geography of the place was adapted to that arch-villain's infamous plot for robbing his young ward. Why, you have only to remember three points to realise how absolutely right I am. Point number one: Whenever Mr. Percival Lake was at home, Miss Calvert could never see her sweetheart. The moment he was supposed to go back to town she found him at the trysting-place in the field ; but always at night, remember, when the disguise, the scar, the black hair, would more easily deceive the young girl. It was only when he had got her money absolutely in his possession that he became more audacious and saw her in London in broad daylight."

"I have always thought that that scar and the thick, black hair meant a disguise," muttered Mason. "Some people are so clever at making up, and Mr. Lake is a little bald and clean-shaved."

"The change of costume was so easy of execution with that convenient little tool-shed in his own shrubbery, secluded from all eyes and, until recently, fitted with a good lock and key, which have since, very ob-

who so far has escaped the vigilance of the police."

"You may be right," murmured Mason, convinced, as I could see, in spite of himself with the firm logic of Skin o' my Tooth's arguments ; "but, as far as I can see, you have not by any means solved our difficulty. It was quite one thing to hunt for a Buckinghamshire yokel, who would be trying to pass a quantity of foreign money and could not speak any language but his own, and quite another to search through the Continent of Europe now for a foreigner, of whose real appearance I presume even your client, his sweetheart, is ignorant."

"You won't have to search through the Continent of Europe, my man," said Skin o' my Tooth, with a jovial laugh. "You just apply—as quickly as you can, too, for the gentleman may slip through your fingers viously, been removed. Why, nothing in the world could be more easy than for an arch-scoundrel like that man Lake to ostensibly leave for town in the evening, carrying his bag, and, walking through his field, to spend the night in the tool-shed, and emerge therefrom in the very early morning as Prince Sierotka; then to repeat this performance whenever the foreign adventurer had to resume his original part of Mr. Percival Lake, Miss Calvert's stern guardian. Add to this point number two—that the man who played the trick on Miss Calvert must have known all about her financial position and the full terms of her father's will, by which she came of age at eighteen."

"That certainly brings it nearer home to Lake than ever. And your third point, Mr. Mulligan?"

"That this so-called foreigner was supposed to have gone up to London from Swanborough very frequently during the week, when he met Miss Calvert in town nearly every day, and helped her to transfer her English securities into foreign money, and yet no one at the Swanborough railway-station had ever seen him before the night of the murder. Then, he wished to show himself, openly, in the company of the platelayer, so that, when he had murdered Stockton and dressed up his body in his own cast-off disguise, everyone should fancy that they recognised in the mangled remains the personality of the Polish Prince. He did the murder at dead of night, of course, and in the privacy of his own fields; he used vitriol where marks of identification might reveal the platelayer; then he murdered Mrs. Stockton and slipped home quietly to bed. I dare say his wife was an accomplice. Some women are very loyal or very obedient to their husbands. But come along, Muggins," he said, suddenly altering the tone of his voice and turning to me; "we shall miss that 6.30 up to London. It must be nearly that now, and Mason will want to think all this over."

"No, I don't, sir," said Mason firmly. "I am going up to town with you, if you will allow me."

"What for?"

"To report myself and to get a warrant for the arrest of Mr. Percival Lake."

* * * * *

Everyone remembers the arrest of Mr. Percival Lake on a double charge of murder. In his safe at his house in Swanborough were found French and Russian notes amounting in value to about £38,000. Tracked to earth, the scoundrel made but a poor defence. Fortunately for his relations, since he was well connected, he died of sudden heart failure during the subsequent magisterial inquiry, and was never committed for trial.

This all happened three years ago. Miss Calvert is married now, and has evidently forgotten her former passionate love for the mysterious Polish patriot.

"SKIN O' MY TOOTH":

HIS MEMOIRS, BY HIS CONFIDENTIAL CLERK.

COMPILED AND EDITED BY
THE BARONESS ORCZY.

III.—THE CASE OF MAJOR GIBSON.

I HAVE always wondered why Skin o' my Tooth was so unpopular in his own profession. He had very few friends among his colleagues, but those he had were certainly very staunch. I have heard it said that his ways were "unprofessional"; certain it is that he avoided actual litigation for his clients whenever that was possible—I suppose that *would* be called unprofessional.

Personally, I never met a man of such varying moods. Over that Swanborough murder case he was alert, uncanny, and irritatingly active; over Major Gibson's case he always looked as if he were going to sleep, and as if any trashy French novel were more interesting than the honour of his client.

Now, I remember when Major Gibson first called upon him and told him his story, I thought to myself: "Here's the prettiest kettle of fish that ever Skin o' my Tooth had placed before him." He was a good-looking man, this Major Gibson; but the day he called at the office he looked as white as a ghost. He began by saying that unless Mr. Mulligan would help him, he had made all arrangements for committing suicide.

I could see that he did not quite know how to begin—Skin o' my Tooth did not evidently come up to the imaginary portrait the gallant Major's imagination had drawn for himself. I must say that my esteemed chief looked particularly fat, pink, and inane that morning.

"I always like to hear the story from the beginning," he said, as he quietly—without asking his client's leave—lighted a huge German long-stemmed pipe. For a moment I thought that the Major was going to make an ass of himself and leave the room, and go and commit suicide, sooner than tell his tale to an ill-mannered Irish lawyer; but he was in a tight hole, and he kept his temper.

"About a month ago," he began at last very abruptly, "I was staying at Belcher Hall, Mr. Everard's place in Rutlandshire. There was a good deal of gambling going on there in the evenings—— I am not a rich man; I disapprove—on principle—of playing games of hazard; nevertheless, I played and lost one night——"

"Dates, please, wherever possible," interrupted Skin o' my Tooth quietly.

"October 18th, 1901," said Major Gibson, whilst I, knowing what would be expected of me presently, made as rapid shorthand notes as my imperfect training would allow. "At about 11 p.m. I at last left the baccarat-table at Belcher Hall, with my last possible cheque on my current account drawn to bearer, and promissory notes amounting to close on £8,000 in the hands of various gentlemen, my fellow-guests in the hospitable mansion of Belcher Hall. I must say that Everard was exceedingly nice to me later on in the billiard-room, when we had a smoke and a drink together. I was a fool, and mistook his kind words for genuine sympathy; I admitted to him that I had lost a great deal more than I could possibly afford, and that there was nothing for it but I must exchange into some Indian regiment, and put off my proposed marriage until I had in some measure retrieved my heavy losses, or if the lady were unwilling to wait, to give her back her word and her liberty. I think Everard must have understood how hard this would be to me. Only a month ago I had become engaged to his wife's niece, Miss Marion Sutcliffe, to whom I was passionately attached. I am not a young man, and I do not

425

fall in and out of love as quickly as some of my contemporaries."

He broke off abruptly; evidently the subject of Miss Marion was still a sore one.

"How long did the interview last—with Mr. Everard, I mean?" asked Skin o' my Tooth quietly.

"At twelve o'clock precisely I left him, intending to go to bed; but as I knew that I should find it very difficult to get to sleep, I strolled into the library, a beautiful room on the ground floor, with deep-mullioned windows. I meant to get a book and then to retire to my bedroom. I remember that the room was quite dark when I went in, as the heavy curtains had been drawn closely across the deep window-recesses. As I did not know where and how to switch on the electric light, I went up to one of the windows, meaning to draw the curtains aside and to let a flood of moonlight into the room. But the garden looked so fine and poetic, and I felt so moody and wretched, that, quite contrary to my usual habits, I sat down in one of the deep window-seats and stared out, mooning, thinking of nothing in particular, into the garden before me. How long I remained there, I cannot tell you. Certain it is that suddenly I became aware that someone was in the library besides myself. I had not heard the door open or shut, and I did not know who the someone was. I only inferred that it was a lady, for I could hear the rustle of a silk gown against the parquet floor as she, in her turn, went up to one of the windows."

Major Gibson paused a moment here, giving me time for the space of thirty seconds at least to stretch out my cramped muscles. Skin o' my Tooth had not said a word; he was looking down at the meerschaum bowl of his long-stemmed pipe, whilst a coy and gentle smile played round the fat corners of his mouth. Major Gibson passed his hand across his forehead once or twice; I know that he was cursing himself for the fool he had been at 1 a.m. on the memorable night of October 18th, 1901.

"I can assure you," he said at last, "that nothing in particular crossed my mind when I heard the rustle of that silk dress, and certainly the next moment I should have made my presence known to the midnight wanderer; but just then I happened to have my head turned towards the garden, and to have caught sight of the figure of a man cautiously making his way towards the library windows, whilst keeping as much as

possible within the shadow of the trees. A second later I had heard a gentle whistle, the window furthest from the one in which I was sitting was opened, then shut, and I realised that the most discreet and prudent thing I could now do was to keep as quiet as I possibly could for the present, and if I were detected later on, to feign a deep and uninterrupted sleep."

"Discreet and prudent," commented Skin o' my Tooth, with a smile. "It is strange how we all differ in the meaning of those two words."

"I am wise, too, now, after the event," retorted Major Gibson a little impatiently. "At the time I did not think I was doing the slightest harm either to myself or to the two who were having this clandestine meeting at this extraordinary hour. Remember, the room was quite dark; the man, whoever he was, had evidently slipped through the window, and no one had drawn the curtains. I heard some hurried whispers, then the man spoke impatiently. 'Have you brought them, anyway?' What the lady replied, I could not hear, but it was evidently satisfactory, for he said quite loudly: 'That's all right—let's have a look.' I remember, it struck me at the time that the midnight interview did not seem particularly tender. It came very soon to an end, too. Curiosity is supposed to be a feminine vice, but I can assure you that at that moment I was positively devoured with curiosity as to who the lady was who could thus risk the whole edifice of her social position for the sake of some individual who was evidently unscrupulous and obviously was none too tender. I again heard the rustle of the dress: the lady was returning to her own room, leaving the man to find his way out alone. I put one finger on the curtain, hoping to catch a glimpse of her, but I only saw the shimmer of a green silk train, as a ray of moonbeam caught it, when she glided out of the room.

"I remembered all the ladies who were staying in the house; I had seen them in the drawing-room before that miserable baccarat party. I remembered, too, that Mrs. Everard, our beautiful hostess, who is very fair, wore a magnificent green satin gown. I also remembered that Marion—my Marion—Mrs. Everard's niece, had looked bewitching in a clinging green frock with a long train. Of course, Marion was out of the question—you will understand that, won't you?—the very thought was preposterous; but Mrs. Everard, my friend's wife, young, pretty—I assure you my head was in a whirl. I had not moved. I had forgotten the man, until a flood of brilliant light startled me from my dream. I pushed aside the curtains. Immediately beneath one of the electric light brackets, which he had evidently just switched on, a man was standing with his back to me; he was examining intently something which he held in his hand. My instinct was to knock him down then and there, like the foul thief he was; but I suppose I must have made a noise when I crossed the room, for he turned before I could reach him. I then saw what he held in his hand. It was the necklet of pearls and diamonds which I had before now seen round Mrs. Everard's neck.

"I really don't think," continued Major Gibson after another little pause, "that I can tell you exactly what happened after that. All I can remember is that I had him on the floor, and that I would have killed him if he had not at last reluctantly given me back that necklet."

"It did not strike you that it might be best to ring for some of the servants, and to give him in charge like the thief he was?" asked Skin o' my Tooth after a while, during which he was contemplating the unfortunate Major through his half-closed lids.

"'He was examining intently something which he held in his hand.'"

"I thought of it for a moment—but——"

"But you did not do it?"

"No."

"Why?"

"Because he swore to make a scandal if I denounced him. I had not *seen* the woman, and I was not *sure*; but there on the floor, close to the door, was a bunch of pink roses which I had given to Marion a few hours ago."

"I see," said Skin o' my Tooth, with a smile. There was silence in the room for a time, whilst I had a chance of cracking my knuckles, which were horribly stiff and cramped.

"I think I can guess what happened after that," said Skin o' my Tooth, at last taking the pipe out of his mouth. The Major did not reply, and he went on: "You sent the thief about his business, and you yourself were discovered five minutes later with that necklet in your hand, unable or unwilling to give an account as to how you had come by it."

Major Gibson nodded moodily.

" I met Everard just outside the library. He caught sight of the necklet in my hand, even before he had recovered from his surprise at finding me there at that hour. He asked me for an explanation. I could give him none—that is to say, I gave him one as near to the truth as I dared, which he, of course, disbelieved. I gave him back the necklet, and he told me at what hour I could get a train back to town. He was supposed to be a friend of mine, but he thought me guilty. You see, he knew how heavily I had lost at cards. I had myself told him that I was sore pressed for money, and might have to break off my engagement, and even leave for India——"

" Will you tell me what lie—I mean explanation—you *did* give Mr. Everard ? " interrupted Skin o' my Tooth quietly.

" I told him that on going into the library late at night, to fetch a book, I had found a man there with Mrs. Everard's necklace in his hand. That I succeeded in getting the necklace from him, but that he, in his turn, succeeded in getting away through the window."

" He naturally asked you why you did not raise an alarm ? "

" He did."

" And also whether you would recognise the supposed thief if you saw him again? Quite so. Your replies not being very lucid, he drew his own conclusions. But forgive my interrupting you. You have not quite finished, I think ? "

" I haven't much more to tell you. It appears that the ladies went up to their rooms soon after twelve, the men staying down in the billiard-room, to smoke. But at last everyone retired, and Everard himself was about to do the same, when his wife—fully dressed still—met him on the stairs, with the news that one of her most valuable necklaces had been stolen. She was putting away the jewels which she had just been wearing, when she noticed that one of the cases was empty. Everard persuaded her to go back to her room, and he himself started on a tour of inspection round the house."

" And met you ? "

" And met me, as you say."

" Then is that all you have to tell me ? "

" That is all. Everard was up in time to see me before I left in the morning—he and Lord Combermury, the colonel of my regiment. Both tried to persuade me to confess, and promised as an inducement, that if I made a clean breast of it to them, and agreed to exchange into some Native regiment

and to break off my engagement with Miss Sutcliffe, the whole matter should be hushed up."

" And you promised—— ? "

" I promised nothing."

" The result being—— ? "

" That the scandal has gone the round of the town. I have been requested to hand in my papers, and in my clubs it has been strongly hinted to me that I should be turned out unless I succeeded in clearing my character."

" And so far you have not attempted to mention the lady's name ? "

" Would I not be branded as a worse blackguard than before, for slandering a woman in order to try and save my own skin ? And I was not *sure*, remember. I did not *know* who the lady was."

" Have you any conviction now ? "

The Major hesitated a moment, then he said quietly—

" No."

II.

THERE was silence in the room for a long time after that. The Major was staring moodily into the fire, and Skin o' my Tooth was puffing away at his old German pipe, smiling gently to himself. Presently he began to hum a tune, and he looked so coy, and fat, and comfortable, no wonder he jarred upon the unfortunate Major's nerves.

" Well, sir ? " said the latter at last very irritably.

Skin o' my Tooth smothered a yawn.

" I was waiting," he said.

" What for ? "

" To hear what you are going to do."

Here the Major swore vigorously.

" Do you think I should be here now," he said, " if I knew ? The few friends I have got left advise a slander action, and I have come to consult you, as someone has told me that you were the ablest man in London in cases of this sort."

" That 'someone' no doubt said to you that you had a jolly bad case, and required an unscrupulous devil like Patrick Mulligan to pull you through," remarked Skin o' my Tooth drily.

I could see from the deep red on the Major's bronzed cheek that my esteemed employer had guessed right.

Skin o' my Tooth settled himself within the depths of his large, shabby, leather arm-chair. He smothered another yawn with an attempt at politeness. He looked, in fact, as if he were getting very tired of the whole thing, and longed to get back to his favourite French novel, the yellow paper cover of which was even now protruding from one of the pockets of his ill-fitting coat.

"A slander action in this case would be a very ticklish matter," he said at last. "Mr. Everard, against whom, I suppose, you would enter it, would plead justification, and you must own that the circumstances of the case are decidedly in his favour. He finds you in a very ambiguous position, and the explanations you give are terribly lame. You might get 'damages one farthing,' which would do you more harm than good, and effectually kill the last shreds of reputation you have got left. But there is one thing, of course, which can put you right, and that is a confession from the lady."

"Impossible!"

"Why?"

"Is it likely?"

"I think so. You have come to me for advice. It is the only one I can give. Some of my more eminent colleagues would no doubt suggest an action. But these same eminent gentlemen will tell you that Patrick Mulligan has no reputation to mar. His ways are tortuous, his means unscrupulous. Perhaps they are right. Are you willing to adopt these ways and means and follow my advice unreservedly? You will scrape through this hole by the skin of your teeth, I tell you, but I will pledge the evil reputation I *have* got that we'll obtain a confession from the unknown lady."

"It would have to be a public one now, I am afraid, to do me any good."

"It will be sufficient. I give you my—— No! I won't give you my word; it wouldn't be much good to you; but ask the most disreputable character in the London slums when Skin o' my Tooth has said 'I'll do it,' whether he is the man to break his word."

No wonder the Major looked a new man. I have seen many a poor chap look like that when once they have had a square talk with Skin o' my Tooth. By Gosh! but he knows how to carry conviction with him; when he talks to a client or to the jury, it's all the same—they run after him like a pack of sheep.

"And now, my dear Major," he concluded, "which day will it be convenient for you to meet Mr. Everard?"

"Meet Everard?" gasped the Major. "I wouldn't care to——"

"Sir," said Skin o' my Tooth, with his gentle smile, "just now I used the word 'unreservedly.' I will not move in this matter unless I possess your entire confidence."

The Major hesitated no longer. Skin o' my Tooth was his last straw.

"You do what you think best," he said doggedly; "but Everard will refuse."

"Wednesday next, shall we say, at 3 p.m.? That will suit you? Muggins, make a note of that."

"Everard will refuse," repeated the Major.

"I think not," said Skin o' my Tooth, with a smile. "Have I your permission to proceed?"

"As you will."

"And you place yourself *unreservedly* in my hands?"

For one brief second the Major hesitated, while his sharp, clear, honest eyes scanned quickly the fat, unwieldy figure huddled up in the armchair, the sleepy eyes with their drooping lids, the ill-fitting, shiny black coat, with that yellow-backed French novel protruding from its pocket.

Skin o' my Tooth sat there, with that coy smile of his playing round the corners of his mouth.

Then the Major, with a sudden, frank gesture, put out his hand and said firmly: "Without reserve."

"Muggins, show the Major out," said my chief, with sudden, obvious alacrity.

When I came back—having shown Major Gibson downstairs—I found Skin o' my Tooth absorbed in his French novel. I waited for awhile; then, as he did not speak, I asked at last: "What am I to do now, sir?"

"Nothing, my boy, nothing," he said airily. "Confine yourself to not being an ass for the rest of the afternoon; that will always be something accomplished. In the meanwhile, you can hand me down 'Burke's Landed Gentry' from that shelf."

I gave him the book he wanted.

Then he added: "By the way, Muggins, copy out your notes on a sheet of parchment and engross them neatly. We may require them in that form later on."

III.

MR. EVERARD, strange to say, was willing enough to meet Major Gibson and his solicitor, and talk the matter over amicably if possible. I fancy he is a decent enough sort of man, and was only too ready to see the end of this unfortunate business; moreover, I don't suppose that he, either, cared to take his chances of defending a slander action. If by any chance Major Gibson did succeed in making his case good, he would get such thundering damages as even Mr. Everard—rich as he was—would not care to pay. It was finally arranged that Major Gibson, accompanied by Mr. Patrick Mulligan and myself, should be at Mr. Everard's house in Park Lane on Wednesday at 3.30 p.m. Of course, Mr. Everard's solicitor would be present; also Lord Combermury, and—by the special request of Major Gibson, as represented by Mr. Mulligan—Mrs. Everard and Miss Marion Sutcliffe.

I had not the least idea, of course, what Skin o' my Tooth was up to, but the whole of that morning, while he was reading his French novel, I saw him smile to himself with that funny, coy, and gentle smile which always meant mischief to his adversaries.

I remember feeling at that interview very like a character in a French play. Everyone wore a frock-coat—except myself. Skin o' my Tooth's was very shabby, and fitted him badly, and from one of the pockets a yellow-backed book protruded very conspicuously.

We were shown into a fine dining-room, oak-panelled, magnificently furnished. There was a large fire in the big open grate, and the two ladies, when we came in (I did not know which was Mrs. Everard and which Miss Sutcliffe), were sitting close beside it.

Skin o' my Tooth put down his hat and drew from his pocket the notes I had made, and carefully copied out and engrossed, of Major Gibson's case. This he placed on a little side-table which stood close to the mantelpiece. Then all the gentlemen sat down round the large dining-table, and the fun began.

Skin o' my Tooth started talking very quietly, I wondering all the time what he was driving at, and how he hoped to benefit the unfortunate Major by this extraordinary comedy; but he went on talking, and I must confess that never in my life had I heard such a fine string of lies so magnificently uttered.

"I must thank you, ladies and gentlemen," he said, "for so kindly acceding to my client's request. He felt, as

"I found Skin o' my Tooth absorbed in his French novel."

I do—as you will, I am sure—that nothing could be more deplorable than the dragging of this unfortunate affair before the public. Major Gibson has been—quite involuntarily, I feel confident, but still grossly—maligned. I will ask you, gentlemen, not to interrupt me just now; you can have your fling at us later on; for the present you must allow me to state positively that Major Gibson is not only absolutely innocent of the ugly charge of theft proffered against him, but is even now the victim of a code of honour as chivalrous as it is misdirected."

Skin o' my Tooth then, with perfect suavity, started a highly coloured account of the incidents in the library at Belcher Hall, as related to him by Major Gibson. The moonlit garden, the dark room, the rustle of the silk skirt, the clandestine meeting. Of the half-dozen people there present, every one of them—except myself—did their best to try and stop him, to sneer at him ; ejaculations, muttered in a whisper, broke out from every side. The ladies looked indescribably shocked and witheringly contemptuous. Mr. Everard looked ready to knock Skin o' my Tooth down, and his legal adviser talked of "extraordinary allegations," of "slander," and "thumping damages." But Skin o' my Tooth sailed serenely on. When the interruptions became too loud, he shouted louder, and that was all.

"Now, gentlemen," he said, "when you have quite done calling me a liar, I can get on all right. I don't blame you. I don't even mind telling you that I called Major Gibson a liar myself when I first heard his tale. You see, he kept telling me that he had no proof, no witnesses to corroborate what he had said. Now, I am not one for believing that there is ever a truth without *any* proof ; and when my client left me, I said to myself there must be some proof, some witness somewhere. Major Gibson did not recognise the lady. Good ! But in that large house and grounds of Belcher Hall, full to overflowing with visitors and servants, someone—I cared not who—*must* have seen that unknown woman in the green gown, or that man ; some trace somewhere would be left of her passage or his, some sign, some indication, whether traced by man or by Fate."

Gradually, as he spoke, I noticed that the attitude of his hearers had become considerably modified. There were no interruptions now, no whispered comments. Mr. Everard and the legal gentleman hung upon my chief's words. The Major himself looked as if suddenly a bright vista of hope had been opened before him. As for the ladies, one looked pale and breathless, while the other, leaning back in her chair, kept up that air of dignified hauteur which some English ladies know how to wear when certain matters which they deem objectionable are discussed before them. In fact, when Skin o' my Tooth paused for a moment and began fumbling in his pockets as if in search of something, this same haughty lady said quietly : "Do you not think, Archibald, that in view of the matters which—er—Mr.—er Mulligan sees fit to discuss here, I and my niece had better go ? "

"I beg a thousand pardons," said Skin o' my Tooth urbanely. "I have finished, I assure you. Please do not go. The matter will interest you both. Have I your permission to proceed ? Many thanks. It is not necessary, I think, for me to dwell here upon the ways and means I employed on behalf of my client. You may imagine that I left no stone unturned."

I was literally gasping, I can tell you. I am a pretty good liar myself on occasions. I would not enjoy Skin o' my Tooth's confidence if I were not. But I had to humbly confess to myself that in face of Skin o' my Tooth's last assertion with regard to those stones, which to my certain knowledge were made of paper and were all yellow-backed, I was only a bungling botcher. But what I could not make out was what all his fumbling in his coat-pockets meant. I thought that he was looking for the notes, which I had written out so neatly, and which he had placed on the little side-table close to the mantelpiece. Not a bit of it. When I made a movement to get them for him, he looked at me, and I understood that I had better sit still and wait.

"I am quite sure," continued Skin o' my Tooth, after a dramatic little pause, during which I noticed that his whole bulky figure seemed as it were to crouch ready for a spring, "that you will understand what a glorious day it was for me and for my client, Major Gibson, when at last my strenuous efforts were crowned with success. No, ladies and gentlemen ! I was *not* mistaken. In that densely populated, magnificent mansion I had unearthed a man who, on that memorable night, was present near enough to the library of Belcher Hall to see the mysterious lady in the green gown give Mrs. Everard's necklace to an unknown thief. This man saw the whole scene from beginning to end. Reasons which I will explain to you presently, but which seemed paramount to him, forced him to silence, until I compelled him to speak. He saw and would know again the man who, like a thief in the night, bullied, then robbed, the woman who was fool enough to ruin her reputation for his sake ; he heard the whispered conversation, saw the necklace pass from her hand to his ; he recognised the mysterious lady in the green gown, and picked up, after she left, something which had belonged to her, which he holds still——"

Skin o' my Tooth was surpassing himself.

"Mrs. Everard, as quick as lightning, had seized the notes and thrown them into the fire."

All of us there felt as if electricity filled the air. I am sure I was shaking with excitement from head to foot ; both Major Gibson and Mr. Everard were as pale as death, and I thought one of the ladies was about to faint. The other, whom I now knew was Mrs. Everard, had risen from her chair ; she was now standing close to the little side-table, almost immediately behind Skin o' my Tooth, who, suddenly dropping his voice and lolling placidly in his chair, said with a gentle smile, in perfectly matter-of-fact tones—

"Unfortunately, misfortune has dogged my steps, or rather those of my poor client. The witness I had so carefully unearthed died a couple of days ago most unexpectedly."

I wondered if I were mistaken, but I certainly thought that I heard a very obvious sigh of relief from somewhere. Certain it is that the spell of excitement under which we all had lain was broken, and one or two ironical comments came from that end of the table where Mr. Everard sat with his legal adviser.

But I knew that Skin o' my Tooth had something up his sleeve. I knew that smile of his.

"However, before the man died, I had succeeded in persuading him to swear an affidavit stating all that he had seen. This affidavit I have brought with me to-day, and——"

Then I knew what he had been driving at all along. He was on the alert, and so was I. In the midst of his neatly told lie, he stopped and pointed to my notes, which were lying on the side-table quite close to the chimney.

"Give me that affidavit, Muggins, my boy," he said.

But before I could reach them, before even anyone else had realised what she was doing, Mrs. Everard, as quick as lightning, had seized the notes and thrown them into the fire, while she turned on Skin o' my Tooth and said defiantly——

"At any rate, that woman's name will now remain a secret for ever."

Then I understood. I cared nothing about burning my fingers, but I did want to rescue the remaining fragments of my notes, as I knew they would be wanted.

Mrs. Everard was glaring at old Skin o' my Tooth as if she were a hungry tigress. If looks could kill, my esteemed employer would have been a dead man then. As it was, he smiled placidly, and taking the fragments of half-burnt paper from me, he quietly smoothed them out and placed them on the table before Mr. Everard; then he once more turned towards the angry lady.

"My dear lady," he said very gently, "I feel that I have behaved towards you absolutely like the cad my eminent colleague here present no doubt will call me. Just at this moment I know that you hate me for the odious comedy I had devised in order to extort an unwilling confession from you. Yes, my dear lady, a comedy and a confession. I don't think that I am the only man here present who knows that the Hon. Thornby Oakhurst, your brother, is the grave thorn in a distinguished family's flesh. That with somewhat impulsive thoughtlessness you tried to be of material assistance to him at a time that he was actually flying from the police and unbeknown to your husband, is only natural. That in trying to shield him and your own family honour, you allowed an innocent man to suffer so severely, is only what, under the same circumstances, most of your sex would have done. Let me in my turn confess to you, and to Mr. Everard, to whom I must also offer my humblest apologies, that the only witness present on that fateful night was Major Gibson himself, and that the affidavit which you hoped to destroy consisted of my clerk's notes of the facts taken under my unfortunate client's dictation. There is no woman's name mentioned throughout its few pages, but I think you will admit yourself that in trying to burn that document, you yourself with your dainty hand have plainly written your own."

It is wonderful with what dignity Skin o' my Tooth can speak when he likes. Mr. Everard looked as if he had some difficulty in standing straight. He did not look at his wife, and she did not attempt to speak. What would be the outcome of this extraordinary scene, I could not conjecture. Evidently Skin o' my Tooth was satisfied, for without another word he bowed to everyone, and, with Major Gibson, left the room, followed by my humble self. As I passed out of the door, I gave a final look round at the actors whom we had left on the stage. Mr. Everard had gone up to his wife, who had fallen sobbing into a chair. Miss Sutcliffe was kneeling beside her, trying to comfort her, and Lord Combermury and the solicitor looked as if they wished themselves safely out of the way.

*   *   *   *   *

I must say Mr. Everard behaved very well in the matter; both he and Lord Combermury made it their business to see that no shadow of a stain remained on Major Gibson's reputation, though Mrs. Everard's name has, of course, never been mentioned.

It all happened more than a year and a half ago, and everyone has, of course, heard of Colonel Gibson's gallant defence of Elands Drift, with his handful of men. He was married to Miss Sutcliffe about a month ago, and Mr. and Mrs. Everard gave a magnificent reception in their fine house in Park Lane in honour of the bride and bridegroom.

I suppose there was supper served in the room in which we had sat on that day.

Skin o' my Tooth was not asked to the wedding or to the reception. He would not have gone, anyhow.

"SKIN O' MY TOOTH":

HIS MEMOIRS, BY HIS CONFIDENTIAL CLERK.

COMPILED AND EDITED BY
THE BARONESS ORCZY.

IV.—THE DUFFIELD PEERAGE CASE.

IT was through the merest coincidence that Skin o' my Tooth got mixed up with this remarkable case, which brought him suddenly into such great prominence before the public, and was really the foundation-stone of his subsequent more fortunate career. In those days—it seems very long ago now—money was often very tight at the Finsbury Square office ; it was spent as soon as earned, for Skin o' my Tooth never learnt its value, principally, I think, because he never exerted himself to earn it. The gentle art of self-advertisement was totally unknown to him, even in its most elementary stages, and had I not made friends with the sub-editor of the *Surrey Post*, and got him to insert that excellent puff, beginning : " Mr. Patrick Mulligan, the most eminent and learned lawyer on criminal cases, is now in our midst," etc., etc., no doubt the Duffield Peerage Case would have drifted into other far less competent hands, and Heaven only knows what the upshot of it all would have been.

We had gone down to Guildford in connection with the Wingfield Will Case, and finding the sweet little Surrey town peculiarly attractive, Skin o' my Tooth had decided to stay on for a few days, and, under the pretence that he would feel lonely, he insisted on my remaining with him. We had spent a week of delightful idleness, and my chief had devoured a large supply of his favourite French novels, when the murder of Mr. Sibbald Thursby, a noted solicitor of Guildford, threw the whole town into a veritable state of uproar. From the very first the wildest rumours were circulated on the subject of this appalling tragedy, and it became really difficult to sift the real facts from the innumerable surmises and embellishments indulged in by the imaginative reporter of the *Surrey Post*. The truth, however, as far as I ultimately succeeded in gathering it for the benefit of my chief, who seemed interested in the case, was briefly this :—

Mr. Sibbald Thursby had an office where he transacted his business in Guildford High Street, but he lived in a tiny house just outside the town, on the Dorking Road ; his household consisting of himself and a man and his wife named Upjohn, who shared the duties of cook, gardener, maid and man of all works between them. On Friday last the Upjohns went upstairs to bed as usual at 9.30 o'clock, leaving their master at work in his study on the ground floor. This room had windows opening out on to the small garden at the back, and also a little conservatory leading to it. Mr. Thursby always bolted the windows and locked the conservatory the last thing before going to bed. The Upjohns heard someone knocking at the front door some ten minutes after they went upstairs, but both having already got into bed, they seem to have been too lazy to get up. Whether Mr. Thursby himself let his belated visitor in or not, they could not say, for they heard nothing, and very soon were both sleeping the sleep of the just.

But next morning, when Mrs. Upjohn went into the study, she was horrified to find her master lying on his side across the threshold of the conservatory door ; his clothes — the clothes he was wearing the night before—were covered with blood, his face was obviously that of the dead. Upjohn, summoned by his wife's screams, quickly ran into Guildford for the doctor and the police : the former pronounced life to be extinct, Mr. Thursby's throat having been cut from ear to ear, obviously with the short, curve-bladed knife found in the conservatory. There had been no time even for a short struggle for his life on the part of the unfortunate solicitor. According to the theory immediately formed by the police, he had been attacked with extraordinary suddenness and fury, practically at the very moment when he was opening the conservatory door in order to let the assassin in. The latter must at once have gripped his victim by the throat, smothering his screams, and only used the knife when the poor man was already senseless. In falling backwards, Mr. Thursby had seized the *portière* curtain and dragged it down with him in his fall, otherwise nothing was disturbed in the room. The windows were found carefully bolted; the lamp even had been extinguished. The few little articles of silver and bits of valuable china in the cabinets were left untouched; the unfortunate man's watch and chain, the loose cash in his pocket, were found intact; and to the police the crime seemed as purposeless as it was mysterious.

At the inquest, which was held on the following Tuesday, a verdict of "Wilful murder against some person or persons unknown" was returned, and the public had perforce to rest satisfied that everything was being done to throw light upon this tragic and awful affair. But gradually a rumour, more persistent and positive, and less vague than others, began to find general credence. The *Surrey Post* had brought the news that a lady—a stranger to Guildford—had gone to the police to request the return of certain papers which had been in the charge of Mr. Sibbald Thursby, and for which she held a receipt signed by him. Rumour went on to assert that a search was made for these papers, and that they had not been found, but that one of the constables, when he was carefully surveying the room where Mr. Thursby was murdered, had discovered a handful of ashes of burned papers in the grate. Twenty-four hours later, the news had spread throughout England like wildfire that the lady whose papers had so unaccountably disappeared claimed to be the lawful wife of the Earl of Duffield, and that those papers were of paramount importance to the legal aspect of her claim and that of her son.

Skin o' my Tooth had stayed on at Guildford all these days, chiefly because the case interested him from the very first; with his unerring instinct in criminal matters, he had scented a mysterious complication, long before the many rumours anent the lady claimant had taken definite shape.

"I imagine Lord Duffield won't enjoy this washing of all his family linen in public, which seems to me quite inevitable," he said

to me one morning, when he had read his *Surrey Post.*

We had just finished the excellent breakfast provided by the Crown Hotel, and Skin o' my Tooth had suggested the advisability of my running up to town to get him a batch of French novels, when one of the waiters came up to our table, with a great air of importance and mystery, and holding a card upon a salver.

"His Lordship is in his carriage," he murmured with the respect befitting so important an event, "and desires to have a few minutes' interview with Mr. Mulligan."

I glanced at the card, which bore the name "The Earl of Duffield," while Skin o' my Tooth quietly intimated to the waiter that he would see his Lordship in the sitting-room.

Lord Duffield was a stout, florid, jovial-looking man of about fifty, decidedly military and precise in his dress and general bearing, but at the present moment obviously labouring under a strong emotion which he was making vigorous efforts to conceal.

"Mr. Mulligan, I believe," he said.

"That is my name," replied Skin o' my Tooth. "To what can I ascribe the honour of this visit?"

"I read your name in the local papers, Mr. Mulligan, but of course I had heard of you before, in connection—er—with criminal cases. The present instance—but," he added, looking somewhat dubiously at my humble personality, "this gentleman——?"

"My confidential clerk, Lord Duffield. You need have no fear of speaking before him."

Satisfied on that point, Lord Duffield sat down, then he said abruptly—

"It is about this murder of Sibbald Thursby. The turn this affair has taken forces me to place the matter, as far as I am concerned, into the hands of a lawyer. Our own family solicitor is too old and has never had any experience of this sort; whereas you——"

"I am entirely at your disposal."

"To make the matter clear to you, I shall have to take you back some thirty years, when I, a young subaltern in a Line regiment quartered in Simla, had no prospects of ever inheriting this title and property. When I was barely twenty, I fell in love, like the young fool I was, with a noted beauty of Simla, a Miss Patricia O'Rourke, whose reputation already at that time was none too enviable. After a brief courtship, I married her, in the very teeth of strenuous opposition on the part of all my friends; and less than six months after my marriage I had undoubted proofs that Miss O'Rourke was of more evil character than even Simla had suspected, for at the time she married me she had a husband still living—a man named Henry Mitchell, as great a blackguard, I believe, as ever trod the earth.

"Half crazy with grief and the humiliation of it all, I at last succeeded in obtaining sick leave, and soon sailed for England, determined, if possible, to turn my back for ever on the woman who had blighted my life, and on the scene of my folly and my shame.

"Well, Mr. Mulligan, I dare say that experience has taught you that grief at twenty is soon forgotten. Within a year of that saddest period of my life, my uncle, the late Earl of Duffield, lost his only son, and I became his heir. He obtained for me an exchange into the Coldstream Guards, and soon after that I married Miss Angela Hutton, the daughter of America's great copper king. The following year my uncle died, I inherited the title and property, and then my son Oswald was born, and I became a widower.

"In the meanwhile, Miss O'Rourke, or Mrs. Mitchell, had disappeared from Simla. No one knew where she had gone to; some of my friends thought that she was dead.

"I was obliged to tell you all this, Mr.

"She was horrified to find her master lying across the threshold of the conservatory door."

Mulligan," resumed Lord Duffield after a slight pause, "so that you may better understand my position at the present moment. Remember that I have been during all these years under the firm impression that my marriage with Patricia O'Rourke was an illegal one, and that our son born of that union was not legitimate. I had what I considered ample proofs that Henry Mitchell was alive at the time that she married me. When I taxed her with the crime of bigamy, she not only did not deny it, but calmly told me to go my way if I liked. Now, after thirty years, she has once more appeared upon the arena of my life. Not only that, but she has come forward with a claim — a strong claim for herself and her son. She has obtained affidavits, sworn to by people of unimpeachable position, testifying to the death of Henry Mitchell in Teheran— where he had settled down in business— three clear days before her marriage to me."

"After thirty years?" commented Skin o' my Tooth in astonishment.

"She went to see Sibbald Thursby, who, as you know, perhaps, was the most noted lawyer in Guildford. He was a very old and very intimate friend of mine. She put all the facts before him and showed him all her papers. He came and told me himself that the affidavits were perfectly *en règle*, duly signed and witnessed by the British Consul in Teheran ; one had been sworn by Dr. Smollett, a leading English medical man, who attended on Henry Mitchell in his last illness."

"But why thirty years ? "

"Well, it appears that she had all along been morally convinced that Henry Mitchell had died *before* our marriage ; but she had lost trace of him for some months, and had been unable to obtain the necessary proofs to convince me of his death. However, when I left her, she resolutely set to work to obtain these proofs ; but by the time she had succeeded, some years had elapsed, and she also had lost sight of me. She did not know that Lieutenant Adrian Payton had become the Earl of Duffield, you see. A mere accident revealed this fact to her, and, immediately realising her duty to her son, she then set sail for England."

"Mr. Thursby, I understand, as a lawyer, thought well of the lady's claim ? "

"He thought that there could be no two opinions on the subject."

"There usually are, though, in law," said Skin o' my Tooth, with a smile.

"Yes ! And you may be sure that I did not mean to allow my son Oswald to lose his rights and become nameless without a struggle. But Sibbald Thursby had shown me the affidavits which my wife—I suppose I must call her that—had given in his charge, and I am bound to confess that her case seemed remarkably clear. Still, I meant to fight to the bitter end— then——"

"Then ? And now ? "

"Now ? Have you forgotten what has happened ? Sibbald Thursby has been murdered, and those same papers have been stolen or destroyed."

"According to you, by whom ? " asked Skin o' my Tooth quietly.

"Ah ! Heaven only knows ! Look at me, Mr. Mulligan. Am I capable of such a crime ? And yet public opinion has already built a veritable scaffolding of base insinuations against me and my son Oswald. My wife has gathered round her a veritable army of partisans ; the London papers utter scarcely veiled accusations, and the people of this county cut me in the street."

"But what about your son, Viscount Dottridge, I mean ? "

"What about him, Mr. Mulligan ? I tell you there is an infamous conspiracy against him. He went out on the afternoon preceding Sibbald Thursby's death to pay a visit to some friends about twenty miles the other side of Guildford. He was on his bicycle, and rode home late in the evening. Just outside Guildford his tyre punctured badly ; he was still five miles from Duffield, so he elected to have that puncture mended in the town sooner than walk his machine home. He left his bicycle at Rashleigh's, in the High Street, then thought he would kill time by having a chat with Sibbald Thursby. He went round to " The Cottage." It was then a little before ten. He knocked at the front door, but receiving no answer, he went away again and went for a stroll in the lanes until his machine was mended. He called for it at Rashleigh's at a quarter past ten ; it was then ready, and he rode home."

"Yes. And—— ? "

"And while he stood for a moment irresolute upon Sibbald Thursby's doorstep, a couple of workmen saw him, and have informed the police of this fact. If you have read the local paper this morning, Mr. Mulligan, you will have noticed that they announce 'Sensational Developments in the Guildford Mystery.' That sensation will be, I take it, that my son Oswald will be accused of having murdered Sibbald Thursby, in order to destroy the papers which would have robbed him of his inheritance."

"Of which crime you assert that he is innocent. Pray do not misunderstand me. Mine is at present an open mind ; I have only followed the case very superficially. Since you have honoured me with your confidence, I will, of course, go very fully into the matter. Your position from a legal point of view is secure for the moment. Failing the proofs that Henry Mitchell was dead at the time of your marriage with Miss Patricia O'Rourke, your proofs that he only died *after* the marriage hold good and make your position unassailable. In that way, the murderer of Mr. Sibbald Thursby has certainly done you—or, rather, your son—a good turn, for the lady may perhaps never succeed in getting her proofs together again. Teheran is such a long way off, and the creditable English witnesses are probably dead or dispersed by now. But, of course, there is public opinion, and no doubt you yourself cannot estimate at the present moment how far it will force your hand."

Lord Duffield groaned.

"'You would not care to name a figure—without prejudice—— ?'"

"At present," he said, "I only seem to care about the danger to my son Oswald."

"Quite so ; and if you will allow me, I will now at once see the detective-inspector in charge of the case, and you may rest assured that everything that can be done, will be done to throw daylight upon these unfortunate events."

Lord Duffield seemed as if he would like to prolong the interview. He looked to me as if he had something on his mind which he could not bring himself to tell, even to his lawyer. Skin o' my Tooth, with his keen insight, also noted the struggle, I am sure, for he waited silently for a moment or two. However, after a brief pause, Lord Duffield rose, shook hands with my chief, nodded to me, and with a few parting instructions he finally left the room.

II.

I DON'T suppose that even Lord Duffield realised how very strong public opinion was already against him in this matter. The lady—small blame to her—had made it her business to let the whole town know the full history of her case, and I must say that, as it now stood, it did not redound to the credit of the noble lord and his son. The detective-inspector, on whom Skin o' my Tooth called that same afternoon, was quite convinced that Lord Duffield and his son had planned and executed the destruction of the documents. The murder, he admitted, might not have been intended, but merely committed as an act of self-defence, when the noble thieves had found their friend awake and alert, instead of in bed, as they had supposed. There was no doubt that Viscount Dottridge was seen to loiter round "The Cottage" at about ten o'clock at night. The Upjohns were firm in their statement that they had heard a noise at the front door at about that time. The theory of the police was that the young man had then gone round to the garden and tried the conservatory door ; Mr. Thursby, hearing a noise, had gone to see what the noise was, and was probably gripped by the throat before he could utter a scream.

"Personally, Mr. Mulligan, I have very little doubt that his Lordship was in this game, somehow," concluded the detective-inspector at the end of our interview with him ; " but I think you will agree with me that the position is remarkably difficult. What in the world am I to do? Duty is duty, and there must not be one law for the rich and another for the poor. The matter can't be hushed up now. Lady Duffield—I suppose she is that, really—won't allow the matter to rest. As long as she remains in the country, she will keep public opinion well stirred up. I wish she could be persuaded to leave the matter alone now. Even if we succeed in proving a charge of murder against Viscount Dottridge, it won't give her son any better chance to make good his claim, will it, sir ? "

"Certainly not," replied Skin o' my Tooth ; " and you have put the matter in a nutshell. As you say, it would be far better if the lady vacated the place and left you a free hand to hush up the scandal or not, according to the discretion of your chiefs."

It was clear from this interview that the detective-inspector did not know how to act. Torn between his respect for the title and position of the Earl of Duffield, and his own sense of duty in view of the many proofs in favour of Viscount Dottridge's guilt, he was certainly inclined to wait, at any rate until public opinion literally forced the hand of his chiefs.

But in the meanwhile, Skin o' my Tooth had announced to me his intention of seeing the lady who seemed to be the real centre of the many tragic events of the past few days.

We walked round to the " Duffield Arms," where we understood that she was staying, and two minutes later we were shown into the private sitting-room which she occupied at the hotel.

I must say that I looked with some interest at the woman round whom such exciting events seemed to have gathered. Though she must have been nearly fifty years of age certainly, there was even now a wonderful amount of fascination about her entire personality, and a power of magic in her blue eyes. Her son, whom she introduced to us as Viscount Dottridge, was with her when we came into the room, and it was quite impossible not to be struck immediately with the distinct resemblance which he bore to his father. Legally or not, this young man was undoubtedly the son of the Earl of Duffield—Nature had taken special care to prove that fact, at any rate ; and my sympathies immediately went out to him and to his beautiful mother, for there was no doubt that Luck had treated them very roughly.

She received my chief very graciously, and, bidding him be seated, she listened with a smile to what I may term the presentation of his credentials.

" I am Lord Duffield's legal adviser in this matter," he said ; " but I think I may safely say that I am the friend of both parties. Whilst I serve my client to the best of my ability, I have every desire— believe me—to be of service to you and to your son."

She shrugged her shoulders.

" I have been a fool, Mr. Mulligan," she said. " I ought never to have parted with those papers. Now I fear that no one can help me."

" Surely you are wrong. There is no reason why the lost papers should not be replaced. It certainly may take some years and——"

" Money," she interrupted impatiently,

"which I have not got. Those who murdered Mr. Thursby and stole the papers knew what they were about. They have left me absolutely helpless; and even if the perpetrator of the dastardly outrage were punished with the full rigour of the law, I should still see my son ousted from his rights."

"Would you mind telling me the exact contents of the papers you considered most valuable to the furtherance of your cause?"

I thought she looked at him a little suspiciously then; but evidently reassured by his genial smile, she said—

"There were two sworn statements made— one by a Dr. Smollett, who was a well-known English doctor in Teheran, the other by an English nurse named Dawson; both these persons were with Henry Mitchell at the time of his death, and remembered all the circumstances connected with it. Dr. Smollett is dead now. As for the nurse, I have lost sight of her for ten years; it is very doubtful if I could ever trace her."

"But surely these statements were made before the resident British Consul at Teheran?"

"Oh, yes! of course they were. Sir William Courteen was Consul at the time. He subsequently became Governor of the Gold Coast, and died, if you remember, some three years ago."

"Fate has indeed dealt harshly with you," murmured Skin o' my Tooth with genuine sympathy.

"To tell you the truth, it never struck me at first that Lord Duffield would contest my just rights. When I understood that Mr. Thursby was a personal friend of my husband's, I left my papers in his hands, thinking that no doubt he would show them to Lord Duffield, who, feeling the unimpeachable justice of my claim, would resign himself to the inevitable and give willingly to my son, and his, what, after all, is his due."

"That being a very unlikely contingency now, Lady Duffield, might I ask you what you intend to do?"

"Failing my rights, Mr. Mulligan, which I suppose from what you say will now never be granted to me, I can always fall back on that barren enjoyment—revenge. Yes, revenge!" she added with sudden vehemence. "He would deprive me of my position and leave my son nameless? I tell you, Mr. Mulligan, that with Heaven's help I will so rouse public feeling against him that, when his son has been hanged for the murder

of Sibbald Thursby, he in his turn will have to flee this country as a pariah and an outcast, for no honest man henceforth will shake him by the hand."

She had spoken with so much vindictive fury that I felt a cold shiver creeping down my back. Skin o' my Tooth, smiling blandly, was obviously smitten by the fire of her magnificent blue eyes.

"I think," he said, "you will reconsider your very severe mandate."

"Never."

"Surely, if my client realised that you had certain undoubted claim upon him—I only speak without prejudice; but you have a son, and revenge, though sweet, might not prove very useful in his career."

"I never looked upon it in that light," she said coldly, and rising from her chair, as if she wished to end the interview.

"You would not care to name a figure?" suggested Skin o' my Tooth insinuatingly— "without prejudice——"

For the first time during the interview she turned to her son and seemed to consult him with a look, but he shook his head very energetically.

"Not now," she said to Skin o' my Tooth, and then, with a charming smile, she intimated that she wished the interview to cease.

"You will, in any case, always find me at your service," concluded my chief blandly, as we finally took our leave.

III.

As the days wore on, the mystery around the Guildford tragedy seemed to deepen more and more. We had another interview with Lord Duffield, at which his son—the only son he would acknowledge—was present, and I must say that seeing those two men, typical of the English, country-bred, but high-born gentlemen, it was almost impossible to conceive that they could lend their hand to the dastardly murder of an old friend. Skin o' my Tooth had received overtures on the part of the claimants, who seemed to have finally realised that revenge was but sorry pleasure, and expressed themselves ready to accept a monetary compromise in return for their permanent residence out of England.

To my intense astonishment, Lord Duffield fell in readily with this arrangement, which, after all, was nothing but a bribe, and first gave me the idea that perhaps he and his son had something on their conscience. It is quite certain that a constrained feeling seemed to exist between father and son.

Undoubtedly I often caught Lord Dottridge casting furtive glances at his father, and once or twice Lord Duffield looked long and searchingly at his son, then sighed and turned his head away.

I don't pretend to any deep insight into human nature, but it certainly struck me that these two men had begun almost to suspect one another. And no wonder! Who else but they had any interest in destroying the papers which would have made good the cause of the claimants? And I had seen the detective-inspector that morning, and knew that the police, forced into it by public opinion, egged on by the claimants, and convinced that they held sufficient proofs, had at last decided to apply for a warrant for the arrest of Viscount Dottridge.

That same afternoon Skin o' my Tooth at last obtained leave to go over "The Cottage." The police—who always resent outside interference in such matters—had so far, on some pretext or other, always refused permission. But my chief was on his mettle. Lord Duffield had promised him £10,000 if he succeeded in elucidating the mystery and in averting the disgrace which threatened him and his son. To-day, at last, Skin o' my Tooth was able, not only to make a vigorous effort towards obtaining that substantial reward, but also to indulge his passion for ferreting out the mysteries which lurk around a crime. I don't think I ever remember seeing his weird faculties more fully in evidence than over the elucidation of the Guildford tragedy - that faculty which literally made him *feel* the criminal even before he held any clue to his guilt.

The late Mr. Sibbald Thursby had been buried the day after the inquest, but in his house everything had been left just as it was the night of the appalling tragedy. The Upjohns had gone, refusing to sleep another night in a place where so terrible a murder had been committed, and as we let ourselves in by the front door our footsteps echoed weirdly within the deserted house. We were accompanied by two constables who, however, took but little interest in Skin o' my Tooth's wild ramblings through the tiny garden, the conservatory, and the study. It seemed as if he expected the ground to give him the final key to the mystery, of which he already had studied the lock; he was walking along with his eyes glued to the floor, his hands buried in the capacious pockets of his ill-fitting coat, and every now and then I could hear him muttering to himself—

"There must be a bit, only a bit—there always is."

Then at last he seemed to have found what he wanted, for he darted forward towards a fine large palm, all dead and dry now for want of water, which stood in an ornamental pot close to the grate. Inside the pot, and covered with dust and mud, there glimmered a piece of paper. Skin o' my Tooth seized it as if it had been a most precious piece of jewellery; then furtively he thrust it in his pocket, and signed to me to hold my tongue, as the constables had just come into the room.

After this short episode, Skin o' my Tooth expressed himself satisfied with all he had seen, and together we returned to the hotel.

Once alone in the privacy of our sitting-room, he took the dirty piece of treasure from his pocket, carefully knocked the dust out of it, and then spread it out smoothly before him on the table.

"You mayn't think it, Muggins," he said, "but this piece of dirty paper is worth an earldom and a good many other things besides, including the life of a man, who without this wee scrap would very probably have ended on the gallows. It is also worth £10,000 to me."

Eagerly I looked over his shoulder. The scrap of paper was about the size of my hand, and had obviously been torn off another larger sheet. The words I could decipher were: ". . . ry Mitchell . . . anuary 22nd, 1871 . . . my presence," and lower down, what was evidently a signature written in a different hand, ". . . nor Dawson."

"And what is it, sir?" I asked.

"What an ass you are, Muggins!" he said impatiently. "Can't you see that this is all that is left of one of the affidavits which proved that Henry Mitchell died on the 22nd of January, 1871, or three days before Adrian Payton married Patricia O'Rourke? The signature is that of the nurse Dawson, who swore this particular affidavit."

"But it's no use in this state, is it, sir?"

"Oh, yes, Muggins. An affidavit is always useful, even in this condition. You look out a train for me. Early to-morrow morning I am going up to town with this scrap of paper."

He would not tell me anything more then, and the next morning he went up to town and stayed away all day. I saw the detective-inspector in the afternoon, who told me that the warrant for the arrest of Lord Dottridge was actually out, but that he had had a wire in the morning from Scotland Yard " to await further instructions."

"I fancy," he added with a grin, "that Mr. Mulligan has not deserved his nickname this time. He can't get Lord Dottridge out of this hole, not even by the skin of his teeth."

In the evening, however, Skin o' my Tooth came home, dead tired and triumphant. I met him at the station, and together we immediately proceeded to the police-station.

"I have been waiting to see you, Mr. Mulligan," said the inspector. "We cannot delay any longer, and to-night we must execute the warrant against Lord Dottridge."

"You can throw that warrant into the fire, inspector," replied Skin o' my Tooth quietly, "and to-morrow you can apply for another. You'll have to be pretty quick, too, as I fancy your game smells a rat already and may yet slip through your fingers."

"What do you mean?"

"Only this. When you kindly allowed me to view the scene of the interesting murder case you have had on hand, it was my good fortune to come across this interesting document."

And Skin o' my Tooth once more carefully unfolded that dirty scrap of paper on which he had set such store.

"What in the world is this?" asked the inspector.

" 'This piece of dirty paper is worth an earldom.' "

"That is the very question put to me under the same circumstances by my clerk, Mr. Alexander Stanislaus Mullins. This paper, inspector, is all that is left of one of the affidavits which were to prove the legality of certain claims made by a charming lady and her son. You will notice the signature, '. . . nor Dawson.' I may tell you that the lady in question had lost sight since ten years of nurse Dawson, who attended upon her husband in his last illness. This same illness occurred thirty years ago. We have no official knowledge as to when this affidavit was filed, beyond the fact that it was more than ten years ago; but if you will examine very carefully the paper on which it was written, you will notice a remarkably interesting fact."

And Skin o' my Tooth held up that dirty scrap of paper against the lamp, allowing the light to show through it. In the extreme corner, the water-mark, "C. & Sons," became clearly visible.

"Looking through the list of English paper-makers," continued my chief, quietly pointing at this with his thick finger, "I came across the name of Clitheroe and Sons, of 29, Tooley Street, London. This afternoon I interviewed the manager of that firm, who informed me that the lettering of the water-mark in this particular bit of paper indicated that it was manufactured by Clitheroe and Sons in 1899."

"I don't understand," gasped the inspector, staring with all his might first at the dirty bit of paper and then at the unwieldy, bulky figure of Skin o' my Tooth, as he quietly revealed the key to the mystery which had so long puzzled the astute detective.

"Yet it is very simple," he said, with one of his bland smiles. "Personally, I had suspected it all along, from the moment that I first saw Lord Duffield and his son, and realised that they had—if I may so express it —not the brains to carry out so daring a crime successfully. Had that very amiable, but not otherwise brilliant, young man committed that murder, believe me, he would have left plenty of evidence of his guilt. The fact that you yourself, in spite of your acumen, had been unable to really bring the crime home to him, showed me that a cleverer head than his, and a subtler mind, had been at work : but until you favoured me with a permission to view "The Cottage," I had not a single indication on which to work. When I first saw the lady, I realised that hers might have been the head ; my instinct told me that her son's was the hand ; but there seemed such a total lack of motive, the whole theory seemed so topsy-turvy, that I hesitated even to follow it up. Then you courteously allowed me to view the scene on which the crime itself was committed. At once the fact struck me very forcibly that whoever had come on that fateful night to steal the affidavits knew where to lay his hand on them. Nothing in the room or in the desk had been disturbed, and yet obviously the murderer would turn down the lamp as low as possible immediately his nefarious deed was done, lest the light from the windows should reveal his presence. Then, again, you know, no doubt as well as I do, how seldom it is that a murderer does not leave a single trace or clue behind him. That is most fortunate in the cause of justice, otherwise many crimes would remain unpunished. I reckoned in this instance that a man after committing what I presupposed would be his first crime, would necessarily have his nerves very much on the jar. His hand, presumably, would shake, and in tearing up the papers by the very much subdued light of the lamp, and in the presence of his victim lying dead on the floor, it is impossible, I say, that some scrap should not have escaped his trembling hands —you know how paper flutters—and lodged itself momentarily out of sight, ready to reappear as a damning witness against him."

The inspector was silent. I could see that he was hanging breathless upon Skin o' my Tooth's lips. And I, too, saw it all now before me, even before my chief gave us the final explanation of his unanswerable logic.

" In ascertaining the fact that this paper was manufactured two years ago, whilst purporting to have been written on and signed more than ten years previously, it became clear to me that the affidavits setting forth Miss Patricia O'Rourke's, *alias* Mrs. Henry Mitchell's, claim were a pack of forgeries. From this conclusion to the understanding of her clever plan was but a quick mental problem. After all, it was simple enough. Having forged the documents, she entrusted them to Sibbald Thursby. Then her son chose his opportunity, the best he could find, to steal and destroy them. After that she hoped so to rouse public indignation against Lord Duffield by openly accusing him of the theft that he would either throw up the sponge altogether and recognise her rights, or at worst pay her a handsome compensation to clear out of the country and leave him alone. Remember, she all but succeeded. You yourself suggested this alternative as the simplest solution of the difficulty, and Lord Duffield was quite ready to fall in with these views."

" But as it is," suggested the inspector at last, " do you think we shall be able to bring the crime home to these people ? They seem to have been very clever."

" You could bring the accusation of forgery and fraud undoubtedly home to her. You *might* succeed in proving the murder against her son, but I don't think that you will get a chance of doing either."

" Why not ? "

" I think you will find your birds flown already."

" That would be tantamount to an acknowledgment of guilt, and then we could overtake them wherever they may have fled."

" It certainly is an acknowledgment of guilt, as you say," concluded Skin o' my Tooth, rising from his chair and stretching his great, loose limbs ; " but personally, I do not think that you will overtake them if they have succeeded in making good their escape."

Skin o' my Tooth's prophecy proved to be correct. The detective-inspector, I think, has remained convinced to this day that my esteemed employer was not altogether innocent in the matter of the escape of Mrs. Henry Mitchell and her son from the clutches of the law. They had left for London that very evening, and thence had gone to Dover, where all trace of them had ostensibly vanished. I believe that their lucky escape from justice cost Lord Duffield a pretty penny, but, of course, he felt that enough family dirty linen had been washed in public, and he was willing to pay a good sum to save even an illegitimate son from the gallows.

"SKIN O' MY TOOTH":

HIS MEMOIRS, BY HIS CONFIDENTIAL CLERK.

COMPILED AND EDITED BY

THE BARONESS ORCZY.

V.—THE CASE OF MRS. NORRIS.

I HAVE always known Skin o' my Tooth to hold the axiom that justice is invariably on the side of the cleverest lawyer. I might as well at this point record the fact that he held the learned gentlemen of the Bar in complete and withering contempt. "They are a necessary evil in the High Courts," he would say ; but then, to my esteemed employer, everybody in a court of law, from the judge downwards, was " a necessary evil." He would have liked some arrangement by which he could have argued out a criminal case with another lawyer ; that side to win who got the best of the argument.

I can recall one or two very narrow shaves, where a judge and jury's decision really seemed a matter of tossing a halfpenny; it might go either way, and my chief fully deserved the nickname which the public had now universally bestowed upon him. But, of the many interesting cases with which Skin o' my Tooth was associated after the Duffield peerage case had brought his name so prominently before the public, none, I think, seemed at the first glance so intricate, and demonstrated his weird gifts more marvellously than the case of Mrs. Norris.

She was a pale, delicate-looking woman—I should say not more than twenty-five years of age, and no doubt among her own friends would be called pretty. Of course, when Skin o' my Tooth saw her in Holloway, she was evidently worn out with sleepless nights, and half crazy with the horror of the position in which she found herself. Her speech was very incoherent, and the curious mixture of self - accusations and vigorous protestations of innocence, together with the marked obstinacy of her general attitude, would have irritated any man less devoted to his calling than Skin o' my Tooth.

The facts, as far as they were known to the police and the public, and as far as Mrs. Norris herself was willing to admit, were briefly these :—

On Thursday, April 17th, the inhabitants of Shirland Mansions, Maida Vale, were startled at eleven o 'clock at night by loud screams proceeding from one of the flats. Very soon the door of No. 22 was thrown violently open, and Mrs. Norris, who occupied the flat with her husband, came out on the landing loudly calling for help.

To the neighbours, who immediately responded to her call, she seemed like one demented ; her eyes were starting out of her head, her face was livid, and with trembling fingers she was pointing towards her own apartments, whilst, in answer to every query, her quivering mouth murmured repeatedly—

" In there—in the sitting-room ! "

At last, Mr. Daniell, from No. 23, less nervous and excitable than the other neighbours, made up his mind to ascertain what it was that had so completely shattered Mrs. Norris's nerves. One glance into the sitting-room, where the electric light was fully turned on, told him the whole gruesome tale. The body of Mr. Norris was lying on the floor, with his throat cut. There was no doubt that he was dead—the body was rigid, the face livid, whilst the eyes stared up at the ceiling with a look of infinite terror ; in his hand the unfortunate man held, tightly clutched, the razor with which evidently he had put an end to his life.

Following Mr. Daniell's example, a few of the neighbours had crowded into the small flat ; a young fellow from No. 20, who owned a bicycle, suddenly bethought himself that perhaps a doctor or the police would be needful at this juncture, so he went off, leaving a select few to gaze awestruck and helpless at the rigid body, and to offer wellmeant but wholly ineffectual comfort to the half-crazed young widow.

It was, of course, very late in the night

when at last the detective-inspector from the station, accompanied by two constables and the police divisional surgeon, came in response to the call from the cyclist. After that, the crowd of eager and inquisitive neighbours had perforce to retire within the precincts of their respective flats.

From the very first the general public refused to believe in the suicide theory. The morning papers already on the following day threw out vague hints of possible sensational developments. The coroner's inquest held on Monday only confirmed what already everyone had suspected—namely, that Mr. Norris had been murdered. The doctor declared that the wound in his throat had not been caused by the sharp razor found clutched in the dead man's hand—it had been inflicted by a much blunter instrument. Now, no knife of any kind was found upon the scene of the tragedy, but a few drops of blood were noticed by the detective-inspector upon the earthenware sink in the kitchen, showing that the murderer had washed his hands and his instrument there. Probably after that he found the razor in the dressing-room, and placed it in his victim's hand in order to raise the question of suicide.

But it was the examination of Mrs. Norris which furnished the truly sensational element of the tragedy. She repeated before the coroner what she already had told the police—namely, that on the fateful night she had been out to dine with a friend in the neighbourhood of Swiss Cottage, she came home at eleven o'clock at night, and going straight into the sitting-room and turning on the electric light, she saw her husband lying on the floor, dead. Horrified beyond measure, she had screamed for help. She, too, had at first believed in the theory that Mr. Norris had for some unaccountable reason committed suicide : certainly he had no enemy, to her knowledge, and she professed herself quite unable to throw any light upon the mysterious affair.

It appears, however, that her attitude when originally questioned by the police was so strange, her confusion and excitement so manifest, that Mason, the detective who had charge of the case, set to work to immediately verify her statements. He saw the friend with whom Mrs. Norris had dined the evening of her husband's death, but he also ascertained that she left that friend's house at half-past nine o'clock.

Pressed by the coroner, now she seemed absolutely unable to give any account as to how she spent her time between 9.30 and 11 p.m. She had walked about the streets, she said ; but as the night of the 17th had been pouring wet, this statement was, to say the least, peculiar. Unfortunately for her, no one in the Mansions had heard her come in ; the outside doors not being closed until 11.30, anyone could come in or go out easily unperceived.

The owners of the other flats in the same building could not give the police much help in the matter. One statement in connection with the Norrises, however, was quite unanimous among all witnesses—namely, that the quarrels between husband and wife amounted to positive scandal. According to Mr. Daniell, at No. 23, scarcely a day passed in the Norris *ménage* without a domestic squabble. It was generally supposed that the young wife's extravagance and love of dress, and the husband's ungovernable temper, were the causes of this disunion. On the very night of Mr. Norris's death, Mr. and Mrs. Wyatt, in the flat immediately below his, heard at half-past ten o'clock at night the sound of a scuffle overhead. So loud was it that Mrs. Wyatt suggested that her husband should go upstairs and intervene, as she was quite sure Mr. Norris was murdering his wife.

I don't think that anyone could blame the police for the course they adopted in this very mysterious affair : they arrested Mrs. Norris on a charge of murdering her husband. Brought before the magistrate, she pleaded "Not guilty," and repeated her story with wonderful obstinacy — she had dined with a friend, and from 9.30 to 11 had walked about the streets alone. Her whole manner on that subject was confused in the extreme. That there was something here which she wished to hide, was apparent to everyone. But the lie told against her, of course ; and were it not for the fact that the magistrate was a peculiarly humane and kindly man, who took pity on her lonely position, and remanded her so that she might obtain legal advice immediately, there is no doubt that she would at once have been committed for trial.

II.

It was at this point that Mrs. Norris's relations approached Skin o' my Tooth, with the view that he should undertake her defence. The case had interested him from the first, and he was quite ready to give the unfortunate woman the benefit of his great skill.

We saw her in Holloway. She was obviously very pleased to have legal advice, and seemed inclined to be less reticent than she had been hitherto.

"I may have acted very thoughtlessly, Mr. Mulligan," she said ; "but I had no one to advise me ; and really, I have been half crazy with this horrible accusation hanging over me."

"I think you were very foolish to make such a secret of how you spent your time between 9.30 and 11 on that fateful night ; an *alibi* in a case like yours is imperative. I hope that you have quite made up your mind to be absolutely frank with me."

"I am afraid that when you hear how simple the explanation is, you will think me worse than foolish."

"It doesn't matter what I think at this point," remarked Skin o' my Tooth drily.

"After I left my friend at 9.30," she began, speaking, I thought, with strange nervousness, "I went on to see another friend, in Hamilton Terrace, with whom I stayed until nearly eleven o'clock."

"As you say, it is extremely simple," said Skin o' my Tooth, who had noticed her curious and constrained manner, and was looking at her through his thick and fleshy lids. "The *alibi* is quite perfect. Of course, your friend will corroborate this statement."

She hesitated very palpably ; then she added—

"I took a hansom to go home—no doubt the cabman can be found."

"No doubt ; but it was a dark night, and the cabman may not be able to identify you accurately. Still, it is additional evidence, your friend's being, of course, the most valuable. Will you give me her name and address, so that I may communicate with her immediately ?"

Again Mrs. Norris hesitated visibly for a moment before she replied—

"Lady Ralph Morshampton, 196, Hamilton Terrace."

Her attitude was a puzzle to me, and I could see that Skin o' my Tooth was both mystified and vexed. However, he dropped that point for the moment, and questioned Mrs. Norris of the probable motive for the murder.

"The police tell me that the rooms had evidently been searched through and through, possibly for money or valuables. Do you know of anything that may have tempted a murderer ?"

"Nothing," she replied most emphatically. "We were in very modest circumstances ; we never kept money in the house, beyond a sovereign or so, and we had no valuables of any kind."

"And you cannot account for the wild search which was evidently made through the rooms for something ? You know that the dressing-bag was turned inside out, the drawers emptied ; even the books in the bookcase were disturbed."

"I don't understand it," she replied, with a return of that strange nervous wilfulness which was so unaccountable, and which had already so much prejudiced her case ; "I cannot account for it in any way."

With marked impatience Skin o' my Tooth rose to go. I could see that he was within an ace of throwing up the case, for it was clear, of course, that Mrs. Norris was not absolutely frank, even with him. But the case had gripped him, and this additional puzzle only aroused his further interest in it ; it seemed literally to bristle with mysteries. He controlled his rising temper for the moment and took leave of his client, promising to call again early the next morning.

"Why does that woman lie to me ? " he said savagely, the moment we were outside. "She knows or guesses the motive of that murder, I'll swear. Is she guilty herself, after all, or is she shielding a friend ? And what in Heaven's name has Lady Ralph Morshampton to do with it all ? "

I, of course, could not answer these intricate questions, and we returned to Finsbury Square in silence. We found that during our absence from the office the boy had introduced a visitor into Skin o' my Tooth's private room.

"A lady, sir," he explained. "She wouldn't give her name, and she wouldn't wait here, so I had to show her in."

I followed my chief into his private office, where the visitor was waiting. She was a lady very elegantly dressed, who rose with languid grace to greet Skin o' my Tooth as he entered.

"Mr. Mulligan ? " she asked.

"That is my name," replied my chief, as he drew an easy-chair forward for her and seated himself at his desk, viewing his elegant visitor with more than professional interest.

She seemed a little troubled at what to say next, and looked across at me somewhat doubtfully.

"My confidential clerk," explained Skin o' my Tooth. "As trustworthy as myself. Still, if you wish it, he can go."

"Oh, no ! not at all. Since he has your confidence, I have nothing more to say. I did not leave my name with your office

" ' In there—in the sitting-room ! ' "

boy, Mr. Mulligan, as I would wish, as far as possible, that my interview with you should remain confidential. I am Lady Ralph Morshampton. No doubt you know my husband by name; and I came to see you about a matter connected with the murder of a Mr. Norris, in Shirland Mansions."

"Indeed!" commented Skin o' my Tooth.

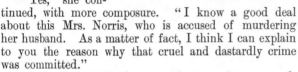

"'I can explain to you why that cruel crime was committed.'"

"Yes," she continued, with more composure. "I know a good deal about this Mrs. Norris, who is accused of murdering her husband. As a matter of fact, I think I can explain to you the reason why that cruel and dastardly crime was committed."

"Indeed!" repeated my employer, quite unmoved.

"As a matter of fact, Mrs. Norris was in my house only an hour or so before she committed that awful crime. She was pursuing a policy of blackmail against me, Mr. Mulligan; and finding that her poor husband would not be a party to that ignoble policy, she made him its victim."

"I don't quite understand."

"I must try to make it quite clear. Before my marriage, Mr. Mulligan, I was on the stage; and as it happened, just before I was engaged to Lord Ralph Morshampton, a villainous scandal was circulated amongst my envious colleagues, coupling my name with that of Adam Norris, a young dramatic author of much promise. Fortunately that scandal never reached the ears either of the Marquis of Camberley, my father-in-law, or of the exalted society of which I was about to become a member. I was the daughter of a gentleman, and had always acted in Shakespearian drama only. Society, after my marriage, tolerated me from the first, but now, after strenuous efforts on my part, it has finally accepted me. I have a position within its circles which many envy. In the meanwhile, Adam Norris also married. Through some unaccountable carelessness on his part, which amounts practically to a sin, his wife got to know of that old and buried scandal anent himself and me. He had been fool enough to keep my letters. I believe they were distinctly compromising. I really had not remembered them at all, but Mrs. Norris having caught sight of them once by accident, bethought herself of doing a bit of illicit traffic with them. She was inordinately fond of finery and gaiety, passions which her husband's somewhat modest position would not allow her to indulge in. She wrote to me one day offering to sell me my old letters for a couple of thousand pounds and a few introductions in good society. Now, Mr. Mulligan, I am the wife of a very rich man, with plenty of money at my command with which to gratify any passing whim. In this case it was my whim to pay money down and regain possession of those letters sooner than allow my husband and my friends to know of their contents. I wrote to Mrs. Norris asking her to come and see me on Thursday evening, the 17th. She came at about ten o'clock, and we had a short interview, in which it was agreed between us that I should give her

£4,000, and no introductions, in exchange for the letters. I must tell you that she informed me then that she had not got the letters. Her husband had them still; but she seemed to think that she would have no difficulty in obtaining possession of them. I could not tell you exactly at what hour she left me," concluded Lady Ralph Morshampton coldly, "but I imagine that she went straight home—well—and that she had some difficulty in persuading her husband to give up those letters. What do you think yourself, Mr. Mulligan?"

"I was merely wondering, Lady Morshampton, whether you are really convinced in your own mind that Mrs. Norris actually murdered her husband?"

"I really have not given that subject a thought. I merely came to you to-day because I thought that probably she would have given you her own version of her interview with me, and that you might take it into your head to cite me as a witness on her behalf. You will see for yourself, I am sure, that this would do your client no appreciable good; on the contrary, it would furnish the prosecution with a strong additional weapon against her—a motive."

"You forget, Lady Morshampton," retorted Skin o' my Tooth, taken aback in spite of himself at this extraordinary display of callousness and egoism, "you forget that citing you as a witness would also give me an additional motive in my client's defence."

"I don't understand."

"The question of time."

"Oh! that is very vague," she retorted placidly, "I did not wish the servants to know of Mrs. Norris's visit; that is why I had fixed the hour ten o'clock, when they were all at supper. I was on the watch for her and opened the door to her myself. I let her out when our interview was over—I could not tell you at what time that was—and I am quite sure that none of the servants even knew that she had been in the house."

"But your husband?"

"Lord Ralph was in the smoking-room when Mrs. Norris called. I heard him go out a quarter of an hour or so later, and he certainly did not come in until after she left."

"Therefore, if I cite you as a witness——"

"You do so at Mrs. Norris's risk and peril," said Lady Ralph Morshampton, rising from her chair, and cooler than any cucumber. "I tell you that I could not swear positively at what hour she left me, and I know that she took a hansom lower down the road. I live in Hamilton Terrace, so it was only five minutes' drive at most. I think," she added finally, as she moved gracefully towards the door, "that I have succeeded in convincing you that it would be more prudent to leave my name out of this case altogether, have I not? Perhaps, after all, Mrs. Norris was wise and did not mention her visit to me, in which case there is no harm done, as I know I can rely on your discretion. By the way, I have not got those letters yet; will you tell Mrs. Norris that the bargain still holds good? Thank you so much. Good morning, Mr. Mulligan. A very wet spring, is it not? Let us hope we shall have fine weather for the Coronation. Don't trouble to see me down. I shall get a hansom outside."

When she had gone, Skin o' my Tooth turned to me with a heavy grunt.

"For Heaven's sake, Muggins," he said, "let's have some air! Open those windows. Even the slushy London air is preferable to the moral atmosphere this elegant lady has left behind her."

III.

WE saw Mrs. Norris in prison that same afternoon. The interview was somewhat stormy, as Skin o' my Tooth was furious with her. Nothing enrages him so much as a want of absolute confidence on the part of a client, and I am quite sure that in this instance he would have thrown up the whole case and let Mrs. Norris literally go hang, but for the fact that the ever-increasing mysteries in connection with it had roused all his passion for what was interesting in the history of crime.

There was no doubt that Lady Ralph Morshampton's narrative had added fresh mystery to this already bewildering case. Mrs. Norris, sternly questioned by Skin o' my Tooth, corroborated it in every detail. The reason why she had so obstinately held her tongue on the subject was because she felt convinced that her attempt at blackmailing, and her avowed interest in obtaining possession of certain letters belonging to her husband, would furnish the prosecution with an additional terrible weapon against her. Moreover, she felt instinctively—and there her instinct did not err—that Lady Ralph Morshampton would prove a bitter enemy whom it would be unwise to drag into the case more than was absolutely necessary.

"I did not dare tell anyone, Mr. Mulligan," she pleaded pathetically. "Don't be hard upon me. I was quite convinced that something would turn up to prove that I did not commit that awful crime. I don't believe now that justice can err quite to such an extent."

"You certainly have done your level best to damage your own case," growled Skin o' my Tooth, somewhat mollified ; " but now tell me, at what time did you leave Lady Ralph Morshampton ? "

"It was just before eleven. I took a hansom, and told the driver to put me down at the corner of Elgin Avenue. Shirland Mansions are just a few yards further on."

"But what about the letters ? "

"I haven't got them, Mr. Mulligan. Just before the inquest, and before I was accused, I looked for them in their accustomed place, but they had gone."

"Where was their accustomed place ? "

"Between some books in the bookcase. I don't think that my husband attached much importance to them. Anyway, I knew that I could easily get at them at any time."

"The police did not find those letters, I know," said Skin o' my Tooth to me, later in the day. "It is clear, therefore, that the murderer succeeded in getting hold of them, and clearer still that the crime was committed in order to obtain possession of them. Now, if Mrs. Norris speaks the truth, she was with Lady Morshampton until close on eleven, when she went straight home."

"Perhaps, after all," I suggested, "Mr. Norris committed suicide, and his wife, on coming home, merely hunted for the letters, and not finding them in their accustomed place, turned the room topsy-turvy before giving the alarm."

To my astonishment, Skin o' my Tooth did not receive my suggestion with the scorn which I feel sure it deserved, and which he usually bestows upon my attempts in that direction. It was clearest of all to me that my esteemed employer was completely at sea for the moment.

"You shall find out for me, Muggins, whether Mrs. Norris did speak the truth or not. I give you two days to do it in, and mind you don't mention the subject to me during that time. You know how to set to work, of course ? "

"I think I do, sir. In any case, I will have an advertisement ready for all the daily papers to-morrow, and police notices all over the town, for the hansom-cabdriver who drove a lady from Hamilton Terrace to the corner of Elgin Avenue on Thursday, April 17th, at about 11 p.m."

"That's all right, Muggins. You are not quite such an ass as you look. Fire away, then ; and, whatever you do, don't speak to me for two days."

The next morning my advertisements were in every paper and my notices all over the town. Twenty-four hours after that, I knew the name, address, and number of the cabman who drove a lady at the hour, on the day, and to the destination I had mentioned. Unfortunately he had not seen the lady's face, and certainly would not know her again.

In the meanwhile, life at the office was anything but pleasant. Skin o' my Tooth was in one of those tempers of his during which it was not good to talk to him. That he had got some fixed idea in his mind about that murder, I was then already quite sure. I knew the symptoms so well. For all the world like a great frowsy hound smelling blood, he sat for hours curled up in his armchair, smoking his long-stemmed German pipe, whilst even his beloved French novels were discarded. Every now and then I would see that weird and cruel spark flash in his lazy, blue eyes. Then I knew that the tracker of blood was on the scent, that he held a clue, and that his mind had already solved the problem which would bring the murderer of Mr. Norris inevitably to justice.

I told him the result of my investigations when the two days had elapsed. It was then ten o'clock in the morning, and we had both just arrived at the office.

"Sit down, Muggins," he said. "I expect a visitor."

I could see that he was very excited. He went himself to the door, when presently a heavy step was heard in the passage. Skin o' my Tooth's visitor was a big, burly fellow, wrapped from head to foot in a huge overcoat. The word "cabby" seemed to be written all over his rubicund countenance. He had a copy of the *Daily Mail* in his hand, to which he was pointing somewhat anxiously as he walked into the room.

"You're the gent, ain't you, sir," he asked presently, "who put this 'ere advertisement in the *Mail ?* "

"Yes. I did put that advertisement in ; and I got your letter this morning, so you see that I was expecting you."

"Ah ! " remarked Cabby, with a grin of satisfaction. "It says 'ere that you'd give 'un a fiver reward. What you want to know is 'oo drove a gent from 'Amilton Terriss to somewhere near Helgin Havenue on the hevening of April 17th ? "

"That's it exactly."

"Now, I drove a swell from top of Carlton 'Ill to the corner of Helgin Havenue and Maida Vale at about a quarter past ten on that night. It was pourin' wet; and when I 'ad dropped 'im, I went in to the 'Lord Helgin' for a drink. Now, about three-quarters of an hour later, that same swell picked me up again just as I was turning into Maida Vale, and I took 'im back to 'Amilton Terriss."

"You don't know to what number?"

"No. I don't; but

"'You're the gent, ain't you, sir, who put this 'ere advertisement in the *Mail*?'"

I'd know that swell again if I saw him. 'E gave me five bob each way. I thought 'e looked as if 'e'd been drinking when 'e drove home—his clothes were all anyhow. 'E 'ad on a silk comforter round his neck, which 'e left in my cab."

"I suppose you won't mind throwing that comforter in with the most valuable inform-

ation you have been good enough to give me," suggested Skin o' my Tooth, "and for which I shall have much pleasure in handing you the promised £5 note?"

A broad grin illuminated the worthy old cabby's countenance. He drew from his pocket a large coloured silk muffler, which he placed on the desk. Then he stretched out a very large and very grimy fist towards the crisp banknote which Skin o' my Tooth was holding out towards him.

"I am mighty glad, sir, that my heffort of memory is worth all that to ye," he said sententiously.

"Not to me, cabby," said Skin o' my Tooth, with a smile, "but to an unfortunate woman whom your excellent memory has saved from the gallows."

"Lor'! it ain't a case of murder, is it? I don't like that."

"Remember that you told this young gentleman here and myself that you would know the swell again," said Skin o' my Tooth sternly.

"Yes. I would," replied Cabby, scratching his shaggy old head, "but I don't like to be mixed up with p'lice and things."

"Must do something for your £5 note, eh?"

"Well, sir, p'r'aps you're right."

He was inclined to be loquacious, but Skin o' my Tooth, having got what he wanted, was eager to be rid of him. I showed the amiable cabby out. I was longing to ask my chief a hundred questions. I found him sitting beside his desk, carefully examining the coloured silk muffler.

"There are stains on it, Muggins," he said quietly. "I am in luck to-day."

"But I don't understand, sir. What was

the advertisement about, and who was 'the swell' who drove from Hamilton Terrace to Elgin Avenue and back?"

"Why, Muggins, you are even a bigger ass than I took you to be. The swell, my boy, was Lord Ralph Morshampton, the murderer of Adam Norris."

"But——"

"I suspected it the moment I saw that very elegant, very egoistical woman of the world, but I was afraid that it would be very difficult to prove. It was, no doubt, all settled between him and his wife, and Lady Ralph arranged that the interview between herself and Mrs. Norris should take place at a moment when it would be most convenient for my lord to tackle the unfortunate dramatic author; this insured the wife being safely out of the way. I don't suppose for a moment that murder was premeditated. Lord Ralph Morshampton probably lost his temper, and finding Adam Norris obdurate, knocked him down."

"But what made you think of it all, sir?"

"Only this, Muggins, that when people tell me a lie, I immediately look about me for the motive which made them tell that particular lie. Lady Ralph Morshampton, if you remember, told me that her husband is a very rich man, and that she had plenty of money at her command with which to gratify any passing whim. Now, that is not true. Lord Ralph Morshampton is a younger brother of the present Marquis of Camberley. His father, the late Marquis, left each of his sons an annuity of three thousand pounds a year, payable out of the estate.

"My inquiries into Lord Ralph Morshampton's financial position, as compared with the lie his wife had told me, gave me the first inkling—call it intuition if you will —of the possible state of the case, for clearly Lady Ralph could not indulge in the luxury of buying those letters for four thousand pounds, however eager she might be to possess them; her appointment with Mrs. Norris, therefore, was a feint, either in order to gain time, or in order to devise some other means of gaining possession of those letters. After that, Muggins, taking it absolutely for granted that the murder *was* committed for the sake of those letters, it became easy enough to reduce the number of people interested in their possession to three; there was Mrs. Norris, who wanted to sell them, and Lady Ralph Morshampton, who wished to destroy them. Putting aside the question that the murder was really far too gruesome and horrible for any woman of

refinement to have committed, it soon became an established fact that the two ladies were actually together at 196, Hamilton Terrace at the time that the murder was being perpetrated. You remember that the people in the flat below the one occupied by Mr. Norris heard the noise and scuffle at half-past ten. There then loomed before me the question of Lord Morshampton, the husband. I made inquiries among the servants at Hamilton Terrace and among the neighbours, and learned that he was passionately fond of his wife, and ever eager to hide her past history before his relatives and friends; he too, then, would have a motive—far stronger than any, since it concerned the woman he loved—to bury for ever a scandal which might injure her position in society. Having got the motive, I soon sought for proof. I remembered that Lady Morshampton herself had said said that her husband left the house at a quarter past ten. I surmised that he would go to Shirland Mansions to see Adam Norris, and that since he would not have much time at his command, he would go there in a cab. I advertised in the terms you know already, and got this morning the very proof I sought for. You see, the whole matter became child's play once I had a clue."

"It was instinct, sir," I said, with genuine admiration, "marvellous intuition."

"Call it reflection, my boy, and you'll be about right. You see, the moment those letters were destroyed, the Morshamptons' name slipped, as it were, right out of the case. My lady was right when she concluded that I could never have cited her on Mrs. Norris's behalf. She was quite ready to see the unfortunate woman go to the gallows, and to swear anything that would achieve that end. That is why I am inclined to think that she planned the whole thing, while her husband was but half willing. Now, Muggins, run along and take this muffler to Scotland Yard. Mrs. Norris comes up before the magistrate to-morrow. Poor woman! she has had a narrow shave; but what a fool she has been!"

Mrs. Norris was discharged by the magistrate.

Everyone remembers, no doubt, the awful sensation caused by the suicide of Lord Ralph Morshampton in his house in Hamilton Terrace. As there is always a special law for those in his position, the whole matter of his guilt in the murder of Adam Norris was most effectually hushed up by the police, and the public never got to know the name of "the swell" who drove to Shirland Mansions at a quarter past ten on that fatal night.

XX

The Experiences of Loveday Brooke, Lady Detective

C.L. PIRKIS

The Experiences of Loveday Brooke, Lady Detective.

By C. L. PIRKIS, Author of "Lady Lovelace," &c. &c.

A PRINCESS'S VENGEANCE.

"THE girl is young, pretty, friendless and a foreigner, you say, and has disappeared as completely as if the earth had opened to receive her," said Miss Brooke, making a résumé of the facts that Mr. Dyer had been relating to her. "Now, will you tell me why two days were allowed to elapse before the police were communicated with?"

"Mrs. Druce, the lady to whom Lucie Cunier acted as amanuensis," answered Mr. Dyer, "took the matter very calmly at first and said she felt sure that the girl would write to her in a day or so, explaining her extraordinary conduct. Major Druce, her son, the gentleman who came to me this morning, was away from home, on a visit, when the girl took flight. Immediately on his return, however, he communicated the fullest particulars to the police."

"They do not seem to have taken up the case very heartily at Scotland Yard."

"No, they have as good as dropped it. They advised Major Druce to place the matter in my hands, saying that they considered it a case for private rather than police investigation."

"I wonder what made them come to that conclusion."

"I think I can tell you, although the Major seemed quite at a loss on the matter. It seems he had a photograph of the missing girl, which he kept in a drawer of his writing-table. (By-the-way, I think the young man is a good deal 'gone' on this Mdlle. Cunier, in spite of his engagement to another lady.) Well, this portrait he naturally thought would be most useful in helping to trace the girl, and he went to his drawer for it,

intending to take it with him to Scotland Yard. To his astonishment, however, it was nowhere to be seen, and, although he at once instituted a rigorous search, and questioned his mother and the servants, one and all, on the matter, it was all to no purpose."

Loveday thought for a moment.

"Well, of course," she said presently "that photograph must have been stolen by someone in the house, and, equally of course, that someone must know more on the matter than he or she cares to avow, and, most probably, has some interest in throwing obstacles in the way of tracing the girl. At the same time, however, the fact in no way disproves the possibility that a crime, and a very black one, may underlie the girl's disappearance."

"The Major himself appears confident that a crime of some sort has been committed, and he grew very excited and a little mixed in his statements more than once just now."

"What sort of woman is the Major's mother?"

"Mrs. Druce? She is rather a well-known personage in certain sets. Her husband died about ten years ago, and since his death she has posed as promoter and propagandist of all sorts of benevolent, though occasionally somewhat visionary ideas: theatrical missions, magic-lantern and playing cards missions, societies for providing perpetual music for the sick poor, for supplying cabmen with comforters, and a hundred other similar schemes have in turn occupied her attention. Her house is a rendezvous for faddists of every description. The latest fad, however, seems to have put all others to flight; it is a scheme for alleviat-

455

ing the condition of ' our sisters in the East,' so she puts it in her prospectus; in other words a Harem Mission on somewhat similar, but I suppose broader lines than the old-fashioned Zenana Mission. This Harem Mission has gathered about her a number of Turkish and Egyptian potentates resident in or visiting London, and has thus incidentally brought about the engagement of her son, Major Druce, with the Princess Dullah-Veih. This Princess is a beauty and an heiress, and although of Turkish parentage, has been brought up under European influence in Cairo."

" Is anything known of the antecedents of Mdlle. Cunier ? "

" Very little. She came to Mrs. Druce from a certain Lady Gwynne, who had brought her to England from an orphanage for the daughters of jewellers and watchmakers at Echallets, in Geneva. Lady Gwynne intended to make her governess to her young children, but when she saw that the girl's good looks had attracted her husband's attention, she thought better of it, and suggested to Mrs. Druce that Mademoiselle might be useful to her in conducting her foreign correspondence. Mrs. Druce accordingly engaged the young lady to act as her secretary and amanuensis, and appears, on the whole, to have taken to the girl, and to have been on a pleasant, friendly footing with her. I wonder if the Princess Dullah-Veih was on an equally pleasant footing with her when she saw, as no doubt she did, the attention she received at the Major's hands." (Mr. Dyer shrugged his shoulders.) ''The Major's suspicions do not point in that direction, in spite of the fact which I elicited from him by judicious questioning, that the Princess has a violent and jealous temper, and has at times made his life a burden to him. His suspicions centre solely upon a certain Hafiz Cassimi, son of the Turkish-Egyptian banker of that name. It was at the house of these Cassimis that the

MDLLE. CUNIER.

Major first met the Princess, and he states that she and young Cassimi are like brother and sister to each other. He says that this young man has had the run of his mother's house and made himself very much at home in it for the past three weeks, ever since, in fact, the Princess came to stay with Mrs. Druce, in order to be initiated into the mysteries of English family life. Hafiz Cassimi, according to the Major's account, fell desperately in love with the little Swiss girl almost at first sight and péstered her with his attentions, and off and on there appear to have passed hot words between the two young men."

" One could scarcely expect a princess with Eastern blood in her veins to sit a quiet and passive spectator to such a drama of cross-purposes."

"Scarcely. The Major, perhaps, hardly takes the Princess sufficiently into his reckoning. According to him, young Cassimi is a thorough-going Iago, and he begs me to concentrate attention entirely on him. Cassimi, he says, has stolen the photograph. Cassimi has inveigled the girl out of the house on some pretext—perhaps out of the country also, and he suggests that it might be as well to communicate with the police at Cairo, with as little delay as possible."

" And it hasn't so much as entered his mind that his Princess might have a hand in such a plot as that ! "

" Apparently not. I think I told you that Mademoiselle had taken no luggage— not so much as a hand-bag—with her. Nothing, beyond her coat and hat, has disappeared from her wardrobe. Her writing-desk, and, in fact, all her boxes and drawers, have been opened and searched, but no letters or papers of any sort have been found that throw any light upon her movements."

" At what hour in the day is the girl supposed to have left the house ? "

" No one can say for certain. It is conjectured that it was some time in the afternoon of the second of this month—a week ago to-day. It was one of Mrs. Druce's big reception days, and with a stream of people going and coming, a young lady, more or less, leaving the house would scarcely be noticed."

"I suppose," said Loveday, after a moment's pause, "this Princess Dullah-Veih has something of a history. One does not often get a Turkish princess in London."

"Yes, she has a history. She is only remotely connected with the present reigning dynasty in Turkey, and I dare say her princess-ship has been made the most of. All the same, however, she has had an altogether exceptional career for an Oriental lady. She was left an orphan at an early age, and was consigned to the guardianship of the elder Cassimi by her relatives. The Cassimis, both father and son, seem to be very advanced and European in their ideas, and by them she was taken to Cairo for her education. About a year ago they 'brought her out' in London, where she made the acquaintance of Major Druce. The young man, by-the-way, appears to be rather hot-headed in his love-making, for within six weeks of his introduction to her their engagement was announced. No doubt it had Mrs. Druce's fullest approval, for knowing her son's extravagant habits and his numerous debts, it must have been patent to her that a rich wife was a necessity to him. The marriage, I believe, was to have taken place this season ; but taking into consideration the young man's ill-advised attentions to the little Swiss girl, and the fervour he is throwing into the search for her, I should say it was exceedingly doubtful whether ——"

"Major Druce, sir, wishes to see you," said a clerk at that moment, opening the door leading from the outer office.

"Very good ; show him in," said Mr. Dyer. Then he turned to Loveday.

"MAJOR DRUCE, SIR !"

"Of course I have spoken to him about you, and he is very anxious to take you to his mother's reception this afternoon, so that you may have a look round and ——"

He broke off, having to rise and greet Major Druce, who at that moment entered the room.

He was a tall, handsome young fellow of about seven or eight and twenty, "well turned out" from head to foot, moustache waxed, orchid in button-hole, light kid gloves, and patent leather boots. There was assuredly nothing in his appearance to substantiate his statement to Mr. Dyer that he "hadn't slept a wink all night, that in fact another twenty-four hours of this terrible suspense would send him into his grave."

Mr. Dyer introduced Miss Brooke, and she expressed her sympathy with him on the painful matter that was filling his thoughts.

"It is very good of you, I'm sure," he replied, in a slow, soft drawl, not unpleasant to listen to. "My mother receives this afternoon from half past four to half past six, and I shall be very glad if you will allow me to introduce you to the inside of our house, and to the very ill-looking set that we have somehow managed to gather about us."

"The ill-looking set ?"

"Yes ; Jews, Turks, heretics and infidels—all there. And they're on the increase too, that's the worst of it. Every week a fresh importation from Cairo."

"Ah, Mrs. Druce is a large-hearted, benevolent woman," interposed Mr. Dyer ; "all nationalities gather within her walls."

"Was your mother a large-hearted, benevolent woman ?" said the young man, turning upon him. "No! well then, thank Providence that she wasn't ; and admit that you know nothing at all on the matter. Miss Brooke," he continued, turning to Loveday, "I've brought round my hansom for you ; it's nearly half past four now, and it's a good twenty minutes' drive from here to Portland Place. If you're ready, I'm at your service."

Major Druce's hansom was, like himself, in all respects "well turned out," and the indiarubber tires round its wheels allowed an easy flow of conversation to be kept up during the twenty minutes' drive from Lynch Court to Portland Place.

The Major led off the talk in frank and easy fashion.

"My mother," he said, "prides herself on being cosmopolitan in her tastes, and just now we are very cosmopolitan indeed. Even our servants represent divers nationalities: the butler is French, the two footmen Italians, the maids, I believe, are some of them German, some Irish; and I've no doubt if you penetrated to the kitchen-quarters, you'd find the staff there composed in part of Scandinavians, in part of South Sea Islanders. The other quarters of the globe you will find fully represented in the drawing-room."

Loveday had a direct question to ask.

"Are you certain that Mdlle. Cunier had no friends in England?" she said.

"Positive. She hadn't a friend in the world outside my mother's four walls, poor child! She told me more than once that she was 'seule sur la terre.'" He broke off for a moment, as if overcome by a sad memory, then added: "But I'll put a bullet into him, take my word for it, if she isn't found within another twenty-four hours. Personally I should prefer settling the brute in that fashion to handing him over to the police."

His face flushed a deep red, there came a sudden flash to his eye, but for all that, his voice was as soft and slow and unemotional, as though he were talking of nothing more serious than bringing down a partridge.

There fell a brief pause; then Loveday asked another question.

"Is Mademoiselle Catholic or Protestant, can you tell me?"

The Major thought for a moment, then replied:

"'Pon my word, I don't know. She used sometimes to attend a little church in South Savile Street—I've walked with er occasionally to the church door—but I couldn't for the life of me say whether it was a Catholic, Protestant, or Pagan place of worship. But—but you don't think those confounded priests have——"

"Here, we are in Portland place," interrupted Loveday. "Mrs. Druce's rooms are already full, to judge from that long line of carriages!"

"Miss Brooke," said the Major suddenly, bethinking himself of his responsibilities, "how am I to introduce you? what rôle will you take up this afternoon? Pose as a faddist of some sort, if you want to win my mother's heart. What do you say to having started a grand scheme for supplying Hottentots and Kaffirs with eye-glasses? My mother would swear eternal friendship with you at once."

"Don't introduce me at all at first," answered Loveday. "Get me into some quiet corner, where I can see without being seen. Later on in the afternoon, when I have had time to look round a little, I'll tell you whether it will be necessary to introduce me or not."

"It will be a mob this afternoon, and no mistake," said Major Druce, as, side by side, they entered the house. "Do you hear that fizzing and clucking just behind us? That's Arabic; you'll get it in whiffs between gusts of French and German all the afternoon. The Egyptian contingent seems to be in full force to-

MAJOR DRUCE'S HANSOM.

day. I don't see any Choctaw Indians, but no doubt they'll send their representatives later on. Come in at this side door, and we'll work our way round to that big palm. My mother is sure to be at the principal doorway."

The drawing rooms were packed from end to end, and Major Druce's progress, as he headed Loveday through the crowd, was impeded by hand-shaking and the interchange of civilities with his mother's guests.

Eventually the big palm standing in a Chinese cistern was reached, and there, half screened from view by its graceful branches, he placed a chair for Miss Brooke.

From this quiet nook, as now and again the crowd parted, Loveday could command a fair view of both drawing-rooms.

"Don't attract attention to me by standing at my elbow," she whispered to the Major.

He answered her whisper with another.

"There's the Beast—Iago, I mean," he said; "do you see him? He's standing talking to that fair, handsome woman in pale green, with a picture hat. She's Lady Gwynne. And there's my mother, and there's Dolly—the Princess I mean—alone on the sofa. Ah! you can't see her now for the crowd. Yes, I'll go, but if you want me, just nod to me and I shall understand."

It was easy to see what had brought such a fashionable crowd to Mrs. Druce's rooms that afternoon. Every caller, as soon as she had shaken hands with the hostess, passed on to the Princess's sofa, and there waited patiently till opportunity presented itself for an introduction to her Eastern Highness.

Loveday found it impossible to get

BESIDE THE BIG PALM.

more than the merest glimpse of her, and so transferred her attention to Mr. Hafiz Cassimi, who had been referred to in such unceremonious language by Major Druce.

He was a swarthy, well-featured man, with bold, black eyes, and lips that had the habit of parting now and again, not to smile, but as if for no other purpose than to show a double row of gleaming white teeth. The European dress he wore seemed to accord ill with the man; and Loveday could fancy that those black eyes and that double row of white teeth would have shown to better advantage beneath a turban or a fez cap.

From Cassimi, her eye wandered to Mrs. Druce—a tall, stout woman, dressed in black velvet, and with hair mounted high on her head, that had the appearance of being either bleached or powdered. She gave Loveday the impression of being that essentially modern product of modern society—the woman who combines in one person the hard-working philanthropist with the hard-working woman of fashion. As arrivals began to slacken, she left her post near the door and began to make the round of the room. From snatches of talk that came to her where she sat, Loveday could gather that with one hand, as it were, this energetic lady was organizing a grand charity concert, and with the other pushing the interests of a big ball that was shortly to be given by the officers of her son's regiment.

It was a hot June day. In spite of closed blinds and open windows, the rooms were stifling to a degree. The butler, a small, dark, slight Frenchman, made his way through the throng to a window at Loveday's right hand, to see if a little more air could be admitted.

Major Druce followed on his heels to Loveday's side.

" Will you come into the next room and have some tea ? " he asked; " I'm sure you must feel nearly suffocated here." He broke off, then added in a lower tone: " I hope you have kept your eyes on the Beast. Did you ever in your life see a more repulsive-looking animal ? "

Loveday took his questions in their order.

" No tea, thank you," she said, " but I shall be glad if you will tell your butler to bring me a glass of water—there he is, at your elbow. Yes, off and on I have been studying Mr. Cassimi, and I must admit I do not like his smileless smile."

The butler brought the water. The Major, much to his annoyance, was seized upon simultaneously by two ladies, one eager to know if any tidings had been received of Mdlle. Cunier, the other anxious to learn if a distinguished president to the Harem Mission had been decided upon.

Soon after six the rooms began to thin somewhat, and presentations to the Princess ceasing, Loveday was able to get a full view of her.

She presented a striking picture, seated, half-reclining, on a sofa, with two white-robed, dark-skinned Egyptian maidens standing behind it. A more unfortunate sobriquet than " Dolly " could scarcely have been found by the Major for this Oriental beauty, with her olive complexion, her flashing eyes and extravagant richness of attire.

" ' Queen of Sheba ' would be far more appropriate," thought Loveday. " She turns the commonplace sofa into a throne, and, I should say, makes every one of those ladies feel as if she ought to have donned court dress and plumes for the occasion."

It was difficult for her, from where she sat, to follow the details of the Princess's dress. She could only see that a quantity of soft orange-tinted silk was wound about the upper part of her arms and fell

MRS. DRUCE.

from her shoulders like drooping wings, and that here and there jewels flashed out from its folds. Her thick black hair was loosely knotted, and kept in its place by jewelled pins and a bandeau of pearls; and similar bandeaus adorned her slender throat and wrists.

" Are you lost in admiration ? " said the Major, once more at her elbow, in a slightly sarcastic tone. " That sort of thing is very taking and effective at first, but after a time —— "

He did not finish his sentence, shrugged his shoulders and walked away. Half-past six chimed from a small clock on a bracket. Carriage after carriage was rolling away from the door now, and progress on the stairs was rendered difficult by a descending crowd.

A quarter to seven struck, the last hand-shaking had been gone through, and Mrs. Druce, looking hot and tired, had sunk into a chair at the Princess's right hand, bending slightly forward to render conversation with her easy.

On the Princess's left hand, Lady Gwynne had taken a chair, and sat in converse with Hafiz Cassimi, who stood beside her.

Evidently these four were on very easy and intimate terms with each other. Lady Gwynne had tossed her big picture hat on a chair at her left hand, and was fanning herself with a palm-leaf. Mrs. Druce, beckoning to the butler, desired him to bring them some claret-cup from the refreshment-room.

No one seemed to observe Loveday seated still in her nook beside the big palm.

She signalled to the Major, who stood looking discontentedly from one of the windows.

" That is a most interesting group," she said ; " now, if you like, you may introduce me to your mother."

" Oh, with pleasure — under what name ? " he asked.

" Under my own," she answered, " and please be very distinct in pronouncing it, raise your voice slightly so that everyone of those persons may hear it. And then, please add my profession, and say I am here at your request to investigate the circumstances connected with Mdlle. Cunier's disappearance."

Major Druce looked astounded.

" But—but," he stammered, " have you seen anything—found out anything ? If not, don't you think it will be better to preserve your incognita a little longer."

" Don't stop to ask questions," said Loveday sharply ; " now, this very minute, do what I ask you, or the opportunity will be gone."

The Major without further demur, escorted Loveday across the room. The conversation between the four intimate friends had now become general and animated, and he had to wait for a minute or so before he could get an opportunity to speak to his mother.

During that minute Loveday stood a little in his rear, with Lady Gwynne and Cassimi at her right hand.

" I want to introduce this lady to you," said the Major, when a pause in the talk gave him his opportunity. " This is Miss Loveday Brooke, a lady detective, and she is here at my request to investigate the circumstances connected with the disappearance of Mdlle. Cunier."

He said the words slowly and distinctly.

" There ! " he said to himself complacently, as he ended ; " if I had been reading the lessons in church, I couldn't have been more emphatic."

A blank silence for a moment fell upon the group, and even the butler, just then entering with the claret-cup, came to a standstill at the door.

Then, simultaneously, a glance flashed from Mrs. Druce to Lady Gwynne, from Lady Gwynne to Mrs. Druce, and then, also simultaneously, the eyes of both ladies rested, though only for an instant, on the big picture hat lying on the chair.

Lady Gwynne started to her feet and seized her hat, adjusting it without so much as a glance at a mirror.

" I must go at once ; this very minute," she said. " I promised Charlie I would be

MR. CASSIMI

back soon after six, and now it is past seven. Mr. Cassimi, will you take me down to my carriage ? " And with the most hurried of leave-takings to the Princess and her hostess, the lady swept out of the room, followed by Mr. Cassimi.

The butler still standing at the door, drew back to allow the lady to pass, and then, claret-cup and all, followed her out of the room.

Mrs. Druce drew a long breath and bowed formally to Loveday.

" I was a little taken by surprise," she began——

But here the Princess rose suddenly from the sofa.

" Moi, je suis fatiguée," she said in excellent French to Mrs. Druce, and she too swept out of the room, throwing, as she passed, what seemed to Loveday a slightly scornful glance towards the Major.

Her two attendants, one carrying her fan, and the other her reclining cushions, followed.

Mrs. Druce again turned to Loveday.

" Yes, I confess I was taken a little by surprise," she said, her manner thawing slightly. " I am not accustomed to the presence of detectives in my house ; but now tell me what do you propose doing ; how do you mean to begin your investigations—by going over the house and looking in all the corners, or by cross-questioning the servants ? Forgive my asking, but really I am quite at a loss ; I haven't the remotest idea how such investigations are generally conducted."

" I do not propose to do much in the way of investigation to-night," answered Loveday as formally as she had been addressed, " for I have very important business to transact before eight o'clock this evening. I shall ask you to allow me to see Mdlle. Cunier's room—ten minutes there will be sufficient—after that, I do not think I need further trouble you."

" Certainly ; by all means," answered Mrs. Druce ; " you'll find the room exactly as Lucie left it, nothing has been disturbed."

She turned to the butler,

who had by this time returned and stood presenting the claret-cup, and, in French, desired him to summon her maid, and tell her to show Miss Brooke to Mdlle. Cunier's room.

The ten minutes that Loveday had said would suffice for her survey of this room extended themselves to fifteen, but the extra five minutes assuredly were not expended by her in the investigation of drawers and boxes. The maid, a pleasant, well-spoken young woman, jingled her keys, and opened every lock, and seemed not at all disinclined to enter into

SHE SWEPT OUT OF THE ROOM

the light gossip that Loveday contrived to set going.

She answered freely a variety of questions that Loveday put to her respecting Mademoiselle and her general habits, and from Mademoiselle, the talk drifted to other members of Mrs. Druce's household.

If Loveday had, as she had stated, important business to transact that evening, she certainly set about it in a strange fashion.

After she quitted Mademoiselle's room, she went straight out of the house, without leaving a message of any sort for either

Mrs. or Major Druce. She walked the length of Portland Place in leisurely fashion, and then, having first ascertained that her movements were not being watched, she called a hansom, and desired the man to drive her to Madame Céline's, a fashionable milliner's in Old Bond Street.

At Madame Céline's she spent close upon half-an-hour, giving many and minute directions for the making of a hat, which assuredly, when finished, would compare with nothing in the way of millinery that she had ever before put upon her head.

From Madame Céline's the hansom conveyed her to an undertaker's shop, at the corner of South Savile Street, and here she spent a brief ten minutes in conversation with the undertaker himself in his little back parlour.

From the undertaker's she drove home to her rooms in Gower Street, and then, before she divested herself of hat and coat, she wrote a brief note to Major Druce, requesting him to meet her on the following morning at Eglacé's, the confectioner's, in South Savile Street, at nine o'clock punctually.

This note she committed to the charge of the cab-driver, desiring him to deliver it at Portland Place on his way back to his stand.

"They've queer ways of doing things—these people!" said the Major, as he opened and read the note. "Suppose I must keep the appointment though, confound it. I can't see that she can possibly have found out anything by just sitting still in a corner for a couple of hours! And I'm confident she didn't give that beast Cassimi one quarter the attention she bestowed on other people."

In spite of his grumbling, however, the Major kept his appointment, and nine o'clock the next morning saw him shaking hands with Miss Brooke on Eglacé's doorstep.

"Dismiss your hansom," she said to him. "I only want you to come a few doors down the street, to the French Protestant church, to which you have sometimes escorted Mdlle. Cunier."

At the church door Loveday paused a moment.

" Before we enter," she said, " I want you to promise that whatever you may see going on there—however greatly you may be surprised—you will make no disturbance, not so much as open your lips till we come out."

The Major, not a little bewildered, gave the required promise ; and, side by side, the two entered the church.

It was little more than a big room ; at the farther end, in the middle of the nave, stood the pulpit, and immediately behind this was a low platform, enclosed by a brass rail.

Behind this brass rail, in black Geneva gown, stood the pastor of the church, and before him, on cushions, kneeled two persons, a man and a woman.

These two persons and an old man, the verger, formed the whole of the congregation. The position of the church, amid shops and narrow back-yards, had necessitated the filling in of every one of its windows with stained glass ; it was, consequently, so dim that, coming in from the outside glare of sunlight, the Major found it difficult to make out what was going on at the farther end.

The verger came forward and offered to show them to a seat. Loveday shook her head—they would be leaving in a minute, she said, and would prefer standing where they were.

The Major began to take in the situation.

" Why they're being married ! " he said in a loud whisper. " What on earth have you brought me in here for ? "

Loveday laid her finger on her lips and frowned severely at him.

The marriage service came to an end, the pastor extended his black-gowned arms like the wings of a bat and pronounced the benediction ; the man and woman rose from their knees and proceeded to follow him into the vestry.

The woman was neatly dressed in a long dove-coloured travelling cloak. She wore a large hat, from which fell a white gossamer veil that completely hid her face from view. The man was small, dark and slight, and as he passed on to the vestry beside his bride, the Major at once identified him as his mother's butler.

" Why, that's Lebrun ! " he said in a still louder whisper than before. " Why, in the name of all that's wonderful, have you brought me here to see that fellow married ? "

" You'd better come outside if you can't keep quiet," said Loveday severely, and leading the way out of the church as she spoke.

Outside, South Savile Street was busy with early morning traffic.

" Let us go back to Eglacé's," said Loveday, " and have some coffee. I will explain to you there all you are wishing to know."

But before the coffee could be brought

" WHY, THEY ARE BEING MARRIED ! "

to them, the Major had asked at least a dozen questions.

Loveday put them all on one side.

" All in good time " she said. " You are leaving out the most important question of all. Have you no curiosity to know who was the bride that Lebrun has chosen ? "

" I don't suppose it concerns me in the slightest degree," he answered indifferently ; " but since you wish me to ask the question—Who was she ? "

" Lucie Cunier, lately your mother's amanuensis."

" The —— ! " cried the Major, jumping to his feet and uttering an exclamation that must be indicated by a blank.

" Take it calmly," said Loveday ; "don't rave. Sit down and I'll tell you all about it. No, it is not the doing of your friend Cassimi, so you need not threaten to put a bullet into him ; the girl has married Lebrun of her own free will—no one has forced her into it."

" Lucie has married Lebrun of her own free will ! " he echoed, growing very white and taking the chair which faced Loveday at the little table.

" Will you have sugar ? " asked Loveday, stirring the coffee, which the waiter at that moment brought.

" Yes, I repeat," she presently resumed, " Lucie has married Lebrun of her own free will, although I conjecture she might not perhaps have been quite so willing to crown his happiness if the Princess Dullah-Veih had not made it greatly to her interest to do so."

" Dolly made it to her interest to do so ? " again echoed the Major.

" Do not interrupt me with exclamations ; let me tell the story my own fashion, and then you may ask as many questions as you please. Now, to begin at the beginning, Lucie became engaged to Lebrun within a month of her coming to your mother's house, but she carefully kept the secret from everyone, even from the servants, until about a month ago, when she mentioned the fact in confidence to Mrs. Druce in order to defend herself from the charge of having sought to attract your attention. There was nothing surprising in this engagement ; they were both lonely and in a foreign land, spoke the same language, and no doubt had many things in common ; and although chance has lifted Lucie somewhat out of her station, she really belongs to the same class in life as Lebrun. Their love-making appears to have run along smoothly enough until you came home on leave, and the girl's pretty face attracted your attention. Your evident admiration for her disturbed the equanimity of the Princess, who saw your devotion to herself waning ; of Lebrun, who fancied Lucie's manner to him had changed ; of your mother, who was anxious that you should make a suitable marriage. Also additional complications arose from the fact that

your attentions to the little Swiss girl had drawn Mr. Cassimi's notice to her numerous attractions, and there was the danger of you two young men posing as rivals. At this juncture Lady Gwynne, as an intimate friend, and one who had herself suffered a twinge of heartache on Mademoiselle's account, was taken into your mother's confidence, and the three ladies in council decided that Lucie, in some fashion, must be got out of the way before you and Mr. Cassimi came to an open breach, or you had spoilt your matrimonial prospects."

Here the Major made a slightly impatient movement.

Loveday went on : " It was the Princess who solved the question how this was to be done. Fair Rosamonds are no longer put out of the way by 'a cup of cold poison '—golden guineas do the thing far more easily and innocently. The Princess expressed her willingness to bestow a thousand pounds on Lucie on the day that she married Lebrun, and to set her up afterwards as a fashionable milliner in Paris. After this munificent offer, everything else became mere matter of detail. The main thing was to get the damsel out of the way without your being able to trace her—perhaps work on her feelings, and induce her, at the last moment, to throw over Lebrun. Your absence from home, on a three days' visit, gave them the wished-for opportunity. Lady Gwynne took her milliner into her confidence. Madame Céline consented to receive Lucie into her house, seclude her in a room on the upper floor, and at the same time give her an insight into the profession of a fashionable milliner. The rest I think you know. Lucie quietly walks out of the house one afternoon, taking no luggage, calling no cab, and thereby cutting off one very obvious means of being traced. Madame Céline receives and hides her— not a difficult feat to accomplish in London, more especially if the one to be hidden is a foreign amanuensis, who is seldom seen out of doors, and who leaves no photograph behind her."

" I suppose it was Lebrun who had the confounded cheek to go to my drawer and appropriate that photograph. I wish it had been Cassimi—I could have kicked him, but—but it makes one feel rather small to have posed as rival to one's mother's butler."

" I think you may congratulate yourself

that Lebrun did nothing worse than go to your drawer and appropriate that photograph. I never saw a man bestow a more deadly look of hatred than he threw at you yesterday afternoon in your mother's drawing-room; it was that look of hatred that first drew my attention to the man and set me on the track that has ended in the Swiss Protestant church this morning."

"Ah! let me hear about that—let me have the links in the chain, one by one, as you came upon them," said the Major.

He was still pale—almost as the marble table at which they sat, but his voice had gone back to its normal slow, soft drawl.

HE WAS STILL PALE.

"With pleasure. The look that Lebrun threw at you, as he crossed the room to open the window, was link number one. As I saw that look, I said to myself there is someone in that corner whom that man hates with a deadly hatred. Then you came forward to speak to me, and I saw that it was you that the man was ready to murder, if opportunity offered. After this, I scrutinised him closely—not a detail of his features or his dress escaped me, and I noticed, among other things, that on the fourth finger of his left hand, half hidden by a more pretentious ring, was an old fashioned curious looking silver one. That silver ring was link number two in the chain."

"Ah, I suppose you asked for that glass of water on purpose to get a closer view of the ring?"

"I did, I found it was a Genevese ring of ancient make, the like of which I had not seen since I was a child and played with one, that my old Swiss bonne used to wear. Now I must tell you a little bit of Genevese history before I can make you understand how important a link that silver ring was to me. Echallets, the town in which Lucie was born, and her father had kept a watchmaker's shop, has long been famous for its jewellery and watchmaking. The two trades, however, were not combined in one until about a hundred years ago, when the corporation of the town passed a law decreeing that they should unite in one guild for their common good. To celebrate this amalgamation of interests, the jewellers fabricated a certain number of silver rings, consisting of a plain band of silver, on which two hands, in relief, clasped each other. These rings were distributed among the members of the guild, and as time has gone on they have become scarce and valuable as relics of the past. In certain families, they have been handed down as heirlooms, and have frequently done duty as betrothal rings—the clasped hands no doubt suggesting their suitability for this purpose. Now, when I saw such a ring on Lebrun's finger, I naturally guessed from whom he had received it, and at once classed his interests with those of your mother and the Princess, and looked upon him as their possible coadjutor."

"What made you throw the brute Cassimi altogether out of your reckoning?"

"I did not do so at this stage of events; only, so to speak, marked him as 'doubtful' and kept my eye on him. I determined to try an experiment that I have never before attempted in my work. You know what that experiment was. I saw five persons, Mrs. Druce, the Princess, Lady Gwynne, Mr. Cassimi and Lebrun all in the room within a few yards of each other, and I asked you to take them by surprise and announce my name and profession, so that every one of those five persons could hear you."

"You did. I could not, for the life of me, make out what was your motive for so doing."

"My motive for so doing was simply, as it were, to raise the sudden cry, 'The enemy is upon you,' and to set every one of those five persons guarding their weak point—that is, if they had one. I'll draw your attention to what followed. Mr. Cassimi remained nonchalant and impassive; your mother and Lady Gwynne exchanged glances, and then both simultaneously threw a nervous look at Lady Gwynne's hat lying on the chair. Now as I had stood waiting to be introduced to Mrs. Druce, I had casually read the name of Madame Céline on the lining of the hat and I at once concluded that Madame Céline must be a very weak point indeed; a conclusion that was confirmed when Lady Gwynne hurriedly seized her hat and as hurriedly departed. Then the Princess scarcely less abruptly rose and left the room, and Lebrun on the point of entering, quitted it also. When he returned five minutes later, with the claret-cup, he had removed the ring from his finger, so I had now little doubt where his weak point lay."

"It's wonderful; it's like a fairy tale," drawled the Major. "Pray, go on."

"After this," continued Loveday, "my work became very simple. I did not care two straws for seeing Mademoiselle's room, but I cared very much to have a talk with Mrs. Druce's maid. From her I elicited the important fact that Lebrun was leaving very unexpectedly on the following day, and that his boxes were packed and labelled for Paris. After I left your house, I drove to Madame Céline's, and there, as a sort of entrance fee, ordered an elaborate hat. I praised freely the hats they had on view, and while giving minute directions as to the one I required, I extracted the information that Madame Céline had recently taken on a new milliner who had very great artistic skill. Upon this, I asked permission to see this new milliner and give her special instructions concerning my hat. My request was referred to Madame Céline, who appeared much ruffled by it, and informed me that it would be quite useless for me to see this new milliner; she could execute no more orders, as she was leaving the next day for Paris, where she intended opening an establishment on her own account.

Now you see the point at which I had arrived. There was Lebrun and there was this new milliner each leaving for Paris on the same day; it was not unreasonable to suppose that they might start in company, and that before so doing, a little ceremony might be gone through in the Swiss Protestant church that Mademoiselle occasionally attended. This conjecture sent me to the undertaker in South Savile Street, who combines with his undertaking the office of verger to the little church. From him I learned that a marriage was to take place at the church at a quarter to nine the next morning and that the names of the contracting parties were Pierre Lebrun and Lucie Cuénin."

"Cuénin!"

"Yes, that is the girl's real name; it seems Lady Gwynne re-christened her Cunier, because she said the English pronunciation of Cuénin grated on her ear—people would insist upon adding a *g* after the *n*. She introduced her to Mrs. Druce under the name of Cunier, forgetting, perhaps, the girl's real name, or else thinking it a matter of no importance. This fact, no doubt, considerably lessened Lebrun's fear of detection in procuring his licence and transmitting it to the Swiss pastor. Perhaps you are a little surprised at my knowledge of the facts I related to you at the beginning of our conversation. I got at them through Lebrun this morning. At half-past eight I went down to the church and found him there, waiting for his bride. He grew terribly excited at seeing me, and thought I was going to bring you down on him and upset his wedding arrangements at the last moment. I assured him to the contrary, and his version of the facts I have handed on to you. Should, however, any details of the story seem to you to be lacking, I have no doubt that Mrs. Druce or the Princess will supply them, now that all necessity for secrecy has come to an end."

The Major drew on his gloves; his colour had come back to him; he had resumed his easy suavity of manner.

"I don't think," he said slowly, "I'll trouble my mother or the Princess; and I shall be glad, if you have the opportunity, if you will make people understand that I only moved in the matter at all out of—of mere kindness to a young and friendless foreigner."

The Experiences of Loveday Brooke, Lady Detective.

By C. L. PIRKIS, Author of "Lady Lovelace," &c. &c.

DRAWN DAGGERS.

"I ADMIT that the dagger business is something of a puzzle to me, but as for the lost necklace—well, I should have thought a child would have understood that," said Mr. Dyer irritably. "When a young lady loses a valuable article of jewellery and wishes to hush the matter up, the explanation is obvious."

"Sometimes," answered Miss Brooke calmly, "the explanation that is obvious is the one to be rejected, not accepted."

Off and on these two had been, so to speak, "jangling" a good deal that morning. Perhaps the fact was in part to be attributed to the biting east wind which had set Loveday's eyes watering with the gritty dust, as she had made her way to Lynch Court, and which was, at the present moment, sending the smoke, in aggravating gusts, down the chimney into Mr. Dyer's face. Thus it was, however. On the various topics that had chanced to come up for discussion that morning between Mr. Dyer and his colleague, they had each taken up, as if by design, diametrically opposite points of view.

His temper altogether gave way now.

"If, " he said, bringing his hand down with emphasis on his writing-table, "you lay it down as a principle that the obvious is to be rejected in favour of the abstruse, you'll soon find yourself launched in the predicament of having to prove that two apples added to two other apples do not make four. But there, if you don't choose to see things from my point of view, that is no reason why you should lose your temper!"

"Mr. Hawke wishes to see you, sir," said a clerk, at that moment entering the room.

It was a fortunate diversion. Whatever might be the differences of opinion in which these two might indulge in private, they were careful never to parade those differences before their clients.

Mr. Dyer's irritability vanished in a moment.

"Show the gentleman in," he said to the clerk. Then he turned to Loveday. "This is the Rev. Anthony Hawke, the gentleman at whose house I told you that Miss Monroe is staying temporarily. He is a clergyman of the Church of England, but gave up his living some twenty years ago when he married a wealthy lady. Miss Monroe has been sent over to his guardianship from Pekin by her father, Sir George Monroe, in order to get her out of the way of a troublesome and undesirable suitor."

The last sentence was added in a low and hurried tone, for Mr. Hawke was at that moment entering the room.

He was a man close upon sixty years of age, white-haired, clean shaven, with a full, round face, to which a small nose imparted a somewhat infantine expression. His manner of greeting was urbane but slightly flurried and nervous. He gave Loveday the impression of being an easy-going, happy-tempered man who, for the moment, was unusually disturbed and perplexed.

He glanced uneasily at Loveday. Mr. Dyer hastened to explain that this was the lady by whose aid he hoped to get to the bottom of the matter now under consideration.

"In that case there can be no objection to my showing you this," said Mr. Hawke; "it came by post this morning. You see my enemy still pursues me."

As he spoke he took from his pocket a

big, square envelope, from which he drew a large-sized sheet of paper.

On this sheet of paper were roughly drawn, in ink, two daggers, about six inches in length, with remarkably pointed blades.

Mr. Dyer looked at the sketch with interest.

"We will compare this drawing and its envelope with those you previously received," he said, opening a drawer of his writing-table and taking thence a precisely similar envelope. On the sheet of paper, however, that this envelope enclosed, there was drawn one dagger only.

He placed both envelopes and their enclosures side by side, and in silence compared them. Then, without a word, he handed them to Miss Brooke, who, taking a glass from her pocket, subjected them to a similar careful and minute scrutiny.

Both envelopes were of precisely the same make, and were each addressed to Mr. Hawke's London address in a round, school-boyish, copy-book sort of hand—the hand so easy to write and so difficult to bring home to any writer on account of its want of individuality. Each envelope likewise bore a Cork and a London postmark.

The sheet of paper, however, that the first envelope enclosed bore the sketch of one dagger only.

Loveday laid down her glass.

"The envelopes," she said, "have, undoubtedly, been addressed by the same person, but these last two daggers have not been drawn by the hand that drew the first. Dagger number one was, evidently, drawn by a timid, uncertain and inartistic hand—see how the lines wave and how they have been patched here and there. The

person who drew the other daggers, I should say, could do better work: the outline, though rugged, is bold and free. I should like to take these sketches home with me and compare them again at my leisure."

"Ah, I felt sure what your opinion would be!" said Mr. Dyer complacently.

Mr. Hawke seemed much disturbed.

"Good gracious!" he ejaculated; "you don't mean to say I have two enemies pursuing me in this fashion! What does it mean? Can it be—is it possible, do you think, that these things have been sent to me by the members of some Secret Society in Ireland—under error, of course—mistaking me for someone else? They can't be meant for me; I have never, in my whole life, been mixed up with any political agitation of any sort."

Mr. Dyer shook his head. "Members of secret societies generally make pretty sure of their ground before they send out missives of this kind,' he said. "I have never heard of such an error being made. I think, too, we mustn't build any theories on the Irish post-mark: the letters may have been posted in Cork for the whole and sole purpose of drawing off attention from some other quarter."

"Will you mind telling me a little about the loss of the necklace?" here said Loveday, bringing the conversation suddenly round from the daggers to the diamonds.

"I think," interposed Mr. Dyer, turning towards her, "that the episode of the drawn daggers — drawn in a double sense —should be treated entirely on its own merits, considered as a thing apart from the loss of the necklace. I am inclined to believe that when we have gone a little further into

HAD BEEN JANGLING A GOOD DEAL.

the matter we shall find that each circumstance belongs to a different group of facts. After all, it is possible that these daggers may have been sent by way of a joke—a rather foolish one, I admit—by some harum-scarum fellow bent on causing a sensation."

Mr. Hawke's face brightened. "Ah! now, do you think so—really think so?" he ejaculated. "It would lift such a load from my mind if you could bring the thing home, in this way, to some practical joker. There are a lot of such fellows knocking about the world. Why, now I come to think of it, my nephew, Jack, who is a good deal with us just now, and is not quite so steady a fellow as I should like him to be, must have a good many such scamps among his acquaintances."

"A good many such scamps among his acquaintances," echoed Loveday; "that certainly gives plausibility to Mr. Dyer's supposition. At the same time, I think we are bound to look at the other side of the case, and admit the possibility of these daggers being sent in right-down sober earnest by persons concerned in the robbery, with the intention of intimidating you and preventing full investigation of the matter. If this be so, it will not signify which thread we take up and follow. If we find the sender of the daggers we are safe to come upon the thief; or, if we follow up and find the thief, the sender of the daggers will not be far off."

Mr. Hawke's face fell once more.

"It's an uncomfortable position to be in," he said slowly. "I suppose, whoever they are, they will do the regulation thing, and next time will send an instalment of three daggers, in which case I may consider myself a doomed man. It did not occur to me before, but I remember now that I did not receive the first dagger until after I had spoken very strongly to Mrs. Hawke, before the servants, about my wish to set the police to work. I told her I felt bound, in honour to Sir George, to do so, as the necklace had been lost under my roof."

"Did Mrs. Hawke object to your calling

"I HOPE YOU UNDER-
STAND"

in the aid of the police?" asked Loveday.

"Yes, most strongly. She entirely supported Miss Monroe in her wish to take no steps in the matter. Indeed, I should not have come round as I did last night to Mr. Dyer, if my wife had not been suddenly summoned from home by the serious illness of her sister. At least," he corrected himself with a little attempt at self-assertion, "my coming to him might have been a little delayed. I hope you understand, Mr. Dyer; I do not mean to imply that I am not master in my own house."

"Oh, quite so, quite so," responded Mr. Dyer. "Did Mrs. Hawke or Miss Monroe give any reasons for not wishing you to move in the matter?"

"All told, I should think they gave about a hundred reasons—I can't remember them all. For one thing, Miss Monroe said it might necessitate her appearing in the police courts, a thing she would not consent to do; and she certainly did not consider the necklace was worth the fuss I was making over it. And that necklace, sir, has been valued at over nine hundred pounds, and has come down to the young lady from her mother."

"And Mrs. Hawke?"

"Mrs. Hawke supported Miss Monroe in her views in her presence. But privately to me afterwards, she gave other reasons for not wishing the police called in. Girls, she said, were always careless with their jewellery, she might have lost the necklace in Pekin, and never have brought it to England at all."

"Quite so," said Mr. Dyer. "I think I understood you to say that no one had seen the necklace since Miss Monroe's arrival in England. Also, I believe it was she who first discovered it to be missing?"

"Yes. Sir George, when he wrote apprising me of his daughter's visit, added a postscript to his letter, saying that his daughter was bringing her necklace with her and that he would feel greatly obliged if I would have it deposited with as little delay as possible at my bankers', where it could be easily got at if required. I spoke to Miss Monroe about doing this two or three times, but she did not seem at all inclined to comply with her father's wishes. Then my wife took the matter in hand— Mrs. Hawke, I must tell you, has a very firm, resolute manner—she told Miss Monroe plainly that she would not have the responsibility of those diamonds in the house, and insisted that there and then they should be sent off to the bankers. Upon this Miss Monroe went up to her room, and presently returned, saying that her necklace had disappeared. She herself, she said, had placed it in her jewel-case and the jewel-case in her wardrobe, when her boxes were unpacked. The

"SHE CAME IN 'THE COLOMBO,' ACCOMPANIED BY HER MAID."

jewel-case was in the wardrobe right enough, and no other article of jewellery appeared to have been disturbed, but the little padded niche in which the necklace had been deposited was empty. My wife and her maid went upstairs immediately, and searched every corner of the room, but, I'm sorry to say, without any result."

"Miss Monroe, I suppose, has her own maid?"

"No, she has not. The maid — an elderly native woman — who left Pekin with her, suffered so terribly from sea-sickness that, when they reached Malta,

Miss Monroe allowed her to land and remain there in charge of an agent of the P. and O. Company till an outward bound packet could take her back to China. It seems the poor woman thought she was going to die, and was in a terrible state of mind because she hadn't brought her coffin with her. I dare say you know the terror these Chinese have of being buried in foreign soil. After her departure, Miss Monroe engaged one of the steerage passengers to act as her maid for the remainder of the voyage."

"Did Miss Monroe make the long journey from Pekin accompanied only by this native woman?"

"No; friends escorted her to Hong Kong—by far the roughest part of the journey. From Hong Kong she came on in *The Colombo*, accompanied only by her maid. I wrote and told her father I would meet her at the docks in London; the young lady, however, preferred landing at Plymouth, and telegraphed to me from there that she was coming on by rail to Waterloo, where, if I liked, I might meet her."

"She seems to be a young lady of independent habits. Was she brought up and educated in China?"

"Yes; by a succession of French and American governesses. After her mother's death, when she was little more than a baby, Sir George could not make up his mind to part with her, as she was his only child."

"I suppose you and Sir George Monroe are old friends?"

"Yes; he and I were great chums before he went out to China—now about twenty years ago—and it was only natural, when he wished to get his daughter out of the way of young Danvers's impertinent attentions, that he should ask me to take charge of her till he could claim his retiring pension and set up his tent in England."

"What was the chief objection to Mr. Danvers's attentions?"

"Well, he is only a boy of one-and-twenty, and has no money into the bargain. He has been sent out to Pekin by his father to study the language, in order to qualify for a billet in the customs, and it may be a dozen years before he is in a position to keep a wife. Now, Miss Monroe is an heiress—will come into her mother's large fortune when she is of age —and Sir George, naturally, would like her to make a good match."

"I suppose Miss Monroe came to England very reluctantly?"

"I imagine so. No doubt it was a great wrench for her to leave her home and friends in that sudden fashion and come to us, who are, one and all, utter strangers to her. She is very quiet, very shy and reserved. She goes nowhere, sees no one. When some old China friends of her father's called to see her the other day, she immediately found she had a headache and went to bed. I think, on the whole, she gets on better with my nephew than with anyone else."

"Will you kindly tell me of how many persons your household consists at the present moment?"

"At the present moment we are one more than usual, for my nephew, Jack, is home with his regiment from India, and is staying with us. As a rule, my household consists of my wife and myself, butler, cook, housemaid and my wife's maid, who just now is doing double duty as Miss Monroe's maid also."

Mr. Dyer looked at his watch.

"I have an important engagement in ten minutes' time," he said, "so I must leave you and Miss Brooke to arrange details as to how and when she is to begin her work inside your house, for, of course, in a case of this sort we must, in the first instance at any rate, concentrate attention within your four walls."

"The less delay the better," said Loveday. "I should like to attack the mystery at once—this afternoon."

Mr. Hawke thought for a moment.

"According to present arrangements," he said, with a little hesitation, "Mrs. Hawke will return next Friday, that is the day after to-morrow, so I can only ask you to remain in the house till the morning of that day. I'm sure you will understand that there might be some—some little awkwardness in ——"

"Oh, quite so," interrupted Loveday. "I don't see at present that there will be any necessity for me to sleep in the house at all. How would it be for me to assume the part of a lady house decorator in the employment of a West-end firm, and sent by them to survey your house and advise upon its re-decoration? All I should have to do, would be to walk about your rooms with my head on one side, and a pencil and note-book in my hand. I should interfere with no one, your family life would go on as usual, and I could make my work as short or as long as necessity might dictate."

Mr. Hawke had no objection to offer to

"CUT THE CARDS AGAIN, PLEASE.

this. He had, however, a request to make as he rose to depart, and he made it a little nervously.

"If," he said, "by any chance there should come a telegram from Mrs. Hawke, saying she will return by an earlier train, I suppose—I hope, that is, you will make some excuse, and—and not get me into hot water, I mean."

To this, Loveday answered a little evasively that she trusted no such telegram would be forthcoming, but that, in any case, he might rely upon her discretion.

Four o'clock was striking from a neighbouring church clock as Loveday lifted the old-fashioned brass knocker of Mr. Hawke's house in Tavistock Square. An elderly butler admitted her and showed her into the drawing-room on the first floor. A single glance round showed Loveday that if her rôle had been real instead of assumed, she would have found plenty of scope for her talents. Although the house was in all respects comfortably furnished, it bore unmistakably the impress of those early Victorian days when aesthetic surroundings were not deemed a necessity of existence; an impress which people past middle age, and growing increasingly indifferent to the accessories of life, are frequently careless to remove.

"Young life here is evidently an excrescence, not part of the home; a troop of daughters turned into this room would speedily set going a different condition of things," thought Loveday, taking stock of the faded white and gold wall paper, the chairs covered with lilies and roses in cross-stitch, and the knick-knacks of a past generation that were scattered about on tables and mantelpiece.

A yellow damask curtain, half-festooned, divided the back drawing-room from the front in which she was seated. From the other side of this curtain there came to her

the sound of voices—those of a man and a girl.

"Cut the cards again, please," said the man's voice. "Thank you. There you are again—the queen of hearts, surrounded with diamonds, and turning her back on a knave. Miss Monroe, you can't do better than make that fortune come true. Turn your back on the man who let you go without a word and ——."

"Hush!" interrupted the girl with a little laugh; "I heard the next room door open—I'm sure someone came in."

The girl's laugh seemed to Loveday utterly destitute of that echo of heart-ache that in the circumstances might have been expected.

At this moment Mr. Hawke entered the room, and almost simultaneously the two young people came from the other side of the yellow curtain and crossed towards the door.

Loveday took a survey of them as they passed.

The young man—evidently "my nephew, Jack"—was a good-looking young fellow, with dark eyes and hair. The girl was small, slight and fair. She was perceptibly less at home with Jack's uncle than she was with Jack, for her manner changed and grew formal and reserved as she came face to face with him.

"We're going downstairs to have a game of billiards," said Jack, addressing Mr. Hawke, and throwing a look of curiosity at Loveday.

"Jack," said the old gentleman, "what would you say if I told you I was going to have the house re-decorated from top to bottom, and that this lady had come to advise on the matter."

This was the nearest (and most Anglicé) approach to a fabrication that Mr. Hawke would allow to pass his lips.

"Well," answered Jack promptly, "I should say, 'not before its time.' That would cover a good deal."

LOVEDAY TOOK A SURVEY OF THEM AS THEY PASSED.

Then the two young people departed in company.

Loveday went straight to her work.

"I'll begin my surveying at the top of the house, and at once, if you please," she said. "Will you kindly tell one of your maids to show me through the bed-rooms? If it is possible, let that maid be the one who waits on Miss Monroe and Mrs. Hawke."

The maid who responded to Mr. Hawke's summons was in perfect harmony with the general appearance of the house. In addition, however, to being elderly and faded, she was also remarkably sour-visaged, and carried herself as if she thought that Mr. Hawke had taken a great liberty in thus commanding her attendance.

In dignified silence she showed Loveday over the topmost story, where the servants' bed-rooms were situated, and with a somewhat supercilious expression of countenance, watched her making various entries in her note-book.

In dignified silence, also, she led the way down to the second floor, where were the principal bed-rooms of the house.

"This is Miss Monroe's room," she said, as she threw back a door of one of these rooms, and then shut her lips with a snap, as if they were never going to open again.

The room that Loveday entered was, like the rest of the house, furnished in the style that prevailed in the early Victorian period. The bedstead was elaborately curtained with pink lined upholstery; the toilet-table was befrilled with muslin and tarlatan out of all likeness to a table. The one point, however, that chiefly attracted Loveday's attention was the extreme neatness that prevailed throughout the apartment—a neatness, however, that was

carried out with so strict an eye to comfort and convenience that it seemed to proclaim the hand of a first-class maid. Everything in the room was, so to speak, squared to the quarter of an inch, and yet everything that a lady could require in dressing lay ready to hand. The dressing-gown lying on the back of a chair had footstool and slippers beside it. A chair stood in front of the toilet table, and on a small Japanese table to the right of the chair were placed hair-pin box, comb and brush, and hand mirror.

"This room will want money spent upon it," said Loveday, letting her eyes roam critically in all directions. "Nothing but Moorish wood-work will take off the squareness of those corners. But what a maid Miss Monroe must have. I never before saw a room so orderly and, at the same time, so comfortable."

This was so direct an appeal to conversation that the sour-visaged maid felt compelled to open her lips.

"I wait on Miss Monroe, for the present," she said snappishly; "but, to speak the truth, she scarcely requires a maid. I never before in my life had dealings with such a young lady."

"She does so much for herself, you mean—declines much assistance."

"She's like no one else I ever had to do with." (This was said even more snappishly than before.) "She not only won't be helped in dressing, but she arranges her room every day before leaving it, even to placing the chair in front of the looking glass."

"And to opening the lid of the hair-pin box, so that she may have the pins ready to her hand," added Loveday, for a moment bend-

"I NEVER SAW A ROOM SO ORDERLY."

ing over the Japanese table, with its toilet accessories.

Another five minutes were all that Loveday accorded to the inspection of this room. Then, a little to the surprise of the dignified maid, she announced her intention of completing her survey of the bed-rooms some other time, and dismissed her at the drawing-room door, to tell Mr. Hawke that she wished to see him before leaving.

Mr. Hawke, looking much disturbed and with a tele-gram in his hand, quickly made his appearance.

"From my wife, to say she'll be back to-night. She'll be at Waterloo in about half an hour from now," he said, holding up the brown envelope. "Now, Miss Brooke, what are we to do? I told you how much Mrs. Hawke objected to the investigation of this matter, and she is very— well—firm when she once says a thing, and—and——"

"Set your mind at rest," interrupted Loveday; "I have done all I wished to do within your walls, and the remainder of my investiga-tion can be carried on just as well at Lynch Court or at my own private rooms."

IN A STATE OF GREAT EXCITEMENT.

"Done all you wished to do!" echoed Mr. Hawke in amazement; "why, you've not been an hour in the house, and do you mean to tell me you've found out anything about the necklace or the daggers?"

"Don't ask me any questions just yet; I want you to answer one or two instead. Now, can you tell me anything about any letters Miss Monroe may have written or received since she has been in your house?"

"Yes, certainly. Sir George wrote to me very strongly about her correspondence, and begged me to keep a sharp eye on it, so as to nip in the bud any attempt to communicate with Danvers. So far, how-ever, she does not appear to have made any such attempt. She is frankness itself over her correspondence. Every letter that has come addressed to her, she has shown either to me or to my wife, and they have one and all been letters from old friends of her father's, wishing to make her acquaintance now that she is in England. With regard to letter-writing, I am sorry to say she has a marked and most peculiar objection to it. Every one of the letters she has received, my wife tells me, remain unanswered still. She has never once been seen, since she came to the house, with a pen in her hand. And if she wrote on the sly, I don't know how she would get her letters posted—she never goes outside the door by her-self, and she would have no opportunity of giving them to any of the servants to post except Mrs. Hawke's maid, and she is beyond sus-picion in such a matter. She has been well cautioned, and, in addition, is not the sort of person who would assist a young lady in carry-ing on a clandestine corre-spondence."

"I should imagine not! I suppose Miss Monroe has been present at the break-fast table each time that you have received your daggers through the post—you told me, I think, that they had come by the first post in the morning?"

"Yes; Miss Monroe is very punctual at meals, and has been present each time. Naturally, when I received such unpleasant missives, I made some sort of exclama-tion and then handed the thing round the table for inspection, and Miss Monroe was very much concerned to know who my secret enemy could be."

"No doubt. Now, Mr. Hawke, I have a very special request to make to you, and I hope you will be most exact in carrying it out."

"You may rely upon my doing so to the very letter."

"Thank you. If, then, you should re-ceive by post to-morrow morning one of those big envelopes you already know the look of, and find that it contains a sketch of three, not two, drawn daggers ——"

"Good gracious! what makes you think such a thing likely?" exclaimed Mr. Hawke, greatly disturbed. "Why am I to be persecuted in this way? Am I to take it for granted that I am a doomed man?"

He began to pace the room in a state of great excitement.

" I don't think I would if I were you," answered Loveday calmly. " Pray let me finish. I want you to open the big envelope that may come to you by post to-morrow morning just as you have opened the others—in full view of your family at the breakfast-table—and to hand round the sketch it may contain for inspection to your wife, your nephew and to Miss Monroe. Now, will you promise me to do this ? "

" Oh, certainly ; I should most likely have done so without any promising. But — but — I'm sure you'll understand that I feel myself to be in a peculiarly uncomfortable position, and I shall feel so very much obliged to you if you'll tell me —that is if you'll enter a little more fully into an explanation."

Loveday looked at her watch. " I should think Mrs. Hawke would be just at this moment arriving at Waterloo; I'm sure you'll be glad to see the last of me. Please come to me at my rooms in Gower Street to-morrow at twelve—here is my card. I shall then be able to enter into fuller explanations I hope. Good-bye."

The old gentleman showed her politely downstairs, and, as he shook hands with her at the front door, again asked, in a most emphatic manner, if she did not consider him to be placed in a " peculiarly unpleasant position."

Those last words at parting were to be the first with which he greeted her on the following morning when he presented himself at her rooms in Gower Street. They were, however, repeated in considerably more agitated a manner.

" Was there ever a man in a more miserable position ! " he exclaimed, as he took the chair that Loveday indicated. " I not only received the three daggers for which you prepared me, but I got an additional worry, for which I was totally unprepared. This morning, immediately after breakfast, Miss Monroe walked out of the house all by herself, and no one knows where she has gone. And the girl has never before been outside the door alone. It seems the servants saw her go out, but did not think it necessary to tell either me or Mrs. Hawke, feeling sure we must have been aware of the fact."

" So Mrs. Hawke has returned," said Loveday. " Well, I suppose you will be greatly surprised if I inform you that the young lady, who has so unceremoniously left your house, is at the present moment to be found at the Charing Cross Hotel, where she has engaged a private room in her real name of Miss Mary O'Grady."

" Eh ! What ! Private room ! Real name O'Grady ! I'm all bewildered ! "

" It is a little bewildering ; let me explain. The young lady whom you received into your house as the daughter of your old friend, was in reality the person engaged by Miss Monroe to fulfil the duties of her maid on board ship, after her native attendant had been landed at Malta. Her real name, as I have told you, is Mary O'Grady, and she has proved herself a valuable coadjutor to Miss Monroe in assisting her to carry out a programme, which she must have arranged with her lover, Mr. Danvers, before she left Pekin."

" Eh ! what ! " again ejaculated Mr. Hawke ; " how do you know all this ? Tell me the whole story."

" I will tell you the whole story first, and then explain to you how I came to know it. From what has followed, it seems to me that Miss Monroe must have arranged with Mr. Danvers that he was to leave Pekin within ten days of her so doing, travel by the route by which she came, and land at Plymouth, where he was to receive a note from her, apprising him of her whereabouts. So soon as she was on board ship, Miss Monroe appears to have set her wits to work with great energy ; every obstacle to the carrying-out of her programme she appears to have met and conquered. Step number one was to get rid of her native maid, who, perhaps, might have been faithful to her master's interests and have proved troublesome. I have no doubt the poor woman suffered terribly from sea-sickness, as it was her first voyage, and I have equally no doubt that Miss Monroe worked on her fears, and persuaded her to land at Malta, and return to China by the next packet. Step number two was to find a suitable person, who, for a consideration, would be willing to play the part of the Pekin heiress among the heiress's friends in England, while the young lady herself arranged her private affairs to her own liking. That person was quickly found among the steerage passengers of the *Colombo* in Miss Mary O'Grady, who had come on board with her mother at Ceylon, and who, from the glimpse I had of her, must, I should conjecture, have been absent many years from the land of her birth.

You know how cleverly this young lady has played her part in your house—how, without attracting attention to the matter, she has shunned the society of her father's old Chinese friends, who might be likely to involve her in embarrassing conversations; how she has avoided the use of pen and ink lest ——"

"Yes, yes," interrupted Mr. Hawke; " but, my dear Miss Brooke, wouldn't it be as well for you and me to go at once to the Charing Cross Hotel, and get all the information we can out of her respecting Miss Monroe and her movements—she may be bolting, you know?"

"I do not think she will. She is waiting there patiently for an answer to a telegram she despatched more than two hours ago to her mother, Mrs. O'Grady, at 14, Woburn Place, Cork."

Dear me! dear me! How is it possible for you to know all this."

"Oh, that last little fact was simply a matter of astuteness on the part of the man whom I have deputed to watch the young lady's movements to-day. Other details, I assure you, in this some what intricate case, have been infinitely more difficult to get at. I think I have to thank those 'drawn daggers,' that caused you so much consternation, for having, in the first instance, put me on the right track."

"Ah—h," said Mr. Hawke, drawing a long breath; " now we come to the daggers! I feel sure you are going to set my mind at rest on that score."

"I hope so. Would it surprise you very much to be told that it was I who sent to you those three daggers this morning?"

"You! Is it possible?"

"Yes; they were sent by me, and for a reason that I will presently explain to you. But let me begin at the beginning. Those roughly-drawn sketches, that to you suggested terrifying ideas of blood-shedding and violence, to my mind were open to a more peaceful and commonplace explanation. They appeared to me to suggest the herald's office rather than the armoury; the cross fitchée of the knight's shield rather than the poniard with which the members of secret societies are

supposed to render their recalcitrant brethren familar. Now, if you will look at these sketches again, you will see what I mean." Here Loveday produced from her writing-table the missives which had so greatly disturbed Mr. Hawke's peace of mind. " To begin with, the blade of the dagger of common life is, as a rule, at least two-thirds of the weapon in length; in this sketch, what you would call the blade, does not exceed the hilt in length. Secondly, please note the absence of guard for the hand. Thirdly, let me draw your attention to the squareness of what you considered the hilt of the weapon, and what, to my mind, suggested the upper portion of a crusader's cross. No hand could grip such a hilt as the one outlined here. After your departure yesterday, I drove to the British Museum, and there consulted a certain valuable work on heraldry, which has more than once done me good service. There I found my surmise substantiated in a surprising manner. Among the illustrations of the various crosses borne on armorial shields, I

" SO SOON AS SHE WAS ON BOARD SHIP."

found one that had been taken by Henri d'Anvers from his own armorial bearings, for his crest when he joined the Crusaders under Edward I., and which has since been handed down as the crest of the Danvers family. This was an important item of information to me. Here was someone in Cork sending to your house, on two several occasions, the crest of the Danvers family; with what object it would be difficult to say, unless it were in some sort a communication to someone in your house. With my mind full of this idea, I left the Museum and drove next to the office of the P. and O. Company, and requested to have given me the list of the passengers who arrived by the *Colombo*. I found this list to be a remarkably small one; I suppose people, if possible, avoid crossing the Bay of Biscay during the Equinoxes. The only passengers who landed at Plymouth besides Miss Monroe, I found, were a certain Mrs. and Miss O'Grady, steerage passengers who had gone on board at Ceylon on their way home from Australia. Their name, together with their landing at Plymouth, suggested the possibility that Cork might be their destination. After this I asked to see the list of the passengers who arrived by the packet following the *Colombo*, telling the clerk who attended to me that I was on the look-out for the arrival of a friend. In that second list of arrivals I quickly found my friend—William Wentworth Danvers by name."

"No! The effrontery! How dared he! In his own name, too!"

"Well, you see, a plausible pretext for leaving Pekin could easily be invented by him—the death of a relative, the illness of a father or mother. And Sir George, though he might dislike the idea of the young man going to England so soon after his daughter's departure, and may, perhaps, write to you by the next mail on the matter, was utterly powerless to prevent his so doing. This young man, like Miss Monroe and the O'Gradys, also landed at Plymouth. I had only arrived so far in my investigation when I went to your house yesterday afternoon. By chance, as I waited a few minutes in your drawing-room, another important item of information was acquired. A fragment of conversation between your nephew and the supposed Miss Monroe fell upon my ear, and one word spoken by the young lady convinced me of her nationality.

That one word was the monosyllable 'Hush.'"

"No! You surprise me!"

"Have you never noted the difference between the 'hush' of an Englishman and that of an Irishman? The former begins his 'hush' with a distinct aspirate, the latter with as distinct a W. That W is a mark of his nationality which he never loses. The unmitigated 'whist' may lapse into a 'whish' when he is transplanted to another soil, and the 'whish' may in course of time pass into a 'whush,' but to the distinct aspirate of the English 'hush,' he never attains. Now Miss O'Grady's was as pronounced a 'whush' as it was possible for the lips of a Hibernian to utter."

"And from that you concluded that Mary O'Grady was playing the part of Miss Monroe in my house?"

"Not immediately. My suspicions were excited, certainly; and when I went up to her room, in company with Mrs. Hawke's maid, those suspicions were confirmed. The orderliness of that room was something remarkable. Now, there is the orderliness of a lady in the arrangement of her room, and the orderliness of a maid, and the two things, believe me, are widely different. A lady, who has no maid, and who has the gift of orderliness, will put things away when done with, and so leave her room a picture of neatness. I don't think, however, it would for a moment occur to her to put things so as to be conveniently ready for her to use the next time she dresses in that room. This would be what a maid, accustomed to arrange a room for her mistress's use, would do mechanically. Now the neatness I found in the supposed Miss Monroe's room was the neatness of a maid—not of a lady, and I was assured by Mrs. Hawke's maid that it was a neatness accomplished by her own hands. As I stood there, looking at that room, the whole conspiracy—if I may so call it—little by little pieced itself together, and became plain to me. Possibilities quickly grew into probabilities, and these probabilities once admitted, brought other suppositions in their train. Now, supposing that Miss Monroe and Mary O'Grady had agreed to change places, the Pekin heiress, for the time being, occupying Mary O'Grady's place in the humble home at Cork and vice versâ, what means of communicating with each other had they arranged? How was Mary O'Grady to know when she might lay aside her assumed rôle and go back to her mother's house. There was no denying the necessity for such communication; the difficulties in its way must have been equally obvious to the two girls. Now, I think we must admit that we must credit these young women with having hit upon a very clever way of meeting those difficulties. An anonymous and startling missive sent to you would be bound to be mentioned in the house, and in this way a code of signals might be set up between them that could not direct suspicion to them. In this connection, the Danvers crest, which it is possible that they mistook for a dagger, suggested itself naturally, for no doubt Miss Monroe had many impressions of it on her lover's letters. As I thought over these things, it occurred to me that possibly dagger (or cross) number one was sent to notify the safe arrival of Miss Monroe and Mrs. O'Grady at Cork. The two daggers or crosses you subsequently received were sent on the day of Mr. Danvers's arrival at Plymouth, and were, I should say, sketched by his hand. Now, was it not within the bounds of likelihood that Miss Monroe's marriage to this young man, and the consequent release of Mary O'Grady from the onerous part she was playing, might be notified to her by the sending of three such crosses or daggers to you. The idea no sooner occurred to me than I determined to act upon it, forestall the sending of this latest communication, and watch the result. Accordingly, after I left your house yesterday, I had a sketch made of three daggers or crosses exactly similar to those you had already received, and had it posted to you so that you would get it by the first post. I told off one of our staff at Lynch Court to watch your house, and gave him special directions to follow and report on Miss O'Grady's movements throughout the day. The results I anticipated quickly came to pass. About half-past nine this morning the man sent a telegram to me saying that he had followed Miss O'Grady from your house to the Charing Cross Hotel, and furthermore had ascertained that she had since despatched a telegram, which (possibly by following the hotel servant who carried it to the telegraph office), he had overheard was addressed to Mrs. O'Grady, at Woburn Place, Cork. Since I received this information an altogether. remarkable cross-firing of tele-

grams has been going backwards and forwards along the wires to Cork."

"A cross-firing of telegrams! I do not understand."

"In this way. So soon as I knew Mrs. O'Grady's address I telegraphed to her, in her daughter's name, desiring her to address her reply to 115a Gower Street, not to Charing Cross Hotel. About three-quarters of an hour afterwards I received in reply this telegram, which I am sure you will read with interest."

Here Loveday handed a telegram—one

" A CROSS-FIRING OF TELEGRAMS."

of several that lay on her writing-table—to Mr. Hawke.

He opened it and read aloud as follows:

"Am puzzled. Why such hurry? Wedding took place this morning. You will receive signal as agreed to-morrow. Better return to Tavistock Square for the night."

" The wedding took place this morning," repeated Mr. Hawke blankly. " My poor old friend! It will break his heart."

" Now that the thing is done past recall we must hope he will make the best of it."

said Loveday. "In reply to this telegram," she went on, "I sent another, asking as to the movements of the bride and bridegroom, and got in reply this:"

Here she read aloud as follows:

"They will be at Plymouth to-morrow night; at Charing Cross Hotel the next day, as agreed."

"So, Mr. Hawke," she added, "if you wish to see your old friend's daughter and tell her what you think of the part she has played, all you will have to do will be to watch the arrival of the Plymouth trains."

"Miss O'Grady has called to see a lady and gentleman," said a maid at that moment entering.

"Miss O'Grady!" repeated Mr. Hawke in astonishment.

"Ah, yes, I telegraphed to her, just before you came in, to come here to meet a lady and gentleman, and she, no doubt thinking that she would find here the newly-married pair, has, you see, lost no time in complying with my request. Show the lady in."

"It's all so intricate—so bewildering," said Mr. Hawke, as he lay back in his chair. "I can scarcely get it all into my head."

His bewilderment, however, was nothing compared with that of Miss O'Grady, when she entered the room and found herself face to face with her late guardian, instead of the radiant bride and bridegroom whom she had expected to meet.

She stood silent in the middle of the room, looking the picture of astonishment and distress.

Mr. Hawke also seemed a little at a loss for words, so Loveday took the initiative.

"Please sit down," she said, placing a chair for the girl. "Mr. Hawke and I

"IT'S ALL SO INTRICATE—SO BEWILDERING," SAID MR. HAWKE.

have sent for you in order to ask you a few questions. Before doing so, however, let me tell you that the whole of your conspiracy with Miss Monroe has been brought to light, and the best thing you can do, if you want your share in it treated leniently, will be to answer our questions as fully and truthfully as possible."

The girl burst into tears. "It was all Miss Monroe's fault from beginning to end," she sobbed. "Mother didn't want to do it—I didn't want to—to go into a gentleman's house and pretend to be what I was not. And we didn't want her hundred pounds——"

Here sobs checked her speech.

"Oh," said Loveday contemptuously, "so you were to have a hundred pounds for your share in this fraud, were you?"

"We didn't want to take it," said the girl, between hysterical bursts of tears; "but Miss Monroe said if we didn't help her someone else would, and so I agreed to——"

"I think," interrupted Loveday, "that you can tell us very little that we do not already know about what you agreed to do. What we want you to tell us is what has been done with Miss Monroe's diamond necklace—who has possession of it now?"

The girl's sobs and tears redoubled. "I've had nothing to do with the necklace —it has never been in my possession," she sobbed. "Miss Monroe gave it to Mr. Danvers two or three months before she left Pekin, and he sent it on to some people he knew in Hong Kong, diamond merchants, who lent him money on it. Decastro, Miss Monroe said, was the name of these people."

"Decastro, diamond merchant, Hong Kong. I should think that would be sufficient address," said Loveday, entering it in a ledger; " and I suppose Mr. Danvers retained part of that money for his own use and travelling expenses, and handed the remainder to Miss Monroe to enable her to bribe such creatures as you and your mother, to practise a fraud that ought to land both of you in jail."

The girl grew deadly white. " Oh, don't do that—don't send us to prison!" she implored, clasping her hands together. " We haven't touched a penny of Miss Monroe's money yet, and we don't want to touch a penny, if you'll only let us off! Oh, pray, pray, pray be merciful!"

Loveday looked at Mr. Hawke.

He rose from his chair. " I think the best thing you can do," he said, " will be to get back home to your mother at Cork as quickly as possible, and advise her never to play such a risky game again. Have you any money in your purse? No—well then here's some for you, and lose no time in getting home. It will be best for Miss Monroe—Mrs. Danvers I mean—to come to my house and claim her own property there. At any rate, there it will remain until she does so."

As the girl, with incoherent expressions of gratitude, left the room, he turned to Loveday.

" I should like to have consulted Mrs. Hawke before arranging matters in this way," he said a little hesitatingly; " but still, I don't see that I could have done otherwise."

" I feel sure Mrs. Hawke will approve what you have done when she hears all the circumstance of the case," said Loveday.

" And," continued the old clergyman, " when I write to Sir George, as, of course, I must immediately, I shall advise him to make the best of a bad bargain, now that the thing is done. ' Past cure should be past care;' eh, Miss Brooke? And, think! what a narrow escape my nephew, Jack, has had!"

XXI

The Romance of the Secret Service

FRED M. WHITE

THE MAZAROFF RIFLE.

(A Complete Story).

NEWTON MOORE came into the War Office in response to a code telegram and a hint that speed was the essence of the contract. Sir George Morley plunged immediately into his subject.

"I've got a pretty case for you," he said. "I suppose you have never heard of such a thing as the Mazaroff rifle?"

Moore admitted his ignorance. He opined that it was something new, and that something had gone wrong with the lethal weapon in question.

"Quite right, and it will be your business to recover it," Sir George explained. "The gun is the invention of a clever young Russian, Nicholas Mazaroff by name. We have tested the weapon, which, as a matter of fact, we have purchased from Mazaroff. The rifle is destined to entirely revolutionise infantry tactics, and, indeed, it is a most wonderful affair. The projectile is fired by liquid air, there are no cartridges, and, as there is practically no friction beyond the passage of the bullet from the barrel, it is possible to fire the rifle some four hundred times before recharging. In addition, there is absolutely no smoke and no noise. You can imagine the value of the discovery."

"I can indeed," Moore observed. "I should very much like to see it."

"And I should like you to see it of all things," Sir George said drily; "indeed, I hope you will be the very first to see it, con-sidering that the gun and its sectional plans have been stolen."

Newton Moore smiled. He knew now why he had been sent for.

"Stolen from here, Sir George?" he asked.

"Stolen from here yesterday afternoon by means of a trick. Mazaroff called to see me, but I was very busy. Then he asked to see my assistant, Colonel Parkinson. He seemed to be in considerable trouble, so Parkinson told me. He had discovered a flaw in his rifle, a tendency for the projectile to jam, which constituted a danger to the marksman. Could he have the rifle and the plans for a day or two, he asked? Naturally, there was no objection to this, and the boon was granted. Mazaroff came here an hour ago, and when I asked him if he had remedied the defect, he paralysed me by declaring that he knew nothing whatever about the caller yesterday; indeed, he is prepared to prove that he was in Liverpool till a late hour last night. Some clever rascal impersonated him and got clear away with the booty."

"I presume Colonel Parkinson knew Mazaroff?"

"Not very well, but well enough to have no doubt as to his identity. Naturally, Parkinson is fearfully upset over the business; indeed, he seems to fancy that Mazaroff is lying to us. Mazaroff generally comes here in a queer, old Inverness cloak, with

483

ragged braid, and a shovel hat with a brown stain on the left side. Parkinson swears that he noticed both these things yesterday."

"I should like to see Mazaroff," Moore replied.

Sir George touched a bell, and from an inner room a young man, with a high, broad forehead, and dark, restless eyes, emerged. He was badly dressed, and, sooth to say, not over clean. Newton Moore's half-shy glance took him in from head to foot with the swiftness of a snapshot.

"This is the Russian gentleman I spoke of," said Sir George. "Mr. Newton Moore."

"Russian only in name," said Mazaroff swiftly. "I am English. If you help me to get my gun back I shall never be sufficiently grateful."

"I am going to have a good try," Moore replied. "Meanwhile, I shall require your undivided attention for some little time. I should like to walk with you as far as your lodgings and have a chat with you there."

Moore had made up his mind as to his man. He felt perfectly convinced that he was speaking the truth. He piloted Mazaroff into the street, and then took his arm.

"I am going to get you to conduct me to your rooms," he said. "And I am going to ask you a prodigious lot of questions. First, and most important—does anyone, to your knowledge, know of the new rifle?"

"Not a soul; I had a friend, a partner two years ago, who saw the thing nearly complete, but he is dead."

"Your partner might have mentioned the matter to somebody else."

"He might. Poor Franz was of a convivial nature. He did not possess the real secret."

"No, but he might have hinted to somebody that you were on the verge of a gigantic discovery. That somebody might have kept his eye upon you; he might have seen you coming from and going into the War Office."

Mazaroff nodded gravely. All these things were on the knees of the gods.

"At any rate somebody must have known, and somebody must have impersonated you," Moore proceeded. "You haven't a notion who it was, so I will not bother you any further in that direction. I have to look for

a cool and clever scoundrel, and one, moreover, who is a consummate actor."

"Cool enough," Mazaroff said drily, "seeing that the fellow actually had the impudence to pass himself off on my landlady as myself, and borrow my hat and Inverness —the ones I am wearing now—and cool enough to return them."

All this Mazaroff's landlady subsequently confirmed. She had known, of course, that her lodger had gone to Liverpool on business, and she had been surprised to see him return. The *alter ego* had muttered something about being suddenly recalled; he had taken off a frock coat and tall hat similar to those Mazaroff had used to travel in, and he had gone out immediately with the older and more familar garments.

"You had no suspicions?" Moore asked.

The landlady was fat, but by no means scant of breath. It was the misfortune of a lady who had fallen from high social status that she was compelled to inhabit a house of considerable gloom. Furthermore, her eyes were not the limpid orbs into which many lovers had once looked languishingly. Was a body to blame when slippery rascals were about?

"Nobody is blaming a body," Newton Moore smiled. "I don't think we need trouble you any more, Mrs. Jarrett."

Mrs. Jarrett departed with an avowed resolution to "have the law" of somebody or other over this business, and a blissful silence followed. Mazaroff had stripped off his hat and coat.

"You must have been carefully watched yesterday," Moore observed. "I suppose this is the hat and cloak your double borrowed?"

Mazaroff nodded, and Moore proceeded to examine the cloak. It was just possible that the thief might have left some clue, however small. Moore turned out the pockets.

"I am certain you will find nothing there," said Mazaroff. "There is a hole in both pockets, and I am careful to carry nothing in them."

"Nothing small, I suppose you mean," Moore replied as he brought to light some dingy looking papers folded like a brief. He threw the bundle on the table, and Mazaroff proceeded to examine it languidly. A puzzled look came over his face.

"These are not mine," he declared. "I never saw them before."

There were some score or more sheets fastened together with a brass stud. The sheets were typed, the letterpress was in the form of a dialogue. In fact the whole formed a play-part from some comedy or drama.

"This is a most important discovery," Moore observed. "Our friend must have been studying this on his way along and forgot it finally. We know now what I have suspected all along—that the man who impersonated you was by profession an actor. That is something gained."

Mazaroff caught a little of his companion's excitement.

"You can go farther," he cried. "You can find who this belongs to."

"Precisely what I am going to do," said Moore. "It is a fair inference that our man is playing in a new comedy or is taking the part of somebody else at short notice, or he could not have been learning this up in the cab. I have a friend who is an inveterate theatre-goer, a man who has a pecuniary interest in a number of playhouses, and I am in hopes that he may be able to locate this part for me. I'll see him at once."

Moore drove away without further delay to Ebury Street, where dwelt the Honourable Jimmy Manningtree, an old young man with a strong taste for the drama, and a good notion of getting value for the money he was fond of investing therein. He was an apple-faced individual with a keen eye and a marvellous memory for everything connected with the stage.

"Bet you I'll fit that dialogue to the play like a shot," he said when Moore had explained his errand. "Have some breakfast?"

Mazaroff proceeded to examine it languidly.

Moore declined. Until he had identified his man, food was a physical impossibility. Hungry as he was he felt that the first mouthful would choke him. He took up a cigarette and lay back in a chair whilst Manningtree pondered over the type-written sheets before him.

"Told you I'd name the lady," he cried presently. "I don't propose to identify and give the precise name of the character, because you'll be able to do that for yourself by following the play carefully."

"But what is the name of the play?" Moore asked impatiently.

"It is called 'Noughts and Crosses,' one of the most popular comedies we have ever run at the Thespian. If you weren't so buried in your stories and your medicine mysteries at the War Office, you might have seen all about it in last Monday's papers. Go and see the show—I'll give you a box."

"Then the play was produced for the first time on Saturday night," Moore was panting and eager on the scent at last. 'Also, from what you say, the Thespian is one of the theatres you are interested in?"

Manningtree executed a wink of amazing slyness. The Honourable Jimmy was no mean comedian himself.

"I believe you, my boy," he said. "I've got ten thousand locked up there, and I shall get it back three times over out of 'Noughts and Crosses.' If you like to have a box to-night you can."

"You're very kind," Moore replied. He laid his hands across his knees to steady them. "And, as much always wants more, I shall be greatly obliged if you will give me the run of the theatre. In other words, can I come behind?"

"Well, I don't encourage that kind of thing as a rule," Manningtree replied, "but as I know you have some strong reason for the request, I'll make an exception in your favour. I don't run my show for marbles, dear boy. I shall be at the Thespian at ten, and then, if you send round your card, the thing is done. Only I should like to know what you are driving at."

Moore smiled quietly.

"I dare say you would," he said. "Later on perhaps. For the present my lips are sealed. No breakfast, thanks—I couldn't swallow a mouthful. Only don't fail me to-night as you love your country."

A brilliant audience filled the Thespian. The stalls were one flash of colour and glitter of gems. The comedy was lively and sparkling, there was a strong story on which the jewels were threaded.

From the corner of his box Moore followed the progress of the play.

The first act was nearing its close. There were two characters in the caste still unaccounted for, and one of these must of necessity be the man Moore was after. The crux of the act was approaching. A thin, dark man stood on the stage. In style and carriage he had a marked resemblance to Mazaroff. He came to the centre of the stage and laid a hand on the shoulder of the high comedy man there.

"And where do I come in?" he asked gently.

It was a quotation, the first line of the play-part spread out on the ledge of the box before Moore. He gave a gasp. He saw a chance here that he determined to take. As the curtain fell on the second act he sent round his card. A little later and he was in Manningtree's private room.

"Who is the man playing the part of Paul Gilroy?" he asked.

"Oh, come," Manningtree protested. "You're not going to deprive me of Hermann. He has made the piece."

"I am going to do nothing of the kind," Moore replied. "We don't make public anything we can possibly keep to ourselves. Only Hermann has some information I require, and there is only one way of getting it. Tell me all you know about that man."

"Well, in the first place, he is a German with an American mother. He seems to have been everything, from a police spy up to a University Fellow. He speaks four or five languages fluently. A shady sort of a chap, but a brilliant actor, as you are bound to admit. Wait till you see him in the last act."

"He has all what you call the 'fat,' I presume?"

"He is on the stage the whole time. Five-and-twenty minutes the act plays. Take my advice and don't miss a word of it."

"I am afraid I shall miss it all," Moore replied in a dropping voice. "I am afraid that I shall be compelled to wander into Mr. Hermann's dressing-room by mistake. In an absent-minded kind of way I may also go through his pockets. Don't protest, there's a good fellow. You know me sufficiently well to be certain that I am acting in high interests. Say nothing, but merely let me know which is my man's dressing-room."

"You're a rum chap," Manningtree grumbled, "but you always manage to get your own way. You are running a grave risk, but you will have to take the consequences. If you are caught I cannot save you."

"I won't ask you to," Moore replied.

Manningtree indicated the room and strolled away. The room was empty. Hermann's dresser had disappeared, knowing probably that his services would not be required for the next half-hour. There was a quick tinkle of the bell, and the curtain drew up on the last act. Moore from his dim corner heard Hermann " called," and the coast was clear at last.

Just for a moment Moore hesitated. He had literally to force himself forward, but once the door had closed behind him his courage returned.

Hermann's ordinary clothing first. It hung up on the door. For some time Moore could find nothing of the least value, to him at any rate. He came at length to a pocket-book, which he opened without ceremony. There were papers and private letters, but nothing calculated to give a clue. In one of the flaps of the pocket a card, an ordinary visiting-card, had been stuck. It bore the name of Emile Nobel.

Moore fairly danced across the floor. He hustled the pocket-book back in its place and flashed out of the room. Nobody was near, nobody heard his chuckle. The whole atmosphere trembled with applause, applause that Moore in his strange way took to himself. He had solved the problem.

The name on the card was one perfectly well known to him. Every tyro in the employ of the Secret Service

He came at length to a pocket-book, which he opened without ceremony.

Fund had heard of Emile Nobel. For he was perhaps the chief rascal in the Rogues' Gallery of Europe. Newton Moore knew him both by name and by sight.

Stolen dispatches, purloined plans, nothing came amiss to the great, gross German, who seemed to have been at the bottom of half the mischief which it was the business of the Secret Service to set right. Moore had never come in actual contact with Nobel before, but

felt pretty sure that he was going to do so on this occasion. He was dealing with a clever coward, a man stone deaf, strange to say, but a man of infinite resources and cunning. Added to all this, Nobel was a chemist of great repute. The Secret Service heard vague legends of mysterious murders done by Nobel, all strictly in the way of business. And Nobel had this gun—Moore felt certain of that. Hermann had accomplished the theft, doubtless for a substantial pecuniary consideration.

Nobel must be found.

Moore saw his way clearly directly. It was a mere game of chance. If Hermann really knew Nobel—and the possession of the latter's visiting-card seemed to prove it—the thing might be easily accomplished. If not, then no harm would be done.

Moore made his way rapidly past the dark little box by the stage-door into the street. Then he whistled softly. A figure emerged from the gloom of the court.

" You called me, sir," a voice whispered.

" I did, Joseph," Moore replied.

" One little thing and you can retire for tonight. Take this card. In a few minutes you are to present it—as your own, mind—to the keeper of the stage-door yonder. Take care that the door-keeper does not see your face, and address him in fair English with a strong German accent. You will ask to see Mr. Hermann, and the stage-door keeper will inform you that you cannot see him for some time. You are to say that you are stone deaf, and get him to write what he says on paper. Then you leave your card for Mr. Hermann saying that you must see him on most important business to-night. Will he be good enough to come round and see you? That is all, Joseph."

Then Moore slipped back into the theatre. He had the satisfaction of hearing the message given, and his instructions carried out without a hitch. And a little later on he had the further satisfaction of hearing the stage-door keeper carry out Joseph's instructions as far as Hermann was concerned. Had Nobel's address been on the card all this would have been superfluous. As the address was missing, the little scheme was absolutely necessary.

There was just a chance, of course, that Hermann might deny all knowledge of Moore's prospective quarry, not that Moore had much fear of this, after the episode of the borrowed cloak and the play-part. Hermann stood flushed and smiling as he received the compliments of fellow comedians. Moore watched him keenly as the stage-door keeper delivered the card and the message.

"Most extraordinary," Hermann muttered. "You say that Mr. Nobel was here himself. What was he like?"

"Big gentleman, sir, strong foreign accent and deaf as a post."

Hermann looked relieved, but the puzzled expression was still on his face.

"All right, Blotton," he said. "Send somebody out to call a cab for me in ten minutes. Sorry I can't come and sup with you fellows as arranged. A matter of business has suddenly cropped up."

Moore left the theatre without further delay. His little scheme had worked like a charm. All lay clear before him now. Hermann had important business with Nobel, he knew where the latter was staying, he was going unceremoniously to conduct Moore to his abode. And where Nobel was at present there was the Mazaroff rifle. There could be no doubt about that now. Naturally the up-shot of all this would be that both the conspirators would discover that someone was on the trail, but Moore could see no way of getting the desired information without alarming the enemy. Once he knew where to

look for the thimble he felt that the search would be easy. Also he was prepared for a bold and audacious stroke if necessary.

With his vivid and delicate fancy, it was only the terrors conjured up by his own marvellous imagination that terrified him. He was one bundle of quivering nerves, and the power of the cigarettes he practically lived on jangled the machine more terribly out of tune.

But there was a sense of exultation now; the mad, feline courage Moore always felt when his clear, shrewd brain was shaping to success. At moments like these he was capable of the most amazing courage. He had a presentiment that success lay broadly before him.

A cab crawled along the dingy street at the mouth of the court, leading to the stage-door of the Thespian. Moore hailed it and got in. "Don't move till I give you the signal," said he, "and keep the trap open."

The cabman grinned and chuckled. This was evidently going to be one of the class of fares that London's gondoliers dream of but so seldom see. Presently the cab, bearing Hermann away, shot past.

"Follow that," Moore cried, "and when the gentleman gets out slacken speed, but on no account stop. I will drop out of the cab when it is still moving. There is a sovereign for you in any case, and there is my card in case I should have a very long journey. Now push her along."

It *was* a long journey. Neither cab boasted horse-flesh of high calibre, and after a time the pursuit dawdled down to a funeral procession.

Near the flagstaff at Hampstead Heath the first cab stopped and Hermann descended. Moore's cab trotted by, but Moore was no longer inside. If Hermann had any suspicion of being followed, it was allayed by this neat stroke of Moore's.

Hermann hurried forward, walking for half an hour until he came to a long new road at the foot of the hill between Cricklewood and Hampstead. Only one of the fairly large houses there seemed to be inhabited, the rest were in the last stages of completion. The opposite side of the road was an open field.

The houses were double-fronted ones with

a large porch and entrance hall, and a long strip of lawn in front. Hermann paused before the house which appeared to be inhabited, and passing up the path opened the front door and entered, closing the big door behind him. In the room on the left-hand side of the hall a brilliant light gleamed, but no glimmer showed in the hall itself. Beyond a doubt Emile Nobel was here.

Moore followed cautiously along the drive. He softly tried the front door, only to find the key had been turned in the lock.

"They are alarmed," he muttered; "the covey has been disturbed. By this time Nobel and Hermann know that they have been hoaxed. Also they will have a pretty good idea why. If I am any judge of character, audacity more than pluck is Hermann's strong point. He will leave Nobel in the lurch as soon as possible. If I could only hear what is going on! But that is impossible."

Moore could hear nothing beyond the murmur of Nobel's heavy voice, Hermann of course responding with signals. For a long time this continued.

Meanwhile Moore was not altogether idle. He had marked Hermann's unsteady eye and the weakness of his mouth. He sized him up as a man who would have scant consideration for others where his own personal safety was concerned.

"Anyway I'm going on that line," Moore muttered. "If Hermann discovers that he has been hoaxed without betraying his knowledge to Nobel, he will be certain to say nothing to him, but will as certainly abandon him to his fate. Nobel's deafness will be an important factor in this direction. Hermann's walking into the house as he did seems to indicate the absence of servants here. That will be in my favour later on.

Doubtless Nobel has taken this house as a blind—much safer than rooms in London, anyway. There is probably little or no furniture here, so that Nobel can slip off at any time. And now to see if I can find some way of getting into the house."

Whilst Moore was working away steadily

Over a table a ponderous German was bending.

with a stiff clasp-knife at a loose catch in one of the panes of the hall window, a conversation much on the lines Moore had indicated was taking place inside.

The hall was comfortably furnished, as was also the one sitting-room, where the brilliant light was burning. Over a table littered with plans and drawings a ponderous German was bending. He had a huge head, practically bald, a great red face, and cold blue eyes, and his mouth was the mouth of a shark. There was no air of courage or resolution about him, but a suggestion of diabolical cunning. A more brilliant rascal Europe could not boast.

Nobel looked up with a start as Hermann touched him.

"You frightened me," he said. "My nerfs are not as gomb letely under gontrol as they might be. Is anything wrong, my tear friendt?"

"Wrong?" Hermann cried. "Why, you sent for me."

Nobel shook his head, for he had not heard a word.

"I was goming to see you to-morrow," he said. "I should have come to-night, but you were engaged at the theatre. Eh, what?"

Hermann turned away to light a cigarette. His hands shook and his knees trembled under him. He had been hoaxed; in a flash he saw his danger before him. Perhaps he had been tracked and followed here. And Nobel knew nothing of it. He was not going to know, either, if his accomplice could help it.

"I came to warn you," he touched off on his fingers.

"Oh," Nobel cried, "there is tanger, then? You have heard something?"

Hermann proceeded to telegraph a negative reply. He had seen nothing whatever; only the last few hours he had a strong suspicion of being followed. He discreetly omitted to remark the absolute conviction that he had been shadowed this evening. He had deemed it his solemn duty to come and warn Nobel, seeing what compromising matter the latter had in his house.

"You are a goot boy," Nobel said, patting Hermann ponderously on the shoulder. "By the morning I shall have gomitted all the plans of that weapon to my brain. Then I will destroy him and the plans. After, I go to Paris, and you shall hear from me there. Meanwhile there is branty and whiskey."

Hermann signalled that he would take nothing. It was of first importance that he should return to London without delay. He had come down there at great inconvenience to himself. As a matter of fact every sound in the empty house set his nerves going like a set of cracked bells. Moore had only just time to plunge into the darkness as the front door opened and Hermann came out. Moore smiled grimly as he heard the lock turned, and saw Hermann hurrying away.

Things had fallen out exactly as he had anticipated. Hermann had told his big confederate nothing. He meant to abandon him to his fate. Nobel was in the house, where he meant to remain for the present. Hermann had given him no cause for alarm.

It was going to be a case of man to man; brains and agility against cunning. Doubtless Nobel was not unprepared for an attack. There would be nothing so clumsy as mere fire-arms—there were other and more terrible weapons known to the German, who was a chemist and a scientist of a high order.

But the thing had to be done and Moore meant to do it. There was no need for silence. He worked away at the window catch, which presently flew back with a click and the sash was opened. A moment later and Moore was in the hall. As he dropped lightly to his feet it seemed to his quick ear that a deep suppressed growl followed. There was darkness in the hall with just one shaft of light crossing it from the room beyond, where Moore could distinctly see Nobel bending over a table. The low growl was repeated. As Moore peered into the darkness he saw two round spots of flaming angry orange, two balls of flame close together near the floor. He gave a startled cry that rang in the house, then paused as if half fearful of disturbing Nobel. But the latter never moved. He would never hear again till the last trumpet sounded.

The flaming circles crept nearer to Moore. He did not dare to turn and fly. He saw the gleaming eyes describe an arc, and then next moment he was on his back on the floor, with the bulldog uppermost.

A fierce flash of two rows of gleaming teeth were followed by a stinging blow on the temple, from which the blood flowed freely. Then the dog's grip met in the thick, fleshy part of the shoulder. As the cruel saws gashed on Moore's collar-bone he felt faint and sick with the pain.

But he uttered no further cry; he knew how useless it was. There was something peculiarly horrible in the idea of lying there in sight of help and yet being totally unable to invoke it.

Moore's hand went up to his tie slowly. From it he withdrew a diamond pin, the shaft of which, as is not uncommon with valuable pins, being made of steel. His hand thus armed, crept under the left forearm of the bulldog, until it rested just over the strongly-beating heart. With a steady pressure Moore drove the pin home to the head.

There was one convulsive snap on Moore's collar-bone, then the teeth relaxed. A shudder, a long-drawn sigh, and all was still. Some minutes passed before Moore had strength to recover his feet. A queer, hysterical laugh escaped him as he raised the carcase of the dog in his arms. A sudden strength possessed him, a sudden madness held him. With the dog in his arms, he staggered into the room where Nobel was so deeply engrossed, and flung the carcase with a crash upon the table.

A frightened cry came from Nobel as he staggered back. His great red face grew white and flabby, his blue eyes were filled with tears. He looked from the carcase on the table to the slight man with the blood on his features. On the table lay the object of Moore's search, the Mazaroff rifle.

"A ghost!" Nobel cried. "A ghost! Ah! what does it mean?"

Next moment he was on his back on the floor.

Moore pointed to the rifle and the drawings on the table.

"Those," he signalled upon his fingers.

"I do not understand," he muttered.

"Not now," Moore replied. He was proficient with that code used by the deaf. More than once he had proved its value. "But you hope to understand that rifle before morning. I have come to take it away. You need not trouble to go into explanations. I am perfectly aware how you and Hermann managed the thing between you."

"My servants," Nobel muttered, "will——"

"You have no servants, you are quite alone in the house."

Nobel smiled in a peculiar manner, and, as if to disprove the statement, laid a finger on the electric bell. At the same time he seemed to be caressing his nostrils with a handkerchief. Moore was conscious of a faint, sweet smell in the air, and the next minute a giddy feeling came over him. A terrible smile danced in Nobel's eyes.

Some infernal juggling was at work here. Moore glanced towards the electric bell. Then he saw that the white stud was no longer there—there was nothing but a round hole, through which doubtless some deadly gas was pouring. With a handkerchief held to his face, Moore snatched up the plans from the table and crushed them into the heart of the fire. He gripped the Mazaroff rifle by the barrel, and held it over Nobel's huge head.

"You scoundrel," he muttered, "you are trying to murder me. Open the windows, open the windows at once, or I will beat your brains out."

Nobel understood enough of this from Moore's threatening gesture to know that he had been found out and what was required of him. With his huge, flabby form trembling like a jelly, he pulled up the curtains and opened one of the windows. It was close to the ground, the lawn coming up to the house. In a sudden paroxysm of rage, Moore's left hand shot out, catching Nobel full on the side of his ponderous cheek.

There was an impact of flesh on flesh, and Nobel went down like a magnificent ruin. As he staggered to his feet again he caught a glimpse of a flying figure hurrying at top speed down the road.

"My kingdom for the Edgware Road and a cab," Moore panted. "I'm going to collapse, I'm played out for the present. Thank the gods there is a policeman. Hi, Robert, Robert. Here's a case of drunk and incapable for you. And, whatever happens to me, don't lose my rifle. Give me your arm, don't be too hard upon me, and we shall get to Cricklewood Police Station all in good time."

He gripped the Mazaroff rifle by the barrel, and held it over Nobel's huge head.

XXII

A Warning in Red

VICTOR L. WHITECHURCH and E. CONWAY

A WARNING IN RED.

THE STORY OF A RAILWAY MYSTERY.

By Victor L. Whitechurch and E. Conway.

Illustrated by Max Cowper.

"YES," said the Colonel, as he lit another cheroot, "many a man when he is in action is simply mad for the time being, and fights like a demon because he sees red."

"Sees red?" I asked, with a start.

"Don't you know what I mean?"

"No."

"Ah, it's a curious psychological problem that I've experienced myself. I was leading a cavalry charge at Joonpore, and suddenly the enemy, the country, everything seemed to fade away into a blood-red mist that blinded me with colour—I could see nothing else. And then the mad desire came upon me to slash and slay. They told me afterwards that I behaved like a fury, and I can believe it, for I've seen many a man in the same condition. It only comes in battle, I believe. That's the only time you can 'see red.'"

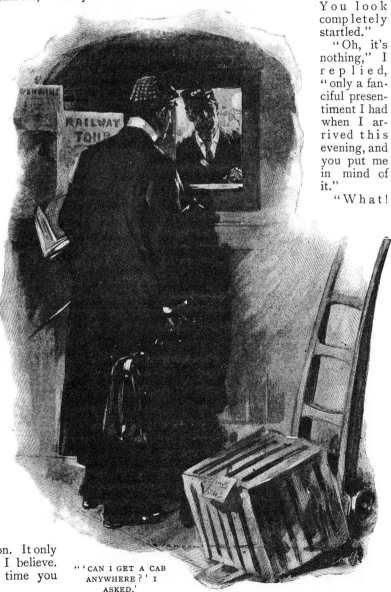

"'CAN I GET A CAB ANYWHERE?' I ASKED.'

"Are you sure?"

"Yes. But what's the matter, Forbes? You look completely startled."

"Oh, it's nothing," I replied, "only a fanciful presentiment I had when I arrived this evening, and you put me in mind of it."

"What!

495

you don't mean to say you saw red," asked the Colonel, with a laugh.

" Not in your sense of the word, Colonel ; and you'll only laugh at me if I tell you. It's a mere fancy, that's all."

"Well, drown your fancies in a whisky and soda, and then get a good night's rest after your journey. That's the best thing for you, Forbes. But if you like to tell me what's upset you I won't laugh at you."

So in the end I told him about the strange effect I had experienced in alighting at the station. I had come down from town to spend a couple of days with Colonel Ward at Manningford. Although I had known him for many years, and had often seen him at his club, it was the first time I had ever been to stay at his country house. He expected me by a late train, but judgment being given in a case in which I was professionally engaged as solicitor rather earlier than I had expected, I was able to get away from town in the afternoon, and reached Manningford station about six o'clock. I had not thought it worth while to wire, as I had determined to take a trap if it was far to walk, and surprise him.

Manningford was a tiny little country station, I was the only passenger who alighted, and one solitary official, who seemed to combine the offices of station-master, porter, and ticket-collector, met me on the platform.

" Tickets, please," he said, gruffly.

I gave him my ticket. As I did so, the train in which I had been travelling glided off the platform, and I caught a glimpse of the red tail-light showing in the fading day.

Grasping my Gladstone bag, I was about to depart, when the idea struck me that I would ask the stationmaster about a conveyance. He had retired to his office and was standing at the ticket-issuing window, which was open. He had lit the lamp inside, as the office was rather dark.

" Can I get a cab anywhere ? " I asked.

He looked up. He was a red-faced man with red hair, and the strong light showed his colour vividly. In accordance with the rules of the railway company he served, he was wearing a red tie.

" No," he said, rather shortly. Perhaps I was staring a little rudely at his illuminated countenance.

" But," I persisted, " surely there is some conveyance to be had near, isn't there ? "

" You can hire a dog-cart at the Star, " he said.

" Where is that ? "

" Cross the line and go out on the other side of the station. Turn to the right, and it's about five minutes' walk."

And he slammed down the window.

I went on to the platform once more, and slowly crossed the line. I say slowly, because the *red* colour of my surroundings began to grow upon me. The station itself was painted a chocolate colour of a reddish tinge. The tiles bordering the flower beds were of a deep red colour, enclosing for the most part scarlet geraniums. Looking down the line I caught the crimson rays of the setting sun reflected upon the rails, and glancing in the opposite direction noticed that the red light on the up starting signal was burning brightly. It was a strange, indescribable sensation that attacked me, this predominance of blood-red colouring ; and I gave a little shiver as I walked to the inn, which was a good quarter of a mile from the station, though apparently the nearest house. A two-mile drive brought me to the Colonel's, and after dinner his mention of " seeing red " recalled what had happened.

" Well," said Colonel Ward, as he bid me good-night, " I won't laugh at you, because I'll admit that we're none of us accountable for peculiar brain sensations at times. Monk, the stationmaster, isn't exactly a beauty to look at, is he ? But he's a capital official. You've been overworking yourself lately, Forbes, and you must take things easy. Good-night, old chap. Pleasant dreams. I hope your red sensation is not the preliminary to a nightmare."

The next morning, as we were sitting at breakfast, a servant burst into the room with a very frightened expression, and told the Colonel that a man wanted to see him at once. He was absent for about a quarter of an hour, when he returned in great agitation.

" Great heavens ! " he exclaimed, " my poor friend Geoffrey Anstruthers has been murdered—killed on the line when coming down from town last night. Your blood-red impression had something in it, perhaps, Forbes."

" Tell me about it, Colonel."

" I will. It's upset me dreadfully. Poor Anstruthers was my nearest neighbour, living about a mile off in that big white house you noticed between the station and my place. We were the greatest of friends, for although he was a very peculiar man we got on thoroughly. The poor fellow was to have met you at dinner here to-night."

"How did it happen?"

"Well, they tell me his body was discovered by the side of the line near Barton—about midway between London and Manningford. A platelayer found it early this morning. There were marks of a struggle and a couple of knife stabs, and he seems to have been attacked and killed in the train and then thrown out.

"Have you any idea if there was a motive for the crime?" I asked.

"Unfortunately, yes," said the Colonel. "Poor Anstruthers was a man of most eccentric habits, and one of his fads was that he would bank nowhere but at the Bank of England, and that he would pay nobody by cheque. He also settled all his accounts once a quarter only, and the tradesman who asked for an earlier settlement, or the servant or labourer who demanded monthly or weekly wages, was sure to be dismissed by him. Regularly every quarter he went up to London and drew several hundred pounds in gold out of the Bank of England, bringing it back in an ordinary brief bag. I often warned him that he was doing a very foolish thing, but he only laughed at me.

"Yesterday he went up to town for this purpose. His servants thought that as he had not returned last evening by his usual train, which arrives at 10.15 p.m., he was staying the night in town. But evidently some blackguard got hold of his movements. Poor old Anstruthers!"

"Is anything being done yet?" I asked.

"I hardly know," said the Colonel; "I think his nearest relations are abroad. At all events I'm the greatest friend he had,

and I'm going to take the matter up. I shall go to Barton by the next train."

"I'll come with you," I said.

"That's very kind of you, Forbes; your assistance will be most valuable, for I know your hobby—railways. It might help us."

We finished our breakfast quickly

"'MY FRIEND GEOFFREY ANSTRUTHERS HAS BEEN MURDERED ON THE LINE COMING DOWN FROM TOWN LAST NIGHT!' HE EXCLAIMED."

and drove into the station. On my way I asked the Colonel a few particulars concerning the train by which Anstruthers had travelled the night before. It ran as follows:—

London (dep.) ...	... 8.45	p.m.
Muggridge (stop)	... 9.10	,,
Barton (stop) ...	... 9.37	,,
Manningford (stop)	... 10.15	,,
Porthaven (arrive)	... 10.30	,,

So that the only stops between London and Manningford were Muggridge and Barton. The body, so the Colonel had heard, had been found about two miles on the London side of Barton.

The red-faced stationmaster was in his office when we arrived at the station.

"Sad job this, Mr. Monk," said the Colonel.

"Terrible, sir. It regularly upset me when the down train brought the news this morning. Poor Mr. Anstruthers! I knew him well, sir. I'd seen him go up in the morning, and wondered why he didn't come back by the 10.15 as usual. Are you going by the up train?"

"Yes. We're going to Barton to inquire into this awful affair. Two first returns, please."

The stationmaster reached to his rack for the tickets. Now, as often happens in small country stations where the supply of

tickets to various stations on the line is limited and becomes exhausted, he did a very common thing. Selecting two blank tickets he dipped the pen into ink and wrote on their respective halves, "Manningford to Barton," "Barton to Manningford," and the fare, 7s. 8d.

Then he passed them through the window and I took them up. He had written the names in *red ink !*

"I hope they'll catch the wretches, sir," said the stationmaster a few minutes afterwards, as he opened our carriage door for us.

Arrived at Barton, we took a trap and drove to the scene of the tragedy. The body, we were told, had been removed to an inn close by the railway, but at my request we went first to the line, as I was anxious to see the exact spot where Mr. Anstruthers had been thrown out of the train. We found a local policeman and two platelayers at the place, which was in a cutting. One of the latter told us that he was the man who had discovered the body.

"He was lyin' just here, gentlemen," he said, pointing to the six-foot way between the two lines of metals.

"Of course he was dead when you found him?" I asked.

"Yes, sir, but it's my opinion he wasn't altogether dead when they threw him out."

"Why?"

"'Cause he seemed to have moved afterwards. One of his arms was just restin' on the down rail."

"Well?"

"Well, sir, he couldn't ha' fallen like that in the first place, cause the wheels o' the train would ha' cut his arm."

"Stop a minute," I said. "What time did you find him here?"

"'Tween three and four this mornin', sir."

"And he was thrown out about 9.30 the night before?"

"Yes, sir."

"Was that train the last down one?"

"The last passenger train, sir."

"Was there a down goods train after that?"

"Yes, sir, between half-past one and two."

"Ah, then, why didn't *that* train crush his arm?"

The question staggered the platelayer and the policeman too. They evidently hadn't thought of this.

"I s'pose 'e must ha' bin alive when the goods train passed, and moved afterwards," said the platelayer presently, and the policeman entered a note to that effect in his pocket-book.

"What are you driving at?" said the Colonel.

"Never mind yet," I answered. Then, turning to the platelayer again, I said, "He was stabbed, wasn't he?"

"Yes, sir."

"Where?"

"In the chest, sir."

"Any blood-stains?"

"Yes, sir. He was wearin' a white weskitt, and it was quite red when I turned him over."

"He was lying on his back, then?"

"Yes, sir."

"Well, where are the blood-marks on the stones here? Have you cleared them up?"

"*There wasn't*

"I HASTILY DREW THE SCRAP OF PAPER FROM MY POCKET-BOOK AND COMPARED IT WITH THE TICKET."

none," said the man.

"Strange!" I murmured to myself, as we left the spot.

"You'd make a good detective, Forbes," said the Colonel.

"Not a bit of it," I replied. "It's simply because there is a mystery connected with my hobby—railways. That's what makes me a little extra sharp."

"A *mystery?*" said the Colonel.

"Yes," I replied, "more than you think. But now let's see the poor fellow."

Mr. Anstruthers was lying on a bed at the inn, just as they had found him. The neighbouring police inspector was there, very imposing and important. The Colonel gave his card, and we were allowed to see the body.

It was a gruesome sight, and my friend turned away to ask some questions of the inspector. I looked at the dead man carefully. There were signs of a struggle. His clothes were torn, and one of his hands was tightly clenched. Then I saw what, apparently, the wily country police had passed undiscovered—a shred of paper clasped in his hand. Without exciting the inspector's attention, I wrested the fingers open and drew from them a tiny scrap of torn paper, evidently clutched by a dying hand. It bore the following in writing:—

"ord—on."

It was such a tiny scrap, such an insignificant thing to go upon, but I slipped it into my pocket-book nevertheless.

THE TINY SCRAP OF PAPER TAKEN FROM THE MURDERED MAN'S HAND.

"Come," said the Colonel, "I can't stand this any longer. Well, inspector, I hope you'll get the villain."

"Ah, we're on the track," said the officer, sagaciously. "They got out at Barton, that's about it; and we'll have 'em yet."

"Do you want to see anything else, Forbes?" asked the Colonel.

"Yes. I should like to see the doctor who examined the body."

"It's Dr. Moore," said the policeman. "He lives at Barton."

So we called on Dr. Moore on our way to the station. He declared that he had seen poor Anstruthers at six o'clock in the morning, and was positively certain that he must then have been dead *seven or eight hours.* The mystery was thickening.

Passing on to the platform at Barton, we had to show our tickets. As I took mine back I gazed at it in a listless sort of way, when suddenly I gave a start. The last three letters of "Manningford"— where had I seen them? That peculiar elongated "o" and the curiously tailed "d"—Ah! I remembered!

Hastily I drew the scrap of paper from my pocket-book, and compared it with the ticket. The "ord" was in the same handwriting! It was part of the words "Manningford station."

In a moment a clue flashed across my mind, and I searched for a porter.

"Is there any official about the station with whom I can have a word? It's about an urgent matter."

"Yes, sir; Mr. Smart, the district superintendent is here; he came down about that murder. You'll find him in the stationmaster's office."

"Come with me, Colonel," I cried, turning to the office.

Hastily I introduced myself to Mr. Smart, telling him my errand was connected with the murder.

"Tell me," I asked, "is there any train from Manningford to London after 10.15?"

"Only a goods," he said.

"Exactly. What time does it leave Manningford?"

"About midnight."

"And Barton?"

"It stops here for shunting. Generally starts on about 1.45 a.m."

"Mr. Smart, can you lay your hand on the men who worked that train last night?"

He consulted some return sheets.

"Driver Power and fireman Hussey," he murmured. "They're on the Slinford branch to-day—they don't often run on the main line—and brakesman Sutton. He works a goods back to Porthaven to-day. He'll arrive there in half an hour."

"Does he always work main line trains?"

"For several months past he has."

"He's the man then, Mr. Smart. It's of the utmost importance that you should wire to Porthaven to have him closely watched. I'll explain presently."

The district superintendent hastily scribbled a line on an official telegraph form and rushed out with it. When he returned I said—

"Have you any of the company's detectives at hand?"

"Yes, two," he answered.

"Bring them then, and come along."

"My dear fellow," said the Colonel, who had been patiently silent up to this point, "*what* does it all mean?"

"Yes," said the superintendent, "I'm in a fog."

"I hear the down train coming in," I cried. "We must all return to Manningford—quick, sir—I'll explain everything in the train."

A few minutes, and the Colonel, the superintendent, and his two detectives and myself were in the train bound for Manningford.

"Now, sir?" said Mr. Smart.

"Well," I replied, "we're going to arrest the murderers, or one of them I think, at all events."

"And who's that?"

"Monk, the stationmaster at Manningford," I answered.

"*Monk?* Impossible. Why, the murder occurred forty miles away."

"No," I replied, "it occurred at Manningford station last night shortly after 10.15. Listen. Poor Anstruthers came down from town, got out of the train, and was done to death by the stationmaster, who was *alone on the station*, for the sake of his money. In the struggle the murdered man clutched a letter that Monk had written and was probably carrying in his breast pocket. This scrap of it I found in his hand just now. It is in Monk's hand-writing. Look!" and I compared it with

the ticket.

"But how about the body being found where it was?" asked the Colonel.

"It was taken there afterwards, probably in Sutton's brake van, and thrown out. This would account for two facts: first, that no blood was found on the permanent way, although Anstruthers had bled; and, secondly, that his arm was lying on the down rail. The down goods had passed before he was thrown from the up goods brake van. That's my theory, gentlemen. Here we are at Manningford, and the least you can do is to arrest the stationmaster on suspicion."

The latter was on the platform when we arrived. I noticed he gave a start as he saw so many of us get out of the train. The superintendent went up to him.

"Mr. Monk," he said, "a very painful duty brings us here. These two gentle-men are members of our police force, and they will have to detain you on suspicion."

"Of what?" gasped Monk, his red face growing paler.

"Of participation in the murder of Mr. Anstruthers last night."

"But he was killed in the train," said the stationmaster.

"That remains to be proved. At all events we are going to detain you, and to search your house."

"I won't submit to it," began the man; but he subsided when a pair of handcuffs were slipped over his wrists. Then we all repaired to his little house, just across the road. Again he proved turbulent, but it was no use. With skele-ton keys one of the detectives opened a box in his bedroom.

"'I WON'T SUBMIT TO IT,' SAID THE MAN; BUT HE SUBSIDED WHEN A PAIR OF HANDCUFFS WERE SLIPPED OVER HIS WRISTS."

"Ah!" he exclaimed, as he drew out a brief bag, "this seems rather heavy. No wonder. It's full of money."

"That's Anstruthers' bag," exclaimed the Colonel.

The wretched man saw the game was up, but, wretch that he was, he exclaimed—

"It's not me—it's Sutton—the brakesman of the up goods train. He had as much to do with it as I did. He took the body away ; and he's got a lot of the gold."

"All right," said the superintendent, "we're seeing after him. You have to thank this gentleman," pointing to myself, "for unravelling the mystery."

"Curse you !" yelled the stationmaster at me.

Sutton turned against Monk, and between the two of them the whole story came out. Monk's accounts were short, and he owed money all round—the usual story—racing. He had half planned to murder Anstruthers several times, and at last the opportunity presented itself. He was the only passenger to alight that night, and Monk noticed that the guard had not observed him. So he asked him to step into his office for a moment under pretence of something, and then went for him. There was a struggle, but Monk was the stronger man. In this struggle Anstru-

thers had grasped the bit of paper, but without the other's knowledge.

Then came the disposal of the body. Sutton was a man of doubtful character, and Monk knew enough about him to ruin him if he disclosed certain cases of goods stealing. So, when the goods train came along, he gave Sutton twenty pounds, and promised him another thirty to take the body in his van and pitch it out so that people would think Anstruthers had been murdered in the train. It was the easiest thing possible on a dark night to halt the train with the brake van opposite Monk's office, and to slip the body in without driver or fireman knowing anything about it.

The sequel was the gallows for Monk, and fifteen years at Dartmoor for Sutton.

"There was something uncanny after all, Forbes," said the Colonel, after dinner on that eventful day, "about your blood-red impression of Manningford station and its master !"